TONAL ALLEGORY IN THE VOCAL MUSIC OF J. S. BACH

TONAL ALLEGORY

IN THE VOCAL MUSIC OF J. S. BACH

Eric Chafe

Bach.

UNIVERSITY OF CALIFORNIA PRESS   BERKELEY LOS ANGELES OXFORD

The publication of this book was made possible in part by generous grants from the National Endowment for the Humanities and the American Musicological Society.

University of California Press
Berkeley and Los Angeles, California
University of California Press, Ltd.
Oxford, England
© 1991 by The Regents of
the University of California

Library of Congress
Cataloging-in-Publication Data

Chafe, Eric Thomas, 1946–
Tonal allegory in the vocal music of
J. S. Bach / Eric Chafe.

    p. cm.

Includes bibliographical references and index.

ISBN 0-520-05856-9

1. Bach, Johann Sebastian, 1685–1750.
Vocal music.   2. Vocal music—History
and criticism.   3. Bach, Johann Sebastian,
1685–1750—Symbolism.   4. Tonality.   I.
Title.

ML410.B13C47   1991
782.2'2—dc20   90-40050
                                    CIP
74546   MN

Printed in the United States of America

9 8 7 6 5 4 3 2 1

CONTENTS

This book considers the figurative use of tonality and its association with theology in the music of J. S. Bach. Although the topic has appeared in various forms in the Bach literature since the nineteenth century, it has never been treated at any length. The term "tonal allegory" has been chosen to broaden the frame of reference for the subject. The figurative dimension of musical thought, theology and hermeneutics (or the science of interpretation generally), and the philosophy of art meet in this shared concern with allegory. Allegory expresses the spiritual life, a way of thought in music, and in the other arts, as well as in religion, and it is fundamental to my argument that tonality acts as a central, if not the central, means by which music becomes allegorical.

I treat allegory here as a mode of thought and expression rather than as a system, although of course it has systematic features. The search for systems of allegory—in the application of music-rhetorical figures and the "reading" of key characteristics, for example—has often been and is still confused with the search for meaning in art. In the area of tonality, even though it has always expressed some truth, it has ultimately failed miserably. The problem for the modern scholar is compounded by the attempts of some authors in the seventeenth and eighteenth centuries to present key characteristics as though they could be systematized. The desire to do this reflects both the passion for categorization that characterized the age of reason and the dominance of the aesthetic of a word-engendered music. The attempt to develop a style that would render music a reflection of rational thought is, in fact, one of the most important features of the emergence of baroque music, one that had far-reaching and enduring consequences for music history and theory. Nevertheless, it was recognized even at the time that allegory is pluralistic and rhetoric flexible. Music, and particularly its tonality, resists wholesale rational understanding. Among Bach's contemporaries, Johann Mattheson and Johann David Heinichen took opposite positions on key characteristics. In 1711 Mattheson published one of the most famous of all presentations of the subject, providing for each of the twenty-four major and minor keys a series of extramusical associations. Heinichen, in contrast, denied the validity of this approach. At the same time Mattheson was careful to qualify his general remarks on the subject, so as to avoid giving the impression that key characteristics could be systematized, while Heinichen in many ways—such as his description of the flat keys as "enharmonic" and the sharp keys as "chromatic"—left the door open to traditional key associations.[1] Both men shifted the responsibility onto the composer's shoulders, where it belongs. Modern scholars, faced with the impossibility of systematizing the allegorical use of key and noting that many composers have ignored this aspect of music, have evaded the issue as a subject of serious investigation.

Such evasion is impossible in the study of Bach's music. Even the most obvious general questions have seldom been asked, however, perhaps because they will not admit of similarly general answers. In Bach's oeuvre, for example, a little more than two-thirds of the cantatas begin and end in the same key. This quantity provides evidence for tonal closure as the norm, while tonal openness clearly operates as significantly more than an exception. Explanations of this situation that depend on "facts," such as the consistent beginning and ending of the secular cantatas in the same key because the brass instruments that contribute to their often festive atmosphere are best suited to particular keys, or on such aspects as haste of composition or the incidence of parody, fall short of the mark. Many of the most carefully planned compositions feature open key structures, and many cantatas that feature highly modulatory schemes reflecting inner antithesis are closed tonally. Valid explication must rest on the particular intent behind the observable features, tonal or otherwise, of the individual work. The reasoning generally must consider the original function of the work as something more than an autonomous musical structure.

Put simply, change of key within many cantatas reflects or allegorizes the spiritual development, its relation to established doctrine, personal experience, and the like. As such, it often introduces design of a kind that is relatively unfamiliar to modern listeners, who have assimilated post-eighteenth-century tonal theory and a more secular outlook. To deepen our appreciation of Bach's work, then, we must expand our conception of tonality and musical allegory by including archaic features and beliefs, some of which may appear at first to be both erroneous and aesthetically irrelevant. It is neither possible nor desirable, however, to disregard the later history of tonal theory, as though ignorance of Richard Strauss somehow helped us to understand Bach. The question goes beyond the fact that we cannot live in the past and centers instead on our willingness that the past live in our lives. This book thus advocates the revival or reawakening in modern interpretation of

1. See the discussion of these matters in Chapter 3.

the pluralistic stance of traditional hermeneutics. The attempt to understand past art by placing ourselves along a continuum of present and past rather than by forming a system or applying a method is hardly new to humanistic scholarship. Nevertheless, it has not had a large following in professional Bach studies, where an understandable fragmentation of interests has characterized the field for forty years. It may now be necessary to glory in our amateur standing as we integrate such subjects as historical theory and eighteenth-century Lutheranism into Bach interpretation.

I have found it necessary, then, to take up the subject of tonal allegory from several different perspectives, while focusing on the interpretation of musical allegory in the works themselves. At times my approach may appear rather distant from Bach's own probable extramusical ideas and even further from the habitual concerns of the modern reader. This is one of the chief hazards for anyone attempting work of this kind. The extent and detail of the musicological explanation necessary to understand what Bach and his contemporaries understood directly and intuitively demonstrate our distance from the world of his thought. This book attempts to aid readers in recognizing that world and comprehending the masterpieces rooted in it. That the intensity of the composer's musicoallegorical vision permits us to experience the essentials of that world with a particular vividness constitutes the major argument of this study. I even go so far as to hypothesize, in Chapter 2, that the musicotheological worldview in Bach's works is linked to a form of "identity projection" on Bach's part. Such an idea is not, of course, to be confused with the idea of self-expression that we have inherited from classic-romantic aesthetics. The word *expression* was, however, used by some baroque theorists. In fact, Athanasius Kircher's *stylus expressus* (objective categories of style, as opposed to the personal traits of style he called *stylus impressus*) reminds us that the baroque period linked expression and allegory in a way that Walter Benjamin reestablished in modern criticism. It would be naive simply to assume that the objective allegorical devices of Bach's text setting offer direct and immediately understandable reflections of his inner life, but we must not ignore that possibility.

This book was written for and is dedicated to the community of Bach scholars, from whom directly or indirectly I have benefited beyond measure. Most of the ideas I present here have been constructively criticized by my colleagues. Specifically, comments from Alfred Dürr several years ago challenged me to think carefully about the "Actus Tragicus" and a number of the cantatas discussed in Chapters 5 through 9. I acknowledge with pleasure the great service to Bach scholarship provided in Dr. Dürr's many sane and comprehensive publications on the composer. The origins of my thinking on the subject of Bach's tonality go back to a seminar held by Christoph Wolff at Toronto two decades ago, in which the subject of tonal organization in the *Passions* was taken seriously. A perceptive suggestion made by Leo Treitler led to the hypotheses on instrumental usage in the *St. Matthew Passion* presented in Chapter 12. Paul Brainard very generously provided a critique of many details in my discussion of the *St. John Passion*. Friedhelm Krummacher provided me with the original parts and his score of a cantata by Christian Ludwig Boxberg. Michael Marissen helped to survey modulations in the Bach cantata recitatives, and Scott Milner assisted in the preparation of the bibliography. I gratefully acknowledge the support given by Brandeis University in the form of a Mazer Faculty Grant and a Bernstein Faculty Fellowship. Both sources provided financial support; the latter also freed me for a semester of concentrated work on the final preparation of the manuscript. Finally, I acknowledge permission from Mr. William Scheide and the Bachhaus Eisenach to reproduce photographs of the Haussmann Bach portrait and the Bach goblet.

TONAL ALLEGORY IN THE VOCAL MUSIC OF J.S. BACH

CHAPTER ONE

Theology and

Tonal Allegory

in the Music

of J. S. Bach

In 1950, for the two-hundredth anniversary of Bach's death, Friedrich Smend published his highly influential *J. S. Bach bei seinem Namen gerufen* (Johann Sebastian Bach called by his name). Smend dealt here with one piece only, the *Canon Triplex a 6 voc.* that Bach holds out toward the viewer in the famous Haussmann painting (see Illus. 1). Smend, recognizing that this canon had symbolic significance, made extravagant and detailed claims for its meaning, most of which centered on its spelling of "BACH" in the number alphabet.[1] He saw numerology and symmetry as means by which Bach signed the extramusical content—both personal and theological—of his works.[2] Smend's title implied, further, that his abstract numerical findings provided a key to Bach's mind. Scholarship founded on the same, usually silent, premise continues unabated; countless Bach pieces have been subjected to numerological interpretations. The reader of this literature is dogged by doubts concerning the validity of the authors' methods and conclusions, and of the practical value of identifying numerical features that can never be discerned by a listener.

Number symbolism exemplifies what Manfred Bukofzer called the "unity of sensual and intellectual understanding" and of the audible and inaudible in baroque music.[3] Interest in such abstract issues seemed absurd to many aestheticians and philosophers of art in the nineteenth century, for whom the visual quality that made the work into a sign, its "appearance" as opposed to its "essence," was irrelevant to its value.[4] This dismissive attitude toward the abstract—toward allegory—

---

1. Friedrich Smend, *J. S. Bach bei seinem Namen gerufen* (Kassel, 1950).

2. Others who shared this view were Wilhelm Werker, *Studien über die Symmetrie im Bau der Fugen und die motivische Zusammengehörigkeit der Präludien und Fugen des Wohltemperierten Klaviers von J. S. Bach* (Leipzig, 1922); and Martin Jansen, "Bachs Zahlensymbolik, an seinen Passionen untersucht," *Bach-Jahrbuch* 34 (1937): 96–117.

3. In his studies of baroque allegory: Manfred Bukofzer, *Music in the Baroque Era* (New York, 1947), p. 369; "Allegory in Baroque Music," *Journal of the Warburg Institute* 3 (1939–1940), 1–21.

4. The nineteenth-century viewpoint is summarized in Walter Benjamin, *The Origin of German Tragic Drama*, trans. John Osborne (London, 1977), pp. 159–74.

ILLUS. 1.   J. S. Bach at age 62. Painting by Elias Gottlieb Haussmann, 1747. Reproduced by permission of William H. Scheide

has never been seriously challenged by Bach scholarship, which has tended to ignore the perennial dichotomy between the historical and the aesthetic approach to art. The result has often been the elevating of abstract historical features of the works to the level of essential qualities.

In 1955, however, one Bach lover raised a momentous outcry. Theodor Adorno felt that musicology had falsified the picture of Bach, had in effect called the composer by the wrong name. Adorno's article "Bach Defended Against His Devotees" began, "The view of Bach which prevails today in musicological circles corresponds to the role assigned to him by the stagnation and industriousness of a resurrected culture," and it concluded, "Perhaps the traditional Bach can indeed no longer be interpreted. If this is true, his heritage has passed on to composition, which is loyal to him in being disloyal; it calls his music by name in producing it anew."[5] Between the two passages lies a great deal of polemic concerning what

5. Theodor W. Adorno, "Bach Defended Against His Devotees," in *Prisms*, trans. Samuel Weber and Shierry Weber (Cambridge, Mass., 1981), pp. 135–46. Adorno ("Bach Defended," p. 145) makes the following comment: "Of course, there is also the possibility that the contradiction between the substance of Bach's compositions and the means for realizing it in sound, both those available at the time and those accumulated since, can no longer be resolved. In the light of this possibility, the much discussed 'abstractness' of sound in the *Musical Offering* and the *Art of the Fugue,* as works in which the choice of instruments is left open, acquires a new dimension. It is conceivable that the contradiction

Bach means to us, who he really was, how he must be performed and analyzed. Every aspect of our conception of the composer is provocatively and provokingly called into question. The article is severely antihistoricist, taking issue with the reduction of Bach's music to "formula and symmetry, the mere gesture of recognition." Musicologists, Adorno said, exalted "appearance" in Bach and ignored "essence." To Adorno, Bach's "essence" consisted in Enlightenment freedom, subjectivity, and autonomy displayed in the "dynamic" (modern, expressive) features of the music, while its "appearance" was made up of the "static" (archaic, abstract) qualities of the "old theological order." Adorno even maintained that the instruments available to Bach were inadequate to realize the advanced motivic and dynamic character of the music.

Between 1955 and 1969 Adorno changed his position significantly, no longer directly linking essence with the dynamic and appearance with the static. The "specific essence" of Bach consisted, rather, in the relation between the static and the dynamic aspects. Moreover, he no longer held that the appearance, the sonorous "surface," of the work had to reveal its dynamic qualities, as demonstrated by analysis.[6] This change perhaps stemmed in part from the conspicuous success of performances of Bach using period instruments. Adorno, then, came to admit that historicist and modern approaches to Bach can be combined. Nevertheless, his criticism that musicology overemphasizes the "static" in Bach's work remains as valid today as it was in 1955.

Bach scholars have largely ignored that criticism; indeed, in the three decades since Adorno first published his article, many of the tendencies he decried have amplified enormously. The music invites widely disparate approaches and techniques. Divergence between positivism and historicism on the one hand and aesthetics and interpretation on the other has, moreover, been a feature of Bach studies for several decades, encouraging specialization even within the former categories. Yet it is axiomatic that the works and their interpretation must always stand at the center of study, as simultaneously the source and the goal of all investigative activity. Their power and directness eclipse historicist commentary and al-

---

between music and sound-material—especially the inadequacy of the organ tone to the infinitely articulated structure—had already become visible at the time. If this were the case, Bach would have omitted the sound and left his most mature instrumental works waiting for the sound that would suit them." And Carl Dahlhaus ("Analytische Instrumentation: Bachs sechsstimmiges Ricercar in der Orchestrierung Anton Weberns," in *Bach Interpretationen*, ed. Martin Geck [Göttingen, 1969], pp. 197–206) concludes that "Webern's instrumentation [of Bach's six-part Ricercar] is therefore not to be taken as an expansion; what it makes palpable is, rather, that the idea of a truly adequate instrumental representation of the Ricercar exists in the no-man's-land between what in Bach's time was not yet possible and in ours is no longer so" (my translation). See also Chafe, "Allegorical Music," *Journal of Musicology*, 3 (1984): 342–44, n. 8.

6. Theodor W. Adorno, *Aesthetic Theory*, trans. C. Lenhardt, ed. Gretel Adorno and Rolf Tiedemann (London, 1984), p. 301. A sensitive handling of Adorno's views on the performance of Bach's music can be found in Laurence Dreyfus, "Early Music Defended Against Its Devotees: A Theory of Historical Performance in the Twentieth Century," *Musical Quarterly* 69 (1983): 297–322.

most call into question the necessity of interpretive mediation. Although baroque music is unalterably wedded to outside significance, it speaks compellingly to those who do not know—and in many cases do not wish to know—anything of what is signified, who respond solely to the organization of patterns in sound. Whether or not this purely musical attitude diminishes the work of art, as Hans-Georg Gadamer suggests, the music without its historical trappings undeniably remains a lasting expressive force.[7] The human need to understand the works historically, however, requires that we deal with the issue of how Bach can be at once an archconservative and the most advanced musical mind of the age, how he can embody simultaneously the spirit of the seventeenth-century baroque and that of the eighteenth-century Enlightenment. The historicist approach is wholly inadequate here: its ceaseless piling up of data only points up the distance between the age in which Bach lived and ours, perhaps documenting the miraculous fact that (great) art transcends its time but doing nothing to show how. It reminds us continually of what art is *not*.[8]

This study attempts to deal with the historical issues by focusing on a widely admired quality of Bach's work that is closely related to its enduring value: its fusion of the emotional and intellectual in music. Of the two—*sensus* and *ratio,* in the terms of Bach's time—the emotional may seem much the more self-sufficient and more fundamentally "Bach," for the "modern" view, which actually descends from Bach's own time, holds that the sensuous side of music has a fuller and more immediate impact than the intellectual.[9] Bach, however, seldom permitted the sensuous aspect to determine the course of his music, to anything like the extent that many of his contemporaries did in their compositions. Even the earliest Bach criticism recognized that this characteristic set Bach's works apart from the "easier" mode of his time.[10] He keeps *sensus* and *ratio* distinct. Their relationship might be described as contrapuntal, in that their differentiation itself underlies the many general assessments of Bach that marvel over their simultaneity. This paradoxical situation soon confronts anyone who engages with the music. Virtually all musicians and scholars agree that Bach's music develops its opposite sides extensively and seemingly independently.

7. See Hans-Georg Gadamer, *Truth and Method* (New York, 1975), p. 73.

8. This should not be taken as a polemic against the findings of historical scholarship or the necessity of understanding the distance that separates Bach and his world from the present age (see, for example, Wolfgang Hildesheimer, *Der ferne Bach* [Frankfurt, 1985], and Ulrich Siegele, *Bachs theologischer Formbegriff und das Duett F-Dur* [Neuhausen, 1978], p. 7). Because, however, the works bridge that distance with remarkable ease, their "historical" features must not be allowed to dominate our understanding or our researches.

9. Johann Mattheson's *Orchestre* treatises, especially *Das beschützte Orchestre* (Hamburg, 1717) and *Das forschende Orchestre* (Hamburg, 1721), frequently take up the subject of sense versus intellect; the subtitle of *Das forschende Orchestre, Sensus Vindicae,* indicates Mattheson's position.

10. See Hans T. David and Arthur Mendel, eds., *The Bach Reader* (New York, 1966), pp. 238–52, 254–57, 260–63, 266–68.

The dualism of emotion and intellect, like that of historical and universal and Adorno's static/dynamic and archaic/modern dichotomies, contains a sense of juxtaposition and balance.[11] These pairs are, in fact, only a few of a spectrum of dualisms in Bach's works ranging from obvious juxtapositions that are very deliberately employed allegorically, such as that between Italian and French styles, to the simultaneity of harmonic and contrapuntal thought that Adorno took to lie at the root of Bach's "duality of mind."[12] The very idea of abstraction as it is often applied to Bach's late works such as *The Art of Fugue* contains a form of dualism: technique and expression constitute the extremes of an allegorical continuum that is embedded in the work, and the separation of the two elements makes us more than ordinarily conscious of their simultaneity. An intense sense both of overlap and of opposition in the music creates a tremendous spiritual power that transcends, not merely the notes and their relationships as pure sound, but the expressive character of the work. As Adorno put it, Bach's "genius of meditation [evokes] an objective, comprehensive absolute."[13] Adorno's belief that Bach's music could not be adequately realized in his own time still seems true of the music's spiritual quality—which, of course, is not limited to the church music or, indeed, to any religious intent at all. This attitude, which is indebted to nineteenth-century aesthetics, stands in stark contrast to the historicist attempt to locate the spiritual character of Bach's work in abstract features. The divergence between the aesthetic and the historicist approach is probably sharper with respect to Bach's work than to that of any other composer.

The theological aspect of Bach's work is apparently a more difficult matter for the modern secular spirit to deal with than has usually been acknowledged. Too often scholars either dismiss it in a passing phrase—for example, calling it a "music of faith" without attempting to define that term—or simplistically reduce it to the terms of number symbolism. We have long since weathered the assault on Bach's spirituality that Friedrich Blume launched in the 1960s, and a new interest in theological features of Bach's work has arisen.[14] Blume's challenge, which is symptomatic of the modern secular viewpoint, has not, however, been answered any

11. Adorno, "Bach Defended," pp. 139–46.
12. Adorno, "Bach Defended," p. 138. Adorno's view that this quality allied Bach inextricably with the Enlightenment (as opposed to the "old theological order") raises doubts; its succeeds, however, in separating Bach spiritually from the picture that still survives whenever musicological commentary is dominated by the delineation of static, abstract elements in the music, which is quite often.
13. Adorno, "Bach Defended," p. 138.
14. Friedrich Blume, "Outlines of a New Picture of Bach," *Music and Letters* 44 (1963): 218. A selective list of literature between 1960 and 1986 emphasizing theological features of Bach's work can be found in Eric Chafe, reviews of Howard Cox, ed., *The Calov Bible of J. S. Bach* (Ann Arbor: UMI Research Press, 1985); Robin Leaver, ed., *J. S. Bach and Scripture: Glosses from the Calov Bible Commentary* (St. Louis: Concordia Publishing House, 1985); and Jaroslav Pelikan, *Bach among the Theologians* (Philadelphia: Fortress Press, 1986), in *Journal of the American Musicological Society* 40 (1987): 345, n. 8. For more recent literature see the bibliography of the present work.

more than Adorno's has. The rediscovery of the Bach Bible and the recent increase in research into historical theology relevant to Bach are important contributions to our understanding of Bach, but even more important is the question of the nature of religious experience in the early eighteenth century and how the music and the theology interacted in Bach's work. Beneath this topic lies the philosophical one of the role of allegory in baroque music. This study attempts to counter the sense that the spiritual quality of Bach's music can never descend from the elevated sphere of aesthetic speculation, or, worse, that it is mere empty panegyric. It suggests instead that the dualism so prominent in Bach's work is related to Bach's intense participation in a vision, essentially aesthetic, of a heteronomous rather than autonomous art, of—to quote Adorno again—"allegorical expression heightened to the utmost."[15] Any study of Bach's music that aims at the integration of theological and musical concerns must, then, accord a high place to the concept of baroque musical allegory.

Those musicians who have recognized the allegorical principle have generally understood it purely as the means whereby music, usually through musical figures, designates extramusical ideas. Manfred Bukofzer, for example, addressed the issue of musical allegory entirely in the terms of rhetoric, referring to the writings of Bach's predecessor in Leipzig, Johann Kuhnau. Kuhnau's view of composition was bound up with the idea of what he called "gute Raison [durch die Music]," meaning a logical correspondence between music and the world of ideas.[16] Kuhnau made clear that music composed in this manner employed a concept as intermediary in "aim[ing] at an analogy" with what was to be represented. Bukofzer then used Goethe's famous contrast between allegorical and symbolic art to develop a purely intellectual concept of baroque allegory and to contrast it with the expression of emotion in the music of the classical period.[17] Although many writers have described the shift between these two eras in terms of other general qualities such as

---

15. Adorno, "Bach Defended," p. 141.

16. Bukofzer, "Allegory," pp. 1–21; Johann Kuhnau, Preface to *Texte zur Leipziger Kirchen-Music* (Leipzig, 1710), reprinted in B. F. Richter, "Eine Abhandlung Joh. Kuhnau's," *Monatshefte für Musik-Geschichte* 34 (1902): 148–54; *Musicalische Vorstellung Einiger Biblische Historien* (Leipzig, 1720), in *Denkmäler deutscher Tonkunst* 4 (1901), ed. Karl Päsler, pp. 120–23.

17. "There is a great difference, whether the poet seeks the particular for the general or sees the general in the particular. From the first procedure arises allegory, where the particular serves only as an example of the general; the second procedure, however, is really the nature of poetry: it expresses something particular, without thinking of the general or pointing to it. . . . True symbolism is where the particular represents the more general, not as a dream or a shadow, but as a living momentary revealtion of the Inscrutable. . . . Allegory changes a phenomenon into a concept, a concept into an image, but in such a way that the concept is still limited and completely kept and held in the image and expressed by it, [while symbolism] changes the phenomenon into the idea, the idea into the image, in such a way that the idea remains always infinitely active and unapproachable in the image, and will remain inexpressible even though expressed in all languages." Cited in René Wellek, *A History of Modern Criticism, 1750–1950.* Vol. 1, *The Later Eighteenth Century* (Cambridge, 1955) p. 211; see also Gadamer, *Truth and Method,* pp. 68–70.

dramatic/nondramatic style or level of psychological complexity, Bach scholars have implicitly endorsed Bukofzer's distinction.[18]

One such view divides art types into those whose forms are taken from outside the field of art (allegory) and those whose forms are internal. In this view Bach's concept of form (*forma*) as split from content (*materia*) was allegorical, since its starting point was numerological: it spelled out theological concepts through the lengths and proportions of its sections.[19] The form is worked out first in numerical terms by analogy to God's creation of the universe with number, weight, and measure. The composition is then realized in stages that are conceived as motion from the universal (now meaning the word of God—i.e., isolated words of theological character—spelled according to the number alphabet) to the specific musical detail.[20] There is much to be said for taking Bach's music as the realization of a general concept—Goethe's "allegorical" art—but the attempt to lock that perception into such a detailed scheme and associate it with number symbolism remains highly speculative. In this endeavor and in related pastimes involving a search for what Adorno called "formula and symmetry" the distance between expression and significance is widened to a degree that, if it does nothing else, illustrates just how much the traffic will bear in this area. The major difficulty with such a conception, apart from the arbitrariness of the numerology, is its one-sided involvement with the static, permutational dimension of composition. The current vogue for number symbolism regularly approaches the limits of abstraction, routinely turning the work into a sign. Whether or not this process is securely documented as a major part of Bach's intent, its focus is overly narrow. In exalting the connections between music and rhetoric to the level of a method by which the meaning of the works can be read, it ignores the fact that Bach's contemporaries generally adopted a more flexible approach to rhetoric—as did Bach himself in the majority of the works.[21] Moreover, it sidesteps its own avowed concern with the relationship between musical and theological content in Bach's works.

18. Bukofzer, "Allegory," p. 20–21: "The counterblast to baroque music took precisely the form of the discovery how to express feelings *without the intervention of the intellect*. Music no longer *meant* this or that emotion; it *was* itself the immediate expression of that emotion. This transition from the notion 'it means' to that of 'it is' marks the transition from the baroque style to its successor, the classical-romantic style."

19. Siegele, *Bachs theologischer Formbegriff*, p. 7.

20. Siegele, *Bachs theologischer Formbegriff*, pp. 7–12.

21. See, for example, Johann Mattheson's treatment of the subject in *Der Volkommene Kapellmeister* (Hamburg, 1740), pp. 235–44. The pieces in which analyses of all kinds that are directed toward static qualities work best are primarily canons and shorter pieces of permutational character, such as the Sinfonia in F minor and the F major duet. As such it is questionable that they can be taken to illustrate Bach's overall conception of form. Nevertheless, there is a strong sense that such pieces do deal in concentrated form with an aspect of Bach's compositional thinking that pervades his work. See also Chafe, "Allegorical Music."

If the word of God was truly the starting point in Bach's conception of composition, musical scholarship should employ an interpretive method that was contemporary with Bach and that would have encompassed any existing number symbolism. Such a method was provided by Kuhnau, who explicitly linked allegory and hermeneutics in sacred composition. This approach to the question of meaning in religious art not only became associated with the music and its interpretation in Bach's own time but in the nineteenth century, through its link with romantic aesthetics, came to be allied with philosophy. Modern philosophical hermeneutics offers an ideal means by which to tackle the disparity between the historical and the universal in Bach's work.[22]

Kuhnau's approach was the practical one of the composer. Several of his predecessors and contemporaries, however, generalized and metaphysically oriented the analogy between music and theology. Their work supports the view of allegory as underlying the baroque musical style. That is, if music operates as a signifier it becomes more patterned; its surface mirrors the rationalism of its time. Countless distinctive features of baroque musical style—terraced dynamics and orchestration, figures, instrumental idioms, objective style and affective categories, key characteristics, hierarchical perceptions of tonality, sequences, even barlines, to name but a few—flow from the idea of a heteronomous art, from *oratio* rather than *harmonia* as the dominant principle of composition and the basis of aesthetics.[23]

In its profusion of referential elements the baroque musical style parallels the imitation of nature that dominated the arts from the sixteenth to the mid-eighteenth century.[24] This profusion seems to invite a search for allegorical meaning. The purpose of this study is not to insist that Bach's music can be appreciated only through an understanding of its background of baroque orthodox Lutheranism with Enlightenment influence. It is, rather, to articulate Bach's particular version of the allegorical vision that was shared by all the arts of the age. No one can say to what lengths Bach intended to carry musical allegory, and of course he was not thinking in extramusical terms every time he sat down to compose. As a believing Christian, however, who was very close to a Lutheran baroque metaphysical tradition in musical thought, he would have seen music, and the other arts, as having theological significance.[25] The Enlightenment no doubt weakened the ties between theology and music; still, Bach's music more than any other fulfills the ideals of this metaphysical tradition. It may, in fact, have been the very complexity of Bach's eighteenth-century language and of his particular harmonic-tonal genius that made

22. The basic work dealing with this subject is Gadamer's *Truth and Method.*
23. *Dichiaratione della lettera stampata nel quinto libro de suoi madrigali,* in *Scherzi musicali . . . raccolti da Giulio Cesare Monteverdi* (1607), reprinted in G. Francesco Malipiero, *Claudio Monteverdi* (Milan, 1929), pp. 83–84; trans. in Oliver Strunk, *Source Readings in Music History* (New York, 1950), pp. 411–12.
24. Wellek, *A History of Modern Criticism,* pp. 14–18.
25. This metaphysical tradition was largely a seventeenth-century phenomenon and was epitomized in the works of Andreas Werckmeister.

such an achievement possible. Kuhnau put forth a highly interesting allegorical concept of composition, yet his music does not embody this concept to nearly the extent that Bach's does. Bach was hardly alone, even in the mid-eighteenth century, in incorporating theology into his music, but he is unique in the complexity of the interaction between music and theology and in its susceptibility to analysis.

Although the link with a seventeenth-century view of art and theology will for many lend support to the view of Bach as a traditionalist, his concern with allegory does not in fact create any conflict between archaic and modern styles in his music. The *stile antico,* the galant style, and the conservative seventeenth-century manner combine harmoniously with many other techniques on Bach's expressive palette. It is meaningless to ask whether Bach is "really" traditional, modern, expressive, rationalistic, or whatever: he transcends such narrow categories.[26]

The dualism of expression and convention in Bach's work demands that allegory be conceived of philosophically, as a form of expression, rather than mechanically, as a mode of designation. The unquestioning, mechanical view of allegory—the approach to allegory that was denigrated by nineteenth-century aesthetics—leads to an exclusive focus on abstract elements of Bach's music. The philosophical approach instead aims at an understanding of just what the use of allegory meant to Bach. This method arrives inevitably at the notion of a theological aesthetics—that is, an extensive analogical relationship between art and religion—as a fundamental aspect of the Lutheran baroque tradition.

Walter Benjamin's study of German tragic drama in the seventeenth century focuses on allegory as its main expressive device.[27] Benjamin rehabilitated allegory within the framework of modern aesthetics and thereby demonstrated how much of the religious character of nineteenth-century aesthetics derived from an earlier period. As Gadamer put it, we can now recognize the dogmatic element in the late eighteenth- and early nineteenth-century "aesthetics of experience."[28] Through its influence on modern philosophical hermeneutics Benjamin's work has made possible a closer union of the historical and aesthetic approaches to art. Benjamin did not write directly on either Bach or baroque music, but his ideas lie behind those of Adorno, especially Adorno's idea of "allegorical expression."

Study of the character of Bach's Lutheranism as it is manifested in his church music may in fact be the easiest route to the universal qualities of his work, what Benjamin called the "truth content."[29] Granted, concepts such as truth content,

---

26. And just as Bach's style cannot be defined by any one of these ideas, his compositional process cannot be locked into either the kind of sequence proposed by Siegele (*Bach's theologischer Formbegriff*) or the written-down stages uncovered by modern source studies (the latter question has been considered in Chafe, "J. S. Bach's *St. Matthew Passion*"). The two are not incompatible, of course, but taken separately neither qualifies as a description of composition, either in conception or practice.

27. Benjamin, *The Origin,* pp. 159–235.

28. Gadamer, *Truth and Method,* p. 73.

29. Benjamin, *The Origin,* p. 182.

appearance/essence, and symbolic art could not have been part of any seventeenth- or early eighteenth-century aesthetics. Bach's time may seem to demand the more rationalistic character of allegory that Benjamin called a "corrective to art."[30] Such terms do, however, have the virtue of suggesting that rationalistic baroque allegory has an aesthetic side. Although we may not make explicit use of these admittedly rarefied and largely evaluative aesthetic terms, we can still recognize that the "dichotomy of sound and script" which Benjamin showed to be central to the philosophical understanding of allegory is as relevant to Bach's work as it is to baroque literature.[31]

Allegory and Musical Hermeneutics

The period of Lutheran orthodoxy, with its need to interpret Scripture in accordance with established dogmatic principles, led to the emergence of hermeneutics as a systematic study which brought to the fore the issue of the role of reason versus that of faith, revelation, and the Spirit. As we have seen, some musicians of the Lutheran tradition perceived a close analogy between music and this developing study of hermeneutics. We can in fact approach the meaning of tonal allegory for Bach by outlining the role of allegory, first in the metaphysical tradition of music theory that coincides with the period of Lutheran orthodoxy, and then in Luther's hermeneutics. This logical rather than chronological order is appropriate for Bach, since Bach's particular form of musical hermeneutics involved in several respects an identification with Luther's principles that was probably intuitive but nevertheless went beyond anything that was provided for him in the metaphysical tradition. That is, Bach's starting point as a composer was the conception of music as *oratio,* but out of the specific character of musical allegory in the Lutheran tradition he developed his own musicotheological devices. Bach's theological library, with its unusual emphasis on Luther's writings, attests to his interest in Luther's thought, but the full extent of that interest is documented only in the works themselves.[32]

Bach's use of Luther's theology in his development of musical devices provides us with the closest analogy of aesthetics we have from the period. An age of word-dominated music and a Lutheran metaphysical tradition of music theory would inevitably have connected music with hermeneutics, even in the area of composition. Kuhnau's 1709–1710 preface to a cycle of Leipzig church cantatas, without unfolding a systematic alignment of music with hermeneutics made clear the importance

---

30. Benjamin, *The Origin,* p. 176.
31. Benjamin, *The Origin,* pp. 174–77. Terry Eagleton (*Walter Benjamin* [London, 1981], pp. 3–24), for example, shows how the sound/script rupture operated in English literature (especially the novel) from Milton, Bunyan, and Defoe to Stern.
32. See Leaver, "Bach und die Lutherschriften."

of hermeneutics for the church composer.[33] Kuhnau speaks of the *sensus, scopus,* and *pondus* of the text and uses such expressions as "in sensu proprio" (in the literal sense) and "in sensu figurato" (in the figurative sense). The procedure that Kuhnau calls "gute Raison durch die Music" takes as its basis the manifold shades of meaning brought out by comparing various translations of Scripture. Its outcomes in composition range from dramatic devices of great immediacy to highly abstract procedures that Kuhnau could justify only as stimulating the composer's powers of invention and as speaking to those with "inquiring minds."[34]

Many of Kuhnau's allegorical devices as outlined both in the preface to the cantatas and that to his *Biblical Histories* involve tonal-harmonic procedures—chromatic tones, modulation, and the like—that play expressive as well as structural roles.[35] Kuhnau was aware that modulation could affect the listener in subtle, less than conscious ways; for example, he describes his use of shifting keys to represent Laban's deceit, and he wrote of another composer who, for programmatic purposes, had deliberately ended his sonata with a weakening of the tonic.[36] Clearly, Kuhnau applied a form of tonal hermeneutic to his understanding of music.

In the appendix to his *Musicae mathematicae* Andreas Werckmeister took a more speculative approach to the use of hermeneutics to join theology and music.[37] Medieval hermeneutics identified four senses of Scripture: the literal/historical, the allegorical, the tropological or moral, and the anagogic or eschatological. Werckmeister entitled his appendix "Von der Allegorischen und der Moralischen Music" (On allegorical and moral music), to indicate that at the deepest level musical meaning is theological and that it is to be uncovered by a practice analogous to hermeneutics. (Compare the statement by Martin Opitz, the founder of modern German poetry, that poetry originated as a "hidden theology.")[38] Werckmeister's two hermeneutic senses have clear correlates in Lutheran church music, including that of Bach: the allegorical sense is seen in the focus on the church and on institutional

---

33. Kuhnau's preface documents his pragmatic perspective on the setting of sacred texts; it is reprinted in Richter, "Eine Abhandlung." See commentaries on Kuhnau's Preface in Arnold Schmitz, *Die Bildlichkeit der wortgebundenen Musik Johann Sebastian Bachs. Neue Studien zur Musikwissenschaft I* (Mainz, 1950), pp. 26–28, and Chafe, "Key Structure," p. 39–40, 51–52.

34. Kuhnau, reprinted in Richter, "Eine Abhandlung," p. 153.

35. Kuhnau, reprinted in Richter, "Eine Abhandlung"; Chafe, "Key Structure," pp. 39–40.

36. Kuhnau, preface to *Biblische Historien,* p. 123. Kuhnau describes the sonata as dealing with an incomplete recovery from illness and specified as such by its composer. He remarks, "Allein so viel ich daraus urtheilen konte, so waren Worte und Noten mit guter *Raison* gesetzet. Die Sonata gieng aus dem *D.moll.* Und in der *Gique* liesse sich immer die *Modulation* in dem *G.mol* hören. Wenn nun endlich das *Final* wider in das *D.* gemacht wurde, so wolte das Ohr noch nicht *Satisfaction* haben, und hätte lieber die Schluss-*Cadence* im G. gehöret."

37. Andreas Werckmeister, *Musicae mathematicae hodegus curiosus* (Frankfurt and Leipzig, 1686), pp. 141–54.

38. Martin Opitz, *Buch von der Deutschen Poeterey* (Brieg, 1624), ed. Cornelius Sommer (Stuttgart, 1970), p. 12.

and doctrinal concerns, and the tropological sense in the focus on the individual and the personal crisis of faith.[39]

Werckmeister's treatment also holds more than a suggestion of the sort of fundamental artistic dualism we discussed above. He finds the key to musical significance in the basic tonal material, outlining many correspondences between the notes of the harmonic series and events and objects, both natural or historic and cosmic-theological. Prominent among these correspondences is an allegorical scheme that covers salvation history, from the Lutheran "hidden God" signified by the fundamental tone, through the Creation (the lowest octave), the Old Testament period with the prefiguring of Christ (the next octave, divided by the fifth), the New Testament period (the third octave) with Christ (major thirds signifying his divine and minor thirds his human aspects), the Trinity (the major triad), and the necessity of dissonance in the earthly life (the out-of-tune seventh partial), to anticipation of the life to come (the clarino octave). In keeping with the pluralistic attitude of the old hermeneutic tradition, none of these meanings is fixed and immutable. In some cases, however—above all, that of the harmonic triad as the symbol of the Trinity—the theological association was overwhelmingly compelling, seeming to justify the extensive analogy between music and theology.

Both Werckmeister's speculative approach and Kuhnau's pragmatic program for allegorical composition affirm a kind of thought we may call the allegorical mentality. This bent exists, of course, in all ages and cultures, but in very few is it more widespread than in the Lutheran baroque of the seventeenth and early eighteenth centuries. From this perspective we will be justified in taking the tonal patterns we find in Bach's work to indicate Bach's perception—whether intuitive or studied does not matter—of what, following the old tradition, we can call the *scopus* of his texts. Scopus, named by Kuhnau as one of the aspects of textual interpretation the church composer must understand, serves as a central concept of the tradition to which Bach belongs, the so-called precritical hermeneutics of the sixteenth to the eighteenth century.[40] Scopus refers to the author's deep purposes or "intention," embracing not merely the text's literal meaning (the sensus) but also its broader theological significance (presumably what Kuhnau means by *pondus*). This latter includes, for the modern historian, the network of beliefs under which the text was created and to which it refers.

---

39. Elke Axmacher ("Bachs Kantatentexte in auslegungsgeschichtlicher Sicht," in Petzoldt, ed., *Bach als Ausleger der Bibel*, pp. 15–32) indicates that interpretation according to the four senses of Scripture remained alive in Protestant hermeneutics into Bach's time and can be observed in his texts; at the same time one of the characteristic changes that took place in such poetry in Bach's time was the emancipation from the four senses (p. 17).

40. Minear ("J. S. Bach and J. A. Ernesti") argues for Bach's adherence to the older hermeneutics in contrast to the position of his younger colleague, the "founder of enlightenment hermeneutics," Ernesti, and suggests that this fundamental difference in outlook lay behind their confrontation. See Hans W. Frei, *The Eclipse of Biblical Narrative* (New Haven, 1974), pp. 17–50, for a survey of precritical hermeneutics; on Kuhnau's use of the term *scopus*, see Schmitz, *Die Bildlichkeit*, pp. 26–28.

The first principle of Lutheran hermeneutics was a belief in the unity of the Old and New Testaments as the historical narrative of God's plan of salvation and the revelation of the fulfillment of his design in the New Testament; Christ was thus the subject of the entire Scriptures. Exegetical techniques such as figural interpretation and the characteristically Lutheran "analogy of faith" clarified these doctrines—essentially, by relating them to basic simplifying patterns in which antithesis constituted a major element—so that not only obscure passages but even conflicting ones were made to harmonize under the fundamental saving truths of the New Testament.[41] The meditative goal of church music replicated that of such exegesis: to unite the outer (literal/historical) and the inner (spiritual) aspects of any text. Thus the narrative of redemption in the Old and New Testaments was seen as analogous to the struggle between flesh (or sin, as exemplified in the old, fallen man, Adam) and spirit (the new, risen man, Christ) within the modern Christian. This analogy expresses the relationship between the individual and the vast unity of scriptural history, between the overarching and continuing scale of great historical epochs and the internal dynamic of faith. As Luther put it in comparing the destruction and rebuilding of Jerusalem to the roles of Law and Gospel in the individual:

> Faith must be built up on the basis of history, and we ought to stay with it alone and not so easily slip into allegories, unless by way of metaphor we apply them to other things in accordance with the method [analogy] of faith. So here Jerusalem can allegorically be called our conscience, which has been taken and laid waste by the terror of the Law and then set free out of the remnant and the sprouts, and the restored conscience is saved by the Word of the Gospel, through which we grow up into mature manhood by the knowledge of God (cf. Eph. 4:13). Such allegory must be used in accordance with the Word of the Law and the Gospel, and this is the explanation of different matters by the same Spirit. . . . This is the summary of Scripture: It is the work of the Law to humble according to history, externally and internally, physically and spiritually. It is the work of the Gospel to console, externally and internally, physically and spiritually. What our predecessors have experienced according to history externally and physically, this we experience according to our own history internally and spiritually.[42]

Luther called this principle for understanding the Scriptures the "analogy of faith."[43] It bridged the gap between the intellectual/historical and the personal,

---

41. Heinrich Bornkamm, *Luther and the Old Testament*, trans. Eric W. Gritsch and Ruth C. Gritsch, ed. Victor I. Gruhn (Philadelphia, 1974), and Jaroslav Pelikan, *Luther the Expositor: Introduction to the Reformer's Exegetical Writings*, companion volume to *Luther's Works* (St. Louis, 1959), give excellent accounts in English of Luther's hermeneutic principles.

42. Martin Luther, *Lectures on Isaiah, Chapters 1–39*, trans. Herbert J. A. Bouman, vol. 16 of *Luther's Works*, ed. Jaroslav Pelikan (St. Louis, 1969), p. 327.

43. Frei, *Eclipse*, p. 39; Bornkamm, *Luther and the Old Testament*, pp. 92–94; Chafe, "Luther's 'Analogy of Faith.' "

faith-giving aspects of Scripture. The Christocentrism of Scripture displays the downward motion of tribulation, Law, and death followed by its opposite, growing faith through Christ and the Gospel—the pattern to Christ's incarnation, death, and burial followed by his resurrection and ascension. Any number of scriptural accounts could be interpreted as displaying this sequence.

It was Luther's great achievement to unite the so-called spiritual senses of Scripture—the allegorical, tropological, and eschatological—with the literal/historical in a new Christocentrism. He likened the individual before faith to the individual of the Old Testament; Christ's coming to Israel and the church parallels his coming to the individual in faith and, ultimately, as judge. As Luther never tired of stating, the conflict between the Law as flesh and the Gospel as spirit was not merely historical. The contemporary Christian would still suffer and struggle under the Law until he was ready to receive Christ and the Gospel, to exchange his life of active righteousness of the Law and good works for the passive righteousness of grace and faith.[44] Historical narrative is thus infused with the personal and contemporary, and internal religious struggle is simultaneously given a suprapersonal, universal dimension.

These ideas are particularly valuable for the interpretation of many Bach cantatas, as we will see in Chapter 4 in relation to the "Actus Tragicus." In a general sense the scopus of virtually any Bach sacred text is faith, and it often happens that the tonal plan allegorizes this inner, spiritual side as a hidden device under the external, musical forms which can be said to represent the doctrinal aspect of the text.

Luther based this theology on scriptural exegesis and commentary. Allegory, not in the traditional but in a deeper sense, played a fundamental role. Luther interpreted antithesis in the Scriptures, in passages such as "The spirit is willing but the flesh is weak" (Matt. 26:41) and "An alien work is done by him so that he might effect his proper work" (Isa. 28:31), as the theology of the cross. Joy was "hidden" in tribulation, life in death, Gospel in Law, and the like. Although Luther opposed the widespread use of allegorical interpretation, he nevertheless called the prevalence of figurative language in Scripture a manifestation of "God's allegorical work," the cross.[45]

The theology of the cross or "theology of faith" was for Luther the only true theology. He often spoke of faith as dynamic, in the initial process of reception and recognition of faith and in the individual's later experience of faith. Luther's theology emphasized first of all the necessity of tribulation and acknowledgement of sin

---

44. Martin Luther, "Two Kinds of Righteousness" (ca. 1519), trans. Lowell J. Satre, vol. 31 of *Luther's Works*, ed. Harold J. Grimm (Philadelphia, 1957), pp. 297–306; here Luther calls the two kinds "alien" and "proper" righteousness, but in his *Commentary on St. Paul's Epistle to the Galatians*, rev. and ed. Philip S. Watson (London, 1953) he refers to them as "active" and "passive."

45. See Martin Luther, *Early Theological Works*, ed. and trans. James Atkinson (Philadelphia, 1962), pp. 233–34; Walther von Loewenich, *Luther's Theology of the Cross*, trans. Herbert J. A. Bouman (Minneapolis, 1976), p. 128.

in conjunction with "faith in opposition to experience," yet it also recognized that faith could create in the individual "hidden possessions" such as joy and comfort. Luther spoke of the "hiddenness" of faith and of Christian life under the cross; of the "hidden" God, who "dwells in darkness," who cannot be apprehended directly, who is "greater than His word," and even of the "hidden" church of Christ.[46] In a word, Lutheran theology is nothing if not allegorical. This quality has two facets: the simpler designative aspect, and the deeper, primary, expressive one. The latter embodies an all-pervasive sense of inverted or hidden significance. It expresses the meaning of life, unifying and giving focus to the fragmented surface of designative allegory. These two facets, the designative and the expressive, can be seen to parallel the doctrinal and personal sides of theology as well as the objective or technical and subjective or expressive sides of affect.

Bach's tonal planning bears a conceptual relationship to Luther's hermeneutic principles.[47] A pattern of tonal catabasis (descent through the circle of fifths, modulation in the direction of increasing flats) followed by anabasis (ascent; modulation toward increasing sharps) often has a unifying effect on the allegorical detail similar to that of Luther's "analogy of faith" on designative allegory. Bach probably developed the pattern intuitively, rather than as a studied feature of his musical Lutheranism. Nevertheless, indications can be found that Bach fully understood the connection to theology. Artists of the baroque period had means of expressing basic relationships between art and transcendent meaning even if the writers on music, having no aesthetics as we understand it, did not. In literature one such means was the poetic epigram. Making extensive use of paradox, conceit, antithesis, and the like, it compressed fundamental concepts into concentrated patterns.[48] The nearest equivalent in Bach's oeuvre is the allegorical canon, that is, the canon whose compositional enigma is bound up with a "metaphysical" inscription and whose musical procedures represent a microcosm of the allegorical devices of baroque musical style.

Bach headed two canons with the word *Symbolum*. At the most literal level the word identified the inscriptions by means of which the musical puzzles were to be resolved, but of course Bach also intended an echo of the wider use of the word in Lutheranism.[49] Both inscriptions are theological. The first, *In Fine videbitur cujus toni. Symbolum. Omnia tunc bona, clausula quando bona est* (At the end you will see the

46. Von Loewenich, *Luther's Theology of the Cross*, pp. 15–17, 21, 36, 77, 114–17; Paul Althaus, *The Theology of Martin Luther*, trans. Robert C. Schulz (Philadelphia, 1966), pp. 30, 278.

47. Chafe, "Luther's 'Analogy of Faith,'" pp. 98–101.

48. On the epigrammatic tradition see Josef Schmidt, Introduction to Angelus Silesius, *The Cherubinic Wanderer*, trans. Maria Shrady (Mahwah, N.J., 1986), pp. 11–33. As Schmidt indicates, in Lutheran Germany collections of seemingly antithetical passages were published under the term *paradoxa* ("God wills that all men should be saved" [1 Tim. 2:1] versus "Few are chosen" [Matt. 20:16]); these were intended to "instruct and familiarize the reader with basic concepts of faith in highly condensed form" (p. 14).

49. See Chafe, "Allegorical Music," pp. 347–56.

mode. Symbol. All's well that ends well), is a general expression of Lutheran eschatology. The second reads *Symbolum. Christus Coronabit Crucigeros* (Symbol. Christ will crown the crossbearers). One of the books in Bach's library, Heinrich Müller's *Apostolische Schluss-Kette* (1687), bears a portrait of its author holding the motto "Crux Christi nostra Gloria"; in a medallion below appears the scriptural quotation "Als die Traurigen aber allezeit frölich," headed "Symb[olum]" and identified as "2 Cor. 6 v. 10."[50] As we saw, Luther had described such antitheses in biblical phrases as signifying the theology of the cross, whose basis was the inverted nature of God's revelation. The cross represents both death and resurrection, a life of suffering and one of fulfillment (hence the future tenses of Bach's inscriptions). For Müller and for Bach, as for countless others, the *Symbolum* expresses the central doctrine of Christian life and of Lutheran hermeneutics: faith in the cross of Christ as the foundation of all hope for salvation.

Behind the designation of Müller's scriptural quotation as a symbol lies the idea that it summarizes the meaning of Scripture, that is, its Christocentrism, its interpretation according to the analogy of faith. The musicohermeneutic equivalent of Müller's *Symbolum,* the "Christus Coronabit Crucigeros" canon utilizes a large body of musical devices to point to the world of interrelated theological ideas that lies behind the *Symbolum* (Ex. 1). These techniques, which of course belong to the hermeneutic of Bach's work as a whole, are: (1) inversion; (2) descent juxtaposed with ascent; (3) chromaticism juxtaposed with diatonicism; (4) major/minor and sharp/flat antitheses; (5) tritonal distance between the sharp and flat chordal extremes; (6) notation of only sharp accidentals; (7) reservation of sense of key until the end; (8) notation of only the descending half of the canon, leaving the remainder to be derived via the *Symbolum*; (9) the perpetual, circling effect; (10) the diatonic, tonally secure ground bass (often designated *fundamentum* at the time); and (11) the symbolism of the capital letter *C,* which appears three times in the inscription.

Only the inscription survives for the other *Symbolum* canon. That inscription, however, makes clear that the lost music was a modulating canon, that is, one whose key becomes definite only at the end.[51] Tonality is often difficult to pin down in the midst of musical events, and Bach's use of a sequence of keys that leaves the final key in doubt until the end might be seen as an allegory of Luther's idea that faith is often hidden from the individual. The ascending/descending primary tonal pattern of the "Christus Coronabit Crucigeros" canon echoes Luther's analogy of faith. In "In Fine videbitur cujus toni," by contrast, Bach may have employed a pattern he used in a number of cantatas to suggest the gradual growth of faith, that of tonal anabasis ending in a new key, usually one higher along the circle of fifths.

50. Leaver, *Bach's Theological Library,* p. 110.

51. A canon of this type is discussed in connection with Bach's inscription in Chafe, "Allegorical Music," pp. 353–54.

EXAMPLE 1.   *Canone Sopr'il Soggetto. Symbolum.* "Christus Coronabit Crucigeros"

The idea of seeking out meaning is itself specified in another of his canons, in the theological inscription "Quaerendo invenietis" (Seek and ye shall find).[52] The intellectual character of the features discussed above differs in both spirit and intent from anything that would have been called a symbol in the nineteenth century. Yet the primary aesthetic goal of a symbol is to evoke the desire for unity, and the degree of concentration and overlap of the details, and the simultaneity of the antithetical ideas in the work, evoke this desire just as unmistakably as it does a sense of the impossibility of attaining such a union by the fragmented means of rationality.

52. This "Canon a2" is from the *Musical Offering*.

The idea of division healed inheres in the theological use of the word *symbol* in the baroque period. Most familiar was the idea of symbol as creed, for example, the *Symbolum Nicenum* or *Credo*. Divine meaning was contained in Scripture, the object of faith, from which the creeds were drawn to summarize the basic articles of belief. Originally meaning a divided token (as a sign of membership), by the seventeenth and early eighteenth centuries the word *symbol* had come to signify an expression of divine meaning, which was of necessity split from the object that bore the meaning. It was generally defined as we would define *allegory*, that is, to refer to the kind of meaning that is indicated in or by the object or work, as opposed to the more recent usage of meaning embodied in and inseparable from the work itself.[53] In other words, it indicated heteronomous rather than autonomous art. Still, through the theological symbol that sense of dividedness was overcome, just as in the creed the believer, in grace through faith, transcends the present world. In the *Symbola* Bach allegorizes this transcendence. He retains to the full the dominance of antithesis—the clearest possible statement that the exaggeratedly visual and abstract qualities in music are signs for something that does not exist in the present life, are reminders of the theological finiteness of the rationalistic allegorical style.[54] Bach's use of the word *Symbolum,* then, suggests a metaphoric, aesthetic dimension to his canon writing, permitting us to take the canons as statements about the nature of meaning and the relationship between art and theology. A number of the Bach canons tend, in fact, to make connections between basic aspects of the tonal material of music—the triad, diatonicism, chromaticism, modulation, and enharmonicism—and a broader sense of theological meaning.[55] No matter what the inscription, however, all the canons are based on antithesis: inversion, contrary motion, retrograde, major/minor and sharp/flat contrasts, and the like. Subjects such as mi contra fa, "concordia discors," cross/crown, and beginning/ending emphasize the idea of the theology of the cross; they fit the dialectical view of art. One precept of Lutheran hermeneutics, the *analogia scripturae sacrae* (the part interpreted in the light of the whole), suggests the view of the *Symbola* of Müller and Bach as affirmations of Lutheran theology, in the form of compressed antithetical statements—even, in the case of the canons, as statements about fundamental qualities of art as well. In the next chapter we will attempt, by applying hermeneutics to the so-called Bach goblet—another symbolic object relating to tonality—to explore these connections in greater detail.

A running theme of the present study will be the notion of tonality as the level of allegory that represents stages of the inner, spiritual life. The concept was intro-

---

53. See Arnold Schering, "Bach und das Symbol. 3. Studie: Psychologische Grundlegung des Symbolbegriffs aus Christian Wolffs *Psychologia empirica," Bach-Jahrbuch* 34 (1937): 89.

54. Adorno ("Bach Defended," p. 138), in discussing the power of Bach's music to evoke an "objective, comprehensive absolute," makes the remark that "this absolute is evoked, asserted, postulated precisely because and only inasmuch as it is not present in physical experience."

55. Chafe, "Allegorical Music."

duced above with the mention of the tonal plan of catabasis followed by anabasis. In order to show how the scale of that tonal pattern expands according to that of the work, it may be amplified briefly here through reference to the *St. Matthew Passion*. In Part One of that work, Bach makes prominent modulations to deep flats (especially F minor) that are triggered by Jesus' predictions of Judas's betrayal and Peter's denial. The second of these expands to the events at Gethsemane, centered, of course, on Jesus' spiritual anguish in anticipation of the crucifixion. In both cases extended modulation back to sharps (E major in particular) aligns with events that have potentially redemptive meaning. Through prolonged tonal anabasis Bach moves through nearly the entire tonal range of the *Passion*—four flats to four sharps. The narrative of events leading to the close of Part One does not merely allegorize the change from Christ's torment before the Father in Gethsemane to his acceptance of the "cup" and the subsequent outbreak of his capture. It deals simultaneously with the dynamic of redemption at another level, that of the powerful impact of personal guilt ("Was ist die Ursach," in F minor) followed by an increasingly positive attitude that concludes with a fuller understanding of the meaning of the Passion and its potential value for man ("O Mensch, bewein," in E major). This pattern, which involves a deeper interpretation of "O Mensch" than the one usually derived from its first line alone, might be called the tropological sense of the *Passion*—and it is represented by Bach's tonal design.

Inner and Outer Structures

The idea that Bach's church music deals with both faith and dogma is generally accepted; but the idea that Bach recognized the dualism of internal and external and deliberately allegorized it is not widely accepted, or perhaps acceptable, to most. Musical scholarship has not widely adopted the concept of systematically differentiated levels of meaning. The Schenkerians discuss levels of musical structure, but they are not concerned directly with aesthetic issues and they do not deal with either the question of conscious intent or the possibility that the levels can serve allegorical purposes. Gustav René Hocke, among others, does argue convincingly for a "depth aesthetics" in analogy with depth psychology, and he has done much to base it historically and conceptually in the art of the sixteenth and seventeenth centuries.[56]

The issue is whether Bach distinguished—whether intuitively or self-consciously does not matter—intrinsic and extrinsic aspects of his work and intentionally differentiated them. This notion is less "modern" than it appears. Some Schenkerian theorists, seeking antecedents of the master's ideas, have seen in Christoph Bernhard's *stylus gravis* and *stylus luxurians* categories the distinction between a

56. Gustav René Hocke, *Manierismus in der Literatur* (Hamburg, 1959), p. 10 and passim; see also *Die Welt als Labyrinth* (Hamburg, 1977).

deeper tonal-contrapuntal level and a surface level.[57] And already in 1592 Lodovico Zacconi spoke of intrinsic and extrinsic "effects" of music, meaning the conceptual differentiation of the harmonic, contrapuntal design of the work according to the *ars perfecta* of the high Renaissance from the performance graces of the late sixteenth century.[58] Zacconi believed the *ars perfecta* had attained its peak in the generation before his own and that the composers of his day had only to add ornaments to the perfect style.

Zacconi's formulation represents simultaneously the last phase of Renaissance sensualism and the beginning of the fragmented, allegorical, and rationalistic character of baroque music. It belongs, more firmly than has been realized, with the first discussions of style, affect, figures, and the like as objective categories. Athanasius Kircher gave these categories their quintessentially baroque form in his *stylus expressus,* which he opposed to *stylus impressus,* or the Renaissance view of style, according to which distinctions were drawn on the basis of personal and individual characteristics rather than clearly separated musical styles.[59] Zacconi's division of musical effects, while it does not reveal the baroque passion for classification, goes beyond Renaissance theorists' tendency to locate the climax of musical achievement in their own day. For Zacconi the written style had ceased to develop; the "improvements" were incapable of notation, improvised and variable from performance to performance, while the notation, like the intrinsic style, remained frozen in its objective purity and perfection. In addition, Zacconi's terms foreshadow the baroque *stile antico/stile moderno* division and anticipate the kind of aesthetic dualism Adorno perceived in Bach.

Although Zacconi's terms, unlike Adorno's, do not bear the weight of the traditions of aesthetic philosophy, they may be taken as meaningful historico-aesthetic

57. Christoph Bernhard, "Tractatus compositionis augmentatus, MS treatise, reprinted in Joseph Müller-Blattau, *Die Kompositionslehre Heinrich Schützens in der Fassung seines Schülers Christoph Bernhard* (Kassel, 1963), pp. 42–43; Helmut Federhofer, *Beiträge zur musikalischen Gestaltanalyse* (Graz, 1956), pp. 61–77.

58. Lodovico Zacconi, *Prattica di Musica,* vol. 1 (Venice 1592), fol. 8–9.

59. See Athanasius Kircher, *Musurgia Universalis* (Rome, 1650), p. 581, on the distinction between *stylus expressus* and *stylus impressus.* Also Erich Katz, *Die musikalischen Stilbegriffe des 17. Jahrhunderts* (Freiburg, 1926); Edward Lippman, "Stil," in *Die Musik in Geschichte und Gegenwart,* cols. 1302–50. The familiar categories into which Kircher divides the *stylus expressus* are found throughout the *Musurgia* (see pp. 243, 309, 543–44, 581, 614, etc.). Cf. Giuseffi Zarlino's well-known statement, "Stile non si puo insegnare, perche viene dalla Natura" (*Sopplimenti Musicali* [Venice, 1588], p. 309). A few writers, notably Pietro Pontio (*Ragionamento di Musica* [Parma, 1588], facsimile ed., ed. S. Clerycx, [Kassel, 1959], and Thomas Morley (*A plaine and easie introduction to practical musicke* [London, 1597], facsimile ed. [London, 1937]), begin to speak for the first time in the late sixteenth century of objective style categories. But the traditional view of Zacconi's position is that he represents the *stylus impressus* (cf. Katz's interpretation of the passage from the *Prattica di Musica,* pt. 2, in which Zacconi discusses the styles of several Renaissance musicians [Katz, *Die musikalischen Stilbegriffe,* p. 17]), and Claude Palisca so characterizes him: "the apogee of sensualism in musical theory and criticism" (Palisca, "The Beginnings of Baroque Music: Its Roots in Sixteenth-Century Theory and Polemics," Ph.D. diss., Harvard University, 1953).

categories for the description of baroque music. Unlike earlier styles, the baroque—in a highly suggestive parallel with philosophy—developed a feeling for the split between the external, material sides of art and the internal, spiritual, and expressive sides. Renaissance art predicated the unity of inner and outer structures; architecture, for example, numerically reconciled *ratio* or abstract proportion, reflecting the divine harmony, with *sensus* or perspective.[60] The baroque intensified the concern with the relationship of *sensus* and *ratio* but saw it as the split between inner perception and outer or objective reality. This view went some way toward overturning the conviction that the intrinsic aspect of music represents, or at least aspires to, a higher, eternal, unchanging level. The recognition of a split soon led to the baroque emphasis on *sensus* as internal, subjective, and *ratio* as external. From that point it was a relatively short step to the complete reversal: *sensus* as the intrinsic aspect.

Perfection was no longer, it seemed, an attainable goal of art, and baroque art readily acknowledged its imperfection in countless ways. Just intonation was abandoned even as a theoretical goal, and harmonic purity yielded to distorting expressive devices. Moreover, there almost seems to have been resistance to the inevitable association of the full range of major and minor keys with the concept of the perfect, closed circle. At first the word *circle* appears more as the key, or Ariadne's thread, to a practical method of modulation then as a full-blown theoretical concept, and until well into the seventeenth century many of the tempered intervals seem to be viewed as necessary evils, providing us, in Werckmeister's words, with a "mirror and representation of our mortality and imperfection in this life."[61] The first presentation of the circle in print recognizes "difficult" and "unusable" keys, as well as tonal "extremes" that still fall short of being enharmonically equivalent.[62]

Despite rapid alterations in these perceptions—for example, Johann David Heinichen's 1728 revision of his 1711 book—the notion of difficult and imperfect keys remained an important part of baroque theory, not as a sign of failure to rationalize the maze of keys but as an inevitable consequence of the sense of compromise the circle involved. Only with the generation of Mattheson and Heinichen is *sensus* finally elevated above *ratio* and the circle of keys becomes a fully articulated, visualizable presence, giving final definition to the tonal material of music and replacing a great deal of the sense of imperfection and loss of modal variety with what would soon become a ubiquitous musical symbol of resolution and completeness in its own right. The circle of keys would also ultimately become transparent, los-

60. Rudolf Wittkower, *Architectural Principles in the Age of Humanism* (New York, 1971), pp. 101–54; Wittkower includes a section entitled "Musical Consonances and the Visual Arts" (pp. 117–26), in which some of the issues that are shared by Renaissance musicians and architects are explained.

61. Werckmeister, *Musicae mathematicae,* p. 141.

62. Johann David Heinichen, *Neu-erfundene und Gründliche Anweisung* (Hamburg, 1711), pp. 261–67.

ing the materiality and artificiality that kept it from being taken for granted in the baroque.[63]

To sum up: Renaissance art united the notions of intrinsic and abstract, divine orders and saw the inner aspect as objective, whereas the baroque exaggerated the split between inner and outer, reversing the relationship of intrinsic and extrinsic to *sensus* and *ratio* and admitting increasing imperfections into the intrinsic qualities of art as the intrinsic became subjective. Although the baroque continued to pay lip service to the old idea of perfection, circles became ellipses—in Kepler's cosmology as well as in church architecture—and the boundaries of tolerance for the nonharmonic relation were steadily extended in music. As Monteverdi had foreseen, *Oratio* replaced *Harmonia*.

If, as René Wellek has observed, "subjective and baroque rarely go hand in hand," that is due to an extraordinary determination to "hide" the subjective within the mass of allegorical detail—hence its internal character.[64] Baroque art flaunts the secular character of structure instead of relying on a belief in eternal proportions pervading the material and serving as a conceptual guide to composition. The association of the French overture, the most pompous genre of the age, with both secular and divine majesty at once asserts the "divine right" and creates an unbreachable split between the divine and the mortal by admitting to a purely worldly conception of the divine. (Luther objected strenuously to the notion that divine plurals in Scripture such as "Let us make man" could be associated with the "royal we.")

It was the externalizing, the rationalizing of proportion and structure, the display of "formula and symmetry"—that is to say, allegory—that caused the shift. Even number symbolism—insofar as it existed in any way beyond the purely incidental—played a role completely different from that of intrinsic proportion in the Renaissance. Now number was rationalized and allegorical, entirely external to the music—esoteric, perhaps; intrinsic, never. The eight-, twelve-, and sixteen-bar ritornelli, the mechanical rhythm and meter of many pieces, and the like constituted an external parade of numbers and proportions, the image of rational thinking rather than divine order. And the emphasis on forming and manipulating patterns derived from the developing analogy between music and language that absorbed the theorists.

To the end of his life Bach remained solidly within this secular tradition. We confirm this in two canons from the *Musical Offering* that explicitly represent

---

63. The circle of keys was described most creatively at its earliest stage as a full-blown theoretical concept: i.e., in Heinichen's *Neu-erfundene und gründliche Anweisung,* his *Der General-Bass in der Composition* (Hamburg, 1728), in which the concept is broadened in scope and several archaic aspects within the earlier treatment are excised, and Mattheson's *Kleine General-Bass Schule* (Hamburg, 1735).

64. René Wellek, "The Concept of Baroque in Literary Scholarship," in *Concepts of Criticism,* ed. Stephen G. Nichols, Jr. (New Haven, 1963), p. 112.

worldly glory: "Per augmentationem, contrario motu" (with the addition by Bach, "As the notes increase, so may the fortune of the king") and "Per tonos" (to which Bach added, "And as the modulation ascends, so may the glory of the king"). Both canons show a disparity between the external signs of the glory and the affect, an explicit opposition between sound and script. In the first the dichotomy occurs between the usual significance of the "majestic" double-dotted rhythms and an unmistakably melancholy tone; in the second it occurs between the rising "all-encompassing" modulations and their deliberate registral finiteness.[65] In both cases the minor, chromatic character of the theme itself is if anything amplified, not overcome. Bach seems here to underscore in a baroque manner what Benjamin calls the "disproportion between the unlimited hierarchical dignity with which [the monarch] is divinely invested and the humble state of his humanity."[66]

In the final analysis it is not his authority but his humanity that is the source of the ruler's redemption. Analogously, it is not the rationalistic and worldly but the expressive quality of art ("Gemüthsbewegung" as the "Finis" of music, according to Kuhnau) that gives the work its universality.[67] Adorno takes the simultaneity of static and dynamic, archaic and modern in Bach to represent the fundamental conflict of a "romantic," expressive and subjective "essence" that exists within the constraints of a conventional, theological "appearance."[68] Adorno's application to Bach of Benjamin's "conflict of convention and expression"—in his commentary on the C sharp minor fugue of the *Well-Tempered Clavier,* Book I, for example—brings out the idea of dualistic "allegorical expression heightened to the utmost," which appears in such works as the "Actus Tragicus" as the double levels of overall plan: the symmetrical image of Scripture, and the downward-/upward-curving dynamic of faith. Thus it is clear that the dynamic and subjective can be rationalized as readily as can the objective.

The two levels of planning can, of course, be related not only to the general division between the dogmatic/external and the personal/internal in theology but also to the official conflict of orthodoxy and pietism that sprang up within Lutheranism in the seventeenth century and with which Bach presumably had to deal at or close to the time he composed the "Actus Tragicus."[69] In baroque Lutheranism the externalization and objectification of the split between doctrinal-intellectual and personal-spontaneous intensified the awareness of their distinctness from one an-

65. Chafe, "Allegorical Music," pp. 361–62.
66. Benjamin, *The Origin,* p. 170.
67. Kuhnau, reprinted in Richter, "Eine Abhandlung," p. 150.
68. Adorno, "Bach Defended," pp. 140–41, 144.
69. On the "Actus Tragicus," see Chapter 4, below. The famous conflict that resulted presumably from Bach's associations with the pietistically inclined superintendent Frohne and the Orthodox pastor Eilmar at Mühlhausen is set forth by Philipp Spitta (*Johann Sebastian Bach,* trans. Clara Bell and J. A. Fuller-Maitland [reprint, New York, 1951], pp. 358–64).

other just as musical style theory in the seventeenth century polarized the strict church style, *stylus ecclesiasticus ligatus,* and the free instrumental style, *stylus phantasticus.* Although, obviously, imagination and structure, freedom and constraint existed together in all works, the objective classifications seemed to externalize and rationalize all aspects, including affect itself. Even the "free" toccatas and recitatives are often rigidly formulaic, reflecting an almost cynical attitude toward the rhetoric of spontaneity and making it difficult to pin down in terms of style—modern or otherwise—what is "really" free, for style itself is a form of law. To the artist in the Lutheran tradition freedom, by analogy to theology, is not free will but grace, its source divine. Owing to the unavoidable human perspective, however, practically every aspect of a work can be thought of as rationalistic. This seemingly pessimistic view lies at the core of theological aesthetics, for another aspect does exist and the baroque denies our ability to name it, denies its human origin, asserts that the most we can do rationally is to allegorize it.

And Bach does allegorize feeling throughout his work. The considerable extent to which he represents rationally aspects of composition that might be taken for direct expression serves as testimony to an intensely Lutheran and allegorical outlook. The pattern of dualism has application at many levels, from Bukofzer's "polarity" of treble and bass and Adorno's "conflicts"—all of which reduce to a simultaneity of harmonic and contrapuntal thinking—to mixed styles in individual movements and double forms of planning in multi-movement works. The emphasis frequently laid on symmetrical structure in the "Credo" of the *Mass in B minor,* for example, only distorts our perception of the plan of the work if account is not also taken of the division of the work into a Trinitarian dynamic of three crescendi in instrumentation. Each begins with one of the basic Lutheran divisions of the work—"Credo"/"Patrem," "Et in unum Dominum," "Et in Spiritum Sanctum"—and increases, movement by movement, until it reaches a climactic movement for full orchestra.[70] The prevailing belief in the intimate if noncausal relation-

<hr />

70. Friedrich Smend, "Luther und Bach," *Bach-Jahrbuch* 37 (1947): 37, and in *Bach-Studien,* ed. Christoph Wolff (Kassel, 1969), pp. 169–70. On the validity of the present viewpoint on the "Credo" rather than Smend's, see Luther's unequivocal division of the creed into three articles—creation, redemption, and sanctification—corresponding to the three persons of the Trinity, in both the small and large catechisms (*The Book of Concord,* trans. and ed. Theodore G. Tappert [Philadelphia, 1959], pp. 344–45, 411–20). The systematic increase in sonority, voice by voice, from one to seven parts above the rhythmically unvarying quarter-note bass in the *stile antico* "Credo in unum Deum" provides the sense of creation and crescendo all at once in unmistakable fashion; the progression through this movement and the ensuing crescendo to full instrumentation in the "Patrem omnipotentem" is one from archaic and severe to modern and festive as well. The parallel with the succession of the *stile antico* "Confiteor" and the jubilant, modern "Et resurrectionem" draws attention to the articles "Credo" ("I Believe") and "Confiteor" ("I acknowledge") that are joined by the use of Gregorian chant, as if Bach, in producing a "Catholic" Mass, were even pointing to the infant baptism shared by the Lutheran and Roman Catholic churches. Likewise, the recall of the climactic move from the "Crucifixus" to the "Et resurrexit" at the "Confiteor"/"Et resurrectionem" junction could be interpreted according to Luther's view that baptism was a reenacting of the death and resurrection of Christ via the descent/ascent pattern of immersion

ship between the rationalistically planned and the affective is revealed in dynamic patterns at all levels of the music, like the baroque swirls in the alchemical pot; it is the dynamic that *moves,* and it may be presented in hidden as easily as in overt form.

The most natural representative of the realm of the hidden is tonality, the perception of which remains in flux until the cadence. The listener is moved from one level to another while his or her attention is occupied with the surface details. Key levels act as ideal means for representing stages of the spiritual life, which cannot be perceived as easily as actions but which form the point of unity for them all. Tonality resists the fragmentation of existence. Its essence is motion; it is to some degree subjective but, although hidden and even abstract, it is never subordinate.

The suggestion that Zacconi's intrinsic/extrinsic dualism comes in the baroque to be represented above all in the dualism of harmony-tonality-counterpoint versus the figured ornamental surface of musical style merits further study; it is not presented here as hard fact. It does, however, seem clearly to relate to Bukofzer's dualism of "continuo homophony" and "harmonic" counterpoint as an evolved, late baroque form of treble-bass polarity, as well as to the basic dualism of harmonic and polyphonic thought that Adorno sees as the root of Bach's "duality of mind."[71] Works such as the "Actus Tragicus" and the *Symbolum* canon on the theology of the cross provide evidence that Bach recognized the allegorical value of "hiding" conspicuous shifts of tonal direction, which so often coincide with the most highly charged affective moments. In the canon the upward, "proper" direction is hidden—not notated—and in the "Actus Tragicus" the movement that represents the individual expression of faith and the beginning of tonal ascent is set in the very dark key, B flat minor, nadir of the tonal design. Ultimately, as we will see, it is its tonal plan, not its symmetry, that makes a work such as the "Actus Tragicus" a truly chiastic cantata.

and emergence from the water. Clearly, both Smend's symmetrical plan and that according to the traditional Lutheran divisions are capable of generating both musical and theological interpretation. The point, then, is that Bach is aware of dual aspects of planning, which we take to be the largest scale of the static/dynamic dualism in his work.

71. Bukofzer, *Music in the Baroque Era,* pp. 221, 277; Adorno, "Bach Defended," p. 138.

CHAPTER TWO

B-A-C-H:
What's in
a Name?

The Bach Goblet: A Hermeneutic Approach

Around the mid-1730s, perhaps for his fiftieth birthday, in 1735, or his appointment as Saxon court composer in 1736, Bach was presented with a glass goblet, which has survived and is now in the Bachhaus in Eisenach (Illus. 2). The goblet is bordered on the base and cup with vine leaves and grapes, and on it is inscribed a dedication to the composer. One side wishes Bach long life: "VIVAT JSB"; Bach's monogrammed initials are intertwined with their mirror image. On the reverse side appears a six-line poem—or, rather, part of a poem—whose meaning has never fully been determined. At the beginnings of lines one to three and in the middle of line six appear segments of the twelve tones of the chromatic scale arranged in groups of four, starting and ending with the four that spell Bach's name: B flat, A, C, B natural (H). The pattern in line two can be interpreted as the inversion of B-A-C-H down a minor third or as its retrograde a major third lower, and the pattern in line three is generated by rotation (repetition) of the main B-A-C-H figure. If we consider each note as representing a single syllable, then the poem breaks into six lines of seven, seven, eight, eight, seven, and seven syllables (fig. 1).

Musicological investigation of the goblet has until now concerned itself primarily with the question of the goblet's donors and how their names may be hidden in the two pitch series, G–G sharp–F–F sharp and E–D sharp–D–C sharp.[1] The text seems to indicate more than one donor: the verb in line two, *ruffet,* is imperative

1. Charles Sanford Terry, "A Bach Relic," *The Musical Times* 76 (1935): 1075–78; Conrad Freyse, "Ein Bach-Pokal," *Bach-Jahrbuch* 33 (1936): 101–8; Friedrich Schnapp, "Das Notenrätsel des Bach-Pokals und seine Deutung," *Bach-Jahrbuch* 35 (1938): 87–94; Friedrich Smend, *Joh. Seb. Bach: Kirchen-Kantaten,* Vol. 6, *Vom 8. Sonntag nach Trinitatis bis zum Michaelis-Fest* (Berlin, 1947), pp. 7–8; Conrad Freyse, "Die Spender des Bach-Pokals," *Bach-Jahrbuch* 40 (1953): 108–18; Friedrich Smend, "Der Pokal im Eisenacher Bach-Museum," *Bach-Jahrbuch* 42 (1955): 108–112; Conrad Freyse, "Noch einmal: Der Bach-Pokal," parts 1, 2, *Bach-Jahrbuch* 43 (1956): 162–64; 44 (1957): 186–87; Otto Friedrich Schulze, "Ein Bach-Pokal im Eisenacher Bach-Museum," *Musica* 21 (1967): 261–64; Joachim Fenner, *Aussage-möglichkeiten barocker Musik untersucht und dargestellt an verschiedenen Orgelwerken Johann Sebastian Bachs und am sogenannten Bachpokal* (Kassel, 1972).

ILLUS. 2   The Bach goblet of ca. 1736. Reproduced by permission of the Bachhaus, Eisenach

FIGURE I.   Poem engraved on the Bach goblet

plural, and lines four and five contain the plurals *ihnen* and *ihr*. The verb in line three, however, *hofft,* is apparently declarative singular, not imperative.[2] Easily the most felicitous of the various solutions proposed was provided by Friedrich Schnapp in 1938 and amplified by Joachim Fenner in the late 1960s.[3] Schnapp suggested that the retrograde motion of the second group of tones implied the name Krebs, that is, "crab," the terms for backwards or *cancrizans* motion. In the years preceding the donation of the goblet Bach had taught two brothers named Krebs. We learn from testimonials and reports that the elder brother, Johann Ludwig, was a favorite of Bach's. He left Leipzig after nine years first as Bach's pupil and then as his close associate. A famous pun quoted at the end of the eighteenth century was attributed to Bach: "Only one crab has been caught, and from only one brook (*Bach*)."[4] Johann Tobias was enrolled at the Thomasschule; a third brother, Johann

---

2. This is not a settled issue, however. Conrad Freyse ("Ein Bach-Pokal," p. 104) maintained that both *ruffet* and *hofft* were singular, while Fenner, for example, assumes that *ruffet* is plural (*Aussagemöglichkeiten barocker Musik,* p. 170).
3. Schnapp, "Das Notenrätsel," pp. 91–92; Fenner, *Aussagemöglichkeiten barocker Music,* pp. 154–86.
4. David and Mendel, eds., *The Bach Reader* pp. 331–32.

Carl, was too young at that time to study with Bach. Krebs senior had studied under Bach at Weimar. Fenner suggests that the Krebs family presented the goblet to Bach and advances the following reading of the poem:

B A C H, theurer Bach!
Carl, Tobias, ruffet, Ach!
Johann Ludwig hofft auf Leben,
So du ihnen nur kanst geben,
Drum erhör ihr sehnlich Ach!
Theurer B A C H, Bach.[5]

Johann Ludwig hopes, presumably, for the life of a musician trained by Bach; his brothers are urged to cry out "Ach," perhaps beseeching the composer for similar instruction. (We might add that just as the crab lives in the brook and its four-note pattern derives from B-A-C-H, so its expression, "Ach," is to be found in B-A-C-H and can be spelled in tones.) A partial withdrawal by Bach from the office of church composer during the 1730s, if only in spirit, could have motivated the gift and could explain its immediate message, especially the reference to "life that only you [Bach] can give."

Researchers have also considered the patterning of the notes themselves and their possible combinations. Nothing in the nature of a canon has ever been uncovered. Rather, it has been found that several combinations of the three four-note groups in various permutations, mostly involving retrograde and inverted forms, constitute intelligible sequence patterns comprising the full chromatic scale. If we confine ourselves to chordal sequences that fit Bach's known style—as Schnapp, for example, did not—we find few possible combinations (Ex. 2).[6]

5. Fenner, *Aussagemöglichkeiten barocker Music,* p. 170.

6. Schnapp ("Das Notenrätsel," pp. 92–94) provides an appendix of eighteen combinations in two to four parts, derived from the tones on the goblet. Some examples involve transposition in one or two parts, while others contain highly implausible sequences involving seventh chords (e.g., No. 18) and chord juxtapositions (No. 13: F sharp, D minor, A flat, E minor, including enharmonic spellings of the first and third chords). In fact, as my Ex. 2 indicates, the greatest number of different chromatic tones that can be used to generate patterns of four three-part chords is eleven. Bach's own examples of chromatic writing involving the patterns of the Bach goblet also involve eleven tones that are generated in fugal imitation; he obtains the twelfth by means of sequential extension (see pp. 59–61, below). In using the terms of twelve-tone theory (O = Original; I = Inversion; R = Retrograde; RI = Retrograde Inversion) to designate manipulations of the Bach goblet patterns in examples 2 and 3 I am aware of the anachronism involved. I do not suggest that Bach thought in those terms (even though his canons demonstrate the relevance of at least the first three to his work). Since, however, B-A-C-H produces only two basic interval patterns (its inversion and retrograde forms, for example, are identical except for the transposition that results from starting on a different tone: B flat for the inversion, B for the retrograde), a fact that the donors of the goblet appear to have understood, these concepts provide the most accessible well-known means of illustrating how such patterns are generated.

EXAMPLE 2.   Patterns using permutations of the tone sequences of the Bach goblet

This inscription presents us with a puzzle that is unique within the corpus of Bach's canonic works in that the text, which normally gives meaning to the patterning of the tones, here contains the tones themselves as (presumed) substitutes for words. We have therefore two unknowns rather than one, and no fixed point of reference such as a certain knowledge of the donors' names. Nothing in either the notation or the poem suggests either transposition of the patterns or any rhythmic modification—for example, augmentation or diminution—such as is usual in the Bach canons. The words and the tones, as well as the monogram, however, clearly project the idea of reversal—the general principle of antithesis that rules in virtually all Bach's canons. Because the three four-note segments are a major third apart from one another several consonant patterns must be ruled out—for example, the B-A-C-H pattern sounding with the retrograde of the G–G sharp–F–F sharp group (F sharp–F–G sharp–G)—for the successive major thirds form cross relations. A few suggestive combinations can be formed, such as that of the inverted

EXAMPLE 3.　　　Combinations based on the tone patterns of the Bach goblet

and retrograde forms of the whole series separated by one quarter note (almost!), and the introduction of the tones that spell out the word *Ach* as a separate idea here and there (Ex. 3); but many of the combinations that first present themselves—most of them involving cross relations—are clearly unacceptable on historical grounds, not to mention the unsuitability of the twelve-note series itself as a theme. Although some other ingenious combinations have been suggested, it is quickly apparent that without making arbitrary decisions we cannot create a canon, even a very short one.[7] Have we then exhausted the meaning of the inscription, or can we by some other means expand on what it tells us about the name Bach?

In fact, pre-Enlightenment pluralistic hermeneutics, which extended—with substantial changes, of course—from the Middle Ages to the early eighteenth century offers other interpretations of the significance of the goblet inscription.[8] It would be senseless to attempt to revive this science in the late twentieth century, given the subsequent development of aesthetics and the needs of our fundamentally secular age. Nonetheless, I will try to construct a modern equivalent as a model to show how the different kinds of meaning treated by disparate branches of scholarship can be related to one another. A particular advantage of this approach is the generation of different kinds of ideas ranged along a continuum from the basis of tangible objects and incontestable facts to the upper reaches of rarefied aesthetic speculation. Hermeneutics encourages the quest for an explanation of the elusive meaning of life; the quest constitutes the purpose of art.

The first level of meaning to be found in the Bach goblet deals with the identity of the donors and the functional-occasional aspects of the object; these facts constitute the literal-historical sense. A second set of referents for the words *ruffet, Ach* and *hofft auf Leben* in particular introduces an allegorico-theological sense that, although obvious, has not been mentioned in musicological commentary. The specifically musical features of the enigma and their affective qualities are equivalent to the third, or tropological sense, while aesthetic interpretation of the basic patterns and their meaning corresponds to the fourth, or eschatological sense.

On the literal-historical level the goblet's inscription yields as much meaning as we might reasonably expect. The donors wish Bach long life and, presumably because they are no longer in contact with him, call out "Ach." Overall, the poem

---

7. As might be expected, disagreement arose among some of the scholars who attempted to create such pieces. The perpetual canon advanced by Freyse ("Spender," pp. 108–18) was criticized by Smend ("Der Pokal," pp. 108–12), who upheld Schnapp's viewpoint. Freyse ("Noch einmal," pp. 163–64) justifiably argued that the chord sequences advanced by Schnapp and Smend were unhistorical and could have arisen only in the period after Reger. Fenner (*Aussagemöglichkeiten barocker Musik,* p. 170) makes complex numerical arguments in support of the chord sequence C minor, E major, D minor, F sharp major, without considering the question of the plausibility of the sequence itself.

8. See Gerhard Ebeling, "Hermeneutik," in *Die Religion in Geschichte und Gegenwart,* 3rd ed., vol. 3, ed. Kurt Galling (Tübingen, 1957), pp. 242–49.

expresses admiration for his art and a desire to continue to enjoy its benefits. Light-hearted play animates this reading, and the "Ach" seems tongue in cheek. The tones themselves cry out for Bach's attention; and Bach's name, standing at their head, symbolizes the composer's mastery. Following from this, the last lines of the poem can now be interpreted as beseeching the composer to provide more artistic and spiritual manna, even, perhaps, more church music. Such an entreaty from his pupils, set in the language of musical notes, came at a time when Bach's regular production of new church music might have fallen off somewhat, when, in the 1730s, the composer had turned to publishing instrumental music and consolidating the large church works of the preceding decade. We may remember that as early as 1728 Picander, in the preface to a set of cantata texts, had invited Bach to set them to music, a request that can be interpreted as an attempt to reinterest Bach in an area from which he appears to have withdrawn, disaffected. At the beginning of the 1730s Bach sought a new position and expressed to the Leipzig town council his dissatisfaction with the performing resources available for church music. During this decade his peace of mind was disrupted by his former pupil Johann Adolf Scheibe, so that by 1739 Bach was able to describe the performance of a *Passion* as a burden.[9] If it was during this period in his life that the composer underlined in his copy of Calov's Bible the commentary on Matthew 5:24–26 that deals with justifiable anger toward one's adversaries in professional matters and the many passages in Ecclesiastes that counsel patience in worldly dealings, then the tone of the words *ruffet, ach* may be interpreted as a reference to Bach's living "under the cross," as it were, in Leipzig.[10]

This last remark brings us to the second, allegorico-theological level of meaning of the inscription. Any reading of the poem that reaches outside its immediate historical context evokes a more serious, expressive tone that is similar to the tone of the cantatas. A characteristic element of Lutheran theology in Bach's time is the idealized Christian who, in the cantatas and countless devotional poems, calls out "Ach" in tribulation, hoping for eternal life; the text of the poem, unusual in an everyday context, in this reading takes on a significance familiar from contemporary theology. The authors wish for salvation both for Bach and for themselves. The "Ach" thus expresses the theology of the cross, Luther's basic definition of the theology of faith, of the necessary tribulation endured in the present life through faith in Christ and hope for the future life of fulfillment. Only such an interpretation can give meaning to the otherwise peculiar occurrence of the words *hofft auf Leben* in conjunction with a segment of the descending chromatic scale. The de-

9. See David and Mendel, *The Bach Reader,* pp. 119–26, 137–49, 152–58, 162–63, 237–51.
10. See Cox, *The Calov Bible,* pp. 423–37, 445. See also Chapter 4 of the present study.

scending chromatic scale appears throughout Bach's work in close association with the immediate expression of the tribulation that signifies the hope of future fulfillment, but in the religious sphere only; otherwise the chromaticism is merely associated with lamentation. Antithesis of this nature—hope linked to lamentation—is the very soul of musical representation of the theology of the cross, and is well known from many Bach cantatas, beginning with "Nach dir, Herr, verlanget mich" (No. 150). Such antithesis is by no means usual, however, in settings of purely secular texts, except where parody is intended.

The structure of the B-A-C-H poem has been shown to be of the chiastic type of symmetry: that is, the two central lines have the same rhyme scheme and meter; they are then framed by the second and fifth lines, ending with "Ach," and these in turn framed by the first and sixth, ending with "Bach."[11] Poetic forms of this type appear in the two arias of the *St. Matthew Passion* that deal specifically with the cross, "Gerne will ich mich bequemen, Kreuz und Becher anzunehmen" and "Komm, süsses Kreuz."[12] The former of these arias is derived from a sermon of Heinrich Müller in which the *Becher* is equated with the cross;[13] this symbolism unquestionably underlies one of the layers of meaning in the goblet. That is, while an aspect of life, victory, and success is certainly intended in the "VIVAT" address to the composer, we cannot fail to recognize the alternate symbolism suggested in the line *ruffet, Ach*. In the *St. Matthew Passion* Christ's drinking of the cup of *Todesbitterkeit* is the means of salvation for mankind; this is stated in the arioso "Der Heiland fällt vor seinem Vater nieder, dadurch erhebt er mich und alle von unserem Falle hinauf zu Gottes Gnade wieder," which features the simultaneous antithesis of melodic descent and ascent. "Gerne will ich mich bequemen," immediately following this movement, uses the chiastic poetic structure to represent something like Luther's idea of man's becoming "conformable to Christ in His suffering," a central theme of his Passion theology.[14] Thus, in addition to its obvious secular, occasional significance, the goblet invokes three symbolic associations within the Christian tradition: first, the cup of Gethsemane, the vessel of sin and bitterness accepted by Jesus in obedience to God's will; second, the sacramental chalice which, as we are told in "Gerne will ich mich bequemen," has been sweetened for man through Jesus' sacrifice; and finally, the eschatological goblet of the heavenly meal of the afterlife. These four levels of meaning—one literal and three "spiritual"—provide a major impetus for our interpretation of the object according

11. See Freyse, "Ein Bach-Pokal," p. 104.
12. Smend, "Luther und Bach," pp. 35–36.
13. Axmacher, *"Aus Liebe,"* p. 174.
14. Martin Luther, *A Meditation on Christ's Passion* (trans. of *Ein Sermon von der Betrachtung des heiligen Leidens Christi* [1519]), in vol. 42 of *Luther's Works,* ed. Martin O. Dietrich (Philadelphia, 1969), pp. 7–14. See Axmacher's analysis of the theological content of Picander's text and the degree to which it moves away from the idea of suffering as *Strafleiden* (God's judgment for man's sin), in *"Aus Liebe,"* pp. 174–75.

to the pluralistic layered approach to deciphering meaning offered in traditional hermeneutics.[15]

A number of Bach cantatas represent the stages of meaning in terms of three- or four-fold chronological sequence that covers past, present, and anticipated events. In many such works an effective progression from tribulation to joy is aligned with the chronological sequence as its tropological dimension: the dynamic of faith. The *ruffet, Ach/hofft auf Leben* antithesis of the goblet poem expresses the cornerstone of this sequence: a life of tribulation lived in hope of the afterlife. The progression from the earlier, literal-historical stage to anticipation of the final, eschatological state is a vitally important one which, within the theological aesthetics of the Lutheran baroque, is a metaphor for the articulation of meaning in art—that is, the continuum that extends from conventional-technical aspects to those of universal significance. Hermeneutics, with its separate levels, likewise fills a role that is closely analogous to the separate branches of art history and criticism, from the purely historical to the more rarefied domain of aesthetics. In a significant number of cantatas this progression from the literal to the abstract is paralleled by an ascending tonal progression, and these works will be taken up in later chapters. We may note, however, that in one of the most interesting of these works, Cantata 61, "Nun komm, der Heiden Heiland," a particular symbolism involving a goblet informs the eschatological goal as expressed in the final chorale, "Komm, du schöne Freudenkrone."

From the standpoint of anticipating the crown of the afterlife we might compare the goblet inscription to the "Christus Coronabit Crucigeros" canon. In it the continual rotation and overlap of descent and ascent as well as chromatic and diatonic elements allegorize the simultaneous juxtaposition of suffering and fulfillment that pervaded the Lutheran spiritual life. It is an aural equivalent to the intertwining of Bach's initials with their mirror image, the whole surmounted by a crown in the best-known form of Bach's monogram (as reproduced, for example, on the covers of the volumes of the New Bach Edition). In the form in which Bach's initials appear on the goblet the capping of the insignia with a crown is absent. It is possible that this detail is the equivalent of the future tense of the canon; that is, the hoped-for crown has a theological meaning, just as it does in many cantatas.[16] In this respect the structural pattern of reversal found in the poem on the Bach goblet and in

---

15. Axmacher ("Bachs Kantatentexte," pp. 16–17) indicates the indebtedness to the four levels of several Bach texts in which the transformation of the tears of earthly tribulation into the *Freudenwein* of the joyful anticipation of the afterlife is related to the four senses of Scripture. The most powerful instance, especially in light of its influence on the structure of Bach's work, is not mentioned by Axmacher. In the penultimate movement of Cantata 21, "Ich hatte viel Bekümmerniss in meinem Herzen," the *Weinen* of Part One is transformed into the *Wein* of joy ("Verwandle dich, Weinen, in lauteren Wein").

16. Fenner, *Aussagemöglichkeiten barocker Musik,* p. 159; Smend, *Kirchen-Kantaten,* p. 19.

the monogrammed initials, as well as in the transposed inversion and retrograde contained in the tones G, G sharp, F, F sharp, all point to the dualistic meaning invoked by the varied associations of the goblet: secular/sacred, present life/ afterlife, tribulation/fulfillment. Likewise, the expressions in lines two and three— calling out "Ach" and hoping for life—reveal that the baroque *Lebensgefühl* itself is rooted in antithesis, just as are all the above-mentioned features; the principle of antithesis, therefore, provides a vital key to deciphering the meaning of the goblet.

We can interpret more fully the ideas of symmetry and antithesis as they are embodied in the goblet inscription and Bach's monogrammed initials if we consider for a moment the title pages of a few of the theological books in Bach's library.[17] On them we frequently find symmetry in the form of illustrative engravings on the topics that come closest to symbolizing the content of the books, and these engravings are sometimes summed up in one or more mottoes that make use of antithesis. Spener's *Schola Pietatis*, for example, has medallions in each corner of a symmetrically-arranged page, each with a motto and a symbolic object: "Die Sünd leg ab" (upper left, with a drinking glass); "und Glauben hab" (upper right, with a communion chalice); "So blüht im Grabe" (below, to the left of a sarcophagus, with a skull); "Des Himmels Gabe" (lower right, with a hand holding a crown). August Pfeiffer's *Antimelancholicus* has the figure of Melancholicus seated between the figure of Christ on one side and those of an armed antagonist, a seductress, and a demon on the other, while below the medallions contain mottoes from Scripture of the antithetical type that Luther described as signifying the theology of the cross: "Ich habe solches offt gehöret, ihr seyd allzumahl Leidige Tröster" and "Ich hatte viel Bekümmernüsse in meinem Herze, aber deine Tröstungen ergetzen meine Seele."[18] Perhaps the most typical of these emblems is that in Pfeiffer's *Evangelische Schatz-Kammer*, which pictures Christ on one side holding the cross and a book of Scripture (i.e., the Gospel) and Moses on the other hiding the two tablets of the Law; the two figures hold out *geistliche Schau-Groschen* before the kneeling figure of a pilgrim, and the title of the book refers to the respective roles of Law and Gospel within Lutheran theology. In all these emblems the antithetical character of the theology of the cross predominates: suffering and tribulation in this life (*Ach*) versus the promise of fulfillment in the next (*hofft auf Leben*). And on many of the title pages the printer represents his initials in exactly the same form of reverse monogram as Bach's on the goblet.[19] Despite the convention of symmetry in all forms of

17. These are reproduced in facsimile in Leaver, *Bach's Theological Library*, see especially pp. 95, 102, 110, 148.

18. See n. 15 above; also the discussion of Bach's "Ich hatte viel Bekümmernis" in Chapter 5.

19. For monogrammed initials similar to Bach's, see Leaver, *Bach's Theological Library*, pp. 90, 121, 128–29, 133, 149.

baroque art, formal balance seems to express—via its frequent conceptual connection with antithesis and its resolution—a fundamental aspect of the Lutheran view of life and the role of the individual therein.

Our expanded interpretation of the B-A-C-H poem now has the donors referring to the spiritual power of Bach's music in terms of the basic Lutheran beliefs they shared with the composer. The force of these beliefs can be seen in one block of underlinings in Bach's Calov Bible found in the book of Ecclesiastes, which contains the greatest number of such markings in any book of Bach's Bible.[20] Ecclesiastes is especially interesting in this regard, for it is the most pessimistic, virtually nihilistic book of the Bible, ringing countless changes on the theme of the futility of hope for an afterlife. Yet Bach usually underlines, not the extraordinarily harsh text itself, but Calov's commentaries. The reason for this seems clear. Because it is based on the negative tone of Ecclesiastes, the commentary reiterates the fundamental doctrine of Luther's theology of the cross: the patient endurance of suffering, persecution, worldly injustice, and the like (after the model of the Christ of the Passion), and the necessity of leaving the outcome of events both worldly and spiritual in God's hands.[21] Bach's inner life—of which we now have a few more indications in the underlined passages of his Bible—was largely regulated according to such beliefs.

The goblet's inscription suggests that Bach's music was perceived by his contemporaries as a force for spiritual regeneration. Luther placed music next to theology in this respect, a configuration that is echoed in music treatises and prefaces of the time and that formed the basis of the metaphysical tradition of music theory in the seventeenth century in which connections between music and hermeneutics are affirmed. In this light the third sense—the musico-tropological, or affective level—takes us deeper into the significance of the goblet inscription for its musical as opposed to purely textual analysis. In an age in which the highest aim of music was repeatedly defined as the moving of the affections, the very tonal material of music was colored with preexistent significance. Within this frame of reference the notes B flat, A, C, B natural could be taken to serve as a kind of key to the chromatic "material" of music as defined in the newly emergent circle of keys and exhibited in all its glory in the *Well-Tempered Clavier*.

Neither Bach nor his pupils could have overlooked the association between the musical spelling of the composer's name and the variable pitch of the gamut contained in its first and last tones—B flat/B natural—used to mutate from one hexachord to another. Further, the variable pitch formed the pattern fa/mi in the soft (flat) and hard (sharp) hexachords, respectively—that is, B flat/A followed by C/B

---

20. Cox, *The Calov Bible*, pp. 423–37.
21. See the passages cited at the end of Chapter 4, below.

natural. The change from B flat to B natural in D minor or G minor suggests the shift from minor to major, with corresponding theological and affective associations. Luther, for example, described the mi/fa semitone as analogous to the Gospel and the other tones to the Law, for the Gospel gave the law its meaning; furthermore, he called the Dorian mode an analogue of the "poor weak sinner" because of its use of the variable B fa/mi.[22] As if by extension of this association of chromaticism with human weakness, the chromatic tonal material of music was described in the seventeenth-century Lutheran metaphysical tradition of music theory as an analogy of "our incompleteness and imperfection in this life."[23] In the goblet inscription Bach's name is extended to generate the chromatic scale. The other tones descend through the diatonic pitches of the gamut, each one followed by a sharpened pitch—G, G sharp, F, F sharp, E, D sharp, D, C sharp—with a change of direction taking place at the diatonic mi/fa, F to E. To the various suggestions of the cross—the cruciform or chiastic plan of the poem, the cross relations and the idea of chromatic descent—we add the choice of sharps rather than flats for the other chromatic tones ("sharp" in German is *Kreuz*, cross); thus the pattern of Bach's name—fa followed by mi—is retained throughout the sequence.

Bach also produced a canon on the mi/fa juxtaposition, entitled *Mi Fa et Fa Mi est tota musica*, the "tota musica" conveying the comprehensiveness of solmization and the gamut that constituted its underlying tonal framework.[24] Smend observed that in the dedicatory inscription Bach's acrostic of the names of dedicator (BACH) and dedicatee (FABER) seems to equate the two, further noting that the letters F, A, B (flat), E added up to fourteen, as do B, A, C, H (the R signified repetition [*Repetatur*], not a pitch).[25] That both names form the solmization syllables fa mi fa mi, the expressly designated subject of the canon cannot be missed; this, the solmizational, more than the numerical aspect, is the most obvious level of equivalence between the two. These factors form a background for the associations of the tones B-A-C-H; not only was it possible to translate the name Bach into tones but the name itself was "melodic." Johann Gottfried Walther tells us this in his music lexicon in the entry for J. S. Bach, where he attributes the discovery of the melodic nature of the name to Bach himself.[26] The name was melodic in an interesting manner, for it made use of the variable mi/fa that signified the "poor weak sinner," yet it moved, potentially at least, from flat to sharp and from minor to major, like the

22. Luther's comments on music are widely quoted. See Paul Nettl, *Luther and Music*, trans. Frida Best and Ralph Wood (New York, 1948), pp. 42–43, 75–76; W. E. Buszin, "Luther on Music," *Musical Quarterly* 32 (1946): 80; Christhard Mahrenholz, *Luther und die Kirchenmusik* (Kassel, 1937); Friedrich Blume, *Protestant Church Music: A History* (New York, 1974), pp. 5–14.

23. Werckmeister, *Musicae mathematicae*, p. 141.

24. See Chafe, "Allegorical Music," pp. 358–61.

25. Smend, *Kirchen-Kantaten*, pp. 10–11.

26. Johann Gottfried Walther, *Musicalisches Lexicon* (Leipzig, 1732), p. 64; trans. in David and Mendel, *The Bach Reader*, p. 46.

"Christus Coronabit Crucigeros" canon, which introduces (incidentally) the tones of Bach's name when it moves from flat to sharp and minor to major harmonies toward the end.[27]

Thus the musicoallegorical associations of the name BACH, extended to the full chromatic spectrum, confirm the theological associations brought out earlier. In view of this interpretation, the inscription perhaps suggests that no hidden canonic piece was ever contrived by the donors for Bach—and posterity—to find; certainly no such discovery is needed for the goblet to yield its meaning. Rather, the poem was probably a cleverly arranged expression of some of the ways Bach conceived of chromaticism in terms of traditional theory. The patterning of the tones probably descends from Bach himself. The goblet is a created allegorical object just as much as the system of tempered intervals and chromatic tones to which it refers. It represents the finite, earthly state in expectation of redemption from without.

The third sense teaches us that in order to grasp Bach's conceptualizing of tonal relationships we need to work with historical theory. One particularly important facet, to be introduced in the following chapter, is the survival within the emerging circle of keys of the hexachord theory, which gave meaning to the spelling of the composer's name in tones and provides affective connotations for broad tonal procedures under the rubrics *durus* and *mollis*. Bach's retention of such archaic features was not, of course, a studied, intellectual procedure, as it is for the modern researcher. But for us to comprehend what was purely intuitive for the composer we must first recognize that baroque theory construed tonal relationships very differently from the way the more familiar concepts of post-Rameau "functional" harmony do. The most important conceptual differences between the two are the result of the great aesthetic shift from the baroque to the classic-romantic periods. Baroque music is heteronomous—that is, allegorical and word generated—and the theory reflects that fact. The historico-allegorical devices we have come to recognize as such do not, of course, constitute the meaning of the music. Some are completely routine (the Phrygian cadence), others inaudible (large-scale tonal anabasis and catabasis), still others deeply and immediately affective (enharmonic changes); all these devices are allegorical and thus fall under the allegorist's control.

The fourth and final level of interpretation moves out of the realm of the historical and gives us a different slant on Bach's chromatic language. This eschatological sense exhibits a fascinating correspondence to what is probably the most successful example in the twentieth century of a criticism combining historical and universal aspects of art: Walter Benjamin's "philosophical criticism," as he called it, or his "aesthetic of redemption," as Richard Wolin has styled it.[28] Benjamin's approach

27. See the tone sequence B flat, A, [D], C, B at the end of the fourth measure of the second part in Ex. 1.

28. Benjamin, *The Origin*, 182; Richard Wolin, *Walter Benjamin: An Aesthetic of Redemption* (New York, 1982).

offers a justification to our use of medieval hermeneutics and historical theory. A sometime teacher of Adorno and a strong, if indirect and posthumous presence in the latter's picture of Bach, Benjamin developed his compelling and formidably erudite system of thought within the context of his investigation of a form of Lutheran baroque literature that had died as far as modern appreciation was concerned, crushed under its own weight. This form, the German tragic drama of the seventeenth century (*Trauerspiel*) was so concerned with extraartistic significance, meaning that lay outside itself—mainly the emblematic, theological perception of events, people, and objects—that its inherent qualities could no longer be perceived. It did not fit the pattern of classical tragedy, for the hero's death was presented as relating to a truth beyond the story itself, which rendered both the story and its characters inconsequent, mere signposts to a higher cosmic-theological reality. Even the hero's corpse was an emblem comparable to the labeled *disiecta membra* on the baroque operating table.[29] Life itself was devalued so that it could point toward a future of greater meaning. Benjamin's book is therefore a philosophy of allegorical meaning in baroque art, in particular its Lutheran manifestation. It is a "theological aesthetics" in that allegory is seen as the ideal expressive device of what might be termed "eschatological" art—that is, an art that places so much of its intended meaning outside itself that it projects a dualism, a conflict between its meaning as an autonomous, self-contained art reveling in its own devices and expression and its intended purpose as an art pointing beyond itself. The two aspects of the dualism were described by Benjamin as the correlatives of the spiritual quality of life according to the Lutheranism of seventeenth-century Germany, where the central doctrine of "faith in opposition to experience" robbed life of its immediate significance, producing in its great men an intense baroque melancholia.[30]

The *Trauerspiel* is as fully allegorical as art can be; everything in it exists for the indirect allegorical meaning supplied and controlled by the author. It appeared that once these predetermined meanings had been uncovered by the reader the work ceased to have value. The critical approach to such a genre is, to use Benjamin's metaphor, the "mortification" of the works, the stripping of historical meaning layer by layer, in order to expose what, if anything, in the work is of lasting value. This process recognizes the historical features of the works for what they are, something whose meaning for the composer and his audience has weakened if not disappeared altogether. Thus the first stage of Benjamin's program for criticism is to focus on the historical, the manifest and visible in the works under consideration, at first for its own sake, but then more and more in dialogue with the hidden, universal qualities.[31]

29. Benjamin, *The Origin,* pp. 215–20.
30. Benjamin, *The Origin,* pp. 138–42.
31. Benjamin, *The Origin,* p. 182.

We do not, of course, judge Bach's work after the manner of the *Trauerspiel*; it is far from dead, and the only "redemption" it needs is a continuing tradition of interpretation in performance and criticism. Interpretation of the goblet inscription according to this fourth, eschatological, sense treats the historical character of chromaticism as a device that the composer utilizes merely as a feature of the appearance of the work. Inasmuch as the historical condition and its characteristic affective state are not conceived as the final or deepest level of meaning, the chromatic style that was virtually exclusively linked to the expression of lamentation will be liberated more and more from that role by future generations of listeners. The tremendous enriching of the harmonic tonal vocabulary of music that Bach's work brought about transformed the archaic figural associations through a new complexity of the conception of affect. The new complexity is apparent in many examples where Bach makes conspicuous use of chromaticism, for example, in the opening chorus of Cantata 78, "Jesu, der du meine Seele," the "Et expecto resurrectionem" of the *Mass in B minor,* and the "Christus Coronabit Crucigeros" canon. As the goblet inscription does, such examples place chromaticism in a context whose primary allegorical subject matter is redemption, as if the chromaticism itself, displayed as allegory, is "redeemed."[32] Redemption is present in Bach's works in the sense that his chromaticism prefigured future tonal practices, even if later composers took some time to recognize Bach as a kindred spirit.

B-A-C-H in Some Instrumental Works

In a 1950 article Schönberg jokingly referred to Bach as the first "composer with twelve tones," which, in light of the goblet inscription, is not an inappropriate statement. We might conclude that the donors of the goblet, like Schönberg two centuries later, recognized Bach's mastery of the "hidden mysteries of tone relations," his ability to move at will in the musical labyrinth of tones.[33] Schönberg's remark brings to mind the paradoxical character of Webern's striving to realize the inner content of Bach's *Ricercar* with extensive motivic and orchestral resources at the same time that his own music was moving in the opposite direction of the greatest concentration and abstraction. In the *String Quartet* Opus 28 Webern even invokes the name of Bach to reduce drastically the combinatorial possibilities of the twelve-tone row. Webern's row begins, like the series of tones on the goblet, with B flat, A, C, B, and derives the rest of the tones from the first four. Not only

32. See Benjamin, *The Origin,* pp. 232–35, for a discussion of the idea of allegorical reversal.
33. Arnold Schönberg, "Bach," in *Style and Idea,* ed. Leonard Stein with trans. by Leo Black (Berkeley and Los Angeles, 1975), pp. 393–97.

the viewpoint on composition as *ars combinatoria,* an expression used by the most allegorical-minded of baroque theorists, but the sharp division between that conception and music's expressive resources is a link between the modern mind and the allegorical mentality of the baroque.[34] Schönberg further wondered at the fact that Bach could produce highly intricate permutational compositions full of contrapuntal artifice, as well as pieces that seemed to have none at all. He felt, typically, that a "hidden mystery" must underlie the pieces of the latter category: that is, they must be founded on some as yet undiscovered unifying contrapuntal devices. And he juxtaposed music of contrapuntal-permutational character such as Bach's with music founded on "developing variation." Since we know that Adorno, as if in response to Schönberg, linked developing variation to Bach as the hidden "essence" beneath the archaic figural "appearance," we will now consider a few chromatic works in which these ideas are confronted. I have chosen works—Sinfonia No. 9 from the *Inventions and Sinfonias* and Contrapuncti III, VIII, IX, and XIX (the quadruple fugue) from *The Art of Fugue*—whose chromatic material relates to the patterns on the Bach goblet.

Sinfonia No. 9

The extraordinarily allegorical character of the F minor sinfonia is underscored by its main thematic material: both the descending chromatic tetrachord, which occupies the role of an ostinato figure, and a second line, featuring the rising minor third/falling semitone—or "Ach"—motive (transposed), recall the goblet inscription. When treated in sequence, the second of these ideas forms the intervallic pattern of the tones B-A-C-H, which appears once at pitch (measure 17, right at the center of the piece, in Fig. 2). In key association, descending chromatic tetrachord, and ostinato character this piece represents the melancholia that for Benjamin constituted the primary expressive character of the allegorical mentality, a spiritual link to the seventeenth-century baroque.

A Smend-type approach to the sinfonia would emphasize a division between the twenty-one measures in which the primary thematic material appears (that is, ten repetitions of a two-bar unit, the last extended one bar for the final chord) and the fourteen measures of episodic material.[35] The sinfonia features some fairly obvious numerological features mostly involving the numbers seven and five, the factors of

---

34. Knowledge itself is defined in these terms in Athanasius Kircher's treatise, *Ars Magna Sciendi Sive Combinatoria,* whose separate categories exactly parallel Kircher's approach to musical style. The unmistakable parallel between Kircher's work and Benjamin's exposition of the baroque allegorical mentality can be seen in the tremendously emblematic illustrations in all Kircher's treatises. See Jocelyn Godwin, *Athanasius Kircher: A Renaissance Man and the Quest for Lost Knowledge* (London, 1979), for a collection of these illustrations.

35. Ulrich Siegele (*Bachs theologischer Formbegriff,* pp. 37–38) indicates some of the same interpretations that I bring out here. Such an interpretation must point out how obvious these devices are, as is the permutational nature of the *Sinfonia in F minor.*

the overall total of thirty-five bars. There are ten thematic entries and five episodes in the ratio of 2:1, and the corresponding measure totals of thirty-five, twenty-one, and fourteen give a ratio of 5:3:2. The theme appears in five different keys and five forms of contrapuntal permutation. The twenty-one bars consist entirely of contrapuntal permutations of the opening two-bar unit (in addition to shift of key and mode). We sense a predetermined meaning, which remains unchanging throughout the piece and projects the static quality that Adorno called "appearance." Interpretation of the number twenty-one would emphasize it as a multiple of seven and three, cosmic and Trinitarian numbers that confirm the eternal, while fourteen is the multiple of seven and two, representing a mixture of the universal and the human, imperfect. Then the tenfold repetition of the basic unit might be interpreted as representing the Law (the Ten Commandments), adding to the idea of strictness suggested in the contrapuntal permutations themselves, and linking up with the role of the Law within Lutheran theology, humbling man with the consciousness of his mortality and sin (the descending chromatic tetrachord and "Ach" motives). The fourteen bars of episodic material, variational and free in character, must then signify the subject, Bach himself; the spelling B-A-C-H appears in the central episode. The "Ach" theme, whose sequential extension generates the B-A-C-H pattern, contains fourteen tones; the chromatic ostinato in its most typical form, ten.

The thematic material and its traditional rhetorical associations fit with the numerological aspects. The *pathopoeia* and its link to ideas of death, lamentation, the cross, and the like, is obvious in the ostinato. In the "Ach" line the motives draw heavily on the mi contra fa pattern. In particular, the ending of the "Ach" theme introduces the melodic tritone to reach the upper octave. This line ascends only slowly and with difficulty at first, then suddenly leaps upward. The following melodic descent of a sixth required for resolution of the tritone suggests the inability to maintain a goal attained by such radical means. We may note that the purposeful character of the rising sequences in the episodes opposes the inevitability of the descending chromatic ostinato of the basic unit. The dynamic here is highly suggestive of Lutheran dogma regarding the efficacy of human works and achievements. Likewise, the harmonic progressions of the sinfonia at times exhibit a highly tortured character. This is particularly evident in passages such as the first half of measure four, where the third melodic line (in the lowest voice) introduces an augmented fifth (D flat) against the A of the descending ostinato. In combination with the chromatic escape figure that resolves the note through B to C, and the fact that the resolution is to an unstable six-four chord that moves immediately to another dissonance, the effect created strains the harmonic logic. The D flat suggests, but cannot be interpreted as, a C sharp, which would strain the logic still further.

Despite such inner tensions and harmonic dissonances, the piece moves at a pace of great rhythmic regularity and control, largely as the result of the inexorable character of the ostinato and its cadences. The structure of the piece was designed to exhibit many correspondences, as if nothing new can be introduced. As shown in Figure 2, the piece features a highly permutational character in the larger groupings of thematic entries and episodes as well as in the contrapuntal combinations. An element of fugal design is incorporated in the succession of elements as well as the exposition (mm. 1–8), in which the "Ach" theme (like the ostinato) appears in all three voices in the tonic/dominant/tonic pattern. After this point a major segment of the piece, moving through A flat and E flat to the dominant (mm. 9–19), is repeated down a fifth (and with parts inverted) as measures 22–32, returning to the tonic for the final presentation of the theme with the ostinato in the bass (mm. 33–35). The correspondence can be carried further back, to include measures 7–10 as the equivalent of 18–21. The only variations in the design are the two-bar free episode in the exposition (mm. 5–6), which modulate from the dominant back to the tonic, and the doubling of the fourth episode (mm. 20–23 = 2 × mm. 9–10) by immediate transposition down a tone to enable the repetition of measures 9–19 down a fifth (mm. 22–32). As a result of the transposition the thematic entries that precede and follow this episode exhibit a semitonal relationship—C minor and D flat—which Bach underscores by placing the ostinato in the soprano both times: this is, perhaps, the indication of the mi/fa sequence in the ambitus. In such a highly planned structure a detail such as the first turn to major for the A flat appearance of the themes (mm. 11–12) is enormously expressive, in this case suggesting the affect of hope, which is otherwise for the most part denied in the piece. Bach underscores the importance of this entry by returning the ostinato to the bass (making thereby a strong cadence to the new key), and he models the final appearance of the themes (mm. 33–35) on the pattern of this passage.

Having reported all this factual matter, we note that such an extensive degree of conscious control over the material of the work is one of the hallmarks of allegorical composition; the numerological, permutational, and structural aspects of such pieces are finite in number; they can be totaled and their meaning assessed. In a commentary of this kind, which fails to provide a complete explanation, we have an intensified sense of all that is historical and—Benjamin would say—subject to death. By stressing the historical aspect we accomplish the first stage of "philosophical criticism": "mortification" of the work.

Adorno's interpretation, on the other hand, would have to indicate dynamic individuated aspects that take precedence over the static contrapuntal character and constitute the expressive essence of the piece. Its focal point would be the process of variation, even within the theme itself, something that is, in fact, discernible in the many subtle interrelationships among its elements. Focusing on just one of these elements—the "Ach" motive and its transformations—we see that Bach has taken pains to expand its expressive character, at least for the first twenty bars (Ex. 4).

FIGURE 2.   Sinfonia in F minor: theme entries and episodes separated

mm. 1–2

mm. 3–4

mm. 7–8

mm. 11–12

mm. 13–14

FIGURE 2   *continued*

mm. 5–6

mm. 9–10

mm. 15–17

FIGURE 2   *continued*

mm. 18–19

mm. 24–25

mm. 26–27

mm. 31–32

FIGURE 2   *continued*

mm. 20–23

mm. 28–30

FIGURE 2   *continued*

mm. 33–35

EXAMPLE 4.   Sinfonia in F minor: Variational patterns derived from the initial melodic figure

This is achieved largely by widening and contracting the intervals of the theme. In this piece, however, we remain within the sphere of works dominated by allegory, such as canons; even the variational side has a calculated character. This is, no doubt, the result of the didactic purpose of the sinfonia.[36] Nevertheless, neither the permutational nor the variational aspect of this piece can be elevated to the status of essence with respect to the other. Rather, it is the interaction of the two that gives the piece its special character; that the allegorical and permutational element dominates makes the few places that are expressive almost by virtue of their rarity, such as the modulation to A flat major, all the more meaningful. This piece offers, in fact, an instance of the frequent sense of dichotomy in Bach between abstract and audible orders, both of which exist together, in manifold relationships throughout his work. The main point is not that critical commentators should learn to discount the great many "paper correspondences" that exist in Bach but to recognize that the dichotomy between "sound" and "script" is central to the understanding of his work.

The Art of Fugue: Contrapuncti III, VIII, IX, and XIX

If any of Bach's works seems to make the direct claim of confronting the "historical" and the "universal" it is *The Art of Fugue*. Hans Heinrich Eggebrecht has characterized much of the work as dealing with the subject of objective being (*Sein*) versus human existence (*Dasein*): at times Bach seems to be saying "It is"; at others "I will"; at still others "I am"; while the final fugue is the eschatological "I will be."[37] The author of this remarkable paralleling of the four senses perceives the "I am" as an expression of the human condition as described in Christian (Lutheran) terms, the very terms that appear on the Bach goblet when it is interpreted according to its theological references, which he links specifically to chromaticism. Moreover, Eggebrecht explicitly denies the "signature" aspect favored by Smend ("I, BACH, composed this") as the meaning of the B-A-C-H tones, while retaining it for other numerical aspects of the work.[38] In this, as in his recognition of the role of

36. As Bach's title page indicates, the collection is directed toward "lovers of the clavier, and especially those desirous of learning," providing "upright instruction"; David and Mendel, *The Bach Reader*, p. 38.

37. Hans Heinrich Eggebrecht, *Bachs Kunst der Fuge: Erscheinung und Deutung* (Munich, 1984), p. 70.

38. Eggebrecht, *Bachs Kunst der Fuge*, p. 15. Nonetheless, Eggebrecht sees the Contrapunctus designation of the fourteen fugues (including the undesignated quadruple fugue) as Bach's means of signing the work: "Ich, BACH, habe dies Komponiert, das heisst: Ich identifiziere mich mit diesem Werk und mit seiner Aussage" (p. 58). Speaking generally of Bach's name appearing in *The Art of Fugue*, Erich Bergel (*Bachs letzte Fuge* [Minden, 1986], p. 195) makes the following remark: "Das B-A-C-H in seiner 'Kunst der Fuge' ist nicht nur ein persönliches autobiographisches Bekenntnis, sondern es ist ein Symbol, dessen Chromatik er selber mit den Worten 'Christus Coronabit Crucigeros' gedeutet hat." See n. 27, above.

abstract qualities (especially number) in relation to a larger expressive totality, Eggebrecht comes closer, perhaps, than any other recent interpreter of Bach's music to dealing with the issues raised by Adorno. In his view, *The Art of Fugue,* from the resemblance between the inversion of the main theme to Luther's chorale on Christian existence, "Aus tiefer Not," to the sense that a substantial part of the work was conceived with the B-A-C-H in mind, expresses Bach's perception of the nature of human existence in the most elevated terms.[39]

Chromaticism first appears in a thoroughgoing way in *The Art of Fugue* in Contrapunctus III, introduced in the fifth bar as countersubject to the main theme. This encroachment of chromatic tones in many places throughout *The Art of Fugue* has great significance at all levels of interpretation and, as Eggebrecht maintains, is intimately related to a "B-A-C-H sphere" of tones that forms the third theme of the quadruple fugue (i.e., the four that spell Bach's name with the addition of C sharp and D).[40] The tones involved are, of course, the ones that constitute the chromatic tetrachord in D minor. On its first appearance the four notes in Bach's name—C, B, B flat, A—initiate a line that descends from the final D of the theme, pivots around the note G sharp, and mirrors the descent by a return from A to D via the notes B, C, C sharp [D] (Ex. 5). The descent pattern fa, mi, fa, mi corresponds in terms of solmization syllables to B-A-C-H, while the ascent reverses the pattern: mi, fa, mi, fa. The patterns suggest those of the melodic minor scale in descent and ascent respectively. In its preserving the melodic directional qualities of raised and lowered tones the melodic minor scale can be considered the descendant of the Dorian mode with variable B fa-mi that Luther compared to the "poor weak sinner." That is, the raised sixth and seventh degrees can be interchanged with the lowered forms, as Bach does extensively in this piece, to produce a wavering, uncertain quality. The exchange between raised and lowered semitones characterizes much of *The Art of Fugue* and can be seen in the ingenious shifting of mi and fa in the theme of the "Canon in augmentation and inversion" as well as in much secondary counterpoint throughout the collection. In fact, Bach's play with the directional tendencies of accidental semitones is at least as significant and conscious a technique—and certainly as all-pervasive—as the inversion of themes and whole pieces. Possibly the idea of descent followed by ascent in the countersubject of Contrapunctus III was intended to suggest the dualism of human existence versus hopes for a future life, as in the "Christus Coronabit Crucigeros" canon, and as suggested in the association of descending chromaticism with the words *hofft auf Leben* of the goblet inscription. In episodic development of this idea the four-semitone pattern is used in descent only, but with a diatonic ascent from dominant

---

39. Eggebrecht, *Bachs Kunst der Fuge*; see especially pp. 46–52.
40. Eggebrecht, *Bachs Kunst der Fuge,* pp. 10–18.

EXAMPLE 5. *The Art of Fugue*: countersubject of Contrapunctus III

EXAMPLE 6. Excerpt from *The Art of Fugue,* Contrapunctus III

EXAMPLE 7. Excerpt from *The Art of Fugue,* Contrapunctus III

to tonic as its counterpoint (Ex. 6). This pattern, which sets up cadential sequences following the circle of fifths and sometimes changes from minor to major, suggests, perhaps, the hopeful character of the reversal. But the chromatic wavering is the dominant device in generating the affect in this piece; both the syncopated rhythm and the chromaticism of the countersubject find their way into the theme itself, so that at times even the stability of the cantus-firmus–like voice is undermined (Ex. 7).

The two triple fugues, Contrapunctus VIII and XI, are, of course, intimately related, and the second of these pieces, as is well known, introduced as its third subject a long sequential line of eighth notes generated by the intervallic pattern of the B-A-C-H tones, which themselves begin the answering voice (Ex. 8). In Contrapunctus VIII this theme does not appear as such, but a very closely related theme—sometimes called its inversion—enters at the end of measure thirty-nine and is present throughout most of the remaining 150 bars of the fugue. The first theme of Contrapunctus VIII features the four-tone chromatic descent, C, B, B flat, A, but transforms its meaning. Despite the chromaticism and the wide range of the melodic descent, this theme, largely by virtue of the melodic leaps and emphasis on diatonic tones, projects a very positive character (Eggebrecht calls it the *lebensvolle* theme) (Ex. 9). If we knew that Bach had the goblet inscription in mind, we would conclude that he had devised this theme of fourteen tones as a means of making the chromatic descent fit with the idea expressed in the words *hofft auf Leben*. The second theme, also with fourteen tones, is a varied and inverted form of *The Art of Fugue* theme. It is often called a "sigh" or *sospiro* theme, because of the rests that interrupt its continuity; it has the same rhythm as the "Ach" theme of Sinfonia No. 9 (Ex. 10). The eighth-note theme in Example 8 often appears to bind these two principal subjects when all three ideas are combined. Whether this last theme is a subject or countersubject is an unsettled question; it enters as a counterpoint to the first *lebensvolle* subject of the fugue, a subject that has already been presented in the traditional pattern of tonic and dominant entries. The combination of these two ideas relates to the antithetical *ruffet, ach/hofft auf Leben* of the goblet inscription, in that the eighth-note theme generates sequential versions of the *ruffet, ach* pattern, that is, the inversion/retrograde of B-A-C-H. At times the counterpoint in this fugue forms combinations that are very close to the abstract patterns of the goblet, although isolating these among the tremendous variety of patterns would be just as pointless as listening for them specifically. A few are given here to prove the point (Ex. 11).

The tremendously expressive content of a piece such as the great four-part triple fugue, Contrapunctus XI, despite the great burden of its complex chromaticism and rhetorical gesture, gloriously transcends its own figural machinery. This piece and Contrapunctus VIII are principally related by the inversion in the former of all the themes of the latter. In Contrapunctus XI the themes enter in a more logical order. The variant of *The Art of Fugue* motive begins the work, now in its recto form, expanding to a twenty-seven bar section in D minor. In the second section the ascending form of the *lebensvolle* theme is heard in a context of raw linear chromaticism in both ascending and descending forms; the juxtaposition of the two at the beginning is especially suggestive of the kind of reversal presented in the "Christus Coronabit Crucigeros" canon. In this section the descending four-note chromatic pattern of Contrapunctus III returns, accompanied by its ascending counterpoint, and even this material is inverted (Ex. 12). In the second half of this section the chromaticism is virtually confined to its descending form, as the *lebensvolle* theme changes back to descent. Finally, for the reappearance of the inverted form of the first theme against this chromatic background, Bach devised an appoggiatura accompaniment that accentuates the *sospiro* character of the theme; and in the midst of this counterpoint emerge references to the B-A-C-H theme to come (Ex. 13). The section then closes on a positive F major cadence.

The third and final section of Contrapunctus XI is a remarkable contrapuntal tour de force occupying over half the fugue; in it the three themes are all presented in

EXAMPLE 8.   Third theme of *The Art of Fugue,* Contrapunctus XI

EXAMPLE 9.   First theme of *The Art of Fugue,* Contrapunctus VIII

EXAMPLE 10.   Second theme of *The Art of Fugue,* Contrapunctus VIII

EXAMPLE 11.   Excerpts from *The Art of Fugue,* Contrapunctus VIII

original and inverted forms, in triple counterpoint, and, in the case of *The Art of Fugue* theme, in simultaneous mirror inversion. All this is a further realization of possibilities suggested in Contrapunctus VIII but not completed there (the three themes were combined in triple counterpoint in uninverted form only). The systematic aspect of the peroration in Contrapunctus XI surely represents, at one

EXAMPLE 12.   Excerpts from *The Art of Fugue,* Contrapunctus XI

(a)

(b)

(c)

EXAMPLE 13.   Excerpt from *The Art of Fugue,* Contrapunctus XI

level, a stage along the way to the contrapuntal climax Bach is supposed to have carried out in the quadruple fugue: combination and note-for-note inversion of four themes in all four voices.[41] Yet, although there is a decidedly permutational

41. The source for this information is the obituary of Bach composed by C. P. E. Bach and J. F. Agricola in the months following Bach's death; it was published by Lorenz Mizler in 1754. See Hans Joachim Schulze, ed., *Bach-Dokumente.* Vol. 3. *Dokumente zum Nachwirken Johann Sebastian Bachs, 1750–1800* (Leizpig, 1972), p. 86; also David and Mendel, *The Bach Reader,* p. 221. For an explanation of the incomplete state of the quadruple fugue, see Christoph Wolff, "The Last Fugue: Unfinished?" *Current Musicology* 19 (1975): 71–77.

EXAMPLE 14.   Related themes from *The Art of Fugue,* Contrapunctus XI

(a)

(b)

(c)

cast to Contrapunctus XI, it is offset by a free-sounding, variational side that is largely owing to two features, the generalized linear chromaticism and, above all, the B-A-C-H material. The latter appears in three different forms: (1) that of the B-A-C-H pattern, generating ascending lines; (2) the descending pattern of Contrapunctus VIII, which generates inversion of B-A-C-H but is not strictly the inversion of the first pattern; and (3) a rising form that generates the B-A-C-H pattern but begins with a rising minor third and falling semitone—that is, the "A-C-H" interval pattern of Sinfonia No.9. Of these three patterns numbers 2 and 3 are inverted forms of one another, while the B-A-C-H pattern is, in fact, not inverted (Ex. 14). When it enters, the eighth-note B-A-C-H theme makes a striking effect in low register above the ascending form of the *lebensvolle* theme. As it continues, ever rising in pitch and entering in successively higher voices, the impression is created of something much more significant and dynamic than the scalar chromaticism that earlier accompanied the second theme. Once again the combinations suggested in the goblet inscription are present, especially that of B-A-C-H with the rising semitone idea that would indicate the idea of reversal suggested in *hofft auf Leben* (Ex. 15). This latter idea is now suggested in the ascending form of the second theme as well, which for musical reasons has lost one of its semitones.

The unfinished quadruple fugue itself confronts and combines practically all of these issues, its three themes suggesting in their numerical, symbolic, and musical features the qualities of being, will, and existence that Eggebrecht proposes. While it is tempting to suggest that the incomplete ending of the fugue is somehow connected to the composer's intention to represent an eschatological sense, that would

EXAMPLE 15.   Excerpts from *The Art of Fugue,* Contrapunctus XI

EXAMPLE 16.   *The Art of Fugue*: excerpt from the first section of the quadruple fugue

be going too far.[42] In the first theme, the seven tones, whole- and half-tone motion, reverse symmetry, and pure diatonicism all symbolize the cosmic, unchanging, ontological perspective—all that, were it all there was, would remain static and archaic in character. Bach, however, soon introduces chromaticism into the counterpoint (mm. 15–18); and when the theme is inverted (beginning in m. 21) he not only introduced chromaticism resembling B-A-C-H in the other two voices but provides the B-A-C-H tonal material, in jumbled order, in the theme itself (Ex. 16). All three sections of the fugue, in fact, utilize linear chromaticism, mostly in the pattern of four ascending tones.

The second theme of the quadruple fugue makes an obviously soloistic impact on its first entrance. Since its first seven tones of upbeat character are overlapped with the cadence of the first section, the long line of forty-one notes (the numerical equivalent of J. S. Bach) seems to emerge from the close of the fugue. It then

42. From time to time this idea has been proposed in one form or another. See, for example, Ludwig Prautzsch, *Vor deinen Thron tret ich hiermit* (Neuhausen-Stuttgart, 1980) pp. 120–28, 169–86. The hypothesis advanced in the last source cited in the preceding note, however, suggests that Bach's death prevented his clarifying his intention for the print with regard to a work that was probably almost complete.

pushes dynamically upward to its climax, B flat, which in itself was perhaps intended to have emblematic quality as the first tone of the composer's name. After combining this second theme with the first in tonic, dominant, and relative major (the very keys, d, a, F, suggesting the first three tones of the main theme), the movement turns to G minor, in which the final entry of the second theme beginning on B flat in the bass is combined with the first theme in stretto in both *dux* and *comes* forms, the first in G *major* (i.e., with B natural) and the second in G minor (with E flat). The ending of this section in G minor can be considered a form of catabasis that allows Bach's name to begin the third section on the correct tone and creates the sense of return to D minor via the change from B flat to B and the additional tones, C sharp–D. Eggebrecht sees these two tones as the composer's representation of his hopes of reaching the *Grundton,* conceived in religious terms, a plausible allegory that is reflected in the reversal of the fa/mi tones of Bach's name to mi/fa.[43]

In terms of the tonal content of the entering voices in the third, B-A-C-H, section of the quadruple fugue the expansion of the "B-A-C-H sphere" to six semitones creates a spectrum of eleven semitones between any two successive entries of the theme. And Bach arranges the series to encompass all twelve tones. This he does in several different ways, each of which involves an ascending line of four semitones (Ex. 17). In the entries of the theme in the exposition (mm. 197–98 and 205–6), the ascending semitone C sharp–D is continued upward with D sharp–E (D sharp is the "missing" twelfth tone between the theme and its answer). In the stretto between theme and answer the D sharp–E semitone is provided by means of a sequential repetition of the cadence of the theme a tone higher (mm. 220–21). When the theme is answered by its inversion, the "missing" pitches are different ones (F sharp–G–A), so Bach places a four semitone ascent (F sharp–G–G sharp–A) in the bass against the theme (mm. 211–13), thereby supplying the required tones. And for the final appearance of the theme, now preceded rather than followed by its inversion, the chromatic motion is particularly intense, involving a free appearance of the B-A-C-H pattern at the fifth below in the tenor (mm. 224–26). Here the four semitone ascent appears in the bass as counterpoint to the theme at pitch, while the tenor provides three of the four remaining semitones. Now Bach allows the chromatic ascent in the bass to move up to the twelfth tone before the theme ends (m. 228).

In all this there is a sense that Bach was intent on providing all twelve semitones between theme, answer, and counterpoint. And, in addition, it is noteworthy first that the four-note chromatic ascent is always associated with the B-A-C-H theme itself, either as extension or counterpoint, never with its answer or inversion, and second, that the four pitches are, in every case but one, the inverted/retrograde

43. Eggebrecht, *Bachs Kunst der Fugue,* p. 15.

(a)

(b)

(c)

(d)

(e)

form of the *hofft auf Leben* pattern from the Bach goblet (C sharp–D–D sharp–E). The one case where the pattern is transposed is the one where the tones in their descending form are already contained within the answering inversion of the theme (mm. 213–15). And for the final appearance of the theme the C sharp–D–D sharp–E pattern appears, as we said, in the bass as counterpoint to the theme. Thus the third segment of the quadruple fugue presents all three patterns from the goblet inscription, the third, *hofft auf Leben*, in inversion only and in close association with the B-A-C-H tones themselves. Rather strikingly, the association via the goblet of these passages—B-A-C-H/*hofft auf Leben*, Bach hopes for life—contains the same eschatological quality as Eggebrecht's suggestion of Bach's striving to reach the *Grundton*.

The preceding discussion may well recall Schönberg's remarks about Bach as the first "composer with twelve tones" and his mastery of the "hidden mysteries" of tone relations, something that, in fact, is disclosed in a purposive manner in *The Art of Fugue*. But these mysteries are not to be found in the raw patterns of the goblet inscription. Unlike those commentators who have struggled to find something "canonic" in the goblet puzzle, Bach was neither interested in producing bizarre harmonic progressions simply because they happened to utilize the pitch material on the goblet nor was he content to give much attention to the routine, sequential patterns that can be formed from some of the patterns. Nevertheless, it is possible, especially in light of recent knowledge, that composition of much of *The Art of Fugue* probably began in the late 1730s, that a connection existed between the goblet (as a challenge) and the chromatic fugues of the set: primarily numbers III, VIII, and XI, in addition to the quadruple fugue.[44] A tracing of some of the interconnections between these four pieces suggests a form of allegory related to the role of B-A-C-H in the work as a whole.

All the foregoing suggests that Bach intended a grand design related to the full emergence and development of the B-A-C-H subject in the quadruple fugue. The context for this feature of the work is, of course, the places where chromaticism is most evident. In Contrapunctus III the chromaticism exists primarily in the form of a counterpoint to the main theme indicating the dualism of melodic descent followed by ascent; but all the developments deal with the chromatic descent of four tones. In Contrapunctus VIII this descent is made into a new theme of positive character; but still chromatic descent dominates the piece. In Contrapunctus XI this new theme is inverted in the context of conspicuous antithesis of chromatic descent and ascent; the secondary counterpoint of Contrapunctus III returns and is inverted also. Then, in all three sections of the quadruple fugue the chromatic ascent alone is used, its quintessential form being the particular relationship to the B-A-C-H theme of the third section. In Contrapunctus XI the B-A-C-H theme

---

44. On the dating of *The Art of Fugue,* see Christoph Wolff, "Zur Chronologie und Kompositionsgeschichte von Bachs Kunst der Fugue," *Beiträge zur Musikwissenschaft* (1983): 130–42.

gradually reveals its relationship to the third theme of its counterpart, the three-part triple fugue, Contrapunctus VIII. The eighth-note theme of the earlier fugue on the same material is shown in Contrapunctus XI to be the mirror form of what might be called an A-C-H theme. Only in the four-part fugue does the precise relationship between the B-A-C-H subject and these other two related forms emerge. And the dominance of the ending of this fugue by these three versions of the third theme produces a dynamic, variation-like interaction that places the first, "sigh" theme and the second, chromatic theme in a new light. The three themes suggest the three ideas that are confronted on the Bach goblet: *ruffet ach* (the *sospiro* theme), *hofft auf Leben* (the *lebensvolle* theme) and, of course, B-A-C-H.

The sense of progression within these fugues, and its relationship to the emergence of the name Bach, has a counterpart within the collection as a whole. That is, from Contrapunctus III through the three-part triple fugue, Contrapunctus VIII,, and the four-part triple fugue on the same material plus the name Bach, Contrapunctus XI, to the incomplete quadruple fugue, in which the name Bach appears as a more genuine subject in its own right (not generated by other material) it is possible to perceive a quasi-allegorical thread running through the work. This is manifested in the change from emphasis on the descending form of the four-tone chromatic idea in Contrapunctus III and VIII to the simultaneity of both in Contrapunctus XI and the focus on the ascending form only in the quadruple fugue. The "Ach" material and the more generalized chromaticism of the "Bach-sphere" represent the general human condition, "Bach" its specific manifestation. The individual, first taken simply as a representative of humanity in general, leaves here an emblem of his subjective independence.

Such a pronounced sense of design is a characteristic feature of "allegorical" art, even when, as is certainly *not* the case here, the work offers little else to later ages. The closing words of Benjamin's study of the *Trauerspiel* convey the spirit:

> In the ruins of great buildings the idea of the plan speaks more impressively than in lesser buildings, however well preserved they are; and for this reason the German *Trauerspiel* merits interpretation. In the spirit of allegory it is conceived from the outset as a ruin, a fragment. Others may shine resplendently as on the first day; this form preserves the image of beauty to the very last.[45]

These words, and Benjamin's study as a whole, urge the detailed study of allegorical intent from a philosophical standpoint as a vital means of probing the meaning of the works, even though the endeavor seems to fragment them even further. Recognition of the grandeur of the design and the elevated quality of the ideas that are dealt with, allegorically, is confirmation of the striving for universality that animated the spiritual life.

45. Benjamin, *The Origin*, p. 235.

The name Bach is thus two-dimensional. On the one hand there is the powerful historical sense of the composer whose very name is rich in traditional associations of allegorical-theological character. Yet on the other hand stands the strong-willed individual who was capable of playing with convention, symmetry, and gesture throughout his work, not in a joking manner but in a way that shows his independence in the face of convention. It is fitting that *The Art of Fugue* should have been the work in which these sides were symbolically confronted for the last time, and that the work should, by pure historical accident, have been left open-ended. The broken-off quadruple fugue recalls the same situation that Adorno invoked when he suggested that Bach might have become conscious of a split between the historical and the "universal" in his own work. Eggebrecht presumably intends something of the same kind when he refers, somewhat obliquely, to the eschatological meaning of the quadruple fugue and the appropriateness of the substitution of the chorale "Vor deinen Thron tret' ich hiermit," even though the latter has no musical connection to *The Art of Fugue*.[46] The romantic story of the intervention of Bach's death in the completion of the work is a last dramatic reminder of the interaction of the historical and finite with the striving for universal, future-oriented communication. The fact that, in all probability, neither the romantic picture nor Adorno's interpretation coincides perfectly with the historical facts surrounding the composition of *The Art of Fugue* does not affect their value as a meaningful part of the work's reception history. In fact, they affirm a certain distance between aesthetic truth and pure historicism, a distance that is accurately measured by the hermeneutic approach.

Although much of *The Art of Fugue* is canon-like, with a decidedly static permutational side, it nevertheless changes almost kaleidoscopically in ways that demand close listening; it offers many variational devices that are based on the fragmentation of the theme, "subjective reflection" as Adorno called it, viewing such subtle intricacy as the product of Bach's "genius of meditation."[47] The latter devices draw the player and listener into a created world of correspondences in which static hierarchical features illuminate and are illuminated in their turn by the free play of the individual consciousness, however slight the scope allotted to it. This is as true in its way of this work as it is of the relationship between festive court orchestra and feeble violino piccolo in the third movement of the First Brandenburg Concerto, in which some of the weightiest structural moments are entrusted to the equivalent in terms of sonority to what can only ironically be called the "poor weak sinner" of the name Bach. In terms of Wellek's juxtaposition of "subjective" and "baroque,"[48] Bach's is an art that is no longer explained by such a historical epithet, but in its unique ability to provide a mirror in tones of the hope within human anxiety, the redemption of a chromaticism burdened with its assigned significance, it is truly for all time, neither historical nor timeless exclusively, but rooted clearly in the one even as it unmistakably evokes the other.

46. Eggebrecht, *Bachs Kunst der Fuge*, pp. 34–40.
47. Adorno, "Bach Defended," pp. 138–39.
48. Wellek, "The Concept of Baroque," p. 112.

CHAPTER THREE

Aspects of

Tonal Theory

in the

Early Eighteenth

Century

The Circle of Keys

We must now make an excursion into the realm of tonal theory as it existed when Bach's early cantatas were written. Our aim will be to discover some of the associations tonal elements may have had for Bach, as well as the purely musical basis for his tonal planning. If not the most forward-looking composer of his time, Bach was the most advanced, a quality that, as Theodor Adorno stresses, paradoxically bears the most intimate relationship to his love for the archaic.[1] The comprehensiveness of his harmonic-tonal vision, epitomized in his great legacy for posterity, the *Well-Tempered Clavier,* distinguished him from his contemporaries. If "well-tempered" tuning, called by Adorno a "monument to musical rationalism," was the basis of Bach's harmonic daring, then the principal conceptual-theoretical basis of his work in general was the circle of keys, the major theoretical achievement of the age. The *musicalischer Circul* must be viewed, in light of what preceded it and its becoming a commonplace in later music, as more than a historical product of the early eighteenth century. It was first presented in 1711 by Johann David Heinichen and intended to rationalize and systematize the most important tendencies and achievements in tonality of its age.[2] In fact, the *musicalischer Circul* can be considered a symbol for the Janus-faced aspect of musical thought of its time.

Heinichen's *Neu-erfundene und gründliche Anweisung* is particularly important for the present study on several counts. First of all, it integrates the concepts we know as "relative" major/minor keys and the subdominant and dominant sides of the key and includes a full statement concerning degrees of nearness in tonal relationships, their practical use in modulation, and their conceptual basis in the circle itself. At the same time Heinichen's discussion of these important matters, although generally "modern" and iconoclastic in spirit, preserves a number of ideas that descend

1. Adorno, "Bach Defended," pp. 139–42.
2. Heinichen, *Anweisung,* pp. 261–67.

from traditional modal–hexachordal theory. Heinichen knew the work of both his teacher, Kuhnau, and Kircher on the circle of fifths.[3] The work of no one single theorist from this period, however, fully represents the transitional nature of all branches of tonal theory that resulted from an increasingly acute sense of the inadequacy of traditional concepts to describe contemporary practice. The more important German treatises from the end of the seventeenth and the first two decades of the eighteenth centuries all preserve somewhat different versions or perceptions of how modal and hexachord theory can be accommodated to the new musical styles. The very fact that some of Heinichen's ideas, such as his description of the sharps and flats as "chromatic" and "enharmonic" respectively and the sense of degrees of "chromaticism" and "enharmonicism" as keys approach or move away from the *extremum chromaticum* and *extremum enharmonicum,* were deleted in his 1728 revision and expansion of the book (now called *Der General-Bass in der Composition*) makes them all the more interesting for us. It must be emphasized that tonal theory was in a state of flux in the early eighteenth century and exhibited what we perceive as a strange conjunction of modern and archaic elements. Present-day study of Heinichen's and other contemporary treatises tends to overlook those aspects that have not remained part of our post-Rameau theory. As Walter Benjamin's criticism teaches us, however, it is often the historical, the "dated" and "dead" aspects, that provide us with the easiest ingress to the "truth content," even if only through the process of "mortifying" the works, that is, stripping away the historical by recognizing it for what it is.[4] By developing a feel for the concerns and modes of expression of the theorists of this period—for it is possible that we cannot systematize their views to our satisfaction—we will learn how to rationalize many of the otherwise recalcitrant aspects of Bach's tonal planning.

The pattern of Heinichen's circle of keys is easily presented and remembered, for it is symmetrical in the sense that each ambitus follows the same order: for C major/A major the arrangement is F, d, C, a, G, e.[5] Heinichen rejects the sequence of keys that moves entirely by thirds—d, F, a, C, e, G (a sequence that constitutes successions of movement keys in a number of Bach's most consciously planned cantatas, such as Nos. 61, 12, 186, 27, 104)—because the major third relationship is not considered to be a close one. Heinichen differentiates his circle from earlier ones in its presentation of both major and minor keys in the most natural ordering of relative major and minor pairs a fifth apart. Johann Mattheson, however, disagrees with Heinichen's circle, and in his *Kleine General-Bass Schule* of 1735 he asserts that, rather than key signatures, the relative consonance or dissonance of the interval between adjacent keys must take precedence as the measure of tonal relationship.

3. Heinichen (*Anweisung*, p. 261; *Der General-Bass*, p. 840) states that he learned of earlier circles, including that of Kircher, from Kuhnau; Kircher's circle appears on pp. 462–63 of the *Musurgia*.

4. Benjamin, *The Origin*, p. 182.

5. Heinichen, *Anweisung*, pp. 261–62.

His arrangement, likewise, has no major thirds but features minor thirds and perfect fifths between adjacent keys: A flat, E flat, c, g, B flat, F, d, a, C, G, e, b, and so on.[6] As a result, his circle is not symmetrical as Heinichen's is; that is, the arrangement of the ambitus is not the same for every major or minor key, although it does preserve the sense of relative major/minor pairing. Heinichen seems to have formed his concept with some consideration for tradition. He preserves (perhaps accidentally) two important "historical" features: the subdominant and mediant keys are polarized as they are in the circular ordering by perfect fifths (*F, C, G, d, a, e*); and each major key is adjacent to the key of its supertonic. The merging of scalar (stepwise) and tonal (by fifths) ordering of keys underlies the earliest and longest-lived arrangement of the modes in the seventeenth century, the one that was still the basis of Mattheson's famous set of key characteristics in 1713.

In the mainstream sixteenth-century view the circular ordering of tones according to fifths had been subordinate, in both theory and practice, to mode, or scalar organization. Music was composed in a mode rather than in a system, at least until the most advanced music of the second half of the century.[7] Yet the learning of music with the aid of solmization inevitably threaded a tonal sense through the music, and the sense of relationships and antitheses between certain modes sometimes expressed underlying tonal (hexachordal) aspects. The syllables of the hexachord were not, of course, related to *ut* as tonic, as in modern solmization, nor were the modes thought of in this way. Nonetheless, the identity of syllable names and interval patterns at different pitch levels encouraged people to hear much music in terms of fourth and fifth parallels. Other suggestive aspects of Renaissance tonality—the appearance of only flat signatures, the different roles and characters of the sharps and flats generally, the greater number of flats in the lower voices in cases of conflicting key signatures, and, only later, the presence of F clefs in the lowest register, C clefs in the middle, and G clefs in the highest parts—invite the conclusion that baroque tonal procedures could have been reconciled without too much difficulty with hexachordal practice. From this vantage point the development of the circle of keys is most easily comprehended.

Before the seventeenth century the only comparable symbol of tonal comprehensiveness was the medieval-Renaissance gamut with its three types of hexachord, within which the various modes were grouped. The move to the "musical circle" as the new conceptual model for the tonal spectrum of music came about through the reduction of the modes at each transpositional level (hexachord) and the ordering of the three hexachords of the gamut under a single ambitus of six keys. Since Heinichen states explicitly that his discovery of the natural scheme of key relation-

---

6. Johann Mattheson, *Kleine General-Bass Schule* (Hamburg, 1735), p. 131.
7. On the use of the concept of *System* in the analysis of Monteverdi madrigals, see Carl Dahlhaus, *Untersuchungen über die Entstehung der harmonischen Tonalität* (Kassel, 1968), pp. 257–86.

ships of the ambitus led him to the presentation of a full circle of keys, we must now consider just what underlies the concept of ambitus.[8]

The Concept of Ambitus

Heinichen's adoption of the traditional modal term "ambitus" to designate the six closely related keys that were subsumed under a single tonic and his laying out the keys around a circle derive from the early-seventeenth-century concept of the six modes "system" (or twelve, including the plagal forms), whose final notes were ordered according to the keynotes of a single hexachord.[9] In much early-seventeenth-century music there was a sense that a circular arrangement underlay the six tones that formed the modal keynotes—F (fa), C (ut), G (sol), D (re), A (la), E (mi)—with the fa and mi closing the system.[10] There was also the sense that the system could be extended on either or both ends with B flat (fa) and B (mi) forming a larger system of two or three hexachords. Heinichen surely chose the term *ambitus,* which literally means "a circle," for its sense of a closed tonal range, a system, or, as Mattheson defined the word, the *Sprengel einer Tonart.*[11] In his manuscript *Fundamenta Compositionis,* Heinichen's teacher, Johann Kuhnau treated the modes while retaining their traditional names of Dorian, Phyrgian, and so on, as comprising complexes of cadences, usually on six scale degrees for each mode. The mode itself thus became comparable to a system in which a hierarchy has been established (with Kuhnau the word *system* means "key signature level," as it does for Heinichen and Mattheson).[12] Kuhnau clearly attempted to follow modal theory in giving first place among the cadences to the traditional three degrees (final, confinal, and median) and retaining a variety of cadence types, such as Phyrgian and plagal, under a multiplicity of Latin headings. There is not yet, however, a fully articulated sense of the grouping of keys *at different key signature levels* under one tonic (i.e., subdominant, dominant, etc.), or any attempt to organize the entire spectrum of modes and cadences into a still more comprehensive order.

---

8. Heinichen, *Anweisung,* pp. 261–62; *General-Bass,* pp. 837–40.

9. Bernhard, *Tractatus compositionis augmentatus,* p. 97; for other references to *Systema der Octav, Systematibus transpositis, Systemate duro, Systemate molli* and the like, see pp. 44, 56–58, 59–61. It seems clear that Bernhard uses the word *Systema* in both modal (octave species) and tonal (hexachord) senses. In light of the overlap of the modal with ambitus, Heinichen's transferral of ambitus to the tonal sphere is understandable (Bernhard, p. 91, No. 3: "Ist also die *Octave* und die darinnen begriffene *Soni* dasjenige worinen ein *Modus* beruhet, und wird solche *Octave* mit denen dazu gehörigen *Sonis* bey denen *Musicis* ambitus genennet"; cf. the reference to *Systema der Octav,* p. 56).

10. This question will be taken up in my forthcoming book, *Monteverdi's Tonal Language* (New York: Schirmer Books, 1992).

11. Mattheson, *Der vollkommene Kapellmeister,* p. 66.

12. Johann Kuhnau, *Fundamenta Compositionis* (MS, Leipzig, 1703), chapter 5, "Von denen Modis insgemein, und deroselben Ambitu, Clausulis und Repercussio"; Kuhnau defines *ambitus* in the traditional modal sense.

The most important difference from Kuhnau's in Heinichen's ambitus-within-circle idea is that the six keynotes, formerly grouped under a single key signature level, are reduced to two modal types, with one of each type at all three levels that once represented the hexachords: tonic (plus the relative minor), subdominant (plus the supertonic), and dominant (plus the mediant). In the sixteenth and early seventeenth centuries, the six tones that served as *voces* in solmization and then as finales in modal theory were grouped under the single hexachord (system), whereas Heinichen now describes his *ambitus* as consisting of three *systemata*. It is as if the ambitus has in this respect replaced the gamut, and the circle has become a spectrum of transposable gamuts. However, the most important point is that all six keys are now related hierarchically to one key from the central major/minor pair.

All earlier systems were, of course, too narrow in tonal range to deal with seventeenth-century music, which is founded in the frequent transposition not of simply the hexachord but of the entire gamut.[13] For example, in 1672, Lorenzo Penna, in his *Li Primi Albori Musicali* gives circles of cadences—each designated *circolo* (circle) or *ruota* (wheel)—organized by fifths. The *cadenze ordinarie* are formed on the six tones of the natural hexachord from E (mi) to F (fa), while the others are called *cadenze estravaganti per b.b. molle* and *estravaganti per li* ♯♯ respectively (there are also four *cadenze communi alli* ♭♭, & ♯♯, or enharmonic cadences). But this presentation is an extension of the tuning circles of single notes, such as Kircher's, and does not imply the existence of keys at all levels. (Penna's circles of cadences do, however, allow for a series of characteristic chord progressions for each cadence, which he gives in figured bass, that increase the sense of modulation.) In fact, Penna's scheme of transposition, based on hexachord mutation, goes only to three sharps and flats, while his circles themselves use key signatures of only two sharps or flats.[14] Heinichen takes pains to point out that his circle is different from earlier ones in that the others were not circles of *keys* and did not encompass key relationships.[15] That Penna discusses transposition via the hexachords (with the major Ionian and Mixolydian modes in signatures up to three sharps and flats), the modes, and the circles in widely separated sections of his treatise indicates the incomplete state of theoretical understanding of tonal relationships throughout most of the seventeenth century. For the first time, Heinichen's circle and ambitus integrate a theoretical understanding of all three branches of tonal thinking into one concept

---

13. A major stumbling block in Dahlhaus's analyses of Monteverdi madrigals (*Untersuchungen,* pp. 257–86) is his limiting of their tonal range to a single system rather than a three-system (or three-hexachord) gamut. As a result the system shifts far too often, parallel transposed passages must be considered to be in different modes, and the like, all of which undermine the often brilliant analyses. In fact, it appears that the tonal range in these works is expanding to two or three systems simultaneously without the sense of a center of gravity that one predominant mode would provide.

14. Lorenzo Penna, *Li Primi Albori Musicali* (Bologna, 1672), pp. 174–83 (circles of cadences); pp. 26–29 (transposition); pp. 120–28 (modes).

15. Heinichen, *Anweisung,* p. 261.

based on key-signature levels as the measure of tonal distance. His statement that the *musicalischer Circul* renders the modes obsolete is revealing of the fact that the difference between tonal and modal relationships consists in the presence or absence of different key-signature levels.[16]

The idea of mode, at least as the governing concept of composition, weakened in the early seventeenth century to the extent that works such as many of Monteverdi's madrigals were perhaps composed more with the above-mentioned concept of the system of modes in mind. The system of modes relegated precise modal definition to a secondary role, represented chiefly by cadence degrees without the sense of modulation as we know it, with the three minor modes (or cadence degrees) offering the possibility of raised thirds at cadences (phrase endings) in a kind of triple Tierce de Picardie effect (all of Penna's and Kuhnau's cadences are given in this form). Often a cadential spectrum, rather than modal unity, produced a wide chordal variety without a single dominant mode—what Jacques Handschin and Dahlhaus refer to as a modal "society."[17] This situation obviously denied the sense of relative majors and minors sometimes created in the music by falling third progressions and increased that of modal ordering by fifth levels. In fact, circle of fifths progressions—including those built entirely on major chords—are common in some tonally advanced music from the late sixteenth and early seventeenth centuries, such as the Lassus *Prophetiae Sibyllarum* and Vicentino's madrigals. Yet since none of these degrees was a bona fide mode or key according to either the traditional or emerging tonal-harmonic paradigms, any kind of incipient circle of keys, while allowing circles of *cadences,* especially in major, was denied at first as the next step in music theory after the circle of tones.[18] The concept of system had to be united with the concept of mode in such a manner that the latter would lose some of its autonomy: that is, its cadences, which now represented other modes, would have to follow a pattern compatible with the overall arrangement of modes themselves. The profusion of cadences within the single mode in patterns such as Kuhnau's did not lead to a larger ordering of both the modes and their secondary cadences into a circle that was symmetrical for all keys (or nearly so) until Heinichen's ambitus.

Yet, already in the sixteenth-century "theory" of perfect fourth and fifth species and of modal *proprietates* we can sense from time to time perceptions of the organization of modes in patterns that suggest the merging of the underlying organization by fifths of the tones within the hexachord with the more overt one among the hexachords themselves. Thus the Lydian mode was sometimes characterized as

16. Heinichen, *Anweisung,* p. 267.
17. Jacques Handschin, *Der Toncharakter: Eine Einführung in die Tonpsychologie* (Zurich, 1948), p. 260; Dahlhaus, *Untersuchungen,* p. 259.
18. Penna, *Albori,* pp. 174–83.

"soft" and related to the soft hexachord by virtue of the B flat; its upper species of fourth, fa/ut, was called *mollar* and considered to be characteristic of the soft hexachord. Likewise, the Phrygian mode was called "hard" and related to the *cantus durus* through its lower *dural* species of fourth, mi/la, that characterized the hard hexachord.[19] When Glarean explains the meaning of a common adage of the sixteenth century that opposed Dorian and Phrygian in terms of the fifth species of the two modes, one can perceive this relationship in terms of the presence or absence of the tritone and the B-quadro, and hence of the juxtaposition of elements characteristic of two different hexachords. Likewise, Glarean berates his own time for its "weakness" in preferring the Lydian mode with the B flat to the mode without it.[20] Luther himself made a similar juxtaposition between tones on F (for the Gospel) and G (for the Epistle), as an expression of the difference between Christ, the "friendly Lord, whose sayings are dear," and Paul, whose words are *ernst* and *gravitätisch*.[21] There is even the sense sometimes of a relationship between Mixolydian (also related to the *cantus durus*) and Phrygian and between Lydian and Dorian (the modes traditionally "corrected" with B flat).[22] Such tonal perceptions are not, perhaps, fundamental to Renaissance theory. They do indicate, however, that the tonal perceptions of the seventeenth and eighteenth centuries had a good deal of tradition behind them, despite our treatment of baroque tonal procedures and theory that has largely given precedence to subsequent developments, and not always with good reason.

The old concept of the mi/fa, which by the early seventeenth century had become the Phrygian cadence as the harmonic-tonal means of identifying a particular system, remained throughout the entire period as the device to signal the ambitus in a single progression bringing together the flat/sharp extremes. This very familiar progression, although usually considered to derive from the minor mode—iv^6 to V—was clearly associated with the ambitus centered on major and minor together.

19. Carl Dahlhaus, "Die Termini Dur und Moll," *Archiv für Musikwissenschaft* 12 (1955): 289–91.

20. Heinrich Glarean, *Dodecachordon* (Basel, 1547), trans., transcription, and commentary Clement A. Miller, *Musicological Studies and Documents,* vol. 6 (Rome, 1965), 1: 129–30, 132.

21. Luther's remarks on the tones for the *Deutsche Messe* were recorded by his friend and collaborator, Johann Walther, and printed in Michael Praetorius, *Syntagma Musicum* I (Wolffenbüttel, 1619), pp. 451–52: "Christus ist ein freundlicher HERR, und seine Rede sind lieblich, darumb wollen wir *Sextum Tonum* zum Evangelio nehmen, und weil S. Paulus ein ernster Apostel ist, wollen wir *Octavum Tonum* zur Epistel ordnen."

22. See Maria Rika Maniates, *Mannerism in Italian Music and Culture, 1530–1630* (Chapel Hill, 1979), pp. 178–92, "Chromaticism," where the influence of hexachordal thinking on the modes is discussed. Some sixteenth-century writers, Nicolaus Listenius, for example, link particular modes with one or another of the hexachords almost as a matter of course: Lydian with the soft hexachord, Dorian with the natural, Mixolydian and Phrygian with the hard. Maniates comments (pp. 178–79) that Listenius's "perspicacious analysis suggests that the hexachord system is fast becoming an integral part of sonorous and harmonic character. If a composition in the Lydian mode can be defined as belonging to the soft hexachord, then by converse logic, a composition that mixes the soft and natural hexachords can be defined as belonging to the Lydian and Ionian modes. The approach exemplified by Listenius will have a great impact on later modulatory practices in chromatic music."

This association is borne out by its frequent occurrence at the close of movements in the relative minor in preparation for the major tonic, as well as the tendency of penultimate sections within extended single movements—for example, several movements from the Brandenburg Concertos, the last movement of the Italian Concerto, and numerous "B" sections of da capo arias—to close in the mediant (Phrygian) key immediately before returning to the tonic.[23] The sense of distance in these progressions is related to both Heinichen's and Mattheson's avoidance in their circles of the major third relationship. As we have said, Heinichen's layout of the individual ambitus of any key along his circle places keys that in the older theory would have represented fa and mi, for example, A flat and G minor in the C minor/E flat ambitus, at the outer limits, no doubt an unintentional act but nonetheless a meaningful one in terms of its reflecting the role of tradition in baroque tonal planning.

We may consider for a moment an important instance of Bach's making reference to these ideas for allegorical purposes, although it is not necessary, of course, to conclude that his understanding came from any one theorist. The brief chorus set twice to the words "Jesum von Nazareth" in the *St. John Passion* (and repeated several times thereafter to different texts) is built on the chords of the ambitus of the particular key in question in circle of fifths order, ending with the Phrygian cadence (see Chapter 10, Ex. 71). The choruses themselves are transposed throughout the *Passion* in an interlocking pattern of fourths and thirds. Given John's picture of Christ as the divine Logos, the Cosmic Christ, Bach's device has a striking resonance with the ancient idea of Christ as Creator-Logos binding all things together into a cosmic system, or *systema*.[24] Intuitively, Bach perceived a connection between the closed, circular ambitus and the more general concept of the system from which the ambitus descended. This is not an isolated reference in Bach's work to symbols of tonal comprehensiveness to allegorize counterparts in the world of ideas—the meaning that is preserved in the general use of *gamut* in English. The canon *per tonos* dedicated to Frederick the Great, referred to in Chapter 1, is another such piece, mirroring the circle of keys in minor, and the presence of the twelve tones of the chromatic scale on the Bach goblet yet another. The huge progressions through successive key signature levels—four flats to four sharps—in Part One of the *St. Matthew Passion* represent the idea of comprehensiveness. And, apart from the *Well-Tempered Clavier,* Bach arranges some of his collections into patterns that reflect aspects of the contemporary historical view of tonality.

23. In several of the Brandenburg Concertos the move to the mediant key seems to correspond to the modulation furthest from the tonic, and the return to the original key is made without a modulation (in the opening movement of the second concerto the return to F major after a strong A minor cadence is made with all the instruments playing in octaves to emphasize the tonic).

24. On the ideas of the Cosmic Christ and the universe as system, see Jaroslav Pelikan, *Jesus through the Centuries* (New Haven, 1985), p. 65.

The most strikingly "historical" of all the concepts in Heinichen's first discussion of the circle is that of the sharps and flats as *genus chromaticum* and *genus enharmonicum,* respectively, for these ideas did not survive even the 1728 revision of the book. Despite the fact that in one form or another they appeared in a great deal of music theory up to this point, they were quickly on the way out. When Heinichen calls C minor "more enharmonic" than G minor, because it is closer to the *extremum enharmonicum* of his circle, B flat minor, one senses that he is speaking of tonal qualities. In using the ancient genera names he clearly replaces the traditional medieval-Renaissance genera, *cantus durus* and *mollis,* which had been increasingly used by the preceding generations of German theorists to signify major (*dur*) and minor (*moll*). The use of traditional genera names for major and minor keys emphasized the reduction of modes to two basic types while recognizing the wide tonal distance between tonic major and minor keys.

Since these ideas are germane to an understanding of Bach's tonal procedures, we will now investigate the concept of musical genera, according an important place to the following general observation of Carl Dahlhaus that arose from his survey of the changing meanings of the terms *durus* and *mollis*:

> [In the seventeenth and early eighteenth centuries] the logical relationship between mode and transposition scale was reversed: up to the seventeenth century the transposition scales (*cantus durus* and *cantus mollis*) represented genera (*Tongeschlechter*), the modes (e.g., C-Ionian and A-Aeolian) represented the species (*Tonarten,* keys). Since then we treat the modes as genera (the Ionian mode as the major "genus," the Aeolian as the minor) and the transposition scales as species: C major [*dur*] and A minor [*moll*] as keys.[25]

Dahlhaus's statement is indicative of more than the evolution of musical terminology or shift of theoretical viewpoint. It is, in fact, of great importance for seventeenth- and eighteenth-century music and points to a major reorientation of tonal thought and practice during that period: the reduction of the modes, by this time twelve in number, to two types, based on their thirds and associated triads, and their merging with the hexachords to form a new tonal spectrum. This new order was larger in that it comprised up to twenty-four keys and utilized far more frequent and extensive shifts of system (key-signature level, i.e., modulation), but it sacrificed the greater subtlety of modal variety. This did not happen all at once, and it was certainly not complete by 1600. Nor, despite the basic truth of

25. Dahlhaus, "Die Termini," p. 291 (author's translation).

Dahlhaus's broad statement, were all the anomalies cleared up even by 1700. Andreas Werckmeister, one of the strongest advocates in the later seventeenth century of the new major and minor modes and the use of the terms *dur* and *moll* to describe them, still called the note A flat and the chord of A flat major, A *moll,* and the chord of A minor, A *dur,* as did most of his predecessors. Werckmeister spoke, without intending any contradiction, of the *two* modes, *dur* and *moll,* as Ionian and Mixolydian on the one hand and Dorian and Aeolian on the other.[26] That the significance of the words *durus* and *mollis* was altered to correspond with the reduction of the modes to two basic types has tended to obscure the fact that much baroque music was composed with a sensitivity to tonal *style* that was far greater than ours. Although it operated within a narrower framework, it preserved a stronger sense of the different characters of modulatory direction, of the shift from sharps to flats, the degree of sharpness or flatness of the music, and, it goes without saying, of modal distinctions. This situation was particularly intense in Germany where the conflict between the double use of the words *dur* and *moll* took place; in Germany both the Lutheran metaphysical tradition in music theory and the central place of the chorale in composition made traditional patterns of thought persist long after they had ceased to influence composition vitally elsewhere.

When in several places in the *St. Matthew Passion,* for example, Bach underscores the change from a region of sharps to one of flats with some conspicuous musicoallegorical device, he is recognizing an ancient perception of the sharps and flats as genera, subsuming change of mode as a secondary, attendant phenomenon (species). Therefore, it is insufficient and possibly inaccurate as well to describe such passages in terms of key alone. Composition in genera (i.e., according to sharp and flat key areas) is an important aspect of tonal planning; it has a history before Bach, of course, and it is reflected in the theory of the time. In 1650 Athanasius Kircher, for example, distinguished between *mutatio toni* (change of mode within the system) and *mutatio modi* (change of mode and system, or key-signature level); only the latter introduces shift of genus.[27]

Many theorists of the late seventeenth and early eighteenth centuries have their own means of treating the sharp and flat keys and tones as genera, ways that usually retain the sense of *cantus durus* and *mollis.* In 1708 Johann Gottfried Walther, for example, follows his teacher, Werckmeister, in using *dur* and *moll* for major and minor. Yet he employs the term *molle* for all flat tones in the chromatic scale, while

26. Werckmeister, *Musicae mathematicae,* pp. 120, 124. Similar instances from Werckmeister and other seventeenth- and early eighteenth-century German theorists are cited in Dahlhaus, "Die Termini," pp. 293–96; Walter Atcherson, "Key and Mode in Seventeenth-Century Music Theory Books," *Journal of Music Theory* 17 (1973): 205–33; Joel Lester, "Major-Minor Concepts and Modal Theory in Germany, 1592–1680," *Journal of the American Musicological Society* 30 (1977): 208–57; "The Recognition of Major and Minor Keys in German Theory, 1680–1730," *Journal of Music Theory* 22 (1978): 65–103.

27. Kircher, *Musurgia,* p. 672.

reserving *durum* for the "enharmonic" sharps; that is, E flat is E *molle,* F sharp is *Fis,* F double sharp is *Fis durum,* A sharp is A *durum,* E sharp is E *durum,* and so on. Behind the multiplicity of Walther's genera—*genus diatonico-chromaticum, chromatico-diatonicum,* and the like—lies an extraordinary sensitivity to harmonic style and tonal range, characteristic of the age generally. In the same year Gasparini, having illustrated "all" the keys, the sixteen most commonly used ones, refers to the remote ones as five (!) "others of the enharmonic or chromatic genus that might occur in the course of modulation (B flat minor, B major, C sharp minor, E flat minor and F sharp major); he names "transposition through every key *and genus* as essential to the good organist."[28] Here the word *genus* is associated with the extremes of tonal range, the less usable keys. Thomas Balthasar Janowka was the first, in 1701, to present all twenty-four keys with their Latin names, major and minor, and refers to the six most rarely used keys—B flat minor, B major, D flat, E flat minor, F sharp, and G sharp minor—as *chromatico-diatonico* as opposed to the eighteen that were *diatonico-chromatico.* He retains *durus* and *mollis* for sharp and flat respectively: "Ex B tonus minor Generis Chromatico-Diatonico-Mollis" (B flat minor); "Ex Cis tonus minor Generis Diatonico-Chromatico-Duri" (C sharp minor); "Generis Diatonici puri ex C tonus Major" (C major), and so on (the boundaries for the change from *diatonico-chromatico* to *chromatico-diatonico* are keys with signatures of four flats or sharps). Like Werckmeister, Johann Adolf Scheibe described enharmonic modulations as bringing about the change of both genus and key, the move being to a new key, which is absolutely unrelated to the original one in nature as well as scale.[29] Not everyone was in complete agreement with these uses of the Greek genera names, however. Mattheson explained, and condemned, what he felt was an all-too-common error, that of calling sharps chromatic and flats enharmonic. The note C sharp was called chromatic because it divided the interval C–D; D flat was called enharmonic because it divided the chromatic interval C sharp–D. Mattheson was careful to state that this view was held even though C sharp and D flat were the same note on the keyboard; that is, the sense of genera was conceptual and not merely allied with tuning concerns.[30]

The important sense of difference between the two modulatory directions and between the sharps and flats themselves was, of course, inherited from traditional hexachord theory, in particular the different primary roles played by the sharps and flats in Renaissance music; the former as *subsemitonia modi* were used frequently at

28. Johann Gottfried Walther, *Praecepta der musicalischen Composition* (MS, 1708), ed. Peter Benary (Leipzig, 1955), p. 66; F. Gasparini, *L'Armonico pratico al cimbalo* (1708), trans. Frank S. Stillings, ed. David L. Burrows, as *The Practical Harmonist at the Harpsichord* (New Haven, 1963), pp. 73–77, 95.

29. Thomas Balthasar Janowka, *Clavis ad thesaurum magnae artis musicae* (Prague, 1701), s.v. "Tonus"; Johann Adolph Scheibe, *Compendium Musices* (MS), ed. Peter Benary in *Die deutsche Kompositionslehre des 18. Jahrhunderts,* Jenaer Beiträge zur Musikforschung, vol. 3, ed. Heinrich Besseler (Leipzig, 1961), pp. 72–73.

30. Johann Mattheson, *Das neu-eröffnete Orchestre* (Hamburg, 1713), pp. 56–57.

cadences and not necessarily in fifth-related situations. The latter, used for hexachord mutations, transpositions, and correction of augmented and diminished intervals, always related to fifth-related tonal situations (Edward Lowinsky's "chain reaction" modulations are characteristic of the use of flats more than of sharps).[31] When Monteverdi spoke of three affective states as musical *termini—molle, temperato,* and the one he claimed to introduce for the first time, *concitato*—he might well have been making a connection between the Greek affective genera (*humile, temperato, grande*) and the tonal character of sixteenth-century music as expressed in the three tonal genera, *cantus mollis, naturalis,* and *durus.*[32] This was a music in which there were virtually no sharp key signatures and in which modulation in our tonal sense took place much more often and characteristically in the flat direction. When Monteverdi states that he found no examples of the *concitato* genus in sixteenth-century music, he is perhaps referring to more than repeated sixteenth notes on the violin. A tradition that links Monteverdi's use of that term to Greek genera names is reflected in Kircher's using the expression "in canto duro sive *incitato.*"[33] There is certainly no mistaking the fact that the *stile concitato* appears overwhelmingly in sharps, or that the systematic use of the sharp direction in musical composition is first opened up in the seventeenth century.

Key-signature changes in seventeenth-century music often point to tonal events that were conceived in a broader framework than that of our major and minor. The significance of historical features such as the ambiguity as to the relative importance for composition of mode and genus, or the opening up of the sharp keys can hardly be overestimated; these were probably the two most important steps toward the modern major/minor tonality that developed around 1700. Still, there is no sense in either Monteverdi or Bach that modulation in the sharp direction was associated with dramatic shifts as there is in the sonata principle of the later eighteenth century. There *is,* however, a traditional perception that the sharps and flats produced completely different effects. For Lorenzo Penna key signatures and, hence, modulations were conceptualized as the successive changing of mi into fa and vice versa; the flat was called b molle because it rendered the composition "soft, sad or languid." Likewise, the introduction of the b-quadro or of sharps changed

31. Edward Lowinsky, *Secret Chromatic Art in the Netherlands Motet* (New York, 1946); *Tonality and Atonality in Sixteenth-Century Music* (Berkeley and Los Angeles, 1961); "Secret Chromatic Art Reexamined," in *Perspectives in Musicology,* ed. Barry S. Brook, Edward O. D. Downes, and Sherman Van Solkema (New York, 1972), pp. 91–135.

32. Claudio Monteverdi, preface to *Madrigali Guerrieri et Amorosi . . . Libro Ottavo* (Venice, 1638), facsimile in *Tutte le opere,* vol. 7, pt. 1, ed. G. Francesco Malipiero; trans. in Oliver Strunk, *Source Readings in Music History* (New York, 1950), pp. 413–15.

33. Kircher, *Musurgia,* p. 639. I have discussed this question in detail in two forthcoming publications: "Aspects of *durus/mollis* Shift and the Two-System Framework of Monteverdi's Music," *Schütz-Jahrbuch 1990* (Kassel: Bärenreiter, 1991) and *Monteverdi's Tonal Language* (New York: Schirmer Books, 1992).

notes from fa to mi and rendered the composition harsh (*aspra*) or hard (*duro*).[34] Mattheson's preface to his famous presentation of key characteristics acknowledges as much for the early eighteenth century.[35]

I use the words anabasis and catabasis in discussions of Bach works in recognition that the qualities associated with the hexachords and the accidentals extended to modulation as well. In England William Turner, for example, in his *Sound Anatomiz'd* of 1724, described the difference between sharps and flats as follows (comparing two chromatic scales, one notated in sharps, the other in flats):

> In the second Bar of the upper Staff, you see the Flat placed before B, which contracts the Tone of it half the Way towards A, underneath which, in the lower Staff, the Sharp is placed before A, which extends the Tone of the same, half the way towards B, both which demonstrate to your View, the different Quality of each; and altho' they bear the same Proportion, yet are they different in nature of sound; for the extending of Sounds, make them yield a cheerful Tone to the Ear; and when they are contracted, they appear Melancholy; which may be illustrated by the Comparison of different Ideas, in any things that are supposed to Rise, or Fall, which needs no farther Explanation to those who understand the Distinction between being lifted up, and cast down, etc.[36]

Although Turner is speaking mainly of sharps and flats as accidentals within a basically diatonic framework, he and other writers of the time expressed in various ways the different affective qualities of sharp and flat keys, pitches (*voces acutae* and *graves*), and tonal directions that I have associated with anabasis and catabasis.

These qualities are easily seen in countless compositions of the seventeenth century, of which those madrigals of Monteverdi's fifth and sixth books with key signature changes may be mentioned, such as "Zefiro torna e 'l bel tempo rimena" of book six. Within this conceptual world it was, then, a perfectly natural thing for Lully, in Act Two of *Alceste,* to modulate downward by fifths—A minor, D minor, G minor, C minor—through a succession of scenes dealing with the death and burial of the heroine. Heinrich Biber, in his *Missa Alleluia,* modulates downward from the tonic, C major, to a A minor for the "Et incarnatus" and to F for the "Crucifixus." Within the latter movement, dominated by the text *passus et sepultus est,* he modulates further by thirds—D minor and B flat—touching on F minor toward the end. Such devices are legion in baroque music. Buxtehude, in his sevenfold cycle of cantatas addressing the parts of Christ's body on the cross, begins in C

---

34. Penna, *Albori*, pp. 34–35.
35. Mattheson, *Das neu-eröffnete Orchestre*, pp. 232–33.
36. William Turner, *Sound Anatomiz'd, in a Philosophical Essay on Music* (London, 1724), facsimile ed. (New York, 1974), pp. 49–50.

minor (*To his Feet*) and moves upward (i.e., sharpward) through the circle of fifths—C minor, E flat, G minor, D minor, A minor—until the sixth cantata (*To his Heart*) in E minor. This cantata, because of its special affective associations, is set with accompaniment of viola da gamba choir instead of the violins of the other cantatas. Then, for the seventh cantata (*To his Face*), whose text is the hymn on which the chorale "O Haupt voll Blut und Wunden" is based, Buxtehude returns suddenly to C minor, for the dual purpose of closing the cycle tonally and of expressing the sorrow of the Passion and the focus on the wounded head of Christ by means of the return catabasis. The progression upward to the heart is one of increasing intensity. Christ's heart is a traditional emblem of salvation (rising tonal progression), while the sight of his face in agony, his head bowed down, marks a change comparable to Turner's distinction between being "lifted up and cast down." If Bach did not know Buxtehude's work as he planned the *St. Matthew Passion* with its two basic keys, E minor and C minor, at least his plan took shape within the same framework of tonal thought.

Heinichen's unusual terminological usage for the sharp/flat genera suggests the importance to him of the sense of tonal distance that the reduction to two modal types might at first have seemed to supplant. His concept of modulation by means of *toni intermedii* (the intervening keys along his circle) offers, for example, several ways of getting from A minor to A major—including short cuts—but no suggestion that tonic major and minor keys are the same, or that modulation from the one to the other can be made instantly as an immediate affective device such as became common in later periods. In contrast to the use of major and minor modes on the same keynote, relative major and minor in Bach's work provide one of the most significant of all immediate tonal relationships and the most prevalent means of modulation by stages. This is exactly the situation in Bach's early cantatas, several of which contain conspicuous progressions from minor to relative major. When, as in Cantata 21, the shift from C minor to C major is the most significant tonal-allegorical device, the *toni intermedii* of the intervening movements are absolutely essential to the move, and the major and minor modes, although given enormous structural emphasis and parallelism, are widely separated. The shift is, in fact, momentous and dramatic, but it relies on memory and intellectual grasp, on our perception of gradual stages of affective change, rather than immediate impact. The sense of time represented in this way is allegorical—horizontal, successive, and rationalistic—and the meaning is reconstructed in stages rather than presented instantaneously with a transformational modulation, after the manner of the classical period. We are prepared for the change, first in the turn to the relative major (E flat), then in the move up to G minor with an affect of consolation, and, finally, in the F major tenor solo, which anticipates but in no way undercuts, the triadic triumph of the C major finale. We might even say that the approach to eternity and the Apocalypse in this kind of thinking is a measured, stage-by-stage affair, recalling the dialectical, analytical odes of Andreas Gryphius, in which the progress of

EXAMPLE 18.   *Clavierübung,* Part Three: excerpt from the F major duet

the soul toward eternity is virtually divested of all mystery. The overall minor/major shift is a function of the flat/sharp motion, in the more generalized sense of *mollis/durus.*

The situation just described holds true even in compositions in which the major and minor modes are immediately juxtaposed, such as the highly permutational F major duet from Part Three of the *Clavierübung,* where the tonic major and minor confront each other within the central segment of a layered structural symmetry. While of great (and obvious) allegorical significance, this is not a dramatic device, even though the minor form is a note-for-note inversion of the major (Ex. 18). The music remains in F minor and C minor throughout the whole of the following section, a transposition in invertible counterpoint of the D minor/A minor music that preceded the central major/minor juxtaposition. While the permutational, quasi-canonic nature of this piece is exceptional, the idea of modulation to the flat side of the key, with or without introduction of the tonic minor, is not. It is a vital aspect of tonal planning in a considerable number of cantatas, and it operates in a large number of individual movements as well.[37] That major and minor represent shift of genera here (in the post-1700 sense indicated by Dahlhaus) must not obscure the fact that the central juxtaposition is a focal point for the larger shift of genera (sharp/flat) that is more common in Bach's work. The interpretation of the F major duet as a representation of the cross seems perfectly accurate (although we do not need the numerical proofs of Bach's intent).[38] The idea of dual genera is exactly

37. See, for example, the discussions of the trio "Wenn meine Trübsal als mit Ketten" from Cantata 38 and the duet "Die Armut, so Gott auf sich nimmt" from Cantata 91 (Chapter 6, pp. 176–79, Chapter 7, pp. 219–21).

38. See G. Friedemann, *Bach zeichnet das Kreuz: Die Bedeutung der vier Duetten aus dem dritten Theil der Clavierübung* (Pinneberg, 1963); Siegele, *Bachs theologischer Formbegriff.*

appropriate to such theological themes as the incarnation and dual natures of Christ and the sense of divided worlds.

The larger observation that the major and minor modes are rarely, if ever, dramatized by Bach might seem to be contradicted here and there in his work. In Cantata 71, "Gott ist mein König," a work of predominantly festive character with several movements in the tonic, C major, the sixth movement, the chorus "Du wolltest dem Feinde nicht geben, die Seele deiner Turteltauben," is set in C minor, preceded and followed immediately by festive C major movements. Here, as in dance doubles and variation movements, the major and minor modes are juxtaposed without any *toni intermedii*. In this chorus, however, the C minor seems to function with a flat, modal character, which is particularly evident in the striking appearance of unison choral writing at the end of the movement in imitation of psalm-tone usage.[39] The human entreaty of the deity in this movement and, perhaps, the sensuousness of *Turteltauben* rather than the reference to *Feinde* prompted the flat minor mode. Even though the two modes are set side by side, the juxtaposition is less dramatic than that in Cantata 21 where the major and minor modes are widely separated. Likewise, the long harpsichord cadenza of the Fifth Brandenburg Concerto, having settled on a dominant pedal, moves to the tonic minor (d) as if to prepare for a dramatic return to D major. Bach, however, does not make the return to D coincide with the return of the final ritornello that, with its prominent arpeggio theme, would set the major mode in high relief. Instead, he introduces the tonic major early, before the harpsichord figuration subsides, providing seven measures

---

39. Spitta apparently bases his description of the affect of this movement (*Johann Sebastian Bach,* p. 350) on the fact that it is in the tonic minor; we read that it represents "a terrible expression of suppressed pain," that "Bach has coloured the tone-picture much too darkly," that "the composer has here overshot the mark," for the text "contains only metaphorically a prayer for protection from the violence of the enemy; and for this prayer . . . a calm trustful sentiment is the only fit one." Although Spitta's analysis of the meaning of the text is basically correct, are his comments on Bach's ready susceptibility to texts of lamentation appropriate? In another highly triumphant *Ratswechsel* cantata in C major, BWV 119, "Preise, Jerusalem, den Herrn," Bach cast the central aria, "Die Obrigkeit ist Gottes Gabe, ja selber Gottes Ebenbild. Wer ihre Macht nicht will ermessen, der muss auch Gottes gar vergessen: wie würde sonst sein Wort erfüllt?" in G minor. And this movement, too, has been misinterpreted, to the extent that some have said that Bach intended a caricature of worldly authority, a view that Alfred Dürr rightly questions as the intrusion of a modern political viewpoint on the hierarchical social strata of the eighteenth century (*Die Kantaten von Johann Sebastian Bach* [Kassel, 1971], p. 586). In fact, such interpretations lose force when we recognize that here, as in other places, Bach represents the world of the flesh and human weakness with a modulation to flats, or flat modal coloring. God's *Ebenbild* on earth, as the text makes clear, is human and mortal. Literal-minded interpreters find such passages, with their shift of genus, the opposition in this case of both major/minor and *durus/mollis,* difficult. And the motion to flats is more meaningful still in the context of the basic descent/ascent plan that Bach uses throughout the *Ratswechsel* cantatas (see Chapter 6). That is, the flat-minor mode in Cantatas 71 and 119 contributes to the idea of descent—a reminder of the human weakness of the rulers. That the sense of descent in some instances extends to the tonic minor (e.g., Cantatas 95, 70, 9) rather than the dominant minor (Cantatas 106, 20, 127, 119) or to another key such as the supertonic or even the simple relative minor seems less important than the fact, manner, and degree of descent, whether it is gradual or sudden and transformational (Cantata 121 and the like).

of figuration that eliminate any possibility that the return to major will make a dramatic impact.

The important decision not to dramatize the relationship between tonic major and minor modes may be related to the fact that the *dominant* major and minor are juxtaposed in a number of cantatas as well as in the F major organ *Pastorale*. This device often causes the minor dominant to represent the subdominant side of the key rather than serving as a foil for the major dominant, as it often is in the music of the classical period. Thus in the F major *Pastorale* Bach juxtaposes the second movement in C major with the third in C minor, the succession framed by movements in F. Undoubtedly his intent was for the minor and major dominants to represent a contained dualism dealing with the meaning of the incarnation. The plan is comparable to the appearance of dominant minor and major in the F major Cantatas 20 and 127, where the dualism is bound up with meditation on death and resurrection.[40] All this is a sign, of course, that, although the genera (key-signature levels) and modes (major and minor) had now been merged for the first time, the older sense of distinct tonal levels with indistinct or generalized modal definition, the possibility of several modes at a single level, was still alive, and Heinichen's discussion, despite the reduction to two modes, provides a sense of the role of key signature levels per se in tonal planning.

Before modes and genera were merged, modulation, or the shift of mi to fa and vice versa, was conceptualized by solmization. When the shift was made suddenly the result was often a mi contra fa or *relatio non-harmonica*, as Kuhnau describes it: "*Sondern hat Lust zum Gesetz des Herrn*. There, in consideration of the adversative conjunction, 'sondern,' [the music] should proceed in a completely different key, with mi transformed into fa, or fa into mi."[41] As is well known, relationships of this kind are used extensively by Monteverdi, in *Orfeo* above all, to allegorize extreme emotional states. Tonal expansion in the seventeenth century, with its greatly increased tendency toward systematization, necessitated the introduction of more such relations than formerly, providing for their integration to a greater extent; tonal antithesis became more common and acceptable. The model of the gamut and the mi contra fa remained, however, and served as an important device of tonal planning for Bach. The keys of numerous collections in the seventeenth and eighteenth centuries, including the original versions of the *Inventions and Sinfonias* and the *Eight Little Preludes and Fugues,* were organized according to the keynotes of the gamut, while the presentation of key relationships and signatures in

---

40. These cantatas are discussed in Chapter 6, pp. 164–67.

41. Kuhnau, reprinted in Richter, "Eine Abhandlung," p. 152 (author's translation). Kuhnau is commenting on his setting of the second verse of the first Psalm, which begins with the words, "Sondern hat Lust zum Gesetz des Herrn." The text of his commentary in German reads "Da soll es bey Erwegung der *Conjunctionis adversativae* kî îm, *Sondern,* gantz aus einem andern *Tono* gehen, und das Mi in Fa, oder das Fa in Mi verwandelt werden."

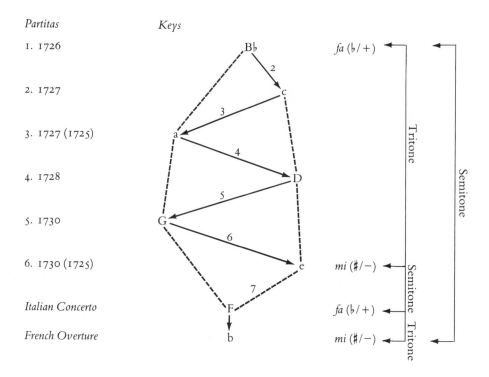

Partitas	Keys
1. 1726	
2. 1727	
3. 1727 (1725)	
4. 1728	
5. 1730	
6. 1730 (1725)	
Italian Concerto	
French Overture	

FIGURE 3.   Parts One and Two of the *Clavierübung*: a schematic representation of the plan of fa/mi relationships among the eight keys. The dates in parentheses after Partitas 3 and 6 are those of earlier versions found in the second *Notebook for Anna Magdalena Bach*; the *French Overture* was transposed to B minor from an earlier C minor version.

some treatises also reflected the medieval system. For the organization of Parts One and Two of the *Clavierübung* Bach utilized the keynotes of the gamut, ordered now to provide patterns of mi (E minor, B minor) and fa (B flat, F major) as the cornerstones (Fig. 3). Even though the musical circle might appear to have replaced the gamut entirely, its earliest presentations with such notions as extreme keys and the like indicate that concepts of the older system remained alive in it.

If a modulation such as that between the "Confiteor" and the "Et expecto resurrectionem mortuorum" of the *Mass in B minor*—with its elements of flat/sharp and minor/major shift—can be taken as a metaphor for a broad human dynamic, it is not (despite its thrilling effect) comparable to that of the transition to C major for the last movement of Beethoven's Fifth Symphony (which possesses an enormous sense of causality suggesting the human overcoming of boundaries). Rather, with all its enharmonicism and lack of build-up for the D major, it suggests the miraculous—divine intervention—or, as Tovey put it, an assertion "that faith is mere reason unless it can put its trust in miracles."[42] In this famous modulation Bach uses genera as they were understood in the earlier eighteenth century (Ex. 19). Both the "Confiteor" and the "Et resurrectionem mortuorom" are in sharps. But the introduction of the tone B flat right after the end of the former movement in A (a mi contra fa) suddenly opens up the realm of enharmonic music. The key, however, is deliberately left in abeyance so that the enharmonicism can be experienced per se; only at the very end of this exceptional passage do we sense some preparation for D and the contrast of the minor and major modes. No doubt the whole span can be considered a tonal ellipse, or parenthesis, from A to D. The sense of descent followed by ascent is strong. Bach undoubtedly intended for this passage to recall the earlier and much less extravagant move from the ending of the "Crucifixus" to the "Et resurrexit," with its introduction of the flat subdominant of the triumphant D major. Baptism (the "Confiteor") was considered within Lutheranism to be both a reenactment of Christ's death and resurrection and a prefiguring of the individual's own death and resurrection (through the catabasis of immersion followed by the anabasis of emergence in a new state). Baptism was the key to the afterlife, and Bach's joining of the "Confiteor" and the "Et resurrectionem" makes that fact unmistakably clear. The tonal sense, or key, is suspended in the enharmonic passage, probably as an allegory of the timeless state of the sleep of death articulated within Lutheran eschatological thought. Enharmonicism is a form of tonal style that is defined in terms of sharp/flat conflict. Werckmeister, for example, describes an enharmonic modulation from E major to F minor as a "great metamorphosis in the harmony," a place where "in an instant one passes from one genus to another."[43] That such a device is uniquely appropriate for the anticipation of resurrection is suggested in Werckmeister's allegorical writings on music, when he calls tempered music a "mirror and image of our mortality and incompleteness of this life" and the clarino register of the trumpet an anticipation of the life to come.[44] His language recalls St. Paul's famous description of resurrection, of transformation in an instant, and the like (1 Cor. 15:51–52).

Finally, we note that when used systematically as an allegorical device, composition with the concept of the sharps and flats as genera can, like many other aspects of music, extend well beyond the audible and into the more abstract region Walter Benjamin calls "script." That is, the shift between flat and sharp regions may not be audible as such (setting aside the question of absolute pitch), or may not be as strikingly dramatized as modulations that do not bring about that shift (just as minor/major shift is often not dramatized). And this disparity between the audible and the inaudible is a vital aspect of some works, especially those in which highly abstract

42. Donald Francis Tovey, *Beethoven*, ed. Hubert J. Foss (London, 1944), p. 43.
43. Andreas Werckmeister, *Harmonologia Musica* (Frankfurt and Leipzig, 1702), No. 67, facsimile ed. (Hildesheim and London, 1970).
44. Werckmeister, *Harmonologia Musica*, No. 72; *Musicae Mathematicae*, p. 145.

EXAMPLE 19. *Mass in B minor*: transition between the "Confiteor" and "Et expecto resurrectionem mortuorum"

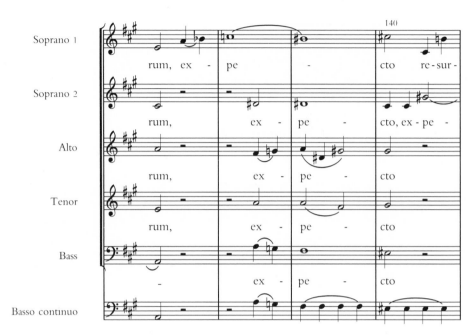

EXAMPLE 19   *continued*

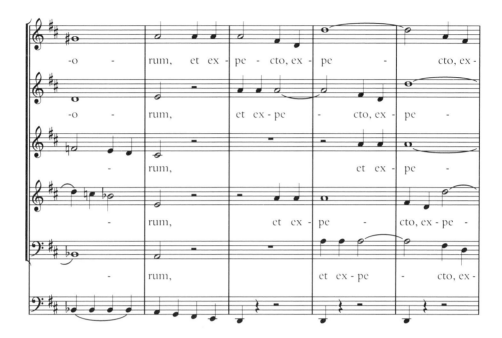

designs seem to conflict with dramatic qualities. The *St. John Passion* provides what is easily the most outstanding instance of this conflict. Its visually oriented plan of sharp, flat, and natural key signatures reflects a set of theological concerns that derive from the more abstract side of the Johannine thought world, while at another level the more readily audible and dramatic musical qualities of the work relate directly to the physical events. The two aspects intersect frequently, of course, but are conceptually separate. And that separation is essential to our interpretation of Bach's musicotheological vision of the work and our recognition of its marked difference from the *St. Matthew Passion* in respect to the treatment of sharp and flat genera.

Key Characteristics

The foregoing remarks have by no means exhausted the traditional modal-hexachordal residue within baroque tonal theory. For us the best-known treatment of these ideas in early-eighteenth-century music theory is, ironically, the conflict between Mattheson and Johann Heinrich Buttstedt—ostensibly over solmization—but eventually encompassing many other issues, such as the relative roles of sense and intellect (*ratio*), the modes, the dissonance or consonance of the perfect fourth, the roles of melody and harmony in composition.[45] Mattheson's treatise, *Der neu-eröffnete Orchestre,* initiated this controversy in 1713, just two years after Heinichen's opus, and his title, like Heinichen's, claimed the virtue of newness. Yet the most famous passage in his treatise has remained his discussion of the key *proprietates,* which is not only traditional in conception but takes as the basis of its ordering the presentation of mode put forth by Banchieri in 1605 and widely repeated in music theory for a century afterward. In fact, it was only supplanted by the widespread acceptance of the circle of keys.[46] Banchieri discussed eight modes, for the first time mixing transposed modes with untransposed in a way that suggests the breakdown of the traditional relationship of transposition to mode. After Dorian D comes G minor as transposed Dorian but also as a mode in its own right (Hypodorian). Banchieri's grouping orders the eight keys in pairs—d and g, e and a, C and F, d (minor, or Aeolian) and G (Mixolydian)—suggestive of an early stage in the merging of modal and hexachordal considerations. This merging was probably connected with its popularity. It was repeated throughout the seventeenth century, with the only modification, though a widespread one, being the replacing of the initial Dorian D with D minor and the D minor (no. seven) with D major. Mattheson not only repeats this idea, but continues the organization of keys in pairs throughout his second set of eight commonly used keys: A and E major, B minor and F sharp minor, B flat and E flat, C minor and F minor.

Mattheson's discussion of the keys has held a certain fascination for musical exegetes because of his definite statements on key characteristics. Several scholars have hoped to find a key to the reading of affect in Bach's works, and some have attempted to apply his ideas to the *Well-Tempered Clavier* and the *St. Matthew Passion,* missing the point made explicitly by Mattheson himself that such tonal qualities were to be sought by the musician in a quasi-empirical manner.[47] Mattheson will not allow that either major/minor or sharp/flat qualities be taken as sole guides to *proprietas,* and his introductory remarks reject (by confirming the existence in his time of) the notion that the sharps are "hard, fresh, and gay," the flats, "soft, tender," and the like. This unsentimental attitude applies to the use of theoretical writing throughout the whole period: its value for us is not that we apply it slavishly (Mattheson uses the term *knechtisch* along with *pedantisch* to condemn such an attitude toward rhetoric), but rather that we use it to develop our own understanding.[48] Despite Mattheson's cautions, however, and Heinichen's outright rejection

45. On the Mattheson/Buttstedt controversy see Beekman Cannon, *Johann Mattheson: Spectator in Music* (New Haven, 1947), pp. 134–45.

46. Adriano Banchieri, *L'Organo Suonarino* (Venice, 1605), p. 41. See also Atcherson, "Key and Mode," pp. 216–19; Mattheson, *Das neu-eröffnete Orchestre,* pp. 60–62.

47. Mattheson, *Das neu-eröffnete Orchestre,* pp. 231–53.

48. Mattheson, *Der Volkommene Kapellmeister,* pp. 241, 235.

of the idea of key characteristics,[49] Mattheson's presentation, like the writings of Werckmeister, indicates that in principle a hermeneutic of tonal devices is possible, but, paradoxically, it cannot be founded in a theoretical presentation such as Mattheson himself provided. Rather, we must survey the oeuvre in question, using theory to unlock its secrets, but, in fact, text setting is a more reliable means of access by virtue of its more direct indication of allegorical associations. The error of rejecting the notion of tonal hermeneutics because it is not sufficiently scientific is greater than that of its uncritical and indiscriminate application, for it constitutes a rejection of one of the greatest spiritual and artistic impulses of the age: allegory.

Some of Mattheson's key characteristics—E minor (Phrygian), F minor—are those traditionally observed in most baroque music, while others are very close to common Bach usages, his discussion of C minor in particular.[50] Yet it is evident that Mattheson, while unable to free himself from the traditional *Proprietas-lehre* against which his wrath bursts out every now and again, is more interested in key characteristics as the subject of more sophisticated enquiry than what was provided by tradition. He clearly recognizes the reality of the phenomenon but is unable to account for it in terms other than those of the early-eighteenth-century empiricist music theorist willing to trust his senses more than traditional doctrine or mathematical precepts. It seems clear that key characteristics in the baroque were influenced by a variety of different factors, some of which were subtly related to each other, such as tuning, traditional modal usage and *proprietates,* hexachordal theory, and instrumental characteristics. The appearance of Mattheson's and Heinichen's books at the time of Bach's Weimar cantatas points to the changes in traditional tonal perceptions in the first two decades of the century, forcing musicians to come to terms with the incredibly forceful and direct, but in many respects brutally simple, tonal style of the new Italian concerto.

49. Heinichen's polemic, from *Der General-Bass in der Composition* (no doubt intended as a response to Mattheson's presentation in *Das neu-eröffnete Orchestre*), is discussed in George Buelow, *Thorough-Bass Accompaniment according to Johann David Heinichen* (Berkeley and Los Angeles, 1966), pp. 270–72. Heinichen gives four basic conditions for the composer's choice of a particular key: (1) inclination or temperament of the composer; his preference for a certain key; (2) the unavoidable changing of a mode in which one has frequently expressed the affect of joy or sadness; (3) necessity, because of instrumental capacities and limitations one must frequently use a key against one's will; and (4) the range of singers' voices.

50. Mattheson, *Das neu-eröffnete Orchestre,* p. 244; "C minor is an exceedingly lovely, but at the same time sad key; if it should happen that the first of these qualities tends to predominate and one becomes too easily satiated with the sweetness, then it would not be bad if one endeavored to animate this by means of a somewhat lively or fluent *Mouvement;* otherwise one might easily become sleepy with its mildness. But if it is to be a piece that has to promote sleep, one can disregard this remark and soon achieve the goal in a natural manner" (author's translation). We think immediately of the answering chorus, "So schlafen uns're Sünden ein" from the dialogue "Ich will bei meinem Jesu wachen" of the *St. Matthew Passion,* the two burial choruses of the two *Passions,* the aria "Die Seele ruht in Jesu Händen" from Cantata 127, the setting of "Mit Fried' und Freud' " from the "Actus Tragicus," and many other instances from Bach's work.

The importance of all this for the composition of a work such as the *St. Matthew Passion* is greater than the relative dryness of the theoretical discussions would suggest and is reflected in the different types of tonal relationship within the work, according to which distinctions of mode, ambitus, and genera are all important categories. The result is a very complex tonal spectrum that preserves many historical tonal perceptions. The opening key, E minor, for example, is a traditional key of lamentation, descended from the Phrygian mode and still identified with it in most baroque treatises. It was linked to the *cantus durus* even in the sixteenth century and, according to Dahlhaus, was the key that opened the sharp system in the seventeenth century.[51] In the *St. Matthew Passion* E minor represents the primary key, associated in several crucial places with something like the stations of the cross and juxtaposed several times with the work's second key, C minor. In one important place (Jesus' death), Bach uses his version of E Phrygian instead. In the opening chorus ("O Lamm Gottes unschuldig") the key is joined with its relative major to suggest the dualisms of guilt versus innocence and physical event versus Christian meaning that are basic to the Passion. And several times in Part One the E minor is set in opposition to E major as well. E major, on the other hand, is juxtaposed also to E flat (the chorale "Erkenne mich, mein Hüter" and its transposition, "Ich will hier bei dir stehen") and, by virtue of its role as the sharp extreme of the *Passion,* to its opposite number, F minor. In introducing the F flat that marks the flattest tone in the *Passion* ("Finsternis") Bach was no doubt aware of its enharmonic relationship to E; it marks the full theological circle of the *Passion,* the redemption of darkness and flats, Golgotha as allegory of salvation. Likewise, the key of E flat connects to its relative minor, and the two act as dual centers of the second ambitus of the *Passion,* the key area of the Mount of Olives and the burial; it is used in "Sehet, Jesus hat die Hand" as the key of a counter-dialogue to the opening chorus and set in opposition to E flat minor, the flat modulatory limit within the recitatives ("Mein Gott, warum hast du mich verlassen?"). All these relationships form a center, expanding to the other tonal relationships in the *Passion.* Some of these are the ones we know as subdominant, dominant, relative major/minor, and the like, based on the ambitus concept; such a relationship, for example, is the trial scene as a hard E minor tonal region, in which the subdominant, A minor, is relatively soft, and the dominant, B minor, relatively hard. Other relationships, however, are the result of a mi contra fa shift within a single genus, e.g., E major/ minor, or from one genus to another, E minor/C minor. Others are the result of Bach's systematic and concentrated presentation of the musical circle of the *Passion* (from F minor through *toni intermedii* at all successive key-signature levels to E major), while still others may be associated with the enharmonic character of flats (the

51. Dahlhaus, *Untersuchungen,* p. 280.

end of the arioso "Erbarm es! Gott" and the recitative before "Ach, Golgatha"). It is clear that Bach's plan for the *Passion* took shape within such tonal concepts as these. No doubt the variety of possible tonal associations has something of the labyrinthine character of pre-circular tonality, but it is also the source of our conception of tonal planning as an enormously important component of the creative process. It also seems to confirm what we take to be the most significant facet of Mattheson's view of key *proprietates*: although keys may have many inherited and perhaps even intrinsic meanings, many others can be sought out and, by extension, created in the work itself.

CHAPTER FOUR

The "Actus Tragicus"

Bach's Cantata 106, "Gottes Zeit ist die allerbeste Zeit," an astonishing masterpiece of musical and religious art, crowns his earliest period. One of its most compelling features is its allegorical design. The highly detailed and purposive "Actus Tragicus" permits elaborate musicotheological explication; yet its unusual directness and appealing simplicity of tone have always won it popularity. Its chiastic design, that is, the symmetrical framework with its pivotal confrontation of Law and Gospel, is familiar even to those who know little more of the cantata. The "Actus Tragicus" exhibits an extraordinary degree of integration at several other levels as well, especially those of textual organization, motivic interrelationships, and tonal plan. These patterns in the work are displayed on two levels that are mirrored by the symmetrical framework on the one hand and, on the other, by the more dynamic aspects of the work, an important focal point for which is the tonal plan. This dualism is considered to be deliberate on Bach's part—the simultaneous representation of Word and Spirit, we might say. As a result, the work strongly evokes that sense of those inner and outer structures described in Chapter 1. Through the relationship between such levels and the idea of hermeneutic senses, much of the text can be understood simultaneously in terms of historical narrative, spiritual dynamic, and presentation of dogma. The interaction between these levels in the "Actus Tragicus" parallels Luther's hermeneutics, remarkably closely, with its concepts of internal and external clarity and its combining the traditional four senses of scriptural interpretation into one, the literal-prophetic.[1] The notion that

1. Martin Luther, *The Bondage of the Will* (*De servo arbitrio*, 1525), in *Luther and Erasmus: Free Will and Salvation,* trans. and ed. Philip S. Watson (Philadelphia, 1969), pp. 99–334. On the dual sense of Scripture that we are arguing exists in the "Actus Tragicus," see pp. 158–69 ("Scripture, with Its 'Internal' and 'External' Clarity, as the Test of Truth"); internal clarity is the understanding of Scripture by the light of faith, while external clarity is the kind of understanding that can be taught to others (e.g., via hermeneutics).

Bach may have undergone a personal conflict between pietism and orthodoxy at Mühlhausen and the meaning of his references to the "goal" of a "well-regulated church music" gain new life as we come to understand the musicotheological character of this early masterpiece. The "Actus Tragicus" cannot be called Bach's profoundest church work from either the musical or the theological standpoint—his cantata style had not developed fully—but it stands as one of the most remarkable and prophetic syntheses of theological and artistic intentions in the whole of music.

The Text

The juxtaposition of biblical mottoes with chorales and the absence of freely composed madrigal texts (either recitatives or arias) assign the "Actus Tragicus" to the pre-Neumeister cantata type, which Bach virtually abandoned after his Mühlhausen period (1707–1708). The solos, instead of serving as immediate expressions of the idealized, contemporary Christian, represent scriptural personages; knowledge of the original context is often essential to an understanding of their religious meaning. One important characteristic of such works, therefore, must be the preservation of the objective historical character of the Scripture. Successions of such texts may then offer a panorama of scriptural viewpoints—some personal, others dogmatic—on the chosen subject, which for the "Actus Tragicus" is that of death. Alfred Dürr describes such cantatas as "troped-motto cantatas."[2] Chorales introduced at carefully chosen points add the church's perspective to the series of biblical mottoes.

The text of the "Actus Tragicus" exhibits two forms of large-scale organization. The first, symmetry, is in part pointed up by analogous sets of correspondences in the musical structure. Antithesis acts a pivotal role here, indicating the subject of the work to be "death under the Law versus death under the Gospel."[3] The second ordering, a chronological one, is seen in the four solos and central fugue/solo/chorale complex between the prologue and doxology. First, three Old Testament texts move forward in time from Psalm 90 through Isaiah and the book of Jesus Sirach (Ecclesiasticus). The last of these texts initiates another threefold sequence: an Old Testament text, a New Testament text, and a chorale text within the central movement. Yet another triad with a very similar pattern of textual sources (Psalm 31, Luke 23, chorale) follows the centerpiece. The chronology passes through the stages of the history of Israel to the coming of Christ, his death on the cross, and the era of the Christian church. The sequence can also be read as an internal progression from fear of death and acceptance of its inevitability to faith in Christ and in the

2. "Tropierende Spruchkantaten": Alfred Dürr, *Studien über die frühen Kantaten Johann Sebastian Bachs* (Wiesbaden, 1977), p. 212.
3. Dürr, *Die Kantaten,* p. 612.

promise of the Gospel, and, finally, to the willingness of the believer to die in Christ and his church. The chronological progression emphasizes the literal-historical sense of Scripture and parallels the growth in the individual's understanding and faith. As the sequence progresses we move closer to the contemporary believer and his relationship with Christ. Thus, time takes on a double meaning. On the one hand, a vast span of events lies under God's control and can be comprehended by man only through the outline presented in Scripture; on the other, these historical events are experienced as stages in the spiritual life of the individual. History, which is beyond our physical experience, becomes real through faith. The objective is that the goal of history, that is to say, eschatological fulfillment, becomes a reality to the individual; the meanings of death and time in the present life are to be transformed and eschatology is realized. Death, which both separates and, ultimately, unites God's time and man's, is in a literal-historical sense the end of time for man and the gateway to God's eternity, while in the metaphorical or tropological sense it is the ultimate test of faith. According to Luther, the "summary of Scripture" is revealed in the "dynamic" of Law and Gospel as relived within the individual in a process of inner spiritual identification, by "analogy of faith," with historical events. In this sense his dictum that "faith must be built up on the basis of history" forms much of the subject of the "Actus Tragicus."

The history referred to is, of course, that of God's relations with man as recounted in Scripture; that is, it is "salvation history." One of the primary New Testament sources for this ancient idea is the book of Acts, from which comes the biblical motto that introduces the "Actus Tragicus." As delineated by Hans Conzelmann, the history of salvation divides time into three epochs, Israel, Jesus, and the church, the span as a whole reaching from the Creation to the Parousia (Second Coming). Continuity between the three periods is an important feature of salvation history, while "the position of Jesus in the center is, of course, the most significant element."[4] The very old idea of Christ as the turning point in history had special resonance within the Christological interpretive framework of Lutheran hermeneutics. Salvation history, then, provides the conceptual model for the prominent textual sequence Old Testament/New Testament/chorale in the "Actus Tragicus."

We can better understand the intent behind this chronological element if we examine two conspicuous features of the "Actus Tragicus" whose meanings have never been analyzed: the superscript "Actus Tragicus" and the theme of "Gottes Zeit," announced in the prologue. The actus, an oratorio-like dramatic form popular in the seventeenth century, differs from its sister genre, the biblical historia, in

4. Hans Conzelmann, *The Theology of St. Luke,* trans. Geoffrey Buswell (Philadelphia, 1961), pp. 150–51. Buswell uses the less common "redemptive history" to render the German *Heilsgeschichte.*

having a more meditative and less purely narrative emphasis. In the "Actus Tragicus" the subject of meditation is the understanding of death according to the stages of salvation history. "Actus tragicus" is the Latin translation of *Trauerspiel,* the main form of German seventeenth-century drama. These tragic dramas treat of human history and its events as "the Passion of the world," a "slow funeral pageant" representing stages of decline and destruction, all directed to moral purposes via unremittingly allegorical interpretations of both the action as a whole and its individual details.[5] The basic premise is that, ever since the Fall, mankind stands under God's wrath and the judgment of death; self-justification before God is no longer possible, and the way to salvation through faith presents tribulations at every turn. The *Trauerspiel* is the preeminent allegorical genre, a kind of *paysage moralisé,* and both the intensely allegorical design and the underlying spiritual import of the "Actus Tragicus" link it to this genre.

The *Trauerspiel's* extensive use of mottoes promoting the fragmented character of existence as signification, which echoes throughout emblem books for two centuries or more, may seem remote from what we are accustomed to consider the pictoralism of Bach's music and the milder discussion of the purely designative side of musical allegory in Manfred Bukofzer's article on the subject, but they are, in fact, facets of the same urge to expression.[6] Walter Benjamin saw a causal relationship between the Lutheran rejection of the efficacy of good works for salvation and the melancholy state of mind that produced the *Trauerspiel* as the quintessential expression of its attraction to allegorical contemplation.[7] That state of mind saw human existence merely as a testing ground for the future life; this is the meaning of the various descriptions of the world as a "desert," a "hospital," and the like in the Bach cantatas. That same pessimistic view of human history lies behind much of the complex allegorical expression of the "Actus Tragicus," in which the fragmentation and use of formula evoke a sense of mortality, of separation of matter and spirit. As Benjamin put it, the gap between matter and spirit is a "jagged line of demarcation" drawn by death, and its "formal correlative" in art is the antithetical relationship between convention and expression, form in a broad sense and content.[8] "Tragedy" in Cantata 106 has exactly the significance that Benjamin has shown it to have in *Trauerspiel:* "mourning" over the human condition. The detailed, multilayered allegorical design of the work reflects this mourning, especially in its acknowledgment of the limits of the rationalistic-allegorical approach to meaning in art.

If the association with allegory and the *Trauerspiel* brings out all in the expression of Cantata 106 that is human, subject to death, the idea of "Gottes Zeit" deals in

5. Benjamin, *The Origin,* pp. 177–82.
6. Bukofzer, "Allegory."
7. Benjamin, *The Origin,* pp. 138–42.
8. Benjamin, *The Origin,* pp. 166, 175.

just the opposite sphere, conveying a unity of time and worlds. God's time provides the only means of overcoming the tragic human condition of the actus. It thus emphasizes a primary level of antithesis in the work, that between the present life, whose temporality is ideally represented in allegory, and the life of eschatological fulfillment, of time and eternity. Bach's theological library contained a work on this subject, Martin Geier's *Zeit und Ewigkeit*.[9] In this light the terms *Gottes Zeit* and *actus tragicus* can be taken as keys to the broadest and most conspicuous aspects of structure in Cantata 106, the primary connotation of the former being God's control of history, that of the latter man's position in the whole design.

The choral prologue introduces this idea. Its central phrase, "In ihm leben, weben und sind wir [so lange er will]," is taken, except for the bracketed words, from Paul's famous "Areopagus" speech before the Greeks at Athens (Acts 17:28).[10] The speech, inspired by the dedication of the Greek temple to the "unknown God," affirms the universal range of God's rule, which encompasses all nations and reaches from the Creation to the Parousia. It thus suggests the concept of salvation history. The third line of the prologue, "In ihm sterben wir zu rechter Zeit, wenn er will," was perhaps, as Dürr suggests, derived from the line "Meine Zeit und Stund ist, wann Gott will" from the chorale "Ich hab mein Sach Gott heimgestellt."[11] The librettist modified the two quotations in order to set up the antithesis of life and death, both under God's control. The opening line, "Gottes Zeit ist die allerbeste Zeit," already indicates this theme, and the repeated expressions *Zeit, in ihm,* and *Will* in the "Actus Tragicus" and throughout Luther's work strongly suggest God's control of history.[12] In the prologue, however, the threefold division foreshadows the human perspective, the sense of separate eras in the "Actus Tragicus." Luther explains God's time as a simultaneity, to be understood by the individual only through faith.[13]

The chronological ordering of the "Actus Tragicus" is itself directed toward such an understanding, what we might call the tropological view of history. In the manuscript the work is divided (by pauses and double-bar lines) into four segments: (1) sonatina; (2) from "Gottes Zeit" through the fugue complex; (3) from "In deine Hände" through "Mit Fried' and Freud' "; (4) the doxology. This grouping of the work suggests the pattern of the *paysage moralisé* in baroque painting, as exemplified in Nicolas Poussin's paintings of the four seasons.[14] In such a

9. Leaver, *Bach's Theological Library*, pp. 119–21.

10. See Martin Dibelius, "Paulus auf dem Areopag," in *Aufsätze zur Apostelgeschichte* (Göttingen, 1951), p. 29.

11. Dürr, *Die Kantaten*, p. 616.

12. They are encountered most clearly in the passages from Ecclesiastes that Bach marked in his copy of the Calov Bible; see below, pp. 121–23.

13. Althaus, *The Theology of Martin Luther*, pp. 216–17.

14. Willibald Sauerländer, "Die Jahreszeiten: Ein Beitrag zur allegorischen Landschaft beim späten Poussin," *Münchner Jahrbuch der bildenden Kunst* 7 (1956): 160–84.

format several overlapping levels of subject matter are presented simultaneously—for example, the four seasons, four eras of salvation history, four times of day, or four stages in the life of man. The divisions vary from work to work, but the basic idea that different spans of time are experienced in analogous ways is common to them all. The term *moralisé* is used tropologically to relate the outer world and the eras of history to man and his experience.

In the "Actus Tragicus" the tropological understanding of history is evident in the relationship between the movements beginning and ending the chronological sequence—the tenor solo "Ach Herr, lehre uns bedenken, dass wir sterben müssen," and Luther's chorale "Mit Fried' und Freud' "—and the change that takes place between them. Luther's theology of death, as delineated in his commentary on Psalm 90 (traditionally attributed to Moses), is given poetic form in "Mit Fried' und Freud'." The line from Psalm 90 in the tenor solo anticipates in its closing words, "auf dass wir klug werden," the understanding of death presented in "Mit Fried' und Freud'." Death as the "proper work" of Moses and the Law is counteracted in "Mit Fried' und Freud' " by the Gospel of Christ, God's "proper work" of redemption.[15] The psalm itself, which embodies several of the main concepts that underlie the plan of the "Actus Tragicus," indicates this change in focus. In it Luther saw "all the parts of Moses' proclamation combine—the sermon of the Creator, which makes the beginning of the psalm a 'copy of Genesis'; fleeting life and hope of eternal life; law (vss. 1–12) and the promise of Christ (vss. 13–17)."[16] Luther called this psalm "Moses at his most Mosaic" ("Moses Mosissimus"). The turning point from the severity of death that dominates the first half to the prayer that dominates the second, which falls between verses 12 and 13, drew from him his famous analogy of Law and Gospel as antiphonal voices: "The Law says 'In the midst of life we are in death' and the Gospel answers 'In the midst of death we are in life.' "[17] Psalm 90 therefore makes an ideal text to represent the period of the Law, and for the "Actus Tragicus" Bach (or his unknown librettist) chose the pivotal verse 12, "Ach Herr, lehre uns bedenken, dass wir sterben müssen, auf dass wir klug werden."

The Lutheran concept of God's time joins us "in God" with all who have gone before; this is the underlying meaning of "In ihm leben/sterben wir" in the prologue. In his commentary on Psalm 90 Luther attached particular importance to Moses' address to God as a "Dwelling Place" or refuge: "If God is our Dwelling Place—and God is Life—and we are residents in that Dwelling Place, it necessarily

---

15. On the idea of God's "alien" and "proper" work, see Althaus, *Theology of Martin Luther,* pp. 120, 168, 171–72, 258, 279–80.
16. Bornkamm, *Luther and the Old Testament,* p. 164.
17. Bornkamm, *Luther and the Old Testament,* pp. 145–46.

follows that we are in life and will live eternally." He added the historical dimension, which we have come to recognize as vital to the "Actus Tragicus":

> This means that from the beginning of the world to the end of the world God has never deserted His own. Adam, Eve, patriarchs, prophets, pious kings are asleep in this Dwelling Place. If, as I believe, they have not as yet risen with Christ, their bodies are indeed at rest in the grave, but their life is hidden with Christ in God and will be revealed in glory on the Last Day.[18]

At the end of the chronological sequence in the "Actus Tragicus," Luther's concept of the "sleep of death" voiced in the final line of "Mit Fried' und Freud'," "der Tod ist mein Schlaf' worden"—brings out the ultimate meaning of God's time: that of an "eternal moment," a unity reaching from the Creation to the end of history and the beginning of eternity for man. This, too, is expressed in the commentary on Psalm 90:

> Since there is no measuring of time in God's sight, a thousand years before him must be as though it were only a day; for this reason the first man Adam is just as close to him as the last man who will be born before the Last Day, for God does not view time in its horizontal but rather in its vertical dimension. . . . This entire time which exists since the beginning of man's creation will seem to Adam, when he arises from the dead, as though he had slept only one hour.[19]

The "sleep of death" unites our own awaiting of the final awakening with that of all who have preceded us in death; this is the final relationship of man to history, the point where *Zeit* and *Ewigkeit* merge. The placement of "Mit Fried' und Freud' " at the very end of the chronological sequence of the "Actus Tragicus" suggests anticipation of the Parousia, whereas "Herr, lehre uns bedenken" prays for an understanding, through faith, of death. Between these two verses the sequence of texts works on both the historical-chronological and the tropological levels to allegorize the sene of inner change effected through Scripture.

The librettist of the "Actus Tragicus" might have created his text from the biblical references in the chorales, a procedure comparable to that followed in Cantata 21.[20] But a number of the chorale references had been brought together in works of

18. Martin Luther, *Lecture on Psalm 90* (1534–1535), vol. 11 of *Luther's Works,* ed. Hilton C. Oswald (St. Louis, 1976), pp. 84–85.

19. Luther, *Lecture on Psalm 90,* quoted in Althaus, *The Theology of Martin Luther,* p. 416 nn. 50, 52.

20. Helene Werthemann ("Zum Text der Bach-Kantate 21, 'Ich hatte viel Bekümmernis in meinem Herzen,' " *Bach-Jahrbuch* 51 [1965]: 135–43) demonstrates that the librettist of Cantata 21 derived part of the sequence of texts for that work from an eighteen-strophe poem by Johannes Rist, of which the first half deals with sorrow and tribulation, the second with trust and joy.

earlier composers, although, so far as is known, never before in chronological order. Cantata 106 seems to owe something to a cantata by Christian Ludwig Boxberg, "Bestelle dein Haus," in which double biblical quotations are combined with an instrumental chorale melody. When the bass voice announces, "Bestelle dein Haus, denn du wirst sterben" (with a melodic line that is similar to Bach's at the corresponding point of the "Actus Tragicus"), the choir answers with a paraphrase of "Herr, lehre uns bedenken, dass wir sterben müssen."[21] In the "Actus Tragicus" the bass response to the tenor solo "Herr, lehre uns bedenken" unmistakably belongs to an Old Testament voice of authority. In the biblical context, King Hezekiah's time has come, and Isaiah delivers God's message in these words. Luther interpreted this as an answer to one "who was puffed up with his victory and began to be proud of his uprightness and righteousness."[22] According to Luther, the story illustrates the opposition between faith and works and shows how true faith achieves more through prayer than it expects (God granted Hezekiah another fifteen years of life). In his prayer Hezekiah boasted of his works and righteousness. Luther explained that God heard his prayer but "not the works of the prayer"; Hezekiah's prayer was answered because his boasting was done in the knowledge that his victory was achieved through the Word alone. "Bestelle dein Haus" can be considered an answer whose immediate message is severe but also contains a promise.

Continuing from the two preceding movements, the choral fugue "Es ist der alte Bund: Mensch, du musst sterben," for altos, tenors, and basses iterates the theme of the inevitability of death for the third successive time in the cantata, now with an apocryphal wisdom text. This movement caps the Old Testament sequence of Law, prophets, and wisdom books, summing up the meaning of death for the Old Testament, the wisdom that is sought in "Herr, lehre uns bedenken." Ecclesiasticus places an extraordinarily strong emphasis on tradition and history, as its title ("church's book") indicates. Not only does the author of Ecclesiasticus express reverence for the Law, but the preface to the book names the "three divisions of the Hebrew Scriptures: the law, the prophets, and the other writings."[23] Ecclesiasticus devotes chapters to the wonders of Creation and the whole of Israel's history, and these are harmonized with the themes of death, time, and personal salvation through faith and prayer. Its maxim, "Fear of the Lord is the beginning of wisdom," was used by Luther in his explanation of the phrase "auf dass wir klug werden" in Psalm 90.[24] The sense of history that is prominent in the words "Es ist der

21. An excerpt from Boxberg's cantata is quoted in Friedhelm Krummacher, "Die Tradition in Bachs vokalen Choralbearbeitungen," in *Bach-Interpretationen,* ed. Martin Geck (Göttingen, 1969), p. 54.

22. Martin Luther, *Lectures on Isaiah, Chapters 1–39,* trans. Herbert J. A. Bouman, vol. 16 of *Luther's Works,* ed. Jaroslav Pelikan (St. Louis, 1969), p. 332.

23. *The Apocrypha,* in *The New English Bible,* ed. Samuel Sandmel (New York, 1972), p. 115.

24. Luther, *Lecture on Psalm 90,* pp. 129–30.

alte Bund" can be felt in the traditional, rather severe character of Bach's fugue. The word *Bund* undoubtedly suggested to Bach a strict contrapuntal form ("ge-*bund*ener Stil") representing traditional musical wisdom. Against it the fluid solo soprano line adds an expressive personal voice, and the third element, the chorale "Ich hab' mein Sach' Gott heimgestellt," sounded by the instruments alone, adds a quiet background. In its emphasis on faith this chorale represents the Gospel and the Christian church as a collective body, just as the fugue represents the old cove-nant and what Luther might have called the church of Israel. The vocal and instru-mental "choirs" keep basically separate throughout the movement, suggesting Luther's famous antithesis of life and death, while the soprano joins each at times, serving to connect the two.

Luther's commentary on Psalm 90 again provides us with a clue to Bach's intent: "The church has always existed; there has been a people of God from the time of the first person Adam to the very latest infant born." But the church has often been "so hidden . . . that it was nowhere except in the eyes of God. . . . The true church is the one which prays. . . . It is made up of those who move forward in the process of sanctification, who day by day 'put off the old and put on the new man.' "[25] Possibly the absence of text and the backgrounding of "Ich hab' mein Sach' Gott heimgestellt" were intended to indicate the hidden characer of the church of faith. The solo soprano, replacing the missing voice of the ATB choir, represents the individual who has moved forward in the process of sanctification. It links two worlds, one of which has not yet fully been manifested. At the very end of the movement all three elements converge momentarily, and then the soprano's "Ja, komm, Herr Jesu" emerges alone to end the movement. This detail arises from the primary textual source of the soprano solo, Revelation 22:20, the final words in the New Testament. But, as Dürr has shown, the soprano melody quotes from the funeral chorale "Herzlich tut mich verlangen," so we are justified in interpreting the text as a reference to the final line of that chorale, "Ach, komm, Herr Jesu" as well.[26] The chronological sequence finds its midpoint in the soprano solo, with its call to Jesus, which looks forward to the physical incarnation of Christ. Yet, in its reference to the funeral chorale it also represents the contemporary individual seek-ing union with Christ, while the connection to Revelation anticipates the Second Coming. The soprano solo, then, contains a literal-historical, a tropological, and an eschatological level of meaning, while the threefold sequence as a whole re-minds us of what has been called the "circle of Luther's theology: Law, Gospel, faith."[27]

---

25. Luther, *Lecture on Psalm 90,* pp . 88–89. Cf. Luther, *The Bondage of the Will,* pp. 154–58; Althaus, *The Theology of Martin Luther,* p. 191.

26. Dürr, *Die Kantaten,* pp. 615–16.

27. Bornkamm, *Luther and the Old Testament,* p. 120.

From the standpoint of this central movement we can better understand the chronological aspect of the "Actus Tragicus" text. As we have seen, the sequence Old Testament/New Testament/chorale stands for the three periods of salvation history, and the continuity between eras, characteristic of the concept of salvation history which is evident in the various forms of overlap between successive movements and between textual references within single movements, as well as in the fact that one movement generally leads into the next without a break.[28] "In deine Hände" contains a marked triple layer of chronology in that the first part of its text, whose primary utterance is the contemporary individual's expression of faith, is simultaneously an Old Testament text (Psalm 31) spoken by Jesus from the cross in the New Testament (Luke 23). This movement marks the shift of eras, while at the tropological level the third-person "In ihm" of the prologue shifts to the second-person "In deine." "In deine Hände" emerges as a pivotal movement in several ways: the overlap of eras in its text marks both a chronological turning point and a point of integration of the fugue complex, and in its expression of faith it exactly articulates the meaning of the untexted chorale verse "Ich hab' mein Sach' Gott heimgestellt," so the solo must also be taken as a turning point toward faith, completing the desire for integration with Christ that is voiced in the soprano solo. The key to this inegration is the *theologia crucis,* faith in the crucified Christ as the foundation of Lutheran theology.

Next comes a New Testament text of promise: "Heute wirst du mit mir im Paradies sein" (also spoken from the cross in Luke 23 and sung here by the bass as *vox Christi*). In the midst of this movement Luther's chorale "Mit Fried' und Freud' " enters as a cantus firmus; here the eras of the New Testament and the church overlap. After combining with the first three lines of the chorale, the bass solo ends and the final three lines of Luther's chorale have only instrumental accompaniment. These details display a striking sense of intent. Beneath the chorale phrase "getrost ist mir mein Herz und Sinn," the bass solo cadences ("im Paradies sein"), then moves up an octave to cadence a second and last time, overlapping with the continuance of Luther's chorale, while the basso continuo makes what sounds like a melodic reference to the first line of the funeral chorale "Herzlich tut mich verlangen." At this point the chorale text, "sanft und stille," changes to the quiet acceptance of death that marks the end of the sequence on all three levels—chronologically, the era of the church; tropologically, the attainment of understanding of death; but, above all, the point at which the eschatological sense dominates in Luther's "sleep of death." The listener who perceives and participates in the historical identification with the words of Simeon will understand the meaning of Luther's statement

28. The last-named feature is common in Bach's early cantatas, and it appears in the group of solos that precede the fugue complex. The solos that follow the fugue complex have additional elements of continuity: a single, shared time signature and tempo.

that faith enables us to "leap over the historical chasm that is between us and the time of Jesus."[29] Simeon lived to witness God's salvation and the shift of eras caused by the historical incarnation of Christ, while the modern believer, having accepted Christ and the Gospel, understands and awaits death as the gateway to the coming life. To the ideal understanding of faith, the boundary between death and life ceases to exist.

The emphasis throughout the second half of the "Actus Tragicus" on three overlapping periods and the possibility of their being apprehended through faith as one suggests the three stages of revelation and spheres of activity of the Trinity: the Father/Old Testament, the Son/New Testament, and the Holy Spirit/the church. The conclusion of the "Actus Tragicus" expresses this idea not only in its text but in its position: like the prologue, it stands outside the passage of time in the work. The text of this movement was written as a doxology to the chorale "In dich hab ich gehoffet, Herr," a paraphrase of Psalm 31 and the source of the alto solo "In deine Hände." Another well-known line from this psalm, "Meine Zeit steht in deine Hände," points to an underlying relationship between these two passages and the overall meaning of the cantata, that is to say, that resignation to God's will is the key to understanding God's time through faith.

The issue of chronology in the text of the "Actus Tragicus" has been eclipsed in the literature by analysis of the symmetrical plan. The latter is indeed an imposing presence, the meaning of which becomes clear in the light of all that we have been considering. If the chronological aspect of the text suggests the literal-historical sense of Scripture, and the idea of an analogous spiritual progression, the tropological, then the symmetry is closest in spirit to the allegorical sense, turning the work most conspicuously into a sign.

This dimension is centered rather obviously in the tripartite fugue/solo/chorale complex, which, as we have seen, represents the separation between Old Testament/Law, New Testament/Gospel, church/faith, on the one hand, and church of Israel, church of Christ, individual, on the other. Before and after this pivotal grouping appear pairs of solos, the first of each pair a ground bass movement and the second a bass solo. In the ground bass movements individual expression comes to the fore. "Herr, lehre uns bedenken" asks for an understanding of the inevitability of death, in order to attain wisdom; "In deine Hände" is the expression of that wisdom, that is to say, of faith in Christ and complete trust in God. The bass solos represent answers from God appropriate to each stage of salvation history. "Bestelle dein Haus" is the authoritative Old Testament answer, God's message as delivered to Hezekiah by Isaiah; "Heute wirst du mit mir" is Christ's promise from the cross to the dying thief, representing the Gospel of the forgiveness of sins and

29. Von Loewenich, *Luther's Theology of the Cross*, pp. 101–2.

the resurrection. Additional musical parallels between the two sets of solos (see below) justify our viewing the intent as both an expansion of the Law/Gospel antithesis and a representation of the typological prefiguring of events in the New Testament by those of the Old. At the next level out from the center, the tenor solo and "Mit Fried' und Freud' " are related, as we saw earlier. Framing these movements are the prologue and doxology, fully scored choral affirmations of God's glory.

The symmetrical arrangement of movements in the "Actus Tragicus" mirrors the methodological framework of Lutheran hermeneutics: the Christocentrism of Scripture ("Ja, komm, Herr Jesu"), the antithesis of Law and Gospel and their complementary roles in faith (the fugue complex), typological parallels between Old Testament and New Testament figures (the two pairs of solos), the cross ("In deine Hände" and "Heute wirst du mit mir") and the "analogy of faith" (see the discussion of the tonal plan below) as keys to the figurative language of the Bible, and the like. The symmetry can also be seen as offering a synchronic view of Scripture, an ordering of chronological events into a static pattern. This obvious patterning probably represents the Lutheran view of the deterministic nature of history; that is to say, the rhetorical stage known as *dispositio* (preplanning) is projected in the work as a reflection of God's plan of salvation (God disposes).[30]

The Tonal Plan

Luther perceived the history of salvation as two-dimensional for God's revelation is twofold: through the Word of Scripture (the "preached" or revealed God), and through the cross (the "hidden" God). The hidden God "wills the death of the sinner," yet at the same time seeks the salvation of man by means of a plan that achieves its goal indirectly and paradoxically, through Christ's death on the cross.[31] Luther gave special emphasis to the idea of the separation of the Word into Law and Gospel, but also to the recognition that, just as the "hidden" God is "greater than His Word," so the individual must pass beyond the crucially important Word to faith. Luther thus distinguished "grades" of faith, the highest of which was "no longer dependent on the external Word" but was a "constant inner readiness to do God's will."[32]

We have been dealing with the chronological and synchronic aspects of the text of the "Actus Tragicus" as mirroring Scripture. Now we must examine the tonal plan as the focal point for the spiritual dynamic that Scripture effects in the individual.

---

30. On Luther's determinism see Von Loewenich, *Luther's Theology of the Cross,* p. 31; Althaus, *The Theology of Martin Luther,* pp. 274–80. The expression "Man proposes, but God disposes" comes from Thomas à Kempis (*The Imitation of Christ,* ed. Harold C. Gardiner [Garden City, N.Y., 1955], pp. 53–54).

31. Von Loewenich, *Luther's Theology of the Cross,* pp. 28–31.

32. Von Loewenich, *Luther's Theology of the Cross,* pp. 34, 96.

The outline of this plan is descent from E flat (the sinfonia and the prologue sections "Gottes Zeit" and "In ihm leben") through C minor ("In ihm sterben wir" and "Ach Herr, lehre uns bedenken") and F minor ("Bestelle dein Haus" begins in C minor and modulates to F minor; the central complex is in F minor) to B flat minor ("In deine Hände"), followed by ascent through A flat ("Heute wirst du mit mir") and C minor ("Mit Fried' und Freud' ") back to E flat (the doxology). The tonal plan of the work thus allegorizes the pattern of Luther's "analogy of faith" in a manner recalling the "Christus Coronabit Crucigeros" canon (see Chapter 1, above). The text does not give the degree of structural prominence to the *theologia crucis* that we would expect in view of the centrality of the cross in Lutheran thought, but the tonal plan completes the framework of Lutheran hermeneutics with the *theologia crucis* and the "analogy of faith." It is most closely allied, of course, with the tropological level, creating a shape that mirrors Jesus' incarnation, death, and resurrection. At the same time the Christian perceives the "shape of his own life" to be reflected in Bach's structure: the experience of the Law brings the man down (the descending sequence of keys for the Old Testament texts), while the encounter with Christ and "comformity" to his sufferings ("In deine Hände) and the message of the Gospel ("Heute wirst du mit mir") give him the understanding ("Mit Fried' und Freud' ") that ultimately restores him to God ("Glorie, Lob, Ehr' und Herrlichkeit").

The tonal plan of the "Actus Tragicus" pivots around the words in the alto solo "In deine Hände" that were quoted from Psalm 31 by Jesus on the cross. The B flat minor there functions as the turning point of a symmetrical descent/ascent key plan; it is simultaneously the spiritual nadir of the work and the beginning of an ascent that appears in the rising ground bass as a gesture of hope.[33] About this time Johann David Heinichen described B flat minor as the *extremum enharmonicum*, the remotest flat key in the circle (as opposed to the *extremum chromaticum*, B major).[34] The allegory of extremity certainly underlies Bach's use of the key here. Out of all Bach's vocal music, "In deine Hände" is the only movement in B flat minor, and whenever that key appears within a cantata recitative its association is with darkness, the cross, the depths of spiritual torment, and the like.[35] In the "Actus Tragicus" it is in B flat minor that the alto cries out in in extremis, just as in the *St. Matthew Passion* Jesus calls, "Eli, Eli, Lama, lama asabthani" in that key.

Even those musicians who readily accept rationalistic arguments for the theological importance of the movement argue, justly, that not "In deine Hände" but the

33. Walter Blankenburg points out that the Credo of the *Mass in B minor* has a descent/ascent tonal plan that is centered on the Crucifixus. See Walter Blankenburg, *Einführung in Bachs h-moll-Messe* (Kassel: Bärenreiter, 1974), pp. 56–58.

34. Heinichen, *Anweisung*, pp. 261–67.

35. In the *St. John Passion* the narration of the crucifixion is made in B flat minor. See also the opening movement of Cantata 159 on the words "Dein Kreuz ist dir schon gericht't"; Cantata 127/II (Jesus' sufferings); Cantata 102/II ("Herzensdunkel").

fugue complex *sounds* like the center of the work. In fact, Bach did not intend that "In deine Hände" *appear* to be the center: faith is contrary to experience and appearance, especially at the outset. The fugue complex with its obvious juxtaposition of contrasting ideas makes a far more striking movement, a uniquely imaginative *artistic* centerpiece, whereas the role of "In deine Hände" as a center depends on theological explanation. The cross seen as "God's allegorical work" holds the key to the antithesis of faith and experience, the ability to believe despite appearances. Just as God's "proper work" (the Gospel, redemption) is, according to Luther, hidden behind his "alien work" (Law, death), just as faith and the church are hidden behind appearances such as works and institutions and joy is hidden in tribulation, the meaning of "In deine Hände" is hidden under the imposing surface of the work: it is deliberately eclipsed by the prominence of the preceding grouping and is even contradicted by the allegory of darkness and tribulation represented by its own key. Yet the conspicuous upward turn of the ground bass points to faith and justification, not the historical conflict of Law and Gospel, as the true center of Lutheranism. The chronological-tropological theme of Cantata 106 is, then, motion from "historical" to "special" faith, in Luther's sense of those terms.[36] From this standpoint the "Actus Tragicus" is structured, not primarily around the prominent symmetry of movements centered on the conflict of elements and styles, but around the descent from E flat to B flat minor and the returning ascent, a dynamic of faith whose onset comes immediately *after* the Law/Gospel confrontation. This movement, not the fugue complex, completes the "circle of Luther's theology."

It is crucial to this interpretation that the fugue/solo/chorale complex be understood as having an "incomplete" ending, that is, on the dominant of B flat minor, not as a Tierce de Picardie in F minor. Modulation at the end of a movement, although unusual, is not unprecedented in baroque music or, in this case, difficult to sustain. Johann Kuhnau has pointed out that emphasis on the subdominant can weaken the tonic at the ending of a sonata.[37] Virtually every detail at the close of the fugue complex of the "Actus Tragicus" points to a similar conclusion (Ex. 20). The chorale ends with one of the cantata's recurrent melodic elements, the oscillating semitone (death), here between f′ and g′ flat. Simultaneously the three parts of the chorus all move upward in B flat minor scale patterns of an octave or more, then fall suddenly a fifth (in all voices) to end on a diminished seventh chord that functions as V of V in B flat minor. This activity takes place over a repeated-eighth-note pedal on F that unmistakably functions as a dominant. Here, for the first and only time in the movement, the vocal and instrumental choirs are heard together. The soprano has previously been heard with each choir separately, but now its

36. Von Loewenich, *Luther's Theology of the Cross*, pp. 101–2.
37. Kuhnau, Preface to *Biblische Historien*, p. 123.

EXAMPLE 20. The "Actus Tragicus": ending of fugue "Es ist der alte Bund"

entrance, voicing the final prayer of hope, is delayed so as to coincide with the climaxes of the two choirs. The final dissonant chord sung by the chorus (on "sterben") represents—like the dissonance that sounds, then resolves, on the final chord of the *St. Matthew Passion*—the "sting of death." And when all the parts of the chorus make their final ascent, then fall suddenly to this dissonance, there can be no mistaking the allegory of the desire for redemption coupled with man's inability to attain salvation through his own efforts; death is presented as putting an end to human aspirations. The final work of the Law at this point is to identify the nadir of the tonal plan, from which ascent is possible. The individual confronts the true terror of death and God's wrath and uses that terror as the springboard to faith, the "beginning of wisdom." Rhythmically fluid, even improvisational, the soprano line trails off, so to speak, alone and with a decided sense of open-endedness. The final semitone, b′ flat to a′—harmonically a 4–3 melodic progression over the (now silent) bass—demands resolution. And the ground bass supplies that resolution: it contains the B flat minor scale of the fugue ending and the oscillating f′–g′ flat of the chorale ending, as well as an overall motion to the high b′ flat with which the soprano ended. In addition, the oscillating semitone leads to the b′ flat, forming a configuration of pitches (solmized mi-fa-mi-la-re) that is important throughout the work and was probably derived here from the soprano solo of the preceding movement (Ex. 21).

The segment of the "Actus Tragicus" that begins with "In deine Hände" initiates the third segment of the cantata. And after the soprano solo Bach indicated an empty bar with a pause in all parts; the preceding bar, moreover, contains only the final two notes of the soprano solo. These details provide the explanation for the silence that separates the fugue complex from the alto solo and makes continuity between the two particularly crucial. Throughout the "Actus Tragicus" repeated and long-held tones suggest the measurement of time, and this correlation becomes strongest at the ending of the fugue complex, when the lower parts sounding the repeated tones of the F pedal drop out one by one and the walking-eighth-note bass that runs throughout the movement settles on a single repeated tone. This tone, perhaps indicating a heartbeat or ticking clock, presents time in particularly graphic fashion, as lengths of individual life spans. In comparison to this, the soprano line with its triplets and mordents suggests rhythmic freedom. The unmeasured bar, a moment of suspended time, has a mystical, symbolic character. It precedes the awareness of faith as allegorized in the rising of the ground bass from the depths to touch the soprano's b′ flat (see below).

The "Actus Tragicus," then, may be said to bridge the gap between the outer (historical) structure represented in the symmetry of movements and the inner (tropological) structure represented in the tonal plan. The outer structure centers on the antithesis of Law and Gospel (the fugue complex), while the inner pivots around the point of their integration through faith ("In deine Hände"). Throughout the work, points of modulation parallel important affective shifts in the text.

EXAMPLE 21.

(a) Ending of instrumental chorale "Ich hab' mein Sach' Gott heimgestellt"

(b) Ending of fugue "Es ist der alte Bund" (bass part only)

Mensch, du musst ster ben!

(c) Ground bass of "In deine Hände"

The initial turn down from E flat introduces the idea of death: "In ihm sterben wir zu rechter Zeit." At this point the music moves to C minor via downward leaps in the bass that foreshadow "Es ist der alte Bund," chromaticism is introduced, and the tempo slows abruptly. The tenor solo with its descending ground bass suggests the obsessive, melancholy contemplation that Benjamin linked to allegory in the *Trauerspiel;* the repetitive, additive form invokes the sense of allegorical time.[38] Then, for the words "auf dass wir klug werden," the ground bass ceases and the music moves upward purposively to cadence in a positive-sounding E flat. This point, before the C minor ground bass returns to close the movement, conveys the hope that is part of the Psalm text.

"Bestelle dein Haus" modulates downward from the C minor closing of the preceding movement to F minor. Its busy recorder accompaniment was probably intended to represent the idea of "works," while the shift of key may have been intended to convey what Luther, commenting on Hezekiah's situation, called the "weakness of our nature. When it has fought a battle on the left, it falls down on the right."[39] Certainly, the end of the fugue complex suggests acknowledgment of

38. Benjamin, *The Origin,* pp. 163–67.
39. Luther, *Lecture on Isaiah,* pp. 333–34.

weakness: the move toward B flat minor leaves the soprano isolated, without the support of the basso continuo. Here faith, described by Luther as the "entrance into darkness," strikes out on its own. Nevertheless, as Luther added, "Faith is not a leap into a vacuum. It perhaps gropes in the darkness—and precisely there runs into Christ. It moves away from all experience and experiences Christ."[40]

The B flat minor of "In deine Hände" allegorizes this quality of what has been called "faith in opposition to experience."[41] And, as we will see below, the relationship between the ground bass and the alto solo cleverly represents the experience of Christ. But the so-called negative delimitation of faith with regard to objective experience does not tell the whole story. Faith also has a positive side, the felt quality of faith "realized in experience." This positive side is symbolized in the upward tonal motion of the music after "In deine Hände," which was already suggested in the turn to major for "du hast mich erlöset." While "In deine Hände" conveys the important first definition of the faith that "reigns in the deepest darkness," whose words "fight against appearance" (in the conflict between B flat minor and the ascending ground bass, perhaps), the ensuing movements represent the more positive view of faith. In Walther von Loewenich's words, "The subjective element of faith demonstrates itself as trust. To the extent that faith as antithesis of all objective experience desires to show itself efficacious in the subject, it assumes the concrete form of trust. In trust we have the point at which faith and experience intersect."[42]

After "In deine Hände" the music moves upward to A flat for Jesus' promise from the cross, then on to C minor for the entrance of Luther's chorale "Mit Fried' und Freud' " accompanied by the viola da gambas. Led by the As of Luther's Dorian melody, the upward progression continues through G minor to B flat *major* for the start of the third phrase of the chorale, "getrost ist mir mein Herz und Sinn." This phrase closes in C minor. The remaining three lines of "Mit Fried' und Freud' " then continue alone, with more than a hint that the new view of death as "peace and joy" is a "possession" created by faith.[43] Particularly striking is the fact that Bach marked the words *stille* and *Schlaf* (a prolonged tone) to be performed *piano*. This emphasis, in combination with the rocking semitone motion in the gambas (a rather homely symbol of comfort and trust derived from the motion of the cradle), colors the individual tones of the melody and lends an immediacy to the C major sonority at the close of the movement that seems the harbinger of eternity.[44]

---

40. Von Loewenich, *Luther's Theology of the Cross*, p. 106.
41. Von Loewenich, *Luther's Theology of the Cross*, pp. 77–88.
42. Von Loewenich, *Luther's Theology of the Cross*, p. 95; cf. pp. 82–86.
43. Von Loewenich, *Luther's Theology of the Cross*, p. 97.
44. In a number of cantatas in which C minor and C major appear as pivotal elements in the tonal planning (127, 20, 21), C major bears this association.

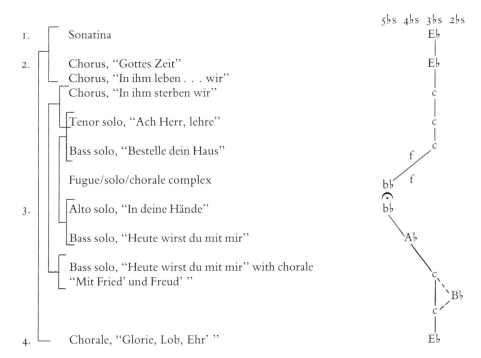

FIGURE 4.   Symmetry and tonal design in the "Actus Tragicus." Brackets indicate structural correspondences between paired solos and key symmetry

The tonal plan of the "Actus Tragicus" can of course be analyzed in symmetrical
terms. The doxology and most of the prologue are in E flat; the sonatina and the
doxology contain modulations to B flat minor (both with Tierce de Picardie) that
somewhat represent in miniature the boundaries of the tonal plan of the work as a
whole. The doxology uses B flat minor for the phrase that deals with Christ as second person of the Trinity ("sei dir, Gott Vater und Sohn bereit"); on the word *Sohn*
the melody leaps up a sixth, from f′ to d″ flat, setting up the cadence to B flat minor
and reminding us of a similar leap in the melody of "In deine Hände." The C minor movements—"In ihm sterben wir" and "Herr, lehre uns bedenken" in the first
half, and "Mit Fried' und Freud' " in the second—are connected by their shared
textual references to Psalm 90 and the Lutheran "sleep of death," and by the fact
that the "rechte Zeit" referred to at the end of the prologue comes to pass in "Mit
Fried' und Freud.' " Throughout his work, Bach preferred C minor for movements depicting the "sleep of death" (e.g., the final choruses of the *Passions*). The
antithetical Law/Gospel relationship of the two bass solos probably underlies the
fact that "Bestelle dein Haus" modulates downward and "Heute wirst du mit mir"
upward (Fig. 4). In all this we perceive that the tonal plan of the "Actus Tragicus" is
as controlled as any other aspect of the work and seems more clearly than any other
to have been intended to follow the inner dynamic of the text.

One striking feature of "In deine Hände" confirms what has been said here regarding its place in Bach's structure: the ground bass and the vocal lines converge three times, in very brief passages of unison writing (Ex. 22). All three convergences precede cadence points. The first appears at the very beginning. The vocal line sings the b′ flat on which the soprano ended in the previous movement. As the ground bass rises to the b′ flat, the alto joins it for four tones that reach across the silence to bridge the gap between movements. The other two instances of this device appear at the point of cadence to the dominant (m. 7) and the point of return to B flat minor (mm. 15–16) after a series of "free" sequences in the bass. This feature is unique for Bach, who otherwise takes great pains to avoid such parallel writing. Here he uses it deliberately to enhance the sense of integration we have stressed, the identification with Christ or the "experience of Christ" made by faith as it "moves into darkness."

The "disintegration" of the end of the fugue complex and the isolation of the end of the soprano solo are countered by the spiritual rebirth of the alto solo, and these details are part of a larger pattern in the solos of the "Actus Tragicus": the reduction or increase of instruments in stages.[45] Throughout Bach's work patterns of this kind often lead to a continuo aria whose meaning, as here, is the intimate relationship between Christ and the believer. In the "Actus Tragicus" the reduction is from the tenor solo with full instrumentation (four real parts), through the bass solo, "Bestelle dein Haus," with basso continuo and recorders only (three parts), to the soprano solo, which, except when it combines with the choirs of voices and instruments, is heard with continuo alone (two parts) and finally with no accompaniment at all. "In deine Hände," with its unisons creating a two-in-one effect, marks the point where increase begins. In "Heute wirst du mit mir," the sequences and chains of suspensions intertwine the two equal-register parts for the words "mit mir in Paradies," the promise of union with Christ that heralds the entrance of Luther's chorale and the return of the viola da gambas.[46]

A similar pattern of instrumentation underlies the chorales. In the fugue complex, "Herzlich tut mich verlangen" is a melodic reference only and "Ich hab' mein Sach' Gott heimgestellt" is untexted; "Mit Fried' und Freud' " is a texted single-voice cantus firmus; and "Glorie, Lob, Ehr' und Herrlichkeit" is fully scored. Moreover, the chorales come into the foreground only after the midpoint of the cantata. Many of the early cantatas thus defer chorale entrances until the major struggles of the individual have been completed. The plan brings out the church's role as sustaining a faith that has been attained through personal, internal struggle.

45. Alfred Dürr has pointed out the same pattern in Bach's early cantatas: *Studien*, pp. 213–16.
46. On the ideas of the union of faith and Christ and of Christ's "indwelling" in the believer, see Von Loewenich, *Luther's Theology of the Cross*, pp. 104–7.

EXAMPLE 22.   The "Actus Tragicus": unison writing in alto solo "In deine Hände"

The unison writing in "In deine Hände" remains the most unusual aspect of Bach's intention. And it connects with the instrumental parts of the sonatina and the doxology, the two other places where (brief) modulations to B flat minor occur. In the doxology, cadential interludes appear between all the chorale lines, and they are all in "three" parts: two obbligato recorders, and a bass line composed of the two viola da gambas moving in parallel octaves. To obtain this texture the basso continuo was omitted, and it seems possible that Bach here, as elsewhere in his music, recognized the octave of the bass as the interval of the Son of God.[47]

47. Andreas Werckmeister, *Musicalische Paradoxal-Discourse* (Quedlinburg, 1707), pp. 92, 100. I have used the association of the octave with Christ to explain the cadence in parallel octaves that appears in the *St. Matthew Passion* on the words "Ich bin Gottes Sohn"; "J. S. Bach's *St. Matthew Passion*," p. 68.

The three interludes that surround the phrases naming the Trinity are additionally set apart by the triplets in the recorders, recalling the threefold groupings of trios with triplets in the "Sanctus" of the B minor Mass. The recorders always play in unison elsewhere in the cantata except for the opening sonatina, where Bach creates a special impression by making the two lines continually separate, then reunite, in yet another form of two-in-one effect. Like the modulations to B flat minor, these combinations with an emphais on "two-in-one" no doubt refer to Christ's position as the second person of the Trinity.

Motivic Interrelationships

The motivic details, more than any other aspect of the "Actus Tragicus," tightly link music and word. Interrelations in much of the musical material parallel the close theological interconnections we have established for the texts. The motivic integration is allegorical in nature, going beyond musical unity and reflecting a theological intent that cannot be so clearly realized by any other means.

Many of the recurrent motivic-thematic and ornamental materials of the "Actus Tragicus" are among the commonest and simplest musical ideas: rising and falling semitone appoggiaturas and descending appoggiatura sequences (a set of changing associations linked to death), oscillating figures, *weben, lebendig, Schlaf,* suggesting the transience of life, rising fifths indicating life and affirmation generally; triads representing God for the ascending major, and contemplation of death, submission to God's will, and the like for the descending minor; held and repeated tones for lengths of time or counting the days; chromaticism to bring death to mind; quickly slurred descending intervals of varying sizes to signify impermanence, perhaps subjectivity, and lines that take their connotations from the chorales from which they were derived. Precise and invariable associations cannot be assigned to these materials, and the extent of their manifold combinations and variations exacerbates the problem of exegesis. Lines such as the ritornello melody from the tenor solo seem to have been put together out of fragments that appear elsewhere throughout the cantata in other combinations; moreover, the signification has deliberately been changed for several thematic ideas (Ex. 23). In addition, many of even the more unusual musical ideas can also be found in many of Bach's early works and in works by other composers.[48] In fact, a central paradox of the work lies in the fact

48. Dürr summarizes the interconnections among Bach's early cantatas in *Studien,* pp. 177–86. I have referred above to an apparent relationship between the "Actus Tragicus" and a cantata by Christian Ludwig Boxberg. A few of numerous instances: the chromatic counterpoint of "In ihm sterben wir" also appears in Cantata 12, on "die das Zeichen Jesu tragen"; part of the "Mensch, du musst sterben" counterpoint of the "old covenant" fugue appears in the first movement of Cantata 21, beginning in measure 15; and the instrumental close of "Bestelle dein Haus" recalls the final movement of "Suonata quarta" of Johann Kuhnau's *Biblische Historien,* which deals with the same Bible story (of Hezekiah's

EXAMPLE 23. Motivic interconnections between the ritornello melody of the tenor solo "Herr, lehre uns bedenken" and other movements of the "Actus Tragicus"

Ritornello melody from tenor solo

(a) Bass solo, "Bestelle dein Haus"

Be - stel-le dein Haus

(b) Alto solo, "In deine Hände"

In dei-ne Hän-de

(c) Tenor solo, "Ach Herr"

be - den-ken dass wir

(d) Sonatina

(e) Fugue, "Es ist der alte Bund"

Es   ist   der   al   te   Bund:

---

sickness and recovery) as does the text of "Bestelle." In light of Kuhnau's use of the chorale melody that is associated with "Herzlich tut mich verlangen" in the "Actus Tragicus" to represent both Hezekiah's illness and recovery, we might postulate a connection. No doubt other such connections exist. These interrelationships themselves, however, are less significant than the allegorical turn of mind that brought them into being and intentionally seeks out such shared material.

EXAMPLE 23   *continued*

(f) Bass solo, "Heute wirst du mit mir"

Heu - te, heu - te   wirst du mit mir

(g) Ground bass of "In deine Hände"

that the more we search for its uniqueness the more of its ideas we find to be common property.

The conflicts and resolutions between simplicity of tone and complexity of musical/extramusical association in the "Actus Tragicus" do not result simply from its admittedly vastly successful fusion of the many elements of Bach's early style and those of musical style around 1700 in general. Nor can we accept the view that eighteenth-century works are not concerned primarily with originality: these works meet modern criteria of originality remarkably well, often despite a superabundance of formulaic aspects. The commonness of the thematic material can perhaps even be taken as intentional, just as can the very difficulty of drawing a line between the composer's original work and the raw material. This amorphousness is the despair of anyone seeking to explicate the meaning of the music completely, for the very simplicity of the thematic material and the complexity of its interconnections inevitably lead to discussion of basics such as scales and intervals rather than demonstrably planned relationships, and promote an atmosphere of allegory.[49]

"Centers" of meaning underlie a great deal of the surface detail of various kinds in the "Actus Tragicus." One such center is the pattern of descent and ascent that determines the tonal plan, the direction of the ground basses, and the themes of several movements. Another is the sequential or chronological order of the text, which controls such aspects as style change and instrumentation. A third underlies the motivic side of the work in general and especially the large number of melodic formulations featuring rising and falling semitones. Much of what is allegorical in nature in the "Actus Tragicus" tends to fragment the work for us, especially because of the high degree of antithesis and differentiation necessary to its theological

49. See Werckmeister, *Musicae mathematicae,* pp. 141–54.

expression. The center of meaning that is voiced throughout the many correspondences in the work can be called the desire for integration, the allegorical longing of the finite for the infinite.[50] The musical relationships of some of these fragmented elements to the chorale "Herzlich tut mich *verlangen*" indicate an additional correspondence between the theological subject matter—longing for death as the gateway to a new existence—and the allegorical character of the work.

Bach's intent in setting "du hast mich erlöset" in the alto solo of "In deine Hände" to a melodic pattern very similar to that heard in the preceding movement to "Mensch, du musst sterben" seems clear (Ex. 24). The meaning is part of the great change that occurs in the alto solo, from an understanding of the inevitability of death as the "old covenant" with Adam to the "new covenant" of justification by faith brought about through Christ's act of redemption. And, as Dürr demonstrates convincingly, in the fugue complex this melodic element is part of a gradual transformation of the countersubject "Mensch, du musst sterben" into a melodic reference to the first line of the chorale "Herzlich tut mich verlangen."[51] A similar set of transformations takes place in the preceding movement, "Bestelle dein Haus," at the line "denn du wirst sterben und nicht lebendig" (Ex. 25). The reference to "Herzlich tut mich verlangen," sung by the solo soprano in the fugue complex, appears in the bass at the end of the "old covenant" fugue, initiating the ascending B flat minor scale that sounds like a hopeful gesture but falls, as we know, to a dissonant final cadence. The longing expressed in the soprano's "Ja, komm, Herr Jesu" and intensified through reference to "Herzlich tut mich verlangen" is a primary factor in the sense of incompleteness experienced at the end of the fugue complex. Under the Law, death is equated with inevitability. The melodic transformations change the meaning of death to a longing for redemption, thus linking "Mensch, du musst sterben" and "du hast mich erlöset."

The thematic interconnections go further and deeper yet. We have seen that the ground bass of "In deine Hände" was made to refer back to elements from the vocal and instrumental choirs at the end of the fugue complex as well as to resolve the soprano's indefinite cadence. It also features a pattern of three intervals that appear separately in several places in the "Actus Tragicus": the rising and falling semitone (mi-fa-mi), a rising fourth (mi-la), then a falling fifth (la-re), a pattern perhaps derived from "Herzlich tut mich verlangen."[52] Even the free-sounding

50. This idea appears in various forms over a fairly wide range of studies of baroque literature. See Arnold Stein, *John Donne's Lyrics* (Minneapolis, 1962), p. 158; Frank J. Warnke, *Versions of Baroque* (New Haven, 1972), pp. 22, 61–62; Fredric Jameson, *Marxism and Form* (Princeton, N.J., 1972), p. 72 ("the distinction between symbol and allegory is that between a complete reconciliation between object and spirit and a mere will to such reconciliation").

51. Dürr, *Die Kantaten*, pp. 615–16.

52. Bach uses a very similar variant of this line of the chorale as the main melodic idea of the tenor aria "Mein Verlangen" in "Komm, du süsse Todesstunde" (Cantata 161), another of his early cantatas on

EXAMPLE 24.

(a) Excerpt from "In deine Hände"

(b) Excerpt from "Es ist der alte Bund"

du hast mich er - lö - set,

Mensch, du musst ster - ben

EXAMPLE 25.   Themes from "Es ist der alte Bund" (a, b, c, d) and "Bestelle dein Haus"
(e, f, g, h) compared

(a)

Mensch, du musst ster - ben,

(e)

denn du wirst ster - ben,

(b)

Mensch, du musst ster - ben

(f)

denn du wirst ster-ben,

(c)

Mensch, du musst ster-ben

(g)

und nicht le - ben-dig,

(d)

Mensch, du musst ster - [ben]

(h)

denn du wirst ster-ben, und nicht le-ben-[dig]

material of the soprano solo derives largely from these elements and others that link it to the tenor solo in particular. The mi-fa-mi-la-re melodic pattern appears in the tenor solo as the words "Herr, lehre uns bedenken, dass wir sterben müssen" are heard for the last time before the text continues with "auf dass wir klug werden" (Ex. 26). Bach creates a number of parallels between the tenor and the alto solo, such as the dropping out of the ground bass and the turn to major when the texts express the understanding that frees man from the inevitable pattern of death ("auf dass wir klug werden" and "du hast mich erlöset"). The motivic connections operate in this context: the understanding of death prayed for in the tenor solo is revealed in "In deine Hände" as the product of faith. The ritornello of the tenor aria uses the rising fourth and falling fifth, joining them to what is probably the most conspicuous direct connection between the two solos: the minor-triad figure that descends from the fifth through the third to the tonic and returns to the fifth (Ex. 27). The triad is itself a motivic/emblematic element in the "Actus Tragicus," and we will return to it later. Use of the semitone, alone or in conjunction with the rising fourth/falling fifth pattern, also occurs throughout the entire work. It first appears near the beginning of the sonatina and it returns conspicuously at "In ihm sterben wir." Here, as at "dass wir sterben müssen," its primary association is death (Ex. 28). In "In deine Hände" the connotation is changed to that of redemption. The semitone is absent from "Heute wirst du mit mir." When it returns, in the oscillation of the viola da gamba figures at the end of "Mit Fried' und Freud'," it has taken on a gentle, comforting character, and when a semitone appoggiatura figure from the tenor solo ("bedenken") appears in the final chorale it is as an ornament to "Die göttlich' Kraft mach' uns sieghaft," that is to say, associated with victory over death.

If the emphasis on the semitone is connected to expressions of the human condition, another equally common musical element, the major triad, comes to serve in the doxology as the emblem of God's time. Often called *triunitas* by theorists of the Lutheran metaphysical tradition, the triad seems to mirror the Deity as no other element can, for its "three-in-one" appears in two forms, the major representing the divinity of Christ, the minor his humanity. This double representation is undoubtedly the correct interpretation of the tonal shift from major to minor at the center of the F major duet from *Clavierübung III* (see Ex. 18).[53] The harmonic triad formed the basis of Werckmeister's allegorical *Anhang,* and Bach, like Werckmeister, produced a canon on the triad that affirmed its expression of universal harmony. The upward-curving symmetrical presentation of the major triad is well known to have been used in works such as "Gott ist mein König" to symbolize

death, which employs material from this chorale as the themes of several of its movements. Dürr, *Die Kantaten,* pp. 448–49. Bach often derives motivic material from this chorale melody; cf. the opening movements of Cantatas 25 and 135.

53. See G. Friedemann, *Bach zeichnet das Kreuz: Die Bedeutung der vier Duetten aus dem dritten Theil der Clavierübung* (Pinneberg im Bans, 1963); Siegele, *Bachs theologischer Formbegriff,* pp. 7–12.

EXAMPLE 26.   Motivic–intervallic relationships between the soprano solo (a, b, c, d) and
tenor solo (e)

(a)

Ja,   ja,   ja komm, Herr Je-su, komm,

(b)

ja, ja, ja,   ja komm,   Ja,   ja, Herr Je-su,   komm!

(c)

ja, Herr Je - su,   komm,   Ja,   ja,   ja, komm, Herr   Je - su,

komm, Herr Je-su, komm!

(d)

ja,   ja, ja, komm, ja, komm, Herr Je - su,

(e)

Ach, Herr!   Herr, leh - re uns   be - den - ken, dass wir

ster - ben müs - sen

EXAMPLE 27.   Head motives of ritornello to tenor solo "Herr, lehre uns bedenken" and
                alto solo "In deine Hände"

Rit. to tenor solo   Alto solo

In dei-ne   Hän-de

EXAMPLE 28.   Semitonal appoggiatura figures in the "Actus Tragicus"

(a) Sonatina

(b) Chorus "In ihm sterben wir"

In   ihm   ster - ben   wir   zu   rech - ter zeit,

(c) Tenor solo

dass wir ster - ben   müs - sen, dass wir   ster-ben müs - sen,

(d) Tenor solo

be - den - ken

(e) Final chorale

Die   gött - lich' Kraft   mach' uns   sieg - haft

God's glory. And the triad has a central place in the "Actus Tragicus," but primarily in its downard-curving shape. The theme of "In deine Hände" offers the clearest presentation of this triadic shape, and the dark and extreme key underscores all we have said regarding the significance of this movement. "Herr, lehre uns bedenken" and "Bestelle dein Haus" give their own versions of the minor triad prominently at the outset. The major triad appears first at the cantata's initial words, "Gottes Zeit," and Bach has arranged the three notes so as to present the image of descent (g'–e' flat) followed by ascent (e' flat–b' flat); the rising fifth links up with the theme of "In ihm leben" that soon follows. The doxology returns to the E flat major triad in Bach's extension and elaboration of the final line of the chorale into a fugal conclusion, "durch Jesum Christum. Amen." In what is for Bach the pre-Leipzig form of this melodic line we have the image of the tonal structure of the entire cantata (Ex. 29). This final emblem of the incarnation and atonement is the quintessential instance of a chiastic theme (in which the central tone, root of the E flat tonic triad, even aligns with the syllable "Chri" in the text, just as the "Actus Tragicus" itself is the paradigm of the chiastic cantata, placing Christ at the center of Scripture, God's time, and the spiritual life of faith.

As we have indicated, however, not all interrelationships of this kind can be proven to have been intended as allegory. It might well be argued that some of them exist primarily as facets of the musicological integration of the piece, and the changing associations are simply incidental results of the sequence of texts. The premise advanced here that an understanding of the whole as exhibited in its conspicuous theological intent gives meaning to such details might be seen as a hermeneutic circle of at least a somewhat vicious kind. We cannot completely exclude that viewpoint, even though the large sense of intent is surely unmistakable in the broadest patterns of text and musical structure, even though the musical unity of Bach's other works from this time (some of which use similar thematic materials) never once generates so conspicuous a sense of correspondence within the work, and even though ideas of transformation, integration, and the like are shared by theology and music and are therefore in keeping in a work of this kind. Were we to tackle this aspect of the "Actus Tragicus" after the ordinary manner of motivic analysis, the results would carry us much further into the realm of speculation regarding the basic philosophical question of baroque music, that of the relative roles of purely musical and musicoallegorical impulses in composition. But it does not illuminate individual works to seek out those elements that can easily be drawn into analogy with theology (or some other set of ideas) without control over the sense of intent as exhibited on the highest levels. When a work is formed from material of very commonplace character, as is the "Actus Tragicus," only explication that deals with the whole can give meaning to the details. For this reason our study has

EXAMPLE 29.   Final chorale line in the last movement of the "Actus Tragicus"

durch   Je - sum Chri-stum,   A   -   men, A - men,

dealt with the work in the broadest terms of musicotheological intent. The evidence of this intent on so many levels and in so many aspects of the "Actus Tragicus" is its most outstanding feature.

The rich interweave of theology and music in the "Actus Tragicus"—so brilliantly illustrative of the epithet "troped-motto cantatas"—supports the suggestion that when Bach referred twice to his goal of a "well-regulated church music" in his dismissal request from Mühlhausen he had an artistic objective in mind.[54] Certainly the "Actus Tragicus," despite its being of an essentially seventeenth-century cantata type, contains hints not only of the depth of the interaction between music and theology throughout Bach's mature work but of many of the specific means by which Bach eventually achieved his goal. This will become clear as we examine several of the Weimar cantatas and Leipzig church works. In particular, the idea of tonal allegory, often exhibited in key structures for entire cantatas, occupied the composers's attention throughout his creative life. The basic premises of Lutheran belief too, as well as the analogy between musical design and hermeneutic principles, continually drew from Bach a form of musicotheological reflection of a profundity that is unique in all of music.

The contents of Bach's theological library and, especially, the underlinings and marginalia in his copy of Abraham Calov's commentated "Luther Bible" show that Bach developed a studied interest in Lutheran theology and that he probably interpreted many of the events of his life in that light. The content of Lutheranism as it appears in Bach's library, and particularly in many of the markings in the Calov Bible, merges unmistakably, and unsurprisingly, with the texts of the church works. In studying this relationship we should, however, bear in mind the viewpoint of Theodor Adorno: that the "office" of church composer stood for Bach in a dialectical relationship to the "dynamic," modern aspects of his work, in which the spirit of the Enlightenment figures prominently. When, therefore, we survey the marked passages in Bach's Bible and note the many places where the suggestion of conflict between human endeavor and the world's reception of it is "resolved" through the Lutheran advice that the outcome be placed in God's hands, we can draw either of two conclusions: that Bach was a believing Lutheran who regulated the inevitable conflicts of life according to religious precepts; or that, as Adorno claims, belief was so difficult for Bach as to involve him in a struggle to remain within what he perceived, at a deeper level, as a restrictive framework. According to this second interpretation, that sense of conflict was much greater than that between artist and public.

We must not take a simplistic or sentimental attitude toward the role of religion in Bach's life. The connection between the composer's beliefs and the intricately musicotheological character of his work may perhaps be supplied by the under-

54. See David and Mendel, *The Bach Reader,* p. 60.

lined passages in his Bible; but the subject will demand very cautious handling. As it happens, the underlined passages often treat the themes that figure most broadly in the "Actus Tragicus": committing one's life to God; God's control of time and history; life and death. They can reasonably be taken as evidence for Bach's perception of the central theme of Lutheran Christianity, and indirectly (and anachronistically) as evidence for the pivotal role in Cantata 106 that we have assigned to "In deine Hände." An important focal point for this theme in the Calov Bible is the book of Ecclesiastes, the *Prediger Salomonis,* which Bach underlined and marked more often and more consistently in a substantive manner than any other book of his Bible. The marked passages themselves, moreover, demonstrate a consistency in that they involve commentary that states and restates the basic themes of Ecclesiastes as they were perceived within the Lutheran tradition. Bach's particular interest in these themes is also evinced in his underlining of that part of the preface that outlines the *Summa* of the book and in his marking of the words *Summa Libri* and an N.B. in the margin. Even the last underlining in Bach's Bible, in the book of James, is of parts of a passage that, as Calov's commentary informs us, states the theme of Ecclesiastes.[55]

As we have said, that theme emphasizes the necessity of leaving the outcomes of both worldly and spiritual affairs in God's hands. Time and again Bach marks passages that iterate this primary "wisdom" and the secondary themes of carrying out the duties of one's "office" without worrying about others or about what the future will bring, of patient endurance of adversities, of the distinction between worldly and spiritual wisdom, and the like. More than once such a passage refers to the fact that those men whose understanding and intelligence are greatest suffer most, because they are frustrated by the lesser abilities of others. There are many hints at Bach's personal situation: for example, the injunction to use one's gifts for the benefit of others even if one does not receive thanks. Always the commentary reminds us that God "sets the clock" and orders things according to this "timetable." If men of great understanding venture into God's realm, as when individuals attempt to control the future, the result is misery. A few quotations from Bach's underlinings will reveal their general tenor:

> Thus joy and sadness, peace and restlessness, fortune and misfortune, death and life lie utterly and completely in God's hands. Therefore it is best that we learn that everyone in his station use with thanksgiving the manifest gifts which God provides and let God reign. . . . Just as no man can be certain at what hour a child will be born or die, thus should we say: Lord God, the highest governance is with You, my life and death are in Your hands; the way I use my life, as long as You allow, I shall dispense with care and thought and give everything over to You. . . . The Lord God has given every man his hour and his measure for our lives and our deaths, all our endeavors, all our labor and work that we perform from our first breath to our last. . . . What is a

55. Cox, *The Calov Bible,* fasc. 141, 273 (trans. pp. 423, 455).

person who now lives or others who are yet to be born? It is already decided in God what shall become of each man—his name and his entire being on earth—from the first moment to the last. With the word "name" let us understand not only his proper name but also name and repute which he may gain from his endeavors and his deeds.[56]

In these passages, expressions such as "My life and death are in Your hands," "as long as You allow," "I shall . . . give everything over to You," "every man his hour," and "measure for our lives and deaths" recall the "Actus Tragicus" directly. The frequency with which Bach marks passages in which expressions such as "alles Gott befehlen" appear is remarkable and illuminates not only the "Actus Tragicus" but a movement such as the chorale "Befiehl du deine Wege" in the *St. Matthew Passion,* which both Spitta and Smend found inappropriate to a *Passion* setting.[57] Bach, however, understood the centrality of this idea to all sacred music as the focal point for the tropological sense—the application to the individual of the events and wisdom of Scripture.

Bach also marked Calov's commentary on Luke 23:46, where Jesus says, "Vater, ich befehle meinen Geist [meine Seele] in deine Hände." Calov completes the passage with the remainder of Psalm 31:6 and concludes it, "Gott gebe, dass wir alle auch also unser Leben beschliessen in beständigem Glauben an unsern Heyland Christum Jesum," which is in effect the prayer that closes the "Actus Tragicus."[58] Another passage marked by Bach expresses the comprehensive theological framework that underlies the cantata. This time Calov's commentary is on the text that Luther believed to be the most important in the New Testament, Paul's Epistle to the Romans (1:17):

> In this argument the path of attaining blessedness is described in its origins; in the most concise statement, that the main cause of blessedness is God whose word and power is the gospel, as the means of blessedness. The effective cause however is Christ, the means on our side is faith which embraces the righteousness of Christ revealed in the gospel which alone belongs to faith. He who is thus vindicated is a sinful man who believes in Christ. The form is the righteousness of Christ which is imputed to us through faith. The final cause is life and eternal blessedness.[59]

In all this we can see that Bach's concerns in composing the "Actus Tragicus" went well beyond the requirements of an occasional funeral cantata. He reached out to touch the central issues of Lutheran Christianity. We know almost nothing of what Bach at the age of twenty-five or so might have acquired or studied of theological works that would have permitted him to enrich the sphere of church music with so enduring a masterpiece. But that the way was prepared for this goal as voiced at Mühlhausen is attested to in Cantata 106 to a degree that leaves room only for wonder.

56. Cox, *The Calov Bible,* fasc. 147, 151, 162 (trans. pp. 425, 427, 430).
57. See below, p. 374; also Chapter 13, n. 17.
58. Cox, *The Calov Bible,* fasc. 244 (trans. p. 448).
59. Cox, *The Calov Bible,* fasc. 153 (trans. pp. 449–50).

CHAPTER FIVE

Tonal Planning

in the

Weimar Cantatas

Although tonal allegory exists in the Mühlhausen cantatas, the "Actus Tragicus" is the only cantata from Bach's earliest group to feature a clearly patterned and purposive overall arrangement of keys in conjunction with detailed planning at other levels. Tonal planning as a recognizable phenomenon organizes a number of individual cantatas only from the Weimar cycle of 1714. This fact and the nature of the planning itself relate to other changes in Bach's cantata composition from Mühlhausen to Weimar, including his adoption of the new Neumeister cantata type in which freely composed recitatives and arias replaced the earlier emphasis on biblical mottoes.

To understand the meaning of this change we must consider a feature of Bach's early cantatas, especially those with allegorical tonal planning, that is common to a number of works from Mühlhausen and Weimar: antithesis. Bach's cantatas from both the Mühlhausen and Weimar periods can be called antithesis cantatas because they are frequently directly structured by such texts as "Dein Alter sei wie deiner Jugend" (BWV 71), "Mensch du musst sterben"/"Du hast mich erlöset" (the "Actus Tragicus"), and "Wir müssen durch viel Trübsal in das Reich Gottes eingehen" (BWV 12).[1] Texts used in this way are, as we have seen, *Symbola,* expressions of fundamental beliefs such as the theology of the cross and Lutheran ideas such as "joy hidden in tribulation."

Although Bach's early cantatas give prominence to texts that express the conflict between a world of tribulation and the hope of redemption, antithesis is presented and resolved differently in the Mühlhausen and Weimar works. Two different, but not mutually exclusive, concepts underlie the treatment of antithesis throughout Bach's work. The first of these is, of course, symmetry. This chapter, however,

---

1. Other examples are "Ich hatte viel Bekümmernisse in meinem Herze, aber deine Tröstungen erquicken meine Seele" (BWV 21) and "Mein Herz schwimmt in Blut"/"Wie freudig ist mein Herz" (BWV 199). See Dürr, *Studien,* p. 213.

deals primarily with the second type, one which treats antithesis successively rather than simultaneously. The conceptual relationship between antithesis and symmetry animating the plan of the "Actus Tragicus" is evident on many of the title pages of the theological works of Lutheran orthodoxy in Bach's library. From them we can immediately see that the symmetry achieves two objectives: it highlights the opposition itself, and it provides a sense of reconciliation at a higher level. These goals, which are clearly the meaning of the "Actus Tragicus," embody Luther's view that scriptural antithesis expresses the theology of the cross. Many oppositions, such as Law/Gospel and flesh/spirit, refer to this basic tenet of Lutheran Christianity. An important, but not exclusive, correlative for symmetry in Bach's work are the diagrams of symmetrical musical structure that appear as crosses.

The symmetry of the "Actus Tragicus" operates in conjunction with and remains conceptually separate from other aspects of the musicotheological design, especially the tonal plan. In this relationship the symmetry stands closer to the theological, dogmatic side of the work, while the other design aspects to varying degrees address the dynamic of change in the individual. Although the distinction is not absolute, it allows the commentator to recognize and avoid interpretations that overlook either one of the two dimensions.

The distinction between the dogmatic and affective, speaking in terms of his texts, belongs to all Bach's work, but in a few cases symmetry highlights the distinction. Symmetry need not affect the tonal allegory at the level of structural planning. For example, Bach utilizes a conspicuous degree of symmetrical planning in the motet "Jesu, meine Freude," with its restricted tonal allegory, to express a double level of antithesis that is already highlighted in the text. The alternation of six chorale verses with five settings of verses from Romans 8 creates an opposition of the kind Luther recognized when he chose opposing modes for the Epistle and Gospel of the German Mass.[2] That is, the chorale, "Jesu, meine Freude," has a personal, even pietist religious orientation, centered on Christ, whereas Romans 8 underscored Luther's Pauline theology and orthodoxy,[3] especially concerning the definition of flesh and spirit that were central to Lutheran theology. At the same time, although Luther contrasted Paul the theologian with Christ the comforter, he called the Epistle to the Romans "the gospel in its purest form."[4] The interweaving of the two texts in Bach's motet, although often creating striking juxtapositions in tone from one section to the next, reconciles the personal-affective and intellectual-dogmatic sides of Lutheranism. Paul's antithesis of flesh (Law) and spirit (Gospel) makes central a fugal movement whose very theme contains the antithesis at both

2. Praetorius, *Syntagma Musicum*, pp. 451–52.

3. The text of "Jesu, meine Freude" was written by Johann Franck and appeared first in the songbook *Praxis Pietatis Melica*, 5th ed. (Berlin, 1653).

4. On Luther's remarks regarding the importance of the Epistle to the Romans, see John Dillenberger, ed., *Martin Luther: Selections from His Writings* (New York: Doubleday, 1961), pp. 18–19.

textual and musical levels. Related correspondences then amplify the opposition throughout the structure of the whole.

The well-known symmetrical structure of the motet both presents and resolves not only Paul's oppositions but those between the two very different kinds of texts.[5] Variation is Bach's mainstay throughout the motet and especially so in a movement such as "Trotz, dem alten Drachen," in which the chorale serves dramatic ends by the most ingenious means. Another dimension of variation involving movements two, six, and ten may be considered here, since its meaning is central to the whole of Bach's work. It has been suggested that the theme of the motet's fugal centerpiece—"Ihr aber seid nicht fleischlich sondern geistlich"—was derived from the Ten Commandments chorale, "Es sind die heil'gen zehn Gebot'."[6] In fact, while the first half of the motet theme, "Ihr aber seid nicht fleischlich," appears to derive from "Es sind die heil'gen zehn Gebot' " (and therefore to represent the association of Law and flesh), its more florid continuation, "sondern geistlich," resembles the first phrase of the chorale "Herzlich tut mich verlangen" (Ex. 30). A funeral chorale itself, "Herzlich tut mich verlangen" is, of course, appropriate within a funeral motet such as this. The chorale melody is never stated explicitly either in the motet or at the center of the "Actus Tragicus." The two halves of the fugue theme are detached from one another and heard in varied forms elsewhere in the work (Ex. 31). And later in the central fugue the "Geist" half is heard—in a form closer to "Herzlich tut mich verlangen"—to the continuation of the text: "so anders Gottes Geist in euch wohnt." Near the end of the fugue the first half of the main theme is put together with this variation to form the composite phrase, "Ihr aber seid nicht fleischlich, so anders Gottes Geist in euch wohnt." This combination states more explicitly the idea that faith ("Gottes Geist") already makes the transition from flesh to spirit possible (Ex. 32). This idea taken from Luther's emphasis on the presence of the Spirit in the flesh through faith underlies the planning (both tonal and otherwise) of many of Bach's works.[7]

The association of antithesis and symmetry remains very important throughout Bach's work, often suggesting that overall symmetrical planning is an image of reconciliation. For example, in Cantata 58, "Ich habe manche Herzeleid," Bach

---

5. Friedrich Smend's 1928 study remains the basis of most later commentary on this aspect of the work ("Bachs Matthäus- Passion," *Bach-Jahrbuch* 25 [1928]: pp. 36–44).

6. Jansen, "Bachs Zahlensymbolik," pp. 97–99. Jansen attributes Smend (source not cited) with the derivation of the closely related theme of "Wir haben ein Gesetz" from the *St. John Passion* from the Ten Commandments chorale and notes that the theme appears ten times in the *Passion* chorus. Smend ("Bachs Matthäus-Passion," p. 41) suggested the relationship between the *turba* chorus and the centerpiece of the motet.

7. Althaus (*The Theology of Martin Luther,* p. 397) quotes Luther: "The Spirit cannot be with us except in material and physical things such as the word, water, in Christ's body, and in these things on earth." Althaus comments further: " 'Spirit' is not a transcendental sphere beyond all earthly history but precisely this history comprehended in God's word. And in this sense it is really important to remain on earth. For we remain most completely on earth precisely when we seek that which is above."

EXAMPLE 30.

(a) Fugue theme from motet "Jesu, meine Freude"

Ihr a - ber seid nicht fleisch - lich, son-dern geist -

- [lich]

(b) First phrase of chorale "Dies sind die heil'gen zehn Gebot"

Dies sind die heil'-gen zehn Ge-bot

(c) First phrase of chorale "Herzlich tut mich verlangen"

Herz-lich tut mich ver - lan-gen

EXAMPLE 31.   Excerpts from the second (a, b, c) and tenth (d, e) sections of the motet "Jesu, meine Freude"

(a)

Es ist nun nichts, nichts, nichts Ver -

-damm-lich-es an de-nen, die in Chri - [sto]

(b)

die nicht nach dem Flei-sche wan - [deln]

EXAMPLE 3 I   *continued*

(c)

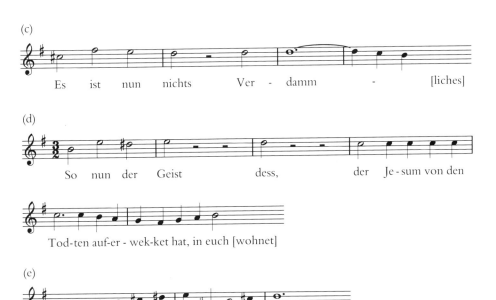

(d)

Es   ist   nun   nichts   Ver - damm   -   [liches]

So   nun   der   Geist   dess,   der   Je - sum von den

Tod-ten auf-er - wek-ket hat, in euch [wohnet]

(e)

um dess wil-len, dass sein Geist in ___ euch woh - [net]

EXAMPLE 32.   Excerpts from the central (sixth) movement of the motet "Jesu, meine Freude"

(a)

so an-ders Got-tes Geist in euch woh - [net]

(b)

Ihr a-ber seid nicht fleisch-lich, so an-ders Got-tes   Geist in euch woh   -   [net]

creates an opposition between patience in adversity (*Geduld*) and the comforting assurance of salvation ("getrost ist mir mein Herz und Sinn") in the outer movements, between the "world" and faith in an inner pair of recitatives, while the central movement, "Ich bin vergnügt in meinen Leiden," voices the reconciliation of the suffering in the world and the benefit of faith. In such a work the symmetrical plan might have been intended to represent the cross, the true theological subject of the text. Cantata 213, "Hercules auf dem Scheidewege," represents the options of Hercules' choice between Pleasure and Virtue by means of both tonal antithesis and symmetrical planning; the latter, as in Cantata 58, brings an element of reconciliation to the work and invites a deeper interpretation of Bach's intent than we might otherwise take. The central segment of the *St. John Passion* (Smend's *Herzstück*) juxtaposes opposites (Law versus Freedom) in the tonal plan as well as in the repetition of choruses in reverse order.[8] The plan of the whole produces a structure that may approximate John's worldview with its famous sets of oppositions (flesh/spirit, below/above, death/life) and its overall concept of cosmic order.

We can adduce many examples of antithesis and symmetry. Although symmetry is real enough in Bach's work, it can easily be overemphasized in musicological writings at the expense of other, more dynamic, aspects. Symmetry works best at the largest structural levels as an allegory of order and reconciliation. Within such a framework, however, the individual movements often exhibit a highly dynamic character that conflicts conceptually with the static nature of symmetry. Freidrich Smend found convincing demonstrations of symmetrical planning in works such as the *St. John Passion, Jesu, meine Freude,* and the "Credo" of the *Mass in B minor.*[9] Much less convincing, however, was his attempt to designate symmetry as a crucial principle of the *St. Matthew Passion.*[10] In addition, his diagramming of the "Credo" as a visual correlative of the cross masked the dynamic element of the work, which is essential to an understanding of its theological content. Accurate interpretation of the "Credo," as well as the "Actus Tragicus," demands that we recognize the simultaneity of both static and dynamic structural conceptions as the composers's intent. Interpretations that stress symmetry often emphasize the dogmatic rather than the personal side of religion and view the cross only as a sign, rather than the expression of Christian life that it was for Luther. Even considering the works purely musically, the focus on "formula and symmetry," as Adorno characterized this musicological tendency, elevates the static above the dynamic features of Bach's work, script above sound.[11]

8. Smend, "Die Johannes-Passion von Bach," *Bach-Jahrbuch* 23 (1926): 105–28.

9. Smend, "Die Johannes-Passion von Bach," "Bachs Matthäus-Passion," and "Luther und Bach," p. 37.

10. Smend, "Bachs Matthäus-Passion," pp. 33–36.

11. Adorno, "Bach Defended," p. 136.

Bach's earliest group of cantatas after Mühlhausen, those for the Weimar cycle of the year 1714, focus on the dynamic side of faith, in a second cantata type that emphasizes a different conceptual pattern for the treatment of antithesis.[12] In these so-called sermon cantatas antithesis is still prominent but is now treated in a successive rather than simultaneous fashion.[13] That is, symmetry now takes second place to a form that presents the theme at the beginning, then develops its features (or contrasts) throughout a succession of movements (usually arias). The sequence often turns from a general congregational focus to a more personal concern for the dynamic of change that takes place within the individual. The most characteristic oppositions in these works often appear between the beginning and the end rather than within a single (often centralized) movement. The Weimar cantatas deal more directly with the affective dimension of religion, a feature that is related to the Neumeister cantata type, with its inevitable emphasis on individual religious experience via the introduction of modern recitatives and arias. Occasionally the tone is pietistic, recalling Luther's emphasis on inner dynamics. Although the older (Mühlhausen) cantata type was capable of representing the dynamic, changing character of Scripture as internalized by the individual, when compared with freely composed arias and recitatives the objective character of the biblical texts never elicited such extremes of expressive intensity from Bach as we find in arias such as "Seufzer, Tränen, Kummer, Not" from Cantata 21. In this last feature the Weimar cantatas of 1714 foreshadow Bach's later achievements.

Within several of these works the pattern of tonal anabasis, or ascent (sharpward motion) through the circle of keys, emerges as a device by which Bach allegorizes sequences of increasingly positive emotions, as well as more internal concerns. Six of the eight surviving cantatas from that year exhibit overall patterned tonal planning to varying degrees, and of the six, five begin and end in different keys. Of these five, four begin in a minor and end in a major key. This open-ended approach to tonal planning reminds us of Bach's second *Symbolum* canon, "Omnia tunc bona quando clausula bona est. In Fine videbitur cujus toni," which suggests a modulatory design in which the final key marks a change from the beginning but provides a satisfactory resolution to the whole.[14] This is exactly the nature of Cantatas 172, 199, 12, 21, and 61, the last two of which exhibit an eschatological character at the end (see below). In fact, two cantatas from Bach's Leipzig period, No.

12. This second pattern might be called *Steigerung,* for its association with the idea of increasing intensity, for example in texture, instrumentation, or contrapuntal complexity, as representing the dynamic quality of music. Christoph Wolff, for example, recognizes it as one of the main ordering principles (symmetry being the other) in several of Bach's collections. In the case of some collections (such as *Canonic Variations on "Vom Himmel hoch")* Bach used both types of organization at different times (Wolff, "Ordnungsprinzipien in den Originaldrucken Bachscher Werke," in ed. Martin Geck, *Bach-Interpretationen* [Göttingen, 1969], pp. 154–64).

13. Dürr, *Studien,* p. 213.

14. The latter part of this *Symbolum* was popularized by Luther (see Nettl, *Luther and Music,* p. 42); on Bach's lost canon, see Chafe, "Allegorical Music," pp. 347–48, 353–54.

27, "Wer weiss wie nahe mir mein Ende?" and No. 156, "Ich steh mit einem Fuss im Grabe," use German versions of the *Symbolum* ("Ende gut, macht alles gut"; "Ist Alles gut, wenn gut das End") in their texts to express this central Lutheran concept; both works end in keys different from those in which they began, No. 27 being an interesting example of an anabasis cantata. Although this new form of tonal planning is not incompatible with symmetry, it represents a greatly increased emphasis on the allegory of spiritual development in Bach's cantatas to this point.

Cantata 150, "Nach dir, Herr, verlanget mich"

We know virtually nothing of the cantatas Bach produced between the Mühlhausen works (1707–1708) and the Weimar works of 1714. It is possible that during that period he composed one surviving cantata, No. 150, "Nach dir, Herr, verlanget mich," a work whose authorship and date remain uncertain.[15] If Alfred Dürr's suggestion for dating this work at Weimar around 1709–1710 is correct, we could posit that it introduces the idea of successive antithesis in a work that stays very close to the Mühlhausen type. This cantata, in quality generally below the level of the Mühlhausen works, remains somewhat anomalous; in some respects it bridges the gap between them and the Weimar cantatas while in others it seems to stand apart from both. Yet, setting these questions to one side, we may discuss the work briefly as an introduction to the more significant Weimar works.

"Nach dir, Herr, verlanget mich" begins with a conspicuous and emblematic chromaticism. An introductory sinfonia almost has the character of variations of the descending tetrachord ostinato, while melodic patterns entering in the bass near the end suggest the first line of "Herzlich tut mich verlangen." The meaning of the chromaticism and the quasi-ostinato element is given in the opening section of the first chorus, which develops the descending chromatic tetrachord polyphonically: *Verlangen* expresses the human condition of the painful feeling of separation from God, the cry of distress so common in the Psalms. There is thus no contradiction when Bach creates a fugue on the descending tetrachord for the closing section of the chorus: "dass sich meine Feinde nicht freuen über mich." Between these two sections two changes of style appear, the first for "Mein Gott, ich hoffe auf dich," which is built on an unchanging harmony, and the second for "Lass mich nicht zu Schanden werden," which is a series of falling fifths. Sequences of falling fifths return at the end of the closing chromatic fugue in association with the words "über mich." From these details we understand the idea of descent—whether in the form of the chromatic tetrachord or the circle of fifths—as the expression of a life of adversity. Hope, on the other hand, is represented by holding on to a harmony—C sharp major—that is relatively sharp (higher on the circle of fifths than the tonic).

15. Dürr, *Studien*, pp. 195–99. Dürr concluded that Bach very probably composed the work around 1709–1710.

I would suggest that this cantata is concerned primarily with hope for redemption within the struggle of the present life, and that this idea underlies the ostinato character of the tonic key throughout large parts of the seven-movement sequence. Departures from the tonic, although few in number, therefore have considerable significance. The primary instance is the fifth movement, a trio aria in D major, "Zedern müssen von den Winden." This movement uses the imagery of cedars bent by the wind to express the idea that the believer must stand firm, placing trust in God despite all that is contrary: "Rat und Tat auf Gott gestellet, achtet nicht was widerbellet." The closing words, "den sein Wort ganz anders lehrt," explain that man must cling to God's Word for safety in a world of tribulation. The D major of this message stands in contrast to the B minor of the world; in the preceding movement Bach begins in B minor with "Leite mich in deiner Wahrheit, und lehre mich," passing an ascending fifth line through all the voices from bass to soprano, with each entrance beginning a fifth higher than the preceding one (B, f sharp, c′ sharp, g′), and turning to D major for the cadence at "lehre mich." This last teaching is given in the following D major movement.

It is vitally important to this allegory that the return to B minor be made so that the cantata ends with the idea of hope in the present life. The movement following "Zedern müssen von den Winden" is a prelude and fugue for chorus, "Meine Augen stehen stets zu dem Herrn" (prelude), "denn er wird meinen Fuss aus dem Netze ziehen" (fugue). It begins in D major with a thematic recollection of the preceding movement but turns to B minor for a series of repetitions of "stets zu dem Herrn." Already in this change we sense the necessity of looking to God in the present life, while the oscillating figures and reiterated fourths in the strings invoke the sense of holding on. The fugue is built on the theme of a rising stepwise fourth (fifth in the answer), but toward the end of the word *Netze* brings forth long descending chromatic lines, with which the movement ends. We have returned to a world comparable to that of the opening movement. The last movement, a ciacona for chorus, completes the idea of hope in the present life. Even more than the previous fugue theme, the ostinato of this movement suggests a foundation of hope in God: the ground bass is a diatonic stepwise ascending fifth that reverses the idea of the chromatic descending tetrachord of the opening movements and the *Netze* idea heard previously. Lines one through six of the text present three sets of antithesis in rhyming couplets, while the remaining two voice God's aid to mankind in overcoming the world through Christ's presence:

Meine Tage in dem Leide
endet Gott dennoch zu Freude;
Christen auf den Dornenwegen
führen Himmels Kraft und Segen;
bleibet Gott mein treuer Schutz,
achte ich nicht Menschentrutz;
Christus, der uns steht zur Seiten,
hilft mir täglich sieghaft streiten.

The structure corresponding to the first six lines consists of a striking series of up-ward modulations: B minor (three statements of the ostinato, line one), D major (three statements, line two, with the key change coming exactly on the word *Freude*), F sharp minor (three statements, lines three and four), A major (one state-ment, line five), and E major (two statements, line six). This tremendous tonal anabasis is of course linked to the teaching expressed in the rising fifths in the fourth movement and is conceptually opposite to the descending fifths in the first chorus and the descending tetrachords. In the first couplet the move up is enhanced by a shift from minor to major, but the second pair stays in minor (the shift from D to F sharp minor appears, with four chromatic semitones on *Dornenwegen*). The up-ward movement indicates that the overall direction takes precedence over the im-mediate details. The sharpward progression is equally underscored by increasing instrumental activity, with half and whole notes at the beginning, quarter notes starting at *Freunde,* eighth notes (and arpeggio figures) for line six, and the E major instrumental interlude that follows it. Within this latter instrumental passage a sin-gle statement of the ostinato reverses the direction both melodically (descending fourth) and tonally (E major back to B minor), just before the final two lines. These last lines are given the most extended treatment by far, and within the final section rhythmic motion moves again from whole and half notes through quarters to eighth notes (*sieghaft streiten*), then closes in half and whole notes again. The alle-gory of the whole is unmistakable: within the B minor that represents the present life, anticipation of God's turning things around prompts sharpward modulation, whereas the presence of Christ helps the individual in the daily struggle of worldly existence.

Anabasis Cantatas

"Nach dir, Herr, verlanget mich," although not among Bach's better composi-tions from this time, features an allegorical design that relates it conceptually to many of Bach's other works. In particular, the differentiation between the nature of human existence on the one hand, and the life toward which faith and hope are directed on the other, runs through much of Bach's work and, beginning with the Weimar cantatas of 1714, is represented quite often by tonal planning. In relation to "Nach dir, Herr" these Weimar compositions exhibit a more dramatic, even ex-travagant, dimension of tonal allegory. Three cantatas from the 1714 cycle open with feelings of fear, guilt, and torment and become more positive as they proceed, eventually ending with the original affective sphere transforming into faith and joy: Cantata 12, "Weinen, Klagen, Sorgen, Zagen," Cantata 21, "Ich hatte viel Be-kümmernis," and Cantata 199, "Mein Herz schwimmt in Blut." Tonal anabasis is most prominent in the first two of these. Compared to the "Actus Tragicus" these cantatas can be said to begin at the point where the individual has already been brought by consciousness of sin to extreme torment.

Cantata 12 particularly emphasizes the Passion as the ultimate source of comfort for the Christian, especially in the first two arias, with expressions such as "Kreuz und Krone sind verbunden," "Doch ihr Trost sind Christi Wunden," and "Ich will sein Kreuz umfassen." The work as a whole centers around the *theologia crucis* (Bach took over the first movement of this cantata as the "Crucifixus" of the *B minor Mass*). The opening key, as in "O Schmerz" of the *St. Matthew Passion,* is F minor, the emotional and tonal nadir of the work. The gradual inner change from torment to joy is made through the following sequence of keys, always rising a third and turning from minor to (relative) major:

CANTATA 12: "Weinen, Klagen, Sorgen, Zagen"

F minor	(1) Sinfonia	
F minor	(2) Chorus:	"Weinen, Klagen . . ."
A flat		Middle Section: "die das Zeichen Jesu tragen"
F minor		"Weinen, Klagen . . ."—da capo
C minor	(3) Rec.:	"Wir müssen durch viel Trübsal"
C minor	(4) Aria:	"Kreuz und Krone sind verbunden"
E flat	(5) Aria:	"Iche folge Christo nach"
G minor	(6) Aria:	"Sei getreu," with instrumental chorale, "Jesu, meine Freude"
B flat	(7) Chorale:	"Was Gott tut, das ist wohlgetan"

Such an arrangement allows Bach to show that even a turn from major to minor (from the fifth to the sixth movements), although it may express the immediate reference to pain and hence appear to be a step backward, belongs to a series of ever more positive affections. The text—"Sei getreu, alle Pein wird doch nur ein kleines sein. Nach dem Regen blüht der Segen, alles Wetter geht vorbei, Sei getreu"— reveals the real direction to lie unswervingly toward faith and comfort, affirmed by the ascent of the tonal plan through successive key signature levels.

The meditative stages of Cantata 12 correspond (for the most part) to the key-signature levels; these are, in fact, very close to the three basic stages outlined by Luther in his *A Meditation on Christ's Passion* (1519).[16] Although we have no incontrovertible evidence of Bach's ever having used this essay, he surely knew it; the dynamic sequence of its meditative program finds parallels throughout his work, in particular in the *St. Matthew Passion*. The contents of the essay are important

16. Luther's sermon is presented in the form of fifteen numbered paragraphs; but the three stages are easily identified in the sermon. Stages 1 and 2 appear in paragraph No. 12, at "*After* man has thus become aware of his sin," and stage 3 appears in paragraph, no. 15, "*After* your heart has thus become firm in Christ" (emphasis added). Elke Axmacher ("*Aus Liebe,*" pp. 18–27) shows how this threefold use (*Nutz*) of the Passion—recognition of sin, comforting the conscience, and model for Christian life— remains the central focus of Passion meditation throughout the seventeenth century.

enough for our understanding of "Weinen, Klagen" that we will summarize them here.

After a few remarks concerning faulty types of meditation on the Passion (such as anger at Judas, lamentation over Jesus' innocent sufferings without perceiving ourselves as the cause), Luther presents his fifteen-point set of instructions in three stages, which can effect a change in man's being, and "like baptism, give him a new birth," "strangl[e] the old Adam," and "mak[e] him conformable to Christ."[17] In the first stage the Christian must view the Passion with a "terror-stricken heart and despairing conscience," recognizing that it is his sins that torture Christ and that he himself must ultimately suffer, "tremble and quake and feel all that Christ felt on the cross." This is, of course, the state of mind represented in the opening chorus, "Weinen, Klagen, Sorgen, Zagen, Angst und Not ist der Christen Tränenbrot, die das Zeichen Jesu tragen," which we would easily recognize even without the connection to the "Crucifixus."

Luther's second stage considers the Passion from the perspective of the resurrection. Its objective is to remove sin from the conscience. In addition to entreating God for faith, we can "spur ourselves on to believe" through recognition that Christ has paid for man's sins out of love; this arouses love of Christ in the heart, and the confidence of faith is strengthened.[18] The first recitative, "Wir müssen durch viel Trübsal in das Reich Gottes eingehen," joins the present life of tribulation to the kingdom to come, and the aria "Kreuz und Krone sind verbunden" is explicitly connected to the Passion in its description of Christ's wounds as the individual's "trust." Then, in "Ich folge Christo nach," the first movement that is entirely in a major key, love prompts the individual to follow Christ and "embrace" the cross ("Ich küsse Christi Schmach, ich will sein Kreuz umfassen") as the individual grows in faith. Finally, the melody of "Jesu, meine Freude," entering as cantus firmus to the third aria, completes this idea of faith with one of the best-known expressions of Jesus-love from the period of Lutheran orthodoxy.

In the third and final stage of Luther's sermon, the individual has, through the foregoing meditative process, received faith; now the Passion must be seen as the center of Christian life. "After your heart has thus become firm in Christ, and love, not fear of pain, has made you a foe of sin, then Christ's passion must from that day on become a pattern for your entire life."[19] Now the individual actively weighs the adverse events of his life against the suffering of Christ; in so doing he can "draw strength and encouragement from Christ against every vice and failing." This idea is developed in the aria "Sei getreu," which urges retaining one's faith through the adversities of life: "Sei getreu, alle Pein wird doch nur ein kleines sein. Nach dem Regen blüht der Segen, alles Wetter geht vorbei, Sei getreu." The final chorale,

17. Luther, *A Meditation on Christ's Passion*, pp. 10–11.
18. Luther, *A Meditation on Christ's Passion*, pp. 12–13.
19. Luther, *A Meditation on Christ's Passion*, p. 13.

"Was mein Gott will," corresponds to the goal of Luther's meditative sequence: through faith the individual can "rise beyond Christ's heart to God's heart," can "grasp him not in his might or wisdom (for then he proves terrifying), but in his kindness and love. Then faith and confidence are able to exist, and the man is truly born anew in God."[20] Starting from the wrathful God who "seeks the death of the sinner," Cantata 12 progresses through Christ to the merciful God who "seeks the redemption of the sinner."[21]

Cantata 12 is the result of much thought and planning both by Bach and his librettist (probably Salomo Franck).[22] By virtue of its descending chromatic tetrachord, its conspicuous use of velar consonants (see below), its emphasis on descent/ascent and minor/major patterns, and its subject matter—the theology of the cross—the cantata is conceptually related not only to the "Crucifixus" but to the "Christus Coronabit Crucigeros" canon. These common devices underscore the extent to which Cantata 12 employs antithesis to suggest the joining of two worlds through the cross of Christ—the present one of suffering and death and the future life of transcendence and fulfillment; this union is expressed in the canon by the three C's of the *Symbolum* and in the cantata by the aria "*Kreuz und Krone sind verbunden, Kampf und Kleinod sind vereint.*" This idea of joining the present and future life, based on the sound of the consonants, has a strong visual correlative in Bach's work. As Friedrich Smend has shown, Bach uses the Greek letter Chi in the score of the *St. Matthew Passion* as the abbreviation for both *Christus* and *Kreuz*.[23] A third association of the Chi is that of the sharp sign (*Kreuz* in German), well known from the "Kreuzstab" cantata, in which the visual cross of Bach's title page (*X-stab*) is translated into the musical motto of a particularly conspicuous C sharp within a G minor context. Like the sharpened note, the cross is a dissonant presence; yet, the direction of transcendence is a sharpward (the "Christus Coronabit Crucigeros" canon notates only sharps), upward progression through the circle of keys, the same direction as the plan of Cantata 12.

In the recitative "Wir müssen durch viel Trübsal in das Reich Gottes eingehen" the antithetical nature of the theology of the cross is represented ingeniously in a dualism of C's. The basso continuo moves from its initial c down an octave to close on low C, while the first violin ascends from its first note—c"—*up* an octave of the C *major* scale, even though the recitative is in C minor (Ex. 33). The registral and tonal conflict expresses the dualism of worlds that are united in the cross, the world of *Trübsal* versus the kingdom of God.[24] In a number of other works Bach treats C

20. Luther, *A Meditation on Christ's Passion*, p. 13.

21. Luther, *The Bondage of the Will*, pp. 197–200.

22. Z. Philip Ambrose, " 'Weinen, Klagen, Sorgen, Zagen' und die antike Redekunst," *Bach-Jahrbuch* 69 (1983): 35–45; Chafe, "Allegorical Music," pp. 350–53.

23. Smend, "Luther und Bach," p. 37.

24. Dürr (*Die Kantaten*, p. 265) sees the dualism of chromatic descending melodic motion in the first movement of Cantata 12 and prominent diatonic ascent in several of the remaining movements as a key

EXAMPLE 33.   Recitative from Cantata 12

to the structure of the work. This is undoubtedly correct; not only "Nach dir, Herr, verlanget mich" but several Bach works featuring chromaticism utilize the same idea. In fact, the idea of chromatic descent is itself reversed already at the A flat major close of the middle section of the opening choral complex of Cantata 12. That an almost identical passage appears in the "Actus Tragicus," on the words "in ihm sterben wir," leads us to conclude that Bach meant to indicate in both places the presence of hope (ascent) within a basic context of tribulation, the same association of the *Ruffet, Ach,/Hofft auf Leben* antithesis on the Bach goblet.

minor and major as keys that represent the fundamental dualism of Christ (the human versus the divine) and the cross (the emblem of suffering and death of this world versus the sign of transcendence). C minor is the burial key of Christ in the *Passions* and the preferred key of the "sleep of death" of Lutheran eschatology; a dualism of two C's must have held compelling associations of Christ for Bach. In the "Christus Coronabit Crucigeros" canon the given notes (those that are notated) constitute a descent pattern of the following harmonies: F sharp major/minor, E major/minor, D major. The descent represents the cross of suffering and death as in the "Crucifixus" and the opening chorus of "Weinen, Klagen." The *Symbolum*, however, reverses the pattern on the tone C of the ground bass, thereby generating the ascending harmonic progression C minor/major, D minor/major, G major. The harmonic content of the canon, represented in the extremes of its first and central chords, outlines a tritone, from F sharp major to C minor, while the key of G major is reserved for the end alone. The three C's of the *Symbolum* signify the union of Christ (Chi), the cross (C minor in conflict with the sharps of cantus durus), and the crown (the turn to major and the upward modulatory direction). As in the *Passions* the dualism of sharps and flats represents the opposition of worlds, the present apparent one of suffering and death and the hidden transcendent one to come; passage from the one to the other is through death in Christ.

The first aria of Cantata 12, "Kreuz und Krone sind verbunden," makes this dualism clear. Throughout this movement, just as in the canon, the identity of the velar consonants—*Kreuz/Krone, Kampf/Kleinod, Christen/Qual*—points up the antithesis that pervades the work at all levels; this is the one complete movement of the cantata whose melodic line cannot be said to reduce to the idea of either descent or ascent. Rather, it utilizes both directions simultaneously—descending sequential patterns of ascending motives, and the like. In all the other movements, however, one or the other direction dominates: in addition to the movements already mentioned, "Ich folge Christo nach" emphasizes ascent; "Jesu, meine Freude" descends conspicuously on its first and last lines; and "Was Gott thut, das ist wohlgethan" ascends at the beginning in a manner recalling "Ich folge Christo nach." One also senses that minor- and major-key movements are paired: two choral movements in F minor and A flat (ending only); two arias in C minor and E flat (the latter of which continues both the idea of textual antithesis and the emphasis on velar consonants from "Kreuz und Krone"); and, finally, two chorales in G minor and B flat. The three key-signature levels point out that the six basic keys of the cantata—despite the seeming disparity between the initial F minor and closing B flat—can be considered to belong to a single ambitus, that of E flat or C minor. Viewed in this light, the three movements in those keys constitute a center presenting Christ as the point of unity (the tonic area) for the cross of the preceding movement (the subdominant region) and the crown of the final chorales (the dominant region). The plan of Cantata 12 can be called chiastic or cruciform in a sense that goes even deeper—perhaps more hidden or symbolic would be the better expression—than that produced by mere symmetry alone.

As the center of the ambitus, "Kreuz und Krone" embodies the symbolic meaning of the work according to the original association of the word *Symbolum*: the two halves of the divided token are reunited. In "Ich folge Christo nach" the individual becomes "conformable to Christ in His suffering," in a personal mystic union. Bach does not use the word *Symbolum* in Cantata 12, but the middle section of the opening chorus speaks of those who suffer as bearing the "sign of Jesus" (*Zeichen Jesu*). This chorus completes the text of "Weinen, Klagen" with the turn to major suggesting the outcome of the preceding suffering. The connection between the *Symbolum* of the chromatic canon, the *Zeichen Jesu* of the cantata, and the chiastic form of the *Symbolum Nicenum* is no coincidence. The cross is the primary theological symbol, uniting two opposed worlds—flat/sharp, minor/major, descent/ascent—while stressing their separateness: the suffering and death of the one versus the transcendence of the other.

Cantata 21, "Ich hatte viel Bekümmernis," first performed eight weeks after "Weinen, Klagen," presents an even wider range of both affective contrast and tonal shift. Part One is absorbed with fear, sorrow, and trouble throughout the course of five movements confined to C minor (the tonic) and F minor; Part Two constitutes a predominantly major-key anabasis, taking the relative major as its point of departure: E flat (recitative and aria duets, Christ comforts the troubled soul); G minor (chorus with chorale, urging comfort to the soul); F (aria expressing the turning of the tears of suffering into the wine of rejoicing); finally, C major (a choral vision of heavenly glory). The cantata demonstrates powerful points of transformation. The first of these is, of course, the turn to major for the second half. Another is the F major tenor aria, in which the play on words, "Verwandle dich *Weinen* in lauterem *Wein*," is reflected in our interpretation of the key of the aria as a tonal *Verwandlung* of the earlier F minor of the tenor aria in Part One, "Bäche von gesalznen Zähren" (the first with full string accompaniment, the second with basso continuo only).[25] But above all the conspicuous contrast between the final choruses of both parts (C minor and C major) gives structural emphasis to an inner transformation, whose outer, historical dimension is, as in the "Actus Tragicus," the Old Testament (Law, constraint, death) versus the New (promise, eschatological fulfillment). The restricted range of minor keys in Part One, the use of Old Testament texts, and the absence of any reference to Jesus, all seem to find their culmination in the C minor permutation fugue, with its ten vocal entries (the Law?) of an archaic-sounding theme based on the descending minor triad (we may well recall the old covenant fugue in the "Actus Tragicus"). And, as in the earlier work, it is succeeded by the personal appearance of Jesus (bass solo as *vox Christi*) in a comforting dialogue with the believer (Soul), now with a decidedly pietistic cast. Likewise, the church enters next (chorale). Finally, a triumphant doxology

25. On the allegorical interpretation of the expression *Freudenwein* in Bach's work, see Axmacher, "Bachs Kantatentexte in auslegungsgeschichtlicher Sicht," p. 16.

EXAMPLE 34.   Cantata 21: themes of closing choruses of Parts I and II

dass er mei-nes An-ge-sich-tes Hül-fe, und mein Gott   ist,

Lob, und Eh-re, und Preis, und Ge-walt sei un-serm Gott von E-wig-keit zu E-wig-keit.

("Lob, und Ehre . . ." Ex. 34), in every sense the reverse of the earlier C minor fugue, celebrates the victory of Christ and the church in an even more all-encompassing supratemporal and eschatological vision ("von Ewigkeit zu Ewigkeit") than that suggested by "Gottes Zeit." The text, drawn from Revelation, symbolically lists the seven attributes of the *Lamm*: "Kraft, Reichthum, Weisheit, Stärke, Ehre, Preis, Lob." Bach concretizes this idea in a theme whose fundamental tones and metric accents every half measure add up to seven before the answering voice enters, as if a half measure early. Nowhere else does Bach create a clearer representation of the upward progression to "somewhere outside of history, to the end of time or to the coincidence of all times."[26]

The tonal character of the ending is foreshadowed within the recitative dialogue that opens Part Two: here the Soul (soprano), in darkness, calls out to Jesus ("mein Licht"), while the violin ascends a (hopeful) major scale against a systematic descent in the bass, an idea similar to that of the first recitative of Cantata 12. Light and darkness express the dualism of the worlds; for the phrase "Bei mir? hier ist ja lauter Nacht!" the strings all drop in pitch with intervals ranging from a tenth to a twelfth, and the soprano cadences in A flat (on "Nacht"); but for the phrase "Brich doch mit deinem Glanz und Licht des Trostes ein!" the soprano turns to C major in a remarkable anticipation of the key of the final movement.

Not all cantatas that represent the dynamic of increasing faith in tonal terms ascend in such immediately recognizable patterns, however. Cantata 199, "Mein Herz schwimmt in Blut," for solo soprano, begins with the individual in a state of extreme tribulation, in C minor. The final aria, "Wie freudig ist mein Herz," expresses the increased faith, similar to that in Cantatas 12 and 21, and ends the can-

---

26. Erich Auerbach, *Mimesis: The Representation of Reality in Western Literature,* trans. Willard R. Trask (Princeton, 1953), p. 45.

tata in B flat, not a great tonal distance from the beginning. Nonetheless, tonal shift is vitally important to the spiritual allegory of this work; instead of developing step-by-step, Cantata 199 wavers among the inner states of fear and torment, hope, repentance, entreaty, sorrow, comfort, and, finally, joy. The progression of the three arias—from C minor ("Stumme Seufzer, stille Klagen") to E flat ("Tief ge-bückt und voller Reue") and B flat ("Wie Freudig")—is upward and increasingly positive. Throughout, the cantata is concerned with the acknowledgment of sin, repentance from a severely humbled state, and therefore "Tief gebückt und voller Reue" cannot mark a conspicuous ascent. The hearing of the *Trostwort* in the midst of sorrow in the following recitative initiates an upward motion from C minor through G minor to an F major chorale for the completion of repentance according to the dynamic expressed in Luther's Passion sermon, of which several crucial ideas are stated in the present work. After acknowledging so much sin in C minor and E flat, the chorale voices readiness to cast sins into Christ's "deep wounds" (Luther's second stage). With this realization attained in the chorale, the individual can him-self "lie down" in these wounds that serve as a resting place (modulation back to E flat), while faith is freed to "soar" and "joyfully sing" the final aria (B flat). As in several other Weimar cantatas, this piece celebrates the central place of the Passion in the dynamic of faith and the linking of spiritual development with tonal shift, primarily anabasis. Cantata 199 illustrates tonal planning as a uniquely powerful presence even when the patterning is less direct.

Elsewhere in the Weimar cycle of 1714 Cantata 61 provides a fairly straightfor-ward, if less pronounced, example of tonal anabasis, making use of relative minor and major keys:

CANTATA 61: "Nun komm, der Heiden Heiland"

A minor	(1) Chorale fantasia in the form of a French overture: "Nun komm, der Heiden Heiland"
C major	(2) Tenor rec.: "Der Heiland ist gekommen"
C major	(3) Aria for tenor and strings: "Komm, Jesu, komm zu deiner Kirche"
E minor	(4) Rec. for basso and strings: "Siehe, siehe, ich stehe vor der Tür"
G major	(5) Aria for soprano and basso continuo: "Öffne dich, mein ganzes Herze"
G major	(6) Chorale with violins: "Amen, amen! Komm, du schöne Freudenkrone"

In this Advent cantata the rising tonal plan represents anticipation and hope in the events surrounding the coming birth of Christ. Although the first recitative begins by announcing that in the literal-historical sense the incarnation has already taken place, the sequence of movements treats the spiritual senses of Christ's coming: that is, to the church (the allegorical sense), to the individual in faith (the tropologi-cal sense), and to the individual awaiting the Second Coming and the joy of the future life (the eschatological sense). The two-octave ascent in the violins at the close of the final chorale expresses the ending words, "deiner wart ich mit Verlangen." This chorale is, in fact, the *Abgesang* of the final verse of "Wie schön leuchtet der Morgenstern," which, along with its companion chorale, " 'Wachet auf!' ruft uns die Stimme," forms a symbolic representation of "Das Himmlische Mahl," by means of the visual arrangement of the lines of each strophe in the shape of a goblet.[27] We are not dealing, however, with a medieval scheme of interpretation, despite the parallels to the four senses. Rather, everything is directed toward the personal dynamic of faith. Bach again uses the device of gradually reducing instrumentation to allegorize an increasingly personal series of affective moments corresponding to the ever nearer relationship to God. The French overture represents the most external stage and the soprano solo (the Soul) the most internal, while the bass recitative—in the role of *vox Christi*—stands apart from the sequence per se, although it encourages the final reduction. Introducing the imagery of night and day from the Epistle (Rom. 13:11–14), the first recitative seems to link the coming of salvation to the brightening of tonality in the cantata, an association for rising key sequences that crops up frequently in Bach and, as we will see in Chapter 9, is expanded greatly in the Christmas Oratorio with exactly the meaning intended in Cantata 61.

In Cantata 182, "Himmelskönig, sei willkommen," for Palm Sunday, three successive arias without intervening recitatives—"Starkes Lieben," "Leget euch dem Heiland unter," and "Jesu, lass durch Wohl und Weh"—form the spiritual core of the work, responding to the words of Christ in the preceding bass recitative—"Siehe, ich komme"—and allegorizing once again the idea of increasingly personal stages of contact with God. The conception seems related to Cantata 61 (the Gospel reading, concerning Jesus' entrance into Jerusalem, is the same for both Sundays): the first movement is overture-like; the single recitative is the *vox Christi* announcing his coming; and, again, Bach uses a rising tonal progression with reducing instrumentation—C major (basso and strings), E minor (alto and recorder), B minor (tenor and basso continuo). Now, however, the series of solos is surrounded by choral and instrumental movements in the tonic, G major. As the work progresses we increasingly recognize that the Passion provides the source of spiritual development for the individual. In particular, the major-key bass solo suggests the vital love between Christ and the individual that belongs to Luther's second stage. Christ's triumphant entry into Jerusalem, represented in the overture style of the opening movement, becomes a personal event; in the first movement the lines "Lass auch uns dein Zion sein! Komm herein! Du hast uns das Herz genommen" voice Christ's coming to the church in terms of the individual "hearts" that it comprises. Later Bach underscores the connection between the worldly and spiritual Jerusalems by his derivation of the theme of the "Himmelskönig sei willkommen"

27. Fenner, *Aussagemöglichkeiten barocker Musik,* pp. 178–179.

EXAMPLE 35.

(a) Chorale "Jesu, deine Passion": beginning of line seven

in dem Him-mel ei-ne Stätt'

(b) Cantata 182: Theme of first chorus

Him-mels-kö-nig, sei will - kom - men, sei will-kom-men,

fugue from the seventh line of the chorale "Jesu, deine Passion" (the seventh movement): "in dem Himmel eine Stätt' [uns deswegen schenke]" (Ex. 35). The text of
the final movement, "So lasset uns gehen in Salem der Freuden," interprets the
individual's accompanying Jesus into Jerusalem in terms of the joy of the person
certain of salvation. Again the emphasis is first on Jesus' coming to the church, then
the tropological advent represented by the three solos, and, finally, the eschatological anticipation of the heavenly Jerusalem in the present life.

The ascending tonal progression through the three arias surely relates to Jesus'
"drawing" all men after him by means of the "lifting up" of the crucifixion; the
final aria states, "Jesu, lass durch Wohl und Weh mich auch mit dir ziehen." In this
B minor aria Bach utilizes an extreme tonal device to represent the double meaning
of the cross—that of this world ("schreit die Welt nur kreuzige") versus the benefit
of faith for the believer. On the word *kreuzige,* which settles on the dominant of the
dominant (a C sharp major chord) through *its* dominant, the bass, undoubtedly to
be harmonized with a diminished seventh chord—B sharp, D sharp, F sharp, A—is
confronted by the Neapolitan sixth chord (G major) of the dominant (F sharp minor) in the vocal line, a chord from the opposite (flat, subdominant) side of the key
(Ex. 36). Although the key of the cantata is G major, by this time we have moved to
the furthest point in the sharp direction; Bach's clash unforgettably presents the
sense of two worlds.[28] The final chorus, "So lasset uns gehen in Salem der
Freuden," while rounding off the cantata in G major with a main theme of conspicuous ascent character, makes very sharp modulations for the text "Er gehet voraus
und öffnet die Bahn," confirming the meaning of the ascending keys in the cantata.

Along with the "Actus Tragicus," these five Weimar cantatas establish many of
the associations for tonal planning that run throughout Bach's cantata oeuvre. In

28. William H. Scheide, *Johann Sebastian Bach as a Biblical Interpreter* (Princeton, 1952), pp. 21–23.

fact, the "Actus Tragicus" remains the quintessential instance of tonal descent followed by ascent, just as Cantatas 12 and 21 are typical of the anabasis pattern. Bach prefers these types whenever he uses a schematic arrangement of keys, which is quite often. But other types exist, and one of them—the catabasis cantata—is also represented among the Weimar cantatas of 1714; for example, Cantata 172, "Erschallet, ihr Lieder." Judging from the number of times he performed it in Leipzig, sometimes repeating the opening chorus at the end, and sometimes transposing it up a tone, this work was one of Bach's favorites.[29] In its original form the cantata begins in C major, the key of the first three movements, then moves down through the relative minor (aria, "O Seelen Paradies") to the subdominant (duet aria, "Komm, lass mich nicht länger warten"; chorale, "Von Gott kommt mir ein Freudenschein"), in which it closes. Again the distance from beginning to end is not great, but the significance of the pattern is unmistakable, not only from interpretation of the work itself but from consideration of catabasis cantatas with the same associations from Bach's Leipzig years. Often the descent represents the coming of the Holy Spirit. The primary set of associations centers around the perspective of the present life as opposed to the anticipation of eternity that usually concludes the anabasis type.

In three of the cantatas for Pentecost the primary biblical idea is found in the verse from the farewell discourse in John: "Wer mich liebet, der wird mein Wort halten, und mein Vater wird ihn lieben, und wir werden zu ihm kommen und Wohnung bei ihm machen." Two cantatas (Nos. 32 and 74) have this verse as the text of the opening movement, and "Erschallet, ihr Lieder" has it as the only recitative. The key ideas are the indwelling of the Father and the Son in the individual heart through the presence of the Spirit and the mutual love between the individual and God.[30] The first of these ideas underlies the opening three C major movements, especially the festive opening chorus and the aria "Heiligste Dreieinigkeit, grosser Gott der Ehren" for bass, three trumpets, and timpani. These movements establish the greatness and majesty of God, while the intervening recitative expresses God's coming to dwell with man by means of descending sequences and a tremendous

29. Dürr, *Studien,* pp. 25–26.
30. Von Loewenich, *Luther's Theology of the Cross,* pp. 104–7.

drop to a final low C. It is clear, then, that downward motion in this work represents God's descent to dwell in man. The middle section of "Heiligste Dreieinigkeit," therefore, moves to the subdominant and colors the modulation to G with so much borrowing from the flat side that it is more G minor than major. The confined scale of the human heart when compared with God is the main impetus for this tonal character: "komm doch in die Herzens-Hütten, sind sie gleich gering und klein." The F major aria duetto, however, crowns the work, owing primarily to the love between the Soul (soprano) and the Spirit within (alto). Longing for the coming of the Spirit is expressed in the highly decorated chorale "Komm, heiliger Geist" that constitutes the oboe line. The obbligato cello line is built mainly around an ostinato pattern that is also derived from the first line of this chorale. These details constitute an allegory of the indwelling and the directing of the individual's will by the Spirit within. The soprano and alto lines comprise a love duet of the type, intimate and pietistic in character, that is known from the duets in Cantatas 21 and 140 as well as from the final duet between Hercules and Virtue in Cantata 213. The subdominant and the key of F in particular seem, as in "Hercules auf dem Scheidewege," to be linked to the soft, loving tone of expressions such as "sanfter Himmelswind," "Liebste Liebe, die so süsse, aller Wollust Überfluss," and "nimm von mir den Gnadenkuss." That is, Bach is deliberately concerned to project a *mollis* character, perhaps remembering Luther's choice of F for singing the Gospel in his *Deutsche Messe,* because, according to Luther, "Christ is a friendly Lord and His Sayings are dear."[31] As in "Heiligste Dreieinigkeit," the F major duet modulates to the dominant minor—now C minor—first for the phrases "ich vergeh', wenn ich dich misse" (Soul), "nimm von mir den Gnadenkuss" (Spirit), then a second time for "sei im Glauben mir willkommen! Höchste Liebe, komm herein!" (Soul) and "ich bin dein und du bist mein" (Spirit) (Ex. 37). In this cantata the intimate relationship existing between God and man with the coming of the Holy Spirit determines the modulations within the first and third arias and the move through the relative minor to the subdominant for the last two movements. The final chorale, with phrases such as "wenn du mit deinen Äugelein mich freundlich thust anblicken" and "Nimm mich freundlich in dein' Arme, dass ich warme werd' von Gnaden," fits perfectly with the increasingly intimate conception of the whole.

In the Weimar cantatas of the following year, 1715, Bach is less interested in tonal planning of the more extravagant systematic kind that had appeared in several of the works from 1714. Already in Cantata 199 and the two cantatas of 1714 that have not been discussed, "Widerstehe doch der Sünde" (No. 54) and "Tritt auf die Glaubensbahn" (No. 152), Bach reduces the performers to solo voices with smaller instrumental forces. Perhaps he was responding to external circumstances, or perhaps this was another means of emphasizing the personal element. It is certainly

---

31. Praetorius, *Syntagma Musicum,* pp. 451–52.

EXAMPLE 37.   Cantata 172: excerpt from duet aria "Komm, lass mich nicht länger warten"

possible that in a number of works Bach restricted the chorus to singing the final chorale because of personnel or other limitations. But the interest in chamber-music–like instrumental sonorities is not the result of limitations but, rather, the reverse. The solo instrumentarium of this relatively small number of works is large, comprising viola d'amore, two obbligato cellos, viola da gamba, and corno da tirarsi, in addition to the recorders that characterize many of Bach's earlier works, and the more usual strings and winds.

In a work such as Cantata 163, "Nur Jedem das Seine," Bach, working within a basic chamber-music framework and utilizing a narrow range of keys, combines tonal allegory with instrumental features to suggest a descent/ascent dynamic that is essential to the idea of spiritual destruction and renewal that belongs to the text. The Gospel for the day (Matt. 22:15–22) provides the idea for the text, especially Jesus' words, "Render therefore unto Caesar the things which are Caesar's; and unto God the things that are God's." The opening B minor aria, "Nur Jedem das Seine," for tenor, oboe d'amore, and strings, identifies "Zoll, Steurn und Gaben" as the due of government and the heart as the property of God alone. The following bass recitative describes God as the source of all goods and gifts, of which only the heart suffices as *Zinsemünze* (coin of the realm), but Satan has damaged the image of God on the coin, rendering it valueless. The recitative begins in E minor and moves downward through C major (*Zinsemünze*) to A minor: "Ach, aber ach! ist das nicht schlechtes Geld?" The meaning of the modulation is unmistakable, since it is introduced with a leap downward in the basso continuo and contains several false intervals to express the devaluing of the coin.

Here Bach provides a movement unique in sonority, the E minor aria, "Lass mein Herz die Münze sein," for bass, two obbligato cellos, and basso continuo. The emphasis on low sonority can be interpreted in relation to the modulation downward in the preceding recitative. Cadence points within the aria are G major, B minor, and D major successively, before the return to E minor; and the D major is a substantial point of arrival: "ach, so komm doch und erneu're, Herr, den schönen Glanz in ihr." With imagery recalling John Donne's famous sonnet, "Batter my heart, three-personed God," the closing E minor section calls for God to "work, melt down, and stamp" ("arbeite, schmelz' und präge") so that the likeness will shine renewed in the heart.[32]

The next two movements are recitative and aria duets for soprano and alto, recalling the Soul/Spirit association of those voices in "Erschallet, ihr Lieder," although here the texts of both parts are the same. The recitative is composed in canonic imitation throughout a series of points of imitation, a very unusual device for Bach, and one that was perhaps intended to represent the desire for integration of flesh and spirit. Beginning in B minor, the text voices the will to give the heart to

---

32. This, the fourteenth of Donne's "Holy Sonnets" (1633), has been widely published. See, for example, A. L. Clements, ed., *John Donne's Poetry* (New York, 1966), p. 86; see also pp. 246–59 for critical viewpoints on the meaning of the metaphoric content of the sonnet.

God, then continues, modulating down through E minor to A minor, with the idea that the flesh struggles against the will. The idea that the world holds the heart captive (B minor) and is hated by the soul serves as a foil for the florid arioso ending (nearly half the recitative), which turns to the love of God and its benefits and establishes D major for the remainder of the cantata: "Wenn ich dich lieben soll, so mache doch mein Herz mit deiner Gnade voll; leer' es ganz aus von Welt und allen Lüsten, und mache mich zu einem rechten Christen." The meaning of the change of key and of vocal register is underscored by the soprano's reaching its highest note in the Weimar cantatas, b". To the soprano and alto of the triple-meter D major duet aria that follows Bach adds in the unison strings the chorale melody "Meinen Jesum lass ich nicht." Although undoubtedly chosen for its text, the chorale melody, with its several descending lines of a fourth or fifth (after beginning with an ascending fourth) adds a wonderful sense of relaxation and fulfillment that helps to express the character of the imitative dialogue between the voices: "Nimm mich mir und gieb mich dir, nimm mich mir und meinem Willen, deinen Willen zu erfüllen." For the final chorale (again in D) Bach notated only the basso continuo with the words "In simplice stylo," a further indication of the dominance of the soloistic conception.

In the four surviving cantatas of the Weimar cycle from 1716 larger performance resources return and, in some works, a larger scale of structural conception as well. Unfortunately, the exact Weimar forms of three of these cantatas are unclear, because Bach reworked them for performances in Leipzig. There are indications, however, that tonal planning played an important role. In one case, Cantata 186, "Ärgre dich, o Seele, nicht," the Leipzig version exhibits a key structure that seems to represent an expanded conception of the Weimar version.[33] This work, to be discussed below in Chapter 8, follows the associations for the sharp and flat modulatory directions that have emerged unmistakably in the Weimar works: upward modulation, now concentrated in Part One of the two-part Leipzig version, is linked with the growth of faith and the hopeful message of the Gospel, while Part Two develops the idea of hope in a world of tribulation, modulating downward to express the reality of the world but still conveying the benefits of faith as the means of transforming the world. The conception is subtler than the very direct schemes of Cantatas 12 and 21, but it is a significant side of Bach's tonal planning, one that underlies, as we saw, the return to B minor in Cantata 150, and one that allows us to interpret correctly the flat-minor ending of the *St. Matthew Passion*.

---

33. The evidence surrounding the existence of a Weimar version is presented in Alfred Dürr, *Kritischer Bericht* to *Johann Sebastian Bach. Neue Ausgabe sämtlicher Werke* (Kassel, 1962), I/1, pp. 89–97, and I/18, pp. 27–55. See also the summary in Dürr, *Studien,* pp. 50–51. Cantata 186 survives only in its Leipzig version, and no indication of the final movement in the Weimar version survives beyond the text of Salomo Franck. In all probability the Weimar version (BWV 186a) contained a sequence of closed movements (the recitatives have survived only in the new ones composed at Leipzig) in G minor, B flat, D minor, G minor, and C minor before the final chorale (perhaps in G minor or C minor). The pattern of an ascending key sequence followed by a descending one is divided between the two parts in the Leipzig version.

CHAPTER SIX

Tonal Planning

in the

Leipzig Cantatas I:

The Image of

the World

Within the richly varied world of the Leipzig cantatas patterned allegorical tonal planning appears in over forty compositions. The principles of tonal planning themselves, however, are ubiquitous and lend significant meaning to many other works. Of the types found in the early cantatas, the descent/ascent pattern dominates, for example, in 2, 9, 20, 25, 38, 58, 86, 87, 91, 95, 98, 127, 167, part of the Christmas Oratorio, and most of the several *Ratswechsel* cantatas. Straight anabasis is generally of a more restricted tonal range than that in Cantatas 12 and 21, for example, in Cantatas 27, 60, 104, 146, 181. Straight catabasis—such as in Cantatas 56, 73, 77, 102, 108, 136, 158, 179—while never covering a wide range of keys, remains a significant presence. There is now a new type of tonal planning, ascent followed by descent (e.g., Cantatas 10, 26, 28, 64, 68, 111, 116, 176, 178, 188). An additional type, which often merges with one or more of the foregoing, emphasizes tonal antithesis rather than progress through the gradual stages of closely related keys (Cantatas 109, 121, 213). In addition, a number of other cantatas, and even some listed above, are hybrids, for they use two or more of the above-mentioned patterns: Cantata 186, "Ärgre dich, o Seele, nicht," for example, emphasizes anabasis in its first part and catabasis in its second; and a composition such as Cantata 148, "Bringet dem Herrn Ehre seines Namens," moves down from D, through B minor, G major to E minor, ends in F sharp minor and can be thought of in terms of more than one type. Other cantatas, such as "Schauet doch und sehet" (BWV 46), suggest one or more different patterns without falling distinctly into any one category, yet the significance of their tonal-allegorical framework is unmistakable. Moreover, the cantatas for a single Sunday may utilize different tonal patterns from year to year, without signaling a shift in theological perspective: three cantatas for the eighth Sunday after Trinity—Nos. 45, 136, and 178—feature, respectively, tonal plans of the descent/ascent, catabasis or descent, and ascent/descent types. Generally the patterning of the keys is clearer when the text exhibits a similar dynamic. For these reasons it is more accurate to think of tonal planning as a principle—that is, tonal allegory—rather than as a set of formal categories. As such it adds a vital dimension to the interpretation of the great majority of Bach's vocal works without necessarily leading to the kind of straightforward patterning of keys that obtains in many of the works discussed here.

Nevertheless, although the cantatas that feature conspicuous tonal planning cover a wide range of themes and affective spheres, one particular set of associations for the sharp and flat directions runs throughout many works: modulation in the flat direction for the world (and its particular attributes, such as tribulation) and the reverse for the anticipation of eternity, the realm of God, and the like. The present chapter deals with cantatas of the descent/ascent type, in which the world is hardly ever absent. But neither this nor any of the other principles of Bach's tonal planning has absolute, objective validity. The value of classifying key structures into types, like that of any attempt to systematize artworks, lies in its potential for illuminating the individual work, for its leading the interpreter closer to the fundamental questions of form, expressive content, and aesthetic value. Knowing that Bach arranged the key successions of the cantatas in a way that joins them to a spectrum of other compositions helps us to understand his musicotheological intent. For this reason, in this and the following chapter, we will take up the works according to their key structure type, reserving the right to intermingle works in different categories from time to time to demonstrate the expressive qualities of the plans themselves and the larger hermeneutic framework used to interpret their meaning.

With relatively few exceptions the movement keys of any given cantata remain within the tonal region of a single ambitus, and of those that do not the great majority remain within a single genus (either sharps or flats). Only the *Passions* utilize the full spectrum of keys of the eighteenth-century circles of sharps and flats that enable us to consider shift of genus as an allegorical device. The *Passions* display these procedures most fully and in greatest detail, providing an array of tonal relationships that are not present in individual cantatas. Some of the relationships within the *Passions*, however, hold true for the whole corpus of cantatas, such as the range of keys for individual movements extending from F minor to E major, with the general associations of worldly tribulation and salvation attached to the two extremes.[1] The general placement of the ambitus of any particular cantata with respect to the

---

1. Bach associates E major in the cantatas with positive qualities—completely contradicting the interpretation for E major given by Mattheson (*Das neu-eröffnete Orchestre*, p. 250)—among which blessedness (Cantatas 8, 60, 124), salvation (Nos. 9, 17, 49, 86, 116, 139), resurrection (Nos. 66, 67, 80, 94, 145), and trust (Nos. 3, 29, 34a, 107, 139, 171, 200) are the most characteristic. B major—Heinichen's *extremum chromaticum*—is, however, extremely rare (Cantatas 45, 49, 139) and never appears as a movement key, whereas G sharp minor appears in recitatives, almost always with negative associations (Cantatas 8, 9, 60, 67, 107, 116). E minor appears frequently, mostly with the association of suffering, sorrow, doubt, pain, fear, and the Passion (Cantatas 4, 7, 20, 32, 60, 75, 81, 84, 88, 91, 92, 100, 109, 135, 138, 147, 155, 158, among others). At the other end of the spectrum B flat minor—the *extremum enharmonicum*—appears only once as a movement key (Cantata 106, "In deine Hände"); and as a key within recitatives it is associated almost always with darkness, the cross, and suffering (Cantatas 2, 13, 21, 23, 29, 46, 47, 48, 52, 54, 78, 93, 102, 105, 127, 134, 146, 159, 186, 199, and others). F minor is the flat

circle of keys is also important, particularly in the case of works in three or more sharps or flats. A few cantatas were conceived in terms of key areas whose tendency toward very sharp or flat modulations is a vital part of the meaning: for example, Cantata 116 is very sharp in tendency, Cantata 102 the reverse. Enharmonic relations are not rare and are always of great allegorical significance. Although they and all other extreme tonal devices are concentrated in the recitatives, they can still have a great effect on the overall plan (see the discussion of Cantata 121, below).

Descent/Ascent Cantatas

Bach's first two cantatas for Rogation Sunday (Leipzig 1724 and 1725) offer interesting examples of tonality reflecting two different aspects of the same Gospel text (John 16:23–30, from Jesus' farewell discourse). Bach begins each of the two cantatas with a dictum sung by the solo basso as *vox Christi* accompanied by strings and oboes. The first of these works, "Wahrlich, wahrlich ich sage euch" (Cantata 86), stresses the predominating message of promise in the Gospel text—"Truly, truly I say to you, that whatsoever ye shall ask the Father in my name, to you He will give it" (verse 23). Bach creates thereby a work pervaded by hope and the assurance of God's aid, set in the bright and uncomplicated key of E major. Although the movements move down tonally through A major and F sharp minor to B minor for the start of the first recitative (no. 4: "Gott macht es nicht gleich wie die *Welt*" [emphasis added]), before returning to E major, the descent in no way offsets the sense of promise. In this work the world, although motivating the descent, does not generate affective associations of its own, and we are probably justified here, as in other E major cantatas, in interpreting Bach's choice of key as a reflection of the place of E major at the upper limit of his tonal spectrum and hence as bearing a very positive association.

The second of these works, however, "Bisher habt ihr nichts gebeten in meinem Namen" (Cantata 87), descends through the minor keys—d, g and c—then ascends with the introduction of a major key—c, B flat, d. In the bass aria, "In der Welt habt ihr Angst," the flattest key, C minor, is associated with the world, while the ascent and major tonality turn suffering into a positive force. Both the key sequence and

---

limit for movement keys but unlike its sharp counterpart, E major, is never used as the key of a whole cantata: its associations are almost invariably anxiety, tears, tribulation, sin, pain, sorrow, care, suffering, and death (Cantatas 3, 12, 14, 18, 20, 21, 47, 48, 54, 55, 56, 57, 70, 78, 89, 102, 105, 112, 131, 146, 186, 187, and others); in this respect its associations are the most fixed. E flat minor appears only once in the cantatas (No. 159) and once in the *St. Matthew Passion,* both times associated with the most extreme torment. C minor appears frequently, and overwhelmingly in association with death and burial (Nos. 1, 20, 27, 48, 56, 57, 58, 73, 82, 91, 94, 95, 102, 106, 109, 127, 135, 138, 156, 161, 186, among others), several times with the mention of the "sleep of death." Other keys are not so firmly connected to their allegorical associations, although F sharp minor and B minor are often linked to the cross and suffering, and D and A major are usually positive, even triumphant. D and C, of course, often appear with trumpets and therefore bear strong associations of triumph, while F major (horns) sometimes has a pastorale association.

the general flat minor tonal region of this cantata are somewhat surprising in light of its predecessor, since they reflect Bach's decision to emphasize at the outset the negative aspect of the Gospel: "Till now ye have asked for nothing in my name" (verse 24). Borrowing from the message of the Epistle as well (James 1:22–27, follow the Word rather than merely hearing it), Marianne von Ziegler's text for Cantata 87 elaborates the opening dictum with emphasis on mankind's neglect of Jesus' Word of promise and of both the Law and the Gospel generally. Bach's tonal plan, realized in the surprisingly intense style of the minor-key arias (especially the G minor), followed by the relaxation offered by the B flat major Siciliano, "Ich will leiden, ich will schweigen," adds an affective dimension that goes beyond the text itself. The message of promise is submerged until the introduction of the major mode in the middle section of the central C minor aria, which is set, like the opening movement for bass: "In der Welt habt ihr Angst [C minor], aber seid getrost [E flat], ich habe die Welt Überwunden [return to C minor]." This second dictum, then, marks the turning point of the cantata, from the anxiety and torment of the world to trust in Christ. The positive tone is more pronounced in the last two movements, the Siciliano aria and the D minor chorale (which ends with the theme this cantata shares with Cantatas 12, 21, and 199, "Seine Liebe macht zur Freuden auch das bittre Leiden"). This antithesis signifies the theology of the cross, which is made explicit in the acceptance of suffering voiced in the B flat aria, "Ich will leiden, ich will schweigen." As in Cantatas 12 and 199, the pattern of discrete stages is clear: the first recitative urges repentance; the G minor aria expresses awareness of guilt and a prayer for forgiveness; in its change of tone, the C minor aria represents the turn to Christ; and the Siciliano voices the believing Christian's willingness to take the Christ of the Passion as his model. The final chorale reflects Luther's belief that recognition of God's love works the change in us.

The theme of suffering turned into joy effects a transformation of a somewhat different kind in Cantata 58, "Ach Gott, wie manches Herzeleid" (presumably for the Sunday after New Year, 1727, but reworked in the 1730s to the version that survives).[2] The work is symmetrical. It begins in C major; the first recitative moves from A minor to F major. After the central aria, in D minor, the second recitative moves back from F major to A minor, and it ends as it began, with a duet in C major. Here the message of the acceptance of suffering is centered within the world that is the subject of the two recitatives, and the key plan is similar (but transposed) to that of Cantata 86. The soprano and bass soloists resemble the personifications of the Soul and Christ that we find in other cantatas. The chorales in the outer movements—the first verse of "Ach Gott, wie manches Herzeleid" and the second of "O Jesu Christ, meins Lebens Licht"—are both sung to the same chorale

2. Dürr, *Die Kantaten*, p. 163.

melody although their characters are entirely different. This difference is underscored in the free poetry sung against the cantus firmus by the bass in each movement and by the contrasted styles of the two settings. The gravely dissonant and somber style of "Nur Geduld, mein Herze" sets up an affective contrast to the exuberant diatonic and triadic emphasis of "Nur getrost; ihr Herzen" (Ex. 38 a & b). Likewise, because the two recitatives deal with the conflict of the world and the life of faith, their modulatory directions are reversed, the one leading down to and the other up from the central aria of faith, "Ich bin vergnügt in meinem Leiden." Their tonal styles, like their respective texts, are also contrasted. The first contains dissonances and modulations to flats for ideas opposed to God's promises (e.g., C minor for Herod's attempt to kill Jesus, followed by D minor for God's warning to Joseph in the dream; down again to G minor for mention of drowning in the Flood, and back up to F major for reiteration of promise); and the second modulates from F up to A minor ending with an arioso expressing longing for the future life, "Ach! könnt es heute noch geschehen, dass ich mein Eden möchte sehen!" Despite the relatively circumscribed range of keys, the tonal character of "Ach Gott, wie manches Herzelied" is planned to the last detail.

The pattern of descent/ascent need not emphasize only the negative side of the world. Cantata 167, "Ihr Menschen, rühmet Gottes Liebe," for the feast of John the Baptist (1723), follows a downward curve from G major (opening aria) through E minor (rec. and arioso) to A minor, then back up to G major (rec. and chorale) to represent the coming of Christ as the fulfillment of God's promise, the way having been prepared by John the Baptist, the last of the prophets. Even the first recitative presents this idea with a descent from E minor through A minor ("der sich in Gnaden zu uns wendet") to D minor ("und seinen Sohn vom hohen Himmelsthron zum Welterlöser sendet"). The return to E minor mirrors the recounting of Jesus' act of redemption: "hierauf kam Jesus selber an, die armen Menschenkinder und die verlor'nen Sünder [rec.] mit Gnad' und Liebe zu erfreu'n und sie zum Himmelreich in wahrer Buss' zu leiten [arioso]." The central A minor duet expresses simply the fulfillment of God's promise on earth ("Was er in dem Paradies und vor so viel hundert Jahren denen Vätern schon verhiess, haben wir Gottlob! erfahren"), and the return ascent in the following recitative leads to a hymn of praise and thanks to God.

The opposition of worldly and divine authority prompted Bach to use tonal descent and ascent in the cantatas written for the changing of the town council in both Mühlhausen and Leipzig. The first of these works for Leipzig, Cantata 119, "Preise, Jerusalem, den Herrn" (1723), is a C major composition of highly extrovert, festive character—with French overture beginning, prominent trumpets and drums and the like. Its central movement, a G minor alto aria with recorders, "Die Obrigkeit ist Gottes Gabe, ja selber Gottes Ebenbild," follows a powerful bass recitative for full orchestra, framed by trumpet fanfares, asserting government as God's representative on earth. Coming after such a display of pomp, the minor key

EXAMPLE 38.   Cantata 58

(a) Excerpt from soprano/bass duet "Nur Geduld"

EXAMPLE 38   *continued*

EXAMPLE 38 *continued*

(b) Excerpt from soprano/bass duet "Nur getrost"

EXAMPLE 38   *continued*

EXAMPLE 38   *continued*

asserts the humanity of the ruling authorities as the tie between them and the community at large. The other *Ratswechsel* cantatas all exhibit to some degree the descent/ascent pattern: 29 (D, D, A, f sharp–*e*, h, D, D, D); 69 (D, b–G, G, *e*–f sharp, b, D); 120 (A, D, b, *G*, D–f sharp, D); and 193 (D, b, *e*, G, D). In most cases the tonal distance covered is not great, but in general the descent is related to God's protection of man ("Denn er versorget und erhält, beschützet und regiert die Welt" [E minor] in Cantata 69), the contrast between the "most high" and his subjects on earth (A major aria, "Halleluja, Stärk und Macht sei des Allerhöchsten Namen" versus B minor aria, "Gedenk' an uns mit deiner Liebe, schleuss' uns in dein Erbarmen ein" in Cantata 29), or an appeal to God (all six *Ratswechsel* cantatas). God's blessings and salvation must be bestowed on the rulers in order for them to provide justice and truth (G major aria, Cantata 120). Bach's picture of the world here is not at all tinged with pejoratives. Within the Lutheran frame of reference it is perfectly consistent; the tonal plan helps to represent a baroque hierarchy with God at the top. The two cantatas that use flat-minor movements (Nos. 71 and 119) point out that wherever the assertion of worldly glory is greatest, it is necessary to bring out there the contrast between the power of the divinely invested ruler and his humanity.

Bach reworked a cantata exhibiting a similar concern with secular authority, "Die Zeit, die Tag und Jahre macht" (BWV 134a, written in 1719 as festive New Year's music for the court of Anhalt-Köthen), as a piece for Easter Tuesday (Cantata 134, "Ein Herz, das seinen Jesum lebend weiss").[3] The first version moves

3. Dürr, *Die Kantaten*, pp. 654–56, 244–46.

downward by thirds from the initial B flat to C minor at the start of the second recitative (no. 5), then back up through the relative minor (aria, no. 6) and a modulatory recitative (no. 7) to B flat (chorus, no. 8). Its allegorical character as a dialogue between Time (*Zeit*) and Divine Providence (*göttliche Vorsehung*), with the former (tenor) directed toward the past and the latter (alto) toward the future, led Bach to utilize the descent/ascent tonal plan.[4] The work is, however, not primarily antithetical in nature—or at least not intensely so—for both past and future are conceived as glorifying the house of Anhalt-Köthen. In the splendid E flat duet (no. 4) slightly different texts are sung simultaneously in a homophonic texture. But in the following recitative Divine Providence modulates from C minor at the outset to an extended arioso in E minor, at the close of which Time enters, returning immediately to the flats (d, C, B flat), in which Divine Providence comes back to close (g). The turn to sharps is clearly aligned with the noble and, we might say, secular qualities of the royal pair ("Klugheit, Licht," "edles Leben," "Glanz") and prayer for the future ("Komm, Anhalt, fleh' um mehre Jahr' und Zeiten"), while the return to flats is associated with their piety and devotion ("Ja, Anhalt, ja, du beugest deine Knie' "). No irreconcilable antithesis is intended, and the following aria emphasizes the "Harmonie der Seelen, die Gott zum Hort and Heil erwählen." The first two closed movements bring out more of the glory of the ruling house; this is mirrored in their two themes, which belong conspicuously to the major-key ascent/descent type that is prominent in "Gott ist mein König." After the E flat duet, however, the cantata emphasizes trust in God. The seventh movement (rec.) is mainly a prayer for God to direct Leopold, sung by Zeit and modulating again into the deeper flats (E flat, c, f); particularly telling is the move to F minor ("auf die bisher dein Gnadenlicht geschienen"), which brings out Leopold's receiving of God's grace—his humanity. Divine Providence closes the recitative, moving up to F for the assertion of God's continuing blessings on princes who live within the prince of life. The descent/ascent plan, completed in the B flat chorus "Ergötzet auf Erden, erfreuet von oben," symbolizes the reconciliation of sacred and secular in the house of Anhalt-Köthen.

When Bach finally, in the 1730s, had the opportunity to complete a religious parody of this cantata that he had begun in 1724, he retained the descent/ascent tonal plan, making it somewhat clearer. Now the ascent/descent themes of the first aria and duet of Cantata 134a served as the image of the glory of the resurrection (just as in the themes of "Gott ist mein König" and the "Et resurrexit" of the *Mass in B minor*) (Ex. 39).[5] The arias were given new texts, the recitatives rewritten, and the third (minor-key) aria of the original was omitted, resulting in a work in which the

---

4. Dürr, *Die Kantaten*, p. 654.
5. See Walter Blankenburg, "Die Symmetrieform in Bachs Werken und ihre Bedeutung," *Bach-Jahrbuch* 38 (1949–1950): 31–32.

EXAMPLE 39.   Cantata 134

(a) Excerpt from aria "Auf, Gläubige"

Auf,   auf, auf, auf,   Gläu - bi - ge!

(b) Ritornello theme of duet "Wir danken und preisen"

three major-key closed movements all contribute to the triumph of the resurrection. Jesus' victory sounds the keynote, while the two extended recitatives (nos. 3 and 5) treat the meaning for mankind of Jesus' Passion and resurrection. Number 3 gives particular attention to the Passion, modulating several times to the deeper flats and ending with a dialogue between the tenor and alto that suggests the association of these voices with "fear" and "hope" as shown in a number of Bach's explicitly allegorical dialogue cantatas. Here, however, the normal association of the alto with fear and the tenor with hope is reversed because of the secular model. After the tenor's recounting of the benefit of the Passion, the alto enters over a slowly rising bass with the message of the resurrection, ending "so hat kein Feind an mir zum Schaden teil" (B flat). Now the alto and tenor modulate alternately in different directions for the closing dialogue: "Die Feinde zwar sind nicht zu zählen" (tenor, F minor); "Gott schützt die ihm getreuen Seelen" (alto, C minor); "Der letzte Feind ist Grab und Tod" (tenor, B flat minor); "Gott macht auch den zum Ende unsrer Not" (alto, E flat). The overall downward direction of the key scheme is clarified both at this point and in the next recitative following the E flat duet. Once again the tenor modulates downward at the outset, to the nadir of the work (c, b flat, f, E flat), while the alto returns to B flat, setting up the final chorus praising God. The move to deeper flats at the beginning of the recitative is associated particularly with the earthly perspective ("Doch würke selbst den Dank in unserm Munde, indem er allzuirdisch ist") that is overcome by Christ's resurrection.

The plans of many of the foregoing works, like that of the "Actus Tragicus," present an approximately equal balance between downward and upward tonal motion. But this is not Bach's most usual procedure. More often the anabasis, as the analogy of redemption and faith, is much more prominent than its opposite: that is, the catabasis may occur quickly, within an early recitative, while the remainder of the cantata is taken up with the return upward.

Among the later chorale cantatas Bach uses this basic descent/ascent type in a quintessential instance of the presentation of Lutheran dogma concerning salvation. Cantata 9, "Es ist das Heil uns kommen hier," presents Luther's doctrine of justification by faith in the form of a theological discussion.[6] After a prologue chorale fantasia, the text relates chronologically the granting of the Law to man, then mankind's sin and inability to fulfill the Law (nos. two and three), Christ's fulfillment of the Law on our behalf (no. 4), the message of justification by faith alone rather than works (no. 5), the replacing of the Law by the Gospel (no. 6), and, finally, our ultimate trust in God (no. 7). The chorale by Luther's contemporary, Paul Speratus, was originally published in fourteen strophes, each headed with the letters from A through O—the Alpha and Omega—and followed by fourteen similarly headed paragraphs that gave the scriptural sources for the doctrinal material in the strophes themselves. The three recitatives, all relatively straightforward and all—exceptionally—for bass, suggested to Whittaker "the preacher elaborating his theories," so concerned with basic doctrine is this entire cantata.[7] In the fifth movement a duet in the form of canons between pairs of instruments and voices sums up the central dictum of justification by faith alone as if to confirm the canonic nature of the subject matter and its scriptural source.[8]

The tonal plan follows the text very closely. The prologue is in E major, announcing salvation through Jesus Christ. But almost immediately the historical narrative begins, with the first recitative sinking to B minor, as an analogue of our sinful, fallen nature under the Law, while the first aria, in E minor, underscores the meaning of the sudden catabasis: "Wir waren schon zu tief gesunken, der Abgrund schluckt uns völlig ein." From this point the music moves sharpward—B minor to A major in the second recitative—to parallel Jesus' fulfillment of the Law for mankind; the message of justification by faith alone confirms the benefit of Jesus' atonement in the A major duet. Next, with its turning to the Gospel and trust in God, the third recitative leads onward to E major, the key of the closing chorale. This recitative summarizes the meaning of Law and Gospel and their role in faith, matching them with tonal shifts: recognition of sin by means of the Law and the humbling of the spirit (F sharp minor to B minor); trust and joy as benefits of the Gospel, strengthening faith (up to A major); anticipation of the future life when God's promise will be fulfilled (a move to the highest key in the work, a G sharp minor cadence); and finally trust in God and the necessity of building on his promise in the present life (E major). Like the "Actus Tragicus," this work emphasizes salvation history in its narration of events related to the historical periods of the

---

6. W. Gillies Whittaker, *The Cantatas of Johann Sebastian Bach*, 2 vols. (London, 1959), 1:502.
7. Whittaker, *The Cantatas*, 1:502.
8. On the association of canon with basic doctrine, see Chafe, "Allegorical Music," pp. 347–49.

Law (first recitative) and time of Christ (second recitative), then its placing them within the faith of the church in the final recitative.

The poles of tonality in this work can be compared to the E minor and E major of the *St. Matthew Passion,* Part One. E minor is the key of the crucifixion drama within the *Passion,* whereas E major marks the end of two long anabases that start from deep flats: the prediction of betrayal (C minor/F minor), leading to anticipation of the resurrection (E); the prediction of Peter's denial and the torment of Gethsemane (C minor/F minor) leading to "O Mensch, bewein" (E). The two keys of E minor and major are juxtaposed structurally several times in Part One, most conspicuously in the betrayal, where, after arriving at E major, the reference to Judas on the word *Verräther* precipitates the downward motion to E minor for "So ist mein Jesus" / "Sind Blitze, sind Donner." Both Cantata 9 and the *St. Matthew Passion* move to E minor for references to the abyss (*Abgrund*) that opens to swallow the sinner. In the *Passion* the subsequent recitative moves back through several *toni intermedii* for the E major ending ("O Mensch, bewein"). Thus the general upward tonal direction of Part One, as expressed in the two great chorale fantasias ("Kommt, ihr Töchter" in E minor and "O Mensch" in E major) and the long anabases, is reflected near the end of the structure in a more dramatic juxtaposition. Fallen man (Judas) is contrasted with man redeemed through consciousness of sin and faith in the atonement.

In his chorale cantata "O Ewigkeit, du Donnerwort" (BWV 20) Bach links a descent/ascent tonal pattern with an even more difficult and incomprehensible subject than death: eternity, and in this case specifically the eternity of hell, which must be envisioned to gain any moral benefits. The supratemporal meditative goal in "O Eweigkeit" suggests structural parallels with "Ich hatte viel Bekümmernis." In Cantata 20 a prominent rising sequence of movements extends from C minor to C major, the latter key now allied with an apocalyptic anticipation of the Last Judgment. Unlike Cantata 21, however, "O Ewigkeit" is concerned not merely, or even primarily, with upward eschatological progression, but with the present reality of sin and the fear of its ultimate consequences. Thus the anabasis of solo movements is contained, stabilized by the three F major chorale settings that all appear at points of great structural prominence (Fig. 5). The church represents the horizontal structure that cuts across the ascent, anchoring the tonality in the present so the Christian can look to his salvation, the concern with the here and now around which, paradoxically, this cantata on eternity is centered.

Unlike his practice in the warmly personal "Ich hatte viel Bekümmernis" with its quality of increasing faith, in Cantata 20 Bach is concerned to reiterate the central message: visualization of an eternity of suffering must impel us to seek salvation at once; fear, rather than comfort, sounds the keynote. Within this restriction imposed by the chorale itself, the rising keys introduce a note of hope for the believer. Nevertheless, the F major recurrences of the chorale (with the apocalyptic voice of *tromba da tirarsi* doubling the soprano), the climax of the rising progression as a ter-

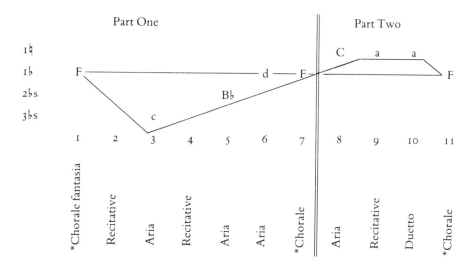

FIGURE 5.   Key structure in Cantata 20, "O Ewigkeit, du Donnerwort"

rifying vision of the Last Judgment, the image of the eternal torment of the rich
man in the final aria, and, of course, the interruption of the ascent itself by the
break between Parts One and Two all check the suggestion of increasingly positive
stages. Neither the anabasis nor the hope it holds for the believer is allowed to dominate the structure.

The keys of C minor and major presented in a structural relationship, as they are
in Cantatas 12, 20, and 21, can be used to signify the divided worlds—human/
divine, flesh/spirit, and so on—that are united in the person of Christ. This idea
extended to the contemplation of eternity in Cantata 20 is developed further in another chorale cantata, "Herr Jesu Christ, wahr' Mensch und Gott" (BWV 127, for
Quinquagesima Sunday 1725). As befits the dualism in its title, the separation of
minor and major by means of *toni intermedii* is far less great in this work. Like Cantata 20, "Herr Jesu Christ" presents the two Christus keys as minor and major
dominants of an F major tonic.

In the opening chorale fantasia Bach uniquely combines two entire chorale melodies: "Christe, du Lamm Gottes" (Dorian G) in the woodwinds and "Herr Jesu
Christ, wahr' Mensch und Gott" (the principal chorale of the work, beginning in F
Ionian, but ending in C Ionian). The latter is heard as soprano cantus firmus, but
diminutions of its first line pervade the other parts as well. Smend has detected the
first line of yet a third chorale—the Phrygian "Herzlich tut mich verlangen"—at
six points in the bass in various transpositions.[9] This chorale with its associations of

9. Friedrich Smend, *Joh. Seb. Bach: Kirchen-Kantaten*, 2d ed., 6 vols. (Berlin, 1950), 6:42.

both death and the Passion ("Herzlich" is a funeral hymn, but the chorale "O Haupt voll Blut und Wunden" was sung to the same melody) provided Bach with an ideal means of emphasizing the dualisms of God and man, the relationship of individual death to Christ's cross and Passion. As is evident in countless compositions, Bach's interpretation of the modal characters of his chosen chorales influences his tonal planning and harmonic-tonal devices. Thus, near the close of the chorale fantasia, as "Herr Jesu Christ" comes to an end, it seems as if the movement will end in C major. Its C Ionian final phrase is preceded by a G Phrygian (C minor) appearance of "Herzlich" in the bass (mm. 65–71), after which the final line of "Herr Jesu Christ"—"du wollst mir Sünder gnädig sein"—brightens the tonality. A nine-bar postlude, however, introduces the last reference to "Herzlich" in C Phrygian (F minor), turning the final cadence to an F major so darkened by flats that it is almost a tonal catabasis. The ensuing recitative links the individual's thoughts on death to the path cleared by Jesus' stoic undergoing of the Passion, closing with an F cadence whose preparation is a cadence to B flat minor ("und diesen schweren Weg auch mich geleitet") and the Neapolitan sixth chord, G flat ("und mir die Ruhe zubereitet"). The C minor "sleep" aria follows, with its first line, "Die Seele ruht in Jesu Händen," recalling the B flat minor aria "In deine Hände" that is the tonal nadir of the "Actus Tragicus." The following recitative/aria/chorale complex centers around a vision of the final awakening that recalls the C major of Cantata 21 and, even more so, that of Cantata 20, with its apocalyptic trumpet calls. Following this unusual hybrid form that is worthy of much closer study than we can give it here, the final choral setting of the last verse of "Herr Jesu Christ" completes the tendency suggested in the opening chorus and brought out in the relationship of the two arias: it closes on a C major chord ("bis wir einschlafen seliglich") after a C minor preparation; the effect intended and achieved is a final brightening in combination with a sense of both incompleteness and expectation.

The tonal plans of Cantatas 20 and 127 both recall that of the "Actus Tragicus": that is, they all move from the major tonic down to the flat or minor dominant and return to the tonic with greater emphasis on major keys and at least a touching of the major dominant along the way. The emphasis on the polarizing (Cantata 20) or juxtaposing (Cantata 127) of the latter keys adds a dimension of antithesis and transformation that is realized more in motivic-referential than in tonal terms in the earlier work. But the theological ideas that are referred to in the "Actus Tragicus" are so central to Bach's church work in general that we find them in other works whose structures are not as fully planned. This is especially true of the cantatas for Sundays in which the theology of death plays an important part, such as the sixteenth Sunday after Trinity, the feast of the Purification, and the third Sunday in Epiphany. In all four cantatas for the last-named occasion the question of will—God's and man's—predominates. This was, of course, the subject of Luther's famous debate with Erasmus, prompting the writing of what he considered his "best theological work," *The Bondage of the Will*.[10]

Cantata 156, "Ich steh' mit einem Fuss im Grab' " (1729), for the third Sunday in Epiphany, is a work that at first does not reveal much conspicuous tonal planning other than its ending in the dominant, C, of its overall F major ambitus. The work deals with spiritual sickness by recalling the story of Hezekiah's receiving the announcement of death from Isaiah, the reference that underlies the bass solo "Bestelle dein Haus" in the "Actus Tragicus." Against the chorale cantus firmus, "Mach's mit mir, Gott, nach deiner Güt'," the tenor solo expresses readiness to die, affirming "ich habe schon mein Haus bestellt." All the ideas of this movement, including "so nimm sie, Herr, in deine Händ'," and "ist Alles gut, wenn gut das End'," are familiar from other cantatas, and some recur throughout the cantata in various forms. The first recitative moves down to D minor, and the following aria continues the descent to the subdominant, B flat major. The distance is not great, of course, but the change to A minor in the succeeding recitative, in which the possibility of recovery is introduced, and the C major of the final chorale—ending "dein Will' der ist der beste"—indicate that Bach is sensitive to the pattern of descent and ascent within such a circumscribed range of keys. The antithetical turning point— B flat to A minor—forms a kind of mi contra fa, leading to an ending that is higher than the beginning.

"Es ist nichts Gesundes an meinem Leibe" (no. 25) also ends in a key different from that in which it began and turns from minor (even modal) to major as well; its first recitative makes the well-known comparison between the world and a hospital. Set in the key of E Phrygian, the opening chorus owes most of its thematic material to the chorale melody "Herzlich tut mich verlangen," whose first line is quoted in augmentation twice in the basso continuo and the entire chorale, two phrases at a time, in the upper winds (three recorders and cornetto!). Two themes are derived from the chorale and developed both separately and together as fugues. The first closely follows the outline of the first line, and the second is similar to the variants in the "Actus Tragicus" and Cantata 161. As in those works, the intrinsic meaning here is the longing for redemption. The melody accompanying the text that compares the world to a hospital, sin to physical illness, and Jesus to a physician leads down to A minor in the first recitative. The interval of a falling fifth, developed from "Herzlich" in the main theme of the first movement, returns prominently in the following D minor aria, "Ach, wo hol' ich Armer Rath," the nadir of the work and the turning point to faith (the aria is in two parts without da capo, the second section beginning "Du, mein Arzt, Herr Jesu nur weisst die beste Seelenkur"). Another recitative expresses the turn to Jesus with a modulation to C major, in which are set the soprano aria with full instrumentarium, "Öffne meinen schlechten Liedern, Jesu, dein Genaden-Ohr," and final chorale, "Ich will alle

10. Dillenberger, ed., *Luther: Selections*, p. 167.

meine Tage." As we might expect, these latter movements anticipate eternity; in keeping with the personal relationship between the believer and his "physician," the text of "Öffne dich" seems almost to voice the hopes of the musician:

Öffne meinen schlechten Liedern,
Jesu, dein Genaden-Ohr!
Wenn ich dort im höhern Chor
werde mit den Engeln singen,
soll mein Danklied besser klingen.

The great emphasis in Lutheranism on God's severe, watchful, and judgmental character forms an immediate obstacle to the expression of a personal relationship between God and the individual. Although God's other side—his forgiving, merciful, and loving nature—is seen as the source of blessings for mankind and ultimately dominates, the reality of God's punishment for sin is never taken lightly. In addressing this theme a number of Bach cantatas exhibit tonal allegory in conjunction with other conspicuous allegorical devices. Of these, Cantata 135, "Ach Herr, mich armen Sünder," is made up of a descent/ascent plan of relatively narrow range in the keys of the closed movements (E Phrygian, C major, A minor, E Phrygian), while featuring many tonal inflections in these movements and a considerably wider range of modulation in the recitatives to intensify the antithesis between the torment of sin and fear of God's judgment (descent) on the one hand and the comfort of God's love (ascent) on the other. The opening chorale fantasia opposes the two by presenting each phrase of the cantus firmus in two successive forms: (1) the chorale (sung to the melody of "Herzlich tut mich verlangen" again) in unison violins and violas without basso continuo supporting imitative chorale-derived lines for two oboes; (2) the chorale in the bass of the chorus doubled by basso continuo, including trombone, with strings doubling the chorus and the oboes now omitted. The trombone symbolizes God's judgmental nature, while the *bassetchen* texture that alternates with it probably represents God's love (as it does in a number of arias from the cantatas and, above all, in "Aus Liebe" from the *St. Matthew Passion*). Even though the chorale cannot modulate in the bass Bach uses tonal direction to express lines such as "Ach Herr, wollst mir vergeben [mein Sünd] and "dass ich mag ewig leben." In the first instance he precedes the bass entry on C by entries on A, D, and G in the upper voices, then carries the downward motion into flats to the beginning of the following phrase, which completes the idea ("mein Sünd"); in the second instance he modulates to B minor (with Tierce de Picardie) above the sustained final tone of the cantus firmus. The modulation to C minor (for falling tears) in the first recitative, wide-ranging descending lines ("sonst versink ich in den Tod"), and flat modulations ("der grossen Seelennot," "Liebster Jesu") in the first aria, juxtaposition of flats and sharps in the second aria (G minor for "Das Trübsalswetter," modulation upward for "ändert sich," and sharps for "die Feinde müssen plötzlich fallen, und ihre Pfeile rückwärts prallen") all illustrate, along with other similar modulatory features, Bach's detailed concern for tonal allegory.

Another cantata dealing with God's judgment, "Herr, gehe nicht ins Gericht" (BWV 105) utilizes rhythmic and metric devices in conjunction with the antithesis of chromaticism/diatonicism to present the complexity of the Lutheran life. The most prominent dimensions of the allegorical treatment are the shift from repeated eighth- and sixteenth-note *tremulante* figures—the symbol of anxiety—to the ornamental thirty-second-note violin roulades and spirited horn themes of the penultimate movement, the B flat aria "Kann ich nur Jesum mir zum Freunde machen." Modulation to deep flats plays a very important role in the passage of the initial chromatic G minor of the opening chorus to the B flat aria. C minor, F minor, G minor, and B flat minor (in connection with the sinner's *Demut* before God) prepare for the B flat cadence of the first recitative, which sets up the E flat aria "Wie zittern und wanken." Following the aria an accompanied recitative moves through stages from B flat major to F minor, A flat, and B flat minor ("So mag man deinen Leib, den man zu Grabe trägt, mit Sand und Staub beschütten"—the nadir of the work) before making the reversal to E flat that prepares the B flat aria. Perhaps the most interesting allegorical device in the work, however, is the summarizing of the stilling of the sinner's *Gewissensangst* in the final G minor chorale, "Nun, ich weiss, du wirst mir stillen mein Gewissen, das mich plagt." Bach utilizes a fivefold alternation between common time (**c**) and compound quadruple meter ($\frac{12}{8}$), along with corresponding changes in the note values of the string accompaniment—sixteenths, triplet eighths, duplet eighths, quarter/eighth patterns in triplet division of the beat, and, finally, straight quarter notes—to indicate the stages of change (Ex. 40). A number of these rhythms had appeared in earlier movements. The texture alternates full choral lines with interludes for violins and viola without basso continuo, and "Wie zittern und wanken" is another *bassetchen* aria. Furthering the tonal plan, the first phrase of the chorale begins on the B flat of the preceding aria and quickly turns to G minor with the chromatic tetrachord ostinato in the bass (this device and the chorale melody itself are shared by Cantata 78, "Jesu, der du meine Seele"); for the ending of the cantata (coinciding with the turn to quarter notes) the strings play a harmonized version of this ostinato, unaccompanied and ending on G major. Cantata 105 is, therefore, a descent/ascent cantata in which the tonal element is not the most prominent feature of the musical allegory. But the idea of motion downward to the deeper flats, then upward to the relative major (the one movement that abandons the *tremulante* idea) is a vital part of the hope that comes from trust in Jesus.

On August 3, 1725, one week after the first performance of Cantata 105 (on July 25), Bach produced another cantata in which many of the same theological issues reappear. Although Cantata 46, "Schauet doch und sehet, ob irgendein Schmerz sei," is not a descent/ascent cantata, it exhibits a considerable degree of tonal alle-

EXAMPLE 40.   Cantata 105: rhythmic and metric shifts in the final chorale

gory, in addition to containing another of the rare *bassetchen* arias and featuring interludes without basso continuo between the lines of the final chorale. Besides
these features "Schauet doch" represents the dichotomy of the wrathful and merciful God by the contrast in instrumental sonority between its two arias: bass voice,
trumpet, and strings for the B flat aria "Dein Wetter zog sich auf von weiten" (no.
3); two recorders and unison oboes da caccia without basso continuo for the G minor "Doch Jesus will" (no. 5). Cantata 46 is full of warning against sin, a theme
arising from the day's Gospel (Jesus' prediction of the destruction of Jerusalem).
The text adopts the familiar device of ranging throughout the Scriptures to find
parallel narratives of destruction as the outcome of God's wrath against sin: Sodom
and Gomorrah, Jerusalem in the time of Jeremiah as well as in 70 A.D., and the
Flood. In keeping with Luther's dictum "faith must be built up on the basis of history" and his choice of the destruction and rebuilding of Jerusalem as an analogue
of individual spiritual humiliation and elevation, the fourth movement of
"Schauet doch" turns the images of destruction into a warning for the eighteenth-
century believer.

Jeremiah's words lamenting the fall of Jerusalem establish the sinner's plight in
the extended opening movement (D minor), after which the first recitative and aria
treat the imagery of the sinful "city" under immanent judgment and destruction by
God. These two movements represent the idea of spiritual annihilation with modulations into deep flats. Within the framework of a G minor beginning and ending

the first recitative modulates to C minor, F minor, and B flat minor in the first half. C minor is the main cadence point ("durch deine Schuld"), after which the recitative moves toward F minor, completing a comparison of the soul to Gomorrah in the words "Du wurdest wie Gomorra zugerichtet, wiewohl nicht gar vernichtet. O besser wärest du in Grund zerstört." At this point the continuation of the line, "als dass man Christi Feind jetzt in dir lästern hört," interrupts the motion to F minor, and a pattern of unsettling seventh chords is established for the remainder of the recitative. The text tells us that the allegory of spiritual destruction is not complete. The following aria with its representation of God's wrath and its effect on mankind completes the move to F minor. In B flat, "Dein Wetter zog sich auf von weiten, doch dessen Strahl bricht endlich ein," represents the beginning of judgment by modulating to the dominant, F, within the first section (for "Strahl"); the dotted rhythms, *concitato* style, and trumpet figures all underscore the reigning affect. But in the middle section Bach contrasts this idea and man's "Untergang," moving first to G minor (man's inability to bear God's wrath), then to F minor ("und dir den Untergang bereiten"); the trumpet drops out, and, as the music becomes pianissimo, the *tremulante* bass figures inevitably change their character from the *concitato* style to the anxiety we know from Cantata 105 and the arioso "O, Schmerz" from the *St. Matthew Passion*. The second recitative clarifies the meaning of the modulations in its move from F major to C minor, drawing the moral, "Weil ihr euch nicht bessert und täglich die Sünden vergrössert, so müsset ihr alle so schrecklich umkommen."

Compared to such an extreme warning the G minor *bassetchen* aria "Doch Jesus will," with its emphasis on Jesus' protection of the pious from the judgment of sin, might be said to mediate between the flat modulations and the D minor tonic. The instrumentation certainly signifies God's merciful, loving side as manifested in Jesus. Interestingly, the melody of the final chorale begins and ends in what might be considered Phrygian A (A with a one-flat key signature, presumably to end with a Phrygian cadence to an A major chord). Perhaps after some change of mind regarding the mode and system of the final chorale, Bach created a setting in the two-flat system (indicated as such) that remains very much on the flat (subdominant) side of its final cadence to D (with Tierce de Picardie).[11] Before the very end the tonality does not indicate that the chorale will end on D; in fact, some of the cadences even suggest the flat side of G minor (the final phrase itself emphasizes C minor at the beginning). Bach's effect and intent recall Kuhnau's description of a passage that

---

11. The melody begins and ends on A (ambitus c' to d''). Except for passing tones all the B's are flattened; the melody has no E flats and one E. The cadence tones are C, A, C, B flat, A, E, G, and A. See the remarks on Bach's treatment of the Phrygian mode on pp. 221–23. As Robert Marshall points out (*Kritischer Bericht* to *Johann Sebastian Bach. Neue Ausgabe sämtlicher Werke* I/19 [Kassel: 1989], p. 156) the two parts of this chorale that are autograph have key signatures of two flats while those of the copyist were written at first with one flat (suggesting that the lost original score had a one-flat signature), then amended to two flats.

suggests incomplete recovery from illness: the emphasis on the subdominant is so extended that the ear is not satisfied with the final cadence as a tonic.[12] The chorale is a prayer from sinful mankind to God asking not to be judged according to their sins but rather in light of Jesus' sacrifice. In its instrumentation (the recorders and oboes da caccia that are associated with God's merciful side) and final D major chord this cantata suggests a hopeful outcome while remaining within the sphere of the awareness of sin. The work follows neither the descent/ascent nor the straight descent plan. The unmistakable musicotheological expression at the end is created not so much by the overall key plan as by the modulations and tonal character of the individual movements, a characteristic shared by many cantatas whose key structures are not pronouncedly patterned.

In those cantatas that have movements in major and minor modes on the same keynote Bach normally presents the minor mode before the major to emphasize the ideas of ascent and transformation. One descent/ascent cantata, however, reverses that procedure. "Christus, der ist mein Leben," Cantata 95, was written for the sixteenth Sunday after Trinity, the Gospel for which tells of the raising of the youth at Nain (Luke 7:11–17). To highlight the juxtaposition of death and resurrection within the context of faith, Bach presents the first verses of no less than three different chorales in an introductory complex of movements, separated only by recitatives. Two of these—"Christus, der ist mein Leben" and "Mit Fried' und Freud' ich fahr dahin" (with a connecting tenor recitative)—comprise the opening movement, the former in a sharp, major key (G) and in triple meter, the latter in a flat, minor key (G Dorian) and in quadruple meter. Although the two hymns share words and ideas, "Christus, der ist mein Leben" emphasizes the joyful view of death in a lively setting that takes its cue from the words *Leben, Gewinn,* and *Freud,* whereas the somewhat archaic style of "Mit Fried' und Freud' " seems more in keeping with *Fried', sanft und stille,* and *Schlaf* in Luther's text. Consciously formulated or not, Bach's underlying conception thus owes much to the opposite attributes of *durus* or *mollis* as associated with both sharp/flat and major/minor tonal polarities. We are not dealing, however, with a positive/negative affective polarity; Bach's choice of these two verses was made, at least in part, because the last line of "Christus, der ist mein Leben"—"mit Freud' fahr' ich dahin"—connects one chorale to the other. The tenor recitative joins the two chorales without a break, measuring the tonal distance between the two modes by modulatory stages and providing us as well with the allegory of their relationship. A pronounced catabasis (both tonal and melodic) from G major to C minor marks the turn from the perfect triad and meter associated with the perfect (Christ) to the imperfect (mortality). The tenor solo starts as a *jubilus*-like extension of the chorale "Mit Freuden, ja, ja mit Herzenslust will ich von hinnen scheiden" and moves to Bach's preferred key for

12. See above, p. 11.

the "sleep of death" on the words "der Erde wieder in ihren Schoss zu bringen." Here the catabasis represents Christian understanding of the duality of death and life as it is already introduced in the antithetical but complementary motivic material that pervades "Christus, der ist mein Leben."[13] Having accepted this truth, the Christian is free from worldly cares ("Mit Fried' und Freud' ").

In the next recitative the abjuration of false desires leads upward from D minor to the D major chorale "Valet will ich dir geben," the fifth and sixth lines of which— "Im Himmel ist gut wohnen, hinauf steht mein Begier"—voice the hope that underlies the return anabasis. *Valet* retains, rather conspicuously, the duality of ascending and descending motives from "Christus, der ist mein Leben." After this point the antitheses of sharp and flat and anabasis/catabasis are no longer necessary. The following recitative does not modulate widely, and the subsequent aria (the only one in the cantata) stays in D. The first verse of yet a fourth funeral hymn closes the work in G, the cantata as a whole giving the unmistakable impression of the church's ever-present support and comfort for the believer. Although "Christus, der ist mein Leben" is not a true chorale cantata, Bach makes his four funeral hymns into the mainstays of his structure, thereby uniting individual and doctrinal emphases. They, rather than the single aria, embody the duality that lies at the heart of Cantata 95. Thus surrounded and supported by the church, the soloist of the aria expresses his readiness to face death. Melodic anabasis and catabasis are heard several times on individual words and phrases of the final recitative and chorale, in particular in the high first violin line at the beginning of the chorale ("Weil du vom Tod erstanden bist") and the counterbalancing descent of a twelfth in the final line of the bass ("drum fahr' ich hin mit Freuden" again), in which the duality of direction and the positive association of catabasis are reaffirmed one last time.

If the uniting of the divine and the human worlds in the person of Christ underlies Bach's juxtaposition of major and minor in several works, a lesser degree of tonal antithesis in conjunction with a highly antithetical point of modulation allegorizes the human response to the mystery of the incarnation in Cantata 121, "Christum wir sollen loben schon" (for the second Christmas feast, December 26, 1724). Dürr has pointed out that the six-movement cantata divides into two halves, the first (nos. 1–3) dealing with the incomprehensible wonder of the incarnation and man's inability to penetrate the unfathomable ways of God, and the second (nos. 4–6) with the human response to the incarnation.[14] The cantata begins and ends in the two-sharp system, its opening and closing movements based on Luther's paraphrase of the medieval hymn "A solis ortus cardine," which begins as if in the first,

13. The opening movement of Cantata 95 presents the main instrumental motive in rhythmically identical ascending and descending forms that answer one another between the winds and strings; the quadruple-meter recitative section between the two chorale movements is punctuated by the triple-meter dialogue between the two.

14. Dürr, *Die Kantaten*, p. 123.

EXAMPLE 41.   Cantata 121: ending of first recitative

Dorian, mode and ends in the Phrygian. Bach's settings thus seem, in modern terms, to begin in E minor and end on the dominant of B minor. Perhaps Bach associated the rise in tonal center with the elevation of the flesh: the first aria, in B minor, "O du von Gott erhöhtes Creatur," seems to resolve the modal ambiguity by interpreting the E minor and F sharp as the subdominant and dominant of that key. The third movement, the recitative completing the first half, modulates upward through A major and C sharp minor, then suddenly, on the last phrase, makes an enharmonic modulation down a tritone from F sharp minor to C major ("Gott wählet sich den reinen Leib zu einem Tempel seiner Ehren, um zu den Menschen sich *mit wundervoller Art zu kehren*; emphasis added) (Ex. 41). The following C major aria marks the turn to the human part of the cantata, and stands in a fa relationship to the B minor (mi) of the preceding aria. From here the movements return by stages to the two-sharp system and the closing verse of the original chorale. Through the incarnation of Christ man is raised again to God; Cantata 121 is, therefore, another descent/ascent cantata, but one that turns catabasis into a transformation.

Another Christmas cantata that deals with the meaning of the incarnation is Number 91, "Gelobet seist du, Jesu Christ"; it likewise has a descent/ascent plan and a sudden shift of key area at the center. From its initial key of G major (chorale

EXAMPLE 42.   Cantata 91: ending of recitative (No. 4)

fantasia, "Gelobet seist du"), the sequence moves down through E minor (recita-tive, telling of Jesus' incarnation in terms of the eternal light taking on accursed, damned, and lost humanity), and A minor (aria, "Gott, dem der Erden Kreis zu klein") to an accompanied recitative ending in C minor, "er kömmt zu dir, um dich vor seinen Thron durch dieses Jammertal zu führen!" (Ex. 42). The return ascent is made in an E minor duet that explains the redemptive meaning of the incarnation ("Die Armut, so Gott auf sich nimmt, hat uns ein ewig Heil bestimmt") and a G major chorale ("Das hat er alles uns getan"). The juxtaposition of Jesus' divine and human natures is a key to the harmonic/tonal and stylistic character of this cantata in closer details as well.

The diatonic G major of the opening chorus, with its rushing scales and arpeg-gios, represents an atmosphere of rejoicing ("des freuet sich der Engel Schar"). The first recitative contrasts chorale lines at the original pitch with recitative interpolations that introduce often striking modulations. The two arias make use of dotted rhythms in association with the idea of Jesus' divinity. But the second one—the soprano/alto duet with unison violins—crowns the work, a movement that Bach subjected to rhythmic revisions to increase his emphasis on the dichotomy of Jesus' two natures. The main melody of the violins is a dotted figure whose rhythm (or, perhaps just its notation) Bach sharpened slightly in his revisions, undoubtedly to underscore the reference to the majestic style. The melodic descent of the figure itself was probably associated with the incarnation. In the middle section of the aria this figure is combined with two others in the vocal parts. The first of these is the ascending chromatic tetrachord that has been heard at the end of the preceding movement (on "Jammertal" in C minor), and the second is a melodic pattern whose prominent syncopated rhythm was added in the revision stage and might have been intended to clash with, rather than assimilate to, the dotted rhythms of the instrumental figure. Both these vocal ideas are clearly linked to the first words of the text: "Sein menschlich Wesen [machet euch den Engelsherrlichkeiten gleich, euch zu der Engel Chor zu setzen]."

The tonal aspect is most striking in intent. Bach divides the section into two halves, passing the chromatic tetrachord once through all four voices in each half. In both halves the chromatic line modulates upward a fifth each time it enters, but the first time the modulations are in sharp keys—A minor, E minor, B minor, F sharp minor—and the second time in flats, C minor, G minor, D minor, A minor (Ex. 43). A minor—expressive of the mean between sharps and flats—is common to both and is the key of the middle section. At the juncture of the two sections the keys of F sharp minor and G minor are confronted in a form of tonal mi contra fa. When the text changes at this point, from "machet euch den Engelsherrlichkeiten gleich, euch der Engel Chor zu setzen" (which is emphasized in the vocal lines as the *menschlich Wesen* idea sounds in the instruments) back to "sein menschlich Wesen" as the move to flats is made, the meaning is made fully clear and immediately audible. The ascending modulations represent, of course, the elevation of mankind to the level of the angels by means of Jesus' humanity (the ascending chromatic tetrachord).

Turning to the reverse of the incarnation we find in the D major Ascension *oratorio,* Cantata 11, a complex series of modulations that, because of the length of the work and the variegated character of its text, does not emphasize a continuous progression in a single direction but mirrors the changing directions suggested in the succession of movements. The work exhibits the following sequence of modulations: to the dominant for the initial narrative of the ascension (no. 2, rec.); from A major down through the circle of fifths to a close in A minor for the Christian entreaty for Christ to remain on earth (no. 3, rec., and no. 4, aria, "Ach, bleibe

(a)

EXAMPLE 43   *continued*

etc., to F sharp minor

(b)

EXAMPLE 43   *continued*

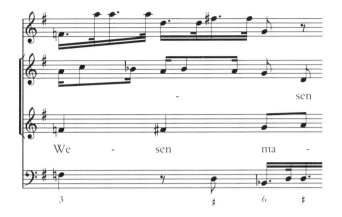

sen   etc., to A minor

We   -   sen   ma   -

doch");[15] back up to F sharp minor for the remainder of the narrative of the ascension (no. 5, rec.); down to D major for a chorale expressing Jesus' rule over the earth ("Nun lieget alles unter dir," no. 6), and the narrative of the two men on the road to Jerusalem who foretell Jesus' return (no. 7, rec.); down to B minor for the recitative beginning "Ach ja! so komme bald zurück" (no. 8), and further down to G major for the recitative and aria, "Jesu, deine Gnadenblicke," the latter without basso continuo to represent the fact that although Jesus is above, love remains as a Christian benefit (middle section, "Deine Liebe bleibt zurücke"). The work is framed by D major choruses.

A paradox that is typical of Bach's work in general is the cantata that urges rejection of the world in the most worldly terms. A perfect example of this type is Cantata 94, "Was frag' ich nach der Welt," another lengthy work in which the full instrumental resources, from the flute down to the basso continuo, all participate in a sound spectrum of dance and concerto-like movements to give the most varied picture of the world in both its splendid and false aspects. The first two movements bring out this antithesis. A chorale fantasia begins with a tremendous ascending line for unaccompanied flute and is dominated throughout by the high, bright flute part and the soprano chorale; it is followed by an aria for bass and basso continuo, "Die Welt ist wie ein Rauch und Schatten," in which the fallen character of the world is represented by an opening arpeggio descent in the basso continuo that

15. In light of the relatively flat (dominant minor) tonal character of this aria within the *Ascension Oratorio* it is significant that the parodied form of the movement in the *Mass in B minor* ("Agnus Dei") is in G minor and is the only movement in flats in the *Mass,* serving almost as a huge plagal cadence, as it were, to the final "Dona nobis pacem"; its character of entreaty to the deity is preserved, of course, in its flat-minor tonality.

constitutes the theme for the piece. The keys are D major and B minor, respectively, and the next two movements carry the sequence of falling thirds to G major and E minor. The G major movement, a chorale setting for tenor and two oboes with troped recitative insertions between the chorale lines, modulates extensively in the recitative sections (e.g., E minor–A minor in the first insertion, down to C minor in the second for "den stolzen Leib auf einmal in die Gruft," and so on), while the chorale lines have to return to the correct pitch. In the tortured alto aria, "Betörte Welt! auch dein Reichtum, Gut und Geld ist Betrug und falscher Schein," the flute is forced to play the most dissonant and difficult nonharmonic intervals in the minor mode, in complete contrast to its role in the opening movement, "Betörte Welt" is the lowest in the descending sequence (D major, B minor, G major, *E minor*), and its middle section—an allegro of florid diatonic character with the words "Jesus soll allein meiner Seelen Reichtum sein"—marks the theological antithesis in the work. After this point Bach reuses the remaining vocal soloists, in ascending order, bass and basso continuo first, in another chorale setting with troped recitative insertions, "Die Welt bekümmert sich." This movement marks a deeper understanding of the world redeemed by Jesus' sacrifice; Bach fits chromatic ascending and descending lines in the basso continuo to the chorale lines only, while the soloist modulates to E major within its last phrase for the anticipation of eternity: "Es ist ja nur ein Leiden dieser Zeit! Ich weiss gewiss, dass mich die Ewigkeit dafür mit Preis und Ehre krönet." The chorale is set in D, but only the last line, concluding the movement, cadences in that key.

To this point the cantata exhibits all the characteristics of the descent/ascent type. Owing to the length of the chorale text, however, and its pejorative characterization of the world, Bach's structure is somewhat more complex, although still open to explication. In keeping with the world's self-image, the aria "Die Welt kann ihre Lust und Freud, das Blendwerk schnöder Eitelkeit, nicht hoch genug erhöhen," for tenor and strings, is in A major, the highest key of the cantata. And the gigue-like character of the aria projects the attractiveness of the world in no uncertain terms, while the following soprano aria, in F sharp minor, begins a falling-third move back to D major for the final two chorale verses; set in Bouree style it rejects the blind World once again. Bach needed to devise a structure to represent both the splendor of the world and its rejection, a plan that leads to fuller understanding of the world but that does not cancel out its enticements. The descent/ascent dynamic within the work (nos. 1–5) constitutes the expression of understanding, while the last three movements contain, respectively, a reminder of the reality of the world's pleasures, a further warning, and a statement of the promise of eternity for those who can resist the world. Behind the tonal structure of the cantata lies an arrangement of the six keys of the ambitus of D major in a pattern of thirds: A, f sharp, D (the last three movements), [D], b, G, e (the first four movements). This device was possibly intended, like the instrumental and dance styles, to represent a comprehensive presentation of all the facets of worldly life.

Although these ideas are easily understandable theologically, the initial anomaly remains. The turn to A major for "Die Welt kann ihre Lust und Freud" breaks the association of sharp keys (especially major ones) with faith, salvation, and the like; and it seems artificial that the words *hoch* and *erhöhen* should have led Bach to contradict the picture of the world presented in "Betörte Welt," even if the preceding recitative does introduce the idea of the world redeemed. Bach's musical allegory confronts the difficulty of representing a negative proposition, a problem that was recognized at the time.[16] Rejection of the world can only be represented (as opposed to being merely stated) if the world is depicted musically, and the depiction itself implies acceptance. Thus in Cantata 52, "Falsche Welt, dir trau ich nicht," Bach utilizes the opening movement of the First Brandenburg Concerto as an instrumental introduction, then brings in the voice immediately with the words "Falsche Welt." Neither here nor in any of the many other similar instances in his work can Bach be considered to reject his own music as too worldly. Nor is it sufficient to say that Bach held (or rejected) the theological view that the world, while fallen, can nevertheless be enjoyed to the full as long as its finite, devalued nature is understood. This view simply separates the composer's religious beliefs from his art (without our knowing that this is correct), eliminates the possibility that the composer might have thought deeply about the question himself, and adds nothing to our understanding of his allegorical procedures per se.

Although drawing logical conclusions on such a question from the works themselves is problematic, it is at least possible to confront the question at the exclusive level of musical allegory. From that standpoint it is clear that Bach uses the forms and styles of instrumental music, concerto and suite, to represent the world in many instances. In Cantata 169 he begins with a concerto first-movement type, and later in the work parodies the second movement of the same concerto as the aria "Stirb in mir, Welt." Cantata 146 likewise begins with a concerto first-movement parody and sets the second movement to the text "Wir müssen durch viel Trübsal." Cantata 35 opens similarly, with the slow movement set to the text "Geist und Seele wird verwirret" (the expression of the inability of human nature to comprehend the deity). From such pieces we might conclude that Bach perceived a parallel dialectical relationship between concerto allegro and adagio types on the one hand and the two sides of the world (its splendor versus its tribulation) on the other. This analogy is not hard and fast either, but it allows us to come closer to the composer's intent in both vocal and instrumental works.

Within the First Brandenburg Concerto, for example, we might perceive such a relationship between, on the one hand, the unusually festive court orchestra whose horns and oboes add great luster to the opening movement and, on the other, the violino piccolo, a voice so weak by comparison that to hear it at all the concert

---

16. Kuhnau, "Eine Abhandlung," p. 152.

listener must sort out a duality of dynamic levels. In the first movement the violino piccolo is almost totally absorbed into the hierarchical orchestral sonority, in which pairs of horns and oboes playing in parallel thirds and sixths project a stately, measured character. But in the slow movement suddenly the formal splendor and pomp give way to the more intimate and intense pathetic emotions of the three soloists, violino piccolo, oboe, and basso continuo. These three stand apart from the string orchestra not only in their roles of individual voices versus accompaniment but also by virtue of the tremendous dissonances that are heard when the orchestra, following the lead of the previous soloist, cadences in its key, only to clash with the entering soloist and its turn toward a new key (Ex. 44). The tonal direction is unmistakably downward, phrase by phrase, from the initial A major sonority to D minor, G minor, and C minor, before the reinterpretation of an A flat as G sharp returns the tonality to D minor. Even the longer sections that make up the main part of the movement modulate downward: the first in D minor and the second in G minor, leading to the chromatic Phrygian approach to the final A major sonority. In its juxtaposition of the sharpest and flattest tonal sonorities of the ambitus this movement can be considered an expansion of the tonal idea behind the Phrygian cadence. The drama of antithesis in the work as a whole, however, is told in terms of the shift from the formal, pompous, and external character of the opening movement to the inward and plaintive adagio, not in the first movement, as is the norm in the classical concerto. And the work mirrors another world altogether from, say, the opening movement of Mozart's D minor Concerto, one that is far more hierarchical in nature. The third movement provides the synthesis or reconciliation, in that both the full court orchestra and the solo violino piccolo are heard for the first time. But it is a reconciliation that emphasizes the opposition between the two parties by assigning the lead to the violino piccolo both in moments of great structural weight and in the only place in the movement where the pathetic character of the preceding movement is recalled (with an emphasis on flats). The first of these situations makes a great impact when, after the full orchestra presents a block of ritornello material, we are left suddenly with the relatively feeble sonority of violino piccolo and basso continuo alone to complete the ritornello. Any sense of an equality that transcends social barriers is out of the question; the formal hierarchy of the court as symbol of the world is ever-present. Yet intrinsic worth and character are preserved for the individual in the face of the striking disparity of resources. The group of symmetrically arranged dances that Bach adds to the concerto proper—including a Polacca of rustic origins—perhaps affirms the role of the court/world as meeting ground of varied, but always hierarchically ordered social sectors.[17]

17. And in this set of movements the violino piccolo once again merges with the violins of the orchestra.

EXAMPLE 44.   First Brandenburg Concerto: beginning of second movement

Oboe 1, 2, 3

Violino piccolo

Violins 1, 2
Viola

Basso continuo

EXAMPLE 44   *continued*

When, in "Falsche Welt, dir trau ich nicht," Bach follows the first movement of this concerto with an immediate turn to D minor in the first recitative, following this in quick succession with modulations to G minor ("unter falschen Schlangen wohnen"), E flat ("Dein Angesicht, das noch so freundlich ist"), and B flat minor ("so muss ein frommer Armer sterben"), an indication of the structure and meaning of the cantata emerges. The relationship between the first and second recitative/aria pairs is one of antithesis: the first pair (in D minor) voices the *jämmerliche Stand* of a world in which only God can be trusted, and the second (B flat) expresses that trust. The move down to the subdominant is associated with God's supportive presence: "Gott ist getreu! er wird, er kann mich nicht verlassen. Will mich die Welt in ihrer Raserei in ihre Schlingen fassen, so steht mir seine Hilfe bei." The idea is similar to the presence of the Spirit in the subdominant aria that ended "Erschallet, ihr Lieder." In the aria "Ich halt' es mit dem lieben Gott," the world is represented by three oboes, moving entirely in homophonic style. This sonority, relating to the introductory concerto movement, had been used by Bach two years earlier, in 1724, in the E minor bass aria "An irdische Schätze das Herze zu hängen ist eine Verführung der thörichten Welt" from Cantata 26 ("Ach wie flüchtig, ach wie nichtig ist der Menschen Leben"). "An irdische Schätze" is written in gavotte style, and its tone is very different from "Ich halt' es mit dem lieben Gott." It is, furthermore, the apex of an ascent/descent cantata, whose plan allegorizes, like several others of its type, the futility of earthly hopes (see the discussion of this type in the following chapter). "Ich halt' es" on the other hand, is another work in which the idea of descent, like the instrumentation, is associated with the world, but a world of peace and comfort owing to faith in God. "Falsche Welt" is one of the simplest of the descent/ascent cantatas, ending with a prayer for God to preserve faith in the individual (F major chorale).

CHAPTER SEVEN

Tonal Planning

in the

Leipzig Cantatas II

This chapter discusses the three remaining types of tonal planning—anabasis, cata-basis, and ascent/descent—along with Cantatas 109 and 38 that deal with the central Lutheran belief of justification by faith. The anabasis cantatas composed in Leipzig are fewer in number than we might expect, considering how many of them Bach composed in his first year at Weimar. This is partly explained by the large number of descent/ascent cantatas among the Leipzig works, and anabasis is very prominent in them. In fact, several cantatas of the latter type end, as we saw, in higher keys than those in which they began and might be grouped in this category as well. Also, other works have similar higher endings but are not discussed here because their plans do not consistently exhibit the features of tonal planning as a whole. The five anabasis cantatas selected for discussion illustrate the major characteristics of this type.

In Cantata 27, "Wer weiss, wie nahe mir mein Ende," a simple ascent by thirds—C minor, E flat, G minor, and B flat—allegorizes the Lutheran desire to die a blessed death. Epitomized in the chorale "Herzlich tut mich verlangen nach einem sel'gen End'," this idea runs through many Bach cantatas, leading to the frequent observation that the composer favored death as a subject. Death seldom fails to call forth special affective treatment by Bach, although some might contend that Bach's response stems from the Lutheran view of death rather than a personal stance. Lutheran eschatology and the doctrine of justification by faith attempted to transform the meaning of death. Taking a dialectical approach that emphasized on the one hand the idea of death as man's punishment for his sins, and on the other the comfort of redemption, the Lutheran view made death into a short sleep from which the faithful would awaken into God's eternity. The anticipation or foretaste of that eternity now so colored death that it was often described as "sweet" (e.g., Cantata 161, "Komm, du süsse Todesstunde"). Within this framework the importance of trust (in the double sense of God's comforting mankind and of man's placing his trust in God) cannot be overestimated. We have seen the idea of trust associated with rising tonal progression in such Cantatas as Numbers 106 and 21. In "Wer weiss, wie nahe mir mein Ende" the ascent and the alternation between minor and major keys can be considered a response to the prayer that ends the opening movement, "mach's nur mit meinem Ende gut," and is confirmed at the end of the first recitative, "denn Ende gut, macht Alles gut." Proof of the centrality of this Lutheran *Symbolum* to Bach's thought is found not only in his giving it canonic status but in his allowing it both here and in Cantata 156 to determine the character of works whose endings are higher than their beginnings. Bach achieves a most impressive *tone* in Cantata 27, moving from the mingling of the individual and pathetic with the message of comfort (opening chorus) to hope, the stilling of worldly desire (akin to the stilling of the *Gewissensangst* in Cantata 105) and, finally, the joy of simple faith.

The joy of simple faith is a key to Bach's treatment of death in all his works. We have seen that the "Actus Tragicus" manages to retain a basic simplicity of utterace that belies and ultimately overcomes the allegorical complexity inherent in the doctrinal emphases. Bach seldom needed such a high degree of allegorical complexity in his later works; its presence in the "Actus Tragicus" signals the transitional character of the work.[1] "Wer weiss, wie nahe mir mein Ende" is far more direct and personal, qualities in Bach's work that, as we saw, came to the fore at Weimar ("Komm, du süsse Todesstunde" is the pivotal piece in terms of the subject of death). Triple meter, often in homophonic textures, links Cantata 161 with Bach's treatment of death and to the Lutheran idea of the "sleep of death." Another tie to death as a subject is the close conjunction of relative major and minor keys. In "Komm, du süsse Todesstunde" all the movements are set either in A minor or C major, without associating positive or negative values to the minor and major modes. Since the key-signature levels do not change among the movements the tonal allegory in such a work might seem to be confined to modulations within the recitatives. In fact, the subtle derivation of the themes of the closed movements from "Herzlich tut mich verlangen" points to the intimate relationship between the two modes, both of which are used to harmonize the Phrygian chorale. At the final cadence of the cantata the E major chord and the settling of the recorder line on the appoggiatura a″–g″ sharp expresses the side of the mode that contains both a historical and a modern aspect. The E major chord is the correct final for the Phry-

---

1. That is, the pre-Weimar form of sacred concerto with its many short, motto-like biblical texts lacked many of the features of musical extension and integration of the later cantata style (da capo arias with ritornello structures, modulatory schemes, *Fortspinnung,* and the like). The principles for extension in individual sections are not in evidence, while those of integration seldom appear in the whole. The structures often appear arbitrary. The plan of the "Actus Tragicus," however, calls for a large-scale integrated structure, yet the means for it are lacking. The problem is solved in the sacred concerto by its extraordinary allegorical interrelatedness. But the message of such a structure is entirely different from that of the later, concerto-derived works, in that it inevitably encourages the fragmentation of the forms into referential elements.

gian mode, yet it sounds like the dominant of A minor. Here, as elsewhere in the Bach cantatas (such as the ending of Cantata 135, the ending of "Wenn ich einmal soll scheiden" in the *St. Matthew Passion,* and the close of Cantata 38) the Phrygian ending allegorizes the nature of the final question regarding death, put in Cantata 161 as a rhetorical question: "Was schad't mir dann der Tod?" This perfect symbol of the faithful anticipation of eternity (E major) from the earthly framework (A minor and the C system) provides a clue to Bach's comforting meditation on death, whether or not he chooses to utilize pastorale and dance (sarabande, Siciliano) elements. Faith and trust are child-like in their simplicity, accepting a meaning that reason would question.

In the case of Cantata 27 Bach uses rising thirds similarly to those of the Weimar cantatas "Weinen, Klagen, Sorgen, Zagen" and "Nun komm, der Heiden Heiland," making a similar progression from the complexity of the opening chorus to the directness of the final chorale. The work emphasizes the church's comforting role in supporting the individual; in the opening chorus not only the chorale but even the troping recitatives are set in triple meter (a unique instance). The ritornello material of this chorus was created to picture the basic antithesis underlying meditation on death. In the first six bars the strings play a descending arpeggio figure above an alternating-octave C pedal and below a duet of pathetic character in the oboes; then, for the remaining six bars the voices are exchanged, and the arpeggio figure appears in the basso continuo, now ascending. Throughout the movement only the descending form will be used until the final ritornello, following "mach's nur mit meinem Ende gut," where the ascending form returns to dominate the ending. Both the devices of quadruple versus triple meter and melodic descent/ascent run throughout the cantata, while the tonal plan indicates the basic upward direction.

The first recitative states that life's only goal is to die a blessed death and enjoy the benefits of faith. This way of thinking suggests the devaluation of life that Walter Benjamin posited as the motive behind allegory in the *Trauerspiel.* The soloist (tenor) voices the willingness to live in constant readiness for death, adding "und was das Werk der Hände thut, ist gleichsam ob ich sicher wüsste, dass ich noch heute sterben müsste; denn Ende gut, macht Alles gut." We cannot know whether Bach really had this kind of faith, but that he knew what it meant is clear from the following movement. In reference to the "work of the hands" the obbligato organ part of the E flat aria, "Willkommen will ich sagen wenn der Tod ans Bette tritt," takes on a personal character that is suggested in the oboe da caccia part as well.[2] The movement retains some of the motivic ideas of the opening chorus in a general way—the slurred duplets of the oboe lines and the alternating-octave pedal, in

2. The oboe da caccia often has a special role in Bach's music related to the affect of love; on its use in the *St. Matthew Passion* see Chapter 12, pp. 348–54.

particular—but the tone of hope dominates and is conveyed from the outset by the rising fifth of the oboe line. These movements, in the three-flat system, are concerned primarily with the acceptance of death, while the last two deal with readiness to leave the world.

Following an accompanied recitative expressing longing for the future life, the G minor bass aria with strings, "Gute Nacht, du Weltgetümmel," alternates the styles of a sarabande-like lullaby ("Gute Nacht") and the *stile concitato* ("du Weltgetümmel"), with the former beginning and ending the aria. In the middle section the words "Ich steh' schon mit einem Fuss" prompt wide-ranging melodic descent by thirds to the open g-string of the violin, while the completion, "bei dem lieben Gott im Himmel" (rather than the expected *im Grabe*) returns to the upper register.[3] Occasional melodic resemblances to the final chorus of the *St. Matthew Passion* (also modeled on the sarabande) and the aria "Es ist vollbracht" of the *St. John Passion* were undoubtedly unintentional but fit entirely with the meaning of the aria. Bach chose the final chorale, "Welt ade! ich bin dein Müde," from its original seventeenth-century setting by Johann Rosenmüller, rather than harmonize it himself, undoubtedly to articulate the simple quality of faith evoked by the harmonies, the antiphonal effect of the low and high voices at the beginning, and the archaic turn from duple to triple proportion for the final phrase ("in dem Himmel allezeit Friede, Freud' und Seeligkeit"). Remembering Bach's reference in his 1730 memorandum to the council to the change in musical style that had taken place since the time of Kuhnau and Schelle, one can imagine that the ending of Cantata 27 represented a form of nostalgia, a yearning for the spirit of a simpler age that was already a thing of the past when the "Actus Tragicus" was composed.[4]

The pastorale cantata from 1724, "Du Hirte Israel, höre" (No. 104), in the anabasis type, presents a different—and seemingly opposed—view of the world and Lutheran eschatology from that of "Wer weiss, wie nahe mir mein Ende." This work moves upward from G major (opening chorus), through B minor (recitative and aria) and D major (recitative and aria) to A major (chorale paraphrase of the Twenty-Third Psalm). Now, however, the theology prompting the tonal ascent is not just the desire to leave the world but a vital aspect of Lutheran eschatology, the foretaste of eternity that is already present for the believer through faith—"Die Welt ist euch ein Himmelreich." Renate Steiger has traced this idea throughout Bach's vocal music in a compelling manner.[5] In Cantata 104 it is clearly expressed in the D major recitative and aria:

Die Weide, die ich mich meine Lust, des Himmels Vorschmack, ja, mein Alles heisse (rec.).

---

3. Cantata 156, "Ich steh' mit einem Fuss im Grabe," has, as we have seen, theological connections to "Wer weiss, wie nahe mir mein Ende."
4. See David and Mendel, eds., *The Bach Reader,* p. 123.
5. Steiger, " 'Die Welt ist auch ein Himmelreich.' "

Beglückte Herde, Jesu Schafe, die Welt ist euch ein Himmelreich. Hier schmeckt ihr Jesu Güte schon, und hoffet noch des Glaubens Lohn nach einem sanften Todesschlafe (aria).

Here the growth of faith represented by tonal anabasis in such Cantatas as Numbers 12, 21, and 199 is linked to the anticipation of eternity as a blessed *Himmelsweide,* and the ascent is neither interrupted nor returned to its original, more earthly perspective. The themes of both arias present a strong sense of upward motion, and the final chorale clearly indicats that the rising tonal progression symbolizes mankind's being led by the shepherd, Christ. The underlying idea of simple trust is expressed perfectly in the second, pastorale aria and the straightforward solidity of the chorale harmonization.

The anabasis patterns prevalent in the tonal planning of the Weimar cantatas turn suffering and acknowledgment of sin into positive values. As Elke Axmacher points out,

> The dialectic of Luther's thought concerning suffering softens in the seventeenth century to an unequivocally positive assessment of suffering. "Wir müssen durch viel Trübsal in das Reich Gottes eingehen" (Acts 14:22) is often quoted as a fundamental statement of the ethical meditation on the Passion, which can now, for the first time, be characterized as an "ethic of suffering."[6]

This change is vital to the interpretation of Bach's cantatas, even though they still exhibit numerous signs of the dialectic relationship between suffering and faith. Cantata 146, "Wir müssen durch viel Trübsal," is such a work, indebted now to the antithetical drama of opposition that characterizes the concerto, the genre from which Bach drew the cantata's first and second movements.

In "Weinen, Klagen, Sorgen, Zagen" Bach had used anabasis to resolve the dialectical character present in the alternation of major and minor, chromatic descent versus diatonic ascent, and the like. And in Cantata 146, Bach relies once more on the device of tonal anabasis. Cantata 146 allegorizes the progression from the tribulation articulated in its first chorus (G minor) to the joy and anticipation of eternity of its final duet, "Wie will ich mich freuen, wenn alle vergängliche Trübsal vorbei," and chorale, "Denn wer selig dahin fähret," both in F major, by a sequence of keys within D minor, whose main outline in the closed movements is the rising-third pattern g, B flat, d, f:

CANTATA 146: "Wir müssen durch viel Trübsal"

D minor   (1) Instrumental introduction arranged for obligato organ and orchestra from the first movement of the Violin Concerto original of the harpsichord concerto, BWV 1052

6. Axmacher, *"Aus Liebe,"* p. 87; author's translation.

G minor	(2) Chorus: "Wir müssen durch viel Trübsal," arranged from the second movement of the above concerto
B flat	(3) Aria: "Ich will nach dem Himmel zu"
G minor–D minor	(4) Rec.: "Ach! wer doch schon im Himmel wär"
D minor	(5) Aria: "Ich säe meine Zähren"
A minor	(6) Rec.: "Ich bin bereit mein Kreuz geduldig zu ertragen"
F major	(7) Duet: "Wie will ich mich freuen"
F major	(8) Chorale: "Denn wer selig dahin fähret"

The extraordinary affect of joy in the duet culminates the longing for eternity that pervades this cantata. And, although the tonal distance from beginning to end is only that from minor tonic to relative major, the combined sense of spiritual ascent and fulfillment at the close is truly impressive. Progressing from the worldly sphere of the concerto, whose subdominant adagio represents the spiritual nadir of mankind's inability to transcend the burden of existence (the theme is based on rising minor triads and falling sevenths doubled between melody and basso continuo), the cantata moves through rejection of the world (major-key violin solo aria), severe antithesis and torment at the dealings of the world, to anticipation of reaping the fruits of seeds sown in tears and of the time when God will avenge earthly sufferings, when tribulation will be replaced by joy and glory. The final vision of this work is prepared by the initial turn to major for the B flat aria, whose ornate violin part acts as a stage in the transformation of the world itself. The tremendous antitheses in the first recitative—which ranges from F minor to F sharp minor, including an enharmonic change—remind us of the extreme torment involved in the rejection of the world. The D minor aria with flute is less immediately and blatantly optimistic but mediates between the world and the hopes to transcend it; the two main sections of the aria represent the antithesis between sowing in adversity and reaping in joy. Following the A minor recitative—with its prominent C major cadence for the *Herrlichkeit* that God will reveal to the elect—the F major duet rests on a secure ground of hope. The acceptance of suffering that has appeared in several other works with structured tonal plans (e.g., "Ich will leiden, ich will schweigen" from Cantata 87 and "Ich bin vergnügt mit meinem Leiden" from Cantata 58) is reserved for the ending of the cantata and the secure establishment of the relative major. Of course, love of the world is not represented but instead the anticipation of eternity by those who live in faith and hope. It is not a vision, like the one that ends Cantata 21; its tone is not one of glory and triumph but of joy and security at the close of a measured series of affections. The work is not really dialectical despite the shift from tribulation to joy, the antithesis of the recitative, and the changes from minor to major. Instead, the increasing sense of security in the meditative progression and the relatively slight tonal distance covered distinguish "Wir müssen durch viel Trübsal" as a perfect example of the *Leidensethik* that is central to Lutheran spiritual life. This is realized eschatology, the growing sense of the "possessions" that faith creates in the individual, of the transformation of present life under the promise of a future one.[7]

All the foregoing cantatas end with the secure expression of joy. But upward progression is not always so easily made. In Cantata 60, "O Ewigkeit, du Donnerwort," alto and tenor soloists, as personifications of Fear and Hope respectively, carry on a dialogue that is resolved only in the penultimate movement, when the voice of Christ (bass) replaces the tenor. Hope alone cannot overcome fear and lead man to salvation; only faith in Christ can achieve this. Cantata 60 is discussed here with the anabasis cantatas, although it shares with the descent/ascent type a sequence of keys that moves from the opening D major down through a recitative ending in G, then up through a B minor duet, a recitative/arioso duet ending in D, and the final chorale in A major. But the descent idea is not central to the work, even though some of the modulations in the first recitative were motivated by such ideas (e.g., A minor for "Ich lege diesen Leib vor Gott zum Opfer nieder"). "O Ewigkeit, du Donnerwort" does not meditate directly on eternity as did Bach's chorale cantata of the same name; this work expresses the fear of death. Nevertheless, although the chorale "O Ewigkeit" supplies only the text of the opening movement and not of the whole cantata as in Cantata 20, it is bound up with the structure of the whole, and especially the idea of ascent. And the ascending sequence of G, b, D, A plays a similar role to that of the same key sequence in Cantata 104, if not so occupied with the foretaste of eternity in the present life.

The dialectic element is now present in the constant doubt and anxiety expressed by Fear and the answering comforting phrases given by Hope. The pronounced simultaneity of opposites, representing the divided soul, requires that the ending express reconciliation or integration. The two solo instruments play highly differentiated parts throughout most of the duet aria "Mein letztes Lager will mich schrecken" (Fear) / "Mich wird des Heilands Hand bedecken" (Hope), while, as Dürr has shown, the vocal parts, which appear thematically contrasted to one another, are in fact related through variation.[8] In addition, forward motion and increasing hope are linked by several factors: the absence of textual da capos in the work; Hope's always having the last word; and, above all, Hope's ability, with its relatively diatonic style, to resolve Fear's chromatic instability.

In the penultimate recitative/arioso movement (no. 4), the angst of the alto part is mirrored in a series of modulations in the sharp direction throughout its first two solos. Beginning in E minor, Fear modulates to F sharp minor, explaining that fear of death tears hope from the heart. Now, with hope gone, the *vox Christi* responds in arioso style with the words of Revelation 14:13, "Selig sind die Toten," in a con-

7. See von Loewenich, *Luther's Theology of the Cross,* pp. 91–107.
8. Dürr, *Die Kantaten,* p. 518.

trasting diatonic style cadencing in D major. Fear enters a second time, modulating upward to cadence first in F sharp minor again, then moving via dissonant and "false" intervals to close on one of the relatively small number of G sharp minor cadences in Bach's work (symbolizing fear of hell and eternal damnation). The bass responds in E major, adding the words "die in dem Herren sterben" to its earlier response. Each time there is a sense of positive upward motion, first from E minor to D major, then from F sharp minor to E major. But the initial motion in both cases is up a whole tone from one minor key to another: E minor to F sharp minor (before closing in D), then F sharp minor to G sharp minor (before the E major cadence). These upward minor progressions are clearly treated as negative, while in each case the move to the major key is treated as the positive completion of the idea. In these passages Fear's envisaging of eternity, while moving upward, serves to intensify the minor-key character of the phrase, exactly the effect created in the ascending canon *per tonos* of the *Musical Offering*. The allegory is of an anticipation of eternity produced by human limitation (Fear), not held in check by the Word and faith, and so turns to images of desolation. The *vox Christi* resolves the fearful tones into the security of understanding that is represented by giving more of the Scripture reading.

Fear enters following the E major, reversing the modulatory direction downward in stages to end on the dominant of E minor ("so schein ich ja im Grabe zu verderben"). The change of direction corresponds to the shift from the fearful anticipation of eternity to that of death and the grave itself. For the third and last time the bass responds, now giving the full quotation from Revelation—"Selig sind die Toten, die in dem Herren sterben, von nun an"—and ending in the E minor that Fear left incomplete. The last three words, "von nun an," are most meaningful for Fear who now, for the first time in the cantata, cadences in a major key (D), ending the movement with the restoration of hope and the words "der Geist kann einen Blick in jene Freude tun." Similar to the idea of the foretaste of eternity of Cantata 104, here the soul can glance into eternity.

Although Hope constantly gives Fear answers of comfort throughout the cantata, only at the end does Fear understand the momentous message, and the work suddenly turns into an anabasis cantata. The famous final chorale, "Es ist genung," is striking both for its initial melodic tritone and its unusually chromatic harmonies. The chorale ends the cantata in A major, a fifth higher than it began. As Dürr indicates, its opening phrase is a distortion of the final four tones of the first phrase of "O Ewigkeit," replacing the tone d″ by d″ sharp, a device that Dürr interprets as "the musical figure of the crossing over [or exceeding] of the realm of life to that of death.[9] This interpretation is certainly correct; it relates to the modulation upward by whole tones (e, f sharp, g sharp) in the preceding recitative, the key of G sharp

9. Dürr, *Die Kantaten,* p. 519–20 (author's translation).

EXAMPLE 45.   Cantata 60, "O Ewigkeit, du Donnerwort"

(a) First movement: beginning of alto chorale

O   E - wig - keit, du   Don - ner - wort,

(b) Beginnings of first recitative and final chorale

O schwe - rer Gang   Es   ist   ge - nung;

EXAMPLE 46.   Cantata 60: ending of final chorale

Soprano
Alto

Tenor
Bass
Basso continuo

Es   ist   ge - nung,   es   ist   ge - nung.

minor signifying there a tonal extreme, an exceeding of the E major that Bach commonly associates with salvation, and with which the bass gives its answering message of comfort. In fact, the idea of sharp ascent in this cantata is announced in the opening phrase of the first recitative, "O schwerer Gang," which distorts the first four tones of "O Ewigkeit" in just the same manner that "Es ist genung" distorts the last four (Ex. 45). The additional sharps make the "schwerer Gang" of course, the way of the cross. Since the direction of transcendence is sharpward, the dissonant D sharp in the final chorale forces the tonality upward to the dominant of A major (third and sixth line endings), enabling the sense of resolution for the final descent to the new tonic on "Es ist genung" (Ex. 46).

In Cantata 60 the ancient association of sharps with the various meanings of the word *durus* is clearly expressed. In Bach's time the word was increasingly used to mean major, although, as we saw in Chapter 3, the older usages—often suggesting hardness or harshness—had by no means disappeared. Mattheson acknowledged an association of sharp key signatures with the qualities of hardness, freshness, and gaiety but took pains to deny that such ideas could be used to explain the affect of any particular key.[10] Nevertheless, he believed in the reality of key characteristics, at least in his earlier writings, and his famous characterization of the keys confirms the traditional associations in a number of respects.[11] Significant for Bach's usage is his calling E major expressive of "a quite deathly sadness full of doubt, most convenient for *extreme* enamorment of helpless and hopeless things, and it has in certain situations such a cutting, separating, suffering, and penetrating quality that it can be compared with nothing but a fatal separation of body and soul."[12] Although it would be a serious mistake to apply such a description too literally, behind Mattheson's rather surprising characterization we can see the ancient linking of sharps to the *cantus durus* and of other deeper sharps to the idea of tonal extremes. Bach's use of E throughout the cantatas has, in the main, a positive set of associations, but it is still close to the idea of an extreme, and a key such as G sharp minor that is generally linked to pejorative associations sometimes appears in company with E. Also, in a very few instances in Bach's work E major is associated with anything but positive ideas; and in these cases it is possible that Bach reverted to something closer to Mattheson's view.[13]

Sometimes the confrontation of extreme sharps and flats suggests the idea of a "separation of body and soul." Such an instance is the first recitative of Cantata 48, "Ich elender Mensch, wer wird mich erlösen." Beginning in E flat, it modulates through F minor, C minor, and A flat to cadence in B flat minor for "Die Welt wird mir ein Siech- und Sterbehaus, der Leib muss seine Plagen bis zu dem Grabe mit sich tragen." Then, on "Allein, die Seele fühlet das stärkste Gift, damit sie angesteckt" Bach makes a shift, via the enharmonic reinterpretation of several tones, to E major (or F flat). Here torment both of body and soul are confronted, a context that suggests the extreme character of E major (Ex. 47).

In the A major cantata "Du Friedefürst, Herr Jesu Christ" (No. 116), a work that in some respects might be called an ascent/descent cantata, but in others just the reverse, E major appears in a context that emphasizes the extreme sharps. The first aria, "Ach, unaussprechlich ist die Not," in F sharp minor, modulates to G sharp minor with much dissonance and chromaticism in its middle section, "Kaum, dass wir noch in dieser Angst, wie du, o Jesu, selbst verlangst, zu Gott in deinem Namen schreien," a reference to the opening chorale, which describes Christ as "ein starker Nothelfer" and ends "Drum wir allein im Namen dein zu deinem Vater schreien." Then, after modulation to E in the first recitative, the E major vocal trio, "Ach, wir bekennen unsre Schuld und bitten nichts als um Geduld und um dein

10. Mattheson, *Das neu-eröffnete Orchestre,* pp. 232–33.
11. Mattheson, *Das neu-eröffnete Orchestre,* pp. 233–53.
12. Mattheson, *Das neu-eröffnete Orchestre,* p. 250 (author's translation).
13. An instance of this kind of E major occurs in the bass aria with obbligato cello, "Wer bist du," from the Weimar cantata, "Bereitet die Wege, bereitet die Bahn" (BWV 132). The cantata exhorts man to seek self-knowledge in his conscience and the Law, both of which will confirm him as "a child of wrath in Satan's net, a false and hypocritical Christian."

unermesslich Lieben," marks the apex of the work, in which the acknowledgment of sin that Luther made central to the dynamic of faith is heard in combination with the slowly descending chromatic tetrachord, broken into "sigh" figures for "um Geduld." In this piece we can see something of the dualistic character of the deeper sharps. The cry of torment to God is all that was *unaussprechlich* in the first aria, while the reference to Jesus' love appeared in the intervening recitative in association with the move to E. The trio divides into four sections, the first, third, and

EXAMPLE 47.　　　Cantata 48: excerpt from first recitative

Violins 1, 2
Viola

Alto

Basso continuo

Die Welt wird mir ein Siech- und Ster - be -

-haus, der Leib muss sei-ne Pla-gen bis zu dem Gra-be mit sich tra-gen. Al-

-lein, die See-le füh-let das stärk-ste Gift, da-mit sie an-ge - stek-ket;

fourth based on the above-mentioned text, the second comprising the B section of the da capo text: "Es brach ja dein erbarmend Herz, als der gefallnen Schmerz, dich zu uns in die Welt getrieben." In the first section the words "um Geduld," imitated between the soprano and alto, set up a falling circle of fifths beginning on G sharp that reaches ultimately to G major, then suddenly turns to B major for "und um dein unermesslich Lieben." In Lutheran theology love is always described as motivating the incarnation (the opening chorale emphasizes the two natures of Jesus: "wahr' Mensch und wahrer Gott"), and the recitative brings out the love of Jesus, the *Friedefürst*, as counterimage to God the judge in the first aria. The second section of the trio provides the image of the incarnation and redemption in a huge descent/ascent pattern that takes the B major close of the preceding section as the dominant of E minor and from there moves down to A minor ("dich zu uns in die Welt getrieben"), before moving in measured stages back up to close in C sharp minor. The first section is repeated, moving once again to G and closing in B major, and a somewhat shortened form serves as the final section, now closing in E. Within the second section the sharpest dissonances describe the pain of humanity as motivating the incarnation.

The basic elements of Luther's Passion Sermon—human tribulation and acknowledgment of sin, prayer, God's judgment, and Jesus' love—underlie the meditative progressions of many of Bach cantatas as well as the *St. Matthew Passion*.[14] As we saw in Cantata 12, these ideas are closely linked to what may be called an allegorical dynamic of increasing faith that goes hand in hand with the rising sequence of keys in its tonal plan. In the case of "Du Friedefürst" the acknowledgment of sin is treated as the apex rather than the nadir of the work as it is, for example, in the F minor arioso dialogue "O Schmerz" from the *St. Matthew Passion*. Acknowledgment of guilt is also linked with Jesus' love in the key design of "Ach, wir bekennen unsre Schuld": that is, the endings of the three main sections turn to B and E major as the text turns to love. Modulation downward, however, is associated with both the human plea for God's forebearance ("und bitten nichts als um Geduld") and the idea that human suffering broke God's merciful heart and prompted the incarnation. Bach begins the preceding recitative in A, with the opening phrase of the chorale "Du Friedefürst" in the basso coninuo ("Gedenke doch, o Jesu, dass du noch ein Fürst des Friedens heissest!"), then transposes the chorale phrase down to D in an unmistakable sign of the merciful side of God that counteracts the F sharp minor and G sharp minor of the preceding aria. After arriving on D the text "Aus Liebe wolltest du dein Wort uns senden" immediately brings in E major, setting up the trio; the effect is very similar to that in Cantata 60. The move from F sharp minor to G sharp minor in the aria represents a false move

14. See the discussions of Luther's sermon in connection with Cantata 12 (pp. 135–37, above) and the *St. Matthew Passion* (Chapter 12, pp. 347 and 348–55).

upward, prompted by fear, while the E major enters as a point of resolution. Acknowledgment of sin is a positive step toward redemption, operating in conjunction with Jesus' work. In this context the octave leap upward of the voices on the opening phrase "Ach, wir bekennen unsre Schuld" and the gradual diatonic descent might suggest, along with the quasi-canonic imitation, the paradoxical nature of Lutheran dogma that holds that the pain of sin is joined to a release from sin. The same dualism underlies the meaning of the E major chorus, "O Mensch, bewein dein Sünde gross," ending Part One of the *St. Matthew Passion,* a movement that is at once a lamento and the culmination of an ascent to E with predominantly positive associations.

The final recitative of "Du Friedefürst" begins in G sharp minor with the words "Ach, lass uns durch die *scharfen* Ruten," moving downward to C sharp minor for "nicht all zu heftig bluten" and continuing downward to end in A as the text prays for peace and the final chorale (in A) prays for spiritual enlightenment and grace. Once again the G sharp minor represents an extreme torment for mankind. As with the progression upward to E major in the *St. Matthew Passion,* the same dualism arises here as the significant modulation to G sharp minor is made.[15] In such places the dualism of *durus* as hard and harsh on the one hand and strong and positive on the other is evident.

The same dualism is found in the final anabasis cantata to be discussed here, "Leichtgesinnte Flattergeister" (No. 181), for Sexagesima Sunday, which moves upward in five movements from E minor (aria), through B minor (recitative ending and aria), to D major (recitative ending and final chorus). The message centers around the Gospel for the day, the parable of God's word as a seed falling on either poor or good soil. Images comparing the human heart to that soil run throughout the work: *Felsenherzen* (no. 2), *Dornen* (no. 3), *guten Lande* (no. 4), *Süssigkeiten schmecket* (no. 4), "ein fruchtbar gutes Land in unsern Herzen zu bereiten" (no. 5). The first two arias (nos. 1 and 3) deal with the qualities of those who reject the Word: in "Leichtgesinnter Flattergeister" Bach has the instrumentarium of flute, oboe, and strings play staccato throughout to represent frivolity, while "Der schädlichen Dornen," which unfortunately lacks one or more instrumental parts, is marked "piano e staccato per tutto."[16] The second recitative (no. 4) marks the shift from disregard of the Word to the positive imagery of the "good land" that brings forth "sweetness," turning to D major for the anticipation of the coming life. In contrast with the light sonority of the minor-key arias, the full instrumentarium of the final chorus in D is augmented by a trumpet part in a joyful prayer for God to preserve his Word, the *Herzens Trost,* for all times.

---

15. The modulation is discussed below, p. 394; see also Ex. 90a.
16. Dürr, *Die Kantaten,* p. 213.

EXAMPLE 48.   Cantata 181: ending of first recitative

The devices of the tonal ascent and turn from minor to major have all been encountered in other cantatas. More interesting here is the manner in which the ascent is initiated at the end of the first recitative. At first the narrative moves downward from E minor, approaching an A minor cadence though its subdominant in "den Schaden nicht versteht noch glaubt." The succeeding arioso then moves sharpward (E minor, B minor) in imitative dissonance-resolution patterns reminiscent of the opening chorus of "Ich hatte viel Bekümmernis," diverting the arrival at B minor to a low D sharp in the bass. Then the chord of the diminished seventh above D sharp and the dominant seventh on G sharp (i.e., dominant functions to E minor and C sharp, respectively) are emphasized; the bass outlines the tones of the latter chord, working its way down to the low B sharp (enharmonically C, the bottom of the normal pitch spectrum). From this point to the final bass f sharp the chromatic notes between b sharp and f sharp appear in a variety of intervals that would have been identified as the music-rhetorical figures *passus duriusculus* and *saltus duriusculus*: diminished octave, diminished fifth, chromatic semitone. Cross-relations occur with some of the changes of harmony. The text throughout this passage refers to the rocks split apart by Jesus' last words, the stone rolled away from Jesus' tomb, and the rock from which Moses brought forth water, ending "Willst du, o Herz, noch härter sein?" (Ex. 48). This ending is but one of the places where Bach associates sharps with the *cantus durus* to allegorize hard-heartedness.[17] As all these works show, the sharps can be *scharf* and *hart,* allegorizing a *schwerer Gang,* but the ascent, once attained, is positive.

Catabasis Cantatas

An emphasis on continuous motion in either the sharp or flat direction does not necessarily indicate either an increasingly hopeful or increasingly despairing series of affections. If that were so, the pattern of tonal catabasis would appear only in works that eventually brought about its reversal. And, although tonal catabasis most often appears in works where the descent is reversed, cantatas exist in which descent has a positive meaning, even descent from a major to a minor key, which happens to be the commonest form of this type. All eight catabasis cantatas to be considered here end in minor, even though six begin in major. In this respect, the Leipzig catabasis cantatas differ from "Erschallet, ihr Lieder," but in several other ways they share a community of ideas with Bach's Weimar work. In them the descent—almost always by thirds—is most commonly associated with some kind of shift from the divine to the human. Thus two cantatas (Nos. 73, 108), like "Erschallet, ihr Lieder," treat the descent of the Spirit; four of the cantatas (Nos. 73, 108, 148, 158) speak of the Spirit (or God) controlling the individual being. Two cantatas (Nos. 102, 158) juxtapose the anticipation of eternity with the necessity of change now. The concept of sinking—either of God's spirit into man or of man into God's will—appears in four cantatas (Nos. 73, 108, 148, 179), and the ability of God to see into the heart in three (Nos. 77, 102, 136). The notion of the flesh or of human incompleteness underlies four of the tonal descent patterns (Nos. 77, 102, 136, 179), and the indwelling of God is prominent in two (Nos. 77, 148). From these general associations we can conclude that Bach chose tonal catabasis when the

17. In the F sharp minor arias, "Auch die harte Kreuzesreise" of Cantata 123 and "Und wenn der harte Todesschlag" from Cantata 124, Bach introduces sharp accidentals and *salti duriusculi* to underscore the hardness. Two instances from the *St. Matthew Passion* (Pilate's sudden modulation on "Hörest du nicht, wie hart sie dich verklagen?" and the biting dissonance followed by an enharmonic change on "und muss viel härter sein" from "Erbarm es Gott") are discussed below (pp. 259–60, 418, and 419).

texts suggested mankind's awareness of the human condition and the need to submit to God's will.

Cantata 179, "Siehe zu, dass deine Gottesfurcht nicht Heuchelei sei," is particularly illustrative of the quality of awareness of the human condition. Its opening movement, in G major, a motet-style fugue with *colla parte* instruments, gives a dictum-like warning against hypocrisy, which is viewed chiefly in terms of a false humanity that disguises arrogant pride; the downward direction of the cantata, ending in A minor, is closely allied to the true humility that acknowledges human sinfulness. The chorus represents this antithesis, where the main theme is continually answered by its inversion. Then a second theme, "und diene Gott nicht mit falschem Herzen" appears in a series of rising-fifth entries—G, D, a, e, b, f sharp—that was undoubtedly intended to suggest the quality of human aspiration. The theme itself contains an internal antithesis between the ascending major triad ("und diene Gott") and the descending chromatic tetrachord ("nicht mit falschem Herzen"). The various themes are then combined, and for the ending of the movement Bach colors the tonality with tones from the flat (minor) side of the key. In later years Bach reused this chorus as the Kyrie of the G major *Missa Brevis,* where the juxtapositions of diatonicism and chromaticism between the first theme and its counterpoint, then of the triadic and chromatic halves of the second theme, were linked to the address to God ("Kyrie" and "Christe") versus the prayer for mercy ("eleison").

In the cantata the following recitative moves to B minor, in a condemnation of widespread hypocrisy. The relationship between the ensuing E minor aria, "Falscher Heuchler Ebenbild können Sodoms Äpfel heissen," and Bach's parodied version from the *Missa Brevis,* "Quoniam tu solus sanctus," underscores the intent of the original form of the aria to represent the appealing appearance, not the falseness, of hypocrisy. As Bach's text tells us, the apple of Sodom symbolized everything that was filthy on the inside and beautiful on the outside ("die mit Unflath angefüllt und von aussen herrlich gleissen"). In the cantata, the ornate instrumental melody of the aria represented the beautiful appearance, and in the Mass, the majesty of Christ. In the cantata, however, the descending tonal plan conveyed the inner truth. The recitative "Wer so von innen wie von aussen ist, der heisst ein wahrer Christ" announces the truth immediately, explaining that humility (*Demuth*) characterizes the true Christian as it did the tax collector in the temple as described in the Gospel, and concluding, "Bekenne Gott in Demuth deine Sünden, so kannst du Gnad' und Hülfe finden." To convey humility the tonality moves downward to cadence in D minor and ends in C major for the "Gnad' und Hülfe."

The ensuing A minor aria, "Liebster Gott, erbarme dich," for two oboes da caccia, soprano, and basso continuo, is the spiritual core of the work, the point at which mankind acknowledges its sinfulness. Within the aria Bach modulates to flat keys three times, first at "lass mir Trost und Gnad' erscheinen" (d minor), then for "Meine Sünden kränken mich" (G minor), and finally in a very striking manner at "hilf mir, Jesu, Gottes Lamm, ich versink' in tiefen Schlamm" (C minor) (Ex. 49). When Bach parodied this aria for the "Qui tollis" of the A major *Missa Brevis,* this passage became "suscipe deprecationem nostram," the aria as a whole expressing the sinful human condition in need of God's aid. For the reworking Bach omitted the basso continuo, replacing it with unison violins and violas in the upper octave, undoubtedly to express increased intimacy; its new key, B minor, became the center of a descent/ascent plan for the "Gloria": A, f sharp, *b,* D, A. The tonal plan of Cantata 179 remains in A minor, however, with the chorale verse "Ich armer Mensch, ich armer Sünder" ending "Erbarme dich, erbarme dich, Gott mein Erbarmer, über mich."

Bach's first cantata for the third Sunday in Epiphany, "Herr, wie du willt, so schicks mit mir" (BWV 73, 1724), is built on a descent from G minor through E flat major to three successive movements in C minor. The image of descent is clearly expressed in the E flat aria, "Ach senke doch den Geist der Freuden dem Herzen ein," in the recitative that modualtes to C minor, ending "Allein ein Christ, in Gottes Geist gelehrt, lernt sich in Gottes Willen senken," in the images of the pain of death pressing the sighs out of the heart and lying down in the dust and ashes that dominate the first section of the C minor aria, and in the line "auch Gott, der heil'ge Geist, im Glauben uns regieret," from the C minor chorale. At issue here is the relinquishing of the self-determining will to God's will, made manifest in the Holy Spirit. God's will, as the opening chorus states, is a "sealed book" to man, its blessings appearing as a curse, and often demanding a life of suffering. The descent plan of "Herr, wie du willt" mirrors man's submission.

In Cantata 108, "Es ist euch gut, dass ich hingehe," anticipation of the Spirit's descent and the relinquishing to it of all self-determination—"Dein Geist wird mich also regieren" (rec.), "Dein Geist, den Gott vom Himmel gibt, der leitet alles, was ihn liebt, auf wohlgebähntem Wege" (final chorale)—prompts a plan of descent from A major (chorus) through F sharp minor (aria) and D major (recitative and aria) to B minor (aria and chorale). Cantatas emphasizing these qualities can also make a return ascent. In Cantata 72, "Alles nur nach Gottes Willen" (1726), for example, after the opening A minor chorus, the second movement, a complex of recitative, arioso, and aria, moves downward from its first words, "O sel'ger Christ, der allzeit seinen Willen in Gottes Willen *senkt.*" The aria, in D minor, emphasizes the weak individual's submission to Christ. The following recitative brings out Jesus' help, through faith, in suffering and oppression; near the end of the phrase "Er stärkt, was schwach" moves to close in G minor as if to illustrate human weakness; but with the final G major chord treated as the dominant of the ensuing C major aria, "Mein Jesus will es tun," the cantata can close in its original key of A minor. Here the flat region is associated with human weakness, the relative major with Jesus' aid.

Cantata 148, "Bringet dem Herrn Ehre seines Namens," moves downward from an appropriately imposing opening chorus in D with clarino through a B minor

EXAMPLE 49.   Cantata 179: excerpt from aria "Liebster Gott, erbarme dich"

aria, G major recitative and aria, to the E minor beginning of the second recitative (no. 5). Within the recitative the modulatory direction is then reversed to end in F sharp minor, the key of the final chorale. Although the reversal and higher ending of Cantata 148 might qualify it for one of the other categories, its textual relationships to several other catabasis cantatas are more significant. Here the descent is associated with increasing intimacy with God, first through the teaching of the church on the Sabbath (no. 2), then, as the close of the first recitative indicates, through God's indwelling in the individual ("Denn Gott wohnt selbst in mir"). The latter idea is expanded in the alto aria with two oboes d'amore and oboe da caccia, "Mund und Herze steht dir offen, Höchster, senke dich hinein! Ich in dich, und du in mich; Glaube, Liebe, Dulden, Hoffen soll mein Ruhebette sein," a sentiment that is very close to that of "Erschallet, ihr Lieder." And the beginning of the second recitative reiterates the prayer: "Bleib auch, mein Gott, in mir" (E minor). The change of direction coincides with the appearance of the Spirit and the anticipation of eternity:

Und gib mir deinen Geist, der mich nach deinem Wort regiere, dass ich so einen Wandel führe, der dir gefällig heisst, damit ich nach der Zeit in deiner Herrlichkeit, mein lieber Gott, mit dir den grossen Sabbat möge halten.

An impressive instance of tonal catabasis in Bach's oeuvre appears in a work whose opening chorus has been much discussed in the Bach literature for its other allegorical qualities: Cantata 77, "Du sollst Gott, deinen Herren, lieben."[18] In this cantata the tonal descent—from G Mixolydian through C major and A minor to D minor—is unequivocally linked to the shift from the sphere of God to that of man; the D minor aria (no. 5) makes the emphasis on the human condition clear: "Ach, es bleibt in meiner Liebe lauter Unvollkommenheit!" Bach left the final D minor chorale untexted, but given the subject of the cantata the intended verse must have been "Herr, durch den Glauben wohn in mir," expressing a desire for God's indwelling once again.[19]

There are too many allegorical details in the opening chorale fantasia to discuss here. Yet two frequently overlooked musical devices are of the greatest importance: the contrast between the spheres of God and man that Bach intended to convey through the flat modulation toward the end of the movement and the notation of the basso continuo in the alto clef—that is, a *bassetchen* line—whenever the cho-

18. See Arnold Schering, "Bach und das Symbol, insbesondere die Symbolik seines Kanons," *Bach-Jahrbuch* 22 (1925): 53–59; Bukofzer, "Allegory," pp. 15–18; Gerhard Herz, "Thoughts on the First Movement of Johann Sebastian Bach's Cantata No. 77, "Du sollst Gott, deinen Herren, lieben," in *Essays on J. S. Bach* (Ann Arbor, 1985), pp. 205–17.

19. Dürr, *Die Kantaten*, p. 423.

rale cantus firmus does not appear in the bass. This latter device, like the similar procedure in the opening chorus of Cantata 135, depicts the two sides that God presents to man, the stern judge and the merciful, loving redeemer.[20] The Epistle for the thirteenth Sunday after Trinity (Gal. 3:15–22) presents this dualism in the form of Paul's juxtaposition of the Law with God's covenant made to Abraham and fulfilled through faith in Christ. This, in combination with the message of the gospel (the parable of the good Samaritan and Jesus' confirming love as the meaning of the Law), inspired Bach to create a chorale fantasia on the Ten Commandments chorale, "Es sind die heil'gen zehn Gebot," in which the canonic nature of the Law is joined to the command to love God and one's neighbor. There are, therefore, levels of dualism in this work—the spehres of God and man, the Law versus love (and faith)—while the paradoxical aspect of the command to love (or to believe) underlies the whole.

Bach derived the means to allegorize these ideas directly from the modal character of the Ten Commandments chorale, which is in G Mixolydian although its third line ends on F and its fifth and last line contains prominent B flats. Bach welcomed this expressive coloring of the melody, dominating the tonal character of the ending of the movement by flats, just as he does in the larger setting of this chorale in *Clavierübung III*.[21] He also anticipates the turn to flats earlier in the movement, in the first interlude. The allegory is the bringing down of man through the Law, which humbles him with the knowledge of his inability to fulfill God's commands. This idea is realized at the structural level through the descending tonal plan, with the *Unvollkommenheit* of the D minor aria providing an explicit statement. Both arias are simple in tone after such a complex opening movement; the D minor aria has an especially simple character. The return of the tromba da tirarsi here, after its playing of the chorale in the opening movement, is a deliberate reminder of the shift; its prominent b″ flats and c″ sharps indicate the realm of imperfect intervals. Although the tonal allegory of this cantata conveys our remaining in the imperfect sphere of human existence, there are nevertheless indications of ultimate hope: the ascent of the bass on the last line of the final chorale is one such. In the opening movement Bach extends the final G of the bass cantus firmus to a ten-bar(!) pedal above which the tromba da tirarsi plays the entire chorale, while the second part of the text is sung for the only time in the movement: "und deinen Nächsten als dich selbst." Here the G minor changes to major for the last two bars, indicating the ultimate reward of love. But the recitative preceding the final aria provides the most striking instance; Bach begins in E minor and contradicts the

20. The *bassetchen* texture is used in the aria "Aus Liebe will mein Heiland sterben" from the *St. Matthew Passion* for a similar purpose (see Chapter 12).

21. The setting from *Clavierübung III* is in G Mixolydian ending in a G minor colored by its subdominant (C minor).

basic modulatory direction of the work by moving up to B minor for a prayer that the individual escape the hard-heartedness of people who pass by those in need ("damit ich nicht bei ihm vorübergeh und ihn in seiner Not nicht lasse"), then closes in an optimistic G major for anticipation of the reward for the future life ("so wirst du mir dereinst das Freudenleben nach meinem Wunsch, jedoch aus Gnaden geben").

In other cantatas the anticipation of eternity may be more prominent still, yet they descend to minor keys at the end. Cantata 186, "Ärgre dich, o Seele, nicht," makes the familiar ascent by thirds—g, B flat, d, F—in its first part, then descends to C minor in Part Two, a movement that expresses joy in the expectation of the afterlife. Bach rounds off the structure with another verse of the F major chorale that ended Part One, but the catabasis in Part Two completes the message given in Part One.[22] In Cantata 158, "Der Friede sei mit dir," Jesus' appearance to the apostles in Jerusalem no doubt prompted the D major beginning of the opening recitative; but the piece modulates immediately to relate the reaction of the anxious individual to Jesus' presence, and the recitative ends in G. The following movement is a soprano/bass duet with an ornate solo violin part, the soprano (doubled by oboe) singing Rosenmüller's "Welt, ade! ich bin dein müde," and the bass a series of troped phrases dominated by longing for eternity ("Salems Hütten") and the heavenly crown. A bass recitative in E minor then gives the key to the descent plan: "Nun Herr, regiere meinen Sinn, damit ich auf der Welt, so lang' es dir mich hier zu lassen noch gefällt, ein Kind des Friedens bin, und lass mich zu dir aus meinen Leiden wie Simeon in Frieden scheiden!" The key ideas here are expressed in the words "regiere meinen Sinn" and "auf der Welt," both expressions indicating that the desire for eternity is contained within a prayer for God's aid in the present life. The cadence at the end of this phrase is to G once again, but the bass descends over an octave and a half; then the arioso continuation repeats the text that ended the preceding aria, but in E minor: "Da bleib' ich, da hab' ich Vergnügen zu wohnen, da prang' ich gezieret mit himmlischen Kronen." The final E minor chorale, "Hier ist das rechte Osterlamm" (a verse of "Christ lag in Todesbanden"), confirms the meaning of the descent and the G major/E minor relationship in the work as the anticipation of eternity in the present life.

Likewise, Cantata 136, "Erforsche mich, Gott, und erfahre mein Herz," makes an overall descent from A major to B minor, the opening chorus with its majestic horn-call theme in a pastorale-style movement creating a picture of an all-powerful but merciful God concerned with the individual being. The first recitative modulates downward at first (B minor, F sharp minor), in keeping with lamentation over the curse that prevents the human heart from bringing forth good fruits. But

22. This work is discussed in greater detail in Chapter 8.

the modulatory direction changes, ending in C sharp minor, with the description of the prevalent hypocrisy of the world and the anticipation of the time of judgment. The F sharp minor aria, "Es kommt ein Tag," elaborates on the idea of coming judgment, and the recitative (no. 4) moves down to B minor, indicating that those who are purified by Jesus' blood and joined with him in faith, although sickened by sin, will escape the *hartes Urteil*. A tenor/bass aria duetto in B minor continues this idea, explaining mankind's *Sünden Flecken* as the outcome of the fall, and Jesus' wounds, the mighty torrent of blood, as the source of purification. The B minor chorale, "Dein Blut, der edle Saft," continues in like manner. Bach wanted the descending plan to emphasize the purification of the soul in the realm of the flesh, and the middle section of the duet, "Allein, wer sich zu Jesu Wunden, dem grossen Strom gefunden, wird wieder rein gemacht," seems to point up this meaning. From a descending-fifth theme of the main section Bach devised a bass pattern of arpeggio ascent through an octave followed by descent; he then passed this through a circle-of-fifths sequence—f sharp, b, e, a, d, G—as if to indicate the positive meaning of the idea of descent.

One last cantata of this type may be considered as an example of Bach's choosing the deeper flat keys to emphasize the urgent need to repent in the present life. Cantata 102, "Herr, deine Augen sehen nach dem Glauben," moves in its first part from G minor to E flat, via a recitative ending in B flat minor ("so geht er ihn ins Herzens Dünkel hin") and the unusually tormented aria, "Weh der Seele, die den Schaden nicht mehr kennt," in F minor. Part Two then returns to G minor for the aria "Erschrecke doch, du allzusichre Seele," and moves to C minor and a series of flat keys in the accompanied recitative "Beim warten ist Gefahr," ending with two chorale verses in C minor: "Heut' lebst du, heut' bekehre dich" and "Hilf, o Herr Jesu, hilf du mir, dass ich noch heute komm zu dir." As these titles indicate, the work is completely admonitory. With virtually no emphasis on the hopeful side of the anticipation of eternity, the ending of the verse "Heut' lebst du"—"So du nun stirbest ohne Buss, dein Leib und Seel dort brennen muss"—envisages the eternal torment of the unrepentant. In this respect it recalls Cantata 20, "O Ewigkeit, du Donnerwort," where the move to flats was connected to a similar attempt to instill fear so that people would live in readiness for death. And the character of "Weh der Seele" brings to mind the character of the first part of "Ich hatte viel Bekümmernis." Those works, however, had introduced tonal anabasis, in one case as the vision of a blessed afterlife and in the other as the means of shocking mankind with the fear of judgment and eternal torment. "Herr, deine Augen," however, makes no attempt to hold out hope to underscore the seriousness of the foremost theme: some members of humanity are so hard-hearted that they cannot recognize their condition and do not feel the torments heaped upon them. The magnificent opening chorus depicts the unfelt blows by a staccato fugue theme, broken twice by rests in the middle of the word *schlägest,* and another fugue theme represents the hard-heartedness of the unrepentant by two leaps of a tritone to sharpened notes for

EXAMPLE 50.   Cantata 102: theme from opening chorus

Sie   ha - ben ein här - ter An - ge - sicht denn   ein Fels

härter and *Fels* (Ex. 50). The severest points of the work come in the first recitative and the F minor aria that follows. After lamenting the loss of both God's image in mankind and the power of his word, the recitative moves to the deep flat-minor keys to illustrate the darkness of heart (B flat minor) that is the final tribulation given by God to the severely unrepentent. After the tortured expressive sphere of "Weh der Seele," the long E flat arioso that closes Part One might be thought to introduce a more hopeful note. Against expectation, the persistent leaps of a seventh (sometimes in descending sequences) in several variants of the first theme, the obstinate repetition of elements within the third theme ("Du aber nach deinem ver-stockten und unbussfertigen Herzen häufest dir selbst den Zorn auf den Tag des Zorns"), and several other similar details, all represent man's despising God's gift of grace (the E flat itself, perhaps). In fact, Cantata 102 is the classic example of Bach's choosing tonal catabasis in conjunction with the flat-minor key sphere to depict the gravity of the human condition.

Ascent/Descent Cantatas

The two most characteristic cantatas of this fourth and last basic type, "Hercules auf dem Scheidewege" (No. 213) and "Wo Gott, der Herr, nicht bei uns hält" (No. 178), will be treated in the following chapters, since they belong to a group of works that treat reason within the context of Lutheranism, a theme that is impor-tant enough to deserve separate treatment. Knowing the association between rea-son and Lutheranism helps in understanding several of the remaining cantatas of the ascent/descent type, however, since it raises such issues as human aspiration in relation to God's glory.

A number of cantatas of the ascent/descent type (e.g., 28, 68, 111, 176) clearly associate upward modulation with God's glory, so that in a sense the upward/downward curve is an image comparable to that of the triadic theme of "Gott ist mein König." In Cantata 28, "Gottlob! nun geht das Jahr zu Ende" (written for the Sunday after Christmas, 1725), the rising sequence praises and thanks God for his past gifts and hopes for continuing blessings. From its initial A minor it ascends through C major (no. 2, chorus), and E minor (no. 3, arioso) to G and D major at the start of the fourth movement (rec.: "Gott ist ein Quell, wo lauter Güte fleusst;

Gott ist ein Licht, wo lauter Gnade scheinet") before returning through C major (no. 4, aria) to A minor (no. 5, chorale). Likewise, Cantata 111, "Was mein Gott will, das g'scheh' allzeit," for the third Sunday in Epiphany (1725), ascends from A minor (opening chorus) through E minor (first aria), to B minor (first rec.), then descends through G major (duet) and E minor (second rec.), back to A minor (ending of second rec. and final chorale). Here one does not sense a sinking into the will of God as in the other cantatas written for this Sunday. Rather, the majesty of God is the central idea, along with the elevating power of his will and the exhortation to the individual to trust in God. The ascent/descent plan provides an emblem of God's glory instead of man's submission, as in Cantata 73.

In Cantata 68, "Also hat Gott die Welt geliebt" (for the second day of Pentecost, 1725), the systematic rise from D minor to C major over the first four movements exults in God's love as manifested in Christ's incarnation. The arias "Mein gläubiges Herze" (F major) and "Du bist geboren mir zugute" (C major) are particularly joyful in tone. Both are parodies based on the Weimar Hunting Cantata (BWV 208), in which the aria "Ein Fürst ist seines Landes Pan" ("Du bist geboren") is one of the most overt of all Bach's paeans to the baroque ruler. The majestic character is evidently transformed into Cantata 68; the simple association of worldly and divine glory through the medium of music is not problematic. But the return to the original key is made in an unusual manner—within a single chorus that begins in A minor and ends in D minor—that reveals "Also hat Gott die Welt geliebt" as a more complicated representation of majesty than the earlier work. This chorus is set up as a double fugue in which the two subjects, "Wer an ihn gläubet, der wird nicht gerichtet" (A minor) and "wer aber nicht gläubet, der ist schon gerichtet" (D minor)—both rather severe in tone—are first heard separately, then in combination. These texts represent the tendency in the Gospel of John toward realized or present eschatology, that is, an eschatology that perceives the division of worlds in terms of above and below rather than present and future. Those who will never be judged already belong to the former world; those who are already judged belong to the latter. The combination section ends in A minor, but Bach sets the rest of the text—"denn er gläubet nicht an den Namen des eingebornen Sohnes Gottes"—continuing from the second phrase and negative in tone, as an appendage ending in D minor. After the two joyful arias no return to D minor could have sounded positive; Bach's ending brings out the Johannine division not only among the peoples of the world but between the worlds themselves in a manner that makes particularly clear the separation of God and man that has no place in the Hunting Cantata. The uncomplicated assertion of secular majesty in the latter work enabled Bach to reuse the music for an assertion of divine majesty. If there is any implication of equivalence in the transfer, it lies only in the ruler's unquestioned authority in his own sphere, a characteristically Lutheran idea. As Cantata 68 makes clear, however, there can be no interpretation of equivalence between the two spheres themselves.

Cantata 26, composed in Leipzig in 1724, illustrates the transience of human qualities with an ascent/descent plan culminating in the central aria, which is characterized by a mocking quality. It is associated here, however, not with the legitimate representatives of God on earth but with human aspiration and worldliness per se. The rapidly ascending and descending scales of the opening chorus of the Cantata, "Ach wie flüchtig, ach wie nichtig," in A minor, suggest the fleetingness of worldly achievement. A C major aria translates this idea into the rising and falling of waves ("So schnell ein rauschend Wasser schiesst, so eilen unser's Lebens Tage"), and a recitative moving from C major to E minor continues the dualism with carefully placed flattened and sharpened tones and tonal directions: "Die Freude wird zur Traurigkeit (B flat), die Schönheit (C sharp) fällt (B flat) als eine Blume, die grösste (B natural) Stärke wird geschwächt (E flat, cadence to C minor), and so on. The recitative closes, "Bald ist es aus mit Ehr und Ruhme, die Wissenschaft, und was ein Mensche dichtet, wird endlich durch das Grab vernichtet." Now a bass aria in E minor, gavotte-like in style and accompanied by three oboes(!), represents the foolishness of resting hopes in the world in a setting so pompous that it borders on the comic. The following recitative moves back down to A minor with tonal devices similar to the earlier one, and the final chorale (A minor) underscores the message of worldly transience. Throughout this cantata the recognition of the futility of human endeavor is always close to the surface.

The Lutheran baroque was not an age of humor and wit compared to the art of earlier and later times; its profundity is never revealed in the kind of cleverness we treasure in *The Marriage of Figaro* or a Haydn quartet, or, for that matter, in Shakespeare, where a deeper sense of wisdom comes from the assertion of purely human qualities. Often the closest it comes to wit is the rustic, even condescending, identification with lower classes that appears in the Peasant Cantata. The well-known earthiness of Luther's language—which Bach shares to a degree—has a directly serious quality that, while emphasizing a common humanity, conspicuously lacks any sense of human transcendence that appears in the best low comedy. Within the Bach cantatas the idea of *Witz* is something entirely different from "wittiness" as we know it; it is generally (as we will see in Cantata 178) a negative quality that conflicts with the established theological order. And this E minor aria is no exception; the extravagance of the three strutting oboes represents not worldly glory but a subtle form of caricature.

The ascent/descent pattern as well as the overall tonal plan of the melodic material of Cantata 176, "Es ist ein trotzig und verzagt Ding," presents a related but ultimately quite different meaning. The melodic line moves up from C minor (opening chorus) and G minor (recitative) to B flat (once again an aria in gavotte-like style, but without any trace of caricature), then returns through G minor (recitative) and E flat (aria) to C minor (chorale). Composed for Trinity Sunday, the cantata conveys through its ascent/descent plan the majesty and incomprehensibility of God, as expressed in the Epistle for the day. The Gospel for Trinity Sunday

(John 3:1–15), which provides the more immediate imagery, tells the story of Nicodemus, prominent man and disciple of Jesus who was, nevertheless, afraid of coming to Jesus by daylight. The contrast between Nicodemus (night) and Jesus (day) is taken up in the first recitative and aria "Dein sonst hell beliebter Schein soll vor mich umnebelt sein," with its ascent from C minor to B flat major. But, as the aria text makes clear, Jesus' glory is *umnebelt* by the darkness; the cantata is set in the deeper flat sphere, returning to close in a modal C minor chorale whose repeated *Stollen* cadence in F minor. The *Abgesang* of this chorale presents a striking ascent/descent melodic curve over the first four of its five phrases, from the initial f′ to g″ and back to f′ for the F minor cadence of the fourth, penultimate phrase. The impression created is that the chorale could end at this point, in the subdominant. The melody of the final phrase, however, leaps up an octave, breaking the melodic continuity of the preceding phrases and cadencing at high pitch with an assertion of the nature of the Trinity, "ein Wesen, drei Personen." In this way the chorale sets God himself apart from his relationship to man, with which the preceding line ends ("der Frommer Schütz und Retter"). Although the shape of Cantata 176 is somewhat related to the symmetrical ascent/descent of the well-known "Gott ist mein König" theme, it is primarily a representation of human qualities.

The fugal opening chorus treats the qualities of the human heart as described by Jeremiah: "Es ist ein trotzig und verzagt Ding um aller Menschen Herze."[23] In German, much more than in English, the attributes described by *trotzig* (stubborn, obstinate, willful) and *verzagt* (discouraging, dejected, timorous) set up an antithesis, the former suggesting human aggression and aspiration, the latter human weakness. And of course the two are ultimately the same. As the second recitative makes clear, Nicodemus's weakness in coming forth only by night can be seen positively—an acknowledgment of human weakness and an inability to comprehend God's ways. Bach's opening theme represents human aspiration with an emphatic ascending minor triad reminiscent of "Bestelle dein Haus" from the "Actus Tragicus" (Ex. 51). The line then rushes upward to the minor ninth (at *trotzig*), but at the peak of its ascent the tone changes to chromatic appoggiatura "sigh" figures that descend in a very different character but that nevertheless suggests an overall symmetrical pattern in its equalling the length of the ascent and descending minor triad conclusion. Bach underscores the antithesis by making the strings play forte concitato-like figures as accompaniment to the first half and sustained piano chords to the second. In the B flat aria short ascent/descent figures of the type used to represent the rainbow in the aria "Erwäge" from the *St. John Passion* appear prominently for "Niemand kann die Wunder thun." Then the first theme of the E flat aria

23. As Dürr (*Die Kantaten*, p. 320) points out, Mariane von Ziegler, librettist of Bach's cantata, interprets the story of Nicodemus's coming forth by night as told in the Gospel for the day (John 3:1–15) as a general human tendency; hence the opening motto from Jeremiah 17:9.

EXAMPLE 51.   Cantata 176: beginning of opening movement

("Ermuntert euch, furchtsam' und schüchterne Sinne") provides another version
of the ascent/descent contour from the opening movement, its first half representing "Ermuntert euch" and its second "furchtsam' und schüchterne Sinne" (Ex.
52). A descending appoggiatura line on *furchtsam* expands in the instrumental interludes until in measures 66–69 it recapitulates the *verzagt* theme (Ex. 51) from the
opening movement above the descending chromatic tetrachord (Ex. 53). The aria
as a whole is not a da capo. For the final section in praise of the Trinity Bach joins
the ascent/descent of the opening chorus and this aria in a very long line that begins
in C minor and ends in E flat and rushes upward, eventually moving beyond the D
flat to E flat before returning downward (Ex. 54). The final chorale returns the idea
of ascent/descent to the appropriate human perspective.

An explicit representation of glory following a different pattern of ascent/descent
is the ascending canon *per tonos* of the *Musical Offering,* which Bach dedicated to

EXAMPLE 52.   Cantata 176: theme of first aria

Er - mun-tert euch, furcht-sam' und schüch-ter - ne _ Sin-ne,

EXAMPLE 53.   Cantata 176: excerpt from first aria

EXAMPLE 54.   Cantata 176: excerpt from final section of first aria

ward' ich dort o - ben mit Dan-ken und Lo -

- ben Va - ter, Sohn und

heil' - gen _____ Geist ___

Frederick the Great with the inscription, "As the modulation ascends so may the King's glory increase" (Ascendenteque Modulatione ascendat Gloria Regis). As is well known, this piece descends to its original key of C minor only in tonal terms, for the pitch keeps rising. The key sequence for one ascending octave is C minor, D minor, E minor, F sharp minor, G sharp minor [A flat minor], B flat minor, and C minor; but with every statement of the theme being answered in canon at the fifth, a secondary sequence—g, a, b, c sharp, e flat, f, g—shadows the first, supplying the accompanying theme on the remaining six tones as well. Therefore, a clear dichotomy exists between rising pitch and returning key. The meaning can only be that of the split between outward, worldly glory—represented by the image in microcosm of the circle of keys—and the inner subjection of all humanity, even kings, to death. The key of C minor, the falling chromaticism of the theme, and, above all, the registral finiteness of a canon that, taken superficially, might seem to represent infinity, all represent the human condition, the "mirror of our incompleteness and imperfection in this life."[24]

Two Cantatas on Faith: BWV 109 and 38

The Gospel for the twenty-first Sunday after Trinity relates a story of faith, the healing of the king's son as told by John (4:47–54). Bach's first two cantatas for this Sunday—BWV 109, "Ich glaube, lieber Herr, hilf meinem Unglauben" (1723), and BWV 38, "Aus tiefer Not schrei ich zu dir" (1724)—reveal fascinating uses of tonality that provide these works with a definite Lutheran *scopus*. "Ich glaube, lieber Herr," in contrast to "Es ist das Heil" (see Chapter 6, pp. 163–64), presents faith in the personal terms of inner conflict, the experience now, rather than the doctrine of faith. In this work tonality, along with other musical elements, allegorizes doubt and uncertainty and their ultimate resolution in faith as a gift of God, granted only after a period of torment. The form is closed tonally, but we do not recognize it as such until the end. This work, then, evaluates the spirit of the theological catch phrase "Ende gut, Alles gut," which we have encountered already in two cantatas (Nos. 27 and 156). Cantata 109 works by antithesis, its opposites represented in terms of sharp and flat keys and tonal directions. Its prologue, in D minor, is followed by a recitative of wavering doubt that moves a tritone from beginning (B flat) to end (E minor); the keys of the tonal extremes of this movement, and of the whole cantata, serve as dual tonal centers in the *St. Matthew Passion*: E minor and C minor (the latter a pronounced melodic and tonal catabasis for "Ach nein! ich sinke schon zur Erden vor Sorge, dass sie mich zu Boden stürzt"). Bach uses shifting (or conflicting) tonal direction in this recitative to great effect. Its seven phrases alternate between positive and negative feelings with regard to faith and God's aid. Bach adopts the unique device of marking dynamics that alternate, phrase by phrase, between forte and piano (Ex. 55). In addition, he associates melodic catabasis and modulation in the flat direction with phrases of fear and hopelessness (the soft phrases), melodic anabasis and sharpward modulation with positive phrases (forte) until the very end, when the recitative turns to E minor for the last two phrases in succession: "Ach nein! es bleibt mir um Trost sehr bange, ach Herr! wie lange?" Up to this point, however, no resolution is possible, and the aria that follows, in E minor, is full of doubt, fear, and torment.

At this point also the very key is in doubt; one chorus has been in a flat key, D minor, voicing the central prayer for faith; a recitative has been tonally unstable; and an aria has been in sharps, E minor, revealing inner torment. The intervening key, A minor, has not been sounded. And Bach—deliberately, I am sure—reverses

---

24. Werckmeister, *Musicae mathematicae*, p. 141 (author's translation).

EXAMPLE 55.   Cantata 109: first recitative (complete)

EXAMPLE 55   *continued*

the relative allegorical meanings of the sharps and flats from the recitative (sharp direction, positive; flat, negative) to the closed movements (flats as positive; sharps as negative). We need some kind of reconciliation to make sense of the figurative use of tonality. The next recitative turns back to D minor (from B minor) with words of trust in Jesus, and an F major aria continues the message of assurance, "Der Heiland kennet ja die Seinen, wenn ihre Hoffnung hilflos liegt. Wenn Fleisch und Geist in ihnen streiten, so steht er ihnen selbst zur Seiten, damit zuletzt der Glaube siegt." The key required to express this last idea, A minor, is now heard prominently in the closing phrases of the aria's middle section, on "damit zuletzt der Glaube siegt." As in Cantata 91, Bach seems to perceive the neutral key of A minor as joining sharps and flats, just as faith joins the worlds of spirit and flesh. At the start of the final chorale Bach makes the strings hold the note A for two bars, even though at first the key appears to be D minor. That is a deception; the chorale ultimately confirms A minor as tonic, thereby placing the foregoing keys within the larger perspective of the ending of the cantata. The allegory is obvious: coming only after a period of torment, faith puts an end to doubt and reveals the true and heretofore hidden meaning of our suffering.

The tonal narrative, so to speak, which Bach sets in parallel with the sequence of textual events in "Ich glaube, lieber Herr," demands that the cantata end in A minor. Bach imparts a jubilant tone to his setting of the old chorale melody via its lively instrumental accompaniment in order to allegorize the resolution it effects. The original context of this movement—the seventh verse of "Durch Adams Fall ist ganz verderbt"—is the raising of man from original sin through trust in God. And the A minor is the highest in a rising series of key notes—d, e, F, a—that reflects the scalar model of a single ambitus. Thus Cantata 109, like several other cantatas, has a plan of anabasis, its central E minor/F major antithesis serving as a kind of mi contra fa, which is intensified here in the style contrast between the E minor and F major arias. In its intense concerto-like character the first of these can be considered an expression of the Italian affective sphere, while its notated conflict between duple and triple subdivisions of the beat (for *wancket* and *zweifelhaftig* in particular) adds to the passionate improvisational style (even a reappearance of the ritornello is notated with triplets where duplets had been used earlier). The F major aria, on the other hand, is a stylized French passepied, in homophonic style with a pair of oboes and no trace of conflict: "Der Heiland kennt ja die Seinen, wenn ihre Hoffnung hilflos liegt." Its middle section introduces, as we said, the victory of faith.

In all the foregoing details "Ich glaube, lieber Herr' discloses an awareness on Bach's part of the uncertainty the believer feels before recognizing his own faith. This idea runs throughout Luther's writings on the way faith is felt. In his *A Meditation on Christ's Passion,* for example, he emphasizes all the points that constitute the dynamic sequence of this cantata—the necessity of prayer for faith (no. 1), the difficulty of belief (nos. 2 and 3), faith as God's work, accomplished through Jesus (nos. 4 and 5), despite the conflict of flesh and spirit within us (no. 5), the fact that "faith rests entirely in the hands of God" (nos. 5 and 6), and finally, the fact that we may often be unaware in our despair that God is working within us, for faith is sometimes "granted openly, sometimes in secret."[25]

If the meaning of Bach's tonal allegory in Cantata 109 is the hidden granting of faith and its overt manifestation only after a period of doubt, the same is true of Cantata 38, "Aus tiefer Not schrei' ich zu dir," of the following year. A chorale cantata based on Luther's well-known hymn, Cantata 38 is a free version of Psalm 130 and sung to the ancient Phrygian melody, which begins as shown in Ex. 56. From two elements of text and chorale melody, with perhaps the additional aid of Luther's commentary on the psalm itself, Bach produced an allegorical structure that is profoundly dependent on tonal directions, using catabasis up to the final verse of the chorale:

CANTATA 38: "Aus tiefer Not schrei ich zu dir"

1. Chorale motet: "Aus tiefer Not," in E Phrygian
2. Recitative ending with Phrygian cadence in A minor (i.e., E Phrygian)
3. Aria: "Ich höre mitten in den Leiden ein Trostwort," in A minor
4. Recitative with chorale cantus firmus in bass: A Phrygian–D Phrygian
5. Trio: "Wenn meine Trübsal als mit Ketten," in D minor
6. Chorale: "Ob bei uns ist der Sünden viel," in E Phrygian

25. Luther, *A Meditation on Christ's Passion,* p. 13.

EXAMPLE 56.   Beginning of chorale "Aus tiefer Not"

Aus tie - fer Not schrei ich zu dir ____

The keys used are similar to those in Cantata 109, but now a falling circle of fifths rather than a rising scalar model determines their arrangement; the final chorale restores the original key.

It seems at least possible that Bach developed the idea for his structure from Luther's conception of Psalm 130 as the cry of a "truly penitent heart that is most deeply moved in its distress." Luther continues, emphasizing that sin and torment must be acknowledged before faith makes salvation possible: "We are all in deep and great misery, but we do not all feel our condition. . . . Crying is nothing but a strong and earnest longing for God's grace, which does not arise in a person unless he sees in what depth he is lying."[26] Bach, like Luther, takes as his starting point the word "deep," to which he adds the dimension of the initial falling fifth of the chorale melody. Bach needed a sustained catabasis to create a tonal analogy to the experience of the "many depths" mentioned by Luther. This need is evident in the development of the melodic material of the aria and trio from the first line of the chorale (Ex. 57). Although the A minor aria stresses hope in the midst of sorrow—and Bach represents it faithfully with melodic lines similar to the final movement of BWV 109 (on *Trostwort* and *sein Wort besteht*)—the overall tonal direction nevertheless continues downward throughout the following two movements. The explanation for this seemingly contradictory procedure is found in Luther's commentary, which emphasizes the "blessing" of "contradictory and disharmonious things, for hope and despair are opposites"; we must "hope in despair" for "hope which forms the new man, grows in the midst of fear that cuts down the old Adam."[27] The catabasis must, of course, be interpreted as a positive force; it is the necessary "other side" of redemption; or, as John Donne, for example, expresses it, "therefore that he may raise the Lord throws down."[28]

The trio of "Aus tiefer Not" presents first the image of our troubles forming the links in a chain that binds us until it is loosened by Christ, then that of the rising of the "morning" of faith amid the "night" of trouble and sorrow. Modulation in the

26. Martin Luther, "Commentary on Psalm 130," trans. Arnold Guebert, in vol. 14 of *Luther's Works,* ed. Jaroslav Pelikan (St. Louis, 1958), p. 189.
27. Luther, "Commentary on Psalm 130," p. 191.
28. Donne's "Hymne to God my God, in my sicknesse" (1623 or 1631) can, of course, be found in many anthologies. The idea expressed in its final line is a very common one in his work and in the poetry of the time.

EXAMPLE 57.   Chorale-derived themes in Cantata 38

(a) Aria "Ich höre mitten in den Leiden": beginning of instrumental ritornello

Oboe 1

Oboe 2

(b) Trio "Wenn meine Trübsal": beginning of ritornello

Basso continuo

(c) Trio: beginning of soprano part

Soprano

wenn mei-ne   Trüb-sal als mit   Ket   -   [ten]

(d) Trio: excerpt from penultimate section

Soprano

wie bald er-scheint des   Tros - tes   Mor   -   [gen]

flat and sharp directions associated with darkness and light respectively appears in several other works as well (e.g., Cantatas 21, 61, the *Christmas Oratorio*). The trio is pervaded by circle-of-fifths motion developed from the chorale-derived themes. Chains of suspensions precipitate a downward motion through the minor keys (d, g, c, f, then B flat [major]; mm. 17–38). The dawning of faith ("Wie bald erscheint des Trostes Morgen"; mm. 70–82), by contrast, reverses the direction upward, until the idea of the "night" of doubt and sorrow turns it back again (mm. 82–94). In this last section, however, the words "Wie bald erscheint des Trostes Morgen" return for a time (mm. 96–111), overlapping and forming a new counterpoint with the "night" melody (which is the same as the *Trübsal* melody at the beginning of the movement). The extension of the *Trostes Morgen* idea is sung to the melody of the ritornello, set to text now for the first time (mm. 96–108). Surely the flats are to be "redeemed" from their pejorative associations. Although on the whole the text of the trio voices a positive message, the absence of a regular da capo means that the movement ends with the "night" image; and the idea of catabasis remains with us through the final ritornello as well.

But Bach's ingenious combinations joined the night of trouble and sorow to the morning of trust. Because the psalm itself and, even more, Luther's exegesis emphasize two ideas at the end, Bach's plan likewise does not allow the prevailing catabasis to reverse itself before the very end. The first idea is the necessity of waiting—through the night watch:

> Therefore the psalmist says: "I wait for the Lord; that is, in this crying and cross-bearing I did not retreat or despair; nor did I trust in my own merit. I trusted in God's grace alone, which I desire, and I wait for God to help me when it pleases Him."
> . . . That is, my soul always has its face directed straight toward God and confidently awaits His coming and His help, no matter how it may be delayed.[29]

As in Cantata 109, Bach's structure delays the full message of help until the last possible moment, the final chorale. The concluding idea of "Aus tiefer Not" is redemption at the hands of God: "That is, with Him alone there is redemption out of the many depths mentioned above, and there is no other redemption. Although our sin is great, yet His redemption is greater."[30] The message of salvation is effected in the final chorale, "Ob bei uns ist der Sünden viel, bei Gott ist viel mehr Gnade." The chorale returns to the original E Phrygian, but not through anabasis, which might, in this case, suggest that salvation was attained by human effort; Luther stresses that we cannot "work our own way out." A transformation suddenly effects the shift of key for the final chorale: the final low D of the aria ritornello is retained in the bass as the chorale begins on an E major chord with the adversitive *Ob* (although). Thus, an initial dissonance in the new key, the D, symbol of *Trübsal* and *Nacht,* is given new meaning by the change.

Perhaps the most fascinating tonal allegory in this cantata appears in a movement that is not based on Luther's text but is derived directly from the Gospel. Between the aria and the trio Bach introduces a recitative that is constructed on the melody of "Aus tiefer Not" as a bass cantus firmus, taking its tonal departure from the preceding A minor aria. Its first *Stollen* is in A Phrygian, beneath the freely composed recitative text, "Ach! dass mein Glaube noch so schwach, und dass ich mein

29. Luther, "Commentary on Psalm 130," p. 192.
30. Luther, "Commentary on Psalm 130," p. 194.

EXAMPLE 58.　　Cantata 38: beginning of second recitative (No. 4)

EXAMPLE 59.　　Phrygian scales on A and D compared

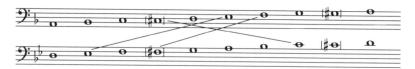

Vertrauen auf feichtem Grunde muss erbauen!" From this point the ground shifts down to D Phrygian for the second *Stollen* and the entire *Abgesang*, for Bach an unprecedented procedure within a single cantus firmus statement (Ex. 58). The beginning justifies the continuing catabasis: despite the *Trostwort* within the foregoing aria, faith remains weak. The second *Stollen* begins, "How often must new signs soften my heart?"—a line drawn from Jesus' words to the father of the healed boy in the Gospel for the day: "Wenn ihr nicht Zeichen und Wunder seht, so glaubt ihr nicht" (John 4:48). The words *neue Zeichen* and *erweichen* suggest the concept of softening, which relates the shift to flats (G minor) to the ancient usage of *mollis* to designate flat keys.

To appreciate how Bach emphasizes the word "signs," we must compare the Phrygian scales of A and D as they were understood in Bach's time (Ex. 59).[31] The variable third degree of the scale is usually used in its sharp form harmonically and in its unaltered form melodically, as in numerous Phrygian chorales such as "Herzlich tut mich verlangen" and "Aus tiefer Not." Here, to maximize the difference between the scale and its transposition, Bach sharpens the third degree, even though it alters the melody significantly; the result is a disparity of three pitches between the Phrygian scales on A and D: E/E flat, C sharp/C, and F/F sharp respectively. Bach then forms the diminished seventh chord on *Zeichen* with the aid of all three of the new signs, one sharp (F sharp), one flat (E flat)—the outer voices—and one natural (C); this, then, is the chord that, with its dominant function, brings about the G minor softening. Since John's Gospel is known as the *Book of Signs,* and since the tonal plan of Bach's *St. John Passion* appears to have been conceived as a form of play on the three musical signs (i.e., sharp, flat, and natural key areas), this important detail in the plan of "Aus tiefer Not" perhaps possesses a wider significance, relating it to Bach's tonal-allegorical procedures in general.

31. Many German music treatises of Bach's time list chorales according to the old modes. There is, of course, a thin line between a close on the dominant in a minor key (especially one of the Phrygian type) and a cadence intended to represent the Phrygian mode itself. Bach merges the two, especially when the cadence expresses a rhetorical question, and the duality or ambiguity regarding complete and incomplete closure is intended (see the final line of Cantata 161, "How then can death harm me?"). The linking of the minor scale (especially the harmonic minor) the Phrygian mode, and a version of the same scale that begins on our dominant to the Hypophrygian can be found in Athanasius Kircher's *Musurgia universalis,* p. 51; Kircher calls the scale of A harmonic minor, Phrygian (and places it in *cantus durus*) and the sequence of E, F, G♯, A, B flat (!), C, D, E (also *cantus durus*), Hypophrygian.

CHAPTER EIGHT

''Schweig' nur,

taumelnde Vernunft'':

Reason contra Faith

in the Cantatas

The title of this chapter, "Schweig' nur, taumelnde Vernunft"—which can be translated as "Silence! tottering (or reeling, even intoxicating) Reason"—is the first line of the soprano aria that is the sixth movement of Cantata 178, "Wo Gott, der Herr, nicht bei uns hält," composed in 1724 for the eighth Sunday after Trinity. It is one of a small number of Bach's works in which the battle cry of the Enlightenment, reason, is directly confronted. Within Bach's church cantatas the word *Vernunft* appears some ten times in nine cantatas. In addition, it crops up in two secular cantatas, in which it is treated somewhat differently. All but the first two of these works—Cantata 152, "Tritt auf die Glaubensbahn," and Cantata 186a, "Ärgre dich, o Seele, nicht," both set to texts of Salomo Franck—were composed in Leipzig.[1]

BWV 152: "Tritt auf die Glaubensbahn" for the Sunday after Christmas, Weimar, December 30, 1714. No. 5, bass recitative: "Was Gott beschlossen hat, kann die *Vernunft* doch nicht ergründen; die blinde Leiterin verführt die geistlich Blinden."

BWV 186 and 186a: "Ärgre dich, o Seele, nicht" for the third Sunday in Advent, Weimar, 1716 (No. 186a); reworked for the seventh Sunday after Trinity with the addition of recitatives and concluding chorales to both parts (No. 186: Leipzig, July 11, 1723). No. 3, bass aria: "Doch, o Seele, zweifle nicht, lass *Vernunft* dich nicht bestricken."

BWV 76: "Die Himmel erzählen die Ehre Gottes" for the second Sunday after Trinity, Leipzig, June 6, 1723. No. 5, bass aria: "Fahr hin, abgöttische Zunft! Sollt' sich die Welt gleich verkehren, will ich doch Christum verehren, er ist das Licht der *Vernunft*."

1. Dürr, *Studien,* pp. 31, 50–51; and *Zur Chronologie der Leipziger Vokalwerke J. S. Bachs, Bach-Jahrbuch* 64 (1957): 5–162; rev. ed. (Kassel, 1976), passim.

BWV 2: "Ach, Gott, vom Himmel sieh' darein" for the second Sunday after Trinity, Leipzig, June 18, 1724. No. 2, tenor recitative: "Der Eine wählet dies, der Andre das, die thörichte *Vernunft* ist ihr Compass."

BWV 178: "Wo Gott, der Herr, nicht bei uns hält" for the eighth Sunday after Trinity, Leipzig, July 30, 1724. No. 6, tenor aria: "Schweig' nur, taumelnde *Vernunft*. Sprich nicht: die Frommen sind verlor'n, das Kreuz hat sie nur neu gebor'n." No. 7, chorale: "*Vernunft* wider den Glauben ficht, auf's Künft'ge will sie trauen nicht, da du wirst selber trösten."

BWV 180: "Schmücke dich, o liebe Seele" for the twentieth Sunday after Trinity, Leipzig, October 22, 1724. No. 4, alto recitative: "Mein Herz fühlt in sich Furcht und Freude; es wird die Furcht erregt, wenn es die Hoheit überlegt, wenn es sich nicht in das Geheimniss findet, noch durch *Vernunft* dies hohe Werk ergründet."

BWV 175: "Er rufet seine Schafen mit Namen" for the third Sunday in Pentecost, Leipzig, May 22, 1725. No. 5, bass recitative: "Ach ja! Wir Menschen sind oftmals den Tauben zu vergleichen: wenn die verblendte *Vernunft* nicht weiss, was er gesaget hatte."

BWV 35: "Geist und Seele wird verwirret" for the twelfth Sunday after Trinity, Leipzig, September 8, 1726. No. 3, alto recitative: "Betracht ich dich, du teurer Gottessohn, so flieht *Vernunft*, und auch Verstand davon."

BWV 197: "Gott ist unsre Zuversicht," a wedding cantata, Leipzig, after 1735. No. 2, bass recitative: "Gott ist und bleibt der beste Sorger, er hält am besten Haus. Er führet unser Thun zuweilen wunderlich, je dennoch frölich aus. Wohin der Vorsatz nicht gedacht, was die *Vernunft* unmöglich macht, das füget sich."

BWV 201: "Geschwinde, geschwinde, ihr wirbelnde Winde," a secular cantata, Leipzig, around 1729. No. 14, recitative of Momus (soprano): "Der Unverstand und *Unvernunft* will jetzt der Weisheit Nachbar sein, man urtheilt in den Tag hinein, und die so thun, gehören all' in deine Zunft."

BWV 213: "Lasst uns sorgen, lasst uns wachen" ("Hercules auf dem Scheidewege"), a birthday cantata for Frederick, Crown Prince of Saxony, Leipzig, September 5, 1733. No. 2, recitative of Hercules (alto): "Und wo? Wo ist die rechte Bahn, da ich den eingepflanzten Trieb, dem Tugend, Glanz und Ruhm und Hoheit lieb, zu seinem Ziele bringen kann? *Vernunft*, Verstand und Licht begehrt dem allen nachzujagen."

Other cantatas deal with closely related themes of reason, such as No. 126, "Erhalt' uns, Herr, bei deinem Wort," in which the bass aria, "Stürze zu Boden schwülstige Stolze," graphically represents the overthrow of arrogant human aspiration. To define a group of compositions on the basis of one word in their texts, therefore, is an arbitrary procedure. Furthermore, Bach's relationship to the Enlightenment cannot be determined on the basis of text setting alone, however ingenious, even profound, it may be. In defense of this approach, however, it must be noted that for the most part the word "reason" is not introduced casually or incidentally into these works. The group as a whole not only shares a number of themes, many of which concern the central issues of Lutheranism and its relation to the Enlightenment, but it contains some of Bach's more carefully planned pieces and therefore points out Bach's primary means of treating what we now think of as conflicting world views. These cantatas constitute probably the smallest manageable number of works in which the conflict of Enlightenment and orthodox values can be considered at different stages of Bach's career and in secular as well as sacred pieces. These cantatas are obviously first divided between sacred and secular works. In the latter (primarily Cantata 213) reason is extolled as a virtue, just the opposite of its role in the former.

The church cantatas alone can be further divided into those whose subject matter places reason in the context of opposition to basic Lutheran dogma, especially the idea of justification by faith, and those that emphasize the positive contexts of God's love and earthly life. Relying on reason to know God or attain salvation is condemned in both contexts, but nevertheless, a much clearer sense of the value of human existence emerges in the second category of church cantatas. As it happens, the first group of church cantatas—Nos. 152, 186, 2, and 178—were composed earlier than the second—Nos. 180, 175, 35, and 197. Cantata 76, "Die Himmel erzählen die Ehre Gottes," stands as an exception and will be discussed later in this chapter. Apart from this, the cantatas will be discussed in approximately chronological order.

The earliest cantata to mention reason, "Tritt auf die Glaubensbahn," introduces the central dogma of Lutheranism: faith is the only path to man's justification before God. A dominant theme among the church cantatas, it is often stated directly and implied when it is not. Let us first consider how reason fits into the Lutheran faith. The above-mentioned cantatas treat reason similarly enough to numerous writings by Luther to allow us to conclude that a negative perspective on reason (and its associated error, philosophy) was little affected by the increasing rationalism of the period of seventeenth-century orthodoxy.[2] Reason is described as leading man into taking offence at God's designs (No. 152) and as the enemy of faith (No. 178); it is associated with blindness and deafness (Nos. 152, 175) and with the flesh rather than the spirit (No. 186). Its most positive attribute is a passive one—it can be illuminated by faith: Christ is described as the light of reason ("Licht der Vernunft") in Cantata 76. Indeed, references to light in several of the cantatas explain that, theologically, reason belongs to the realm of darkness and the flesh rather than of spiritual enlightenment, whereas Luther often describes faith as

2. Luther's thoughts on the role of reason in human existence recur throughout his work. In *The Bondage of the Will,* for example, a section is entitled "Ecclesiasticus 15:14–17. The Foolishness of Reason" (pp. 182–88). See Althaus, *The Theology of Martin Luther,* pp. 64–71, where both the positive and negative views are discussed; also von Loewenich, *Luther's Theology of the Cross,* pp. 65–77.

dwelling in darkness but illuminating reason.[3] The incapacity of reason to comprehend God or his works prompted several cantatas that deal directly with God's glory, such as "Die Himmel erzählen die Ehre Gottes." Other themes associated with reason appear in Bach's cantatas, such as its opposition to the way of the cross (Nos. 2, 178) and the necessity of placing God's Word above reason (practically all the cantatas express this idea in some form). Neglect of the Word gives rise to a characteristic Lutheran notion regarding reason: it is a stumbling block to faith and salvation (No. 152).

Together the foregoing ideas point to the antithetical relationship between faith and reason in Lutheran theology: Scripture is the source of God's Word; Christ is the subject of the Scripture; and whoever understands this can receive the spiritual manna that nourishes faith. Reason stumbles over the fact that God presents himself in the Scriptures "hidden" behind the cross and suffering. The humanity and humility of Christ, his sufferings and ignoble death are the antithesis of all that man expects from the deity. Therefore, reason often leads man to believe that he can come to grasp God through his own resources rather than through the Scriptures. Not accepting the implications of the incarnation, reason wants to build knowledge of God on man's understanding of the wonders of Creation (we would say science and philosophy), wants to see God in his glory rather than his shame.

For Luther this error was central to the very definition of theology, which he divided into two categories: the only true theology, the *theologia crucis,* or theology of the cross, and the false *theologia gloriae,* or theology of glory. The theology of the cross (or the theology of faith) sees things as they are, not as they appear, sees that God's glory, and his proper work (redemption and the Gospel) are hidden behind the shame of the cross, God's "alien work" of suffering, death, and the Law. The theologian of the cross knows that God can only be perceived in suffering, both that of Jesus as his story is told in Scripture and that of the individual himself, while the theologian of glory rejects suffering, the cross, and Christ, in the futile attempt to match wits with God. Luther's famous statement, "Let God be God," runs contrary to the spirit of individualistic self-assertion of the eighteenth century Enlightenment, just as his denial of human free will opposed the humanistic standpoint of Erasmus in the sixteenth.[4]

Cantata 152 clearly states the role of reason in Lutheran orthodox theology. Throughout the first three solo movements of this cantata (nos. 2, 3, and 4, following an introductory sinfonia) Franck—drawing on several Scripture passages—develops the metaphor of a stone. The first texted movement, a bass aria, urges man to step onto the path of faith, for which God laid the stone that upholds the church (Zion), and not to stumble over it. In this movement the exact meaning of

3. Von Loewenich, *Luther's Theology of the Cross,* pp. 83–86; Althaus, *The Theology of Martin Luther,* pp. 70–71.

4. See von Loewenich, *Luther's Theology of the Cross,* pp. 17–24.

EXAMPLE 60.   Cantata 152: vocal melody from first movement

Tritt auf die Glau-bens - bahn, _____

the stone is not specified. Then, in the next movement, the primary referent of the metaphor is given in the simple opening words, taken from the Gospel for the day—"Der Heiland ist gesetzt in Israel zum Fall und Auferstehen!"; these words stand as the symbol for the whole work. The stone has two aspects: as an obstacle to human inclination and as the cornerstone of faith. Jesus' fall is the former since it contradicts the human conception of the deity. Continuing, the recitative declares that in rushing to attack what is now described as this "edle Stein," the "böse Welt" injures itself and falls into hell. For the elect, however, the stone is the source of redemption and salvation. The aria that follows ("Stein, der über alle Schätze," no. 4) sums up this idea in a prayer. Then a recitative gives a full explanation of the theology behind the cantata: "Es ärgre sich die kluge Welt, dass Gottes Sohn verlässt den hohen Ehrenthron, dass er in Fleisch und Blut sich kleidet und in der Menschheit leidet." At issue above all is the humble, low estate in which God revealed himself in Jesus Christ, which is an offence to human reason. The text continues to emphasize that "Die grösste Weisheit dieser Erden muss vor des Höchsten Rat zur grössten Torheit werden. Was Gott beschlossen hat, kann die Vernunft doch nicht ergründen; die blinde Leiterin verführt die geistlich Blinden." The soprano/bass duet that concludes the cantata is a characteristic question-and-answer dialogue between the soul and Christ in which the answers, given by the bass, show the true *Glaubensbahn*: Denial of the self and giving up everything; understanding Christ through faith and not taking offence; finally, proceeding from suffering to joy so that, after tribulation and shame, Jesus will grant the soul the crown. The *Stein* that is the foundation of faith is the fall and rising again of Christ, and the true *Glaubensbahn* is the duplication of this descent/ascent dynamic within the individual, or spiritual humiliation followed by the joy of faith. The melody of the opening aria, with its pronounced descent/ascent shape, describes this dynamic of faith (Ex. 60).[5] The "offence" to reason is caused by its inability to accept the theological paradox that joy comes through suffering, ascent through descent. Ascent alone, whether made solely by God's aid (the Lutheran view) or through man's own effort (the view that became more prominent in the Enlightenment), is a desired end. The necessity of suffering to attain this end, however, seemed to lie in a realm different from that of rationality and human endeavor. In Cantata 152 the

5. Chafe, "Luther's 'Analogy of Faith,'" p. 98.

idea of falling, more than that of rising, is given the greater emphasis. Bach's setting pays great attention to the striking descending lines and leaps, which is in keeping with the function of the work. As a Christmas cantata it deals with the incarnation of Christ, with the initial fall into humanity that was often seen to parallel the fall of Adam, the fall of Christ in Gethsemane, and, of course, the crucifixion; all these were inseparably linked in Luther's incarnational theology.

Cantata 186, "Ärgre dich, o Seele, nicht," a Leipzig reworking of a Weimar cantata, exhibits a powerful structural realization of the issues surrounding the condemnation of reason in orthodox Lutheranism.

Part One

1. Chorus: "Ärgre dich, o Seele, nicht," in G minor
2. Rec. (bass): "Die Knechtgestalt," in C minor–D minor
3. Aria (bass): "Bist du, der mir helfen soll," in B flat
4. Rec. (tenor): "Ach, dass ein Christ so sehr vor seinen Körper sorgt!" in G minor–B flat
5. Aria (tenor): "Mein Heiland lässt sich merken in seinen Gnadenwerken," in D minor
6. Chorale (with instrumental interludes): "Ob sich's anliess', als wollt' er nicht," in F major

Part Two

7. Acc. Recitative (bass): "Es ist die Welt die grosse Wüstenei," in E flat–B flat
8. Aria (soprano): "Die Armen will der Herr umarmen," in G minor
9. Recitative (alto): "Nun mag die Welt mit ihrer Lust vergehen," in C minor–E flat
10. Duet (soprano, alto, with full instruments): "Lass, Seele, kein Leiden von Jesu dich scheiden," in C minor
11. Chorale (same music as no. 6): "Die Hoffnung wart' zur rechten Zeit," in F major

The opening chorus urges the soul not to be offended that the "allerhöchste Licht, Gottes Glanz und Ebenbild" appears to man in lowly servant's guise ("Knechtgestalt"). Above all else, reason cannot accept this appearance of God in the form of the suffering Christ rather than in all the majesty of the creator. The third movement of this work, a bass aria, urges the doubting soul not to allow reason to confuse it, for its helper, "Jacob's light," can be perceived in the Scriptures. In fitting these ideas with the Gospel story of the feeding of the four thousand in the desert, Bach develops a flesh/spirit juxtaposition in the newly composed recitatives. The cantata can thus be said to take a figurative approach to the Gospel narrative, interpreting the desert as the world, the hunger of the crowd as both physical and spiritual need, and Jesus' words as spiritual manna. Cantata 186 is a hopeful work, and the image of Christ as "friendly Lord" counters the warning against reason and the flesh. Christ's taking on of human form for the salvation of mankind constitutes the primary message of Scripture—the "höchste Schatz"—as in Cantata 152, and Scripture is the primary means by which the contemporary believer can encounter Christ. In times of tribulation the believer can "taste and see there how friendly Jesus is," a quality that is revealed in his works of grace, which provide nourishment for the worn-out body and spirit (nos. 4 and 5). The concluding chorale of Part One sums up the idea that Christ is present exactly when he most seems not to be (i.e., in the tribulations of the flesh); the Christian, therefore, should rely on the promise of Scripture.

In keeping with this increasingly positive message, the tonal plan of Part One constitutes an ascent involving primarily the keys G minor, B flat, D minor, and F major for the closed movements. Also, like many of the cantatas that utilize this idea, Part One of "Ärgre dich, o Seele, nicht" exhibits much directional antithesis. In the opening chorus long descending oboe lines are paired with an ascending arpeggio figure in the bass that is then ordered into scalar ascending and descending sequences. In the following recitative the line "Wird dir im Gegentheil die Last zu viel zu tragen, wenn Armuth dich beschwert, wenn Hunger dich verzehrt" calls forth a long descent in the bass and modulation to F minor. The first three (of four) sections in the B flat bass aria cadence in F, E flat, and D minor respectively, probably to represent the increasing doubt and the warning against reason. The second recitative juxtaposes the torment of the world with Christ: the half line "Drum, wenn der Kummer gleich das Herze nagt und frisst" is built on a cadential sequence that falls by step eleven times over an octave and a half, then finally cadences at "so schmeckt und sehet doch, wie freundlich Jesus ist" (Ex. 61). The instrumental parts in the final chorale setting are based on contrary motion: the oboes ascend and the strings descend in alternation. For the interludes between the chorale lines and especially the ending of the movement all the parts play descending scalar lines over a wide range (Ex. 62).

Bach's emphasis on directional duality in Part One makes audible at various levels of the music the antithesis between tribulation and hope that dominated Lutheran spiritual life. In the final chorale the two are continually set in opposition; yet the very solidity of the chorale, the tonal ascent to its F major key, and even the convergence of the upper parts into parallelism at the end suggest a hopeful outcome. In contrast, Part Two begins with what seems like a step backward, reversing the direction of the tonal plan, and placing the greatest emphasis on minor keys: B flat (ending of the first recitative), G minor (aria), E flat (second recitative ending), C minor (aria duetto). After this descent the concluding chorale verse, in the same F major musical setting that ended Part One, restores the perspective with which the first part ended, but only by a sharp tonal contrast with the preceding duet.

EXAMPLE 61. Cantata 186: ending of second recitative (No. 4)

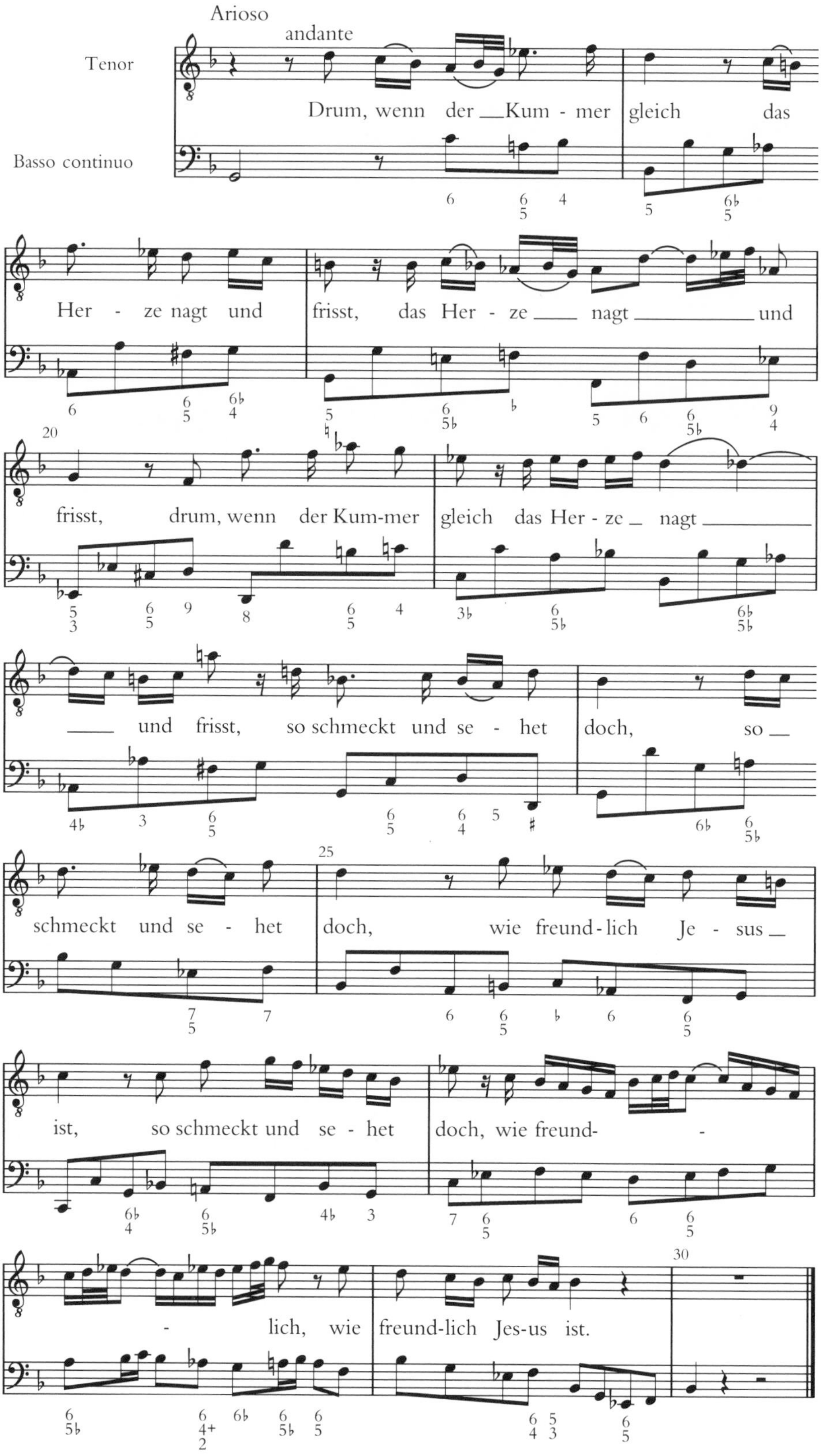

EXAMPLE 62.   Cantata 186: ending of final chorale of Parts One and Two

The meaning, however, is clear: knowing the promise of the Gospel and the nature of Christian existence from Scripture is not enough; it must be lived in the world, for only then does the truth of Scripture fully manifest itself. Part One having shown the true source of faith in the Scriptures, Part Two completes the idea of the *Glaubensbahn* with the nature of the life of faith—life under the cross, so to speak. At the beginning an accompanied recitative for bass and strings announces that when Christians accept God's word in faith "Es ist die Welt die grosse Wüstenei; der Himmel wird zu Erz, die Erde wird zu Eisen." Bach uses the means familiar from the recitatives in Part One to underscore the antithesis between faith in the Word and the resultant withdrawal from the world and between the lamenting of God's people and God's future blessings. The final recitative utilizes the same kind of antithesis several times, all with the general aim of opposing the view of the world as a desert or "vale of tears" *(Jammerthal)* to the promise of Scripture.

However, successive antithesis, suggesting the before and after of faith, or the tribulation of the present life versus the joy and fulfillment of the afterlife, does not represent the fact that the two coexist and even conflict in the believer. Luther himself stressed this in the *simul* of his famous expression "Simul justus et peccator" (at one and the same time justified and a sinner).[6] Simultaneity is the basis of the incarnation and of the life of faith; Luther, therefore, always stressed the presence of the Spirit in the flesh. In Part Two Bach goes an important step further; the two arias develop the idea of simultaneous antithesis. The first of these, on the text "Die Armen will der Herr umarmen mit Gnaden hier und dort; er schenket ihnen aus Erbarmen den höchste Schatz, das Lebenswort," is a highly chromatic piece, featuring a variation of the descending chromatic tetrachord in the violin line against arpeggio descent figures in the basso continuo that suggest an inversion of the figure from the opening chorus (Ex. 63). A second chromatic element is the long scalar ascent followed by an even longer descent; only in the ritornello that frames the movement does the pattern ascend again for the final cadence. The figural aspect of this piece can be interpreted in a number of similar ways; the first half of the ritornello (the descending tetrachord) might be seen to depict "die Armen" and the second half the "umarmen," the ascent/descent pattern might be seen to represent the rainbow as a sign of God's grace, and the like.

Much more important to the interpretation of this movement, however, is Bach's deliberate contraversion of the ordinary rhetorical significance of chromaticism. The primarily diatonic vocal line of this aria is almost completely separate in its melodic and motivic content from the violin line. The meaning of the "Ruffet, Ach"/"Hofft auf Leben" juxtaposition on the Bach goblet is present once again, now in terms of reliance on the *Lebenswort* of Scripture in the midst of a life of tribulation. Likewise, the C minor aria duetto features a simultaneity of opposites: the C minor key and its place at the end of a structural sequence based on tonal descent versus a lively gigue rhythm and a generally uncomplicated and melodically oriented homophonic texture. The text mixes promise, the central message of the work, with the clear indication that fulfillment lies in the future; only then are the "bonds of the flesh" broken:

6. Althaus, *The Theology of Martin Luther,* pp. 242–45.

EXAMPLE 63.   Cantata 186, Part Two: ritornello of aria "Die Armen will der Herr umarmen"

Lass, Seele, kein Leiden
von Jesu dich scheiden,
sei, Seele, getreu!
Dir bleibt die Krone
aus Gnaden zu Lohne,
wenn du von Banden des Leibes nun frei.

Near the end of the movement the chromatic tetrachord returns, now ascending in the bass, beneath the last line of the text. Hope is based on the promise of Scripture but is still within the earthly perspective. Even the final F major chorale verse, "Die Hoffnung wart' zur rechten Zeit," does not alter this perspective. This cantata can be compared with other two-part structures, most notably the two *Passions,* in which Bach utilizes tonal ascent to indicate the direction of redemption early in the work but later moves to flats to suggest a worldly perspective. Thus the *St. Mat-*

thew Passion, for example, moves from E minor to E major in Part One, but the close of the work is in C minor, the flats associated with faith in the present life.

Although reason seems almost casually introduced into Cantata 186, the work in fact deals with all the related issues, and in a manner that allows for interpretation of a wider range of Bach's aesthetics. The G minor aria demonstrates clearly that affective intent cannot be interpreted solely by musical figures. Bach was aware of the general aesthetic role of composition with musical figures (as signposts of the spiritual nature of allegory—the separation of matter and spirit, or intrinsic/extrinsic meaning) to the extent that he could set figures and affect in opposition. Yet he never rejects the figural mode of composition, as later aesthetics sometimes claimed to do. Gluck can produce an aria of lamentation in which simple melodic beauty in a serene F major replaces figural devices altogether, but Bach does not use this device, which is closer to the emerging aesthetics of beauty and the sublime. The one-to-one relationship between musical figures and extra-musical ideas and images in Bach's music creates the impression of a rationalistic "surface" that is often highly detailed. But the affective character of the music is not absolutely bound to this surface. On rare occasions the relationship between figured surface and affect can suggest the dualism of appearance and essence. Such a contraverting of the usual direct relationship between figures and affect was possible for Bach because the direct relationship had existed as a central feature of musical composition for centuries (as a musical manifestation of what is often generally referred to as the "aesthetics of imitation"). The extent of Bach's conscious recognition of the role of the rationalistic element in his own music can, of course, be debated. Nevertheless, it is tempting to posit awareness on Bach's part when we encounter a warning against reason in the text of a work that separates figural rationality and affect.

Since reason, in the Lutheran orthodox viewpoint, cannot encompass the paradoxical idea that redemption can be brought about in suffering and death, it attempts instead to base man's salvation on his direct efforts, on ethical works and achievements. A cantata exemplifying this idea is "Ach, Gott, vom Himmel sieh' darein" (No. 2). One of the descent/ascent cantatas, it moves downward from the opening Phrygian chorale melody in A (harmonized by Bach in D minor) through a D minor recitative in which reason is described as the erratic compass that causes man to deviate from God in all directions, a B flat aria in which God is urged to strike out the false teaching of those who deny or distort his word, a recitative modulating to G minor, in which flat modulations as far as B flat minor are linked to the suffering of the pious. In this recitative a reversal up to F major accompanies God's rescuing and refreshing his own people. The next movement, a G minor aria, states the dialectical message of the *theologia crucis:* "Durchs Feuer wird das Silber rein, durchs Kreuz das Wort bewährt erfunden. Drum soll ein Christ zu allen Stunden im Kreuz und Not geduldig sein." The final chorale returns to the key of the opening movement with a renewed prayer to God to preserve his truth in the face of a people who take offence. In short, this cantata presents exactly the context in which reason is usually invoked, and condemned, and its pattern of descent followed by ascent—even though the range of keys is small—is Bach's typical means of representing the basic dynamic of God's truth in the Lutheran view.[7]

Cantata 178, "Wo Gott, der Herr, nicht bei uns hält," is a chorale cantata whose hymn is based on Psalm 124, in which God's protection is invoked against the ravages of one's enemies. The Gospel for the day warns against false prophets, and the text of the cantata identifies these prophets with the enemies referred to in the psalm. In the final chorale reason is described as fighting against faith, which is emphasized in the aria "Schweig' nur, taumelnde Vernunft." It is surprising, therefore, to find that the tonal plan of "Wo Gott, der Herr" reverses the kind of pattern just described. It ascends first—from A minor through C major, E minor, G major, and B minor (two movements)—then descends through successive movements in E minor and A minor. The aria "Schweig' nur, taumelnde Vernunft" is the penultimate movement in E minor; that is, it marks the turning point from ascent to descent. The purposeful ascent by thirds from A minor to B minor here signifies the upward direction of human aspiration, while the descent represents the overthrow of reliance on reason by faith. This cantata most conspicuously demonstrates Bach's treatment of human aspiration in a religious context.

The opening chorale fantasia in A minor paints a striking picture of man's inability to attain salvation, if left entirely to his own resources. Against an insistent dotted rhythm, Bach sets a long line of descending sixteenths that is the second main theme of the movement, the meaning of which is certainly the fall of secular, human power in the absence of God. As the cantata proceeds it becomes clear that the enemies and the false prophets use independent human aspiration, and reason in particular, as the weapon against faith. In the first recitative, in dialogue with the second chorale verse, "Menschen Kraft und Witz," "Klugheit," and the like, are set in opposition to God's way: "so geht doch Gott ein' andre Bahn: er führt die Seinigen mit starker Hand, durch's Kreuzes Meer, in das gelobte Land, da wird er alles Unglück wenden"; this moves from C major to E minor. The G major aria that follows represents the waves of the "Kreuzes Meer" as it attempts to wreck the ship of faith. Its theme is based on falling thirds, but its rising sequences are associated with the line "mit Ungestüm ein Schiff zerschellen, so raset auch der Feinde Wuth." The middle section moves to the mediant key, B minor; Bach then astonishingly transposes much of this music to G minor. The sudden introduction of an unrelated key a third lower illustrates the text's description of enemies attempting to broaden the realm of Satan and dash the Christian *Schifflein* to pieces.

In "Wo Gott, der Herr" B minor is the highest in a series of rising keys; its juxtaposition with G minor is but one instance of the meaning of conflicting direction in the work, namely that a strong upward movement will precipitate its reverse. The next two movements, both in B minor, voice the antithesis between the raging of

---

7. Chafe, "Luther's 'Analogy of Faith,' " pp. 97–101.

the enemies and the expectation that God will overthrow such violent falsehood. The tenor chorale-aria with oboes d'amore begins with the ravages of the enemies and false prophets perpetrated against the believers in God's name but ends with the assurance that God will uncover the hypocrisy. The melody of its ritornello descends in sequences as well; since it is a chorale setting modulation is limited, but the descent was probably meant to indicate the uncovering to come. To this point the chorale melody has appeared three times descending in pitch by fourths through the soprano, alto, and tenor voices, while it ascends in key signatures through A minor, E minor, and B minor. This simultaneous descent in pitch and ascent in tonal levels represents the false humility of the enemies, called "wolves in sheeps' clothing" in the Gospel. After the tenor chorale, another verse is heard, again in B minor, with troped recitative insertions between the lines, now in a four-part setting with the melody in the soprano, its highest pitch in the cantata. Throughout the entire movement the basso continuo has ascending arpeggio figures in sixteenth notes, twice per measure, for a total of fifty-two times. These surely summarize the overall ascent of the cantata to this point, revealing the aggressive character of human aspiration. When the text describes the baring of teeth ("sie fletschen ihre Mörderzähne") the bass soloist has a decorated form of the ascending figure, but when God's overthrow is predicted the bass introduces a descending form of the idea ("und *stürzen* ihre falsche Lahr").

The stage is set, so to speak, for the E minor aria, "Schweig' nur, taumelnde Vernunft," in which not only the wide-ranging descent of the violin lines but the declamatory tenfold repetition of the words "Schweig', schweig' nur" at the beginning represent the rejection of reason. This aria is the single instance in Bach's cantatas where the exercise of reason is credited with emotion. The association of reason with *Taumel* suggests passion, abandon, headiness, and the like, all of which seem opposed to the *Stricken* mentioned in Cantata 186. With its extravagant leaps and runs, augmented and diminished intervals, strident emphases, syncopations, sudden rests, and generally dramatic expression, Bach's aria certainly is full of *Taumel*. Reason is shown to be surprisingly emotional, a notion underscored by images from earlier cantatas of a blind leader and an errant compass that suggest instability. Reason leads man arrogantly to seek personal goals; its style is dramatic, exaggeratedly emphatic, and not without an element of fear, pointing to the individual's struggle for inner control in details such as the almost hysterical beginning of the vocal line. In contrast, the middle section voices the familiar message of the theology of the cross:

> Sprich nicht: die Frommen sind verlor'n, das Kreuz hat sie nur neu gebor'n. Denn denen, die auf Jesum hoffen, steht stets die Thür der Gnaden offen; und wenn sie Kreuz und Trübsal drückt, so werden sie mit Trost erquickt.

The final chorale—back in A minor—mixes the assertion of God's power over enemies and his aid to the faithful with a final reminder of the opposition between reason and faith and a prayer for illumination from God's "light" ("dein Licht lass uns helle werden").

"Wo Gott, der Herr" and the cantatas discussed thus far assert the orthodox view of reason, although it is paradoxical in its musical representation. A somewhat different, "softened" treatment of reason in the Bach cantatas still rejects reason as the guideline for life but does not insist on the necessity of suffering in the world. Cantata 175, "Er rufet seinen Schafen mit Namen," presents this somewhat different perspective and also features the plan of tonal descent followed by ascent. The subject is once again the notion of being led along the path of faith. The Gospel for the day, John 1:1–11, tells the parable of the true shepherd whose voice is recognized by the sheep, of Christ as the "door" by which one may enter and have life. In the cantata the ability to recognize Christ's voice in faith contrasts with the inability of reason to hear what is said.

In the overall design Christ's voice is represented by two elements, the special instrumentarium of three recorders (nos. 1 and 2) and violoncello piccolo (no. 4), and the descending sequence of keys from G major (no. 1) through E minor (no. 2) to the subdominant C (no. 4). In both these aspects Bach intended to project a *mollis* quality that is specified as such in the third section of the C major aria: "Ich kenne deine holde Stimme, die voller Lieb' und Sanftmuth ist." The idea of an intimate relationship with Christ through faith controls these movements: at the beginning of the sequence Jesus calls his sheep personally, "by name," and at the end the individual answers, "Du wirst im Glauben aufgenommen" (no. 4). The turning point in the work coincides with the words of the Gospel (no. 5), "Sie vernahmen aber nicht, was es war, das er zu ihnen gesaget hatte." The alto serves as Evangelist and an accompanied recitative for bass and strings responds:

Ach ja! Wir Menschen sind oftmals den Tauben zu vergleichen: wenn die verblendte Vernunft nicht weiss, was er gesaget hatte. O Thörin! merke doch, wenn Jesus mit dir spricht, dass es zu deinem Heil geschicht.

After the C major aria the turn to sharps here is sudden, and the cadence to F sharp minor that concludes the characterization of reason marks the distance of a tritone (Ex. 64). Yet, if we can carry the tonal allegory so far, this cadence is more than an antithesis: it is also a part of the upward move to the D major with which the recitative ends ("wenn Jesus mit dir spricht, dass es zu deinem Heil geschicht") and that is the key of the following aria, "Öffnet euch, ihr beiden Ohren," for bass and trumpets. These instruments contrast starkly with the soft instruments used up to that point. The move to D in the recitative is coupled with the idea of salvation and a turn to arioso style; the turn to sharps, at first antithetical in nature, is clarified by these events. The allegory posits that reason alone cannot find the true path, it does not hear the soft instruments and requires the trumpeting of the word of salvation. In fact, the direct address to reason—"O Thörin! merke doch, . . . dass es *zu deinem*

EXAMPLE 64.   Cantata 175: ending of No. 5, recitative

EXAMPLE 64   *continued*

EXAMPLE 64   *continued*

Heil geschicht"—suggests that reason represents human nature and can itself be redeemed, can possess some of the truth as long as it can learn to "open both ears" to Jesus' words.

Faith is presented differently in this cantata than in others, partly because it is based on John's Gospel, which treats many of the great theological themes differently from the other Scriptures. Conspicuous by its absence here, as in the *St. John Passion,* is the emphasis on the tribulation of faith, the cross as symbol of suffering. Although the final aria, "Öffnet euch, ihr beiden Ohren," explains that the cross is the true path of life, the cross is interpreted purely as the emblem of Christ's victory and mankind's participation in Jesus' glorification, just as it is in John: "Gnade, Gnüge, volles Leben will er allen Christen geben, wer ihm folgt, sein Kreuz nachträgt." If carrying the cross after Christ means a life of suffering, it is not stated. Rather, the aria asserts triumph over the forces of evil: "Öffnet euch, ihr beiden Ohren, Jesus hat euch zugeschworen, dass er Teufel, Tod erlegt," and mankind is the beneficiary of Jesus' victory over death and sin. In the first aria we do find the line "Mein Herze schmacht', ächzt Tag und Nacht, mein Hirte, meine Freunde," and the following recitative also expresses some anxiety: "Wo find ich dich? Ach, wo bist du verborgen? O zeige dich mir bald! Ich sehne mich. Brich an, erwünschter Morgen!" The meaning of the whole, however, is that Jesus is close at hand; the prolonged waiting and suffering of Cantata 186 no longer obtain.

Part of the "Johannine" character of this cantata lies in its "realized eschatology," that is, its immediate participation in the realm of the spirit through faith. The final chorale states this directly:

> Nun, werther Geist,
> ich folg' dir;
> hilf, dass ich suche für und für
> nach deinem Wort ein ander Leben,
> das du mir willt aus Gnaden geben.

Dein Wort ist ja der Morgenstern,
der herrlich leuchtet nah' und fern.
Drum will ich, die mich anders lehren,
in Ewigkeit, mein Gott, nicht hören.
Alleluja, Alleluja!

The "other life" given in grace, or the present life of faith based on the Word of God, is akin to the Johannine idea that "Eternity is now."[8] The cry "Brich an, erwünschter Morgen!" and the reference to Christ's Word as the "Morgenstern" express desire for inner light, the illumination of reason. The instrumentation represents the idea of immediacy and suggests personal contact, Christ within us.

This last idea is important for several of the cantatas that deal with reason, in which the high incidence of special instruments (recorders, oboes da caccia, obbligato organ, violoncello piccolo, viola da gamba, viola d'amore) in these cantatas relates to the two ideas of love and the sense of taste.[9] The fairly frequent references to the senses—the blindness and deafness of reason, the tasting of Christ in Scripture, the opening of the ears to Jesus' voice, and the like—are associated with reason and the flesh. At times it may appear that the elevation of the senses above reason is primarily a means of denying the notion that reason is spiritual. However, "taste" has another connotation through the term *Vorgeschmack* (foretaste) in the Lutheran tradition to denote the anticipation of the afterlife in the present.[10] Luther's emphasis on the presence of the spirit in the flesh lies behind all ideas asserting the blessings that follow faith, the "possessions" created by faith, of which love is the most obvious. The subject of love rarely fails to call forth special instrumental sonorities and textures from Bach; we may remember the aria from the *St. Matthew Passion* "Aus Liebe will mein Heiland sterben" for flute, soprano and two oboes da caccia without basso continuo. Love and such related expressions as "sweetness" are justifiably regarded as ideas central to the modification of rigid orthodoxy in the early eighteenth century.[11] Orthodoxy, so dependent on rationality, ironically took the harshest, most dogmatic attitude toward reason, whereas pietism in some respects stood closer to the Enlightenment. Two aspects of pietism that emerge in these cantatas are subjectivity and the idea of "unmediated awareness"—unmediated,

8. Robert Kysar, *John, the Maverick Gospel* (Atlanta, 1976), pp. 84–110.

9. The use of special (i.e., relatively rare) instrumentation in these cantatas was probably not, in all cases, determined by the subject matter. Cantata 152, for example, illustrates Bach's turning to chamber-music textures at Weimar in a number of cantatas; and Cantata 35 belongs to a group of works from 1726 in which the obbligato organ is featured.

10. Von Loewenich, *Luther's Theology of the Cross*, pp. 93–94; Bach's texts from this group illustrate von Loewenich's statement (p. 94) that "the faith that carries through in experience is love." See also August Hermann Francke, "The Foretaste of Eternal Life" (1689), in *Pietists: Selected Writings*, trans. and ed. Peter Erb (Ramsey, N.J., 1983), pp.149–58. Francke refers to the discussion by Johann Arndt, whose major work (*True Christianity*, 1606), was in Bach's library; see Johann Arndt, *True Christianity*, trans. Peter Erb (Ramsey, N.J., 1979).

11. Axmacher, *"Aus Liebe,"* pp. 174–79.

that is, by reason. Metaphors of taste and the other senses and an emphasis on love convey these ideas in the texts, while they are represented in the music largely by means of strikingly sensuous instrumental sonorities.[12]

Thus Cantata 180, "Schmücke dich, o liebe Seele," presents a complex of ideas associated with the foretaste of eternity by pietist writers. One such idea is light: the opening chorus urges the soul to "Lass die dunkle Sünden höhle, komm ans helle Licht gegangen"; the fifth movement describes Jesus as the "Lebens Sonne, Licht der Sinnen." Another is the desire for union with God: in the third movement the individual cries out, "wünsche stets, dass mein Gebeine sich durch Gott mit Gott vereine." The indwelling of Christ was a favorite theme of pietism: the first movement states, "Der den Himmel kann verwalten, will selbst Herberg' in dir halten." The second movement urges opening the heart to Christ; the fourth, sixth, and seventh, love between the individual and Christ: "Die Freude aber wird gestärket, wenn sie des Heilands Herz erblickt, und seiner Liebe Grösse merket" (no. four); "dein treues Lieben" "entzünde du in Liebe meinen Geist" "und deiner Liebe stets gedenke" (no. six); "Lass mich durch dies Seelen Essen deine Liebe recht ermessen" (no. seven).

The subject of the Gospel for the twentieth Sunday after Trinity, the wedding feast for the king's son as a parable of the kingdom of heaven (Matt. 22:1–14), of course invites many figurative references to eating: the "Seelen Essen" mentioned above and the description of Jesus as the "bread of life" being the most conspicuous. Bach's setting creates a sensuous atmosphere with the sonority of two recorders with oboe and oboe da caccia in the fully scored movements, a virtuoso flute part in one aria, violoncello piccolo accompaniment to a solo chorale verse, two recorders as accompaniment to one recitative, and the dance-like characters of the three extended movements. The recitative with two recorders (no. four) juxtaposes fear and joy within the heart: fear is produced when reason fails to comprehend God's work; joy when the soul, taught by the Spirit through the Word, recognizes Jesus' heart and the greatness of his love. Fear appears in a number of Bach cantatas, such as No. 60, "O Ewigkeit, du Donnerwort," in dialogue with hope; although always overcome by hope in such contexts, fear remains the beginning of wisdom when it is fear of God. The two coexist in the individual, and their dialectical relationship resembles that between Law and Gospel. In Cantata 180 fear is aroused by the true perception of reason's limitations. Reason, earthly and finite, plays an almost positive role in the dynamic of faith, for the awakening of fear is in no sense comparable to "leading the spiritually blind into error" (Cantata 152). The aria "Lebenssonne, Licht der Sinnen," sumptuously scored for full orchestra—recorders, oboe, oboe da caccia, and strings—affirms the possibility of spiritual enlightenment in the realm of the flesh.

---

12. Von Loewenich, *Luther's Theology of the Cross,* pp. 93–94; Francke, "The Foretaste," pp. 149–58; Arndt, *True Christianity,* pp. 245–64.

The remaining two sacred cantatas, "Geist und Seele wird verwirret" (No. 35) and "Gott ist unsre Zuversicht" (No. 197), emphasize the transcendence of God's nature and actions over reason. There are no warnings in these works, no condemnation of human qualities, false prophets or teachings, no urging a life of tribulation. Rather, God's transcendence seems to be understood from the start. Man's role in this context is to trust in God, which is entirely the theme of "Gott ist unsre Zuversicht." In "Geist und Seele wird verwirret" the theme of God's "wonder works," derived from the Gospel narrative of the healing of a deaf and dumb man, provides a framework for stating the relationship between God and man, and one that possibly had personal associations. This two-part cantata features the most prominent use of obbligato organ in all Bach's church works: all the closed movements (five out of seven) contain elaborate right-hand parts, and it is probable that an entire concerto was reworked for three of the movements.[13] Large-scale concerto allegros serve as preludes to both parts, while the first aria is the familiar Siciliano slow-movement type, set to the text "Geist und Seele wird verwirret." This setting does not, as is sometimes said, portray God's works, for such an idea would directly contradict the text, but rather illustrates such lines from the following recitative as "Du macht es eben dass sonst ein Wunderwerk vor dir was Schlechtes ist" and "dir ist kein Wunderding auf dieser Erde gleich." The line "Betracht ich dich, du teurer Gottessohn, so flieht Vernunft und auch Verstand davon" also belongs in this context. Surely the references to the senses and faculties of reason, understanding, hearing, speech, and sight are related to the instrumentation of the work. In the first recitative the framework for such references is God's transcendence of everything in Creation; in the second (no. 6, Part Two) it is that of prayer for God to stir the senses and faculties to his purposes: thought, so that God may "sink into the soul"; hearing, so that mankind will not be lost; and speech for the praise of God. Sight is implied in the final aria of longing to be with God.

In the fall of 1726, when this cantata was written, Bach suddenly produced a number of cantatas, and single movements within cantatas, that feature obbligato organ.[14] The reason for this tendency toward a particular instrument has never been fully divined. Although there is no hard evidence, perhaps Bach favored this instrument just at the time that he was endeavoring to reach a wider audience through the publication of the *Clavierübung*. In fact, some of the cantatas and arias with obbligato organ do have a personal quality, such as the aria "Willkommen will ich sagen" for obbligato organ and oboe da caccia from Cantata 27 and the Siciliano "Stirb in mir, Welt" for organ and strings from Cantata 169. The dialogue cantata "Ich geh' und suche mit Verlangen," in which the obbligato organ per-

13. The concerto model has not survived apart from a nine-bar segment of an incomplete reworking for harpsichord (Dürr, *Die Kantaten*, p. 420).

14. These works (Cantatas 27, 35, 49, 146, 169, 170) are listed in Dürr, *Die Kantaten*, pp. 54–56, along with other works with obbligato organ from other years; Dürr advances the possibility that questions of sonority prompted the use of obbligato organ (p. 54).

forms in the concerto-derived sinfonia as well as the final "love duet" between the Soul and Christ, is throughout a work of the most highly pietistic character.[15] As we saw, in its reference to "was das Werk der Hände thut," the first recitative in Cantata 27, immediately before the aria "Willkommen will ich sagen," clarifies the meaning of the obbligato organ. "Geist und Seele wird verwirret" might be considered to state, as does the first recitative of Cantata 169, that worldly pleasure, represented by the instrumental style, is like a *Bächlein* whose source is the mighty torrent of God's gifts to man. That is, Cantata 35 might be viewed as a dramatic form of the "Soli Deo Gloria" that Bach signed on many manuscripts.

The wedding cantata "Gott ist unsre Zuversicht" is the last of Bach's works to refer to reason. Written after 1735, it is chronologically closer to Bach's secular cantata "Hercules auf dem Scheidewege" than to the church cantatas. Like the Hercules cantata, it focuses on the images of *Wege* and *Bahn,* and, like that work, it is intimately related through parody to a Christmas cantata, "Ehre sei dir Gott in der Höhe" (around 1728), a work that has survived only in part. Bach's striking re-working of the aria "O du angenehmer Schatz" as "O du angenehmes Paar" and the aria "Ich lasse dich nicht, ich schliesse dich ein" as "Vergnügen und Lust, Gedeihen und Heil" hints at the intent behind "Gott ist unsre Zuversicht."[16] Above all, unlike the earlier Leipzig cantatas in which the fulfillment of hopes must be deferred, now a more positive viewpoint on the present life prevails.

"Gott ist unsre Zuversicht" attempts to reveal to the joined couple the blessings that follow from complete trust in God. As in several other cantatas reason is introduced in the first recitative, now as a power that can never fathom God's will. The first aria, "Schläfert aller Sorgen Kummer in den Schlummer kindlichen Vertrauens ein," parodied from the Shepherd Cantata of 1725 (BWV 197a), urges a child-like trust of God in a gently melodic pastorale A section, while God's watchfulness over man contrasts sharply with it in the B section. Man's relationship to God as child to father appeared just before the final aria of Cantata 35 also ("und mich als Kind und Erb erweise"). Such a relationship contradicts a reliance on reason, of course, but it also suggests an inherited inner quality that aids man in following the true path. The second recitative of "Gott ist unsre Zuversicht" begins thus: "Drum folget Gott und seinem Triebe. Das ist die rechte Bahn. Die führet durch Gefahr auch endlich in das Kanaan." The words may recall Cantata 178, but God's way is now presented as an impulse rather than as everything that opposes human instinct. The remainder of the recitative and the succeeding chorale make clear that the impulse is love. In keeping with this following of God's path, the first recitative

15. This work (BWV 49) is a dialogue cantata between the Soul (soprano) and its Bridegroom, Christ (bass); the first recitative culminates in a dance-like love duet, beginning "Komm, Schönste, komm und lass dich küssen," and the following soprano aria, "Ich bin herrlich, ich bin schön," uses oboe d'amore and violoncello piccolo to create an atmosphere suitable to the beauty of the soul, as in "Schmücke dich."

16. See Dürr, *Die Kantaten,* pp. 605–8, 114–15.

moves, after the D major opening chorus, to A major, and Part One holds to A major throughout the four remaining movements.

Part Two, on the other hand, begins in the subdominant of G, the key of the two parodied arias, between which the recitative moves still further in the subdominant direction, ending in C major. This emphasis on the subdominant has a counterpart in the Christmas Oratorio, in the first and second cantatas taken separately, and in the first three cantatas as a whole. In that work the subdominant direction is unmistakably associated in several cantatas with the incarnation. Also, in the fourth cantata (largely parodied from "Hercules auf dem Scheidewege") the key of F major relates to the direct focus on the infant Christ. Love for Christ as a child, for his humanity and weakness, expresses mankind's relationship to the Father as well. Above all, the personal nature of the relationship informs these works and carries over into the marital relationship in "Gott ist unsre Zuversicht." Bach's stunning reworking of the two arias from "Ehre sei Gott in der Höhe" creates an atmosphere of love that is seldom so beautifully expressed in his work. "O du angenehmes Paar" is scored for the unique combination of oboe solo, two muted violins, obbligato bassoon, and bass solo with continuo, and "Vergnügen und Lust" for solo violin, two oboes d'amore, soprano, and continuo. In each case Bach changes the instrumental parts of the original (flutes to muted violins, cello to bassoon; oboe d'amore solo to violin solo) and adds one or more parts to the original texture. In "O du angenehmes Paar" the added voice is an oboe line that for much of the time plays the three-note figure accompanying the word *Paar* at the ends of phrases; its character is complementary, sometimes echoing the line endings, sometimes inverting them, and usually furthering continuity between the lines. At times it takes the leading melodic line, usually before major sectional cadences. This addition to the soft instrumentation creates an atmosphere of assurance, the muted violins (perhaps, as elsewhere, a substitute for viole d'amore) allowing the winds to color the sound. The recitative restates God's fatherly caring and the happiness of the pair. Bach then adds to the aria "Vergnügen und Lust" two oboes d'amore, playing an accompaniment comprising pairs of off-the-beat eighth notes throughout the piece, the effect being the inner impulse (*Triebe*) mentioned in Part One.

This aria, and the work as a whole, represents earthly pleasure and joy ("Vergnügen und Lust") as attainable for those who trust in God. Gone is the emphasis on the purification of the soul in tribulation, on the condemnation of human qualities and works. Now the text states explicitly that [God] "wird dir nie bei deiner Hände Schweiss und Müh' kein Gutes lassen fehlen," urging confidence in life. The theology behind such statements is not, of course, irreconcilable with the stricter expressions of orthodoxy in the earlier cantatas, but the shift in emphasis is significant. Although we will not conclude that Bach's outlook shifted during his Leipzig years, the more personal and intimate works with softer instrumentation equally offer the softened viewpoint on reason and associated qualities.

In summary, reason is approached from two sides in the church cantatas. One side emphasizes the strict Lutheran view that reason is a stumbling block to salvation. Reason is condemned and warned against, not without an element of fear for its ability to overcome man. Such a viewpoint, holding to the antithetical seventeenth-century *Lebensgefühl*, assumes that the struggle of faith is ever present. The second approach presupposes a faith already attained and secure and therefore deals with its benefits for the present life. Walther von Loewenich has discussed these coexisting viewpoints in Luther's writings in detail as "faith in opposition to experience" and "faith realized in experience," respectively.[17] The degree of their separation in the Bach cantatas reflects the many years of orthodox/pietist divergence in the century before Bach. In their emphasis on love many of Bach's texts tended to resolve the dialectical character, right on the threshold of an Enlightenment revolution in hermeneutics that would eventually transform theology to the point of rendering the formal pietist/orthodox split irrelevant.[18] Although this revolution was taking place under Bach's eyes, so to speak, it is not likely that he was more than intuitively aware of it.

The illumination of reason emerges in Cantata 76, "Die Himmel erzählen die Ehre Gottes," as part of the broadest theological context in which reason is treated in the cantatas. Written in June 1723 for the second Sunday after Trinity, Cantata 76 is only the second cantata Bach produced after taking up his position in Leipzig. A still more arresting fact is that, along with the cantata for the preceding Sunday, "Die Elenden soll essen" (No. 75), the work is especially long for Bach. Cantatas 75 and 76 both have fourteen movements each, the longest of all the church cantatas. Moreover, their sequences of movements are identical. Each has seven movements before and after the sermon following this pattern: chorus, accompanied recitative, aria, secco recitative, aria, secco recitative, chorale for Part One; then sinfonia, accompanied recitative, aria, secco recitative, aria, secco recitative, chorale (the same music that ended Part One) for Part Two. Although Bach's earlier Leipzig cantatas tend to be longer than his average, the length and parallelism between "Die Elenden soll essen" and "Die Himmel erzählen" have no counterpart elsewhere in Bach's output, which suggests a symbolic intent. The number fourteen immediately invites the speculation that Bach wanted to announce his presence numerologically to each of the two main Leipzig congregations in turn. However, this idea neither explains the parallelism nor does it tell much about the works themselves.

In fact, it is probable that Bach intended to make a musicotheological statement to the Leipzig community on the assumption of his position. Given the Gospel and Epistle texts for these two Sundays, it is likely that Bach (and his librettist) saw an opportunity to bind two weeks together in a comprehensive message of God's love, brotherly love, and the juxtaposition of the present life with hopes for the afterlife. The Epistles for both Sundays, from the first Epistle of John, emphasize

17. Von Loewenich, *Luther's Theology of the Cross*, pp. 77–88, 91–101.
18. The man who has been called the "father of Enlightenment hermeneutics," J. A. Ernesti, was the rector of the Thomasschule with whom Bach had the famous *Praefektenstreit* in the 1730s. Minear ("Bach and Ernesti") contrasts the attitudes of composer and theologian-scholar.

brotherly love, while the two Gospel readings, both from Luke, treat the notion that the lowly of the earth shall enjoy the kingdom of God, the first Gospel reading being the story of Lazarus and the rich man, and the second the parable of the kingdom as the feast to which all were invited from the "highways and byways." Bach emphasizes the Epistle readings more than usual, ending Cantata 76 with four movements that refer directly to John's idea that brotherly love is manifested in deeds, especially in the aria, "Liebt, ihr Christen, in der Tat". Here already we see that the message of Cantata 76 is set apart from the severe inveighing against works that often dominated orthodox Lutheran thought. The underlying theology is not different, of course, but here the emphasis is on the concerns of the present life and love as the keys to worldly existence. This message, so appropriate from the new cantor, unfolds in clearly marked stages when Cantatas 75 and 76 are considered as a continuous theological statement.

The opening chorus of Cantata 75, "Die Elenden soll essen," can be seen to link up with Cantata 76, since there is no reference to the banquet of the afterlife in the Gospel for the first Sunday after Trinity. Part One of Cantata 75, although anticipating the blessings of the future life, juxtaposes poverty and riches to underscore the idea that values are inverted between the kingdoms of earth and heaven. This idea is characteristically expressed in the second recitative (no. 4): "Gott stürzet und erhöhet in Zeit und Ewigkeit. Wer in der Welt den Himmel sucht, wird dort verflucht. Wer aber hier die Hölle übersteht, wird dort erfreut." The following aria, on the text "Ich nehme mein Leiden mit Freuden auf mich. Wer Lazarus' Plagen geduldig ertragen, den nehmen die Engel zu sich," develops this idea in the familiar manner of the cantatas treating the theology of the cross, such as "Ich habe manches Herzeleid" (No. 58). The severity of suffering in this life is offset, however, by the message of trust in Jesus, especially in the aria "Mein Jesus soll mein alles sein" (no. 3).

Part Two of this cantata (No. 75) develops the contrast between *Armut* (particularly the spiritual poverty of man's awareness of his inability to produce *Wachstum* and *Frucht* for the afterlife) and *Reichtum,* with Jesus as the source of the latter (aria "Jesus macht mich geistlich reich"). Self-denial confirms love of God and leads man to God in the afterlife. The second aria, joining faith and love, describes Jesus' giving his spirit to man in almost pietistic terms:

Mein Herze glaubt und liebt.
Denn Jesu süsse Flammen,
aus den' die meinen stammen,
gehn über mich zusammen,
weil er sich mir ergibt.

The final recitative, beginning "O Armut, der kein Reichtum gleicht!" expresses the change that the spirit of Jesus' love works in man.

Thus we might conclude that the symbolism of fourteen movements in this cantata expresses something more than the name Bach. Because of the association to the *A* and *O,* Alpha and Omega, the number fourteen had striking Christological meaning within the Lutheran tradition, especially meaning of the kind that is expressed, for example, in "Mein Jesus soll mein alles sein."[19] This Christological emphasis is strong in Cantata 76 as well. In fact, in both cantatas the first arias describe Jesus in similar terms. Cantata 76 begins with the voice of God as proclaimed in nature and calling mankind to his *Liebesmahl.* The latter idea emphasizes the Lutheran concept of Jesus Christ as both one with the creator God and the impetus for mankind's turning to God: "Hört, ihr Völker, Gottes Stimme, eilt zu seinem Gnadenthron! *Aller Dinge Grund und Ende* ist sein eingeborne Sohn: dass sich alles zu ihm wende."

Immediately after this point the idea of reason is introduced. The second recitative refers to those people who reject God in favor of "eigene Lust," and the aria "Fahr hin, abgöttische Zunft!" rejects them in turn. In the middle section the believer voices his desire to honor Christ in opposition to the contrary way of the world, ending "er ist das Licht der Vernunft." These last words are given particular emphasis at the end of the section as all the parts come to a general pause, the bass moving up chromatically and the voice dropping a diminished fifth to a $^6_3$ chord on A sharp (i.e., V of V, its root a tritone from the C major tonic). After the pause "er ist das Licht der Vernunft" repeats, adagio and cadenza-like, before the da capo (Ex. 65). It is noteworthy that reason is not described as leading man astray. Rather, as the following recitative indicates, God causes man to be "erleuchtet und belebet." The chorale also refers to this illumination: "sein Antlitz uns mit hellem Schein erleucht' zum ew'gen Leben, dass wir erkennen seine Werk, und was ihm lieb auf Erden."

"Auf Erden" marks an important emphasis that is taken further in Part Two, completing the message of Bach's first two Leipzig cantatas. The first recitative after the break prays for God's blessing on the "treue Schar" (i.e., the community of the faithful), for they constitute "heaven on earth" ("Sie ist der Himmel auf der Erden"). The idea of heaven on earth completes the message given in Cantata 75 that anyone seeking heaven in this life is cursed in the afterlife. There is no contradiction, of course; the "treue Schar" is made up of those who do not seek heaven on earth, or as the end of the recitative states explicitly, who must "durch steten Streit mit Hass und mit Gefahr in dieser Welt gereinigt werden." The aria "Hasse nur, hasse mich recht, feindlich's Geschlecht," with its middle section "Christum gläubig zu umfassen, will ich alle Freude lassen," recalls the emphasis of Cantata 75, Part One. The idea of "heaven on earth," however, reveals the other side of faith, its positive benefits for the believer and the community. The remainder of

19. See Klaus Düwel, ed. *Epochen der deutschen Lyrik,* vol. 3, *Gedichte, 1500–1600* (Munich, 1978), pp. 71–75.

EXAMPLE 65.   Cantata 76, Part One: excerpt from aria "Fahr hin, abgöttische Zunft"

Cantata 76 then develops this idea in relation to brotherly love. First a recitative voices the inner change and its source: "Ich fühle schon im Geist, wie Christus mir der Liebe Süssigkeit erweist, und mich mit Manna speist: damit unter uns allhier die brüderliche Treue stets stärke und erneue." This passage newly focuses on the Spirit, love, and sweetness—the ideas running through the arias in Cantatas 75 and 76 where Jesus as Alpha and Omega was the foremost theme, in particular, "Mein Jesus soll mein alles sein" ("und seines Geistes Liebesglut mein allersüsster Freudenwein"). In "Mein Herze glaubt und liebt," love stands beside faith as its affective character ("Denn Jesu süsse Flammen, aus den' die meinen stammen, gehn über mich zusammen"). In the sweetness of love the individual recognizes the presence of the Spirit, and love softens the severity of "faith in opposition to experience" to the point that the injunction against works fades from the center of Lutheran dogma, replaced by its other side, "faith realized in experience."

In keeping with the increased emphasis on love and the experience of the Spirit in "Die Himmel erzählen," Bach once again changes the character of the instrumentation within a cantata. After the militant tone of the trumpets in Part One of "Die Himmel erzählen," he sets the sinfonia introducing Part Two for oboe d'amore, viola da gamba solo, and basso continuo. He then retains the viola da gamba for the recitatives and the continuo aria "Hasse mich recht" and scores the very gentle final aria, "Liebt, ihr Christen in der Tat," for alto with the same instrumental complement as the sinfonia. This aria and the final chorale, "Es danke, Gott, und lobe dich das Volk in guten Taten," focus on the believing community. The intimate, chamber-music nature of Part Two contributes to the message that brotherly love is the basis of worldly life, the means by which mankind gives honor to God. Here, as in the statements he made in his *Orgelbüchlein* and his collection of rules for figured bass ("Dem Höchsten Gott allein zu Ehren, Dem Nächsten, draus sich zu belehren"), Bach seems to proclaim the glory of God and the edification of one's fellow men as the goal of his music.[20] The concept of the "riches" of faith now goes beyond the emphasis on hope for the afterlife amid a life of tribulation, as it is presented in Cantata 75. Significantly, Cantata 76 gives "Glaube, Liebe und Heiligkeit" (rather than *Hoffnung*) as the human qualities by which mankind renders honor to God. Cantata 76 shifts emphasis from the *Essen* of the afterlife to God's *Liebesmahl* as the manna shared by the community. The expression "Wachstum und Frucht" of Cantata 75 likewise assumes new meaning for the present life, for the final chorale of "Die Himmel erzählen" announces prosperity as God's gift to the faithful: "Das Land bringt Frucht und bessert sich." Seen this way the final "Amen" of Cantata 76 rings out as the community's symbolic assent to a message

---

20. See David and Mendel, eds., *The Bach Reader,* p. 75; also Werner Neumann and Hans-Joachim Schulze, eds., *Bach-Dokumente,* vol. 1 (Leipzig, 1963), p. 214. In this light Günther Stiller (*Johann Sebastian Bach and Liturgical Life in Leipzig,* trans. Herbert J. A. Bouman, Daniel F. Poellot, and Hilton C. Oswald [St. Louis, 1984], p. 210) describes Bach's "final purpose" in composition as "Glory to God and service to the neighbor."

embracing the range of basic Lutheran beliefs concerning faith and love as they were given by the new cantor.

In linking Cantatas 75 and 76 as Bach's first musicotheological statement to the Leipzig community, I do not argue that the two cantatas constitute a unit in the sense that applies, for example, to the cantatas of the Christmas Oratorio. Rather, the writing of "Die Elenden soll essen" and "Die Himmel erzählen" might be compared to the procedure Bach followed at the beginning of the chorale cantata cycle of the following year when he produced four chorale fantasias of systematically differentiated types with the cantus firmus successively in each of the four voices of the choir.[21] That is, Bach often thinks on a scale larger than the individual work. So, for example, the change from C major to E minor in Cantata 76 might be thought of as a return to the key with which Cantata 75 began (and abandoned soon after), without our concluding from this that the two works should be performed on the same program. The latter is a possibility, however, that would bring out the fullness of the theological message running through the two compositions.

Returning to the theme of *Vernunft,* it seems now that the context in which such an idea is treated is essential to understanding the idea itself. Within Bach's church cantatas two somewhat different contexts are possible: the condemnation of the world as the realm of the flesh, which is emphasized by the stricter forms of orthodoxy; and the sense of a world transformed by faith, which might be called orthodoxy softened by elements of pietism, particularly subjectivism. The former is more allegorical in nature. As it happens, the cantatas that deal with reason according to the more orthodox viewpoint—Nos. 186, 2, 178—exhibit the more patterned tonal plans. The treatment of reason in Cantata 76, however, relates more closely to that of the later cantatas, a situation that might have additional significance. Bach, arriving in Leipzig after nearly a decade at the reformed court of Köthen, might not have been so close in his thinking to the orthodoxy prevalent in Leipzig. The shift of perspective regarding reason that appears in Cantatas 186, 2, and 178 might then reflect his adjustment to his new circumstances, while the subsequent return to his original viewpoint could reflect changes in Leipzig.[22]

We would misrepresent the Lutheran view of reason if we did not add that Luther's writings on the subject are not entirely derogatory; nor is Bach's treatment of *Vernunft,* as the following chapter will show. Luther's writings, in fact, take a positive stance so long as mankind confines the use of reason to the secular sphere and recognizes it as a gift from God, given to man to manage earthly affairs, but not as a quality that can lead him to equal terms with God. In this light the *Drama per Musica,* "Hercules auf dem Scheidewege" (BWV 213), suggests that Bach, in a work from the 1730s, could deal with secular, Enlightenment values with the same means he uses in his church music and effect something of a reconciliation between the two spheres.

21. Dürr, *Die Kantaten,* pp. 47–48.
22. A similar situation perhaps obtained in the case of the revisions to the *St. John Passion.* See below, pp. 301–4.

CHAPTER NINE

"Hercules auf

dem Scheidewege"

and the

Christmas Oratorio

"Hercules auf dem Scheidewege," BWV 213, is the one composition in Bach's oeuvre that brings together allegorical subject matter, structural symmetry, and tonal allegory in a truly detailed and profound manner. A secular cantata, it belongs to the tradition of allegorical drama produced to glorify a baroque ruler. The subject is the widespread dramatic and pictorial allegory of Hercules' choice between the paths of Pleasure (*Wollust*) and virtue (*Tugend*). This choice, representing the turning point (*Scheidewege* or crossroads) of character development and explicitly linked to Hercules' exploits as a child in Picander's text, was uniquely appropriate to the occasion, the eleventh birthday of Friedrich August II, who had acceded to the electoral throne of Saxony in that year of 1733. This very beautiful cantata has suffered from undue neglect at least in part because Bach parodied most of its movements in the *Christmas Oratorio*; the relationship between the two works has elicited differing viewpoints.[1]

Of all Bach's work, the *Passions* exemplify the fullest and most profound use of tonal allegory. Compared to the *Passions,* only "Hercules auf dem Scheidewege," of all the two hundred cantatas, exercises a wide tonal range embracing movements in both sharp and flat key areas. The broad tonal range of Cantata 213 explains why the *Christmas Oratorio* is the only Bach oratorio other than the *Passions* with much music in keys outside its basic D major ambitus (the fourth cantata, in F major).

---

1. On the relative dating of the two works see Dürr, *Zur Chronologie der Leipziger Vokalwerke,* pp. 107, 109; Walter Blankenburg and Alfred Dürr, eds., *Kritischer Bericht* to *Johann Sebastian Bach. Neue Ausgabe sämtlicher Werke,* II/6 (Kassel, 1962): pp. 162, 214–15; Alfred Dürr, ed., *Johann Sebastian Bach: Weihnachts-Oratorium, BWV 248,* facsimile of the autograph score (Leipzig, 1960), pp. 7, 40. "Hercules auf dem Scheidewege" was first produced in 1733, the *Christmas Oratorio* in the following year, and examining the parodied movements in the autograph score proves that the secular work was written first. The opposite viewpoint, advocated most strongly by Charles Sanford Terry ("The Christmas Oratorio: Original or Borrowed?" parts 1–3, *The Musical Times* 71 [October, November, December 1930]) tended toward circular arguments based on the appropriateness of text-musical relationships that had the effect of devaluing "Hercules."

Although "Hercules" is no longer than some other cantatas, and therefore does not need a broad tonal spectrum, it, like the *Passions,* is a drama, even if a purely allegorical one; the cantatas, however, despite the occasional use of personification, are meditative and do not dramatize immediate external events. The theological ideas in the church cantata subordinate any pictorialism and overt dramatic devices.

Bach's church music is dominated by the perspective of the New Testament, the Gospel, and God's revelation through the cross, whereas his greatest contemporary, Handel, remains spiritually closer to the Old Testament, to event, history, and drama. Both men set the Hercules subject to music, but only Bach's version expresses the unity of musicoallegorical and Lutheran theologial thought, which are based on a form of theological aesthetics. Cantata 213 might lead one to speculate that Bach's operas, if he had written any, would have followed completely different paths from those of Handel. Although one can easily show the allegorical character of the eighteenth-century "opera of affections," Bach's vision in "Hercules" is still older and relates to the allegorical focus found at the very beginnings of baroque music drama. This early emphasis on allegory explains the underlying connections between such works as Monteverdi's *Orfeo* and Emilio de' Cavalieri's *Rapprasentatione di anima, et di corpo,* and the occasional confusion whether the latter is an opera or oratorio; like Bach's cantata, both are forms of allegorical drama, a category central to the baroque Weltanschauung.[2]

The planned symmetry is unmistakable in "Hercules": instrumentation, keys, placing of modulations, a thematic parallel between movements 3 and 11 (Fig. 6). Casting the central aria as a fugue makes it one of a very few fugal arias in Bach's oeuvre. It is common knowledge that Bach places a fugal movement at the center of a symmetrical structure in a number of well-known instances, such as the *St. John Passion* (two choral fugues) and Cantata 106, "Jesu, meine Freude." Typically it signifies Law or covenant opposed to freedom: *Gesetz* versus *Freiheit* in the *St. John Passion;* the *alter Bund* versus the message of the Gospel in the "Actus Tragicus"; the law of the flesh versus that of the spirit in "Jesu, meine Freude." Prominent antithesis in such pieces expands the central idea, and "Hercules auf dem Scheidewege" is unquestionably another of these antithesis cantatas. In this case, however, the most conspicuous confrontation appears well before the central movement. This placement has been criticized on the grounds that the work presents no dramatic conflict after the second recitative (this viewpoint, as we will endeavor to show, misconstrues the nature of the work). The fugal centerpiece of

2. This is a contestable statement. The presence of allegorical characters (e.g., Speranza in *Orfeo*) and of allegorical prefaces to the earliest operas, however, very strongly indicates that in a certain sense the message takes precedence over the drama, and when that happens the work can be called allegorical, even though characters such as Orfeo, Poppea, and Seneca are, of course, more than the representations of human frailty, desire, virtue, and so on. The very idea of affect can be called allegorical in that it emphasizes an abstract quality rather than the representation of character that is much more prominent in Mozart.

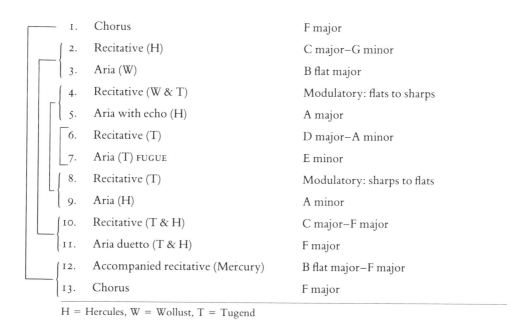

	1.	Chorus	F major
	2.	Recitative (H)	C major–G minor
	3.	Aria (W)	B flat major
	4.	Recitative (W & T)	Modulatory: flats to sharps
	5.	Aria with echo (H)	A major
	6.	Recitative (T)	D major–A minor
	7.	Aria (T) FUGUE	E minor
	8.	Recitative (T)	Modulatory: sharps to flats
	9.	Aria (H)	A minor
	10.	Recitative (T & H)	C major–F major
	11.	Aria duetto (T & H)	F major
	12.	Accompanied recitative (Mercury)	B flat major–F major
	13.	Chorus	F major

H = Hercules, W = Wollust, T = Tugend

FIGURE 6.   Symmetry and tonal design in "Hercules auf dem Scheidewege"

"Hercules," with its stretti and inversions on a theme of ornate melismatic character, perfectly expresses both the discipline and the exhilaration of virtue. Not since Seneca's death scene in Monteverdi's *L'incoronazione di Poppea* had Virtue's name been carved on such a splendid musical triumphal arch. Yet its function in the dramatic structure of the work celebrates the bond between Hercules and Tugend that is already established by the preceding echo aria.

The lasting impression of "Hercules auf dem Scheidewege" is of a structure created not so much to dramatize a conflict as to stand as a monument to Hercules' choice, with the central aria as the crowning element. The symmetry represents the allegorical view of life, the attempt to freeze and analyze the flow of human events, just as symmetry does both in the many da capo opera arias of the period, as in *Orfeo* and the "Actus Tragicus." On either side of the fugal centerpiece Hercules sings arias expressing his choice of Virtue over Pleasure, the first in A major, the second in A minor. The major/minor shift points up Hercules' change in attitude toward Pleasure, which is more important than the mere fact of his choice. Moving from the center the correspondences between movements become more direct musically while their texts grow increasingly antithetical. According to their texts, Pleasure's enticing "Schlafe" aria (B flat) and the duet between Hercules and Virtue (F) should be opposed to one another, but a melodic parallel between their main themes—along with details of instrumentation—connects them in the sphere of affect. Finally, two choruses of the gods (both in F major, homophonic, with horns) frame the whole, putting the earthly events in the broader perspective of their divine significance. One movement stands outside the symmetrical arrangement; it is the accompanied recitative of Mercury, immediately before the final chorus, "Schaut, Götter, dieses ist ein Bild von Sachsens Churprinz, Friedrichs Jugend." Mercury, or Hermes, as the messenger of the gods—whose name forms the root of the word "hermeneutics"—himself represents allegorical meaning in baroque art.

As in the "Actus Tragicus," the tonal plan of "Hercules auf dem Scheidewege" adds to the musicoallegorical structure a dimension that is connected more to the dynamic flow of dramatic events than to the static allegorical meaning. It can be described as a slight catabasis from F to B flat for the first aria, then a sudden anabasis in the second recitative to the A major echo aria, followed by a long, gradual descent from this, the hero's first aria, back to F. The principal stages in the descent are a D major recitative, E minor aria, C major recitative, A minor aria, F major duet, and final chorus. The A major echo aria departs radically from the key of the whole: not only is it further removed along the circle of fifths from its tonic than any other movement we have examined, but it marks a greater conceptual division as well. Bach envisaged Hercules' choice of paths as the opposition of sharp and flat keys, making the two key areas represent separate affective spheres. Juxtaposing the arias in B flat and A constitutes a structural *relatio non-harmonica* and represents the antithesis between Pleasure and Virtue, while the ensuing catabasis, with its gradual, step-by-step nature, resolves the whole in a return to the original key. The keynotes used for the closed movements of the cantata are F, A (major and minor), B flat, and E (minor);[3] the return to F major in "Hercules" through measured key signature changes is a significant allegorical device connected to the resolution of the early confrontation.

Immediately following the introductory chorus of the gods, Hercules voices his goals in Enlightenment terms in the first recitative: the pursuit of reason, understanding, and "light" demands that he follow his innate urge toward living a life of virtue, honor, renown, and glory. These are some of the qualities that are generally rejected for man according to the Lutheran spiritual realm of the church cantatas, or else they acquire a new meaning, such as the Lutheran definition of "understanding," because of their illumination by faith. Singing in flats, Pleasure begins immediately to try to entice Hercules into a life of ease (B flat aria, "Schlafe, mein Liebster" and the following recitative). The sinking move to the subdominant calls up several associations of passivity—the suggestion of a relinquishing of will from Cantata 73, the B flat subdominant of Cantata 156 (acceptance of God's will), and

3. Bach uses these very tones a decade later as the ground bass of the canon "Fa Mi et Mi Fa est tota musica," a piece that defines the tonality of a key by its extremes, the mi and fa tones; Chafe, "Allegorical Music," pp. 358–61.

the descent patterns in Cantatas 38, 179, and so on, plus the association of "sleep" belonging to the flats in such works as Cantata 127 and the *St. Matthew Passion.*

Following this attempt to lull Hercules into the sleep of a life of unbounded pleasure, Virtue confronts Pleasure in a recitative dialogue. Pleasure sings the first half in flats, promising to direct Hercules with "sanften Tritten," roses strewn in his path of comfort. Virtue, answering with a modulation to sharps, and dominating the second half, offers instead a life crowned by success and glory: "Durch Tugend, Müh und Fleiss erhebet sich ein edler Sinn." Now the active course, not the passive, is the nobler. This stance is the opposite of the church music, in which Luther's concept of "passive righteousness" (submission to God's will) is the true course of faith, while "active righteousness" is the erroneous one that relies on good works and human achievement. Yet Virtue, in a Leipzig definition from Bach's time, signified "die wahre Gottes-Furcht, die Sanfftmuth und Gedult, die holde Freundlichkeit, die Anmuth der Gebehrden, die Demuth ohne Schein," all qualities suggestive of the *mollis* sphere of affections.[4]

Since Virtue returns to flats later in the work, it is possible that Bach intends a more complex allegory than the early antithesis suggests, an allegory evident both in the symmetrical structure and even more in the tonal plan of the work. Virtue's extolling human endeavor is seemingly antithetical to the Lutheran devaluation of works for salvation, particularly since both Pleasure and Virtue state that life's goal is *Heil* (salvation). Pleasure counters, "Wer wählet sich den Schweiss, der in Gemächlichkeit und scherzender Zufriedenheit sich kann sein wahres Heil erwerben?" This phrase has exactly the same harmonic turn—an anticipated A minor cadence diverted to the dominant of F sharp minor—that Bach uses in the *St. Matthew Passion* for Pilate's question to Jesus: "Hörest du nicht, wie *hart* sie dich verklagen?" (Ex. 66). Virtue responds, "Das heisst: sein wahres Heil verderben," completing the cadence to F sharp minor. A conflict between Virtue and Pleasure has been set up, which goes beyond simple good/evil correlates to the conflict of the sacred and secular.

Continuing the comparison with the *St. Matthew Passion,* we see that the questions of Pilate and Pleasure are, of course, the same: "Why choose the hard way?" Pilate's question constitutes the modulation to sharps for the trial and sets up the hard character of that scene, through which Jesus remains silent. Bach's alliance of these modulations to the *cantus durus* interpretation of sharp keys seems particularly clear. Pleasure's question is to no avail. Virtue's completion of the cadence lessens the provocative character of the modulation, indicating acceptance of the challenge. Hercules finds support for his choice of the hard path in the dialogue aria with Echo, which we would guess to be the voice of Virtue within him. His question embodies the answer he already knows: "Oder sollte das Ermahnen, dass so

---

4. Johann Georg Hamann, *Poetisches Lexicon* (Leipzig, 1737), s.v. "Tugend."

EXAMPLE 66.

(a) Cantata 213: excerpt from second recitative (No. 4)

(b) *St. Matthew Passion*: excerpt from recitative (No. 43)

mancher Arbeit nah, mir die Wege besser bahnen? Ach! so sage lieber: Ja!" Virtue wins an early and easy victory over the enticements of Pleasure; the pàstorale-like echo aria is in A major, the sharp-key extreme of the cantata. Its character is gentle, effortless, and assured; the only thing needed is a concluding celebratory chorus.

Virtue rejoices in the choice Hercules has made, inviting him (now addressed as "Mein hoffnungsvoller Held!"—i.e., suggesting that his spiritual development is not yet complete) to further his counsel with Virtue. Bach sets the recitative in the two-sharp system, thus assigning to Virtue the change of direction that will eventually lead back to flats. Virtue moves down to G major, then closes in A *minor* with a Tierce de Picardie, and celebrates the young hero's anticipated fame and glory in the magnificently ornate E minor fugal aria. This piece is certainly triumphant, but we may recall the powerful association of E minor with lamentation from its connection to the Phrygian mode. In addition, full inversion of the theme in the basso continuo as the vocal part ends each of the two main sections hints at conflict beneath the surface. In several respects—in particular the elements of the main theme, octave leap, staccato repeated notes, and the *schweben* melisma—this aria recalls the opening chorus of the *St. John Passion,* which casts a marked sense of triumph in a minor-key movement. The *Passion,* however, exemplifies the Johannine theology of the cross, glorification *through abasement,* and we note the descent that takes place on the word *Niedrigkeit* in the middle section. As if to point out the significance of the downward direction to Hercules, the following recitative contains a carefully placed modulatory shift—now from sharps to flats. Beginning in B minor, Virtue cautions Hercules that Pleasure still remains enticing: "Der weiche [!] Wollust locket zwar." Despite the hero's early resolve to a life of virtue, Pleasure is a temptress who must be cast down (D minor ending). This initial crossover back to flats begins to modulate on the word *Verführerin* (temptress).[5] As if responding to Virtue's test of his fidelity, Hercules sings once more of his resolve; the tonic is again A, but the mode is minor, as Hercules, resisting the turn to flats, abjures Pleasure more forcefully: "Ich will dich nicht hören."[6]

The fourth bar of the next recitative of "Hercules," which opens in a neutral C major, begins another modulation to sharps, on Hercules' "Wo du [Tugend] befiehlst, da geh' ich hin" (a move from C to F sharp in the bass). Hercules is now ready to take Virtue as his guide, whatever the direction. But with the next phrase, "Das will ich mich zur Richtschnur wählen," Hercules turns to flats instead, with a cadence to G *minor* on *Richtschnur* (guideline). This precisely placed move confirms Hercules' willingness to follow Virtue, even into the flats that up to now he has rejected. The return to flats closes the "circle" of F major to provide a coherent tonal plan. But for the allegorical structure as a whole it is inconsistent with the meaning that Bach so obviously attached to the original turn to sharps. We must conclude that the motion back to F represents a final reconciliation not merely between Hercules and Virtue but between virtue (spirit) and pleasure (flesh) within Hercules as well. Bach's tonal narrative tells us that, Hercules having rested his trust in Virtue, the shift back to flats is shorn of its negative implications; the hero can soften—to the qualities of "Sanftmut, Geduld, holde Freundlichkeit, Demut ohne Schein," and the like—for the virtuous life is a life of pleasure (small *p*), as the texts of the final movements suggest. In the final chorus Hercules is praised as "*Lust* der Völker, *Lust* der Deinen"; the emphasis has shifted, in other words, from the enticement of *Wollust* (excessive pleasure) to the necessity of pleasure(*Lust*) when it

5. It may be recalled that Johann Kuhnau had described in the preface to his *Biblische Historien* (p. 123) his use of modulation to represent Laban's deceit, calling the device a "Verführung des Gehörs."

6. This point in the drama recalls an interesting parallel situation in the recitative from Cantata 95 in which the modulation from flats back to sharps is made (see above, p. 173). Beginning in D minor the recitative associates the flats with the *falsche Welt* and its *Wollustsalz*: "Nun falsche Welt, nun hab' ich weiter nichts mit dir zu tun [exactly Hercules' attitude towards Pleasure]; mein Haus ist schon bestellt, ich kann weit sanfter ruhn [!], als da ich sonst bei dir, an deines Babels Flüssen, das Wollustsalz verschlucken müssen." The expression *Wollustsalz* sounds the last echo of flats in Cantata 95, the Neapolitan sixth chord, B flat, of a prominent internal cadence to A minor (the neutral crossover point from flats to sharps that Bach invests with allegorical significance in other works as well, notably the two *Passions*). From this point on the modulatory course in Cantata 95 associates the return to sharps with the Christian's resolve to fix his thoughts on heaven rather than the world.

is not carried to excess. While the A major Echo aria represented a foreign presence, a nonharmonic relation within the key of F, and hence an appropriate allegorical device for Hercules' initial rejection of Pleasure, its immaturely formed message, that pleasure and virtue are incompatible, was not Bach's intention.[7] For the hero, virtue comes to encompass pleasure in the second half of the cantata; the A minor aria belongs within the ambitus of F. This development allegorizes the growth of the hero's personality, and the neutral system of A minor probably represents in part Hercules' attaining his independence, his ability to reconcile ideals and necessities. The catabasis, and especially the final return to flats, thus symbolizes a resolution analogous to that of the Lutheran conflict of flesh and spirit that took place in the realm of the flesh via the presence of the spirit. The bond between Hercules and Virtue is renewed and strenghtened at the close of the recitative: "Wer will ein solches Bündniss trennen?"—sung by Hercules and Virtue together (C major) in preparation for the F major duet.

The next movement is a pure love duet, softened by the accompaniment of two violas, without violins; a melodic reminiscence of "Schlafe, mein Liebster" underscores the meaning (Ex. 67). Hercules and Virtue are united (in pleasure) just as Christ and the soul are in the pietistic duet toward the end of Cantata 140, "Wachet auf." After the duet, Mercury, singing to a string accompagnato, explains that the cantata represents the youth of Crown Prince Friedrich, who has begun to fulfill the hopes others had placed on him. With this as the intent of the cantata, the subject of Hercules' choosing virtue and confirming his decision in a second aria was only logical.

The tonal-allegorical dynamic of "Hercules auf dem Scheidewege" relates it to similar devices in the church cantatas and *Passions*. The values of the secular realm, such as reason and good works, which are condemned in the church cantatas, take on the more passive qualities (*Sanftmut, Demut,* even *Lust*) signified in this cantata by the flats, indicating a rapprochement between the two seemingly opposed sets of values. That is, a ruler's taking pleasure in the exercise of virtue and reason is a restatement of the Lutheran idea that good works, which on their own are meaningless, follow from the individual's resignation to God's will through faith (passive righteousness). Love as the manifestation of faith produces good works in the spiritual realm; in the secular sphere the inner inclination to virtue, that is, virtue as pleasure, produces good works. Hercules, in fact, makes no choice; the modulation to sharps is made by Virtue for him. And the questions Hercules puts to the Echo in his A major aria are purely rhetorical, for the Echo is the voice of virtue within him. Hercules exists, as it were, in a state of grace. The reference Virtue

7. The ending of the cantata also introduces the word *Lust* in the Hercules/Virtue duet—"Wie Verlobte sich verbinden, wie die Lust, die sie empfinden"—with a totally positive meaning.

EXAMPLE 67.

(a) Beginning of aria "Schlafe, mein Liebster" (melodic parts only)

Violin 1

Violin 2

(b) Beginning of duet "Ich bin deine"/"Du bist meine" (melodic parts only)

Viola 1

Viola 2

makes to Hercules' salvation (right at the cadence that completes the sharp modula-tion) clearly indicates that "Hercules auf dem Scheidewege," despite its emphasis on such secular values as reason and glory, is based on the same theological aesthet-ics as the sacred cantatas.

As he did in the *St. Matthew Passion,* Bach enhanced the qualities associated with the terms *durus* and *mollis* when used for sharp and flat keys in several of the individ-ual movements of "Hercules." Warm string accompaniment for the B flat aria and F major duet and horns rather than trumpets in the two essentially homophonic choruses impart a soft, pastorale-like aura to the outer regions of the structure, making clear that this F major *mollis* character corresponds to the work's predomi-nant affective sphere. Throughout the cantata a community of words and expres-sions belongs to each of the key regions, just as in the *Passion.* Sleep, rest, pleasure, smooth steps, comfort, contentment, softness, sweetness, ease—all these are used by or about Pleasure, whereas sweat, toil, diligence, labor, achievement, success, and so on, are attributes of Virtue. Such is the case, that is, until the final duet, when for the first time Virtue takes on the qualities that it should have intrinsically but have instead up to that point been associated with Pleasure. While encomia on the beauty of the arias are hardly necessary (they can be found in the literature on the *Christmas Oratorio*), "Schlafe, mein Liebster" has been justly called "the most beautiful slumber-song ever written," for this piece is all gentleness and love.[8] Bach has made Pleasure so convincingly alluring that some prefer its religious set-ting.

8. Whittaker, *The Cantatas,* 2:629.

The movement most comparable to both "Schlafe, mein Liebster" and the duet of Hercules and Virtue in the *St. Matthew Passion* is the B flat aria "Mache dich, mein Herze, rein,"which resembles the former in its pastorale character. Like the duet, an expression of reconciliation, it bears the association of acceptance of Christ, of his finding his "süsse Ruh" in the believer's heart.[9] Perhaps, in fact, the character of "Schlafe, mein Liebster," the association of a slumber song to the infant Christ, brought out in the *Christmas Oratorio,* and the relation of this movement to the love duet of Hercules and Virtue justify viewing Pleasure as equally positive as Virtue, or, more accurately, recognizing that without pleasure virtue is a hollow exercise. Such is the intersection of the Lutheran worldview with the secular sphere of human aspirations in "Hercules." To be sure, Pleasure represents flesh, but humanity is the only basis for salvation; F major is the key associated with this idea, while B flat is perhaps a bit too "weak" or immature. The elevated sharp keys of the spiritual realm, on the other hand, do not constitute man's normal milieu; contact with it may be made, but man must return to the earthly for progress to take place. This is another Lutheran dynamic, underlying such diverse tonal procedures as the modulation upward in Part One of Cantata 186 versus the modulation downward in Part Two, the move up to sharps for the culmination of Part One in both *Passions* versus the endings in deep flats.[10] The early ascent represents the ideal of God's proper work of salvation as it is revealed in Scripture, while the return to flats represents the worldly reality of life.

The very excellence of "Hercules auf dem Scheidewege" surely prompted Bach to turn to it when preparing the *Christmas Oratorio,* whether or not he had planned to reuse its music when he wrote it. Knowing the reuse of "Ich will dich nicht hören" as "Bereite dich, Zion" helps to interpret the earlier work. As is well known, Bach took great care in his parodies to keep the affect of his new text as close as possible to the original, and he did so here. Only the A minor aria contradicts this situation in its change of performance indication, which transforms the affect of the piece. In "Hercules" Bach indicates that the aria be played staccato, yet legato in its counterpart, "Bereite dich, Zion." "Bereite dich" voices an affect opposite to that of "Ich will dich nicht hören": preparation of Zion (the church) for the arrival of her bridegroom, Christ. There is, nevertheless, a parallel between the

---

9. It is, of course, preceded by the arioso "Am Abend, da es kühle war" in which the idea of reconciliation with God as the outcome of Jesus' death is given its definitive expression within the *Passion.* On Bach's use of the pastorale to indicate this kind of meaning, see Steiger, " 'Die Welt ist auch ein Himmelreich.' "

10. The modulation to E major near the beginning of the first part of the *Christmas Oratorio* in conjunction with the anticipation of salvation, followed by A minor for the unredeemed world is another instance of the Lutheran dynamic. A similar dynamic underlies the modulation from E flat up to A major within the first, trinitarian, segment of *Clavierübung III* (the "Prelude," "Kyrie," and "Gloria" settings), followed by the catechism chorales and the stepwise move up to A *minor* in the four duets before the final E flat. Likewise, the modulation from E flat/C minor up to E major in the *Herzstück* of the *St. John Passion* (freedom), then the return to E flat ("In meines Herzens *Grunde)* reflects the dynamic.

contexts in which the two versions of the aria are placed, for in "Hercules" it is followed by a duet of acceptance (even though not of Pleasure per se). But acceptance of Virtue does bring pleasure, which, although clearly recognizable as such in the duet (the thematic parallel to "Schlafe, mein Liebster"), is transformed from the subdominant passivity of the lullaby to a function of virtue.

From Bach's reuse of "Ich will dich nicht hören" as "Bereite dich, Zion" we might conclude that two different layers of affect underlay the original setting. One layer is the adamant rejection of pleasure, emphasized by the staccato articulation. The other is a deeper, latent quality of acceptance that enabled Bach to reuse the aria with a text that expresses the opposite affect. The dualism in "Hercules auf dem Scheidewege" results from a context in which the hero "protests too much." Hercules has not yet understood that his true nature is to reconcile pleasure and virtue; his setting them in opposition in "Ich will dich nicht hören" represents an artificial rejection that masks the true affect. This antithetical quality might be associated with the issues of self-determination and will, which are so conspicuously different in the secular and the religious spheres. In the *St. Matthew Passion,* for example, the dialogue aria for tenor and chorus, "Ich will bei meinem Jesu wachen," matches its affirmative text with an opening motive reminiscent of a horn call; but the key is C minor, the horn is a pathetic oboe solo, and the chorus sings "sleep" music. The affect of this piece, based on these details and its place in the narrative—soon after Peter's insistence that he will never deny Christ, in a move from sharps to C minor—is made up of both the desire to fulfill Christian precepts and the weakness of the flesh.[11] Bach's allegorical plans may profoundly influence the conception of affect in individual movements; and affect can be more complex than we are accustomed to think.

One final question may be asked regarding Hercules' arias: what prompted Bach (and Picander, of course) to put an echo aria—and such an undramatic one—just where he did? It is not a representative aria of this genre; no real question is posed, for the answer is fully known in advance, embodied in the question. The nature of a true echo—a surprise answer, a provocative twisting of the original question into a new meaning—is entirely absent. Virtue has already resolved Hercules' only challenge and left him on a safe pinnacle of sharps, but one on which, as we know, he cannot remain. At this point the music represents the elevated nature of Hercules' choice, his innate nobility of character. Despite the personification, therefore, Virtue, and the Echo, must be taken as an aspect of Hercules himself (in the first recitative Hercules speaks of an *eingepflanzter Trieb* [implanted inclination] toward virtue, splendor, fame, and majesty). Hercules' "ethical consciousness" makes his choice inevitable; the only remaining conflict is the testing of it in the world.

11. The parodied form of this aria that appears in the Köthen *Trauerode,* "Geh', Leopold, geh' zu deiner Ruh,'" expresses the nobility of Leopold, Prince of Anhalt-Köthen, in the ascending part of the theme ("Geh', Leopold") and his death in the remainder ("zu deiner Ruh'").

This quality, suggestive of Enlightenment rather than Lutheran thought patterns, has, in fact, a theological pedigree, which in Bach's time was conceived in terms of the image (*Ebenbild*) of God—specifically of Christ—in the heart.[12] In the *Christmas Oratorio* Bach's parodied version of this aria replaces the Echo with the name of Jesus that is stamped on the heart and gives comfort and assurance of salvation to the believer in times of torment. The preceding chorale/recitative complex ends in C minor with thoughts of death, while the Echo aria follows in C major. The question put to Echo in the later work—whether Jesus' name inspires even the "very smallest seed" of severe terror—refers to the old Adam within man, the legacy of the Fall, which is now eradicated through faith in Christ. The character of the fourth cantata of the *Christmas Oratorio* with its unique emphasis on flats is bound up with this idea. As we will see, Bach treats the Echo aria as a specifically personal element. To the extent that similar ideas are present in the "Hercules" Echo aria, we can interpret the piece as representing Hercules' trust in Virtue, who has made his first decision for him, shown him the ideal, and will now guide him into the more difficult "real" world, where the direction is basically downward. The final message is that complete acceptance of virtue brings joy (*Lust*), or, in the theological sense to which the dynamic of this cantata is indebted, true faith and justification rest on the individual's will becoming one with God's.[13] Bach could not represent the trials Hercules will face in a work of this type, but the return to flats in Cantata 213 stands for the acceptance of God's (Virtue's) will, which necessitates accepting humanity and the weakness of the flesh ("der weiche Wollust locket zwar") as the continuing reality of life. Although not independent of contemporary Enlightenment notions, the highly detailed tonal "narrative" in Bach's "Hercules" owes much of its basic patterns to the Lutheran Weltanschauung. In short, "Hercules auf dem Scheidewege" is a masterpiece of baroque allegory.

The Christmas Oratorio

While it is highly unlikely that Bach wrote the music for "Hercules" planning to use it again later, nonetheless, its tonal contrast of sharp and flat keys was appropri-

---

12. Von Loewenich indicates that in Luther's earlier writings the concept of the *synteresis* is held over from medieval theology and is connected to grace, faith, and salvation (*Luther's Theology of the Cross,* pp. 52–58). *Synteresis* refers to the preservation within the individual of a "seed" or "spark" of "ethical consciousness" from before the Fall; it is described as the "natural" desire for, or inclination toward, salvation, the point of contact for grace within man. Although Luther retained the idea at first, it became more and more incompatible within the development of his *theologia crucis,* for it suggested that salvation could be founded on an inner, human quality. Luther never dealt fully with the problem, and it simply disappears from his later work. Bach would not have had it in mind, of course. The related idea of God's image in man, however, was certainly well known to him, and it appears in a number of his works (Cantatas 163 and 179 are among those discussed in the present study). The first chapter of Arndt's *True Christianity* (pp. 29–32) deals with it directly, as do a number of other places within the treatise (e.g., pp. 247–49), where subjects that became central to pietism, such as the foretaste of eternity and the union with Christ, are discussed. In "Hercules" the equivalent of the *unio mystico* is between Hercules and Virtue.

13. This idea, the very core of Lutheranism, is very closely related to the idea of the image of God in man, the indwelling of the Spirit, and related pietistic ideas, all of which are prominent in the above-mentioned passages from *True Christianity* (see note 12).

ate for the *Christmas Oratorio,* where it would appear for the last time in any vocal work known to us. In contrast, the *Mass in B minor* remains to a much greater extent within the D major/B minor ambitus, the only exception—apart from the very brief appearance of flats within the "Credo"—being the G minor "Agnus Dei." The fourth cantata of the *Christmas Oratorio,* for New Year's Day and the feast of the circumcision, not only borrows most from "Hercules" but stands apart from the other cantatas in more than tonality alone. As Dürr notes, Bach totally omits anything to do with New Year's Day, producing instead a cantata on the name of Jesus.[14] In addition, the work may have had personal meaning for Bach, for it contains two chorales whose melodies were apparently composed by him. One of these closes the cantata. The other is divided; its *Stollen* are set for soprano, in a recitative/arioso dialogue with bass that precedes a parody of the Echo aria from "Hercules," while its *Abgesang* continues the dialogue after the aria, the whole grouping forming a miniature chiasmus. The Echo aria, too, expresses a personal tone, in that Bach transforms it into a dialogue between Christ (Echo) and the believing Soul seeking assurance of redemption (Hercules' part). After this complex the fugue aria from "Hercules" affirms a life dedicated to honoring Christ with a prayer for strength. The element of choice has, of course, no place here, so Bach transposes the two sharp-key arias to fit the F major tonality, chosen, perhaps, to affirm Luther's linking of the "sixth tone" to Christ, the "friendly Lord."[15] The soft character of F major, the pastorale key, as announced in the opening chorus, is the strongest bond between the two cantatas; as the textual modifications reveal, it was partly the fact that Hercules (Friedrich) was a child that prompted the association with the infant Jesus. Neither Hercules nor Jesus has as yet come into his full powers, which will be marked by the conspicuous emblems of glory of the D major trumpets and drums in the final cantata. In contrast to the militant tone of the latter piece Bach uses the word *dämpft* in the fourth cantata rather than the more aggressive *zerbricht* to describe Christ's overcoming the devil. The focus in the fourth cantata on Jesus' infancy thus temporarily suspends the more overtly triumphant tones that accompany his work of salvation elsewhere, seeming—as in the modulation to the dominant minor in the first cantata—to place that work in the future.

The *Christmas Oratorio* as a whole has a more meditative character than the *Passions,* a trait that is manifested in the lower proportion of recitative to chorales and madrigal-texted movements. The fourth cantata is easily the most extreme in this respect; a single verse from Luke—seven bars of recitative in all—narrates the circumcision and christening; otherwise there is no biblical recitative. Bach was free to build the cantata almost entirely from contemplative movements. This part of the oratorio thus resembles in purpose some of the flat-key scenes of the *St. Matthew Passion,* where Bach dominates the recitative by the addition of medita-

14. Dürr, *Die Kantaten,* p. 157.
15. See Chapter 3, p. 71.

tive movements to increase the focus on the person of Christ in his sufferings and inner crises. Apart from Gethsemane and the ending, this character appears most prominently in two scenes where Jesus' silent suffering is emphasized and in both of which Bach uses the viola da gamba, perhaps for its soft sound; in both places chorales in F major ("Wer hat dich so geschlagen" and "O Haupt voll Blut und Wunden") provide the Christian reaction to the figure of the suffering Christ.

In "Fallt mit Danken, fallt mit Loben" this meditative quality is evident above all in the personal tone of the quasi-chiastic grouping of dialogues and chorales around the Echo aria. The first segment of this unit is unique in the entire oratorio for its references both to the Passion (soprano chorale, "der du dich für mich gegeben an des bittern Kreuzes Stamm," sung simultaneously with the bass soloist's fourfold iteration of the plea, "Ach! nimm mich zu dir") and to thoughts of Christ's and the individual's own death, the opposite of the Christmas message. These passages instigate modulations to C minor (the flat extreme of the oratorio), the latter closing the recitative, so that the ensuing C major Echo aria enters as an assurance of redemption that is reminiscent of dialogues in the *Passions*. The juxtaposition of C minor and major within the key of F recalls works such as Cantata 127 or even the F major Pastorale for organ. In this sense "Fallt mit Danken" assumes some of the meaning of flats as representative of the incarnation, the human, rather than the divine side of Christ, the infant and the crucified, mortal being with whom a personal relationship is conceivable. This region of the oratorio is spiritually close to the *Passion,* and the fourth cantata as a whole compares favorably to the flat-key scenes that provide meditative oases within the narratives of Christ's betrayal and capture, his trial and the crucifixion in the *St. Matthew Passion.* The overt expression of victory over death that is lacking in the Passion—but would have followed at Easter—is provided in the *Christmas Oratorio* with the return to sharps for the last two parts.

In a full study of the *Christmas Oratorio,* Walter Blankenburg has drawn attention to the tonal structure of the first three cantatas, which narrate the Christmas story proper.[16] Two cantatas in D major frame one in G major of a pastorale character, the subdominant being unmistakably associated with the incarnation. After the triumphant introductory chorus in D major, the narrative of the events leading to the birth of Christ (the first recitative) moves up to A and E major in anticipation of Christ's birth ("nun wird der Held aus Davids Stamm zum Trost, zum Heil der Erden einmal geboren werden"), until the close of the recitative, where we are suddenly returned to the immediate historical situation of the as yet unredeemed world in the image of Zion weeping ("verlasse nun das Weinen, dein Wohl steigt hoch empor") and a turn to A minor (Ex. 68). The E major close on the last phrase of the

16. Walter Blankenburg, *Das Weihnachts-Oratorium von Johann Sebastian Bach* (Kassel, 1982), pp. 38–41.

EXAMPLE 68.   Part one of the *Christmas Oratorio,* "Jauchzet, frohlocket": ending of first recitative

recitative is thus pressed into a dominant function. The following movements ("Bereite dich, Zion" in A minor; "Wie soll ich dich empfangen?" in E Phrygian) represent Zion before the coming of Christ; then, after a brief recitative narrating the birth, the sequence of movements turns to major and continues upward (G major and D major), closing as it began, joyfully. Bach probably introduced the move to E major in the first recitative for the words "Heil der Erden," whereas its reinterpretation soon after as the dominant of A minor places that *Heil* in the future, an interpretation that is confirmed in the later appearances of A and E major in the oratorio (see below). That Bach associated upward motion to E major with salvation seems established from the conspicuous tonal patterns in both *Passions* as well as in Cantata 9, and even works such as Cantatas 86 and 150.

In the second cantata the subdominant region is related to the announcement of Christ's birth to the shepherds; and this cantata descends from G through E minor (aria, "Frohe Hirten") to its subdominant, C, for the chorale "Schaut hin! dort liegt im finstern Stall." The cantata as a whole can be called another of the descent/ascent type, like its immediate predecessor. The third cantata, however, is much closer to the ascent/descent type; it moves up to A major for the shepherd's chorus, "Lasset uns nun gehen zu Bethlehem," ending in C sharp minor for the idea of the fulfillment of God's promise, then moving up to E major for the meaning of Christ's birth as it was foretold by that key in the first cantata: "Er hat sein Volk getröst't, er hat sein Israel erlöst, die Hülf aus Zion hergesendet und unser Leid geendet." A major remains through a chorale and the parodied form of the duet from "Hercules": "Herr, dein Mitleid, dein Erbarmen, tröstet uns und macht uns frei." The latter key has the association of Christian freedom that "Durch dein Gefängnis" has in the *St. John Passion*; this freedom is generally expressed by the deeper sharps in the *Christmas Oratorio* as it often is throughout the cantatas. The move down passes through F sharp minor (recitative) and B minor (aria) to G major (recitative and chorale) and symbolizes Mary's keeping the words in her heart, as a model that the Christian must emulate to strengthen his weak faith. The move down thus expresses the internalizing of the message of salvation. Once again we encounter the dynamic of an early move into deep sharps associated with the message of salvation followed by descent to the personal concerns of the physical world. The return to D for the repeat of the opening chorus follows a chorale in F sharp minor that comes right after the one in G, that is, the mi and fa within the ambitus of D, whose meaning is surely the idea of Christ as both man (subdominant side) and God (dominant side) that is stated explicitly in the second of the two chorales.

These three cantatas complete the Christmas story and are heard in the week beginning on Christmas Day. The turn to F major for the fourth cantata represents the New Year and the Epiphany with a new key area. The emphasis on flats is, as we saw, associated not merely with the infant Christ but also with the introduction of references to the Passion and a sense of a new personal relationship to Christ. In contrast, the fifth cantata is set in A major, the sharpest area of the oratorio. This cantata, dealing with the Magi's seeking Jesus, is concerned with the imagery of light associated with the spread of salvation to the Gentiles:

Wohl euch! die ihr dies Licht gesehen,
es ist zu eurem Heil geschehen.
Mein Heiland, du, du bist das Licht,
das auch den Heiden scheinen sollen,
und sie, sie kennen dich noch nicht,
als sie dich schon verehren wollen.
Wie hell, wie klar muss nicht dein Schein,
geliebter Jesu, sein! [alto recitative]

Dein Glanz all' Finsterniss verzehrt
[chorale]

Erleucht' auch meine finstre Sinnen
[aria]

Zwar ist solche Herzensstube
wohl kein schöner Fürstensaal,
sondern eine finstre Grube;
doch, sobald dein Gnadenstrahl
in dieselbe nur wird blinken,
wird sie voller Sonnen dünken.
[final chorale]

That is, of course, another aspect of the meaning of the dominant (sharp) region within the oratorio (introduced in the first cantata in the association of *Heil* with the "Stern aus Jacob") as opposed to the "finstre Stall" of the incarnation (subdominant).

If the fifth cantata asserts Jesus' light, the sixth, back in D major, takes the persecution of Herod as an occasion to treat his power over all enemies. The tonal plan follows the principles of its predecessors, but encompasses modulation to both sides of the key in a final expression of the overall power of Christ. The music moves first to the dominant, A, for assertion of that power (aria: "Nur ein Wink von seinen Händen stürzt ohnmächt'ger Menschen Macht"). Then the recitative narrating the visit of the Magi modulates downward by stages from F sharp minor to the subdominant, G, for the chorale "Ich steh' an deiner Krippen hier, O Jesulein, mein Leben." The return to D is made through B minor (aria: "Nun mögt ihr stolzen Feinde schrecken"). But before the final chorale Bach gives us one last suggestion of downward circular modulation, in the recitative "Was will der Hölle Schrecken nun, was will uns Welt und Sünde thun, da wir in Jesu Händen ruhn?" for all four soloists (Ex. 69). The successive seventh chords resemble the effect of

EXAMPLE 69.   *Christmas Oratorio*: penultimate movement

EXAMPLE 69   *continued*

"Eröffne den feurigen Abgrund, O Hölle" from the double chorus "Sind Blitze" of the *St. Matthew Passion*. But the question is rhetorical, as is, in fact, the sense of modulation; the circling ends in D, and, as the final chorale tells us, "Tod, Teufel, Sünd und Hölle sind ganz und gar geschwächt; bei Gott hat seine Stelle das menschliche Geschlecht."

The *St. John Passion*:

Theological Themes

Although there are many fascinating parallels between the *St. John Passion* and *St. Matthew Passion,* the two works are, nonetheless, strikingly different in the way they deal with some fundamental theological questions and the impact that these issues have in turn on the characters and structures of the *Passions.* The differences between them have been described by many commentators from several sides. Among the better known explications are the idea that the *St. John Passion* is a dramatic and its successor a meditative work, the notion that the former setting is more severe, concerned with abstract form, while the latter is more human and expressive; even the dualism of orthodoxy, as expressed in the *St. John Passion,* and pietism, in the *St. Matthew Passion,* has been proposed.[1] While none of these fully explains the contrasted natures of the two works, they all indicate a widespread sense that the differentiation is an intrinsic part of the compositional meaning.

There are a number of reasons why Bach's two *Passions* should exhibit different musicotheological characteristics. The *St. John Passion* might well have been composed before most of the first Leipzig cantata cycle, that is, before Bach had established the long-range goals of his Leipzig church music.[2] The *St. Matthew Passion,* on the other hand, follows the first two Leipzig cantata cycles, and Bach might have intended it to belong to an annual cycle of cantatas of very different character from that of its predecessor.[3] In any case, composing the chorale cantatas must

---

1. See, for example, Nettl, *Luther and Music,* p. 144; Spitta, *Johann Sebastian Bach,* vol. 2, pp. 524–28, 531, 538–39, 546–49, 557, 567; Blume, *Protestant Church Music,* pp. 304–7.

2. Owing to the loss of the composing score of the *St. John Passion,* the dating of its composition is uncertain. The parts indicate 1724 as the date of the first performance; the hypothesis that the work was written in Köthen and might have been first performed in Leipzig in 1723 has not been confirmed and must be seriously doubted in light of Bach's first taking up duties there in June 1723. See Arthur Mendel, *Kritischer Bericht* to *Johann Sebastian Bach. Neue Ausgabe sämtlicher Werke,* II/4 (Kassel, 1974), pp. 24–26.

3. On the dating of the *St. Matthew Passion,* see Joshua Rifkin, "The Chronology of Bach's *St. Matthew Passion,*" *The Musical Quarterly* 61 (1975): 360–81; Chafe, "J. S. Bach's *St. Matthew Passion,* pp. 103–12.

surely have affected Bach's ideas about church music in general; the opening chorale fantasia of the *St. Matthew Passion* seems to have arisen in a climate different from that of "Herr, unser Herrscher." In addition, Jaroslav Pelikan has shown that Bach's two *Passions* can be considered to represent two different theological traditions, the first retaining the view of the early Greek Fathers that emphasized Jesus as Christus Victor, and the second the "satisfaction" theory of redemption put forth by Anselm of Canterbury in the eleventh century.[4] The latter point of differentiation may depend on the change from the religious climate of the reformed court at Köthen to the orthodoxy of Leipzig; the revisions to the *St. John Passion* were perhaps meant to bring it theologically closer to the particular emphases of the *St. Matthew Passion*.[5]

One can also say that the *St. John Passion* expresses many traits particular to the Gospel of John, the Johannine traits, while the *St. Matthew Passion* articulates a more Lutheran theology. Even this characterization can not be entirely satisfactory, for Luther's thought was thoroughly imbued with the spirit of John, his favorite Gospel.[6] Such a singling out of Johannine characteristics would be extraordinary in an age in which the character and theology of individual Gospel accounts were completely dominated by the dogmatic concerns of Lutheran orthodoxy. Any Johannine aspects of Bach's setting must, therefore, be viewed through the lens of contemporary Lutheranism. Thinking of the *St. John Passion* in terms of Bach's direct interaction with the Gospel itself, including his pinpointing many traits that modern scholarship calls characteristically Johannine, helps us not only to understand the work's structure but also to interpret the many different theological emphases carried over from Bach's first Leipzig *Passion* to its successor.

The *St. Matthew Passion* treats in particular the relation of faith to meditation on the Passion, Luther's dynamic of faith as he presented it throughout his writings and particularly in the widely published *A Meditation on Christ's Passion*. As in all his writings on faith, recognition and acknowledgment of sin was the first and most important point in Luther's sermon, and the *St. Matthew Passion* follows this lead. Thus the opposition of guilt and innocence colors the *St. Matthew Passion*, contributing enormously to its often elegiac tone. For an example we have only to think of the opening chorus with its chorale expressing Christ's innocence—"O Lamm Gottes unschuldig"—floating above the antiphonal choral lament urging man to consider his guilt: "Seht!" "Wohin?" "Auf uns're Schuld." The importance of the chorale "O Lamm Gottes unschuldig"—a German version of the Agnus Dei—had already been established in the Lutheran Passion tradition of the seventeenth century for settings of both John and Matthew. This Passion tradition remained vital

4. Pelikan, *Bach among the Theologians*, pp. 89–115.
5. This theme will be taken up in greater detail below, pp. 301–4.
6. Luther, *Selected Biblical Prefaces*, in Dillenberger, ed., *Selections*, pp. 18–19.

in the settings of Sebastiani, Flor, Theile, Strutius, Meder, and others, including, of course, the *St. Matthew Passion,* but it is less pronounced in the *St. John Passion.*[7] From the first aria of the *St. Matthew Passion,* "Buss und Reu knirscht das Sündenherz entzwei," to the recitative before the final chorus, "O selige Gebeine, seht, wie ich euch mit Buss und Reu beweine, dass euch mein Fall in solche Not gebracht," we are asked to consider the Passion for the moral benefits it offers, as a catalyst to repentance. Matthew's picture of Christ as the Man of Sorrows is given a powerful injection of the Lutheran view of his bearing the weight of human sin and of his serving as the model for man. For Luther man's only hope was to become conscious of his guilt and thereby "conformable to Christ in His sufferings," a theme from the Passion Sermon suggested in the aria "Gerne will ich mich bequemen, Kreuz und Becher anzunehmen." As Elke Axmacher has shown, however, the severity of Lutheran thinking regarding suffering softened in the late seventeenth and early eighteenth centuries, so that suffering was described as "sweet" (indicated in the expressions *gerne* and *bequemen*), yet the cup that the Christian must accept contains, we are told in the preceding arioso, all the foulness and stink of man's sin.[8] The dialectical quality remains despite the softening.

The Passion as Trost: *Realized Eschatology*

Remarkably then, no single movement in the *St. John Passion* mentions the guilt/innocence dualism; only in the closing scene of Part One—"Wer hat dich so geschlagen" / "Ich, ich und meine Sünden" and Peter's aria, "Ach, mein Sinn"—is the necessity of penitence emphasized. Meditation in the *St. John Passion* revolves around Jesus' sacrifice as a benefit for mankind; in numerous movements, therefore, Bach (or an unknown librettist) used the Johannine device of inverting the immediate, literal meaning of the narrative events to bring out their soteriological interpretation. The opening chorus addresses Christ in majesty, asking that the modern-day congregation be shown that the Passion, with all its adverse events, represents the glorification of Christ ("Zeig' uns durch deine Passion, dass du, der wahre Gottessohn, zu aller Zeit, auch in der grössten Niedrigkeit, verherrlicht worden bist"). The first chorale introduces Christ's love for man and contrasts Jesus' sufferings with man's "Lust und Freude" in the world. This contrast extends across the break between Parts One and Two in the shift from the A major "Petrus, der nicht denkt zurück" to the A minor (E Phrygian) "Christus, der uns selig macht"; the major indicates Peter's redemption through faith, despite his betrayal, while the minor indicates the suffering that brings about mankind's salvation ("der uns selig macht").

7. See Basil Smallman, *The Background of Passion Music* (New York, 1957), new ed. (New York, 1970), pp. 83, 144, 148–52.
8. Axmacher, *"Aus Liebe,"* pp. 174–75, 178–79.

In the first aria Jesus' bonds are described as loosening man's bondage to sin, his wounds as healing mankind; after the narrative of the scourging, the arioso "Betrachte, meine Seel' " urges man to see his "highest good" in Jesus' sufferings, to consider how the *Himmelsschlüsselblume* (the "primrose," but here a complex metaphor meaning, literally, the flower that is the key to heaven) blooms from the crown of thorns and "sweet fruit" from his "wormwood." In the aria "Erwäge" meditation on the scourging takes up not the idea of human guilt but the fact that the blood on Jesus' back forms rainbow patterns, a sign of the renewal of the covenant made with Noah after the Flood. In the chorale "Durch dein Gefängnis" Jesus' imprisonment sets man free, the prison is the throne of grace. In "Mein teurer Heiland" even the falling of his head in death becomes a nod in answer to the individual's question concerning his redemption, and so on. The positive, redemptive meaning of the Passion is constantly stressed without much emphasis on what comes between Jesus' sacrifice and the redemption it brings about, without, that is, the personal suffering that is essential to Luther's theology. Instead of the message from the *St. Matthew Passion* of our conforming to Christ in his suffering voiced in "Gerne will ich mich bequemen," at the most nearly equivalent spot in the *St. John Passion* the aria "Ich folge dir gleichfalls mit freudigen Schritten" expresses the joy that comes from following Christ, without mentioning what such a following entails. As the second aria of the *St. John Passion*, "Ich folge dir gleichfalls" might be compared with the second aria of the *St. Matthew Passion*, "Blute nur, du liebes Herz," which, like "Buss und Reu," articulates the contemporary individual's tortured state of mind. The major key and bright instrumentation of "Ich folge dir" conveys the uncomplicated affect of joy that is the concomitant of faith.

The text of the *St. John Passion* is clearly concerned with immediate opposition contrasting the suffering of Christ with the ultimate benefit for man—*Stricken/entbinden, Gefängnis/Freiheit,* and the like—rather than the stage-by-stage progression of man's inner development that is more characteristic of the *St. Matthew Passion*. In Lutheran terms we might say that the *St. John Passion* moves much more readily to the second stage of Luther's meditative dynamic, that is, the perspective of the resurrection, under which the spirit leaps from contemplating Jesus' sufferings to focusing on their benefit for man, whereas the *St. Matthew Passion* details the process—successive in nature—by which the opposition is bridged. This immediacy informs much of the work's dramatic character, a quality often emphasized in John, whose literary style is famous for its antitheses, such as light/dark, truth/falsehood, good/evil, freedom/law, above/below, and life/death. John's was the last of the four Gospels to be written, and the concern of the synoptic Gospels over the crisis of the "delay of the Parousia," that is, the expectation that Christ's Second Coming was near at hand—was resolved by John's emphasis on two simultaneously existing worlds and the possibility of passing from the one to the other in the present life. Eternity simply became an alternate sphere, that of the spirit, light, and truth.

The antithesis in the text of the *St. John Passion* counters the features of one world with those of the other, thereby emphasizing their simultaneity. Or, as Luther expressed it in terms of Jesus' sayings concerning his kingdom, "Though physically they are still living upon earth, He sets them in heaven by the power of His kingdom, Word, Spirit and faith."[9] With faith the vehicle of moving to the world above, John's Gospel appealed very strongly to Luther; in fact, he pronounced it "unique in loveliness, and of a truth the principal gospel," largely on the basis of Jesus' words of comfort to the tormented soul.[10] Of course faith is directed to the world above, but the believer must physically inhabit the world below, the source of his experience; in this world the "intersection" of faith and experience is "trust."[11] Among Jesus' sayings in John—many of which are given special settings by Bach—none summed up the character of the Gospel more for Luther than the one we have already considered as the turning point in the descent/ascent cantata, "Ich habe manches Herzeleid": "In der Welt ihr habt Angst; aber seid getrost, ich habe die Welt überwunden."[12] Here the antithesis between the world and Christ's victory is resolved in terms of *Trost,* the benefit for the faithful.

In the *St. John Passion* the idea of *Trost* emerges in two very significant places, first in the E flat chorale "In meines Herzens Grunde" ("Erschein mir in dem Bilde zu Trost in meiner Not"), then in the B minor aria "Es ist vollbracht" ("O Trost für die gekränkten Seelen"). "In meines Herzens Grunde" culminates the symmetrical centerpiece of the *Passion,* the so-called *Herzstück;*[13] the chorale meditates on the crucifixion and the "royal inscription," making an inner association between the two ("dein Nam' und Kreuz allein") that is the crux of the whole work's theology. "Es ist vollbracht" meditates on the meaning of the crucifixion as the completion of Jesus' work. In both places trust is the comfort that the soul enjoys in a world of tribulation. But in "Es ist vollbracht" there is a more direct sense of the antithesis between the world, represented in the elegiac, minor-key beginning and ending sections of the aria based on the melody of "Es ist vollbracht" in the preceding recitative, and Jesus' victory, represented by the triumphant D major middle section, "Der Held aus Juda siegt mit Macht" (Ex. 70). It is Jesus' death that provides the ultimate antithesis between the physical events and their redemptive meaning and its resolution. Immediately following "Es ist vollbracht," the D major

9. Martin Luther, *Commentary on Psalm Eight,* in vol. 12 of *Luther's Works (Selected Psalms I),* trans. and ed. Jaroslav Pelikan (St. Louis, 1955), p. 104.

10. Dillenberger, ed., *Selections,* pp. 18–19.

11. Von Loewenich, *Luther's Theology of the Cross,* p. 95.

12. Von Loewenich, *Luther und das Johanneische Christentum* (Munich, 1935), pp. 15–22.

13. Smend, "Die Johannes-Passion von Bach," p. 115. Although I have adopted Smend's term *Herzstück* to designate the central segment of the Passion, I do not follow the exact boundaries given by Smend (Smend, for example, begins his *Herzstück* before the move to flats that culminates in "Betrachte, meine Seele" and "Erwäge"). The theological reasoning behind my adjusting the boundaries of this segment will become apparent in this and the following chapter.

EXAMPLE 70.

(a) *St. John Passion*: recitative ending

Jesus

Es ist voll - bracht!

Basso continuo

(b) Aria "Es ist vollbracht": beginning of ritornello

Molto Adagio

Viola da gamba

etc.

Basso continuo

(c) Aria "Es ist vollbracht": alto solo beginning

Alto

Es ist _ voll - bracht,

Basso continuo

(d) Aria "Es ist vollbracht": beginning of middle section

Alla breve

Violins 1, 2

Viola

Alto

Der Held aus Ju-da siegt mit Macht,

Viola da gamba
Basso continuo

EXAMPLE 70   *continued*

(cont.)

(e) Ending of aria "Es ist vollbracht"

EXAMPLE 70   *continued*

dialogue aria with chorale, "Mein teurer Heiland" / "Jesu, der du warest todt," gives the transforming message of redemption in Jesus' silent nod of assurance to the believer's question, "Bin ich vom Sterben frei gemacht." The chorale presents the antithesis between Jesus' death and his victory ("Jesu, der du warest todt, lebest nun ohn' Ende") and indicates in a prayer the benefit of Jesus' death ("gieb mir nur, was du verdient").[14] This *Trost,* founded in the anticipation of eternity and its benefits, underlies the emphasis on the juxtaposition of opposites in the *St. John Passion.* As in many cantatas, Bach associates the direction to flats with the world below and to sharps with the world above.

John's Theology of the Cross: The Passion as Jesus' Glorification

In John, Christology, all aspects of the person of Christ, and the theology of the cross are both very closely related to Jesus' glorification. Certain characteristics of

---

14. Just as the chorales "O Lamm Gottes unschuldig," "O Haupt voll Blut und Wunden," and "Herzliebster Jesu" express the primary theological focus of the *St. Matthew Passion* (see Chapter 13), the chorale to which the verse "Jesu, der du warest todt" belongs, "Jesu, deine Passion ist mir lauter Freude," expresses the overall meaning of trust so central to the theology of the *St. John Passion.*

John's Gospel, such as the trial and Jesus' speaking of the crucifixion as the "lifting up" that will draw all men to him, make clear that within John's terms Jesus must be recognized above all as the Messiah in the cross and Passion. This fundamental idea of glorification in abasement, which is completed in "Es ist vollbracht" and related immediately to the *Trost* of the believer in "Mein teurer Heiland," is announced as the goal of the Passion in the opening chorus:

> Herr, unser Herrscher
> dessen Ruhm in allen Landen herrlich ist!
> Zeig' uns durch deine Passion,
> dass du, der wahre Gottessohn,
> zu aller Zeit,
> auch in der grössten Niedrigkeit,
> verherrlicht worden bist.
> (da capo)

This chorus is based on the address to God that frames Psalm 8, on which the opening section was based: "Herr, unser Herrscher, wie herrlich ist dein Name in allen Landen." As Luther's commentary on the opening words of this psalm tells us, the God of the eighth psalm and the Old Testament generally is the same as the God of the Passion—the Word incarnate in the man, Jesus of Nazareth, Son of God.[15] This forms the foundation of Lutheran Christology, which was based on John more than any other Scripture, for only in John does Jesus say explicitly, "He who has seen me has seen the Father," a passage Luther never tired of quoting.[16]

Elke Axmacher describes "Herr, unser Herrscher" as a "singular case" among the choral prologues of the *Passions* of the time.[17] Axmacher draws attention to the Johannine character of the chorus, and in particular to the idea of *Herrlichkeit* (majesty), making the important distinction between the *Herrlichkeit* of God as it is expressed in the A section of the text (lines one and two) and the process of glorification referred to in the middle section. The climactic endings of Bach's two sections are in parallel ("herrlich ist"/"verherrlicht worden bist") and express a basic dualism of the Passion: the identity of the eternal, preexistent God of Psalm 8 (lines one and two) and the incarnate Word, which enters the world of the flesh and is glorified through the crucifixion. The descent/ascent dynamic indicated in "Herr, unser Herrscher" is comparable to John's traditional interpretation of Jesus' life as like the arc of a pendulum whose return upswing begins with the crucifixion.[18] In

15. Martin Luther, *D. Martin Luthers Werke*, vol. 45 (Weimar, 1911), pp. 207–11; *Luther's Works*, vol. 12, pp. 99–101.

16. Althaus, *The Theology of Martin Luther*, pp. 181–93 (see especially p. 182); von Loewenich, *Luther und das Johanneische Christentum*, pp. 20, 35–41.

17. Axmacher, *"Aus Liebe,"* p. 163.

18. Raymond Brown, *The Gospel According to John XIII–XXI*, The Anchor Bible, vol. 29A (New York, 1970), p. 541.

Bach's structure the tonal nadir of the *Passion* is the narrative of the crucifixion (B flat minor), which is followed immediately by the so-called royal inscription over the cross: "Jesus of Nazareth, King of the Jews." From this point to the scene of Jesus' death, in which the arias "Es ist vollbracht" and "Mein teurer Heiland" appear, the basic tonal motion is upward, through the neutral scene of the dividing of the cloak (C major) and into sharps. This represents the point of Jesus' glorification, the lifting up of the cross.

A quotation from the author of the foremost English-language commentary on John, Raymond Brown, clarifies the meaning of the cross as glorification in abasement as it appears in Bach's prologue, and its spiritual connection to the royal inscription:

> The "lifting up" of the Son of Man which will draw all men to him (predicted in xii 32) begins on the cross where Jesus is physically lifted up from the earth. For other men crucifixion would have been an abasement; but because Jesus lays down his life with power to take it up again (x 18), there is a triumphant element in the Johannine concept of crucifixion. It is a death that achieves glorification, and the crucified Jesus is proclaimed as king in the principal languages of the world (xix 19–20).[19]

The Passion in John is a triumph and the Johannine Christ is an all-powerful majestic figure who undergoes the Passion voluntarily, who has complete foreknowledge and remains unaffected by the torments he suffers. Jesus' last words—*tetelestai* in John's Greek, "It is accomplished" or "Es ist vollbracht" in translation—are a cry of victory, totally in contrast to Matthew's account of "My God, why has thou forsaken me." Even the narrative of Jesus' death—"und neigte das Haupt und verschied"—describes a voluntary act.

"Herr, unser Herrscher" is Bach's attempt to express glory and triumph within a movement that has all the outward signs of lamentation—minor key, descending minor triads, chromaticism, throbbing pedal tones, dissonances, and the like. In contrast to "Es ist vollbracht," in which the two main sections divide the present world of physical events from the anticipation of resurrection—"Herr, unser Herrscher" weaves its separate ideas together, subordinating them to an overriding rhythmic motion that comprises the various layers of the bass (eighth notes), strings (sixteenths), and winds (quarter and half notes). The unchanging character of the different ideas creates a powerful sense of inevitability, of inexorability, that permits only awe to emerge from the mechanical patterns. The chorus's monosyllabic shouts of address to God ("Herr"), now on, now off the beat, are not at all

19. Brown, *The Gospel According to John*, p. 541.

personal; even when the call to God breaks into more decorative, almost hopeful, figures, a great distance remains between addressor and addressee. The main ascent in sixteenth notes produces the idea of majesty, even glory, despite the traditional signs of lamentation; but as long as God is presented in such a remote fashion, man has yet to learn the true meaning of the Passion. This is certainly Bach's intention. The *St. John Passion* traces the growth of greater understanding, even of revelation, as it proceeds; the appeal in "Herr, unser Herrscher" to be shown the glorification of Christ is not yet that of the personal appeal to Christ on the cross in "Mein teurer Heiland." The division of the ritornello material of the prologue into two parts—the first over a pedal point and emphasizing diatonic ascent, the second introducing circle-of-fifths harmony and a gradual chromatic descent—mirrors the shift from the eternal, unchanging God to the process of abasement leading to glorification. Later the more hopeful, almost joyful figures appear with the circle-of-fifths harmony at section endings ("Herr, unser Herrscher," mm. 37–39; "dessen Ruhm in allen Landen herrlich ist," mm. 49–58; "verherrlicht worden bist," mm. 86–95), adding optimism to the descending chromaticism, and the circle of fifths will be taken up as the harmonic basis of the "Jesus of Nazareth" choruses, which make up a vital part of the Christological character of the *Passion*.

The opening chorus emphasizes two points to which Bach gives particular symbolic and structural emphasis: the geographical and temporal universality of Jesus' rule—"in allen Landen" and "zu aller Zeit." The former is the message of the multilingual royal inscription, while the latter recurs in the chorale "Ach, grosser König, gross zu allen Zeiten." "Ach, grosser König" is the culminating point of a Christological scene that introduces the trial; the inscription along with the crucifixion is the event on which the final chorale of the *Herzstück* meditates.[20] This chorale, "In meines Herzens Grunde dein *Nam'* und *Kreuz* allein," internalizes the idea of the identity of name and cross (or of Christology and the *theologia crucis*), which animates "Herr, unser Herrscher." The sense of abasement is represented in the B flat minor narrative of the crucifixion, the flat-key extreme of the work, and a few other excursions into deep flats, while the sense of glorification is articulated at the other end of the tonal spectrum, in the E major center of the Passion ("Durch dein Gefängnis") and later with sharps in the arias "Es ist vollbracht" and "Mein teurer Heiland." Bach thus fashions the overall tonal plan of the *St. John Passion* into both a huge sign of the cross and the name of Christ, through associations of symmetry to cruciform and chiastic planning. On the largest scale of any of his works Bach unites in the figure the two theologies of the cross—Luther's idea of the cross of suffering in the present life amid hope for the life to come and John's notion of the cross as the instrument of Jesus' glorification.

20. The scene ending with "Ach, grosser König" will be taken up in the following chapter.

The Christological portrait of Jesus accompanying these ideas combines Jesus' divinity and his humanity, the latter emphasized throughout the *Passion* by minor keys, and the former emerging most strongly in major keys at the point of his death. "Herr, unser Herrscher" is in a minor key, not because it is a chorus of lamentation, which it is not, but because it portrays divinity from the human perspective. Such is the case with the Christological scene that follows, up to "O grosse Lieb" (G minor), which focuses on the power and majesty supposedly signified by Jesus' words "Ich bin's," which are spoken within the context of the humiliation of his arrest. Examining the "Jesus of Nazareth" choruses reveals an extraordinary and highly calculated Christological emphasis in the work, a feature that is only fully apparent when the theology of the work is understood to encompass its musical structure and the various levels of musical allegory in addition to the textual content. The musical allegory of the *St. John Passion* carries the message of the prologue more deeply into the work than the text alone would suggest.

Two of the best-known means by which John emphasizes the identity of Jesus as the Messiah appear within the Passion narrative and are given special treatment by Bach. The first of these is the *Ego eimi* (I am) expression of divine self-revelation that Jesus uses in several places in the Gospel and the second is the royal inscription. The former appears in the *Passion* in one of the three different forms it has in the Gospel, that is, its predicate is implied—meaning "I am he" (*ich bin's*)—whereas the Greek construction, if translated literally, would mean something like "I myself am." Elsewhere in the Gospel the expression is used either with no implied predicate, in which case it is usually taken to express divine self-revelation (a form that has an extensive biblical background), or with a figurative predicate nominative, such as "I am the bread of life," "I am the way, the truth, and the life," and so on.[21] In the *Passion* narrative it is used in the above-mentioned Christological scene, in conjunction with the two short choruses set to the name "Jesus of Nazareth." When the words are spoken the arresting party draws back and falls to the ground, which is usually taken to mean that Jesus has not merely said "I am he" but has revealed himself as the deity. The name "Jesus of Nazareth" identifies the historical personage, and the *Ego eimi* the Christ. The royal inscription, on the other hand, is associated with the ironic proclamation of Jesus' true identity to the world via the crucifixion. Both instances relate to the text of the opening chorus, where the spread of God's name in all lands is associated with the theme of Jesus' glorification in abasement. The inscription is given a special treatment as the subject of the final

21. See Raymond Brown, *The Gospel According to John I–XII*, The Anchor Bible, vol. 29 (Garden City, N.Y., 1966), pp. 533–38.

meditation of the *Herzstück*. It is, however, the "Jesus of Nazareth" choruses that raise the question of Jesus' identity at various adverse points in the narrative, especially those where the antagonism is focused in the choral outbursts from the crowd (*turbae*).

Twelve of the fourteen *turba* choruses of the *Passion* display musical correspondences with others of the set; the two exceptions are those that are not concerned with the trial—"Bist du nicht," addressed to Peter, and "Lasset uns den nicht zerteilen," the chorus of soldiers casting lots for the robe (see Fig. 8, below). The first nine *turbae* of Part Two belong to the real trial scene, which Bach extended to include the tenth chorus, "Schreibe nicht: der Juden König"; this may be an additional reference to the Law through the number associated with the Ten Commandments, as it is in the *St. Matthew Passion.*[22] In the *St. John Passion,* more than in its successor, the series of *turbae* introduces a sense of antithesis to the Christological meaning of the Passion; the choruses of the earlier work not only emphasize antagonism to Christ in their tendency toward violent, agitated affects—chromaticism, the obsessive *kreuzige* rhythm, staccato, eighth-note rhythms, and the like—but their very interrelatedness and the fewer meditative movements make the crowd of persecutors into a presence of great dramatic intensity. All the more reason, then, for us to consider Bach's expressing the ability of faith to perceive the true identity of Christ even within the *turbae* themselves. This is the one means by which the immediacy of antithesis becomes a simultaneity.

Near the beginning of the work, with the arrival of the arresting party, we hear the two very brief and nearly identical choruses with the text "Jesum von Nazareth" (Ex. 71). We saw them associated with one of John's famous *Ego eimi* or "I am" sayings, which appears in the recitative between the choruses, and they are characterized musically by their active sixteenth-note flute part and circle-of-fifths harmony with Phrygian cadence ending. Each chorus encompasses harmonically the full span of chords that compose what the theorist Johann David Heinichen called the ambitus of the key, that is, the progression V–i–iv–VII–III–VI in minor, while the Phrygian cadence—iv^6–V—traditionally signaled the ambitus of either a major or a minor key by the juxtaposition of its flattest and sharpest harmonies. Perhaps Bach intended the circular, all-encompassing harmonic character of the chorus to signify something like John's image of Jesus, who remains apart from the adverse circumstances in which he is placed; the minor key was undoubtedly meant to indicate the incarnate Word, Jesus of Nazareth. In any case, the brevity and distinctness of the "Jesus of Nazareth" choruses help the listener to recall them: later in the *Passion* the music reappears three more times, each time with a different text—five in all. Yet only two of the later appearances have been traditionally

22. Jansen, "Bachs Zahlensymbolik," pp. 96–100; Smend, "Bachs Matthäus-Passion," p. 34.

EXAMPLE 71.   *St. John Passion*: the "Jesum von Nazareth" choruses

(a) No. 2b

EXAMPLE 71 *continued*

(b) No. 2d

EXAMPLE 71   *continued*

recognized for what they are: the fourth, "Nicht diesen, sondern Barrabam" (in answer to Pilate's question "Wollt ihr nun, dass Ich euch der Juden König losgebe?") and the fifth, "Wir haben keinen König denn den Kaiser" (in response to Pilate's "Soll ich euren König kreuzigen?") (Ex. 72); the associations to the idea of kingship are obvious.

The remaining occurrence of the Jesus of Nazareth music—the third of the five within the *Passion*—is remarkable for its four-bar chorus being grafted onto the beginning and ending of a longer chorus, "Wir dürfen niemand töten," which is itself a repetition of the first section of a chorus heard shortly before without the "Jesus of Nazareth" music. That is, the basis of "Wir dürfen niemand töten" (thirteen of its seventeen bars) is the opening section of the chorus "Wäre dieser nicht ein Übeltäter" (thirteen bars). "Wäre dieser nicht" then continues with "wir hätten dir ihn nicht überantwortet" (fifteen bars combining the chromatic fugue theme of the first section with a new one). In "Wir dürfen niemand töten" the thirteen repeated bars are preceded by a half bar from the beginning of "Jesus of Nazareth" and followed by the final three bars of that chorus (Ex. 73).[23] In addition, Bach runs the sixteenth-note flute pattern from "Jesus of Nazareth" through the whole of "Wir dürfen niemand töten." In this way "Wir dürfen niemand töten" is literally embedded within "Jesus of Nazareth," creating the sense that the surface of the chorus is associated with the word *Übeltäter*, while an additional hidden element is given in the "Jesus of Nazareth" music. Such a striking sense of purpose compels us to seek a theological explanation.

Perhaps Bach intended the beginning and ending of "Wir dürfen niemand töten" to represent Jesus as the Alpha and Omega; the first and fourteenth bars, those whose numbers correspond to the places of the *A* and *O* in the German alphabet, frame the thirteen bars from "Wäre dieser nicht ein Übeltäter."[24] In the literal context of the narrative "Wir dürfen niemand töten" is the crowd's response to Pilate's suggestion that Jesus be tried according to Jewish law; its text refers to the Roman rule that took the power of execution away from the Jews. As the beginning of the following recitative indicates, the chorus confirms Jesus' prediction of the means of

23. Werner Breig also notes this occurrence and suggests that Bach originally planned a four-bar chorus for "Wir dürfen niemand töten," the connection to "Wäre dieser nicht ein Übeltäter" coming only later. This is certainly possible; such a change would provide in my opinion an indication of Bach's thinking in theological terms even before the question of musical balance between the two choruses in this scene (perhaps) caused him to extend "Wir dürfen niemand töten" and connect it musically to "Wäre dieser nicht ein Übeltäter." The text of "Wäre dieser nicht" was far too long for it to have been set to the "Jesum von Nazareth" music; Bach's decision to join the music of two other choruses in "Wir dürfen niemand töten" respects both theological and musical exigencies. See Werner Breig, "Zu den Turba-Chören von Bachs Johannes-Passion," in *Geistliche Musik: Studien zu ihrer Geschichte und Funktion im 18. und 19. Jahrhundert,* Hamburger Jahrbuch für Musikwissenschaft, vol. 8, ed. Constantin Floros, Hans Joachim Marx, and Peter Petersen (Laaber: Laaber Verlag, 1985), pp. 65–96.

24. On this occasion with the number fourteen, see above, p. 163; also Chafe, "Allegorical Music," pp. 355–56.

EXAMPLE 72.

(a) Chorus "Nicht diesen, sondern Barrabam"

EXAMPLE 72   *continued*

(b) Chorus "Wir haben keinen König"

EXAMPLE 72   *continued*

his death: crucifixion by the Romans ("Auf dass erfüllet würde das Wort Jesu, welches er sagte, da er deutete, welches Todes er sterben würde"). John refers to Jesus' prediction, "Wenn ihr des Menschen Sohn erhöhen werdet, dann werdet ihr erkennen, dass ich es bin" [*Ego eimi*] (John 8:28). From this it is clear that the chorus refers to the prediction as a whole, not only to Jesus' crucifixion ("Wenn ihr des Menschen Sohn erhöhen Werdet") but to the revelation of his identity that was joined with the lifting up ("dann werdet ihr erkennen, dass ich es bin"). Name (the "Jesus of Nazareth" music) and cross (the goal toward which "Wir dürfen niemand töten" is directed) are joined symbolically once again. But the context of this first reappearance of the "Jesus of Nazareth" music suggests also that a large part of the motive for repeating the music was the issue of Jesus' identity as King (of the Jews), the theme that dominates the ensuing recitative, for the scene culminates shortly after this with two verses of the chorale "Herzliebster Jesu," the first beginning "Ach, grosser König."

As these five "Jesus of Nazareth" choruses thread through the *Passion* in a pattern of transposition that alternately rises a fourth and falls a third (or falls a fifth and rises a sixth)—G minor, C minor, A minor, D minor, B minor—it is clear that they lead toward the crucifixion (the narrative of which immediately follows "Wir haben keinen König") and conceal as their meaning the final ironic inscription over the cross, "Jesus of Nazareth, King of the Jews." The pattern of transposition presumably indicates—like the literal texts of the repeated choruses—that the physical events of the narrative tend downward, toward Jesus' death (the immediate transposition down by a fifth between the choruses that appear in the same scene), while the ultimate direction is upward, suggesting John's perception of the crucifixion as a lifting up. "Jesus of Nazareth" One and Two are in flats, "Wir dürfen niemand töten" and "Nicht diesen, sondern Barrabam" have no key signatures (the latter, in D minor, is part of the move from A minor to flats), while the last of the series, "Wir haben keinen König denn den Kaiser," culminates the central sharp-key segment of the *Passion* and is followed immediately by the judgment of crucifixion—the ending of John's trial—before the turn to flats. Several details in "Wir haben keinen König" suggest that their function is to underscore its place at the end of the series: the flute part is at its highest pitch; the independent instrumental parts and brief antiphonal beginning between chorus and instruments that had been present in "Jesus of Nazareth" One and Two but not in "Wir dürfen niemand töten" and "Nicht diesen, sondern Barrabam" are restored, and there is now a quasi-canonic imitation between chorus and instruments. At the climax of John's trial the conflict between the worldly and Christological meanings of kingship peaks in the comparison here and in "Lässest du diesen los, so bist du des Kaisers Freund nicht" between Jesus and the Roman emperor. And behind "Wir haben keinen König" lies a rejection of the First Commandment, the commandment whose "work" is faith.[25] The repetition of "Jesus of Nazareth" as "Wir haben keinen König" brings together questions of faith, Christology, and Law just at the end of the trial as judgment is passed.

The overarching allegory in the "Jesus of Nazareth" choruses is unquestionably the ability of faith to see the truth through appearances; Bach seems to have used the busy flute part to point to the more important reference to Christ's name hidden in "Wir dürfen niemand töten." And, of course, the continued references to the music that originally accompanied the name of Jesus of Nazareth suggest that Jesus' name carries over a hidden meaning from the first two choruses and is used primarily as a response to questions concerning the King of the Jews. That is, we are meant to understand all repetitions of the chorus as reiterations of the name Jesus of Nazareth in situations where the identity of the King of the Jews is called into question. The message of the royal inscription is thus threaded through the *Passion*. The name Jesus of Nazareth is, of course, an affirmation, associated with a famous Johannine locus of divine self-revelation, while the repetitions of its music all emphasize negatives: "Wir dürfen *niemand* töten," "*Nicht* diesen, sondern Barrabam," and "Wir haben *keinen* König." Bach's device, therefore, suggests Luther's description of Jesus as the Yes hidden behind the No of the Law (the *turbae*).[26]

As if confirming the association of the "Jesus of Nazareth" music to recognition of Jesus' kingship, Bach uses the music yet a sixth time, now in B minor, varied somewhat, and without the flute part, in the *Christmas Oratorio* to the text "Wo ist der neugeborne König der Juden?" (Ex. 74). On the basis of an article written by Gerhard Freiesleben in 1916, this latter chorus has been generally accepted as a parody of the chorus "Pfui dich" from the lost *St. Mark Passion*. While this may be so, it is nonetheless surprising that Freiesleben did not mention the correspondence to the "Jesus of Nazareth" choruses, even though he cites other choruses from the two surviving *Passions* to support his thesis of the Passion-like character of "Wo ist der neugeborne König der Juden."[27] The recognition of Jesus' kingship by the Magi signified, of course, the initial spread of the Word to the Gentiles as well. Repetition with a different text, at least in the *St. John Passion*, signifies the recognition of Jesus' identity as the Messiah by the faithful; we are not far either from Luther's idea of the hidden God who is revealed through faith in the cross of Christ, the point to which the "Jesus of Nazareth" series of choruses leads, or from the foundation of Luther's Christology in John's assertion of the identity of Jesus and the Father.

25. Althaus, *The Theology of Martin Luther*, pp. 141–51.
26. Althaus, *The Theology of Martin Luther*, pp. 58, 407.
27. Gerhard Freiesleben, "Ein neuer Beitrag zur Entstehungsgeschichte von J. S. Bachs Weihnachtsoratorium,"*Neue Zeitschrift für Musik* 83 (1916): 237–38.

EXAMPLE 74.   *Christmas Oratorio,* Part Five: chorus "Wo ist der neugeborne König der Juden"

Yet another chorus in the *St. John Passion* seems to be related to the "Jesus of Nazareth" series, although not so directly. The repetition of the chorus "Kreuzige ihn," transposed from its original G minor to F sharp minor with the text "Weg, weg mit dem, kreuzige ihn," involves an addition of slightly more than three bars at the beginning for the words "Weg, weg mit dem" that did not occur in the earlier chorus (Ex. 75). In the bass an idea similar to the eighth-note bass pattern of "Jesus of Nazareth" recurs, although for the most part the harmonies now follow a

EXAMPLE 74   *continued*

-bor - ne   Kö - nig   der   Ju - den?   wo,   wo?

pattern of ascending rather than descending fifths. The chorus is once again a response to Pilate's presenting Jesus as king: "Sehet, das ist euer König." Perhaps
Bach intended the reversal of the harmonic direction of the "Jesus of Nazareth"
choruses to indicate contradiction. In any case, "Weg, weg mit dem" is followed
by "Wir haben keinen König," the climax of the trial and the "Jesus of Nazareth"
series; this detail adds to the sense of interrelatedness of the choruses in the central
section.

The circle of fifths can also be found in the countersubject of the fugal chorus
"Wir haben ein Gesetz" (F major) and its transposition, "Lässest du diesen los" (E
major), set to the texts "denn er hat sich selbst zu Gottes Sohn gemacht" and "denn
wer sich zum Könige machet, der ist wider den Kaiser," respectively. Particularly
apparent at the close of each chorus where the voices move together in eighth
notes, the circle of fifths sounds a series of harmonies that closely parallels that of
"Jesus of Nazareth" and closes with a Phrygian cadence (Ex. 76). And, like the
"Jesus of Nazareth" series, these two places treat the objection of the Jews to Jesus'
Christological titles. Along with the fact that the two succeeding recitatives begin
with the words "Da Pilatus das Wort hörete" (which Bach sets in identical transposed phrases), this parallel must have aided Bach in developing his plan of the
Herzstück. The circle of fifths is nowhere more prominent, however, than in
"Herr, unser Herrscher," where, in combination with chromaticism, it concludes
the ritornello, as well as the two main sections, with "dessen Ruhm in allen Landen
herrlich ist" and "verherrlicht worden bist," respectively (the latter having a certain motivic resemblance to the bass of "Jesus of Nazareth").

EXAMPLE 75.   *St. John Passion*: beginning of chorus "Weg, weg mit dem, kreuzige ihn"

EXAMPLE 76. *St. John Passion:* ending of chorus "Wir haben ein Gesetz"

The Text Revisions

It is quite possible that the text of the *St. John Passion* did not satisfy Bach's Leipzig superiors as much as its successor did. It appears to be the case that at least once Bach came to a head-on confrontation with the Leipzig authorities over one of his *Passions*—most likely the *St. John Passion*—the performance of which was canceled in 1739. From Bach's response to this situation, it is clear that he anticipated objection to the work on textual grounds and had met such objection before.[28] The musicoallegorical emphasis on John's theology of Bach's masterwork may satisfy us even more than its successor, but to the theologians among its original audience the Johannine characteristics may not have been sufficiently incorporated into the Lutheran framework of repentance. It is suggested here, therefore, that certain of the most important differences between the *St. John Passion* and the *St. Matthew Passion* might not only have occasioned some objection to the earlier work but might also have prompted some of the revisions that the *St. John Passion* underwent during the Leipzig years.[29]

The differing emphases in Bach's two *Passions* are not incompatible either with Luther's theology or with each other, but only the *St. Matthew Passion* provides a well-rounded picture of orthodox Lutheran theology of the late seventeenth and early eighteenth centuries. This theology is reflected in the Passion sermons of the late-seventeenth-century orthodox Lutheran theologian, Heinrich Müller, which served as a primary source for a great many meditative movements, in particular the very theological-sounding ariosi.[30] Perhaps Bach's acquisition of a theological library—including several volumes by Müller—was part of his attempt to produce of body of works in Leipzig that would stand as theological as well as artistic expressions. The musicotheological goal of the Mühlhausen years, developed further at Weimar and interrupted at Köthen, was renewed in full creative maturity in the early Leipzig period. In any case, problems with the text of the *St. John Passion* could have been the result of Bach's not having yet fully accommodated himself to the Leipzig requirements, for practically all the revisions made at varying times in Bach's lifetime—as well as certain of the substitutions of movements—effectively bring the work closer to the theological character of the *St. Matthew Passion*.[31] Al-

28. The documents relating to the canceled *Passion* performance are set forth in Neumann and Schulze, eds., *Bach-Dokumente II*, pp. 338–39; English translation in David and Mendel, eds., *The Bach Reader*, pp. 162–63. It is not known which *Passion* was involved, but only the *St. John Passion* shows signs of text revisions. Dürr (*Zur Chronologie*, pp. 114–15) indicates that the parts show at least two performances of the work can be distinguished between 1735 and 1750, one before and the other after 1742; the *St. Matthew Passion* was also performed at least twice in those years, once presumably in 1736.

29. The revisions are discussed in Mendel's *Kritischer Bericht*, pp. 168–72. The textual revisions have most often been treated from the standpoint of poetic quality, an unlikely concern for Bach (see, for example, Rudolf Wustmann, "Zu Bachs Texten der Johannes- und der Matthäus-Passion," *Monatsschrift für Gottesdienst und kirchliche Kunst* 15(1910): 126–31. Mendel suggests at one point (p. 168) that "it is conceivable that objections in terms of spirituality played a role [in the text revisions]" (author's translation).

30. See Axmacher, "Ein Quellenfund"; "Aus Liebe," pp. 170–85.

31. Alfred Dürr also notes the Johannine character of some of the *St. John Passion* texts and the change in character introduced by the revisions, which he views as having a character of "rationalistic abstraction" in contrast to the concrete pictorialism of the original texts. See Alfred Dürr, *Die Johannes-Passion von Johann Sebastian Bach: Entstehung, Überlieferung, Werkeinführung* (Munich: Deutscher Taschenbuch Verlag; Kassel: Bärenreiter, 1988), pp. 50, 64–65.

though the musical Lutheranism of Bach's early works, particularly the "Actus Tragicus," is very impressive, the change in emphasis from the *St. John Passion* to the *St. Matthew Passion* suggests that Bach made an intensive study of Lutheran texts between composing the two works; the years in Köthen, away from regular church composition, might have weaned him from directly pursuing his early stated goal of creating a "well-regulated church music." The most prominent influences on the text of the *St. John Passion*—Johann Postel's Passion poetry, the Brockes Passion text, and poetry of the Weimar court poet, Salomo Franck—are of a very different type from Luther's or Heinrich Müller's sermons.[32]

Examining the text revisions in the *St. John Passion* reveals that, although they were done at different times, they had a theological and not a literary motivation. "Ich folge dir gleichfalls," for example, is modified so that the goal of following Christ becomes acceptance of suffering—"bis dass du mich lehrest, geduldig zu leiden"—a much closer correspondence to "Gerne will ich mich bequemen" than its original concluding line, "selbst an mir zu ziehen, zu schieben, zu bitten." The text of "Ich folge dir" seems to have been created in the first place with several particularly Johannine expressions in mind; Jesus is called *Leben* and *Licht* just as he is throughout the Gospel, and the choice of the verb *ziehen* reflects the fact that Jesus speaks in John of "drawing" all men to him, especially through the Passion. The revisions change this emphasis altogether: *ziehen* is removed and *Leben* is replaced by *Heiland*.

In the case of the arioso "Betrachte, meine Seel'," the line "Vor deine Schuld den Isop blühn und Jesu Blut auf dich zur Reinigen versprengen" is introduced to replace the images of the *Himmelsschlüsselblumen* and the *süsse Frucht* that emphasized the benefit for mankind of Jesus' sufferings. The added line expresses man's guilt and the process of purification of the individual through Jesus' blood. The rainbow image of "Erwäge" is replaced with the soteriological interpretation of Christ's blood within the context of another reminder of our sin: "es tilgt der Sünden Not." Finally, the line "die ich nun weiter nicht beweine" in the closing chorus is replaced by "um die ich nicht mehr trostlos weine," a qualifying of the suggestion—no doubt developed from John's view of the Passion as a triumph—that weeping is not necessary.[33]

---

32. Mendel, *Kritischer Bericht*, pp. 162–68.

33. This particular revision appears, however, to have been done by C. P. E. Bach (Mendel, *Kritischer Bericht*, p. 171); and the new final line, "Dann eil auch ich verklärt dem Himmel Gottes zu," with its reference to glorification, seems closer than the original to John. But there is, nevertheless, a sense that the revision qualifies, through explanation, the tendency of the original toward realized eschatology in expressions such as "nicht beweine" and "keine Not umschliesst"; that is, the new text places the emphasis on present comfort for weeping rather than eliminating the weeping altogether, and it places the glorification clearly in the future.

Moreover, the modifications of the year 1725, while they were partly motivated by the desire to accommodate the *St. John Passion* to the chorale *Jahrgang,*[34] nevertheless brought out—above all in the substitution of "O Mensch, bewein" for "Herr, unser Herrscher"—the emphasis on acknowledgment of sin that would later dominate the *St. Matthew Passion*. Replacing the final chorale, "Ach, Herr, lass dein lieb' Engelein," with its solid major key and associations of triumph, by the chromatic, modal, and minor-key setting of the German Agnus Dei ("Christe, du Lamm Gottes") was another enormously significant change that allied the work more closely to the elegiac character of the *St. Matthew Passion*. And, of course, in 1725 "Betrachte, meine Seel'" and "Erwäge" were taken out in favor of the aria "Ach, windet euch nicht so, geplagte Seelen," which, as we might expect, brings out the question of man's guilt: "So zählet auch die Menge eurer Sünden." In this case the original, 1724, version of the work is so much preferable that we must assume that Bach decided to revise the texts rather than keep the musical substitution. The dialogue with chorale, "Himmel reisse"/"Jesu deine Passion," was added in Part One, making an internal symmetry of sharp-key settings of verses of this chorale; it is grotesquely out of place, since it meditates largely on Golgotha.[35] But here again, the motive was probably theological; "Himmel, reisse," is the only place in the *Passion* where the first stage of the dynamic of faith in Luther's Passion Sermon—becoming "comformable to Christ in His suffering" through acknowledgment of sin—is truly emphasized: "Sehet meine Qual und Angst, was ich, Jesu, mit dir leide! . . . weil ich in Zufriedenheit mich in deine Wunden senke." Both "Ach, mein Sinn" and its substitute for 1725, "Zerschmettert mich," urge penitence; but "Zerschmettert mich" does so in a more explicit, less poetic manner, and its musical representation of tears is connected to the foregoing recitative (whose text is not from John but was borrowed from Matthew). Bach's ultimate restoration of the original version of the *St. John Passion* may testify to his awareness of the intensity of the original vision that produced the work; his handing the score over to a copyist for completion after ten folios, attests, perhaps, to the impossibility of continued involvement in a project in which the artistic and functional aspects could not be reconciled.

As examination of the theological features of the *St. John Passion* indicates, the work does not have to take a back seat because of the intensity of its musicotheological character. Bach, in the *St. John Passion,* shows uncanny penetration of the structure of John's Passion account and, even more important, of its highly sym-

---

34. Chafe, "Bach's *St. Matthew Passion,*" pp. 109–10.

35. Alfred Dürr, "Zu den verschollenen Passionen Bachs," Bach-Jahrbuch 37 (1949–1950): 89; Arthur Mendel, "Traces of the Pre-History of Bach's St. John and St. Matthew Passions," *Festschrift Otto Erich Deutsch,* ed. Walter Gerstenberg (Kassel, 1963), pp. 37–38.

bolic presentation of the crux of faith in the recognition of the identity of the man Jesus of Nazareth as the Messiah and the crucifixion as the primary means by which this identity is proclaimed to the world. In its own very different way from that of the *St. Matthew Passion,* Bach's first Leipzig *Passion* is a virtuoso piece in the musical allegorizing of theological themes. That it could have been perceived as such at the time is more than doubtful. Nonetheless, the *St. John Passion* projects a theological intent that is surpassed by no other work, and on that account it makes an impressive claim to be considered theology as well as music. The primary basis of Bach's achievement in this work, more than in its successor, is the composer's direct interaction—unmediated so far as we know by extensive theological material—with the Gospel itself.

CHAPTER ELEVEN

The *St. John Passion*:

Tonal Planning and

Musical Structure

Whether his understanding was largely intuitive or carefully studied, Bach's emphasis on particularly Johannine aspects in his *St. John Passion* reflects his sense that John presents a very different view of Jesus and the world from that of the synoptic Gospels. Among these Johannine features none is more pronounced than the overall structure, which bridges the gap between the composer's independent study of the Gospel in seeking a general plan and the Gospel's theological message. Musical form and theological content need not bear any particularly significant reciprocal relationship, of course. But in the *St. John Passion* they do, more so than in any other of Bach's works, largely because John's Passion narrative is itself highly, even at times abstractly, structured.

The Three Divisions and the Symbolic Trial

Bach's plan for the *St. John Passion* reveals a profound understanding not only of the structure of John's account of the Passion but of the very *reasons* John developed his structure in the first place. John's Passion narrative falls into three main divisions, as indicated in Fig. 7: (1) the arrest and interrogation of Jesus (Part One); (2) the trial before Pilate; (3) the crucifixion, death, and burial. John, as modern scholarship believes, manipulated the sequence of events as presented in the synoptic Gospels to arrive at his structure and its symbolic purposes. For example, he places the crucifixion a day earlier than the other Gospels, so that the Last Supper is no longer the passover meal; thus Jesus' death and the killing of the passover lambs take place at the same time, thereby strengthening the sacrificial association of Jesus' calling himself "Lamb of God"; John places the scourging at the center of the trial instead of after Jesus is delivered for crucifixion, narrates Jesus' carrying the

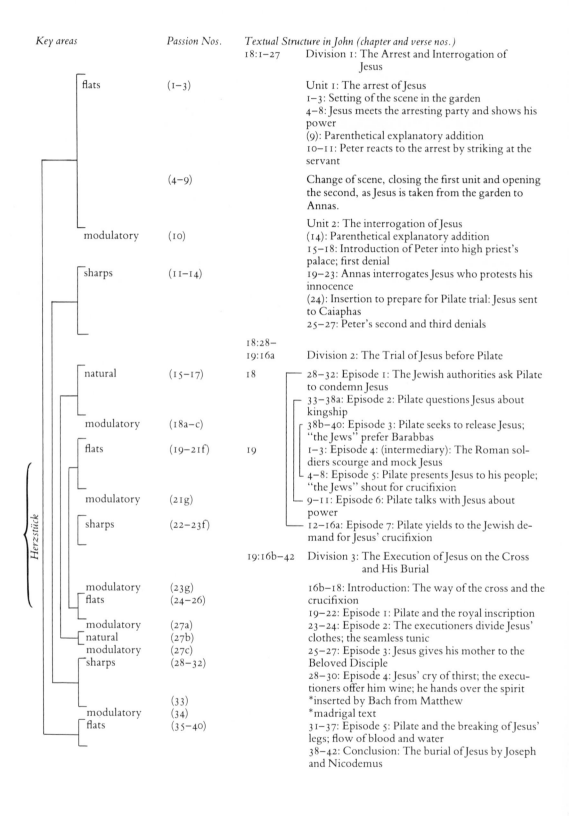

Key areas	Passion Nos.	Textual Structure in John (chapter and verse nos.)
		18:1–27 Division 1: The Arrest and Interrogation of Jesus
flats	(1–3)	Unit 1: The arrest of Jesus 1–3: Setting of the scene in the garden 4–8: Jesus meets the arresting party and shows his power (9): Parenthetical explanatory addition 10–11: Peter reacts to the arrest by striking at the servant
	(4–9)	Change of scene, closing the first unit and opening the second, as Jesus is taken from the garden to Annas.
modulatory	(10)	Unit 2: The interrogation of Jesus (14): Parenthetical explanatory addition 15–18: Introduction of Peter into high priest's palace; first denial
sharps	(11–14)	19–23: Annas interrogates Jesus who protests his innocence (24): Insertion to prepare for Pilate trial: Jesus sent to Caiaphas 25–27: Peter's second and third denials
		18:28–19:16a Division 2: The Trial of Jesus before Pilate
natural	(15–17)	18 28–32: Episode 1: The Jewish authorities ask Pilate to condemn Jesus 33–38a: Episode 2: Pilate questions Jesus about kingship
modulatory	(18a–c)	38b–40: Episode 3: Pilate seeks to release Jesus; "the Jews" prefer Barabbas
flats	(19–21f)	19 1–3: Episode 4: (intermediary): The Roman soldiers scourge and mock Jesus 4–8: Episode 5: Pilate presents Jesus to his people; "the Jews" shout for crucifixion
modulatory	(21g)	9–11: Episode 6: Pilate talks with Jesus about power
sharps	(22–23f)	12–16a: Episode 7: Pilate yields to the Jewish demand for Jesus' crucifixion
		19:16b–42 Division 3: The Execution of Jesus on the Cross and His Burial
modulatory	(23g)	16b–18: Introduction: The way of the cross and the crucifixion
flats	(24–26)	19–22: Episode 1: Pilate and the royal inscription
modulatory	(27a)	23–24: Episode 2: The executioners divide Jesus' clothes; the seamless tunic
natural	(27b)	
modulatory	(27c)	25–27: Episode 3: Jesus gives his mother to the Beloved Disciple
sharps	(28–32)	28–30: Episode 4: Jesus' cry of thirst; the executioners offer him wine; he hands over the spirit *inserted by Bach from Matthew
	(33)	*madrigal text
modulatory	(34)	31–37: Episode 5: Pilate and the breaking of Jesus' legs; flow of blood and water
flats	(35–40)	38–42: Conclusion: The burial of Jesus by Joseph and Nicodemus

Herzstück

cross, and so on.[1] The great scene of Jesus' anguish at Gethsemane is virtually eliminated from the Passion narrative. For our purposes, however, the most striking set of changes concerns the structure of the trial before Pilate. John greatly plays down the role of Jesus' other trial, before the Jewish authorities. Along with the decreased emphasis on Gethsemane, this change means that the first division of the Passion narrative (Part One in Bach's setting) concludes with Peter's denial, a point considerably later in the narrative than the ending of Part One of the *St. Matthew Passion,* while the second is completely taken up with the Roman trial. Even more striking is the structure of the trial itself, which John arranges into a sevenfold shifting of locale back and forth between an inner room of the praetorium, where the dialogues between Jesus and Pilate take place, and the outside court, where the crowd is gathered. The dialogues (confined, of course, to recitative in Bach's setting) approach the elevated themes of the Johannine discourses—power, freedom, truth, the Kingdom above—while the outside parts of the trial—primarily *turbae*—constitute the sheer visceral demand for blood. John's Gospel is famous for what have been called its "typical chiastic patterns," and of these patterns the trial is the best known and the most conspicuous, that is, episode one resembles episode seven, episodes two and six, and three and five are similar, while John shifted the scourging to place it at the center of the trial (episode four), the only scene that involves the *Kriegsknechte* rather than Pilate or the crowd. The abstract quality of John's arrangement is underscored by the correspondence of the seven episodes of John's trial to John's seven signs, seven discourses, and "I am" sayings.[2]

John emphasized the Roman trial for various reasons. We have encountered one of these in examining "Wir dürfen niemand töten": the trial is directed toward the interpretation of Jesus' death as the predicted lifting up, and crucifixion was the Roman method of execution. Also, the secular trial focused on the split between worldly and religious issues. The central question of the trial—Jesus' kingship—has two clearly opposed senses: the spiritual, articulated in Jesus' telling Pilate that his kingdom is not of this world; and the worldly, which climaxes in the crowd's "We have no king but Caesar." The dialogues between Jesus and the representative

---

1. Of the four Gospels only John has Jesus carry his own cross, a detail that is often interpreted as fulfilling the typological prefiguration of the crucifixion in the story of Abraham and Isaac, in which Isaac carried the wood for his own sacrifice. When, in the *St. Matthew Passion,* Bach mentions Jesus' carrying the cross ("Kommt, ihr Töchter"; implied in "Komm, süsses Kreuz") he does so to strengthen the meaning of "O Lamm Gottes unschuldig" in the opening chorus.

2. On this use of the number seven in John, see Brown, *The Gospel of John I–XII,* pp. cxlii, 429–30.

of secular authority (inside) treat elevated, religious subject matter, while the outcries of "the Jews" (outside) force the dominance of worldly, political issues.

Above all, the dramatic and independent structure of the trial before Pilate climaxes John's concerns: the question of Jesus' identity—in particular whether or not he is king (of the Jews)—and what the criteria are for establishing that identity. Throughout the Gospel John uses forensic expressions, such as "witnesses," "law," "testimony," "signs," and "advocate," to the extent that some commentators have suggested that the entire Gospel was conceived as a symbolic trial. The trial is bounded by the demand for crucifixion and the judgment of crucifixion, but between these two places the governor wavers, flirting with the idea of setting Jesus free ("Von dem an trachtete Pilatus, wie er ihn losliesse"). Pilate shies away from "truth"; when Jesus states, "Wer aus der Wahrheit ist, der höret meine Stimme," Pilate answers, "Was ist Wahrheit?" Setting Jesus free proves to be impossible once that action is seen as opposition to the *Kaiser*. While Pilate questions Jesus concerning his kingship, the crowd increasingly opposes Jesus' claims to kingship to the *Kaiser*, which reinforces the worldly interpretation that ultimately causes Pilate to make the death judgment. John's trial ends at this point; the third division of his Passion narrative takes up the crucifixion, Jesus' death, and burial. But in having Pilate place the so-called royal inscription over the cross and his refusing to change its wording, John continues the theme of Jesus' identity. Although Pilate chooses the worldly interpretation, his placing the inscription at all ironically proclaims the truth he has rejected.

In searching for a plan for this part of the *Passion*, Bach was drawn to the idea of musical correspondences between the *turba* choruses, no doubt to represent the unanimity of the crowd and its vivid dramatic presence. Certain textual interrelationships helped him with this idea. First, he saw the opportunity to set in parallel the choruses "Sei gegrüsset, lieber Judenkönig" and "Schreibe nicht, der Juden König, sondern dass er gesaget habe: Ich bin der Juden König," as well as "Kreuzige ihn" and "Weg, weg mit dem, kreuzige ihn." In addition, the narratives following "Wir haben ein Gesetz" and "Lässest du diesen los" both begin with "Da Pilatus das Wort hörete"; Bach gives the two phrases the identical, if transposed, musical setting. These textual parallels might have immediately suggested an integrated substructure extending beyond where the trial ends in John to encompass the crucifixion itself and the royal inscription, to which the crowd responds, "Schreibe nicht, der Juden König." But these textual correspondences do not determine the structure of the finished work, for other structures involving musical repetition might just as easily have been conceived. "Wir haben ein Gesetz," for example, might have been repeated as "Wir haben keinen König"; the two choruses with *Kaiser* references might have been linked in a similar manner; or the "Kreuzige ihn" choruses might have repeated the music of "Jesus of Nazareth" to identify "Nam' und Kreuz," and so on. That Bach was drawn to the particular sets of correspondences in his *St. John Passion* must indicate how compelling he found them as a means to realize his foremost musicotheological intentions.

He certainly meant to create points of culmination and resolution after the narrative of the crucifixion and the royal inscription. Perhaps early on he meant the chorale "In meines Herzens Grunde" to express the joining and internalizing of the two events. He might also have intended for the subsection culminating with this chorale to have a symmetrical (chiastic) structure—a visual realization of the cross and name. While John did not intend his chiastic structures to be visual representations of either the cross or the letter Chi, it is quite possible that symmetry bore this association for Bach.[3] The figurative sense of the cross, symbolizing earthly trial and tribulation, might then have been applied to the trial of Jesus. Bach must also have intended the idea of antithesis and resolution to be conveyed by the symmetrical structure. How Bach decided these issues is, perhaps, not important; interpreting the subsection itself makes his intentions clear.

Bach's equivalent to John's symmetrical trial, the segment Friedrich Smend called the *Herzstück*, comprises, in my reinterpretation of Smend's concept, a flat/sharp/flat tonal grouping in which two choruses of the first key area—"Kreuzige ihn" (G minor) and "Wir haben ein Gesetz" (F major)—are transposed into sharps and heard in reverse order with new texts in the second: now "Lässest du diesen los" (E major) and "Weg mit dem, kreuzige ihn" (F sharp minor). The first chorus from the flat key segment, "Sei gegrüsset, lieber Judenkönig" (B flat), is repeated in the original key after the return to flats in the third section of the *Herzstück*, to the text "Schreibe nicht: der Judenkönig." Further framing the *Herzstück* are the arioso/aria pairing "Betrachte, meine Seel' " (E flat) and "Erwäge, wie sein blutgefärbte Rücken" (C minor) at the outset and the chorale "In meines Herzens Grunde" (E flat) at the close. Bach bases his structure on antithesis, but he shifts what we might call his symbolic trial further along, so that it begins with a meditation on the scourging, the center of John's trial. The center of Bach's structure deals with the climactic ending of John's trial, the final rejection of Jesus in "Wir haben keinen König" and the judgment of crucifixion; and Bach's final segment extends beyond John's trial and into division three, ending with the narrative of the royal inscription and the chorale response, "In meines Herzens Grunde" (Fig. 8). The inscription itself is generally considered the classic example of Johannine irony, for the sign is intended to mock Jesus, but from John's perspective it tells the truth. Bach's extension of the trial to culminate in both the crucifixion narrative and the royal inscription actually brings out a traditional interpretation of John's meaning that is less clearly articulated in the Gospel itself: namely, that the trial has two judgments, both made by Pilate—the first, the judgment of death made under pressure from the crowd and culminating the segment in sharps, and the second,

---

3. Smend, "Luther und Bach," pp. 35–36.

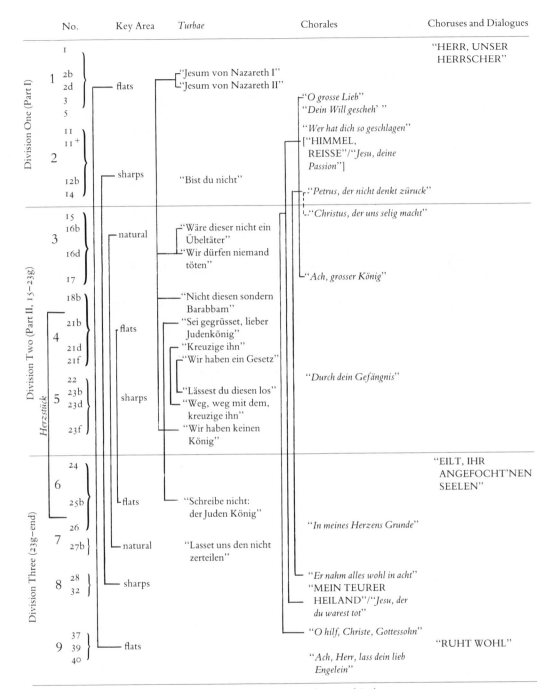

No.	Key Area	*Turbae*	Chorales	Choruses and Dialogues

Division One (Part I)

1 — I, 2b, 2d, 3, 5 — flats

2 — 11, 11+, 12b, 14 — sharps

"HERR, UNSER HERRSCHER"

"Jesum von Nazareth I"
"Jesum von Nazareth II"

"O grosse Lieb"
"Dein Will gescheh' "

"Wer hat dich so geschlagen"
["HIMMEL, REISSE"/"Jesu, deine Passion"]

"Bist du nicht"

"Petrus, der nicht denkt zürück"

Division Two (Part II, 15–23g) — *Herzstück*

3 — 15, 16b, 16d, 17 — natural

4 — 18b, 21b, 21d, 21f — flats

5 — 22, 23b, 23d, 23f — sharps

"Christus, der uns selig macht"

"Wäre dieser nicht ein Übeltäter"
"Wir dürfen niemand töten"

"Ach, grosser König"

"Nicht diesen sondern Barabbam"
"Sei gegrüsset, lieber Judenkönig"
"Kreuzige ihn"
"Wir haben ein Gesetz"

"Durch dein Gefängnis"

"Lässest du diesen los"
"Weg, weg mit dem, kreuzige ihn"
"Wir haben keinen König"

Division Three (23g–end)

6 — 24, 25b — flats

7 — 26, 27b — natural

8 — 28, 32 — sharps

9 — 37, 39, 40 — flats

"Schreibe nicht: der Juden König"

"Lasset uns den nicht zerteilen"

"In meines Herzens Grunde"

"Er nahm alles wohl in acht"
"MEIN TEURER HEILAND"/"Jesu, der du warest tot"

"O hilf, Christe, Gottessohn"

"Ach, Herr, lass dein lieb Engelein"

"EILT, IHR ANGEFOCHT'NEN SEELEN"

"RUHT WOHL"

N.B.: lower case = biblical texts; italics = chorale texts; capitals = madrigal texts

FIGURE 8.   The Structure of the *St. John Passion*

the judgment of Christ as "King of the Jews," the theme of the "Jesus of Nazareth" choruses that has run through the entire trial, now culminating the *Herzstück* in the flat-key area in which it began. Bach's shift removes the trial from exact correspondence to the physical events of the narrative, giving it a more symbolic, and very Johannine, character.

To bring out the message of the inscription as the final judgment, Bach had to overlap the final section of his *Herzstück* with the beginning of John's division three; he made the beginning of division three return to flats, which allowed the music of "Sei gegrüsset, lieber Judenkönig" to repeat as "Schreibe nicht: der Juden König" in its original key, B flat, and the tonal closure of the *Herzstück* to be in E flat. After the central sharp segment closed with the B minor chorus "Wir haben keinen König denn den Kaiser" and the D major narrative of the crucifixion judgment, Bach made the crossover modulation from sharps on the phrase "Und er trug sein Kreuz." The word *Golgatha* now marks the move to flats; the recitative ends in G minor with the arrival at Golgatha, and Bach introduces the beginning of John's division three with the dialogue "Eilt, ihr angefocht'nen Seelen," which interrupts the pattern of repeated choruses. "Schreibe nicht: der Juden König" not only returns to its original key, but it is delayed, separated by "Eilt, ihr angefocht'nen Seelen" from the *turbae* that were transposed to sharps. "Eilt, ihr angefocht'nen Seelen" is set in G minor like the opening chorus of the *Passion*; and it is conceptually related to several opening choruses of hortatory character in other works by Bach: "Kommt, ihr Töchter" (opening chorus of the *St. Matthew Passion*); "Kommt, eilet und laufet" (opening chorus of the *Easter Oratorio*); "Kommet, ihr verworf'nen Sünder" (Bach's new text for the first movement of Handel's *Brockes Passion*). We are sure that Bach was fully aware of the tripartite structure (which he observes in the *St. Matthew Passion* as well) and knowingly overlapped the *Herzstück* with it. The overlap demonstrates the fact that Bach is working on two levels, the literal-historical, which demands that he observe the divisions of the physical narrative, and the spiritual, which carries with it the equally compelling requirement that his structure provide an interpretation of the theological meaning of the events. As we will see, the overall tonal plan of the *Passion* derives from the latter concern, leading to the abstract structuring of the physical events.

The third scene of the *Herzstück* comprises an introductory chorus, a recall of music from its first scene, and a concluding chorale, all of which give structural emphasis to the narrative surrounding the crucifixion and royal inscription. Several factors contribute to Bach's creating a kind of substitute trial extending from the scourging to the royal inscription, apart from its bringing out Pilate's second judgment. "Schreibe nicht, der Juden König" is the last *turba* chorus in the *Passion* to deal with the issues of the trial, and Bach might have wanted to symbolize the Law with this addition to the nine choruses of the trial. But above all the point of culmination that comes in the chorale "In meines Herzens Grunde" brings out the meaning intended in "Herr, unser Herrscher," the "Jesus of Nazareth" choruses, and the inscription: God must be recognized in the crucified Jesus. The "showing" referred to in the opening chorus becomes a physical reality in the ironic inscription, whereas the chorale internalizes its meaning.

The Postel Passion text used by Bach in setting the *St. John Passion* begins with the scourging. This text might have been the impetus for Bach to begin the *Herz-stück* with that incident.[4] In any case, Bach treated the events of the trial before the scourging as a separate scene of decidedly Christological character beginning Part Two. Apart from the framing A minor chorales, "Christus, der uns selig macht" and "Ach, grosser König" (two verses), the scene contains the interrelated *turba* choruses "Wäre dieser nicht ein Übeltäter" and "Wir dürfen niemand töten," the latter, as we saw, being a reappearance of the "Jesus of Nazareth" music as well. Thus, this scene parallels, both structurally and conceptually, the one that follows "Herr, unser Herrscher." In both places a recitative refers to Jesus' knowledge of events to come, both scenes contain the "Jesus of Nazareth" music and two *turba* choruses a fifth apart, and they both end with verses of the chorale "Herzliebster Jesu" (in "Ach, grosser König" the two verses are distinguished from the other chorales in the *Passion* by their running eighth-note bass). It is possible, therefore, to see this scene as a continuation of the Christological message given at the beginning of the work and serving here to introduce Jesus' sufferings, beginning with the scourging.

The decisions to centralize the E major chorale "Durch dein Gefängnis," to repeat the music of "Wir haben ein Gesetz" as "Lässest du diesen los," and to structure the tonal plan of the *Herzstück* in three divisons, flats at the beginning and ending, sharps in the center, were all very closely intertwined. The transfer of music was aided by the fact that both final lines of the two choruses object to Jesus' divine claims, while the ensuing recitatives both begin with the words "Da Pilatus das Wort hörete." The placing of "Durch dein Gefängnis" was carried over from the Postel Passion text, where its aria text articulates the antithesis between Jesus' imprisonment and the freedom it brings for mankind. Bach, however, also saw the possibility of introducing the Lutheran/Pauline idea of Christian freedom—meaning freedom from the Law, as it appears in Luther's famous tract *The Freedom of a Christian*. This idea was the source of another of Bach's most striking instances of symmetrical structure, the motet "Jesu, meine Freude," the center of which—juxtaposing flesh and spirit—is related conceptually to the *St. John Passion*.[5] Bach's turning "Durch dein Gefängnis" into a chorale, by setting Postel's aria text to a

---

4. The evidence for Bach's knowing Postel's text is his taking from that work the aria "Durch dein Gefängnis, Gottes Sohn." Whether or not Bach knew a musical setting of the Postel text is unknown. Johann Mattheson discusses the relative merits of his own setting of the text and the anonymous setting formerly attributed to Handel in Part V of his journal, *Critica musica. Des fragende Componisten/Erstes Verhör/über eine gewisse Passion* (Hamburg, 1724), facsimile ed. (Amsterdam, 1964).

5. Smend, "Bachs Matthäus-Passion," pp. 46–49; Jansen, "Bachs Zahlensymbolik," pp. 98–99.

melody of Johann Hermann Schein, had unmistakable theological meaning. Once the central antithesis had been reinterpreted in this light the juxtaposition of *Gesetz* to both *los* and *Freiheit* provided a striking rationale for expanding the importance of the literal opposition of imprisonment and freedom to the theological opposition of Law and freedom through tonal shift.

The Tonal Plan

When Bach repeated the music of "Wir haben ein Gesetz" as "Lässest du diesen los," he indicated the antithesis by transposing the chorus from flats to sharps. E major was the obvious choice, not only because of a mi-contra-fa relationship to the F of "Wir haben ein Gesetz" but also because the key of E major, the upper limit of the sharp spectrum, has its own associations with salvation in Bach's work. "Wir haben ein Gesetz" is followed by a recitative that modulates to sharps on the phrase "Weissest du nicht, dass ich Macht habe, dich zu kreuzigen, und Macht habe, dich loszugeben." The modulation in this line suggests that crucifixion (the introduction of sharp accidentals) and freedom (the completion of the move to sharps) are joined, an association made explicit by the entrance of "Durch dein Gefängnis" in the key of E major. The recitative itself contains Jesus' significant answer to Pilate, "Du hättest keine Macht über mich, wenn sie dir nicht wäre von oben herab gegeben," which closes in C sharp minor and sets up Pilate's E major cadence on "Von dem an trachtete Pilatus, wie er ihn losliesse." This sequence of tonal events illuminates the thought process that led Bach to devise the tonal plan for the whole *Passion*. That is, associating crucifixion and freedom with one another as well as with power from above resonates strongly with both classic Lutheran and Johannine thought. Within John's frame of reference the cross lifts Jesus up and with him, mankind; for Luther power from above means the supreme knowledge and all-determining nature of God as well as the salvation of mankind resulting from God's sending his Son into the world. For Bach the turn to sharps at this point was no mere rhetorical punning with the double meaning of the word *Kreuz* as cross and sharp (even though he carefully placed the modulations into and out of the sharps to illustrate this connection). Rather, it must be understood as the kind of tonal event that took place, on a smaller scale, in works such as Cantatas 60 and 181: the *schwerer Gang* of the hard upward modulation has a positive outcome.

The principle of sharp/flat antithesis allowed Bach to allegorize the ideas of John's theology in the structure of the *Passion* as a whole. In general, when we examine the roles assigned to the flats and sharps respectively, we find that they bear a striking association to the Johannine worlds of below and above, or the realms of flesh (flats) and spirit (sharps). The scenes of Jesus' capture, scourging, crucifixion, and burial are all in flats, with special modulations into deep flats for the narrative of the crucifixion itself (B flat minor), the reference to Judas (F minor), the Ecce homo (F minor), the interpretation of the fact that Jesus' legs were not broken and the piercing of his side (B flat minor), the chorale "O hilf, Christe, Gottes Sohn, durch dein bittres Leiden" (F Phrygian) and the aria "Zerfliesse, mein Herze, in Fluthen der Zähren" (F minor). Then, Peter's repentance marks the move from flats to sharps, ending in A major, in Part One, "Durch dein Gefängnis" voices the redemptive meaning of Jesus' suffering in E major, the triumphant D major middle section of the aria "Es ist vollbracht"—"Der Held aus Juda siegt mit Macht"— expresses the Johannine view of the crucifixion as a triumph, the D major dialogue "Mein teurer Heiland" interprets even the fall of Jesus' head in death as a voluntary action ("und neigte das Haupt und verschied"), the nod of assurance to the individual of his redemption, and so on. Even Jesus' reference to truth ("Wer aus der Wahrheit ist, der höret meine Stimme") interrupts a structurally important move to flats with a modulation to D major, while Pilate's unbelieving response, "Was ist Wahrheit," begins the change of direction down to flats (it is followed by E minor, A minor, D minor, and, finally, G minor, setting up the E flat that begins the *Herzstück*).

Above all, the sharp/flat antithesis in the tonal plan of the *Herzstück* expresses the idea of conflicting Johannine worlds that are reconciled through the cross. In the *St. Matthew Passion* the key of E major, which is most clearly associated with power from above, culminates two extended progressions that move upward through the circle of keys from F minor, the flat extreme.[6] Likewise, the *Herzstück* of the *St. John Passion* moves, although less regularly, from its starting point in E flat (the arioso "Betrachte, meine Seel' ") up to the E major of "Durch dein Gefängnis" and "Lässest du diesen los," then back to close in the E flat of "In meines Herzens Grunde." Following the G minor ending of the scourging the keys of the closed movements are: E flat, C minor, B flat, G minor, F, E (2), F sharp minor, B minor, G minor, B flat, E flat (a pattern that is, incidentally, very close at the start to the ordering of keys in Heinichen's *musicalischer Circul*).[7]

Bach might even have intended the shape of the ascent followed by descent pattern to suggest a rainbow, to which the aria "Erwäge" at the beginning of the *Herzstück* refers. There the patterns formed by the blood on Jesus' back are described as resembling the rainbow of the covenant with Noah after the Flood. Jesus' sufferings now bring about a second reconciliation with God. From the sixteenth to the eighteenth centuries the traditional image of Christ in majesty portrayed him

---

6. Chafe, "Key Structure," pp. 46–50.

7. That is, the ambitus of the keys of B flat and G minor follow the sequence E flat, C minor, B flat, G minor, F major, D minor. The first cadence in the recitative following "Wir haben ein Gesetz" (F) completes the sequence with a cadence to D minor. This parallel to Heinichen's scheme was presumably incidental on Bach's part. If the move to sharps had continued to parallel Heinichen's musical circle, C major, A minor, G major, E minor, D major, and B minor would have come next; in the *Passion* after the D minor Bach moves at once to A minor and from there to B minor. The recitative thus illustrates that within the flat-key region the keys (and the cadences within the connecting recitatives) are all very closely related, whereas within the modulating recitative tonal ellipses take place.

seated in judgment on the rainbow, a sword protruding from one ear and a lily from the other—symbols of the division of humanity and of worlds that John continually emphasizes. "Luther had seen pictures such as these and testified that he was utterly terror-stricken at the sight of Christ the Judge."[8] In context, the *Herzstück* presents both the sharp and flat extremes (E major and B flat minor), the latter in recitative only. Like the ends of the rainbow, the beginning and ending are closer to the realm of the flesh, whereas the center represents the Johannine interpretation of the cross as a lifting up.

At the center of the *St. John Passion* Bach superimposes Paul's idea of Law and freedom (or Gospel) as flesh and spirit on John's dualism of worlds. The two sides of redemption that Luther linked to the revealed (or preached) and the hidden God are expressed in two chorales. "Durch dein Gefängnis" (E major) expresses the universal message of the Gospel for humanity—"ist uns die Freiheit kommen"; "In meines Herzens Grunde" (E flat) embodies the Gospel message for the individual. The former is known through Scripture, the latter only through the cross and faith (personal suffering as conformity to Christ).[9] In Luther's *Sermon on Preparing to Die* (1519) we learn that the line "Erschein mir in dem Bilde zu Trost in meiner Not" stands for the image of Christ on the cross, which must be impressed on the heart as the counterimage to sin.[10] It is vitally important to Luther's theology, however, that neither Law and Gospel nor flesh and spirit be taken as mere opposites, but, rather, that each pair be correctly understood as facets of a higher unity.[11] The antithesis is greatest at the center of the *Herzstück*, whereas correspondences exist between the outer (flat) regions: the B flat choruses, "Sei gegrüsset, lieber Judenkönig" and "Schreibe nicht: der Juden König"; and the E flat movements, "Betrachte, meine Seel' " and "In meines Herzens Grunde." As in "Hercules auf dem Scheidewege," the idea of opposition is placed within a larger, reconciling context, and the symmetrical ground plan with its return to flats is basic to the representation of this reconciliation. The great culmination in "In meines Herzens Grunde" allegorizes the inner union of name and cross that lies behind the symmetrical structure of the tonal plan.

After the *Herzstück* the move back up to sharps, whose goal is the final assurance of salvation from the dying Christ ("Mein teurer Heiland"), deals with the dynamic of the positive realization of faith in experience.[12] In "Es ist vollbracht" faith

8. Roland Bainton, *Here I Stand: A Life of Martin Luther* (Nashville, Tenn., 1950), pp. 22–25.

9. On Luther's understanding of the "heart" and "depths of the heart," see Althaus, *The Theology of Martin Luther*, pp. 47, 53; on the "revealed" and "preached" God, pp. 20–34, 276. See also von Loewenich, *Luther's Theology of the Cross*, pp. 31–49.

10. Martin Luther, *A Sermon on Preparing to Die,* trans. Martin H. Bertram; ed. Martin O. Dietrich, in vol. 42 of *Luther's Works,* ed. Helmut J. Lehmann (Philadelphia, 1969), pp. 97–115; see especially p. 104.

11. Althaus, *The Theology of Martin Luther,* pp. 251–66, 393–99.

12. Salvation from the dying Christ is likewise symbolized by the move upward in "In deine Hände" in the "Actus Tragicus." Von Loewenich, *Luther's Theology of the Cross,* pp. 93–101; Althaus, *The Theology of Martin Luther,* pp. 55–63.

has changed from opposing objective experience (the B flat minor of the crucifixion) to assuming the concrete form of trust (the line "O Trost für die gekränkten Seelen" sounds like a response to "Eilt, ihr angefocht'nen Seelen").[13] If the G minor introduction to division three, "Eilt, ihr angefocht'nen Seelen," can be said to parallel "Herr, unser Herrscher," with its flat tonality belonging to the region in which the crucifixion as a physical event is narrated, then the continuing ascent to sharps for "Es ist vollbracht" and "Mein teurer Heiland" signifies the meaning of the crucifixion as the salvation offered to mankind. In "Mein teurer Heiland" the message of freedom is personalized. Compared to the words "ist uns die Freiheit kommen" from "Durch dein Gefängnis," "Mein teurer Heiland" speaks in both universal and individual terms: "Ist aller Welt Erlösung da?" followed by "Bin ich vom Sterben frei gemacht?" The two bass dialogues represent aspects of the way of the cross—first as an almost physical urging that the individual "fly with the wings of faith to Golgotha, where his pilgrimage will be fulfilled" ("Eilt"), then as the comforting sense of fulfillment that follows Jesus' victory ("Mein teurer Heiland").[14]

At the expressive height of Jesus' victory in the triumphant middle section of "Es ist vollbracht" (on the words "und schliesst den Kampf") the music abandons suddenly the *stile concitato* and returns to the elegiac tone of the aria's opening section, the soft tone of the solo viola da gamba, the minor key, and the words "Es ist vollbracht." In the vocal line Bach returns not to the melodic line of the opening section, derived from Jesus' words in the recitative, but to the exact melody with which Jesus' words were spoken (see Ex. 70, above). This very dramatic return to the "literal" has a wider significance for the allegorical structure of the *Passion* as a whole. The D major section of the aria confirms Bach's understanding of the triumphant association of John's "It is finished." But equally clear is his conception of the theological purpose of the *Passion,* which, while directly concerned with indicating the benefit for mankind of Jesus' death, is directed toward understanding and the benefit of faith in the present life, not toward the depiction of transcendent splendor. This meaning determined that the key structure of the *St. John Passion* (as well as that of the *St. Matthew Passion*) return to flats in the end. It is the same meaning as Bach intended by modulating into deep sharps in the final movement of Cantata 150, which was followed by a return to the tonic of B minor to emphasize Christ's presence throughout the daily struggle (and ultimate victory) of the present life. The transcendent realm is indicated, but return to the earthly is essential. Related to this idea, the final section of the *St. John Passion* focuses on the deep flat-minor keys. Terror ("Mein Herz"), mourning ("Zerfliesse"), intense prayer

13. Von Loewenich, *Luther's Theology of the Cross,* p. 95.
14. It may be mentioned that the bass solo parts of the two dialogues sometimes have similar melodic material: cf., the melismas on "Eilt" and "Erlösung" (mm. 49–51 and 27–28, respectively).

("O hilf, Christe"), and the "sleep of death" ("Ruht wohl"), all in flat-minor keys, precede the final E flat chorale, in which for the last time some anticipation of eternity is suggested, now from a different perspective. The physical objects of meditation are the piercing of Jesus' side and the burial, both with marked associations of the flesh.

We may never know whether the "necessity" of ending in flats—for the purpose of returning to a solidly earthly perspective—led Bach to devise the abstract plan of flat/sharp/natural key areas for the *Passion,* or vice versa. The sequence of key areas from the *Herzstück* to the end is a very logical one; after the flat-key ending of the *Herzstück* the move up to sharps, for "Es ist vollbracht" and especially "Mein teurer Heiland," belongs to the triumphant character of the Johannine concept of Jesus' crucifixion, whereas the C major chorus of the "Kriegsknechte" represents a neutral area. The turn to flats for the final segment obviously relates to the sphere of the flesh, Jesus' burial, the "sleep of death," and similar ideas. Before the *Herzstück,* however, the sequence of key areas is not always so readily rationalized. The flat-key beginning of the *Passion* can, of course, be said to relate to the earthly perspective of the work, and the modulation to sharps in Part One represents, as it does in the *St. Matthew Passion,* the upward direction of redemption. But the first scene of Part Two, in A minor, seems to have been set in that key area for the double purpose of indicating a measure of antithesis to the A major at the end of Part One, and of providing a second natural key area for the overall symmetry of key areas.

The result of the compositional decisions is highly symbolic, especially since an overall symmetry of key areas led to imbalances in the lengths of corresponding segments. That is, the whole of Part One comprises only two key areas (the first one subdivided into G minor and D minor parts), whereas Part Two has seven. Bach's expansion of the symmetrical sharp/flat antithesis to the tonal plan of the whole *Passion* represents a number of John's major themes at the highest level of structure. The arrangement produces all the possible permutations in the ordering of flat, sharp, and natural key areas—not a startling achievement from a composer who did much the same thing with triple counterpoint. Such abstract preplanning can be viewed as a correlative of John's deterministic worldview, while the symmetrical plan of key areas with the sharpest keys (*Kreuztonarten*) at the center seems unmistakably to join the name and cross of Christ in a huge sign whose ultimate meaning is the inseparability of Christology and the theology of the cross.[15] The four flat-key areas might refer to "the world" in numerological terms, and the three sharp-key areas and the ninefold (3 × 3) division of the work into key areas suggests the world above through Trinitarian symbolism (analogous to the nine divisions of the "Credo" of the *Mass in B minor* and the nine chorales of the first

15. On the relationship between Christology and the theology of the cross in Lutheranism and its indebtedness to John, see Von Loewenich, *Luther und das Johanneische Christenum,* pp. 39–40.

division of *Clavierübung III*).[16] In addition, John regularly uses the word *signs* not only to designate Jesus' miracles but, beyond that, to make them particularly symbolic. In Cantata 38 Bach understood this symbolism and translated it into the musical signs of sharp, flat, and natural. The *St. John Passion* symbolizes Jesus' great "work," the redemption of mankind through the cross.

Modulations between Sharp- and Flat-Key Areas

Although certain basic associations for sharps and flats appear in the *St. John Passion,* this principle obviously cannot hold true for every movement. The necessity of organizing the work into scenes means that the broad pattern must sometimes take precedence over the detail. But in one allegorical use of sharps and flats Bach is consistent: the eight precisely placed changes of key between the nine tonal areas. Three of these are placed on the word *Kreuz* or *kreuzigen* and play with the double meaning of "cross" and "sharp" in German:

1. The move to sharps for the central segment of the *Herzstück* and the *Passion* is made on Pilate's "Weissest du nicht, dass ich Macht habe, dich zu kreuzigen [leap of a tritone from D to G sharp], und Macht habe, dich loszugeben" (cadence in B minor completing the modulation to sharps);

2. The move from this segment to the flats of Golgotha is made on a similarly elliptical modulation on "und er trug sein Kreuz"; and

3. After the close of the narrative of the casting of lots over Jesus' robe—ending with a D minor cadence, "Solches taten die Kriegsknechte"—the move to the final sharp segment is made on the phrase "Es stund aber bei dem Kreuze [leap to a sharp] Jesu seine Mutter und seiner Mutter Schwester" (ending with a transposition of the earlier D minor phrase to E minor to underscore the completion of the modulation).

These places may be compared with narratives from the *St. Matthew Passion* where Bach associates a structural modulation to sharps with the cross and where he simply juxtaposes flat and sharp cadences in the two principal keys of the *Passion* to refer to the crucifixion (Ex. 77).

We saw one other structural modulation in the *St. John Passion* marking two different attitudes toward the meaning of "truth," a classic Johannine reference to the

---

16. In *Clavierübung III,* a work whose symbolism of the numbers three and four seems to determine the arrangement of the whole, the first division (following the prelude) comprises the three *stile antico* "Kyrie" settings in the three-flat system, the three shorter "Kyrie" settings in the natural system, and the three "Gloria" settings, in which a conspicuous ascending motion from F major through G major to A major seems related to the ideas of transcendence and the world above.

EXAMPLE 77.   Sharp/flat crossover modulations in Bach's two *Passions*

(a) *St. John Passion*: modulation to sharps in the *Herzstück*

(b) *St. John Passion*: modulation from sharps to flats in the *Herzstück*

EXAMPLE 77   *continued*

(c) *St. John Passion*: modulation to the final sharp-key segment

(d) *St. Matthew Passion*: modulation to the sharp scene of the crucifixion

(e) *St. Matthew Passion*: excerpt from recitative "Und da sie ihn verspottet
hatten" (No. 55)

division of worlds above and below, and another marking the shift away from the crucifixion to the narrative of the soldiers' casting lots for the robe. Of the remaining three symbolic modulations, one (the final turn to flats) is associated with the outbreak of natural events after Christ's death, in particular the rending of the veil of the temple, from a second passage introduced into the *St. John Passion* from Matthew, perhaps for this very symbolic purpose. In this case we might consider Luther's interpretation of the significance of the veil. Luther explained that the "veil of the Temple was figuratively a sign of the flesh of Christ," and that Christ's passing through the veil (Paul's figurative description of the atonement) signified his "crossing over to the glory of the Father". Thus its rending signified the breakdown of the absolute division between the realms of flesh and spirit, putting an end to the "old way" of sin. Old Testament references to the priest's passing through the veil into the holy of holies constituted typological prefigurations of the "crossover" of the flesh, which was accomplished by Christ.[17] The rending of the veil, which prompted Bach to produce the electric modulatory arioso "Mein Herz," might thus have been intended to signify the opening of a new spirituality in the realm of the flesh (flats)—for man. Certainly, the final flat-key segment of the *Passion* contains the flattest movements in the work—"Zerfliesse, mein Herze" (F minor) and "O hilf, Christe" (F Phrygian)—the latter following from the B flat minor ending of the narrative of the piercing of Jesus' side, a narrative traditionally associated with the flesh via the sacraments. "O hilf, Christe" expresses Luther's incarnational theology in the idea of Jesus' sufferings as mankind's hope.

The two remaining modulations—the first from flats to sharps in Part One and the second from the sharps that close Part One to the A minor (natural) scene that opens Part Two—are both associated with the relationship between Peter and Jesus, which we will examine in some detail, since it raises questions of musicotheological intent that are central to the *Passion*, even if they cannot all be settled.

The shift from flats to sharps in Part One is made very symbolically. Within recitative no. 10 Bach gives us both a musical and even a visual sign of the modulation, which is made on Peter's first denial, "Ich bin's nicht," a G major cadence on which in the score Bach indicated a key signature change, without, however, bringing in a sharp signature (Ex. 78). Peter's cadence and the words "Ich bin's nicht" refer unmistakably to Jesus' earlier "Ich bin's" (*Ego eimi*). Bach sets the words "Ich bin's" to the simplest of all progressions—a dominant/tonic cadence—just as later in the *Passion*, and at several points in the *St. Matthew Passion*, he sets the words "Du sagest's" to this formula.[18] Peter's version of the cadence is subtly different, leaping up to the

17. Luther's figurative interpretation of the veil of the Temple is presented in his *Lectures on the Epistle to the Hebrews* (1517–1518), in his *Luther: Early Theological Works,* ed. and trans. James Atkinson (Philadelphia, 1962), pp. 196–98.

18. In the trial, when Jesus is questioned by Pilate regarding his kingship, he answers "Du sagest's, Ich bin ein König"; the beginning of the phrase is the dominant/tonic progression in G major, and the

EXAMPLE 78.   *St. John Passion:* excerpt from recitative "Derselbige Jünger war dem Hohenpriester bekannt" (No. 10)

third before falling, with an appoggiatura emphasis, to the tonic; its effect is unnec-
essarily emphatic and decorative beside Jesus' simple statement of truth.

The sense of contradiction in Peter's words indicated in this musical and textual
interconnection is a basic aspect of the relationship between Jesus and Peter. This
idea can be traced elsewhere as well. First, the agitated narration of Peter's cutting
off the ear of the high priest's servant is opposed to Jesus' arioso words to Peter:
"soll ich den Kelch nicht trinken den mir mein Vater gegeben hat," which are the
object of meditation in the chorale "Dein Will gescheh." John's Passion narrative
does not include an extended scene in Gethsemane, as does Matthew's, but this latter passage suggests that Bach introduced a contradictory relationship between Peter and Jesus in the *St. John Passion* as well as in the *St. Matthew Passion.* Then, following the narrative of Jesus' delivery to Annas and the aria "Von den Stricken,"
the brief recitative "Simon Petrus aber folgete Jesu nach, und ein and'rer Jünger"
leads to the aria "Ich folge dir gleichfalls," whose melodic line, as has often been
observed, derives from the recitative. The rising scale treated in canon that opens
this aria is a type Bach associates with following Christ in a number of arias: "Ich
folge Christo nach" from Cantata 12, and "Ich folge dir nach" from Cantata 159,
for instance. Following (or being drawn by) Jesus means the "discipleship of suffer-

---

words "Ich bin ein König" a G major arpeggio moving to the lower octave; the character of the phrase is
one of confirmation. In the *St. Matthew Passion* the formula appears in G minor in answer to Judas's "Bin
ich's, Rabbi?" and again in response to Pilate's question concerning kingship (C minor).

EXAMPLE 79.

(a) *St. John Passion*: recitative beginning (No. 8)

(b) *St. John Passion*: beginning of aria "Ich folge dir gleichfalls"

(c) *St. John Passion*: beginning of chorus "Sei gegrüsset" (remaining parts omitted)

ing," following Jesus through cross and Passion.[19] "Ich folge dir gleichfalls" is the first major-key movement in the *Passion* and it suggests the affect of innocent joy rather than suffering. Bach nevertheless musically and tellingly connects it and the trial by making the beginning of the aria remarkably similar to the beginning of the B flat choruses "Sei gegrüsset, lieber Juden König" and "Schreibe nicht, der Juden König" that frame most of the *Herzstück*. The turn of phrase for "mit freudigen Schritten" (m. 3 of the ritornello) reappears for the important expression "Juden König" (Ex. 79). The joy of following Christ brought out in "Ich folge dir," which retains something of the idea of the royal entry into Jerusalem, is the direct result of

19. The Quinquagesima cantatas, and Cantata 159 in particular, are deeply concerned with this question, which arises out of the narrative of Christ's journey to Jerusalem for the Passion.

the Johannine emphasis on Jesus' spiritual kingship and its ultimate benefit for mankind. This idea is directly expressed in the final lines of "O grosse Lieb": "Ich lebte mit der Welt in Lust und Freuden, und du musst leiden!"

The recitative that narrates Peter's admittance to the high priest's palace, his first denial, and the questioning of Jesus, contains the modulation from flats to sharps, beginning in G minor and ending in E major. The specified turning point comes, as we said, on the words of denial. It is not Peter, however, but Jesus who establishes G major with the words, "Siehe, dieselbigen wissen, was ich gesaget habe!" which can be taken at least to include Peter, if not to refer to him specifically. It is also Jesus who closes the recitative on E major, the sharp limit of the work ("Was schlägest du mich?"). From the ensuing chorale, "Wer hat dich so geschlagen" / "Ich, ich und meine Sünden," to the end of Part One the music remains in or close to A major, ending with the F sharp minor aria "Ach, mein Sinn" and A major chorale "Petrus, der nicht denkt zurück." The scene ending Part One, is the only place in the *Passion* where guilt and repentance are acknowledged ("Ich, ich und meine Sünden" and "Ach, mein Sinn").

Two points in the *St. Matthew Passion* that are related to this scene also modulate to sharps to indicate the positive outcome of redemption: the ending of Part One ("O Mensch, bewein") and the scene of Peter's repentance in Part Two (aria "Erbarme dich" and chorale "Bin ich gleich von dir gewichen"). Peter stands, of course, for the individual suffering a crisis of faith, which is the reason all Passion settings emphasize his story and the basis of the "personification" that Spitta discerned in both *Passions*.[20] Peter's G major cadence is a form of denial of Jesus' earlier one in G minor, but the continuing upward motion of the tonal dynamic to the A major that closes Part One nevertheless represents the direction of his redemption.

Like the motion from E minor to E major over the first part of the *St. Matthew Passion,* the striking tonal distance from "Herr, unser Herrscher" to the A major chorale must represent a rising progression. In the 1725 revisions to the *St. John Passion* Bach added to this scene the aria with chorale "Himmel, reisse" / "Jesu, deine Passion ist mir lauter Freude," creating a symmetrical relationship between the two verses of "Jesu, deine Passion" that appear here ("Petrus, der nicht denkt zurück" is the other verse) and the two that appear in the penultimate sharp-key scene ("Er nahm alles wohl in acht" and "Jesu, der du warest tot," the latter heard in dialogue with "Mein teurer Heiland").[21] In making this change Bach might have wanted to create a chorale substructure that would bring the *Passion* closer in spirit to the cycle of chorale cantatas of 1725. The addition certainly brings out the basic

---

20. Philipp Spitta, "Die Arie 'Ach, mein Sinn' aus J. S. Bach's Johannes-Passion," *Vierteljahrsschrift für Musikwissenschaft* 4 (1888): 101–10.

21. See Dürr, "Zu den verschollenen Passionen Bachs," p. 89. The dating of the different versions in this article predates the new chronology and is, therefore, inaccurate. Dürr indicates the framing of the

antithesis we have emphasized in the *Passion,* and it as well links the "joy" of the benefit for mankind of the Passion to the move to sharps. It strikingly confirms the symmetrical key plan. But, beyond these factors, the symmetrical relationship draws attention to the fact that the large-scale motion from flats to sharps that takes place three times within the *Passion*—in Part One (G minor–A major), within the *Herzstück* leading to "Durch dein Gefängnis" (E flat–E major), and from "Eilt, ihr angefocht'nen Seelen" to "Mein teurer Heiland" (G minor–D major)—deals with redemption (Peter's, the general message of salvation for mankind, and the meditating individual's, respectively).

The message of redemption in the *St. John Passion* is most characteristically presented in the three sharp-key scenes of E major, A major, and D major. Although it would be going too far to suggest that a spiritual hierarchy of sharpness is involved, with the extreme of E major associated with Christ alone, the choice of A major rather than E at the end of Part One suggests a subtle level of allegory. We have noted that the recitative in which the move to sharps is made ends with Jesus' words "Was schlägest du mich?" on an unmistakable cadence to E, even though the voice ending on the fifth of the final chord and the lack of a strong dominant/tonic progression in the bass provide the necessary questioning character. The chorale response makes clear that the question, put to makind in general, concerns the responsibility for Jesus' sufferings ("Wer hat dich so geschlagen" and "Ich, ich und meine Sünden"). Speaking metaphorically, we might say that the chorale does not take up the offer of E major, treating the recitative cadence—by hindsight—as the dominant of A. The key of E major might just as easily have followed to confirm Jesus' cadence (as does, for example, the chorale "Erkenne mich, mein Hüter" that follows Jesus' E major in the *St. Matthew Passion*).

At Peter's second opportunity to bear witness to the truth there is another lead-in to E major; the chorus "Bist du nicht seiner Jünger einer?" begins in A and ends in E, but the narrative of Peter's second denial (borrowed from Matthew) emphasizes the leap of a seventh up to D natural on *leugnete,* which turns the cadence on the second "Ich bin's nicht" to A. The character of denial in this D natural is all the more striking in comparison with the upward leap of the soprano to D sharp in the penultimate measure of "Bist du nicht." Finally, as Peter is challenged yet a third time by one of the servants, now with a melody that suggests a compressed version of the last two phrases of the chorus, E major is offered for the third time, but the response "Da verleugnete Petrus abermal" moves to B minor instead (Ex. 80).

Herzstück by the four settings of verses from "Jesu, deine Passion" and these in turn by the larger chorale settings that began and closed the *Passion* ("O mensch, bewein" and "Christe, du Lamm Gottes"). His chorale symmetry takes on new meaning given that we now know that the version he was describing was contemporaneous with the chorale cantata cycle, and it goes hand in hand with the division of the *Passion* into sharp and flat key areas.

EXAMPLE 80.   *St. John Passion*: beginning of recitative No. 12c

The theology of the time—represented, for example, in the Calov Bible—recognized that Jesus' "Ich bin's" expressed all that set him apart from men, which is, of course, the intent behind the shift of mode and key area for Peter's "Ich bin's nicht."[22] The same idea is carried across the break between Parts One and Two, in the chorales "Petrus, der nicht denkt zurück" (A major) and "Christus, der uns selig macht" (E Phrygian, or A minor), which are identical in poetic structure, meter, and rhyme scheme but opposed in content and mode. The minor mode for Jesus and major for Peter reverses our expectations but can easily be rationalized when we consider the role played by "Christus, der uns selig macht." Bach undoubtedly used this chorale for the same reasons that Mattheson gave for his own use of it as prologue to his setting of the Postel text: it summarizes Jesus' sufferings and serves to introduce the ensuing narrative of the sufferings via its final line ("wie denn die Schrift saget").[23] Bach then places the last verse of the same chorale, "O hilf, Christe, Gottes Sohn, durch dein bitt'res Leiden," right at the end of the narrative of the piercing of Jesus' side, so that the two verses frame the story of Jesus' sufferings. The unusually extreme key to "O hilf, Christe," F Phrygian, more than any other detail in the *Passion,* gives the sense of the depths of Jesus' suffering and humiliation. Although "Christus, der uns selig macht" introduces this idea, its first line nevertheless indicates the benefit that accrues to mankind as the result of Jesus' sufferings. Thus, while the beginning of the *Passion* announces the theme of glorification in abasement, the A minor scene that opens Part Two introduces the narrative of the fulfillment of that message, the reality and extent of Jesus' sufferings. The minor key, as in "Herr, unser Herrscher" and "Jesum von Nazareth," represents the descent to *Niedrigkeit* of the incarnate Word, and the major the raising of mankind. The A minor is closer to the adverse events of the physical narrative, as is E minor in the *St. Matthew Passion,* while the A major is a region of anticipated transcendence, like E major in the later work.

Melodic Interrelationships

Yet another dimension of musical allegory relates Peter's denial to Jesus' "Ich bin's," namely, a series of melodic interconnections that runs through a number of the places just discussed. This is a very delicate issue, since it all too easily invokes the concept of leitmotiv, which certainly has no place in Bach's conceptual world. Even the unquestionable musical interrelationships that indicate a strikingly intricate level of allegorical thinking on Bach's part (the "Jesus of Nazareth" choruses, for example) do not involve extending the musical allegory to interconnections be-

---

22. Abraham Calov, *Die Heilige Bibel nach S. Herrn D.MARTINI LUTHERI Deutscher Dolmetschung und Erklärung . . . ausgearbeitet und verfasset von D. ABRAHAM CALOVIO* (Wittenberg, 1681), pp. 914, 918–19.
23. Mattheson, *Critica musica,* p. 12.

tween recitative passages. Recitative is traditionally free and unmotivic, reflecting the momentary, passing words; its formulaic nature practically forbids the idea of large-scale referential content. In some respects the recitative of the *St. John Passion* is even more inclined to the momentary and immediately pictorial than that of the *St. Matthew Passion*. Particularly angular representations of individual words (*Hochpflaster,* for instance) and highly graphic moments stand out: "weinete bitterlich," "geisselte ihn," and the like. At the same time in the *St. John Passion* relationships between recitative formulae are unquestionably present: "wärmete sich," "Da Pilatus das Wort hörete," and a few others. These are incidental in nature. Also, a few melodic connections between recitatives and the arias following them have been suggested: "Simon Petrus folgete Jesu nach" to "Ich folge dir gleichfalls"; "weinete bitterlich" to "Ach mein Sinn" (even more to the 1725 substitute aria "Zerschmettert mich"); "Es ist vollbracht" (recitative and aria).[24] Therefore, the highly developed sense of interrelationship within the *Passion* might be extended, with the appropriate cautions, to certain recitatives. The following discussion is advanced in such a spirit.

Within the recitatives that follow the two "Jesus of Nazareth" choruses the rising fourth of Jesus' words "Ich bin's" is expanded twice in related phrases: first, the Evangelist's "Als nun Jesus zu ihnen sprach: Ich bin's"; then Jesus' "Ich hab's euch gesagt, dass ich's sei" (Ex. 81). Then in the modulatory recitative the maid's challenge to Peter—"Bist du nicht dieses Menschen Jünger einer?"—recalls the second of these places, setting up Peter's first denial. Earlier, the phrase "Da hatte Simon Petrus ein Schwert" had sounded a similar formula, the perfect fourth altered to a tritone. The same kind of rising phrase appeared on "Simon Petrus aber folgete Jesu nach," ending now with a sixth. If we view these modifications as belonging to a single category of melodic formula, it becomes clear that the melodic type in question returns at the following places within the recitatives of Part One (Ex. 82):

1. "Der dem Hohenpriester bekannt war, hinaus"
2. "Da sprach die Magd, die Türhüterin, zu Petro" (see Ex. 78)
3. "Bist du nicht dieses Menschen Jünger einer?" (see Ex. 78)
4. "Solltest du dem Hohenpriester also antworten?"
5. "Da gedachte Petrus an die Worte Jesu"

The melodic formula runs throughout the story of Peter's denial in one or another of these forms, sometimes suggesting a deliberate reference backward, such as when the response to Jesus' words by one of the servants—"Solltest du dem Hohenpriester also antworten?"—is recalled musically later, after Peter's third denial,

24. See Mendel, "Traces," p. 42.

EXAMPLE 81.   *St. John Passion*: excerpts from recitatives 2c and 2e

(a)

(b)

(c)

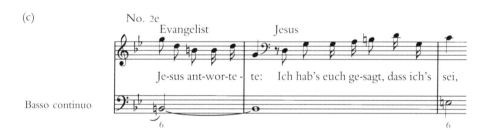

EXAMPLE 82.   *St. John Passion*: excerpts from recitatives Nos. 10 (a and b) and 12c (c)

(a)

EXAMPLE 82   *continued*

(b)

Diener

Soll-test du den Ho-hen-prie-ster al-so ant - wor-ten?

Basso continuo

(c)

Evangelist

Da ge-dach-te Pe - trus   an die Wor-te Je - su,

Basso continuo

on the phrase, "Da gedachte Petrus an die Worte Jesu." The most interesting occurrence, however, appears in the theme of the chorus "Bist du nicht seiner Jünger
einer," where the rising sixth is used at the beginning and the fourth at the end,
with a variety of modifications in between (Ex. 83). The final appearance of the
rising fourth in the bass of the closing bars (resembling "als nun Jesus zu ihnen
sprach: 'ich bin's' ") represents the point at which the key of E is presented to Peter,
and which, as we saw, he avoids. The insistent repetition of the words "Bist du
nicht" in this piece underscores the urgency of the question put to Peter, which
seems to be addressed to all humanity.

EXAMPLE 83.   *St. John Passion*: chorus "Bist du nicht" (No. 12b)

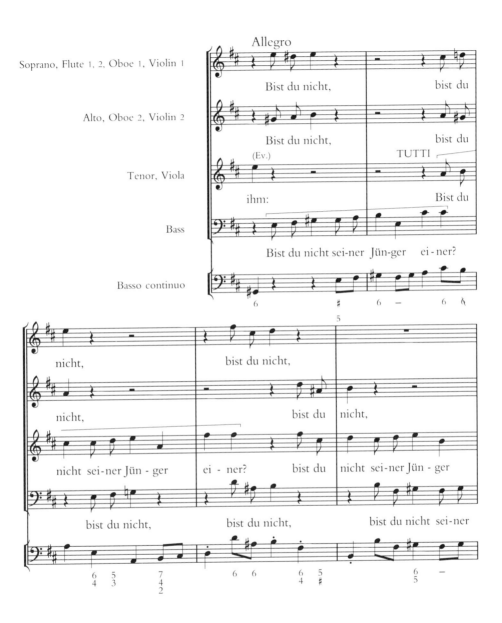

EXAMPLE 83   *continued*

EXAMPLE 83   *continued*

CHAPTER TWELVE

The

St. Matthew Passion:

The Lutheran

Meditative Tradition

It now seems likely that Bach had completed the *St. Matthew Passion*—at least in the earlier version of the work preserved in the copies of two of his pupils—by the spring of 1727, not long after what was perhaps the most intensely creative period in his life—the one that produced the *St. John Passion* (1724) and the two Leipzig cantata cycles (1723–1725).[1] During the latter part of this time he also embarked on the publication of his great cycle of keyboard music, the *Clavierübung*. It also seems likely that after about mid-1725 Bach focused attention on either the *Clavierübung* or the *St. Matthew Passion,* instead of cantatas, for many months. We do not know how long composition of the *Passion* took, but no new *Passion* was performed in the intervening years. In 1725 he had again performed the *St. John Passion* but with modifications both to accommodate it to the chorale cantata cycle and, as was discussed in Chapter 10, to bring it theologically closer to the *St. Matthew Passion,* and in 1726 he performed Reinhard Keiser's *St. Mark Passion* for the first time since his Weimar years.[2] To our knowledge Bach began his collaboration with Picander, at the very latest, by February 1725, and it is possible that plans for the *St. Matthew Passion* were set in motion as much as two years before the presumed date of the first performance in 1727.[3]

Only circumstantial evidence supports this suggestion, such as Picander's publishing in 1725 his first attempt at a Passion poem, the *Erbauliche Gedancken auf dem Grünen Donnerstag,* which he subsequently drew upon for the *St. Matthew Passion* text, and some of the modifications to the *St. John Passion* that clearly anticipate the later work. The major texts that influenced the *St. Matthew Passion*—the sermons

1. Rifkin, "The Chronology."
2. Andreas Glöckner, "Johann Sebastian Bachs Aufführungen zeitgenössischer Passionsmusiken," *Bach-Jahrbuch* 63 (1977): 75–119.
3. Chafe, "J. S. Bach's *St. Matthew Passion*," pp. 103–8.

of Heinrich Müller above all, the above-mentioned Kaiser *Passion,* Picander's ear-lier Passion poem, and, of course, the *St. John Passion* itself—indicate a close collab-oration between Bach and Picander prior to the completion of the *St. Matthew Pas-sion* text.[4] The Leipzig authorities may have directed Bach to Picander, and even to the Müller sermons, hoping that these would provide him with a more orthodox Lutheran viewpoint than is present in the *St. John Passion.* The double-edged char-acter of the revisions to the *St. John Passion* suggest that both the chorale emphasis in the 1725 version and the shift in theological emphasis (both then and later) were early indications of a conception that would be fully realized only in the *St. Matthew Passion.* Hence we can reasonably surmise that the latter work was conceived early on to be part of the chorale cycle, but, like the cycle itself, was not completed in 1725.[5]

This hypothesis, however, is in no way essential to our interpretation of the *St. Matthew Passion* as a work of art, and the question of the work's *Entstehungsge-schichte*—viewed here as of primarily biographical interest—is not our goal. The foregoing statement is necessary because we will give considerable attention to the logical—as opposed to the chronological—inner history of the work. The compo-sitional history of a work can be of great importance when, as a reasonably clear sequence of events, it tells us the composer's intent. In the case of Bach's *Passions* the lack of sufficient written documents such as sketches, composing scores, and the like, does not permit the outlining of such a sequence. Speculation on this sub-ject is most fruitful, therefore, when it tries to understand the work's internal cor-respondences and coherence.

Unfortunately, the most significant work on the *St. Matthew Passion,* that of Friedrich Smend, also a Lutheran pastor and theologian, tended to make the com-positional history the object of musical analysis rather than a means toward the higher goals of interpretation and criticism.[6] In Smend's overall conception a more complex history behind the *Passion* imbued it with greater meaning. The necessity of giving weight to selected movements in relation to the framework of a hypo-thetical compositional chronology forced Smend to juxtapose questionable musi-cal parallels and interrelationships with those of great significance and originality. In his critical assessment of the work Smend, rather than accepting the work as the expression of its composer's intention and of the theology of its time, preferred to explain the presence of some movements as the result of external circumstances, changes of mind, and the like, occurrences for which he had no objective evidence and which he therefore had to justify by analysis and criticism. In addition, Smend

---

4. Picander's *Erbauliche Gedancken* is reprinted in Spitta, *Johann Sebastian Bach,* vol. 2, pp. 873–81; discussions in Spitta, Eng. ed., vol. 2, pp. 506–8; Wustmann, "Zu Bachs Texten," pp. 161–65; Axma-cher, *"Aus Liebe,"* pp. 166–69.
   5. Chafe, "J. S. Bach's *St. Matthew Passion,*" pp. 111–14
   6. Smend, "Bachs Matthäus-Passion."

overlooked the purpose of meditation on the Passion in the tradition established by Luther: (1) recognition and acknowledgment of sin; (2) the growth of faith through love and casting one's sins on Christ; and (3) the Passion as the model for Christian life.[7] Instead, Smend allowed into his argument a more modern view of the Passion as an elevated account of the life of Christ, which adversely affected his judgment of some movements in which the concerns of the troubled and sinful individual conscience come to the fore, such as, "Wenn ich einmal soll scheiden."[8] As a result, much of the intended character of the work seemed to demand an external explanation; the explanation then became a surrogate for meaning.

With the *St. John Passion* Smend achieved greater success; that work was in some respects closer to the modern view of the Passion—it expresses a less strict Lutheran orthodoxy—and Smend saw it as a key to the structure of the later work. Smend's concern for compositional history proved a drawback primarily in his interpretation of two series of movements within the *Passion*: the ten *turbae* of division two and the five chorale verses sung to the melody "Herzlich tut mich verlangen."[9] He based the idea of a *turba* series on the *St. John Passion,* taking over the idea of a symmetrical ordering with a *Herzstück* as centerpiece, claiming in addition that three of the chorales supposedly originated in the Köthen *Funeral Music* of early 1729 and were introduced into the *St. Matthew Passion* at the latest stage of composition.[10] Smend's conception of stages of composition began, rather simplistically, with a group of movements that Rudolf Wustmann had designated as the *frühes Gut* of the work, based on their appearance in earlier versions in Picander's *Erbauliche Gedancken* and on Smend's belief that Bach began with the *St. John Passion* and evolved the *St. Matthew Passion* from it.[11] Smend's standpoint negates the possibility that Bach might have intended his *Passions* to have two very different musicotheological characters. Smend replaced Bach's rational planning with a slower, more evolutionary picture of composition according to which Bach was not so much the architect as the unwitting participant in a process of growth and even chance modifications.

Although Smend's work cannot go uncriticized, his study nevertheless contains much valid observation; examining its main ideas afresh will enable us to renew his quest for meaning. In keeping with the hermeneutic sequence described in Chapter 2, our concept of the way in which the "origins" of a work are investigated might be expressed in the progression from *Quelle* (documentary source) through *Entstehungsgeschichte* (compositional history) and its successor, "compositional process," to *Ursprung* (in Walter Benjamin's sense of the "original idea" or "leap" of the mind), a stage that is accessible to us only in the finished work.

7. Luther, *A Meditation on Christ's Passion,* pp. 8–14.
8. Smend, "Bachs Matthäus-Passion," pp. 60–71.
9. Smend, "Bachs Matthäus-Passion," pp. 16–33, 60–71.
10. Smend, "Bachs Matthäus-Passion," pp. 64–69.
11. Wustmann, "Zu Bachs Texten," pp. 161–65; Smend, "Bachs Matthäus-Passion," pp. 11–12, 16.

Discussion of the structure of the *St. Matthew Passion* can certainly include talk of "origins" and influences apart from strict historical chronology. This chapter proposes, first of all, to restore to music criticism a sense of the true theological purpose of the *Passion* in terms of Lutheran orthodoxy, and, second, to show the derivation of Bach's structure from that tradition. For example, when we consider the three divisions and the articulation of the third division within Part Two in relation to the *St. John Passion,* we find that Bach worked with some of the same problems, in particular the relationship between the beginning of division three and the end of the trial, and found fascinatingly different solutions, interpretation of which tells us much about his intentions for the two *Passions.* The actual order in which these matters presented themselves to him is, by comparison, relatively unimportant.

The *St. Matthew Passion* does exhibit a conspicuous three-divison plan, comprising

1. Part One (the Passion narrative through the arrest of Jesus and the fleeing of the disciples);

2. Part Two up to no. 58d (the questioning of Jesus before the high priest, through the trial and crucifixion, up to the mocking of Jesus on the cross, ending with the *turba* chorus "Andern hat er geholfen" with its E minor cadence in octaves on the words "ich bin Gottes Sohn"); then, after the brief modulatory recitative, no. 58e;

3. The final flat-key segment of the *Passion,* from no. 59 ("Ach Golgatha") to the end (i.e., Jesus' last words, his death, and burial).

The tripartite structure of the *St. Matthew Passion* is like that of the *St. John Passion,* but it does not reflect a dualism between the natural divisions of the physical narrative and the more symbolic, abstract plan as in the earlier work. Now divisions two and three do not overlap, for in the *St. Matthew Passion* the third division does not begin with the arrival at Golgotha as it does in its predecessor. Instead it occurs further along, which allows the series of ten *turbae* to culminate in "Andern hat er geholfen" before the shift of keys and the entrance of a hortatory dialogue. Yet its introductory movements retain the association between Golgotha and division three that prompted the structural overlap in the *St. John Passion:*

1. The arioso "Ach! Golgatha" (presumably inspired by the appearance in Keiser's *St. Mark Passion* of an aria, "O, Golgatha," at the place corresponding to "Eilt, ihr angefocht'nen Seelen" in Bach's *St. John Passion*); and

2. the "introductory" dialogue, "Sehet! Jesus hat die Hand," which is modeled after "Eilt, ihr angefocht'nen Seelen."

The pairing of "Ach! Golgatha" and "Sehet" effects a meditation on the meaning of Golgotha rather than the physical motion to the place of crucifixion. "Sehet" urges the faithful to seek redemption in the crucified Christ. Also, the upward melodic motion and dramatic questioning entrances of the second chorus that appeared in "Eilt" are noticeably tempered in "Sehet": instead of the sweeping scalar line of "Eilt," more meditative slurred duplet sixteenths dominate the melodic character of "Sehet." The earlier dialogue had symbolized the motion toward Golgotha—in the lines "Nehmet an des Glaubens Flügel, flieht zum Kreuzes Hügel, eure Wohlfahrt blüht allda." The words *eilt, Flügel,* and *flieht* suggest, nevertheless, the haste that belongs to the physical narrative. Then, as we saw in the preceding chapter, the sense of forward (and upward) motion in the *St. John Passion* is completed in the second bass dialogue, "Mein teurer Heiland," where the faithful receive the answer to their question concerning redemption. In the *St. Matthew Passion* both the placement of "Sehet" and its imagery also correspond closely to those of "Mein teurer Heiland" in the *St. John Passion*: Jesus is on the cross and one of his final gestures—the outstretched arms in "Sehet," the final nod of his head in "Mein teurer Heiland"—is interpreted as a familiar sign of assurance. "Sehet" thus combines features of both earlier dialogues. Because its meditative character relates more directly to "Mein teurer Heiland" than to "Eilt," it is paired with "Ach! Golgatha," which, as the expression of desolation as the immediate reaction to the crucifixion, is its foil. The Passion sermons of the seventeenth century provide a particularly rich textual background for "Sehet, Jesus," confirming its important role in marking a shift of perspective within the *Passion*; Bach highlighted the shift in perspective by fashioning the movement as a dialogue.[12]

In both *Passions* the articulation of the third division is related to several stages in the way of the cross. These stages do not, however, proceed in the same order in both *Passions*. In the *St. Matthew Passion* division three begins with the acceptance of the cross as a completed idea, which has already been given in "Komm, süsses Kreuz." The third division comes later in the work, after the crucifixion, and is devoted to the ideas of reconciliation and peace to a greater extent than the ending of the earlier work. The scheme that follows outlines the major events surrounding the completion of the message of redemption in the two *Passions,* ordered here according to the sequence that appears in the *St. Matthew Passion*.

1. In both *Passions* a series of ten *turbae* that represent the core of division two closes with reference to the reason for the crucifixion: Jesus has called himself "King of the Jews" ("Schreibe nicht: der Juden König") or "Son of God" ("Andern hat er geholfen"). In both places an ironic truth is intended: "Schreibe nicht" responds to the royal inscription,

12. Axmacher (*"Aus Liebe,"* pp. 79–83) quotes excerpts from several similar texts from the seventeenth-century Passion sermon literature.

while the end of "Andern hat er geholfen" sets the words "ich bin Gottes Sohn" in parallel octaves (interval of the Son, according to Werckmeister);[13]

2. The modulation to flats for Golgotha (*before* the last of the *turbae* in the *St. John Passion,* and *after* in the *St. Matthew Passion*) involves reference to the cross ("Und er trug sein Kreuz"; "Desgleichen schmäheten ihn auch die Mörder, die mit ihm gekreuziget würden"). The movement that represents Golgotha marks a conspicuous culmination of the move to flats ("Eilt"; "Ach, Golgatha");

3. A solo movement in dialogue with chorus gives assurance of redemption ("Mein teurer Heiland"; "Sehet");

4. The meaning of the Passion is internalized ("In meines Herzens Grunde"; "Mache dich, mein Herze, rein").

In the *St. Matthew Passion* this sequence underscores other details to bring out the sense of reconciliation that emerges toward the close. The sequence in the *St. Matthew Passion* may appear more natural because Bach could simplify the overall plan in the absence of a symmetrical key structure. A dialogue before the arrival at Golgotha would interrupt the momentum and undercut the sense of ironic finality of the octave cadence. Therefore Bach delayed the introduction to the third division until after "Andern hat er geholfen," used the brief recitative that followed it to make a modulatory transformation to flats, and pictured the physical progression to Golgotha in the prologue to the entire work, "Kommt, ihr Töchter." This movement is also modeled after "Eilt, ihr angefocht'nen Seelen." Thus the textual relationship between the two dialogues in the earlier work, "Eilt, ihr angefocht'nen Seelen" and "Mein teurer Heiland," the sense that the hastening toward the "Kreuzes Hügel" ("Eilt") is fulfilled in the message from the cross ("Mein teurer Heiland"), is now conflated into "Sehet, Jesus," on the one hand, and, on the other, carried over to the parallel between "Kommt, ihr Töchter" and "Sehet, Jesus." Transferring the "Golgotha" dialogue to the head of the work suggests that the entire *Passion* is a symbolic progression to the cross, where the message of redemption is given as the basis of divison three in "Sehet." At exactly the point in the work where "Kommt, ihr Töchter" "belongs" chronologically, Bach placed the aria "Komm, süsses Kreuz" (apparently derived from the aria "O, süsses Kreuz" in Keiser's *Passion,* where it appears only a short recitative before Keiser's "O Golgotha"). The words *selber tragen* in Bach's "Komm, süsses Kreuz" ("Wird mir mein Leiden einst zu schwer, so hilf du mir es selber tragen") refer back to the opening

13. Werckmeister, *Musicalische Paradoxal-Discourse,* pp. 92, 100, describes the octave as representing the Son; the unison, the Father; and the fifth, the Holy Spirit (on the basis of the proportions 1:2:3); some such idea may underlie the octave leap at the beginning of the "Quoniam" of the *Mass in B minor.*

chorus where Jesus is pictured as carrying the cross ("Sehet ihn aus Lieb und Huld Holz zum Kreuze selber tragen"), a detail that is narrated only by John, not Matthew. Bach worked out the articulation of his points of sectional division and of the introduction to the Passion in dialogue with the *St. John Passion* and Keiser's *St. Mark Passion*, a stage in the conception of the work that had to have involved Picander's willingness to provide texts for Bach according to his (Bach's) needs at these points.

A number of the key ideas in the text of "Kommt, ihr Töchter" are reflected throughout the *Passion*, particularly Part Two, in individual meditative movements and approximately in the order of the prologue:

"Kommt, ihr Töchter"/"O Lamm Gottes"	Meditative Movements
"Seht—Wohin?—auf unsre Schuld"	Chorale verse: "Was ist die Ursach aller solchen Plagen?"; "Ich, ach Herr Jesu, habe dies verschuldet, was du erduldet"; also several other movements up
"O Lamm Gottes unschuldig"	up to "Ach, Golgatha" ("Die Unschuld muss hier schuldig sterben")
"Sehet—Was?—seht die Geduld"	Aria: "Geduld"
"Erbarm' dich unser, o Jesu!"	Aria: "Erbarme dich, mein Gott"
"Sehet ihn aus Lieb und Huld"	Aria: "Aus Liebe"
"Holz zum Kreuze selber tragen"	Aria: "Komm, süsses Kreuz" ("so hilf du mir es selber tragen")
"Kommt, ihr Töchter" "Sehet—Wen?—den Bräutigam" "Seht ihn—Wie?—als wie ein Lamm" "Sehet—Was?—seht die Geduld" "Seht—Wohin?—auf unsre Schuld" "Sehet ihn aus Lieb und Huld"	Aria: "Sehet, Jesus hat die Hand" "Kommt—Wohin? "Suchet!—Wo? ⟩ In Jesu Armen" "Bleibet—Wo?

The foregoing interrelationships significantly help us to understand the musicotheological intent of the *St. Matthew Passion*. What we see in the prologue—*Schuld, Geduld,* and *Liebe,* above all—constitutes the primary meaning of the work. In the *St. John Passion* the chorale prologue, "Herr, unser Herrscher," announced the fundamental vision of glorification in abasement and the Christological focus of the "Jesus of Nazareth" choruses and the royal inscription. Now, in the *St. Matthew Passion,* "Kommt, ihr Töchter" points not only to the physical progression to Golgotha but also to the place where the themes of the prologue—Jesus' innocence versus man's guilt, Jesus' patient suffering, love as the basis of Jesus' sacrifice, and so on—are brought to completion. Through several devices—tonal plan, instrumentation, double-chorus aspects, and a meditative sequence that runs through the arias and ariosi—the events surrounding the crucifixion represent the completion of the message of the entire work as announced in the prologue. A shift in meaning takes place at Golgotha, and from "Komm, süsses Kreuz" to the end of the *Passion* the regular alternation of ariosi and arias back and forth between the two choirs is broken: the meditative movements from this point on are sounded by Chorus One, with special instrumentation (see below). Then the redemption that is offered in "Sehet" and the reconciliation with God articulated in "Am Abend" go along with the personal, inner relationship between the individual and Christ that is symbolized by his burial within the human heart in the pastorale "Mache dich, mein Herze, rein." Directing a meditative series within the *Passion* toward these events appears to have been carefully worked out with the aid of Heinrich Müller's Passion sermons.[14] Focusing events on Golgotha, locale of human desolation, is, as we will see, linked to outstanding events in the tonal plan of the *Passion,* as if to acknowledge the extreme allegorical character of the "place of the skull."

We may now focus more closely on Golgotha's role in the *Passion* as the goal of the events in the prologue, beginning with textual considerations. The theologian Paul S. Minear has listed several instances of madrigal texts present in the *Passion* in which motifs of the Matthean narrative are "rightly identified," at the head of which he places the phrase "Die Unschuld muss hier schuldig sterben" from "Ach, Golgatha."[15] As we saw, the pairing of "Ach, Golgatha" and "Sehet, Jesus hat die Hand" marks the shift that constitutes the double meaning of Golgotha, simultaneously the "Platz herber Schmerzen" (as it is described in Keiser's text) and the turning point to God's proper work of redemption ("Sehet, Jesus"). Needless to say, before "Ach, Golgatha" many texts emphasize guilt, sin, and the need to repent. In addition, the further requirements of Luther's Passion Sermon—becoming conformable to Christ in his sufferings, casting one's sins on Christ, and recognizing that Jesus' sufferings and death were undergone out of love for mankind—are all given a prominent place, as the following summary indicates.

Part One

1. Chorale fantasia: "Kommt, ihr Töchter"/"O Lamm Gottes unschuldig" ("seht auf unsre Schuld")—man's guilt contrasted with Jesus' innocence, exhortation to meditation on the Passion
2. Chorale: "Herzliebster Jesu" ("Was ist die Schuld, in was für Missetaten bist du geraten?")—Jesus' guiltlessness
3. Aria: "Buss und Reu knirscht das Sündenherz entzwei"—guilt and repentance

14. Axmacher, *"Aus Liebe,"* pp. 170–85.
15. Minear, "Matthew, Evangelist, and Johann, Composer," p. 254.

4. Chorale: "Ich bin's, ich sollte büssen"—acknowledgment of guilt

5. Aria with chorale: "O Schmerz"/"Was ist die Ursach" ("Ach, meine Sünden haben dich geschlagen. Ich, ach Herr Jesu, habe dies verschuldet")—acknowledgment of guilt

6. Aria: "Gerne will ich mich bequemen, Kreuz und Becher anzunehmen"—willingness to accept the cross

7. Chorale fantasia: "O Mensch, bewein dein Sünde gross"—exhortation to acknowledgment of sin

Part Two

8. Arioso: "Mein Jesus schweigt"—Christ as model

9. Aria: "Geduld" ("Leid ich wider meine Schuld Schimpf und Spott")—Christ as model

10. Chorale: "Wer hat dich so geschlagen" ("Du bist ja nicht ein Sünder, wie wir und unsre Kinder; von Missetaten weisst du nicht")—man's guilt contrasted with Jesus' innocence

11. Aria: "Erbarme dich"—repentance

12. Chorale: "Bin ich gleich von dir gewichen" ("Ich verleugne nicht die Schuld, aber deine Gnad und Huld ist viel grösser als die Sünde, die ich stets in mir befinde")—acknowledgment of guilt

13. Chorale: "Wie wunderbarlich" ("die Schuld bezahlt der Herre, der Gerechte, für seine Knechte")—Jesus pays for mankind's sins

14. Arioso: "Er hat uns allen wohlgetan" ("sonst hat mein Jesus nichts getan")—Jesus' innocence

15. Aria: "Aus Liebe" ("dass das ewige Verderben und die Strafe des Gerichts nicht auf meiner Seele bliebe")—removal of sin from conscience, Jesus' innocence, love

16. Arioso: "Ja! freilich will in uns das Fleisch und Blut zum Kreuz gezwungen sein"—conformity to Christ, acceptance of the cross

17. Aria: "Komm, süsses Kreuz" ("wird mir mein Leiden einst zu schwer, so hilf du mir es selber tragen")—casting sins on Christ, acceptance of the cross

18. Arioso: "Ach Golgatha" ("die Unschuld muss hier schuldig sterben")—Jesus' innocence bearing the weight of human sin

19. Recitative with chorus: "Nun ist der Herr zur Ruh gebracht" ("Die Müh ist aus, die unsre Sünden ihm gemacht . . . seht, wie ich mit Buss und Reu beweine, dass euch mein Fall in solche Not gebracht.")—acknowledgment of man's guilt, referring to the first aria of the *Passion*

The madrigal-texted movements in the above sequence correspond very closely to the group of texts derived from the Passion sermons of Heinrich Müller.[16] "O Schmerz," "Gerne will ich mich bequemen," "Mein Jesus schweigt," "Er hat uns allen wohlgetan," "Aus Liebe," "Ja, freilich," "Komm, süsses Kreuz," and "Nun ist der Herr" all descend from Müller sermons, along with three movements— "Sehet, Jesus," "Am Abend, da es kühle war," and "Mache dich, mein Herze, rein"—that come after "Ach, Golgatha" and mark the shift away from guilt and sin to thoughts of redemption, reconciliation, and union with Christ. In these movements Picander reworks the orthodox Lutheran Passion theology into an early-eighteenth-century perspective. As Jaroslav Pelikan has shown, the "satisfaction" theory of redemption whose origins go back to Anselm of Canterbury in the eleventh century lies behind this theology.[17] According to this view human nature was so contaminated after the Fall by sin that it was incapable of satisfying the just demand of a wrathful God for its punishment, or in Lutheran-Pauline terms, it was unable to fulfill the Law. Restitution was therefore made on mankind's behalf in the sacrifice of the innocent Christ on the cross; this payment motivated by love satisfied the demand for justice, enabling God to forgive man's sins and to assure his redemption.[18] This theology runs throughout the *St. Matthew Passion* and is especially prominent in those texts that derive from Heinrich Müller.

Although, as Axmacher has shown, Picander's text changes the emphases significantly in a number of movements, lessening the idea of God's wrath and increasing the prominence of love, the imagery of God's court of judgment, of Jesus' payment for man's sin, and the like, remains close to the two models of Luther and Müller in its basic thematic outline.[19] This outline is very important to the structure of the *St. Matthew Passion,* for the central themes are made into a series. If we add to this the aria "Geduld" (one of the most important themes of the Lutheran Passion tradition and one that was also developed from that tradition)[20] we have a sequence that runs closely parallel to the themes introduced in "Kommt, ihr Töchter." Bach articulates the central meaning of these movements in a number of ways: the use of special instrumentation in a number of cases (viola da gamba and oboes da caccia, above all), dialogue treatment, key structure, and musical correspondence with other movements. These devices indicate that Bach and Picander wanted to create a particular form of Lutheran meditative dynamic within the *Passion* (Fig. 9).

---

16. Axmacher, *"Aus Liebe,"* pp. 70–85.
17. Pelikan, *Bach among the Theologians,* pp. 91–101; see also Althaus, *The Theology of Martin Luther,* pp. 202–8.
18. Pelikan, *Bach among the Theologians,* p. 91.
19. Axmacher, *"Aus Liebe,"* pp. 18–27, 171–72.
20. On the textual background for *Geduld,* see below, p. 356.

Luther's Stage	Movement No. and Title	Theological Content of Text	Special Instruments	Textual Background
One	19: "O Schmerz"/"Was ist die Ursach"	Recognition of sin, prompted by meditation on Jesus' sufferings	Recorders, oboes da caccia	Müller
	22: "Der Heiland fällt"	Jesus' acceptance of the cup restores man to God's grace		Müller
	23: "Gerne will ich mich bequemen"	Readiness to accept the cross and cup; Jesus' drinking of the cup has sweetened it for mankind		Müller
Three	34: "Mein Jesus schweigt"	Jesus' silent sufferings as model for mankind	Viola da gamba	Müller
Three	35: "Geduld"	Patient acceptance of suffering	Viola da gamba	Gerhardt?
Two	48: "Er hat uns allen wohlgetan"	Jesus' works of love for man	Oboes da caccia	Müller
Two	49: "Aus Liebe"	Jesus dies for love, not sin; his death removes God's judgment from man's conscience	Oboes da caccia	Müller
Three	56: "Ja, freilich"	Benefit of suffering for man	Viola da gamba	Müller
Three	57: "Komm, süsses Kreuz"	Suffering willingly accepted with Jesus' aid	Viola da gamba	Keiser?
	59: "Ach, Golgatha"	Jesus dies as *Fluch*; horror and degradation of the cross	Oboes da caccia	Keiser?
	60: "Sehet, Jesus hat die Hand"	Seek redemption in Jesus' arms	Oboes da caccia	Müller
	64: "Am Abend"	Evening as time of reconciliation with God; Jesus' cross as means of reconciliation		Müller
	65: "Mache dich, mein Herze, rein"	Purification of the human heart as resting place for Jesus	Oboes da caccia	Müller

FIGURE 9.   The stages of Luther's *A Meditation on Christ's Passion* in the *St. Matthew Passion*

The Oboes da caccia

Bach's use of special instrumentation not only indicates the most important stages of meditation on the Passion but also represents their affective qualities via instrumental characteristics and associations. For example, the oboes da caccia point to the theological uses Luther makes of the Passion: acknowledgment of sin and, with the aid of love, "Tröstung des Gewissens."[21] Together these two stages constitute a faith dynamic that Luther articulates most succinctly in his *A Meditation on Christ's Passion.*

The texts of "O Schmerz" and the answering chorale verse in dialogue, "Was ist die Ursach," correspond closely to Luther's sermon. Luther stresses that the first stage of meditation on the Passion is contemplation of Christ's innocent sufferings that then impel the Christian to recognize the seriousness of his own sin, lead him to become conformable to Christ, to "tremble and quake and feel all that Christ felt on the cross."[22] Both Luther and Müller use the image of the poor sinner before a court of judgment to represent God's wrath in weighing man's sin. This is the scene that lies behind "O Schmerz": Picander's text is a contemplation on Jesus' suffering at Gethsemane that retains the image of God's judgment—"Der Richter führt ihn vor Gericht, da ist kein Trost, kein Helfer nicht"—but does not give as much emphasis to man's fear of God's judgment as Luther demanded. Fear is inferred from the repeated sixteenths of the bass line, but the trembling and quaking is associated with Jesus' spiritual torment rather than that of the contemporary individual; Luther's first stage is presented in the chorale verse from the second chorus. "Was ist die Ursach" states the acknowledgment of sin most fully: "Ach, meine Sünden haben dich geschlagen. Ich, ach Herr Jesu, habe dies verschuldet, was du erduldet." Its low pitch and dark tonal coloring—F minor, beginning on B flat minor and utilizing the Neapolitan sixth at the end of the first phrase on *Plagen*—provide a special sonority to go along with the recorders and oboes da caccia that accompany the tenor arioso. That the latter instruments cease whenever the chorale enters and reenter immediately afterward signals two different kinds of suffering, the one intensely impassioned, the other full of heaviness, as if in response to Jesus' words, "Meine Seele ist betrübt bis an den Tod," on which this movement meditates.

Bach's musical setting adds an affective dimension that Picander could never have foreseen. Although it recognizes with Picander (presumably) that "O Schmerz"/

21. Axmacher, *"Aus Liebe,"* pp. 20–24.
22. Luther, *A Meditation on Christ's Passion*, p. 11. Holborn ("Bach and Pietism," pp. 61–71) discusses the theological content of the *St. Matthew Passion* in relation to Luther's sermon.

"Was ist die Ursach" represents the first stage in Luther's meditative dynamic, it goes beyond Picander in its treatment of the relationship between such moments of affective response to the narrative and the larger theological questions at issue. Bach has his own theological perspective, even toward given texts, expressed in the prominence he gives to particular movements within the structure of the *Passion*. Whether or not Picander's own understanding was much deeper than the texts reveal is yet another issue. There is no question, however, that the plan of the *St. Matthew Passion* revolves around theological as well as musical exigencies; its theological character, therefore, can be read only in a limited way from Picander's text.

Instrumentation is Bach's first means of highlighting those movements that most clearly express the main points of Luther's sermon. In "O Schmerz" the soft-toned oboes da caccia represent God's love, which counteracts his wrath. Axmacher notes that the ending of the arioso introduces thoughts that are not part of Müller's sermon but instead belong to Picander's softened emphasis on the severity of God's judgment.[23] The concluding lines, "Ach, könnte meine Liebe dir, mein Heil, dein Zittern und dein Zagen vermindern oder helfen tragen, wie gerne blieb' ich hier," express an affective response to Christ's sufferings that, if carried out, would halt the Passion.[24] The emphasis has so altered that Jesus' sufferings as the necessary means by which God's justice is satisfied are virtually forgotten. Instead, Jesus inspires love in the believer. The apparently too sudden leap from the contemplation of Christ's sufferings and the acknowledgment of sin to the introduction of the idea of love is derived from Luther's sermon. In it shifting to love as a partial means of "spurring oneself to believe" belongs to the second stage, in which the meditating individual moves from the contemplation of Jesus' sufferings and recognition of sin, learning now to "cast one's sins on Christ," to "see them overcome by His resurrection."[25] One must be aware of sin in a positive fashion; sin must not be allowed to remain in the conscience or it will prove too strong for man and "swallow him up completely." Man cannot live with the terror of guilt for an extended time; he must learn to remove sin from his conscience so that he will "grow in faith," which is the Lutheran aim of meditation on the Passion.

At this second stage in meditating on the Passion the individual is aided by recognizing that Jesus' sacrifice was prompted by divine love for man. Luther stresses that the individual's understanding that fact produces love for Christ, and faith continues to grow. Bach's choice of oboes da caccia for "O Schmerz," like the turn toward love at the end of the arioso, connects the points at which Luther's first two stages are presented. The text of the soprano aria "Aus Liebe" is related directly to that of "O Schmerz" in its juxtaposing the ideas of love and God's judgment, now

23. Axmacher, *"Aus Liebe,"* pp. 171–72.
24. Axmacher, *"Aus Liebe,"* pp. 195–96.
25. Luther, *A Meditation on Christ's Passion*, p. 12.

with the former dominating. The middle section of the aria makes clear that Jesus'
death, motivated by love, causes mankind to be freed from God's judgment: "Aus
Liebe will mein Heiland sterben . . . dass das ewige Verderben und die Strafe des
Gerichts nicht auf meiner Seele bliebe." Throughout Bach's music oboes da caccia
are prominently associated with love in various forms (see, for example, the *Christmas Oratorio,* and Cantatas 1, 16, 46, 65, 74, 180, 186). Besides the oboes da caccia
and the juxtaposition of judgment and love, "O Schmerz" and "Aus Liebe" are
further linked by Bach's placing the chorale verses "Was ist die Ursach" and "Wie
wunderbarlich," in close conjunction with them. These two verses are extracted
from a chorale ("Herzliebster Jesu, was hast du gebrochen?") that is entirely occupied with the themes we are discussing. "Wie wunderbarlich," although not in dialogue with "Aus Liebe," as "Was ist die Ursach" is with "O Schmerz," introduces
the theme of Jesus' paying the sinner's debts ("Die Schuld bezahlt der Herre, der
Gerechte, für seine Knechte") shortly before "Aus Liebe" develops it with the line
cited above. The chorale appears, along with "Er hat uns allen wohlgetan" and
"Aus Liebe," between the two "Lass ihn kreuzigen" choruses (the segment that
Smend viewed as the *Herzstück* of the *St. Matthew Passion*).

Smend was correct in viewing the framing of "Wie wunderbarlich," "Er hat uns
allen wohl getan," and "Aus Liebe" by the two "Lass ihn kreuzigen" choruses as
another *Herzstück,* the center of Jesus' trial in division two.[26] Although freedom
had prompted the antithesis at the center of the *St. John Passion,* love stands at the
center of its successor. The almost ethereal instrumentation of "Aus Liebe" for
solo soprano, solo flute, and a pair of oboes da caccia playing a kind of substitute
basso continuo in parallel thirds, sixths, and tenths is in apposition to the ponder-
ously chromatic *turbae.* It belongs to the very small number of so-called *bassetchen*
arias in Bach's oeuvre.[27] Elsewhere in the *St. Matthew Passion* Bach uses the *bassetchen* idea in dialogues to offset Jesus' capture with the reaction of the Christian community ("So ist mein Jesus nun gefangen"/"Sind Blitze, sind Donner"; "Ach, nun
ist mein Jesu hin"/"Wo ist denn dein Freund hingegangen?").[28] Bach uses the *bassetchen* texture for a variety of purposes in the church music; in Cantata 135, for
example, it stood for the opposition of God's wrathful and loving natures, through

26. Smend, "Bachs Matthäus-Passion," pp. 18, 30, 33.

27. The term *bassetchen* (or *bassetgen*; French: *petit basse*; Italian: *bassetto*) was used by theorists of the
seventeenth and eighteenth centuries to designate basso continuo accompaniment in a register other
than the bass, as well as a bass line that substituted for the basso continuo in the upper register. See F. T.
Arnold, *The Art of Accompaniment from a Thorough-Bass* (London, 1931; reprint, New York, 1965), pp.
224, 233, 373–81. Bach's oeuvre contains several such arias; e.g., BWV 11/10, 46/5, 234/3, etc.

28. The bass line of the soprano/alto duet "So ist mein Jesus" is played by violas and cellos in unison,
while the second chorus interjects with its "Haltet, lasst ihn, bindet nicht." In "Ach, nun ist mein Jesu
hin" the word *Ach* is prolonged in the voice part and accompanied by the upper parts without basso
continuo.

the juxtaposition of low and high bass parts. In the *Ascension Oratorio* (BWV 11) the *bassetchen* texture in the aria "Jesu, deine Gnadenblicke" represents the fact that Jesus' love remains even though he is not physically present. In Cantata 46 an alto aria scored for two flutes and two oboes da caccia likewise omits the basso continuo and substitutes the oboes in unison for a bass line. The meaning of the latter aria is closely bound up with the pastorale association of the winds, and the text speaks of Jesus' lovingly gathering in the pious like sheep and "little chickens" (*Küchlein*); the good shepherd Jesus is a figure to whom the idea of love attaches itself naturally, and both this aria and "Aus Liebe" explicitly represent Jesus as protecting the faithful from the judgment of sin.

This protective aspect provides the necessary link between "Aus Liebe" as representing Luther's second stage and "Sehet, Jesus hat die Hand" as introducing the third, prompting the next appearance of oboes da caccia. In "Sehet" the image of Jesus' gathering in the faithful like "lost chickens" ("ihr verlass'nen Küchlein") is combined with the idea of man's finding rest and salvation in Jesus' arms to create a turning point in the work. "Sehet, Jesus hat die Hand" is so rich a movement that commentators as diverse as Smend and Bruno Walter have both marveled at its moving beyond the adverse events of the narrative to portray the benefit of the crucifixion from the perspective of the resurrection.[29]

The pairing of "Ach, Golgatha" and "Sehet, Jesus" brings the oboes da caccia into the foreground in two movements whose relationship was conceived antithetically. "Ach, Golgatha" is perhaps the most tortured movement in the *Passion,* modulating into the deep flat-minor keys and voicing horror at the physical event. In this piece the drama of human guilt reaches its spiritual and tonal nadir. The arioso exists as a foil for the dialogue aria that follows. Whereas "Ach, Golgatha" describes the horror of the crucifixion in antithetical terms ("der Segen und das Heil der Welt wird als ein Fluch an's Kreuz gestellt"), "Sehet, Jesus hat die Hand," pictures Jesus on the cross as the shepherd, his arms outstretched to gather in the faithful.

The relationship between these two movements is based on Luther's exposition of the meaning of the crucifixion in his tenth sermon on the Passion of his *Hauspostille* of 1545: the cross is accursed (*verflucht*), Jesus dies as a *Fluch* (literally "curse"), bearing the weight of man's sin and God's hatred of sin. Only thus could mankind's debt of sin be paid, could Jesus redeem man from the Law's "curse" as described by Saint Paul ("Christ redeemed us from the curse of the Law, since he

---

29. Smend, "Bachs Matthäus-Passion," pp. 49–53; Bruno Walter, *Of Music and Music-Making,* trans. Paul Hamburger (New York, 1961), pp. 188–89.

became a curse for us," as Luther quoted Paul).[30] The Law is represented symbolically in the *St. Matthew Passion,* as in its predecessor, by the series of ten *turbae* that concludes just before "Ach, Golgatha." The modulation from E minor (the ending of "Andern hat er geholfen") to the flats marking the turning point is effected by a cross relation that juxtaposes the words *Mörder* and *ihm* (i.e., Christ) in a particularly concentrated sharp/flat shift. "Ach, Golgatha" culminates the emphasis in the Passion on guilt versus innocence ("die Unschuld muss hier schuldig sterben"). The antithesis of *Fluch* and *Segen* that is represented broadly in the juxtaposition of "Ach, Golgatha" and "Sehet, Jesus" is derived from Luther's interpretation of Paul and the Heinrich Müller sermon that served as the model for "Sehet, Jesus hat die Hand."

Axmacher points out that Picander's text for "Sehet, Jesus hat die Hand" removes Müller's interpretation of Jesus' outstretched arms as the sign of blessing (*Segen*) that belongs to His priesthood.[31] But Bach's various structural and allegorical devices bring out this meaning much more than Picander's text attempts to do. The shift of key area to flats, and especially the turn to E flat major after the troubled waverings in the deep flat-minor keys of "Ach, Golgatha," the parallel between "Sehet, Jesus" and "Kommt, ihr Töchter," and, of course, the tremendous change in tone between the two meditative movements are all expressions of what in Luther's sermon is described as man "truly born anew in God" as the result of understanding God "not in his might or wisdom, . . . but in his kindness and love."[32] The oboes da caccia are unmistakably linked to Luther's emphasis on love at this stage of the Passion. The overall impact of "Sehet, Jesus" is close to that of the pastorale character of many of Bach's movements in which slurred duplets appear, such as the "Et in terra pax" of the *Mass in B minor.* In terms of Luther's meditative dynamic this is when faith is fully attained, the completion of the second stage.

The role of the oboes da caccia to indicate stages in the Lutheran meditative sequence changes throughout the *Passion.*

1. Accompanying the tenor solo "O Schmerz" along with recorders in a chamber-music texture that features many wide leaps, often of diminished and augmented intervals. Despite its elaborate dialogue setup, this movement is still an arioso, and the instrumental accompaniment is, as in "Er hat uns allen wohlgetan" and "Ach, Golgatha," bound to a preset rhythmic and figural pattern;

---

30. Luther, *Passio, oder Histori vom leyden Christi Jesu, unsers Heylands, Die Zehend Predig* ("Wie Christus ans Creutz geschlagen, und was er dran thun, erlitten und geredt habe, biss er verschiden ist, Matthei am xxvii"), in Luther, *D. Martin Luthers Werke,* vol. 52 (Weimar, 1915), p. 806.
31. Axmacher, *"Aus Liebe,"* p. 180.
32. Luther, *A Meditation on Christ's Passion,* p. 13.

2. As substitute basso continuo in "Aus Liebe," the oboes are linked to the idea of Jesus as the shepherd who is sacrificed out of love for the sheep; that is, the oboes da caccia indicate love as the foundation of the human relationship with Jesus;

3. In "Sehet, Jesus" the oboes sing forth for the first and only time in the *Passion* as melody instruments, conveying not only the pastorale association of Jesus' outstretched arms but the freedom that it brings for the believer; it is here that they come into their own.

Then, in "Mache dich, mein Herze, rein" the oboes sound for the fourth and last time in the work, now reintegrated into the orchestra as doubling instruments for the violins, adding their characteristic soft coloring to one of Bach's most moving pastorales, comparable in character to "Schlafe, mein Liebster" from the *Christmas Oratorio,* where Bach also adds oboes da caccia for a meditation on Mary's love for the infant Christ. Theologically, "Mache dich" and its companion arioso, "Am Abend da es kühle war," both derived once more from Müller, mark the final stage in the atonement. This reconciliation with God is conveyed in the line "Der Friedeschluss ist nun mit Gott gemacht, denn Jesus hat sein Kreuz vollbracht" of the arioso (a strong E flat cadence) and in the aria through the idea of Jesus' resting within the human heart to await the resurrection. Renate Steiger interprets "Mache dich, mein Herze, rein" as exemplifying "realized" or "present" eschatology within Lutheranism, that is, the transformation of the world through faith. "Am Abend" expresses the sense of transformation by linking not only Adam's fall in Eden to Christ's fall in Gethsemane but also the first reconciliation with God, the olive branch brought to Noah after the Flood, to its counterpart in the new covenant of the cross. All these events took place in the evening, which was thereby transformed from the time of darkness and fear to that of peace and reconciliation.[33] The oboes da caccia reach across a wide span of the *Passion* to relate the four stages of Gethsemane, the trial, Golgotha, and the burial in a sequence that brings out the major stages of faith as presented in Luther's Passion sermon: acknowledgment of sin prompted by Jesus' suffering; recognition of love as the cause of Jesus' sacrifice; understanding the resurrection and Jesus' innocent death as the means of conquering the fear of sin; and, finally, the fullness of faith and the transformation of the present life.

In these four places Bach gave six of the movements based on Müller texts important structural positions (in terms of tonal planning, placement, dialogue treatment, and the like) and an instrumental aura that both bound them in a sequence

---

33. Steiger, " 'O schöne Zeit!" pp. 6–11.

and imparted to them a tone suggestive of love. Two of these places—Gethsemane and Golgotha—are set in deep flats, the key area with which the oboes da caccia are most frequently associated in the cantatas. Gethsemane and Golgotha are spiritually related, of course, in that they are the places of human desolation, of Jesus' tormented struggled with the flesh, that is, with acceptance of the cup, of God's will as manifested in the crucifixion (Gethsemane), and of the horror and darkness of the crucifixion itself (Golgotha). The "evening" of Gethsemane and the "darkness" of Golgotha—as well as the spiritual states they represent—are allegorized in the *Passion* by the darkest flat-minor keys—F minor for "O Schmerz" and a modulatory wavering that reaches to touch B flat minor, E flat minor, and even, briefly, A flat minor at Golgotha. Together these places represent the nadirs of Parts One and Two respectively. Just as the oboes da caccia are associated with both suffering and love (the pastorale aspect) in the cantatas, throughout the *St. Matthew Passion* they are associated with a dialectic of guilt and love that is finally resolved at "Sehet, Jesus hat die Hand" into what was for Luther the more important use of the Passion: "Tröstung des Gewissens" (i.e., the benefits of faith and love for the believer).[34]

The Viola da gamba

In the stages of Gethsemane, the trial, Golgotha, and the burial Bach focuses on two of the three primary objects of meditation from the opening chorus, *Schuld* and *Liebe*. They correspond to two of the Lutheran uses of the Passion, recognition of sin (*Sündenerkenntnis*) and comforting the conscience (*Tröstung des Gewissens*).[35] Each appears in relation to its opposite—man's guilt versus Jesus' innocence and God's love versus his demand for justice and punishment. A third use of the Passion in Luther's writings is its exemplary role as expressed in the next section of the Passion sermon: "After your heart has thus become firm in Christ, and love, not fear of pain, has made you a foe of sin, then Christ's passion must from that day on become a pattern for your entire life."[36] As Luther's words reveal, this stage is not part of the meditative dynamic concerned with the growth of faith but, rather, follows that dynamic. It is an actively operating rather than a passively receiving stage, and its theological character has an ethical cast: works are no longer to be feared for now faith is secure.

Clearly, this exemplary role cannot be presented in the *Passion* as if it were the final climactic goal of faith. Although it is clearly recognized in the *St. Matthew*

34. Axmacher, *"Aus Liebe,"* pp. 20–24.
35. The three uses of the Passion in the Lutheran tradition are discussed in Axmacher, *"Aus Liebe,"* pp. 18–27. See also Luther, *Von dem nutz des leidens Christi,* in *Werke,* vol. 52, pp. 228–36.
36. Luther, *A Meditation on Christ's Passion,* p. 13.

Passion and given special instrumentation and structural correspondence, it does not follow the other two stages as it does in Luther's Passion sermon. The special instrumental resource by which Bach articulates the exemplary role is the viola da gamba, in particular the seven-stringed instrument associated with the advanced gamba music of the French baroque. The instrument signals the structural correspondence between the two scenes in which it is used. The first is the narrative of Jesus' punishments at the hands of the high priests, the false witnesses, and Jesus' silence, before the trial, and the second is the story of his sufferings at the hands of the Roman soldiers, after the trial. The narratives of these two scenes are clearly parallel, and Bach augments the correspondence musically by tonal planning, chorales, and even connections between two *turba* choruses.[37]

These two scenes articulate the ethical stage of Luther's meditative scheme naturally and even inevitably, for Luther's treatment of the Passion as a model introduces a different meaning for suffering from that brought out in "O Schmerz." In "O Schmerz" man's torment was the result of his guilt and led to his recognizing his sin and to repentance. Now, however, suffering is innocent, not a judgment by God for sin but a punishment at the hands of worldly, antagonistic forces. Instead of leading to consciousness of guilt and repentance, this kind of suffering must be endured patiently as the cross of the faithful. The ethical quality *Geduld* (patience) characterizes such pain, not the spiritual anguish that dominated the first stage of the faith dynamic. This viewpoint is expressed by the arioso "Mein Jesus schweigt" and the aria "Geduld." These two movements meditate on Jesus' silence before the accusations of the false witnesses who, as the chorale "Mir hat die Welt trüglich gericht't" makes clear, represent the world. Quoting the text in full reveals the exact correspondence between "Mein Jesus schweigt" and Luther's sense of the Passion as model:

Mein Jesus schweigt
Zu falschen Lügen stille,
Um uns damit zu zeigen,
Dass sein erbarmensvoller Wille
Vor uns zum Leiden sei geneigt,
Und dass wir in dergleichen Pein
Ihm sollen ähnlich sein,
Und in Verfolgung stille schweigen.

The expressions "um uns damit zu zeigen," "dergleichen Pein," "ähnlich sein," and "Verfolgung" all show the individual actively modeling himself after Jesus.

---

37. These parallels are discussed in Chapter 13, pp. 385–88; also Ex. 88.

The aria makes clear—in the words "falsche Zungen," "Leid' ich wider meine Schuld" (If I suffer for something other than my guilt), and "meines Herzens Unschuld"—that the torment referred to is not God's judgment but unjust treatment by the false world. Bach's aria texts often refer to patience in tribulation as the foremost quality of the theology of the cross; nowhere else, however, does Bach present it as clearly as here. In this case Picander's model is not Müller, but perhaps a passage from a Passion sermon of Johann Gerhard, cited in another context by Axmacher, which might well have served as a source; it voices the same theological message as "Mein Jesus schweigt" and "Geduld":

Es wil uns auch Christus mit diesem Stillschweigen lehren/ dass man Unrecht und Verleumbdung sol mit Gedult ertragen. Gott und der Zeit mus man viel befehlen/ und erwarten/ biss unsere Unschuld hernach bekannt werde. . . . darumb wil ichs mit Gedult tragen/ meine Sache in der Stille ihm befehlen/ er wird zu seiner Zeit meine Unschuld ans Liecht bringen und für allen offenbar machen.[38]

Neither the version of the *Passion* in the hand of Bach's pupil and son-in-law Altnikol nor the autograph version of the mid-1730s indicates the viola da gamba part for either "Mein Jesus schweigt" or "Geduld." It appears for the first time in both movements in the parts copied soon after the autograph.[39] In "Geduld" the instrument merely plays the bass line as part of the basso continuo; but in "Mein Jesus schweigt" its role is very similar to that of the later arioso "Ja, freilich": a fully chordal part like that of a written-out continuo, accompanying a pair of oboes, and playing chords of up to six notes including the low A' of the seventh string at the final cadence. In "Ja, freilich" the treatment is almost identical, except that arpeggiation is indicated, and a pair of flutes rather than oboes plays the upper parts. Nowhere else in Bach's music does this kind of gamba writing appear; in the oldest version of the *Passion* the gamba parts of "Ja, freilich" and of the following aria, "Komm, süsses Kreuz," were scored for lute solo instead. Only the beginning chords of "Ja, freilich" were written out, however, presumably because the lutenist would create his own chordal continuo.[40] While the change from lute to gamba

38. Johann Gerhard, *Erklärung der Historien des Leidens und Sterbens unseres Herrn Christi Jesu* (Jena, 1611), pp. 155–56, cited in Axmacher, *"Aus Liebe,"* p. 202, in connection with the chorale "Befiehl du deine Wege."

39. The oldest known version of the *St. Matthew Passion* is preserved in two copies made by Bach pupils (after the later version was in existence): (1) MS score made by Johann Christoph Altnikol between 1744 and 1748 (Am. B. 6, 7, Stiftung Preussischer Kulturbesitz, Berlin); (2) incomplete score copied by Johann Friedrich Agricola between 1741 and 1774 (Mus. MS Bach P26, also in the Stiftung Preussischer Kulturbesitz). The well-known autograph score from the 1730s is perserved in the Deutsche Staatsbibliothek, Berlin (Mus. MS Bach P25), and the somewhat later set of parts survives in the Stiftung Preussischer Kulturbesitz (St. 110).

40. See Am. B. 7, fol. 22r.; facsimile edition in Dürr, ed., *Kritischer Bericht* II/5a (1972).

might have been motivated by practical considerations, it is clear that Bach wanted to create a movement of special instrumental character at this point. The textual and other kinds of musical connections between the scenes in which "Geduld" and "Komm, süsses Kreuz" appear leave no doubt that the addition of the gamba to the earlier scene only in the 1740s was meant to emphasize an already existing relationship.[41]

"Ja, freilich" and "Komm, süsses Kreuz" meditate on Simon of Cyrene's helping Jesus to carry the cross. Luther and later theologians called Simon "der erste Nachfolger im Leiden," the model for "ungesuchte Leiden," for suffering that is neither sought for nor brought on by sin.[42] In fact, "Komm, süsses Kreuz" completes the theology introduced in "Mein Jesus schweigt" and "Geduld." Just as the oboes da caccia changed their role through the series of movements that dealt with Luther's dynamic of faith, so the viola da gamba progressively emerges from being a chordal continuo part to being the only fully chordal solo gamba piece in Bach's oeuvre. The piece is unique, something that could not be said even of the lute original.

Both the lute and gamba instrumentations point in the direction of French music, and, although "Komm, süsses Kreuz" is not really in French style, its allemande character and continually dotted rhythms—some of which are sharpened in the last version in similar fashion to those of other, more avowedly French pieces (e.g., the French Overture from *Clavierübung II*)—all suggest that Bach intended the instrumental character to be as prominent as possible. The text refers to the depth of human sorrow, and Bach uses the lowest pitches of the seven-stringed gamba to express this on the words "zu schwer". The affect of "Komm, süsses Kreuz" is, nevertheless, by no means dominated by *Leiden* or even heaviness (despite its three bass-register voices—bass solo, gamba, and basso continuo); instead, the aria represents something closer to Mattheson's description of the Allemande: "a broken, serious and well-worked-out harmony, which represents the image of a contented, satisfied spirit that delights in good order and rest."[43] The relative quietness of the gamba—so often associated, as in the "Actus Tragicus" and the *Funeral Ode,* with meditation on death—serves an important purpose in Bach's design. In "Mein Jesus schweigt" the quiet tone mirrors the text. In "Geduld," however, the middle section of the aria—"Leid' ich wider meine Schuld Schimpf und Spott, ei! so mag der liebe Gott meines Herzens Unschuld rächen"—moves away from the ideal of patient suffering. In fact, although the aria counsels patience, it has a very restless character. The long-held tone in the voice at the reprise only inadequately compensates for the mere five bars of text in this section. Bach wanted "Geduld" to antici-

41. See Chapter 13, pp. 385–88.
42. Axmacher, "*Aus Liebe,*" p. 26.
43. Mattheson, *Der Volkommene Kapellmeister,* p. 232 (author's translation).

pate a state that would only be attained in "Komm, süsses Kreuz," when the dotted rhythm pervading both arias would serve an entirely different affect, and the gamba would cease doubling the basso continuo to take the lead in an exceptional manner. In the latter aria the middle section voices the individual's willingness to let Jesus bear the weight of his suffering: "Wird mir mein Leiden einst zu schwer, so hilf du mir es selber tragen." The cross has become an instrument of benefit for the individual. No doubt the gamba part, with its many cross figures, was intended to represent that instrument.

Like the prominence of love in the theology of the *St. Matthew Passion,* the word "sweet" in "Komm, süsses Kreuz" suggests a move away from the strict theological character of Lutheran orthodoxy, in which suffering remains in a dialectical relationship to redemption. "Ja freilich" expresses what remains of this dialectic by asserting that the more bitter the suffering is, the better it is for the soul ("je mehr es unsrer Seele gut, je herber geht es ein"). Here, and in "Komm, süsses Kreuz," suffering has lost its real character, a situation signaled by the recurrence of the expression "sweet" throughout the *Passion.*[44] In Part One the E major chorale "Erkenne mich, mein Hüter" ends with the lines "Dein Mund hat mich gelabet mit Milch und süsser Kost, dein Geist hat mich begabet mit mancher Himmelslust," clearly associating "sweetness" with the foretaste of heaven allegorized in the E major tonality. Bitterness and sweetness are contrasted in the middle section of the dialogue "Ich will bei meinem Jesu wachen": "meinen Tod büsset seiner Seelen Not, sein Trauren machet mich voll Freuden. Drum muss uns sein verdienstlich Leiden recht bitter und doch süsse sein." This juxtaposition reflects Luther's description of "love" as a "cross and suffering," love that, in Luther's words, is "sweet to its object, but bitter to its subject. For it wishes others everything that is good and gives it to them, but it takes upon itself the ills of all as if they were its own."[45] The text of the next aria, "Gerne will ich mich bequemen, Kreuz und Becher anzunehmen," makes explicit that what is bitter for Jesus is ultimately sweet for the believer, echoing the end of "O Schmerz" ("wie gerne blieb' ich hier"). Its paired arioso, "Der Heiland fällt," clearly expresses Jesus' acceptance of the "cup of death's bitterness" as the source of mankind's redemption:

Der Heiland fällt vor seinem Vater nieder,
Dadurch erhebt er mich und alle
Von unserm Falle
Hinauf zu Gottes Gnade wieder.
Er ist bereit,

44. Axmacher, *"Aus Liebe,"* pp. 178–79.
45. Luther, *Lectures on Romans,* p. 255.

Den Kelch, des Todes Bitterkeit
Zu trinken,
In welchen Sünden dieser Welt
Gegossen sind, und hässlich stinken,
Weil es dem lieben Gott gefällt.

Throughout this movement the strings play descending arpeggios to represent Jesus' "fall." Beneath them in the first section the bass line ascends step-by-step to indicate mankind's return to God's grace. The middle section of "Gerne will ich mich bequemen" elaborates on the bitter/sweet theme, recalling the last lines of "Erkenne mich, mein Hüter": "Denn sein Mund, der mit Milch und Honig fliesset, hat den Grund und des Leidens herbe Schmach durch den ersten Trunk versüsset." The *St. Matthew Passion* develops the sequence *Schmerz, Schuld/Unschuld, Geduld, Liebe, Kreuz* that the opening chorus announces as the subjct of meditation: all stages are touched by the transforming power of God's love in human existence.

CHAPTER THIRTEEN

The *St. Matthew Passion*:

Dialogues, Chorales,

Turbae

In this chapter we will examine three series of movements within the *St. Matthew Passion,* the dialogues, the chorales, and the *turbae.* The dialogues, few in number, are placed so as to mark the turning and focal points for the most important theological issues. Broadly considered, they represent a response to the narrative that is closer to the physical events than that of the chorales; a scene, whether the procession to Golgotha, Jesus' agony at Gethsemane, the betrayal and capture, the image of the crucified Christ, or the burial, always underlies their texts as the subject of meditation. Thus they mix the dramatic with the didactic and hortatory. There are more chorales than dialogues, and they offer a more spontaneous congregational form of meditation. They do not normally mark the large structural divisions, and it is not true, generally speaking, that they divide the *Passion* into scenes. Sometimes they confirm the modulation of keys, and their complex interaction with both the subject matter and structure of the biblical narrative offers an interesting demonstration of the basic planning in the *Passion.* Finally, whereas both the dialogues and chorales are meditative, the *turbae* are not; as the voice of the crowd, and chiefly the persecutors of Christ, their role is primarily dramatic. In this section we will deal with the series of ten *turbae* in division two that are closely associated with Jesus' trial. However, the structure of division two—for many commentators the most problematic part of the *Passion*—cannot be explained simply by the organization of the *turbae.* The division of this segment into scenes according to broad tonal patterns allows the *turbae* series to function as a symbolic presence whose structural importance emerges at a few key places.

The Dialogues

The *St. Matthew Passion* dialogues are meditative movements distinct from the dramatic double-chorus writing of seven of the *turba* choruses and between two others of the crowd in division three ("Der rufet dem Elias" [Chorus One] and "Halt, lass sehen" [Chorus Two]). The double choruses of the work, which are partly symbolic, partly formal in intent, form a background for the dialogues. The symbolic nature of the choruses is manifested, for example, not only in the appearance of antiphony but in the fact that one choir only will voice a certain chorus: the three disciples' choruses from Chorus One ("Wozu dienet dieser Unrat," "Wo willst du," and "Herr, bin ich's"); the chorus of Peter's challengers ("Wahrlich, du bist auch einer von denen") and the duet of the false witnesses from Chorus Two. In addition, in the oldest surviving version of the *Passion* the association of Chorus One with the disciples and Chorus Two with antagonistic forces extends to the antiphonal disposition of parts in the two violin concerto arias that meditate on Peter's repentance and Judas' remorse respectively. In the first of these, "Erbarme dich," the vocal soloist and the orchestral strings sound from Chorus One, while the *concertato* violin plays in Chorus Two, as if reproachfully reminding Peter of his denial. In the second, "Gebt mir meinen Jesum wieder," this arrangement is reversed: the voice and strings are in Chorus Two, the *concertato* violin in Chorus One. Since this kind of alternation was described in the seventeenth century as *kreuzweis* antiphony, Bach may have intended the double-chorus aspect of the *St. Matthew Passion* to signify the cross.[1] All of the remaining *turbae* are set for the two choirs together to provide selectively a heightened degree of unanimity among the persecutors of Christ: the shout for release of Barrabas, both "Lass ihn kreuzigen" choruses, "Sein Blut komme über uns und unsre Kinder," "Wahrlich, dieser ist Gottes Sohn gewesen," and "Herr, wir haben gedacht."[2] Within the double choruses of the trial Bach follows an abstract scheme of alternation in the successive entries of the separate choirs: the first two paired *turbae*, "Er ist des Todes schuldig" and "Weissage uns, Christe," begin with Chorus One; the next two separated double choruses ("Was gehet uns das an" and "Gegrüsset seist du, Judenkönig") begin from Chorus Two and One respectively; and the final two paired choruses ("Der du den Tempel" and "Andern hat er geholfen") begin with Chorus Two. The recitatives are all sung from Chorus One and the chorales all from both choirs together, while the arias and ariosi strictly alternate between the choirs, regardless of text, until "Komm, süsses Kreuz," from which point, as we said, the last three

1. Heinrich Schütz, Preface to *Psalmen Davids* (1619), in vol. 23 of *Neue Ausgabe sämtlicher Werke,* ed. Wilhelm Ehmann (Kassel, 1971); Praetorius, *Syntagma musicum* III (1619), pp. 179–80.
2. Mendel ("Traces," p. 44) describes "Der du den Tempel," "Andern hat er geholfen," and "Herr, wir haben gedacht" as "choruses which begin with from two to four measures of antiphonal music, after which both choruses sing the same four-part texture," and suggests that they were taken over from earlier, single-chorus versions and their beginnings "dressed up" antiphonally. "Herr, wir haben gedacht," however, does not begin with antiphonal separation of the choirs; rather, it begins with both choirs together in seven-part writing, then reduces to four. It is difficult to imagine that Bach would have done this in order to convey the impression of antiphony.

aria/arioso pairs are all in Chorus One: "Ja freilich," "Komm, süsses Kreuz,"
"Ach, Golgatha," "Sehet, Jesus hat die Hand" (a dialogue whose solo part sounds
from Chorus One), "Am Abend," "Mache dich, mein Herze, rein." The four soloists of "Nun ist der Herr zur Ruh' gebracht" (immediately before the final chorus) also sound from Chorus One. Possibly Bach intended the antiphony of the
Passion to emphasize a dualism or dialectic—the antithetical character of faith and
the cross—which finds a resolution in unity at the end.[3]

Although the *St. Matthew Passion* contains eight dialogues, that is, madrigal-
texted movements featuring antiphony between the two choirs, it is logical to
speak of these in terms of the six places they appear in the *Passion*. These six places
constitute the most conspicuous points of structural articulation in the work, appearing as they do at the beginning and ending of both parts, at the midpoint of Part
One, Gethsemane, and at the turning point between divisions two and three in Part
Two, Golgotha. The last two comprise the most prominent appearances of deep
flat keys in the work:

Part One | No. 1: "Kommt, ihr Töchter"/"O Lamm Gottes unschuldig": E minor
No. 19: "O Schmerz"/"Was ist die Ursach": F minor
No. 20: "Ich will bei meinem Jesu wachen"/"So schlafen unser Sünden ein":
C minor
No. 27 a and b: "So ist mein Jesus nun gefangen"/"Sind Blitze, sind Donner":
E minor
No. 29: "O Mensch, bewein dein Sünde gross": E major

Part Two | No. 30: "Ach, nun ist mein Jesus hin"/"Wo ist denn dein Freund hingegangen":
B minor
No. 59: "Ach, Golgatha": A flat
No. 60: "Sehet, Jesus hat die Hand": E flat
No. 67: "Nun ist der Herr zu Ruh' gebracht"/"Mein Jesus, gute Nacht": C minor
No. 68: "Wir setzen uns mit Tränen nieder: C minor

3. The intentionality of this occurrence is debatable: following the principle of regular alternation of
arias between the two choirs, "Komm, süsses Kreuz" would sound from Chorus One, "Ach, Golgatha" would presumably sound from Chorus One by virtue of its being coupled with a dialogue whose
soloists, as in all the other dialogues, sings from Chorus One. It could then be rationalized that "Am
Abend" and "Mache dich, mein Herze, rein" could also sound from the first choir simply because the
dialogue had broken the pattern of alternation. If all this is acknowledged then the focus on Chorus One
toward the end of the work is purely incidental, even though such an emphasis occurs nowhere else in
the work. Yet, in light of other patterns toward the end—the shift to flats, the thinning out of the chorales, the absence of Jesus' speeches—the lessening of antiphonal contrast makes an impact.

In Picander's published text for the *Passion*, all but one of the dialogues are designated as "Zion und die Gläubigen," that is, as dialogues between Zion (the Christian church) and the community of believers. These pieces thus introduce an ancient Christian symbolism that was particularly meaningful in the Lutheran tradition, the identification of the church with the people of Israel and the church of the Old Testament. Such dialogues were common in texts of the time; the Brockes Passion text has several, as does Picander's above-mentioned *Erbauliche Gedancken* (references to this symbolism abound in devotional poetry). In the case of "Kommt, ihr Töchter" the designation is slightly different, "Töchter Zion und die Gläubigen," a designation suggesting that its symbolism is derived from Jesus' address to the women who follow the procession to the cross: "Weep not for me, but for yourselves and your children." Luther referred to this passage often—twice in the Passion sermon—to point out that the Passion was intended to awaken consciousness of sin in the believer, not mere lamentation over Jesus' sufferings or outcry over the treachery of Judas.[4] In "O Mensch, bewein" the meaning of Jesus' words is extended to all humanity.

I have added the chorale fantasia "O Mensch, bewein" to this list of movements although it is not a dialogue because its meaning and E major tonality are bound up in several ways with its structural relationships to other dialogues. In fact, these relationships open our approach to the *Passion* from the largest scale of structural articulation and tonal plan. The two great chorale fantasias mark an overall motion from E minor to E major, and "O Mensch, bewein" (an addition to the *Passion* made only in the mid-1730s) was transposed to fit this key scheme.[5] The change from E minor to major represents the shift from the initital exhortation to meditate on the Passion to a renewed emphasis on Luther's first stage of the beginning of faith, acknowledgment of sin. Given prominence at Gethsemane as well, this theme is voiced in the second dialogue in "O Schmerz" / "Was ist die Ursach?" Between the second dialogue and the chorale fantasia, places where the acknowledgment of sin is emphasized most, Bach moves regularly from F minor through the key signature levels of the circle of keys up to the E major of "O Mensch, bewein." His purpose is to indicate, on the largest scale of tonal anabasis in all his music, the positive value of repentance. The immediate impact of "O Mensch,

4. Luther, *A Meditation on Christ's Passion*, pp. 7–8, 9–10.

5. In the older version of the *Passion* represented in the scores of Altnikol and Agricola (see Chapter 12, n. 39) Part One ends with the E major chorale, "Jesus, lass ich nicht von mir." At the time of the copying of his new score (around the mid-1730s) Bach replaced the four-part chorale setting with the chorale fantasy, "O Mensch, bewein," which had introduced the 1725 version of the *St. Matthew Passion*, in E flat. Bach transposed the movement to E major for its new place. Mendel's belief that "O Mensch" had originally been set in D major at Weimar has been questioned by Dürr (see Mendel, "Traces," pp. 33–35; "More on the Weimar Origin of Bach's 'O Mensch, bewein,' " *Journal of the American Musicological Society* 17 (1964) to II/5, pp. 88, 120).

bewein," however, results from its powerful assertion of E major not long after an earlier cadence to E major turns back down to E minor for the dialogue "So ist mein Jesus nun gefangen" / "Sind Blitze, sind Donner." This change was prompted in part by a desire to compare Judas the fallen man with mankind's hopes for redemption via repentance. The E minor/major juxtaposition also points out that the dialogue "So ist mein Jesus" / "Sind Blitze" voices the very kind of lamentation that Luther inveighed against at the beginning of his Passion sermon. The introduction of the chorale fantasia "O Mensch, bewein" at the end of Part One shifts perspective away from what Luther called "the wrong way to meditate on the Passion."[6] "O Mensch, bewein" seems to restore the true use of the Passion as expressed in Jesus' words to the "daughters of Jerusalem." From this standpoint the dialogues of Part One are very closely connected to mankind's acknowledgment of sin. "O Mensch, bewein" is thus less a lament for mankind's sinfulness than the culminating articulation of Luther's first stage, indicated in its use of all three vocal choirs (including the soprano chorale choir doubled by organ manual that otherwise appears only in "Kommt, ihr Töchter"). The keys of the dialogues in Part One represent some basic tonal associations within the *Passion*: E minor is the key of the crucifixion drama and the first key of the *Passion*; C minor is the second and final key area; F minor and E major are the flat and sharp limits of the circle of keys used for the closed movements of the *Passion*, while E major is the opposite mode to E minor as well.

The dialogue beginning Part Two, "Ach, nun ist mein Jesus hin" / "Wo ist denn dein Freund hingegangen" in B minor, carries over several ideas from "So ist mein

6. Axmacher has noted (*"Aus Liebe,"* pp. 195–96) that "So ist mein Jesus" and three other movements ("O Schmerz," "Gebt mir meinen Jesum wieder," and "Erbarm es, Gott") run contrary to the Lutheran purpose of meditation on the Passion in their voicing a reaction to the Passion as if it were an event taking place before the individual. Such a stance implies a view of Jesus' sufferings that places the dramatic, human qualities of the narrative above their theological significance. Expressions such as "Lasst ihn, haltet, bindet nicht" ("So ist mein Jesus") and "Haltet ein" ("Erbarm es, Gott") express the wish that the events of the *Passion* not take place. This quality of the texts is very closely related to Luther's wrong kind of meditation. That Bach and Picander would have deliberately introduced an incorrect form of meditation to serve as a foil to the correct kind seems very unlikely. But it must be noted that two of the above-mentioned appearances of such meditation involve Judas (as Luther indicated), and both times Bach takes care both to avoid giving a positive meditative response to Judas's actions and to correct the meditative focus soon afterward (a discussion of the events surrounding Judas's remorse and the chorale "Befiehl du deine Wege" appears on pp. 374–78, below). In the case of "Erbarm es, Gott" the transformational character of the enharmonic change at the end marks a pronounced shift of tonal area from sharps to flats that can be taken as a major shift in perspective, away from the exaggerated reaction to the physical events and toward the new interpretation of suffering that culminates at the end of the scene in "Komm, süsses Kreuz." Whether such details were worked out in an atmosphere of delicate theological sensitivity must remain open, of course. But the musical impact of the E minor/major shift from "So it mein Jesus" to "O Mensch" and the sharp/flat transformation in "Erbarm es, Gott" are unmistakable, as is the recession of the physical events in favor of the Christian perspective at both points.

Jesus nun gefangen," such as the textual resemblance in the first lines, the general tonal area, and the omission of basso continuo on the sustained word "Ach." The second chorus, "Wo ist dein Freund hingegangen," is from the Song of Solomon with the traditional typological significance of Solomon's mistress (already an allegorical figure even in Old Testament terms) as the voice of the bride of Christ, the church. This piece therefore links up with "Kommt, ihr Töchter," in which Jesus is spoken of as the *Bräutigam* (bridegroom). This dialogue furthers the continuity between Parts One and Two. After the concern expressed in "O Mensch, bewein" for the contemporary individual, "Ach, nun ist mein Jesus hin" returns with a reminder of the physical events in preparation for the upcoming trial.[7]

"Sehet, Jesus hat die Hand" has already been discussed from the dual standpoint of its introducing division three and its emphasis on the shift of perspective from acknowledgment of sin to *Tröstung des Gewissens*. It derives its most significant allegorical features from (1) its background as a traditional appearance in seventeenth-century Passion sermons; (2) its parallel with "Kommt, ihr Töchter"; and (3) its derivation from "Eilt, ihr angefocht'nen Seelen" and "Mein teurer Heiland."[8] The final segment it introduces, centered on E flat/C minor, is related tonally to Gethsemane, and the arioso "Am Abend" makes this connection more explicit in its reference to the idea that Jesus' "fall" in Gethsemane and the reconciliation brought about by his death constitute a renewal of Adam's fall and the reconciliation with Noah, all of which took place in the evening.[9] Finally, the words *Buss und Reu* of the closing dialogue recitative and chorus, "Nun ist der Herr zur Ruh gebracht," refer to the first aria of the *Passion,* and the "sleep" music and C minor tonality inevitably recall "Ich will bei meinem Jesu wachen." Like the final arioso of the *Christmas Oratorio,* this piece functions as a summary in introducing each of the four vocal solosits in turn.

The dialogues, then, form an integrated set of movements that determine to a great degree the major points of structural and theological emphasis in the *Passion.* They are related in this sense to the articulation of Luther's meditative dynamic together with visualization of the physical events. As such an articulation the dialogues give the work a strong theological character in concert with such devices as

7. For the 1726 performance of Keiser's *St. Mark Passion* Bach added the chorale verse, "So gehst du nun, mein Jesus, hin," at the end of Part One. See Glöckner, "Johann Sebastian Bachs Aufführungen," p. 78.

8. On (1) see Axmacher, *"Aus Liebe,"* pp. 79–83; on (2) and (3) see Smend, "Bachs Matthäus-Passion," pp. 49–53.

9. On the character of the arioso "Am Abend, da es kühle war," see also Werthemann, *Die Bedeutung,* pp. 36–38, 63; Minear, "Matthew, Evangelist and Johann, Composer," pp. 252–53; Axmacher, *"Aus Liebe,"* pp. 180–82. On the change to flats for the ending of the *Passion,* see Smend, "Bach Matthäus-Passion," pp. 49–50; Scheide, *Bach as a Biblical Interpreter,* p. 25. Steiger (" 'O schöne Zeit,' " pp. 6–11) links the shift to flats to the idea of evening and reconciliation, making a connection to Gethsemane.

the set of ariosi and arias with texts based on Heinrich Müller's Passion sermons; the red ink Bach used to write the biblical recitative and his using different scripts for passages in which the fulfillment of Scripture is mentioned;[10] even his (presumably intuitive) separating with the device of modulatory contrast some of Matthew's formula quotations from intercalated narrative.[11] Of the four Gospels Matthew's is most concerned with ecclesiology; this emphasis is reflected in its traditional designation as the church's book and its place at the head of the New Testament. Luther had used Matthew as the basis for the Passion sermon cycles of his *Hauspostille*.[12] The Lutheran oratorio Passion tradition of the seventeenth century most commonly used Matthew's account; the *St. Matthew Passion* is unmistakably part of this tradition. The dialogues in Bach's work, therefore, derive in some respects from a musicotheological tradition, which is expressed in such devices as the chorales ("O Lamm Gottes unschuldig" in particular), the famous eleven statements of "Herr, bin ich's," the canonic writing for the false witnesses, juxtaposing string arias for Peter and Judas (and the reference in "Erbarme dich" to the chorale text traditionally used for Peter's aria, "Erbarm dich mein, O Herre Gott"), using string accompagnato for Jesus and eliminating it for the words "Eli, Eli, lama asabthani," arioso style for the words of institution of the Lord's Supper, and the *concitato* writing for the narrative of the rending of the veil. But Bach incorporated traditional elements on a more fundamental level, and in order to recognize it we must examine the chorales and *turbae* more closely.

The Chorales

Following a traditional pattern, most of the chorales in the *St. Matthew Passion* enter in immediate and direct response to the narrative, often seeming to have been triggered by a single word or phrase: "Ich bin's, ich sollte bussen" enters in response to "Herr, bin ich's"; "Erkenne mich, mein Hüter (i.e., *Hirte*)" refers to "Ich werde den Hirten schlagen"; "Was mein Gott will, das g'scheh' allzeit" comes after

---

10. Bach uses Latin script for the words "Eli, eli, lama asabthani" and a script that is intermediate—but clearly distinguishable—between Latin and the ordinary German script, for the Evangelist's references to the Old Testament predictions of the buying of the Potter's Field and the dividing of Jesus' clothes; a similar script appears for the words of Judas as reported by the Evangelist, "Welchen ich küssen werde, den greifet."

11. The scene at Bethany, the intervention of Pilate's wife in the trial, the narrative of the Potter's Field, and the scene before the high priest are all set apart by modulation to flats. These are all places traditionally interpreted as intercalations: i.e., additions by Matthew to the Passion tradition that is transmitted in Mark. Matthew is famous for his so-called formula quotations—i.e., references to the fulfillment of Old Testament prophecy that are initiated with such a formula as "And all this happened so that the prophecy of——would be fulfilled, which said. . . ." The narrative of the Potter's Field is introduced by such a formula.

12. See *D. Martin Luthers Werke*, vol. 52, pp. 734–827.

"so geschehe dein Wille," and so on. Although in many cases the chorale text was written as a meditation on the Passion, assuring a degree of appropriateness, this fact only insufficiently explains their role in the *St. Matthew Passion*. The most prominent chorales in the work express central concerns of the *Passion*—"O Lamm Gottes" and "O Mensch, bewein" (in elaborate settings) and "Herzliebster Jesu" and "O Haupt voll Blut und Wunden" (in multiple verses). Whereas the first three deal conspicuously with the theme of human guilt versus Jesus' innocence, "O Haupt voll Blut und Wunden" covers a wider range of associations. All the associations derive from a desire for a personal relationship between Christ and the individual—both the Christ who is the good shepherd, rich in benefits ("Erkenne mich, mein Hüter") and the suffering Christ of the Passion ("O Haupt voll Blut und Wunden," "Ich will hier bei dir stehen") who comforts the individual at the moment of death ("Wenn ich einmal soll scheiden").

"O Lamm Gottes unschuldig"

The most traditional chorale within the *St. Matthew Passion*—because of its frequent appearance in seventeenth-century oratorio Passions—is "O Lamm Gottes unschuldig," which Bach distinguishes with its unique setting as a cantus firmus above a double-chorus movement with a da capo aria text. This prominent German troped version of the Agnus Dei, here as well as in other seventeenth-century Passions, expresses the dualism of guilt and innocence, which is further represented in the dialogue of the opening chorale fantasia, in the simultaneity of aria and chorale texts, and in the tonal dualism of E minor (for the double chorus) versus G major (key of the "O Lamm Gottes" melody). As mentioned above, the theme of guilt versus innocence runs through the entire *Passion* until it diminishes in the third division. The E minor tonality of "Kommt, ihr Töchter," in which mankind is urged to consider its guilt, is associated with the crucifixion drama; and the stages of that drama (mostly in E minor) correspond to the places where verses of "O Lamm Gottes" tended to appear in seventeenth-century settings of the Passion according to Matthew:

1. After the *turba* chorus "Er ist des Todes schuldig"
2. After the second "Lass ihn kreuzigen" chorus
3. After the *turba,* "Sein Blut komme über uns"
4. After the words "und überantwortete ihn, dass er gekreuziget würde"
5. After "und fuhreten ihn hin, dass sie ihn kreuzigten"
6. After the words "Desgleichen schmäheten ihn auch die Mörder, die mit ihm gekreuziget waren"

The first and last appearances coincide with the first and last of the *turba* series in division two; the third and fourth mark the ending of the trial proper; the second is

EXAMPLE 84.

(a) First phrase of chorale "O Lamm Gottes" as it appears in the opening
    chorus of the *St. Matthew Passion*

O Lamm Got - tes un-schul - dig

(b) *St. Matthew Passion*: excerpt from chorus "Andern hat er geholfen"

Ist er der Kö-nig Is - ra - el,

linked explicitly with the demand for crucifixion, and the fifth with the way of the
cross. It seems clear, therefore, that the chorale traditionally served to remind man
of his guilt amid the adverse events of the trial and the stations of the cross. Jesus'
innocence was the measure of man's guilt, the mirror in which he might learn to
recognize his sinfulness.

In seventeenth-century Passions a verse of "O Lamm Gottes" often made an especially dramatic impact immediately following the word *schuldig* in the *turba* "Er
ist des Todes schuldig" (see, for example, the Passion settings of Sebastiani, Flor,
and Meder).[13] Bach, however, does not repeat the chorale after its appearance in
"Kommt, ihr Töchter," whose text, as we saw, emphasizes the main theological
points in the *Passion*. One of Smend's most fruitful discoveries was that in the last
of the ten *turbae* the melody of the opening phrase of "O Lamm Gottes" is heard to
the text "Ist er der König Israels"[14] (Ex. 84). As in the opening movement, the
phrase is in G major within an E minor movement. Smend argued that other thematic events in this multisectional chorus were derived from "O Lamm Gottes," as
was the theme of the first *turba,* "Er ist des Todes schuldig" (Ex. 85). Smend's suggestions gain credence in light of the seventeenth-century traditions concerning the
placing of "O Lamm Gottes," which Smend did not discuss, and the hidden character of the "Jesus of Nazareth" series of the *St. John Passion* that we brought out

13. On Luther's interpretation of Christ as *Osterlemlein*, see *Werke,* vol. 52, pp. 812–19; Smallman,
The Background, p. 83.
14. Smend, "Bachs Matthäus-Passion," pp. 19–22.

EXAMPLE 85.

(a) Theme of chorus "Er ist des Todes schuldig" (Soprano 1)

Er ist des To-des schul - dig!

(b) Beginning of chorus "Andern hat er geholfen" (Soprano 2)

An-dern hat er ge-hol-fen

(c) Excerpt from chorus "Andern hat er geholfen" (Soprano 1, 2)

der er-lö - se, er - lö - se ihn nun,

earlier. Bach might well have intended to make more or less oblique references to "O Lamm Gottes" at traditional places in the *Passion* to represent a Christological message hidden behind the adverse events. The lead-in to "Er ist des Todes schuldig" is in E minor, but the chorus begins in G; then, as the outcome of Bach's addition of the minor seventh to the theme (on *schuldig*), the phrase is transposed down the circle of fifths through the soprano, tenor, and bass voices, leading the five-bar chorus to close in G minor (Ex. 86). This modulation, of course, represents the fall of Jesus, reminding us of his anguish at Gethsemane (the first fall before the Father). At the initial judgment of death from the Jewish authorities the fall is represented in a particularly striking manner. When, however, the first phrase of "O Lamm Gottes" is heard behind "Ist er der König Israels," the meaning is no longer hidden but manifested in irony, just as Jesus' identity is in the great octave cadence heard soon afterward. In the *St. John Passion* Bach had used the last of the ten *turbae* of his symbolic trial and the chorale "In meines Herzens Grunde" to complete the symmetry of the *Herzstück* in a response to the royal inscription, thereby indicating the ironic hidden meaning of the "Jesus of Nazareth" choruses. In the *St. Matthew Passion* the closest equivalent to such a symbolic assertion of Jesus' identity is the reappearance of the first phrase of "O Lamm Gottes" within "Andern hat er geholfen."

Part One is distinguished by the appearance in it of eight of the fourteen chorales and all three elaborate settings ("O Lamm Gottes," "Was ist die Ursach," and "O Mensch, bewein"). Like the tonal plan, the progression from the delicate, innocent soprano of "O Lamm Gottes," almost overwhelmed in sonority by the dialogue below, through the dark coloring and low pitch of "Was ist die Ursach" to the solidity of "O Mensch" (now lacking any dialogue aspect), constitutes one of the foremost clues to Bach's intention for the structure of Part One. Part One seems to have been designed to create an imposing affirmative impression (especially at the end) that will not be upheld throughout the work as the sense of life under the cross becomes a reality. Part One not only contains the majority of Jesus' speeches—and hence most of the accompanied recitative—and the most prominent patterns of key structure in the work, the chorale emphasis also suggests that Part One is a self-contained structure with a positive sense of direction. This sense of direction is a deliberate counterpart to the thinning out of the chorales toward the end of the *Passion*; in addition, there is no chorale after the final chorus as there was in the *St. John Passion*. The positive, hidden message of the theology of the cross as presented later in the work is of great allegorical character; it is expressed by opposition in deep flats rather than sharps, as befits the message itself.

Part One includes two verses from two other chorale series as well: the first and third strophes of "Herzliebster Jesu" and two verses of "O Haupt voll Blut und Wunden"—the fifth, "Erkenne mich, mein Hüter" (E major), and sixth, "Ich will hier bei dir stehen" (with exactly the same harmonization, now in E flat). The latter group of chorales is, of course, one of the best-known elements in the *St. Matthew Passion* and the only one that the majority of listeners will instinctively recognize as a series. Smend stressed that "Ich will hier bei dir stehen" was not part of the *Passion* until the surviving autograph score (dating from the mid-1730s) and was indicated in the score by its clef, key signature, and a note by Bach to indicate its position. That it was an afterthought cannot be doubted, even though, as Dürr points out, the incomplete bar at that point in the recitative of the older version suggests that Bach had intended a meditative interruption.[15] A more felicitous insertion could hardly be imagined. "Erkenne mich, mein Hüter" is the culminating point of the first of two extended anabases from deep flats to E major, while the following recitative returns to flats in a highly symbolic fashion, confronting E minor and C minor in Jesus' prediction of Peter's denial and Peter's protestation of loyalty. In the final version, "Ich will hier bei dir stehen" confirms the turn to flats and connects with several major allegorical features of the *Passion,* above all the focus on Will and the conflict of flesh and spirit that pervades Gethsemane. *Erkenne* suggests an appeal to the resurrected Christ rather than to the Christ of the Passion, and "Ich will hier bei dir stehen," by virtue of its context and the transposition down a semitone to flats, evokes the weakness of man and his inability to maintain his resolves.

This last detail points out that the musical context of "Ich will hier bei dir stehen" denies that we can simply interpret the theological intent of the chorale verse according to its text and harmonization alone. The chorale confirms a modulation to flats that has been connected allegorically with the prediction of Peter's denial, featuring minor keys only (C minor and G minor). The shift of key, the transposition of the chorale, and the dropping out of the flutes from the instrumental doubling are perfectly audible, not to mention the move into deeper flat-minor keys after this point. Both this chorale and the dialogue "Ich will bei meinem Jesu wachen" meditate on Peter's and the disciples' statements of good intention, which are not carried out in the narrative. The affirmative opening words, "Ich will," are denied in both cases by the *mollis* character that Bach has variously given to the chorale and the dialogue, a quality especially evident in the sleep music in the second chorus of the dialogue and the minor-key version of an otherwise triumphant head motive in

---

15. Smend, "Bachs Matthäus-Passion," pp. 59–60; Dürr, Introduction to *Kritischer Bericht* II/5a, p. vii; Dürr's alternative hypothesis is that the recitative might have been taken over from an earlier setting of the *Passion*.

the oboe.[16] In contrast to the E flat of "Ich will hier bei dir stehen," the E major of "Erkenne mich, mein Hüter" was prepared by a strong sequence of ascending modulations, including the *concitato* flurry for "Ich werde den Hirten schlagen," all accompanied by the strings and closing emphatically in the key of the chorale itself. The *mollis* character of "Ich will hier bei dir stehen," however, appropriately expresses a personal relationship based on love between Christ and the individual that is as prominent in this piece as in the whole *Passion*. Although it cannot be heard in the chorale, the parallel between this E flat and the E flat of "Sehet, Jesus," much later in the work—each introducing a region of deep flats and following a juxtaposition of E minor with C minor—is a meaningful detail: the intention of remaining with Jesus through his sufferings, denied at the end of Part One, is completed in "Sehet, Jesus." The concluding lines of the chorale, "alsdenn will ich dich fassen in meinen Arm und Schoss," seem to reciprocate the relationship of being held by Christ expressed in the E flat dialogue: "Sehet, Jesus hat die Hand uns zu fassen ausgespannt, kommt—Wohin?—in Jesu Armen sucht Erlösung."

Both "Ich will hier bei dir stehen" and "O Mensch, bewein" were presumably added to the *Passion* at the same time in the mid-1730s. The original chorale ending of Part One (which "O Mensch" replaced) was a simple setting of "Jesum lass ich nicht von mir" (E major), introduced in response to the final words of the narrative ending Part One: "Da verliessen ihn alle Jünger, und flohen." The situation and its chorale response recall Peter's and the disciples' resolve never to deny Christ and the chorale "Ich will hier bei dir stehen." The great attention given to Gethsemane in Matthew as well as the scene of Bethany and the Last Supper make the narrative much longer than in the *St. John Passion*. Thus Part One of the *St. Matthew Passion* cannot end with a positive narrative such as Peter's repentance. Jesus' announcement to the arresting party that the events taking place are the fulfillment of Scripture are followed by the terse report of the disciples' desertion. Nevertheless, it seems probable, in light of the similar tonal dynamic with which Part One of the *St. John Passion* ends, that Bach considered the positive ascending motion at this point a necessary indication of the ultimate goal of the *Passion,* the background against which the final descent to a flat-key ending must be measured. But the closing of the earlier version of the *Passion* with the E major "Jesum lass ich nicht von mir" was overshadowed by the powerful emphasis on the return to E minor for "So ist mein Jesus" / "Sind Blitze," with its clear association to Judas as the exemplification of "fallen man." Bach might well have felt that the narrative of scriptural fulfillment in the following recitative and the simple E major chorale only

16. The theme type that is suggested in "Ich will bei meinem Jesu wachen" is that of a trumpet call, now turned into minor; see, for example, the theme of Dietrich Buxtehude's cantata "Ich bin der Auferstehung" (C major), in *Dietrich Buxtehudes Werke*, vol. 2, ed. Wilibald Gurlitt (Klecken and Hamburg, 1926); reprint, New York, 1977. See also Chapter 9, n. 11.

insufficiently provided a positive sense of completion. His decision to close Part One with "O Mensch, bewein" is brilliant, since it satisfies several different needs within the *Passion*: balancing of "Kommt, ihr Töchter"with a chorale fantasia; providing an E major meditative movement of sufficient scale to counter the E minor dramatic emphasis in "Sind Blitze"; emphasizing the centrality of acknowledgment of sin to the Lutheran meditative sense of the Passion; and even assuring that Part One closes not with a congregational resolve set in opposition to the fleeing of the disciples but with an extended chorale verse summarizing Jesus' ministry. As such "O Mensch, bewein" indicates the meaning of the *Passion* and thus can be said to respond to Jesus' announcement of the fulfillment of Scripture.

This change in the character of the ending enabled Bach to make up for the removal of "Jesum lass ich nicht von mir" by introducing earlier a chorale that relates the question of remaining with Jesus to Peter's avowal of his loyalty ("Ich will hier bei dir stehen"). As the extension and confirmation of Peter's modulation to flats, "Ich will" expresses not a positive assertion of the ability of the Christian community to maintain a resolve that Peter, as we know, will not, but the very inability of the flesh despite its desire and willingness to do so. Throughout this region of the *Passion* Bach emphasizes the idea of will in relation to the weakness of the flesh. And while "Ich will hier bei dir stehen" is linked to the latter, "O Mensch, bewein" closes Part One with a powerful indication that acknowledgment of sin and an understanding of the meaning of Jesus' atonement are the true spiritual gateways to the benefit of the Passion. This series of revisions provides a unique opportunity to study Bach's thought process in operation.

We do not need to know which of the two new chorales was the initial inspiration for these changes. Presumably "O Mensch, bewein" triggered the revisions since Bach, in copying the score, at first passed over the place in the score where "Ich will hier bei dir stehen" would have been entered. Recognition of their interrelatedness, however, is essential. In these revisions, we see that firmly established details of the compositional history can greatly help us to see the meaning of the finished work. As mentioned earlier, Smend, in his desire to uncover more of the process of composition, formed a hypothesis regarding the "O Haupt voll Blut und Wunden" chorale verses that led him away from the principal function of meditative movements in the *Passion*. In the case of the verse "Befiehl du deine Wege" both Spitta and Smend took the position that it was inappropriate to the *Passion,* a viewpoint that must be questioned.[17] The following discussion, leading to a rationalization of the presence of "Befiehl du deine Wege," is necessarily complex since it has to describe in words a process that might have been largely intuitive on Bach's part. It aims to illustrate the nature of certain thought processes that were very logical as

17. Spitta, *Johann Sebastian Bach,* vol. 2, pp. 549–50; Smend, "Bachs Matthäus-Passion," pp. 59–60.

well as the pitfalls of using one's critical judgment as evidence for compositional history.

Briefly, Smend's hypothesis states that Bach, in early 1729, had used the chorales "Erkenne mich, mein Hüter," "Befiehl du deine Wege," and "Wenn ich einmal soll scheiden" in the Köthen funeral music. Only the text of this latter work has survived (with obvious signs that many poetic movements were parodied from arias and choruses of the *St. Matthew Passion* but without any indication of the particular chorales used).[18] Bach then took these verses over into the *St. Matthew Passion*, where they were less appropriate. Smend's argument was bolstered by the fact that Bach normally presents the verses of a chorale in their proper order, whereas the verses of "O Haupt voll Blut und Wunden" appear in the succession 5, 6, 1/2, 9 (although sung to the same melody, "Befiehl du deine Wege" is the first verse of a different hymn and thus does not enter into this discussion). Had Smend known that the chorale cantatas preceded the composition of the *Passion* he would presumably have made even more of this fact. In reality it carries very little weight, since in those works the chorales form the basis of the textual sequence and any altering of the order of verses would make no sense. In the *Passion*, however, the chorales enter in response to situations whose order is determined by an independent narrative. Only when the chorale verses follow the chronological order of the particular *Passion* account is it reasonable to demand that the order be the same. The argument that multiple verses of chorales—even entire chorales of many verses—follow in correct order in many older *Passions* is irrelevant, for they follow immediately after one another in lengthy meditative chains that completely interrupt the narrative. In fact, when Bach repeats chorale verses in this way—for example, verses 1 and 2 of "O Haupt voll Blut und Wunden"—even when only a short recitative intervenes— verses 5 and 6—he respects the correct order. The appearance of verses 1 and 2 in immediate succession might have been a means of emphasizing the beginning of the chorale to make up for the otherwise shuffled order of the verses. Smend's argument is inconsistent in its implication that Bach's original conception, which was supposedly connected to introducing chorales in correct sequence, was no longer important to him in the spring of 1729. We need doubt no further that "Wenn ich einmal soll scheiden" belonged with Bach's conception of the *St. Matthew Passion* from the beginning if we recall that Bach performed Keiser's *St. Mark Passion* both in Weimar (1714) and Leipzig (1726) with his own addition of a setting of "Wenn ich einmal soll scheiden" at exactly the place that it appears in his own work.[19]

The introduction of "Ich will hier bei dir stehen" created a well-known chromatic descent in the ordering of the keys of its verses that did not follow the order in which the verses appear in the *Passion*—no. 54, "O Haupt" and "Du edles Ange-

18. Smend, "Bachs Matthäus-Passion," pp. 59–71.
19. Glöckner, "Johann Sebastian Bachs Aufführungen," p. 80; new ed. of Keiser's *Passion* in *Die Kantate*, No. 152, ed. Hans Grishkat (Stuttgart, 1963).

sichte" (verses 1 and 2) in F, no. 15, "Erkenne mich" (verse 5) in E major, no. 17, "Ich will hier bei dir stehen" (verse 6) in E flat major, no. 44, "Befiehl du deine Wege" in D major, and finally, no. 62, "Wenn ich einmal soll scheiden" (verse 9) in E Phrygian. The descent expresses through pitch levels (perhaps accidentally) the order of verses in the chorale itself: that is, verses 1 and 2 are the highest, 5 and 6 continue the semitone descent, and the last one used, the ninth, is the lowest. Probably more important to Bach than this series aspect, however, were several more obvious facts:

1. The first verse to appear, "Erkenne mich," was in E major and the last, "Wenn ich einmal soll scheiden," in E Phrygian, both of which relate in different ways to the E minor first tonality of the *Passion*;

2. The almost immediate semitone transposition between "Erkenne" and "Ich will" is an easily audible dramatic device;

3. In conjunction with the decreasing number of chorales toward the end of the *Passion* the last ones we hear—and the only chorales at all after the trial—are the first two verses of "O Haupt voll Blut und Wunden" together at the highest pitch of the series (F), then the ninth verse at the lowest pitch (E Phrygian, a fourth lower), and in an unusually chromatic harmonization.

The supposedly inappropriate chorale, "Befiehl du deine Wege," culminates the move to sharps for the trial. The preceding scene, narrating Peter's denial and repentance and Judas's remorse and suicide, is in sharps. The narrative of Peter's denial and repentance had moved from the flats of the preceding scene to A major, culminating with a chorale, just as it does at the close of Part One in the *St. John Passion*. Bach then reverses the modulatory direction for Judas's story. "Was gehet uns das an" is in E minor and "Gebt mir meinen Jesum wieder" is in G. In keeping with the contrast between the fates of Peter and Judas, no chorale follows the narrative of Judas's remorse and suicide. As a result the Peter/Judas scene lacks a definite sense of conclusion. Since the aria "Gebt mir meinen Jesum wieder" is not a truly meditative aria, the necessary theological perspective is lacking. Although the G major tonality and first-movement concerto style of "Gebt mir" may seem optimistic, especially after the deeply felt expression of repentance in "Erbarme dich," the affect intended was undoubtedly a deliberate shallowness, a superficial brightness, like the traditional interpretation of the violin roulades as the rolling silver pieces. "Gebt mir" is another of those movements, like "So ist mein Jesus," in which faulty meditation is introduced. It attempts to recreate the narrative dramatically without, as it appears, a subsequent movement to restore the theological perspective.

Following the aria Bach turned to flats for the subsequent narrative of the buying of the Potter's Field with the blood money, beginning with the word *Blutacker*. He then cadenced in C minor for the end of the scene proper ("als mir der Herr befohlen hat"). The flats continue into the beginning of the trial, culminating in a second C minor cadence for Jesus' response, "Du sagest's," to Pilate's question, "Bist du der Juden König?" This is the last time in the *Passion* that Jesus speaks with the string halo, and it marks his silence throughout the entire trial, the passive, patient suffering of Matthew's Man of Sorrows. The C minor anticipates the key of his burial, linking it to the Potter's Field (i.e., a place for the burial of foreigners), and emphasizing that Jesus' kingship is manifested in his silence, death, and burial. The key of burial is the end point of the continued tonal descent into flats that is the outcome of Judas's betrayal. While the narrative of Peter's repentance moves from the flats of the preceding scene up to A major, that from Judas's dealing with the high priests and his death to the beginning of the trial involves one of the most extensive descent patterns in the *Passion,* from three sharps to three flats.

The trial, however, must return to sharps. In a practical sense, Bach used the modulation to flats to mark a division between two scenes, both of which had to be in sharps. He now uses "Befiehl du deine Wege" to complete the return, following Pilate's reference to Jesus' silence in the midst of persecution: "Hörest du nicht, wie *hart* sie dich verklagen?"[20] "Befiehl du deine Wege" makes up for the lack of a chorale ending for the preceding scene, urging trust in God's will. Axmacher has also argued that "Befiehl du deine Wege" is perfectly in keeping with the theme of Jesus' silent suffering and cites a passage from Johann Gerhard in which the verb *befehlen* is used in this context.[21] In fact, the narrative of the Potter's Field concluding the preceding scene ends, as we saw, with the words "als mir der Herr befohlen hat" (the first C minor cadence), implying that "Befiehl du deine Wege" was triggered in the traditional associative manner and simply delayed (as was, for example, "Erkenne mich, mein Hüter," which, technically speaking, should have followed "Ich werde den Hirten schlagen").[22] The delay of "Befiehl du deine Wege" allows the flats to continue uninterrupted to culminate with Jesus' words while the positive association of the chorale marks the move to sharps. At the same time, Bach avoids the troublesome association of a chorale with Judas's suicide, while maintaining the reference of "Befiehl du deine Wege" to the preceding scene. Judas's actions bring about death and humiliation for Christ (the flats), whereas Jesus' silent suffering accomplishes the positive outcome (sharps). The overall tonal dynamic resembles that of Part One, where the descent into flats is associated with the prediction of Judas's betrayal and Peter's denial, while the principal move to sharps is the outcome of Jesus' accepting the cup at Gethsemane.

20. See Chapter 9, Ex. 66b.
21. Axmacher, *"Aus Liebe,"* pp. 200–202; the passage from Gerhard is cited in another context on p. 356 of the present study.
22. The correct wording of the first line of this verse is "Erkenne mich, mein Hirte"; presumably Bach's *Hüter* is a slip.

The reasoning here is complex, but consistent and logical. In fact, it is worth considering that the subtle intricacy of Bach's intention as manifested in such a situation compares with his continually turning away from obvious devices and solutions in the composing process itself, even in abstract instrumental music when no such allegorical rationale is discernible. In this, as in everything about Bach's work, we must look beyond the superficial explanation before pronouncing judgment, and to do that we must first take the work on its own terms.

"Herzliebster Jesu, was hast du gebrochen"

The three verses of "Herzliebster Jesu" that appear in the *St. Matthew Passion* also go hand in hand with broader structural features of the *Passion* to articulate aspects of the overall musicotheological design. Often remarked is the sudden entrance of the first verse, "Herzliebster Jesu, was hast du gebrochen?" immediately after the opening recitative in which Jesus predicts the crucifixion. The impact of this chorale is bound up with its entering as a questioning of the guilt that has brought about such a *scharf Urteil*. The issues posed by "Was hast du gebrochen?" and "Was ist die Schuld?" are fundamental to understanding the *Passion,* and the remaining verses of "Herzliebster Jesu" and the rest of the *Passion* must provide an answer. These not-so-rhetorical questions introduce the dichotomy between the innocent suffering Christ and the guilt of mankind that has brought about his judgment. The main theme of the prologue has now entered the work at ground level, so to speak.

When we next hear a verse of this chorale, the third "Was ist die Ursach aller solchen Plagen," at Gethsemane (in dialogue with "O Schmerz"), the question of guilt is answered: "Ach, meine Sünden haben dich geschlagen. . . . Ich, ach Herr Jesu, habe dies verschuldet, was du erduldet." Finally, the fourth verse, "Wie wunderbarlich ist doch diese Strafe," sounding in the midst of the trial, between the two "Lass ihn kreuzigen" choruses, completes the message of the atonement: "Die Schuld bezahlt der Herre, der Gerechte, für seine Knechte." This last appearance of a verse of "Herzliebster Jesu" belongs, then, within Smend's *Herzstück*. The full succession of movements framed by the "Lass ihn kreuzigen" choruses completes the answers prompted by the first verse. "Was hast du gebrochen" is echoed in Pilate's challenge, "Was hat er denn Übels getan?" and answered by "Er hat uns allen wohlgetan." This question, now answered, "Aus Liebe will mein Heiland sterben" states the motive for the atonement, the indirect question that pervades "Herz*liebs*ter Jesu" (it is stated explicitly, of course, in the verse "O grosse Lieb," which Bach used in the *St. John Passion*). Following Axmacher's insistence on the importance of love to the theology of the *St. Matthew Passion,* we can interpret love as the point of intersection between the judgmental, wrathful God who punishes sinners and the redeeming God manifested in Christ. The verses of "Herzliebster Jesu" emphasize Jesus' innocent suffering, man's guilt, love as the basis of the atonement, and—in expressions such as "scharf Urteil" and "Strafe"—retain the sense of God's judgment. The two places that mention God's *Gericht*—"O Schmerz" ("Der Richter führt ihn vor Gericht") and "Aus Liebe" ("Dass das ewige Verderben und die Strafe des Gerichts nicht auf meiner Seele bliebe")—make conspicuous reference to love as the means by which judgment is avoided.

Considering the relationship of these verses to the meditative dynamic brought out in Chapter 12, it seems clear that the verses of "Herzliebster Jesu" belong to a series as do those of "O Haupt voll Blut und Wunden." The verses chosen were instrumental for articulating the theology of the Passion. Moreover, the interrelated character of the three verses is reflected musically as well. "Herzliebster Jesu" and "Wie wunderbarlich" are both in B minor, the only widely separated verses of the same chorale in Bach's oratorios to be set in the same key. There are distinct parallels between their harmonizations, especially in the last lines, where *Schuld* is introduced. It has been mentioned that these verses were placed to bring out the relationship between the prediction of the crucifixion at the beginning of the Passion narrative and its coming to the fore in the trial, that the theme of the two "Lass ihn kreuzigen" choruses resembles the pattern of diminished intervals that end the opening recitative (on "gekreuziget werde").[23] The remaining verse of this chorale, however, "Was ist die Ursach," set for Chorus Two in dialogue with the tenor arioso, "O Schmerz," is pitched a tritone lower, in F minor, the traditional key of lamentation, and by far the lowest appearance of any verse of the chorale in Bach's oeuvre. We have already said much about "O Schmerz" in terms of its special instrumentation, its place in the key plan, and its pivotal role in the Lutheran meditative dynamic that appears in the *Passion* as a primary element derived from Heinrich Müller's Passion sermons. The tritone relationship between the verses of "Herzliebster Jesu" is meaningful as a form of mi contra fa between the nadir of human guilt expressed in "O Schmerz" and the crucifixion of the innocent Christ. It is an extension of the relationship between E minor, the key of the crucifixion drama, and C minor, the tonal center of the more meditative scenes of Gethsemane and the burial.

The Turba *Choruses*

As mentioned above, Part One of the *Passion* receives much of its character from the speeches of Jesus, the number and elaborateness of the chorales, and the structural correspondence of these details with the dialogues and tonal plan. Both of the latter increase the focus on Gethsemane as a contrast region of meditation to the crucifixion narrative itself. Division two, on the other hand, is organized into several scenes grouped around the questioning of Jesus by the high priest and the trial

<hr>

23. Charles Sanford Terry, *Bach. The Passions, Book II: 1729–1731* (London, 1928), p. 19.

before Pilate. Running through it are the ten *turbae* from "Er ist des Todes schuldig" to "Andern hat er geholfen." We have Smend to thank for the understanding that these *turbae* constitute a series. However, his idea that Bach originally intended a symmetrical grouping of the whole set, closer to that of the *St. John Passion,* cannot be supported either by means of internal (i.e., analytical) evidence or from any other documents.[24] Clearly, the fifth and sixth choruses—both setting the words "Lass ihn kreuzigen"—form a center to the trial. The special character of the aria that appears between them, "Aus Liebe will mein Heiland sterben," justifies Smend's calling this grouping a *Herzstück.*[25]

This *Herzstück,* however, is neither the center of the entire *Passion* in the same sense as its counterpart in the *St. John Passion* nor a turning point, either of the tonal plan or in Pilate's attitude toward Jesus. Instead, the transposition of the second "Lass ihn kreuzigen" chorus up a major second (the first moves from A minor to the dominant of E minor and the second from B minor to the dominant of F sharp minor) creates a significant push further into sharps. This move is offset by the shift in the opposite direction of the intervening movements: "Wie wunderbarlich" (B minor); "Er hat uns allen wohlgetan" (E minor to C major); "Aus Liebe" (A minor). These details amplify the antithesis between the gravity of the choruses and the ethereal *bassetchen* aria.[26] After "Aus Liebe" the trial continues its course with even greater antagonism, underscoring the fact that division two is characterized by a sense of forward motion—ultimately to the E minor octave cadence on "ich bin Gottes Sohn"—that is interrupted and suspended several times by the scenes of meditation (basically in flats).

Nothing could give a more explicit sense that the flat-key areas run counter to the trial than Bach's leading even the very brief interjection of Pilate's wife to a G minor cadence. The perspective shifts from the adverse physical events to Christian meditation once after the trial proper culminates (between "Sein Blut komme über uns" and the arioso "Erbarm es Gott") and again after the end of division three (between "Andern hat er geholfen" and "Ach, Golgatha"). At both places Bach conspicuously shifts from sharps to flats for scenes in which the meditative viewpoint is emphasized. At the center of the trial such a device is impossible. Bach makes the most of the contrast of modulatory direction in terms of the subdominant (A minor) and dominant (B minor) sides of the key and their juxtaposition in "Aus Liebe" and "Lass ihn kreuzigen."

Clearly, the *turbae* further the course of the adverse events and mark their culminating points. Although Smend spoke to the sense of culmination at the end of division two and emphasized the change at division three, his insistence that the *tur-*

24. Smend, "Bachs Matthäus-Passion," pp. 16–19.
25. Smend, "Bachs Matthäus-Passion," pp. 29–30.
26. See Chapter Twelve, n. 27.

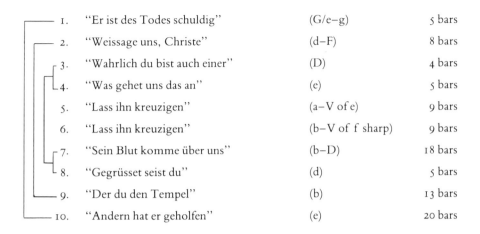

1.	"Er ist des Todes schuldig"	(G/e–g)	5 bars
2.	"Weissage uns, Christe"	(d–F)	8 bars
3.	"Wahrlich du bist auch einer"	(D)	4 bars
4.	"Was gehet uns das an"	(e)	5 bars
5.	"Lass ihn kreuzigen"	(a–V of e)	9 bars
6.	"Lass ihn kreuzigen"	(b–V of f sharp)	9 bars
7.	"Sein Blut komme über uns"	(b–D)	18 bars
8.	"Gegrüsset seist du"	(d)	5 bars
9.	"Der du den Tempel"	(b)	13 bars
10.	"Andern hat er geholfen"	(e)	20 bars

FIGURE 10.   Friedrich Smend's symmetrical arrangement of the *St. Matthew Passion turbae*

bae formed a symmetrical arrangement imposed a static view on the trial and undercut the sense of forward thrust to the crucifixion. Moreover, Smend's contention that Bach composed the *turbae* according to a plan of symmetry similar to that of the *St. John Passion,* changed his mind, yet composed the pieces with a residue of the original idea of symmetry—a plan demonstrated by analytical legerdemain—is unrealistic. If we set forth the *turbae* in order—bracketed here according to Smend's theory of symmetry—it will be seen at once that, with the exception of the two "Lass ihn kreuzigen" choruses, they diverge considerably from one another in their keys and relative lengths (Fig. 10). In addition to the repetition of "Lass ihn kreuzigen," the presence of E minor at the beginning and ending of the series adds a dimension of closure. The first two *turbae* are paired because they appear close together in the same scene. The last two are paired in the same way, but with the additional detail of a clear musical correspondence between similarly texted phrases: "so steig herab vom Kreuz" (in "Der du den Tempel") and "so steige er nun vom Kreuz" (in "Andern hat er geholfen"). Smend may also be correct in suggesting that references to "O Lamm Gottes" appear in the first and tenth of the choruses. In fact, it seems possible that Bach intended the musically related phrases "so steig herab vom Kreuz" and "so steige er nun vom Kreuz" to bind the two final *turbae* of the series together in a musical reference to the melody of "O Haupt voll Blut und Wunden" as well (Ex. 87). Each of these excerpts follows a Christological challenge—"Bist du Gottes Sohn" and "Ist er der König Israel." In

EXAMPLE 87.　　Correspondences and chorale references between "Der du den Tempel
　　　　　　　　Gottes zerbrichst" (a, b) and "Andern hat er geholfen" (c, d, e)

(a)

Bass

Bist du Got-tes Sohn,

(b)

EXAMPLE 87   *continued*

(c)

O Lamm Got - tes un-schul - dig,

Violin 1

Choruses One and Two

Soprano

Ist er der Kö - nig Is - ra - el

Alto

Ist er der Kö - nig Is - ra - el, Is - ra - el

Tenor

Ist er der Kö - nig Is - ra - el, der Kö - nig Is - ra - el

Bass

Ist er der Kö - nig Is - ra - el

(d)

O Haupt voll Blut und Wun-den

Choruses One and Two

Soprano

so stei - ge ____ er nun vom Kreuz, so stei -

Alto

so stei - ge ____ er nun vom Kreuz, ____

Tenor

so stei - ge er nun vom Kreuz, so

Bass

so stei - ge er nun ____ vom

Basso continuo

EXAMPLE 87   *continued*

(e)

Bass

Ich bin Got-tes Sohn.

"Der du den Tempel" the words "Bist du Gottes Sohn" end with a strong cadence to E minor immediately before "so steig herab vom Kreuz," and the bass at this point seems to anticipate the great octave cadence that closes "Andern hat er geholfen." The suggested chorale references, like the octave cadence, might then represent the meaning of the "Jesus of Nazareth" choruses in the *St. John Passion*: a hidden assertion of Jesus' divinity that lies beneath the surface antagonism.

Bach's intention to create a series of *turbae* and to use internal musical relationships to articulate significant theological themes is apparent. "Andern hat er geholfen" stands out as one of the most important culminations in the *Passion,* not only in the above-mentioned features but also because it is the only *turba* chorus in the work to end with a tonic cadence in the key in which it began. Otherwise, "Er ist des Todes schuldig" and "Andern hat er geholfen" are not at all alike, and the musical relationships Smend put forth as correspondences between "Weissage" and "Der du den Tempel" are outrageously contrived, those between "Was gehet uns das an" and "Gegrüsset" only slightly more convincing.[27] In fact, Smend bases his comparison of these choruses on a feature that has nothing to do with symmetry: several choruses mock Jesus directly, in the first person ("Weissage," "Gegrüsset," and "Der du den Tempel"), while the others either speak about him in the third person or belong to the Peter/Judas scene. The octave leaps of the flutes, running sixteenths in the vocal parts, and repeated notes in "Weissage"and "Der du den Tempel" reflect this change in address, while their supposed motivic connections are pure wishful thinking. No correspondences other than those between the two "Lass ihn kreuzigen" choruses can be compared to those of the *St. John Passion,* where they amount to virtual identity, obviating any need to make a case based on analysis.

Although Smend valiantly attempted to draw "Wahrlich du bist auch einer von denen" and "Sein Blut komme über uns" into his symmetrical scheme, they are nonetheless as totally unlike one another as any choruses in the two *Passions*; in addition, "Wahrlich" is the shortest of the set and "Sein Blut" one of the longest. The structural weight required by each chorus determined the relative length of each. "Wahrlich" actually has a longer text than "Sein Blut," but as part of the questioning of Peter, an intermediary stage to the intensity of "Erbarme dich" and the catharsis of "Bin ich gleich von dir gewichen," Bach could not assign it an extended setting. "Sein Blut komme über uns," by contrast, is the culmination of the trial before Pilate, demanding a grave and weighty setting despite its short text. Bach hides a set of fugal entries within the four-part writing at the beginning; the theme—a rising fifth moving up to the sixth and back to the fifth—might even have been conceived as a minor-key distortion of the first phrase of "O Lamm Gottes." In any case, "Sein Blut" points out that, rather than symmetry, there are two major points of culmination within the structure of division two: the ending of the trial, which immediately follows "Sein Blut," and the ending of division two with the pairing of "Der du den Tempel" and "Andern hat er geholfen." These three *turbae* are the longest in division two and the most final sounding. Following both these points we have conspicuous transformations to flats for scenes of meditation, the first made in the enharmonic change at the end of the arioso "Erbarm es, Gott!" and the second made with a powerful nonharmonic relation in the recitative before "Ach, Golgatha."

Assuming that the *turbae* derive their structural significance more from their role in the narrative than from an abstract plan of symmetry, we may consider a correspondence that is far more important than any of Smend's: between the two D minor *turbae,* "Weissage uns, Christe" and "Gegrüsset seist du, Judenkönig," both addressed to Christ (Ex. 88). Of the introduction and five scenes in division two,

27. Smend, "Bachs Matthäus-Passion," pp. 23–29.

EXAMPLE 88.   Correspondences between choruses "Weissage uns, Christe" (a) and "Gegrüsset seist du, Judenkönig" (b), with motivic basis of choral entries and
bass sequence patterns (c)

(a)

EXAMPLE 88   *continued*

(b)

Flute 1, 2, Chorus 1, 2

Soprano, Chorus 1

Soprano, Chorus 2

Basso continuo, Chorus 1, 2

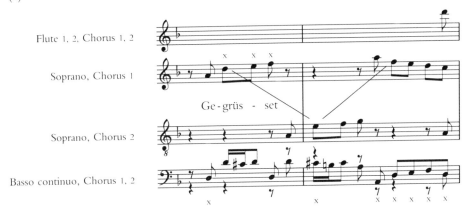

Ge - grüs - set

(c)

only two are in flats (see Fig. 12, below). In addition, of the ten *turbae* only two are in flats, "Weissage" and "Gegrüsset," both in D minor. The two flat-key scenes in which these choruses appear deal, as we saw in Chapter 12, with Jesus' silent suffering at the hands of the crowd, they both meditate on his sufferings with F major chorales, and they both contain an arioso/aria pair in which the viola da gamba appears. Figure 11 illustrates the major points of comparison between the two scenes.

From this it seems clear that Bach never conceived the structure of division two as a symmetry of *turba* choruses. Rather, he divided the *Passion* into scenes and

FIGURE 11.   Parallels between two scenes in the *St. Matthew Passion*

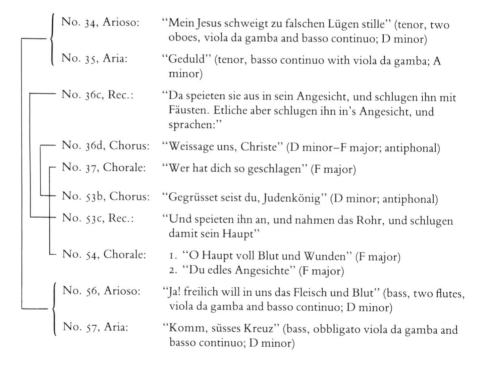

No. 34, Arioso: "Mein Jesus schweigt zu falschen Lügen stille" (tenor, two oboes, viola da gamba and basso continuo; D minor)

No. 35, Aria: "Geduld" (tenor, basso continuo with viola da gamba; A minor)

No. 36c, Rec.:   "Da speieten sie aus in sein Angesicht, und schlugen ihn mit Fäusten. Etliche aber schlugen ihn in's Angesicht, und sprachen:"

No. 36d, Chorus: "Weissage uns, Christe" (D minor–F major; antiphonal)

No. 37, Chorale: "Wer hat dich so geschlagen" (F major)

No. 53b, Chorus: "Gegrüsset seist du, Judenkönig" (D minor; antiphonal)

No. 53c, Rec.:   "Und speieten ihn an, und nahmen das Rohr, und schlugen damit sein Haupt"

No. 54, Chorale: 1. "O Haupt voll Blut und Wunden" (F major)
2. "Du edles Angesichte" (F major)

No. 56, Arioso: "Ja! freilich will in uns das Fleisch und Blut" (bass, two flutes, viola da gamba und basso continuo; D minor)

No. 57, Aria: "Komm, süsses Kreuz" (bass, obbligato viola da gamba and basso continuo; D minor)

searched out a plan that would simultaneously satisfy both the artistic requirement of a coherent structure and the various levels of musicotheological allegory. To a far greater extent than is the case with the choruses of the *St. John Passion* the *turbae* of the *St. Matthew Passion* are bound to their place in the narrative, fulfilling a variety of structural functions that take precedence over their independent interrelationship as a series.

CHAPTER FOURTEEN

The *St. Matthew Passion*:

Theology and

Tonal Allegory

The tonal allegory of the *St. Matthew Passion*, in conjunction with the overall tonal planning, relates countless details to broad theological issues. Affective moments and theological exigencies create one of the most intricate and profound musico-allegorical structures in all of music. In it the composer presents a set of tonal relationships in alignment with what we must view as a form of musical hermeneutics; the tonal plan is an index to the theological intent of the work. In this respect the *St. Matthew Passion* is immensely rationalistic, a compendium of the various tonal procedures used in the cantatas, utilizing almost the full range of major and minor keys in a coherent fashion. Whether by design or not, the work uses twenty-three of the twenty-four major and minor keys (F sharp major does not appear); seventeen serve as the keys of entire movements (save for C sharp major and minor, E flat minor, F sharp, A flat minor, B flat minor, and B major). Thus, the tonal scheme of the work expresses the normal range of the practical circles of keys common in the first quarter of the century and interestingly relates to the contemporaneous theoretical discussions of key relationships.

We cannot approach the interpretation of tonal allegory in the *St. Matthew Passion* expecting that the categories of tonal relationship familiar from post-Rameau theory will always apply; there was no unilateral agreement on these relationships in the first half of the eighteenth century. Still less can we use historical tonal schemes such as Mattheson's presentation of key characteristics as if they could explain a work whose depth probably went beyond the understanding—if not the rationalizing capacity—of any of the composer's contemporaries. In fact, we are thrown back on our own resources, and subjectivity will never be completely avoidable. If we follow Mattheson's pluralistic attitude toward researching key characteristics, rather than blindly adopting his famous set of conclusions regarding the *proprietates* of individual keys, we would see tonal relationships within the *St. Matthew Passion* in terms of Bach's work generally and the text-musical associations both within the *Passion* and related works. We must also take into account both traditional *pro-*

prietates and the newer associations that arose for some keys within the general tonal expansion of the seventeenth and eighteenth centuries.

Almost inevitably, when we seriously question any kind of theoretical fixing of the associations of keys—whether historical or not—and replace it with a more fluid approach, one that is based on the experience of the works themselves combined with an attempt to understand just what it meant to compose with an allegorical view of tonality, we create an illusion of following familiar paths within the maze of the composer's thoughts. This is unavoidable and necessary to the process of interpretation.

Since we have observed that the narrative events surrounding Golgotha have a special importance in the theology of the *Passion,* we can justifiably expect that this importance will be mirrored in the tonal plan. At Golgotha the keys that represent what Heinichen would have called the *extremum enharmonicum* of the *Passion* demand the circle of keys as their underlying conceptual basis. In this introductory arioso to the third division the horror and desolation of the place of the skull call forth from Bach the most extreme manifestation of flat keys in the *Passion*: the keys (or cadence degrees) of D flat, A flat, F minor, B flat minor, E flat minor, even A flat minor are all touched on in this deeply unsettled movement. The nonharmonic intervals in "Ach, Golgatha" continue the character of the modulatory transformation that leads into flats from the final E minor of "Andern hat er geholfen."[1] In fewer than three bars of recitative Bach confronts the sharps and flats in a striking nonharmonic relation that sets the words *Mörder* (murderers) and *ihm* (him, i.e., Jesus) in apposition, the latter given in a D flat harmony that will become the Neapolitan sixth of C minor (Ex. 89). At the same time there is, of course, a sense of continuity from the G major chord with which the recitative begins (relative major or mediant of the preceding E minor) and the C minor with which it ends. The diminished seventh chord on *Mörder* is a form of dominant of G, which could lead to C minor then and there, by moving immediately to a C minor $^6_4$ chord, then to the dominant of C minor. The beginning notes of the recitative recall the melodic turns of phrase that have been linked to "O Lamm Gottes," almost suggesting that the broader role of G as dominant of C minor, linking the beginning and ending

---

1. "Ach, Golgatha" emphasizes the tritone at several places and pitch levels, most notably at the beginning and ending for the words *unsel'ges Golgatha* (G flat–C in bar two; D flat–G in the final measure). The beginning of the arioso sounds the dominant of D flat for three measures, making almost a backward reference to the D flat Neapolitan harmony in the recitative. The E flat minor cadence of the phrase "wird als ein Fluch an's Kreuz gestellt" seems to anticipate the reappearance of the latter key on "Mein Gott, Mein Gott, warum hast du mich verlassen"; the F minor of "Das gehet meiner Seele nah" (the only phrase that refers to the meditating individual) was perhaps introduced with a recollection of the key of "O Schmerz" in mind. And the A flat ending sounds a note of hope that foreshadows the A flat of "Wahrlich, dieser ist Gottes Sohn gewesen." If these quasi-referential features may be admitted into discussion the arioso can be considered to combine the sense of change and uncertainty with hope that underlies its theological significance.

EXAMPLE 89.   *St. Matthew Passion*: recitative No. 58e

Evangelist

Des-glei-chen schmä-he-ten ihn auch die   Mör-der, die mit

Basso continuo

ihm ge-kreu-zi-get wa-ren.

keys of the *Passion* (E minor and C minor), might be extended symbolically to the role of "O Lamm Gottes." In this brief recitative, where the shock of the nonharmonic relation is greatest, the sense of continuity is most essential. The meaning is, of course, the new significance of the cross for mankind, the change from instrument of death and antithesis (the sharps and the word *Mörder*) to the sign of salvation (the flats and the word *ihm*).[2]

This is the major turning point of the *Passion,* where the key of the crucifixion drama, E minor, is given its most momentous cadential point of emphasis in the work ("ich bin Gottes Sohn") and then drops out altogether, along with the sharps, to be succeeded in the recitative by the second key of the *Passion,* C minor. In contrast to the extreme modulatory waverings of "Ach, Golgatha," the dialogue with which it is paired, "Sehet, Jesus," is set in a comforting E flat, and its text, like none other in the *Passion,* pictures Jesus on the cross as if already resurrected and offering salvation to the believer. The following recitative brings back the tone F flat (*Finsternis*) that appeared near the end of "Ach, Golgatha," while the keys of B flat minor and E flat minor return for Jesus' last words, divested now of the string accompaniment. Within this final segment Bach may have intended the tone F flat and the E Phrygian tonality of "Wenn ich einmal soll scheiden" to stand in for the E minor that can no longer appear in conjunction with the crucifixion drama. In

2. A discussion of the significance of this modulation, linking it to the rhetorical concept of the *parrhesia,* appears in Chafe, "Key Structure," p. 51.

any case, from these details we can conclude that the E minor crucifixion drama is inextricably bound to the physical narrative of human guilt that reaches both its lowest point and its transformation at Golgotha. Golgotha and the *Finsternis* surrounding the death of Christ constitute the point of enharmonicism: the F flat and the key of A flat minor are the counterparts of E and the key of G sharp minor that appear in the sharpest region of the *Passion*, near the end of Part One (Ex. 90).

Intuitively, Bach might have mapped out a tonal-allegorical spectrum whose flat and sharp extremes contain a degree of equivalence. It seems possible, therefore, that Bach employed the flat limit of the work with full consciousness of its proximity to the opposite end of the spectrum. That the *Passion* should come full circle at Golgotha seems uniquely appropriate in light of Walter Benjamin's characterization of Golgotha as the turning point of baroque allegory, the end point of the "emptying" process of allegory, a metaphor for the arising of lasting artistic value amid the "ruins" of mechanical allegorical procedures.[3] For Bach Golgotha's spiritual character was most nearly related to the notion that the extreme tonalities were now redeemed by the enharmonically closed circle of keys. As in the brief recitative, antithesis, representing the historical condition, is transcended by the sense of continuity provided by the larger frame of reference. Just as the enharmonic change at the end of "Erbarm es, Gott" marks the transformation of the physical events through their spiritual interpretation, "Ach, Golgatha" and the recitative leading into it signify the events surrounding the transformation of the world.

At or near both ends of the flat/sharp continuum some keys are associated with suffering and tribulation (G sharp minor, F minor, B flat minor, and E flat minor), others with redemption (E major, A flat, and E flat). Both ends of the spectrum introduce acknowledgment of sin and emphasize Jesus' sufferings; these are the inseparable themes that constitute the primary message of the *Passion*, the starting point of meditation. If we can read such an idea into the sharp and flat extremes of the *St. Matthew Passion*, its ancillary perhaps is that salvation can be found in the extremes of Jesus' spiritual and bodily anguish. The flattest keys in the work are the F minor, A flat, and B flat minor of the narrative surrounding the prediction of Judas's betrayal, the A flat of Jesus' words "Meine Seele ist betrübt bis an den Tod, bleibet hie und wachet mit mir," the F minor of "O Schmerz"/"Was ist die Ursach," and finally, the deep flats of "Ach, Golgatha," the B flat minor and E flat minor of Jesus' last words, and the A flat of "Wahrlich, dieser ist Gottes Sohn gewesen." The last of these passages has a different character from the others and must be taken, along with other signs at the end of the *Passion*, as an expression of the need to recognize Jesus' identity in the realm of the flesh. Luther described Jesus

---

3. Benjamin, *The Origin*, p. 232.

EXAMPLE 90.   Sharpest (a) and flattest (b) regions of the *St. Matthew Passion*

(a) Part One, recitative No. 26

(b) Part Two, "Ach, Golgatha" (No. 59)

as the bottom rung on the ladder by which we ascend to knowledge of God; this essential recognition of Jesus' identity takes place in "Wahrlich," the lowest tonal region of the *Passion*.[4] Thus, although the antithesis of flat and sharp key areas is a governing principle behind the tonal design of the *St. Matthew Passion*, the closing of the circle of keys provides the conceptual basis for transcending the antithesis.

Continuing the idea of antithesis Bach chose the keys of E minor and C minor, first and last keys of the *Passion*, as the particular representatives of the sharps and flats, respectively. E minor bears the threnodic associations of its Phrygian ancestor, and the latter is perhaps used for its association with sleep. C minor is particularly linked with sleep in Bach's music, although with Bach it has even more particular reference to the Lutheran concept of the "sleep of death."[5] E minor is the tonic minor of the sharp end of the normal spectrum (E) and C minor is the dominant of the flat (f). Already this statement points out that the first key area of the *Passion* belongs to a region of sharps that is further separated from the sharp end of the spectrum in mode and key signature than its flat counterpart is from the other end; thus, in the *St. Matthew Passion*, the deep flats are more normal than the deep sharps. The *Passion* itself provides the reasons for this situation. E minor is, as we said, the key of the crucifixion drama; as such it is associated with points of lamentation, adverse events, and the like; we might say it is *durus* in the archaic sense of "hard" and "harsh." E major, by contrast, is a key that transcends the physical events of the *Passion*. "Erkenne mich, mein Hüter" pictures the resurrected rather than the suffering Christ, and "O Mensch, bewein," as we have suggested, represents not merely lamentation over man's sin but the goal to which acknowledgment of sin and repentance lead. On the other hand, the flats coincide with regions of meditation on Jesus' sufferings—Bethany, Gethsemane, the two scenes of Jesus' sufferings in division two—and counter the physical events (the narrative of Pilate's wife), anticipate the ending of the Passion (the narrative of the Potter's Field), and, in general, represent the realm of the weakness of the flesh. They are the other side of present life from that of the violent actions of the crucifixion drama. The flats also contain important positive associations by way of the feminine, gentler associations of *mollis* (Bethany, Pilate's wife). The latter predominate at the end of the *Passion* in a wonderful sense of the transformation of the flesh and earthly life through Jesus' death and atonement.

The associations suggested by certain keys resulting from textual connections constitute another category of tonal relationship within the *St. Matthew Passion*. These do not exclude the more general sense of key character that may exist inde-

---

4. Althaus, *The Theology of Martin Luther*, pp. 185–88.
5. See Mattheson, *Das neu-eröffnete Orchestre*, p. 244. The predictions of Judas's betrayal and Peter's denial, the narrative of the buying of the Potter's Field and its prediction in the Old Testament, the narrative following "Komm, süsses Kreuz," and the final shift to flats all juxtapose E minor and C minor in meaningful ways.

pendent of the *Passion*, but in these instances the keys are not extreme and do not bear such firm traditional associations as many of the others. The *Passion* contains, for example, only two movements in F major, both chorales, and both meditate on the sufferings of Christ: "Wer hat dich so geschlagen?" and "O Haupt voll Blut und Wunden." At the same time, Bach may be indicating that F major is a key of sympathy, an association arising from its widespread use for pastorales, such as in Part Four of the *Christmas Oratorio*. The keys of D minor and G minor are connected as a shallower region of flats to the less tormented—even welcome—view of suffering that dominates in movements such as "Komm, süsses Kreuz" and "Gerne will ich mich bequemen." Yet no such association exists for B flat major, which Bach uses for the chorale response to the false witnesses, "Mir hat die Welt trüglich gericht't," and the aria "Mache dich, mein Herze, rein," in which the text urges the human heart to banish the world to purify it for the acceptance of Jesus. Such an interpretation fits well with the sense that the flats are associated with the world of the flesh, which is transformed at the end. This interpretation is based on internal associations that we do not expect to carry over to other works.

G major, for example, functions as a positive presence within the ambitus of E minor: "O Lamm Gottes unschuldig," "Ich will dir mein Herze schenken," and the narrative of the kingdom that closes the words instituting the Lord's Supper. In this last case the key of G can be seen to include the Last Supper, even though the central part of that scene moves into deep flat keys that make up the far-reaching patterns of descent and ascent. The narrative begins in G, and in the chorus "Wo willst du, dass wir dir bereiten, das Osterlamm zu essen" the pastorale character and reference to Osterlamm connect to "O Lamm Gottes." After the excursion into flats for the prediction of Judas's betrayal the words instituting the Eucharist move back to close in G major. The following arioso and aria, "Ich will dir mein Herze schenken," constitute a meditation on the Eucharist that closes the episode in G. We can even read a reference to "O Lamm Gottes" into the main theme of the aria as well as to "Wo willst du"; the continuation of the chorus evokes the melody of "O Haupt voll Blut und Wunden" (Ex. 91). With this reference Bach is probably making the important theological connection between the passover lambs and Jesus as the Lamb of God. If the G major aria "Gebt mir meinen Jesum wieder" seems to contradict this association, we may at least notice that it follows from Judas's words "Ich habe übel getan, dass ich unschuldig Blut verraten habe," where there appears a clear reference to the innocent sacrifice articulated in "O Lamm Gottes."

A minor appears within the *Passion* variously as subdominant to the E minor tonic of the crucifixion drama and as an E Phrygian ("Wenn ich einmal soll scheiden"). Its primary appearances in "Geduld," "Aus Liebe," and "Wenn ich einmal soll scheiden" are associated with a more passive, meditative side of the crucifixion narrative. By contrast, B minor seems to belong to the harder side of E minor: "Ach, nun ist mein Jesus hin," "Sein Blut komme über uns," "Herzliebster

EXAMPLE 91.

(a) First phrase of chorale "O Lamm Gottes" in the form used in the opening chorus of the *St. Matthew Passion*

O Lamm Got - tes un - schul - dig,

(b) "O Lamm Gottes": first phrase in the usual form

O Lamm Got - tes un - schul - dig,

(c) First phrase of chorale "Herzlich tut mich verlangen" ("O Haupt voll Blut und Wunden")

O Haupt voll Blut und Wun - den

(d) Beginning of chorus "Wo willst du" (Soprano 1)

Wo willst du, dass wir dir be - rei - ten das Os-ter-lamm zu —
es - sen, wo willst du, dass wir dir be -

(e) Aria "Ich will dir mein Herze schenken": ritornello beginning

(f) Aria "Ich will dir mein Herze schenken": vocal beginning

Ich will dir mein Her - ze schen-ken,

Jesu" (in its role as response to the *scharf Urteil* that has just been foreseen at the close of the preceding recitative), "Wie wunderbarlich," "Blute nur," the bitterness of "Erbarme dich," and the like. As a final example, the E flat of "Ich will hier bei dir stehen" and "Sehet, Jesus hat die Hand"—whether an intentional connection or not—joins two movements that emphasize remaining with Jesus: "Ich will hier bei dir stehen . . . alsdenn will ich dich fassen in meinen Arm und Schoss" and "Sehet, Jesus hat die Hand uns zu fassen ausgespannt . . . in Jesu Armen sucht Erlösung, . . . bleibet in Jesu Armen." An interpretation based on such a connection would suggest that the individual voices in the chorale intended to remain to take care of Jesus at the point of his death, whereas the dialogue makes clear that it is instead Jesus who looks after mankind.

Further examples of this kind could be easily adduced. The final point, however, is that we react to the individual keys of the work for reasons that cannot be completely schematized, some ancient and relatively unfamiliar, some fitting very well with post-Rameau tonal thinking, and others even subjective and arbitrary. This situation is certainly a relief—heartening in fact—to the interpreter who struggles to articulate his sense that Bach composes with key as with anything else, but who inevitably faces contradictions to any all-encompassing theory of key relationships. Arising from the world of tonal associations aroused by such a work as the *St. Matthew Passion,* however, the closest we can come to a rational reductionist understanding is the situation provided by the circle of keys of the early eighteenth century with its heritage of ancient, often contradictory elements; it is possible that only a substantial philosophical investigation of the concept of the musical circle in the seventeenth and eighteenth centuries could enable us to speak with full authority on the phenomenon of tonal allegory; and such a study we do not as yet have.

Part One

Turning now to Part One of the *St. Matthew Passion,* we recall that the overall tonal motion is from the opening E minor chorale fantasia, "Kommt, ihr Töchter, hilft mir klagen," to the E *major* of its concluding counterpart, "O Mensch, bewein dein Sünde gross." The motion up to E major was planned and purposeful, emphasized by the large portion of Part One that is taken up with two extended progressions from four flats (F minor/A flat) through all the adjacent key-signature levels to four sharps (E major); both of these great tonal anabases deal conspicuously with the issues posed in Luther's Passion sermon. In each case Bach makes the preliminary move down to the deep flat level in a recitative containing a prediction of Christ concerning one of the disciples: Judas's betrayal in the first instance and Peter's denial in the second. In both recitatives a prominent internal cadence to E minor (Jesus) is followed by a key signature change and a turn to flats culminating in a C minor cadence. In this way Bach confronts the beginning and ending keys of the whole *Passion.* The first of these passages, following Jesus' C minor announcement that one of the disciples will betray him, features the F minor chorus "Herr, bin ich's" and the A flat chorale "Ich bin's, ich sollte büssen." It is followed by the further descent to B flat minor for Jesus' prediction of the crucifixion, then the turn upward that will eventually lead to E major for Jesus' prediction of the resurrection and the E major chorale "Erkenne mich, mein Hüter." The beginning, middle, and end of the whole descent/ascent pattern were carefully placed, the initial introduction of flats coming, significantly, on the word "evening" ("Und am Abend satzte er sich zu Tische mit den Zwölfen"). The flat and sharp poles of this extended motion through what is essentially the full tonal spectrum not only of the *Passion* but of the entire cantata repertory are the cross and the resurrection. The corresponding points of chorale emphasis are acknowledgment of sin ("Ich bin's") and a prayer to the resurrected Christ ("Erkenne"), respectively. These movements correspond to the two basic stages of the faith dynamic as presented in Luther's sermon, comprising, as we have said, the basic flat and sharp limits of the *Passion*.

Clearly, Bach planned his first "fall" into deep flats in the *Passion* to coincide with the prediction of Judas's betrayal, which he took as a focal point for the more general acknowledgment of sin by the disciples in "Herr, bin ich's" and the Christian community in "Ich bin's, ich sollte büssen." This descent/ascent segment contrasts the ideas of death and resurrection as well as flesh and spirit in the flat/sharp motion, and in Bach's placing the point of crossover from flats to sharps on the unique arioso words of the institution of the Lord's Supper: F major for the bread, C major for the wine, and G major for Jesus' closing anticipation of the Kingdom of God. The meditative movements "Wiewohl mein Herz mit Tränen schwimmt" and "Ich will dir mein Herze schenken" confirm the turn to sharps, the latter taking up a melodic figure from Jesus' recitative as its opening motive, and completing the Last Supper with a possible reference to "O Lamm Gottes." B minor and D major follow for the ascent to the Mount of Olives. Then Jesus' three predictions—the disciples' anger (F sharp minor), the arrest of Jesus and desertion of the disciples as foretold in Scripture (A major, with *stile concitato*), and the resurrection and Parousia in Galilee (E major)—complete the ascent with the keys that will reappear when some of these events come to pass at the close of Part One. At that point Jesus' A major cadence, completing the phrase "Aber das ist alles geschen, dass erfüllet würden die Schriften der Propheten," immediately precedes the narrative of the disciples' desertion.

Following the arrival at E major predicting the resurrection and the confirmation of that key in "Erkenne mich, mein Hüter," a second, much longer, and more detailed pattern of descent/ascent begins. The focal point for the move down to flats is the recitative following "Erkenne mich," in which Peter protests his loyalty. The major stages are Jesus' prediction of Peter's denial (ending "wirst du mich dreimal verleugnen"), an E minor cadence followed by a key signature change, and Peter's rhythmically identical words "so will ich dich nicht verleugnen," cadencing in C minor, so that the passage parallels the recitative predicting Judas's betrayal. Now the E flat major chorale, "Ich will hier bei dir stehen," confirms the modulation to flats. Its music is that of "Erkenne mich, mein Hüter," transposed down a semitone, providing thereby a measure of tonal distance and antithesis.

Gethsemane is the true spiritual and theological center of Part One of the *Passion*; and Bach recognizes it as such by placing there the dialogues for tenor and chorus "O Schmerz" and "Ich will bei meinem Jesu wachen." The latter, like "Ich will hier bei dir stehen," continues the theme of human resolve that Peter's assertion of loyalty introduces—the conflict of flesh (Peter) and spirit (Jesus). The descent/ascent curve from "Erkenne mich, mein Hüter," down to the A flat of Jesus' words "Meine Seele ist betrübt bis an den Tod" and its F minor response in "O Schmerz," then up to the E major of "O Mensch, bewein" occupies the remainder of Part One, a time span of about half an hour. This span deals significantly with basic Lutheran themes—will, the conflict of spirit and flesh, the theology of the cross, the acknowledgment of sin prompted by meditation on Jesus' suffering, the necessity of the individual's becoming "conformable to Christ in His suffering"; its structure is, in fact, built around them. Although Bach makes the descent to F minor a relatively quick one, the return ascent to E major proceeds in regular stages that parallel Luther's sermon to a considerable extent.

1. A flat, F minor: Jesus' words "Meine Seele ist betrübt bis an den Tod" followed by the tenor arioso "O Schmerz" with chorale "Was ist die Ursach"; the tenor mediates on Jesus' suffering, while the chorale expresses human guilt. Love is introduced in the closing lines of the tenor solo.

2. C minor: tenor aria "Ich will bei meinem Jesu wachen" in dialogue with chorus "So schlafen unsere Sünden ein." This corresponds to Luther's demanding that after recognition of sin we must learn to cast our sins on Christ through faith in the resurrection. The resurrection is not explicitly referred to, but the opening theme in the oboe is a minor-key form of a trumpet call. The middle section introduces the juxtaposition of the ideas of bitterness and sweetness that is developed throughout several later movements.

3. G minor: recitative ending with Jesus' prayer asking that if possible the cup (the necessity of crucifixion) pass from him, but ending with submission to the will of God ("sondern wie du willst"); this recitative is written so as to introduce a flat/sharp parallel with no. 8, below.

4. D minor, B flat: arioso, "Der Heiland fällt vor seinem Vater nieder." The falling arpeggios in the strings are set above a stepwise ascent in the basso continuo, all of which signifies the meaning of the anabasis as a whole: adverse physical events leading down to Jesus' death but with an underlying meaning of ascent to salvation (Ex. 92).

EXAMPLE 92.   Beginning of arioso "Der Heiland fällt"

5. G minor: aria "Gerne will ich mich bequemen, Kreuz und Becher an-
    zunehmen" corresponds to Luther's demanding that the individual be-
    come "conformable to Christ in His suffering," that is, acceptance of
    the way of the cross. This solo thus picks up on the G minor of Jesus'
    recitative, in no. 3, above. The middle section continues the theme of
    bitterness versus sweetness.

6. F major, B flat: Jesus' return to the sleeping disciples: his exhortation to wakefulness rather than falling into temptation (B flat).

7. A minor: Jesus' words "The spirit is willing but the flesh is weak" combines the Lutheran themes of spirit versus flesh, Will, and the theology of the cross (in his exegesis of Paul's Epistle to the Hebrews Luther picked out this phrase as an illustration of how scriptural antithesis signified the theology of the cross.)[6]

8. E minor, ♭ minor: Jesus' prayer and his full acceptance of God's will (no. 24), set by Bach in musical parallel to the earlier prayer in which Jesus prays that the cup pass from him (no. 21); now, however, the ending is a cadence in B minor (Ex. 93).

9. B minor: chorale "Was mein Gott will, das gescheh allzeit," full acceptance of God's will in the chorale confirmation of the move to sharps.

10. D major, F sharp minor, C sharp minor, G sharp minor: Jesus prays, then returns to the disciples and predicts Judas's arrival; G sharp minor is the sharp extreme of the *Passion*, associated here with Jesus' agitation.

11. E major: the arrival of the arresting party

12. D major, A major, D major, G major: the reference to Judas as the betrayer (*Verräter*) prompts a move down to G major, setting up the E minor of "So ist mein Jesus"/"Sind Blitze."

13. E minor: duet "So ist mein Jesus nun gefangen" with double chorus "Sind Blitze, Sind Donner"; lamentation over Jesus' capture with exhortation to the forces of nature to break out and destroy Judas and the captors. We may remember the move from E major to E minor in Cantata 9, where the E minor represented man's fallen state in which the *Abgrund* had swallowed him completely; here the chorus calls out for hell to open up ("Eröffne den feurigen Abgrund, O Hölle").

14. B minor, F sharp minor, C sharp minor: recitative narrating the physical events surrounding the capture and the fleeing of the disciples. Jesus announces the events as fulfilling the Scriptures (A major cadence).

15. E major: chorale fantasia, "O Mensch, bewein dein Sünde gross"; a return, in the opening line, to the emphasis on acknowledgment of sin, emphasizing its positive meaning. "O Mensch, bewein" recounts in all the succeeding lines of its text the story of Jesus' atonement from the incarnation to the crucifixion. It parallels "Kommt, ihr Töchter," marking the change from minor to major.

6. Luther, *Early Theological Works*, pp. 233–34.

If we extract from the foregoing large outline of the ending of Part One several of the main articulating points of the modulatory scheme—the move to flats and its chorale confirmation, the flat/sharp parallel between Jesus' two prayers to the Father concerning his acceptance of the cup, the modulatory crossover point between them, and, finally, the move to sharps and *its* chorale confirmation—we observe an emphasis on will and resolve.

1.   Peter: "so *will* ich dich nicht verleugnen" (modulation to C minor)
2.   Chorale: "Ich *will* hier bei dir stehen" (E flat)
3.   Dialogue: "Ich *will* bei meinem Jesu wachen" (C minor)
4.   Jesus: "Mein Vater, . . . sondern wie du *willst*" (G minor)

EXAMPLE 93   *continued*

5. Aria: "Gerne *will* ich mich bequemen" (G minor)
6. Jesus: "Der Geist ist *willig,* aber das Fleisch ist schwach" (A minor)
7. Jesus: "Mein Vater, . . . so geschehe dein *Wille*" (B minor)
8. Chorale: "Was mein Gott *will,* das g'scheh' allzeit"(B minor)

The course of modulatory events can now be seen to deal substantially with this issue of will, the subject of Luther's famous debate with Erasmus. The question involved—whether or not man has free will—was decided by Luther in the negative; "free" will in man is capable of turning only to evil. While his true course—subjection to the will of God—may involve him in the downward direction of suffering and death, it ultimately guarantees his salvation. Between the two prayers in which Jesus' humanity struggles to accept the cup—God's will as represented by the crucifixion—Bach placed the arioso "Der Heiland fällt," which, as we have seen, explains this dichotomy, while "Gerne will ich mich bequemen" urges the Christian to follow Jesus' model, the model not of such external behavior as self-denial but that of the complete acceptance of the burden that life and God's wrath imposes on mankind. Such acceptance is dependent, of course, on faith and the theology of the cross, and Luther's treatment of will is inseparable from them and is another means of articulating the same basic questions.

Much of the character of Part One results from the twelve speeches of Jesus, compared to the three in the remainder of the *Passion.* Only one of the later speeches—the prediction of the Parousia, early in Part Two—has the extended prophetic character of those in Part One, while the others consist of brief flat-minor utterances: the C minor "Du sagest's" and his last forsaken cry, "Eli, Eli," without the string halo.[7] The earlier, more extended speeches form the backbone of Part One even more than do the *turbae* of Part Two. In them Jesus predicts, in order, the crucifixion, his burial, the spread of the Gospel, Judas's betrayal, the coming kingdom, his capture and the desertion of the disciples, the resurrection and Parousia in Galilee, and Peter's denial—all these before Gethsemane. At Gethsemane the character of the speeches changes to torment, then resolve, agitation awaiting the arrival of the arresting party, finally the speech to the captors concluding with the announcement of the fulfillment of Scripture. These speeches are central to the sense of modulatory causality in Part One. Many of the major key changes, including the shift from flats to sharps in particular, are accomplished by Jesus. In contrast, the flat modulations are made by the Evangelist (Bethany and the Last Supper) and Peter (response to the prediction of his denial). Jesus' modulations from

7. Spitta (*Johann Sebastian Bach,* vol. II, p. 544) gives Carl von Winterfeld as the source of this famous comparison. The dropping of the strings for Jesus' last words is a device that appears in Sebastiani's *St. Matthew Passion* as well.

flats to sharps concern the spread of the Gospel, the institution of the Lord's Supper, and anticipation of the Kingdom of God, and his acceptance of the cup, whereas others of his speeches complete the most substantial motion to deep sharps (prediction of the resurrection, anticipation of his arrest, and the final speech to the arresting party). From all of this we get the unmistakable sense that Jesus is the primary source of upward modulation, while being the suffering victim of the modulations to flats, as it were, the latter brought about by the narrative of the sins of others and the patient, passive sufferings Jesus undergoes. By extension, the upward direction of Part One concerns the meaning of Jesus' sufferings and the Passion as a whole, while the overall downward motion of the *Passion* to its C minor close symbolizes all that he suffers at the hands of mankind.

Part One comprises fewer self-contained scenes in sharps or flats than division two. Instead, the process of tonal motion from sharps to flats and vice versa cuts across the normal boundaries of scenes and binds the events together in terms of their affective qualities and theological significance. The overall motion is upward from E minor to E major. Bach twice expands the upward motion to the scale of progressions through the full practical circle of key-signature levels to signify the Lutheran belief that before ascent to the highest level can be made we must first descend to the bottom level (here associated with the fall of the two disciples who represent mankind). The three flat-key scenes—Bethany, the Last Supper, Gethsemane—all associate the move to flats with a failing of the disciples: (1) their rebuking the woman for her anointing Jesus; (2) Jesus' prediction of Judas's betrayal; (3) Jesus' prediction of Peter's denial. In contrast, Jesus' speeches return to sharps in each case. The second and third descent/ascent patterns have a wider tonal range than the first; throughout the three the progressions increase in length and theological comprehensiveness, the last comprising the entire span of events at Gethsemane.

The narrative of events before Bethany deals with the issues of Jesus' prediction of the crucifixion (ending in B minor) and the plotting against him (moving down to C major for the chorus "Ja nicht auf das Fest"). Bach reserves the first move to flats for Matthew's intercalated narrative of the anointing by the woman of Bethany, introducing the first B flat on *Bethanien* and a cadence in G minor on *Haupt*. As the disciples object to the woman's action Bach makes a restless move to A minor for the beginning of the chorus "Wozu dienet dieser Unrat," then allows the chorus almost to drift into a C minor cadence for the disciples' expression of concern for "the poor," before ending in D minor. The affective quality of the flats within the chorus is unmistakable as the tenor leaps to and sustains an A flat on *Armen* (Ex. 94). However, Bach wants us to understand the meaning of the tonal shift in Matthew's sense, which goes beyond the suggestion of an affect of sympathy in the chorus. Therefore, he repeats the modulation to C minor—including the leap to A flat—in Jesus' subsequent recitative, on "Ihr habet allezeit Arme bei euch," then moves to a cadence in D minor, at low pitch and enhanced by the Neapolitan sixth

EXAMPLE 94.   Excerpt from chorus "Wozu dienet dieser Unrat"

EXAMPLE 94   *continued*

EXAMPLE 94   *continued*

chord, as Jesus explains the significance of the anointing: "Dass sie dies Wasser hat auf meinen Leib gegossen, hat sie getan, *dass man mich begraben wird*" (Ex. 95, emphasis added). Only then does Jesus make a modulation back to sharps to announce that this event will be known wherever the Gospel is preached (E minor cadence).

In this scene there were several possible—and not mutually exclusive— motivations for the move to flats: the feminine aspect, the change of locale (the B flat on *Bethanien*), the fact that the setting is a (presumably evening) meal, like the Last Supper, the sense of this scene as an intercalation. The careful placing of accidentals and cadence points (the G minor on *Haupt* is given slight appoggiatura emphasis) and repeating the modulations of the chorus in Jesus' recitative make clear Bach understands that the primary purpose of the scene in Bethany is to foreshadow Jesus' burial. The word *Armen* can be understood in Matthew's sense of the poor and weak, including even the humanity of Christ. After Jesus' E minor cadence, which matches the significance of Matthew's characteristic word *Evangelium,* the arioso "Du lieber Heiland" (B minor) and aria "Buss und Reu" (F sharp minor) continue the upward motion to the sharpest point of the scene. There is thus a descent/ascent dynamic from the prediction of the crucifixion down through the plotting against Jesus, into flats for Bethany, and back up to F sharp minor for

EXAMPLE 95.   Excerpt from recitative No. 5c

"Buss und Reu" as the idealized Christian responds with an expression of penitence. We may recall the moves to sharps for Peter's repentance in both *Passions,* as well as the E major of "O Mensch bewein." The message of penitence that is the first goal of Luther's Passion sermon was Bach's and Picander's as well. When, in the final dialogue arioso of the *Passion,* the words "Buss und Reu" reappear in the context of acknowledgment of sin ("O selige Gebeine, seht, wie ich euch mit Buss und Reu beweine, dass euch mein Fall in solche Not gebracht"), Bach makes a strong move to F minor, the key of "O Schmerz." The dualistic side of repentance—it is at once both tortured and beneficial (or, as Luther put it, "simul justus et peccator")—underlies its expression in both the deeper flats and sharps in the work.

Immediately following "Buss und Reu" the short narrative of Judas's plotting with the high priests and the offer of thirty silver pieces changes the direction of modulation, just as in Part Two the direction changes from Peter's repentance to Judas's remorse.[8] The scene then concludes with the tortured aria "Blute nur" (B minor). The following scene begins in G, and remains in that key until Jesus' words "ich will bei dir die Ostern halten mit meinen Jüngern" cadence in E minor followed by a key-signature change. The move to flats for the narrative of the Last Supper begins with careful precision on the word *Abend,* as if to underscore its connection to the *Finsternis* of Golgotha and the typological interpretation of evening as the time of fall and reconciliation in "Am Abend, da es kühle war." After Bethany the next two excursions into flats are progressively more sustained. At the same time the affective character of Jesus' pivotal speeches in flats becomes more intense. Noteworthy instances are the delayed minor third in the first violin at the close of "Wahrlich, ich sage euch: Einer unter euch wird mich verraten," the string appoggiaturas on "Du sagest's," and, of course, the *tremulante* character of "Meine Seele ist betrübt bis an den Tod" in the Gethsemane scene. Along with these details the modulations to sharps also receive more attention: in the arioso of the words instituting the Lord's Supper and in the focus of flesh/spirit and will at Gethsemane, with Bach's introduction of parallel recitatives and other details showing strong intent. In terms of the structural impact of these events the third move to flats (Gethsemane) is really the affective center of Part One, as Gethsemane is the theological center. Bach confirms this by placing a pair of dialogues at the culminating point of the deep flats. Thus Bethany and the Last Supper anticipate the events at Gethsemane, just as the first anabasis from F minor to E major is preparatory to the second. Bach's repetition of such purposeful structural-tonal devices at

8. This aspect of the Peter/Judas scene is discussed above (pp. 376–77). It may be noted that the turn downward from Judas's plotting to the prediction of his betrayal is paralleled in the Peter/Judas scene by the move to flats for the buying of the Potter's Field that ultimately leads to C minor. Besides the two arias of the Peter/Judas scene the only aria of the *Passion* lacking a prefatory arioso is "Blute nur, du liebes Herz," undoubtedly because of its association with Judas.

successively larger scales indicates his intention that the sense of fall and extended rise be as comprehensive as possible. The tonal plan deals with the positive theological truth that underlies the inescapable physical reality of the adverse events.

Part Two

The structure of division two may now be presented in toto (Fig. 12). The main points of modulation are carefully placed:

1. The narrative of the false witnesses (No. 31, to flats; we may remember the treatment of the discussion of *Wahrheit* in the *St. John Passion*)

2. The beginning of the *turba* series (up to E minor for the prediction of the Parousia (No. 36a), and the beginning of "Er ist des Todes schuldig," (No. 36b) then down to G minor within the chorus itself for the implications of "Todes schuldig")

3. Peter's denial and repentance (No. 38a, to sharps; again comparable to the *St. John Passion*)

4. The symbolic significance of the Potter's Field (No. 43, to flats), culminating in Jesus' "Du sagest's" at the outset of the trial

5. The modulation to the sharps of the trial on Pilate's reference to "hardness" (No. 43) followed by "Befiehl du deine Wege"

6. The change from the antagonistic *turba*-dominated character of the trial to the meditative character of the following scene (No. 51, to flats)

7. The narrative of the crucifixion itself (No. 58a, to sharps, on "Da sie ihn aber *gekreuziget* hatten"), and

8. The transformation of the cross between "ich bin Gottes Sohn" and "Ach, Golgatha" (No. 58e, the final move to flats)

As for Part One, Bach set division two mainly in sharps, beginning with the B minor dialogue "Ach, nun ist mein Jesus hin" that makes reference to the events at the close of Part One, and ending with the great octave cadence in E minor on "ich bin Gottes Sohn." Because Bach centered the stages of the crucifixion drama in E minor four of the main scenes—the introduction, the Peter/Judas scene (scene 2), the trial (scene 3), and the mocking of Jesus on the cross (scene 5)—had to remain close to E minor and B minor. The above-mentioned parallels between the scene before the high priest and the punishing of Jesus by the Roman soldiers provided the opportunity for musical correspondences that added a sense of the framing of the trial with scenes in flats. The trial itself suggested, by virtue of the repetition of "Lass ihn kreuzigen," an ordering of the *turbae* as a series. While it seems probable that Bach contemplated such a series, it conflicted with the plan of scenes in that the first two *turbae*, "Er ist des Todes schuldig" and "Weissage," appeared within the

FIGURE 12.   *St. Matthew Passion,* Part 2, Nos. 30–58e

No.	Movement
30	ACH, NUN IST MEIN JESUS HIN/Wo ist denn
31	Die aber Jesum gegriffen hatten
32	*Mir hat die Welt trüglich gericht't*
33	Und wiewohl viel falsche Zeugen
34	MEIN JESUS SCHWEIGT
35	GEDULD
36a	Und der Hohepriester antwortete
36b	*Er ist des Todes schuldig
36c	Da speieten sie aus
36d	*Weissage uns, Christe
37	*Wer hat dich so geschlagen*
38a	Petrus aber sass drausen
38b	*Wahrlich, du bist auch einer von denen
38c	Da hub er an zu verfluchen
39	ERBARME DICH, MEIN GOTT
40	*Bin ich gleich von dir gewichen*
41a	Des Morgens aber
41b	*Was gehet uns das an
41c	Und er warf die Silberlinge
42	GEBT MIR MEINEN JESUM WIEDER
43	Sie hielten aber einen Rat
44	*Befiehl du deine Wege*
45a	Auf das Fest
45b	*Lass ihn kreuzigen
46	*Wie wunderbarlich ist doch diese Strafe*
47	Der Landpfleger sagte
48	ER HAT UNS ALLEN WOHL GETAN
49	AUS LIEBE WILL MEIN HEILAND STERBEN
50a	Sie schrieen aber noch mehr
50b	*Lass ihn kreuzigen
50c	Da aber Pilatus sahe
50d	*Sein Blut komme über uns
50e	Da gab er ihnen Barabbam los
51	ERBARM ES GOTT
52	KÖNNEN TRÄNEN
53a	Da nahmen die Kriegsknechte
53b	*Gegrüsset seist du, Juden König
53c	Und speieten ihn an
54	*O Haupt voll Blut und Wunden*
55	Und da sie ihn verspottet hatten
56	JA, FREILICH WILL IN UNS DAS FLEISCH
57	KOMM, SÜSSES KREUZ
58a	Und da sie an die Stätte kamen
58b	*Der du den Tempel Gottes zerbrichst
58c	Desgleichen auch die Hohenpriester
58d	*Andern hat er geholfen
58e	Desgleichen schmäheten ihn auch

N.B.: * = *turba* choruses; lowercase = biblical texts; italics = chorale texts; capitals
= madrigal texts. The strict alternation of CHORUS I and CHORUS II
applies only to madrigal-texted solo movements.

		Keys
	CHORUS I, II	B minor
		modulatory: sharps to flats
		B flat
		ends G minor
————————————	CHORUS II	D minor
		A minor
		ends E minor
		modulatory: sharps to flats
		ends D minor
		D minor to F major
		F major
		modulatory: flats to sharps
		D major
		ends F sharp minor
	CHORUS I	B minor
		A major
		ends E minor
		E minor
		ends B minor
	CHORUS II	G major
		modulatory: sharps/flats/sharps
		D major
		ends A minor
		A minor to V of E minor
		B minor
		E minor
————————————	CHORUS I	E minor to C major
		A minor
		E minor
		B minor to V of F sharp minor
		ends B minor
		B minor to D major
		ends in E minor
————————————	CHORUS II	modulatory: sharps to flats
		G minor
		ends D minor
		D minor
		ends D minor
		F major
		ends A minor
————————————	CHORUS I	D minor
		D minor
		modulatory: flats to sharps
		B minor
		E minor
		E minor
		modulatory: sharps to flats

first flat-key scene rather than in sharps. Bach's solution was to move upward along the circle of keys within this scene—from the flats that are introduced for the narrative of the false witnesses and the B flat chorale (with its references to the world) through D minor for "Mein Jesus schweigt," A minor for "Geduld," and E minor, even B minor (Jesus' words "Du sagest's") for the recitative dialogue with the high priest. His intention was to begin "Er ist des Todes schuldig" in E minor/ G major, bringing in a reference to "O Lamm Gottes," then immediately returning to flats, a move that in itself has great dramatic force. In this way the scene before the high priest traces an ascent/descent curve. The flats at the beginning link the narrative of the false witnesses to Jesus' first punishments with which the scene ends, both places dealing with evil treatment at the hands of the world. The rising series of keys, leading to the sharps, represents the increasingly positive sequence from the didactic role of "Mein Jesus schweigt" and "Geduld" ("Mein Jesus schweigt . . . , *um uns damit zu zeigen*"; emphasis added) to Jesus' prediction of the Parousia. This is the last time Jesus speaks more than a single line in the *Passion* and the first of only three places in Part Two where he speaks at all. It therefore relates to several of Jesus' speches in Part One in which moves to sharps are made in connection with his predictions (the spread of the Gospel, the Kingdom, the resurrection).

The ensuing scene in which the fates of Peter and Judas are narrated had to be in sharps for the double purpose of representing Peter's denial and repentance with a move from flats to sharps (similar to that of the *St. John Passion*) and of pointing out the different character of Judas's remorse by means of tonal motion in the opposite direction. Bach makes the modulation into sharps in the first stages of the questioning of Peter by the onlookers, making it appear that Peter resists the move. The latter is a significant occurrence given the association of flats to the falseness of the world in the preceding scene. The recitative starts out in D minor. Then, as Peter is challenged by the servants, it gradually moves into sharps, reaching the dominant of E minor in the twelfth bar. The main events along the way are B natural on "Magd," which initiates the turn away from D minor, the E flat on "Er leugnete," as Peter attempts to move back to B flat (compare the D natural on "leugnete" in the *St. John Passion* as Peter denies E major), the E natural that enters in the bass beneath his phrase "Ich weiss nicht, was du sagest," giving the lie to his words, and, finally, the A minor and E minor phrases of the Evangelist and servant that confirm the move to sharps (Ex. 96). The chorus "Wahrlich, du bist auch einer von denen" gives a sense of certainty to the words of Peter's challengers and finality to the move to sharps in that it is constructed entirely on a descending D major scale. The change of direction after "Erbarme dich" and "Bin ich gleich von dir gewichen" for the narrative of Judas's suicide indicates, as we saw, the difference between repentance and remorse. Judas's "Gebt mir meinen Jesum wider" has the superficial optimism of movements from the cantatas such as "Leichtgesinnte Flat-

EXAMPLE 96.   Excerpt from recitative No. 38a

EXAMPLE 96   *continued*

tergeister" (BWV 181). The move to flats eventually culminating on Jesus' isolated C minor cadence introduces Jesus' silence throughout the sharps of the trial.

The move into sharps for the trial was delayed, undoubtedly to allow the flats to culminate in Jesus' "Du sagest's." Pilate's question, "Hörest du nicht, wi *hart* sie dich verklagen?" sets up an antithetical relationship between Jesus and his persecutors. Numerous devices throughout the trial then express its hard character: that interrupted cadence at "Barabbam!" with its diminished fifth bass motion substituting for the expected perfect fifth, the chromaticism of "Wie wunderbarlich" (*passus duriusculus* in the old rhetorical terminology), the augmented and diminished intervals (*salti duriusculi*) of "Lass ihn kreuzigen," as well as the transposition of its second appearance further into sharps, the severity of "Sein Blut komme über uns," and the like. Against all this, as we said, the aria "Aus Liebe" stands as an oasis of gentleness.

The second flat-key scene of divison two, from "Erbarm es, Gott" through "Komm, süsses Kreuz," once again associates Jesus as Matthew's suffering servant with the flat keys. It is not a scene in the strict sense of its dealing with a relatively discrete event in the narrative since the shift of location to Golgotha takes place within it. Rather, Bach has created a scene of symbolic musicotheological character in which the transformational character of the initial shift to flats and the point of culmination in "Komm, süsses Kreuz" indicate the beginning of a new way according to which suffering is "sweet"and the cross (symbolized, in all probability by the viola da gamba) is the instrument of benefit for mankind.

Perhaps the two most striking modulations in the entire *Passion* are the last two from sharps to flats, both of which project a strong sense of transformation by virtue of their emphasizing the confrontation of sharps and flats. The first of these involves the entire arioso "Erbarm es, Gott," which presents a concentration of the most arresting tonal events in the *Passion*. The recitative that precedes "Erbarm es, Gott," "Da gab er ihnen Barabbam los; aber Jesum liess er geisseln, und überantwortet ihn, dass er gekreuziget würde," ends the trial with the judgment of crucifixion and the narrative of the scourging in E minor. It was, as we saw, a traditional place for the entering of a verse of "O Lamm Gottes" in the seventeenth-century Passions. "Erbarm es, Gott" is the only instance in the *Passion* where a structural modulation is made within a madrigal-texted movement. Here Bach creates a movement of even greater modulatory wavering and uncertainty than "Ach, Golgatha." The arioso is practically a chain of seventh chords, beginning with a seventh on C, moving first toward flats, then to sharps, and ending, finally, with an enharmonic transformation from sharps (F sharp minor) to flats (G minor)—the only enharmonic change in the *Passion*. With hindsight, we might interpret the first chord of the movement as an enharmonically notated augmented sixth chord in the E minor that ends the trial. More likely, Bach intended it to register as a shock, a *relatio non-harmonica* in terms of the preceding cadence. Here Bach is anticipating the final transformation to flats for the end of the *Passion*.

As a reaction to the scourging and the trial, "Erbarm es, Gott" confirms our view of the trial as a focus for hardness. Near the end of the arioso, at the point where F sharp minor is being established, apparently as the final key, Bach introduces an especially dissonant effect: the (momentary) simultaneity of B sharp in the strings and C sharp in the vocal line on the word "härter" (Ex. 97). Immediately following this device the enharmonic change moves us out of the sharps ("haltet ein!") in one of the most striking shifts of perspective in all music: from the dominance of the physical events to the meditative Christian viewpoint. The device that Andreas Werckmeister had disparagingly called a "grosse Metamorphosis in der Har-

EXAMPLE 97.   Ending of arioso "Erbarm es, Gott"

monie" has never been put into practice more compellingly in another instance of the transforming potential of the circle of keys.[9]

Many performances of "Erbarm es, Gott" pass over this great tonal event in favor of emphasizing the dotted rhythm that supposedly represents the scourging. This kind of performance is testimony to our loss of the sense of tonal allegory along with the religious as opposed to purely dramatic motivation for such outstanding musical events. In fact, the dotted rhythm itself is transformed at the end of this movement, so that no hint of aggressive character is retained when it reappears in the aria that follows, "Können Tränen." Dotted rhythms remain a conspicuous presence throughout the next aria, "Komm, süsses Kreuz," where they combine with the viola da gamba sound and the allemande style to suggest something of a French character after the trial. This detail was quite possibly intended as a counterpart to the pre-trial intensity of the Italian concerto style in "Erbarme dich" and "Gebt mir meinen Jesum wider," a stilling of *Gewissensangst*.[10] In "Erbarm es, Gott" and "Können Tränen" the dotted rhythm mediates between the physical events and their meditative significance, its changing character one of the signs of the coming reconciliation. (The *St. John Passion*, too, has a sense of rhythmic reconciliation at the point of meditation on the scourging. The rhythm of the rainbow figures in the aria "Erwäge" relate to the ostinato-like *kreuzige* figure of the most agitated *turbae* of the *Herzstück*, underscoring the meaning of the cross as the sign of reconciliation under the new covenant.)

Ultimately, however, the greatest point of reconciliation is the turn to E flat major for "Sehet, Jesus," the key that Bach introduces prominently in the arioso of reconciliation, "Am Abend," for the phrase "Der Friedeschluss ist nun mit Gott gemacht, denn Jesus hat sein Kreuz vollbracht." A significant relationship that Bach could not have planned from the start was the introduction of E flat as the key of "Ich will hier bei dir stehen," at which point it bore associations of the weakness of the flesh. Its appearance at the beginning of division three suits the new trans-

9. Werckmeister, *Harmonologia Musica*, No. 72. Axmacher indicates (*"Aus Liebe,"* pp. 195–96), "Erbarm es, Gott" is one of four movements in the *St. Matthew Passion* that "awaken the fiction of direct participation in the Passion events"—i.e., in which the present-day individual seems to intervene to halt Jesus' sufferings, a highly questionable form of meditation, and one expressly condemned by Luther (*A Meditation on Christ's Passion*, pp. 7–8). The enharmonic change at the end of "Erbarm es, Gott," in fact, serves to underscore the shift away from this wrong kind of meditation.

10. I have suggested elsewhere ("Key Structure," pp. 100–102) that Bach's early planning of the *St. Matthew Passion* might have included the idea of a French/Italian juxtaposition of arias in flats and sharps similar to that between the Italian Concerto (F major) and the French Overture (B minor) from *Clavierübung II*. Because in Agricola's incomplete score of the *Passion* only the arias "Erbarme dich," "Gebt mir meinen Jesum wider," and "Komm, süsses Kreuz" appear, attention is drawn to their instrumental characters and national style models, suggesting that some relationship lies behind their selection. The trial is, in fact, framed by two scenes—one in sharps, the other in flats—each of which contains two arias: "Erbarme dich" and "Gebt mir" are Italian-style concerto movements, and "Können Tränen" and "Komm, süsses Kreuz" both exhibit prominent dotted rhythms.

formed view of the flesh and the redeemed world that we have indicated. It may be remembered that E flat was Bach's chosen key to close both the *Herzstück* of the *St. John Passion* ("In meines Herzens Grunde") and the *Passion* as a whole; it is also the key that provides the framework of the world in the third part of the *Clavierübung*.[11] We have indicated that the principle of regular alternation between choirs gives way to Chorus One only for the arias after "Komm, süsses Kreuz," and it is possible that Bach meant to resolve the antithesis for the final segment of the *Passion*. The message of redemption sings forth in "Sehet, Jesus," the recognition of Jesus' divine identity is proclaimed by the soldiers in "Wahrlich, dieser ist Gottes Sohn gewesen," reconciliation with God appears in "Am Abend," and the sense of a close personal relationship with Jesus underlies "Mache dich, mein Herze, rein." At all these points major keys come into the fore, considerably changing the character of the flat ending from its beginning at "Ach, Golgatha."

Within the final flat-key region the only move upward, away from flats, leads to the narrative of Jesus' death and the chorale "Wenn ich einmal soll scheiden" (A minor and E Phrygian). What is indicated in this motion, however, is not the triumph of Jesus' death, as in the move to sharps at the corresponding point in the *St. John Passion,* but the individual's anticipation of his own death, tinged with anxiety. The key of E Phrygian recalls the E minor "first" key of the *Passion* immediately before the narrative of the rending of the veil returns to flats. In the final dialogue recitative, "Nun ist der Herr," and chorus, "Wir setzen uns," Bach returns to C minor and the tone of lamentation over the physical events with which the *Passion* began. The character of "Wir setzen uns" is unmistakably that of the homophonic dance; and its melodic resemblance to the beginning of a Köthen sarabande has even occasioned the suggestion that it had a dance original.[12] But the final cadence, its momentary biting dissonance suggesting the sting of death and its resolution, indicate the perspective of the present world and the reality of death. This last gesture, necessary within the framework of physical events not to be fully transcended until Easter, does not, of course, cancel the progression in understanding that the structure of the *St. Matthew Passion* takes such pains to allegorize; it merely leaves the outcome in the realm of faith.

From details such as these it seems clear that Bach's structure of scenes in division two makes complex but consistent use of tonal allegory to articulate the various characters of the Passion events. This part of the *St. Matthew Passion* is sometimes described as lacking the sense of a self-contained structure that Part One exhibits. There is some truth to this statement, and it draws attention to one of the more important features of the *Passion*: that Bach derived the musical architecture in all its complexity from the structure of Matthew's account as it is interpreted accord-

11. See Chapter 9, n. 10.
12. Terry, *Bach: The Passions*, vol. 1, pp. 51–56.

ing to musicotheological principles, the broadest of which is tonality. Yet Bach does not give the work over to an abstract plan, as might be said of the *St. John Passion*. In the earlier work Bach's intuitive recognition that John is well served by an abstract plan led him to create the structure of signs. Matthew's is a very different treatment. His conception of Jesus as the Man of Sorrows rather than the aloof Messiah king of John's Gospel suggests a structure that follows rather than predetermines the order of the events of the narrative. In the *St. Matthew Passion* and, indeed, in all Bach's work, tonal allegory is a procedure more than a plan.

Abert, Hermann. "Bachs Matthäus-Passion." In *Gesammelte Schriften und Vorträge,* 143–55. Halle: Max Niemeyer Verlag, 1929. 2d ed. Reprint. Tutzing: Hans Schneider, 1968.

Adorno, Theodor W. *Aesthetic Theory.* Translated by C. Lenhardt; edited by Gretel Adorno and Rolf Tiedemann from the second German edition (1977). London: Routledge and Kegan Paul, 1984.

———. "Bach Defended Against His Devotees." In *Prisms,* translated by Samuel Weber and Shierry Weber, 133–46. Cambridge, Mass: MIT Press, 1981.

Althaus, Paul. *The Theology of Martin Luther.* Translated by Robert C. Schulz. Philadelphia: Fortress Press, 1966.

Ambrose, Z. Philip. " 'Weinen, Klagen, Sorgen, Zagen' und die antike Redekunst." *Bach-Jahrbuch* 69 (1983): 34–45.

Angelus Silesius [Johann Scheffler]. *The Cherubinic Wanderer.* Translated by Maria Shrady. Introduction and notes by Josef Schmidt. Mahwah, N.J.: Paulist Press, 1986.

Arndt, Johann. *True Christianity.* Translated by Peter Erb. Ramsey, N.J.: The Paulist Press, 1979.

Arnold, F. T. *The Art of Accompaniment from a Thorough-Bass.* London: Oxford University Press, 1931. Reprint. New York: Dover Publications, 1965.

Atcherson, Walter. "Key and Mode in Seventeenth-Century Music Theory Books." *Journal of Music Theory* 17 (1973): 205–33.

Auerbach, Erich. *Mimesis: The Representation of Reality in Western Literature.* Translated by Willard R. Trask. Princeton, N.J.: Princeton University Press, 1953.

Axmacher, Elke. *"Aus Liebe will mein Heyland Sterben": Untersuchungen zum Wandel des Passionsverständnisses im frühen 18. Jahrhundert.* Neuhausen-Stuttgart: Hänssler Verlag, 1984.

———. "Bachs Kantatentexte in auslegungsgeschichtlicher Sicht." In *Bach als Ausleger der Bibel,* edited by Martin Petzoldt, 15–32. Göttingen: Vandenhoeck und Ruprecht, 1985.

———. "Ein Quellenfund zum Text der Matthäus-Passion." *Bach-Jahrbuch* 54 (1978): 181–91.

Bainton, Roland. *Here I Stand: A Life of Martin Luther.* Nashville, Tenn.: Abingdon Press, 1950.

Banchieri, Adriano. *L'Organo Suonarino.* Venice, 1605.

Benjamin, Walter. *The Origin of German Tragic Drama.* Translated by John Osborne. London: New Left Books, 1977.

Bergel, Erich. *Bachs letzte Fuge.* Minden: Max Brockhaus, 1986.

Bernhard, Christoph. "Tractatus compositionis augmentatus." MS treatise. Reprinted in Joseph Müller-Blattau, *Die Kompositionslehre Heinrich Schützens in der Fassung seines Schülers Christoph Bernhard,* 40–153. Kassel: Bärenreiter, 1963.

Besch, Hans. "Eine Auktions-Quittung J. S. Bachs." *Festschrift für Friedrich Smend,* 74–79. Berlin: Merseburger, 1963.

———. *Johann Sebastian Bach: Frömmigkeit und Glaube.* Kassel: Bärenreiter, 1950.

Blankenburg, Walter. *Einführung in Bachs h-moll-Messe.* Kassel: Bärenreiter, 1974.

———. "Der Harmonie-Begriff in der lutherisch-barocken Musikanschauung." *Archiv für Musikwissenschaft* 16 (1959): 44–56.

———. "Johann Sebastian Bach und die Aufklärung." In Walter Blankenburg, *Kirche und Musik: Gesammelte Aufsätze zur Geschichte der gottesdienstlichen Musik,* edited by E. Hübner and R. Steiger, 163–73. Göttingen: Vandenhoeck und Ruprecht, 1979.

———. *Kirche und Musik: Gesammelte Aufsätze zur Geschichte der gottesdienstlichen Musik.* Ed. E. Hübner and R. Steiger. Göttingen: Vandenhoeck und Ruprecht, 1979.

———. "Die Symmetrieform in Bachs Werken und ihre Bedeutung." *Bach-Jahrbuch* 38 (1949–1950): 24–39.

———. "Der Titel und das Titelbild von J. H. Buttstedts Schrift Ut, mi, sol, re, fa, la . . ." *Die Musikforschung* 3 (1950): 64–66.

———. *Das Weihnachts-Oratorium von Johann Sebastian Bach.* Kassel: Bärenreiter, 1982.

Blankenburg, Walter, and Alfred Dürr. *Kritischer Bericht* to *Johann Sebastian Bach. Neue Ausgabe sämtlicher Werke* II/6 (*Weihnachts-Oratorium*). Kassel: Bärenreiter, 1962.

Blume, Friedrich. "Outlines of a New Picture of Bach." *Music and Letters* 44 (1963): 214–27.

————. *Protestant Church Music: A History*. Translation of *Geschichte der evangelischen Kirchenmusik,* 2d ed. Kassel: Bärenreiter Verlag, 1965. With 3 additional chapters written for the English edition. New York: Norton, 1974.

Bornkamm, Heinrich. *Luther and the Old Testament*. Translated by Eric W. Gritsch and Ruth C. Gritsch; edited by Victor I. Gruhn. Philadelphia: Fortress Press, 1974.

Brainard, Paul. "Bach's Parody Procedure and the St. Matthew Passion." *Journal of the American Musicological Society* 22 (1969): 241–60.

Breig, Werner. "Zu den Turba-Chören von Bachs Johannes-Passion." *Geistliche Musik: Studien zu ihrer Geschichte und Funktion im 18. und 19. Jahrhundert,* Hamburger Jahrbuch für Musikwissenschaft, vol. 8. Edited by Constantin Floros, Hans Joachim Marx, and Peter Petersen, 65–96. Laaber: Laaber-Verlag, 1985.

Brown, Raymond. *The Gospel According to John I–XII and XIII–XX*. The Anchor Bible, vols. 29 and 29A. Garden City, N.Y.: Doubleday, 1966, 1970.

Buelow, George. *Thorough-Bass Accompaniment According to Johann David Heinichen*. Berkeley and Los Angeles: University of California Press, 1966.

Buelow, George, and Hans Joachim Marx, eds. *New Mattheson Studies*. Cambridge: Cambridge University Press, 1983.

Bukofzer, Manfred. "Allegory in Baroque Music." *Journal of the Warburg Institute* 3 (1939–1941): 1–21.

————. *Music in the Baroque Era*. New York: Norton, 1947.

Buszin, W. E. "Luther on Music." *Musical Quarterly* 32 (1946): 80–97.

Buxtehude, Dietrich. *Dietrich Buxtehudes Werke,* vol. 2. Edited by Wilibald Gurlitt. Klecken and Hamburg: Ugrino Verlag, 1926. Reprint. New York: Broude International Editions, 1977.

Calov, Abraham. *Die Heilige Bibel nach S. Herrn D. MARTINI LUTHERI Deutscher Dolmetschung und Erklärung . . . ausgearbeitet und verfasset von D. ABRAHAM CALOVIO*. Wittenberg, 1681.

Cannon, Beekman. *Johann Mattheson: Spectator in Music*. New Haven: Yale University Press, 1947.

Chafe, Eric. "Allegorical Music: The 'Symbolism' of Tonal Language in the Bach Canons." *Journal of Musicology* 3 (Fall 1984): 340–62.

————. "Aspects of *durus/mollis* Shift and the Two-System Framework of Monteverdi's Music," *Schütz-Jahrbuch 1990*. Kassel: Bärenreiter, forthcoming 1991.

————. "Bach's First Two Leipzig Cantatas: A Message for the Community." *A Birthday Offering: Essays in Honor of William H. Scheide*. Kassel: Bärenreiter, forthcoming.

————. "J. S. Bach's *St. Matthew Passion*: Aspects of Planning, Structure, and Chronology." *Journal of the American Musicological Society* 35 (1982): 49–114.

————. "Key Structure and Tonal Allegory in the Passions of J. S. Bach: An Introduction." *Current Musicology* 31 (1981): 39–54.

————. "Luther's 'Analogy of Faith' in Bach's Church Music." *dialog* 24 (Spring 1985): 96–101.

————. *Monteverdi's Tonal Language.* New York: Schirmer Books, forthcoming 1992.

————. Reviews of Howard Cox, ed., *The Calov Bible of J. S. Bach* (Ann Arbor: UMI Research Press, 1985); Robin Leaver, ed., *J. S. Bach and Scripture: Glosses from the Calov Bible Commentary* (St. Louis: Concordia Publishing House, 1985); and Jaroslav Pelikan, *Bach among the Theologians* (Philadelphia: Fortress Press, 1986). In *Journal of the American Musicological Society* 40 (1987): 343–52.

————. "The St. John Passion: Theology and Musical Structure."*Bach Studies.* Edited by Don O. Franklin, 75–112. Cambridge: Cambridge University Press, 1989.

Chemnitz, Martin. *Examination of the Council of Trent,* part I. Translated by Fred Kramer. St. Louis: Concordia Publishing House, 1971.

Clements, A. L., ed. *John Donne's Poetry.* New York: Norton, 1966.

Conzelmann, Hans. *The Theology of St. Luke.* Translation by Geoffrey Buswell of *Die Mitte der Zeit,* Tübingen: J. C. B. Mohr, 1953. London: Faber and Faber, 1960.

Cox, Howard. *The Calov Bible of J. S. Bach.* Ann Arbor: UMI Research Press, 1985.

Crist, Stephen A. "Bach's Debut at Leipzig: Observations on the Genesis of Cantatas 75 and 76." *Early Music* 13 (May 1985): 212–26.

Dahlhaus, Carl. "Analytische Instrumentation: Bachs sechsstimmiges Ricercar in der Orchestrierung Anton Weberns." In *Bach Interpretationen,* edited by Martin Geck, 197–206. Göttingen: Vandenhoeck und Ruprecht, 1969.

————. "Die Termini Dur und Moll." *Archiv für Musikwissenschaft* 12 (1955): 289–91.

————. *Untersuchungen über die Entstehung der harmonischen Tonalität.* Kassel: Bärenreiter, 1968.

Dammann, Rolf. *Der Musikbegriff im deutschen Barock.* Cologne: Arno Volk Verlag, 1967.

————. "Zur Musiklehre des A. Werckmeister." *Archiv für Musikwissenschaft* 11 (1954): 206–37.

David, Hans T., and Arthur Mendel, eds. *The Bach Reader: The Life of Johann Sebastian Bach in Letters and Documents.* Rev. ed. New York: Norton, 1966.

Dibelius, Martin. "Individualismus und Gemeindebewusstsein in Johann Sebastian Bachs Passionen." *Archiv für Reformationsgeschichte* 41 (1948): 132–54.

———. "Paulus auf dem Areopag." *Sitzungsberichte der Heidelberger Akademie der Wissenschaften. Philosophisch-historische Klasse,* vol. 29. Heidelberg: Carl Winters Universitätsbuchhandlung, 1939. Reprinted in Martin Dibelius, *Aufsätze zur Apostelgeschichte,* edited by Heinrich Greeven, 29ff. Göttingen: Vandenhoeck und Ruprecht, 1951.

Dillenberger, John, ed. *Martin Luther: Selections from His Writings.* New York: Doubleday, 1961.

Dreyfus, Laurence Dana. "Early Music Defended Against Its Devotees: A Theory of Historical Performance in the Twentieth Century." *Musical Quarterly* 69 (1983): 297–322.

———. "The Metaphorical Soloist: Concerted Organ Parts in Bach's Cantatas." *Early Music* 13 (1985): 237–47.

Dürr, Alfred. *Die Johannes-Passion von Johann Sebastian Bach: Entstehung, Überlieferung, Werkeinführung.* Munich: Deutscher Taschenbuch Verlag; Kassel: Bärenreiter, 1988.

———. *Die Kantaten von Johann Sebastian Bach.* Kassel: Bärenreiter, 1971.

———. *Kritischer Bericht* to *Johann Sebastian Bach. Neue Ausgabe sämtlicher Werke* I/1, I/18, and II/5. Kassel: Bärenreiter, 1962.

———. *Studien über die frühen Kantaten Johann Sebastian Bachs.* Wiesbaden: Breitkopf and Härtel, 1977.

———. "Zu den verschollenen Passionen Bachs." *Bach-Jahrbuch* 37 (1949–1950): 81–99.

———. "Zur Chronologie der Handschrift Johann Christoph Altnikols und Johann Friedrich Agricolas." *Bach-Jahrbuch* 56 (1970): 44–65.

———. *Zur Chronologie der Leipziger Vokalwerke J. S. Bachs. Bach-Jahrbuch* 64 (1957): 5–162.

———, ed. *Johann Sebastian Bach: Weihnachts-Oratorium, BWV 248.* Facsimile of the autograph score. Leipzig: Deutscher Verlag für Musik, 1960.

———, ed. J. S. Bach, *Matthäus-Passion: Frühfassung, BWV 244b.* Facsimile edition of the copy made by J. C. Altnikol. Johann Sebastian Bach, *Neue Ausgabe sämtlicher Werke,* II/5a. Kassel: Bärenreiter, 1972.

Dürr, Alfred, and Werner Neumann. *Kritischer Bericht* to *Johann Sebastian Bach. Neue Ausgabe sämtlicher Werke,* I/1. Kassel: Bärenreiter, 1955.

Düwel, Klaus, ed. *Epochen der deutschen Lyrik.* Vol. 3, *Gedichte, 1500–1600.* Munich: Deutsche Taschenbuch Verlag, 1978.

Eagleton, Terry. *Walter Benjamin.* London: Verso Editions, 1981.

Ebeling, Gerhard. "Hermeneutik." In *Die Religion in Geschichte und Gegenwart,* 3rd ed., vol. 3, edited by Kurt Galling, 242–49. Tübingen: J. C. B. Mohr, 1957.

Eggebrecht, Hans Heinrich. "Bach—Wer ist das?" *Archiv für Musikwissenschaft* 42 (1985): 215–28.

———. *Bachs Kunst der Fuge: Erscheinung und Deutung*. Munich: R. Piper Verlag, 1984.

Epstein, P. "Ein unbekanntes Passionsortatorium von Christian Flor (1667)." *Bach-Jahrbuch* 27 (1930): 65–99.

Federhofer, Helmut. *Beiträge zur musikalischen Gestaltanalyse*. Graz: Akademische Druck- und Verlagsanstalt, 1956.

Fenner, Joachim. *Aussagemöglichkeiten barocker Musik untersucht und dargestellt an verschiedenen Orgelwerken Johann Sebastian Bachs und am sogenannten Bachpokal*. Edited by Ursula Fenner. Kassel: Private publication, 1972.

Fletcher, Angus. *Allegory: The Theory of a Symbolic Mode*. Ithaca: Cornell University Press, 1964.

Francke, August Hermann. "The Foretaste of Eternal Life" (1689). In *Pietists: Selected Writings,* translated and edited by Peter Erb, 149–58. Ramsey, N.J.: The Paulist Press, 1983.

Frei, Hans W. *The Eclipse of Biblical Narrative*. New Haven: Yale University Press, 1974.

Freiesleben, Gerhard. "Ein neuer Beitrag zur Entstehungsgeschichte von J. S. Bachs Weihnachtsoratorium."*Neue Zeitschrift für Musik* 83 (1916): 237–38.

Freyse, Conrad. "Ein Bach-Pokal." *Bach-Jahrbuch* 33 (1936): 101–8.

———. "Noch einmal: Der Bach-Pokal." Parts 1, 2. *Bach-Jahrbuch* 43 (1956): 162–64; 44 (1957): 186–87.

———. "Die Spender des Bach-Pokals." *Bach-Jahrbuch* 40 (1953): 108–18.

Friedemann, G. *Bach zeichnet das Kreuz: Die Bedeutung der vier Duetten aus dem Dritten Theil der Clavierübung*. Pinneberg im Bans, 1963.

Gadamer, Hans-Georg. *Truth and Method*. Translated from the second German edition (1965). New York: Crossroad Publishing Co., 1975.

Gaffurius, Franchinus. *Practica musicae* (Milan, 1496). Translated and edited by Irwin Young. Madison: University of Wisconsin Press, 1969.

Galilei, Vincenzo. *Dialogo della musica antica e della moderna*. Florence, 1581.

Gasparini, F. *L'Armonico pratico al cimbalo* (1708). Translation by Frank S. Stillings; edited by David L. Burrows as *The Practical Harmonist at the Harpsichord*. New Haven: Yale University Press, 1963.

George, Graham. *Tonality and Musical Structure*. London: Faber and Faber, 1970.

Glarean, Heinrich. *Dodecachordon* (Basel, 1547). Translation, transcription, and commentary by Clement A. Miller. *Musicological Studies and Documents,* vol. 6. Rome: American Institute of Musicology, 1965.

Glöckner, Andreas. "Johann Sebastian Bachs Aufführungen zeitgenössischer Passionsmusiken." *Bach-Jahrbuch* 63 (1977): 75–119.

Godwin, Jocelyn. *Athanasius Kircher: A Renaissance Man and the Quest for Lost Knowledge*. London: Thames and Hudson, 1979.

Grubbs, John. "Ein Passions-Pasticcio des 18. Jahrhunderts." *Bach-Jahrbuch* 51 (1965): 10–42.

Hamann, Johann Georg. *Poetisches Lexicon*. Leipzig, 1737.

Hamel, F. *Johann Sebastian Bach: Geistige Welt*. Göttingen: Vandenhoeck und Ruprecht, 1951.

Handschin, Jacques. *Der Toncharakter: Eine Einführung in die Tonpsychologie*. Zürich: Atlantis, 1948.

Heinichen, Johann David. *Der General-Bass in der Composition* (Hamburg, 1728). Facsimile ed. Hildesheim and New York: Georg Olms, 1969.

———. *Neu-erfundene und Gründliche Anweisung*. Hamburg, 1711.

Herz, Gerhard. "Thoughts on the First Movement of Johann Sebastian Bach's Cantata No. 77, 'Du sollst Gott, deinen Herren, lieben.' " In *Essays on J. S. Bach*, 205–17. Ann Arbor, UMI Research Press, 1985.

Hildesheimer, Wolfgang. *Der ferne Bach*. Frankfurt: Insel Verlag, 1985.

Hocke, Gustav René. *Manierismus in der Literatur*. Hamburg: Rowohlt Taschenbuch Verlag, 1959.

———. *Die Welt als Labyrinth*. Hamburg: Rowohlt Tachenbuch Verlag, 1977.

Hoffman-Erbrecht, Lothar. "Von der Urentsprechung zum Symbol. Versuch einer Systematisierung musikalischer Sinnbilder." *Bachiana et alia musicologica: Festschrift Alfred Dürr zum 65. Geburtstag*. Edited by Wolfgang Rehm, 121–60. Kassel: Bärenreiter, 1983.

Holborn, Hans Ludwig. "Bach and Pietism: The Relationship of the Church Music of Johann Sebastian Bach to Eighteenth-Century Lutheran Orthodoxy and Pietism with Special Reference to the *St. Matthew Passion*." Ph.D. diss., School of Theology at Claremont, Calif., 1976.

Hörner, Hans. *Georg Philipp Telemanns Passionsmusiken*. Borna-Leipzig: Universitätsverlag von Robert Noske, 1933.

Jameson, Fredric. *Marxism and Form*. Princeton, N.J.: Princeton University Press, 1972.

Janowka, Thomas Balthasar. *Clavis ad thesaurum magnae artis musicae* (Prague, 1701). Facsimile ed. Amsterdam: F. Knuf, 1973.

Jansen, Martin. "Bachs Zahlensymbolik, an seinen Passionen untersucht." *Bach-Jahrbuch* 34 (1937): 96–117.

Katz, Erich. *Die musikalischen Stilbegriffe des 17. Jahrhunderts*. Freiburg, 1926.

Keiser, Reinhard. *Markus-Passion. Die Kantate,* No. 152. Edited by Hans Grishkat. Stuttgart: Hänssler, 1963.

Kempis, Thomas à. *The Imitation of Christ.* Edited by Harold C. Gardiner. Garden City, N.Y.: Doubleday, 1955.

Kerman, Joseph. *Contemplating Music: Challenges to Musicology.* Cambridge, Mass.: Harvard University Press, 1985.

Kircher, Athanasius. *Musurgia universalis sive Ars magna consoni et dissoni in X. libros digesta* (Rome, 1650). Facsimile ed. Edited by Ulf Scharlau. Hildesheim: Georg Olms, 1970.

Kluge-Kahn, Herthe. *Johann Sebastian Bach: Die verschlüsselten theologischen Aussagen in seinem Spätwerk.* Wolfenbüttel: Möseler, 1985.

Kroyer, Theodor. "Die barocke Anabasis." *Zeitschrift für Musik* 100 (1933): 899–905.

Krummacher, Friedhelm. "Die Tradition in Bachs vokalen Choralbearbeitungen." In *Bach-Interpretationen,* edited by Martin Geck, 29–56. Göttingen: Vandenhoeck und Ruprecht, 1969.

Kuhnau, Johann. *Fundamenta Compositionis* (Leipzig, 1703). MS in the Deutsche Staatsbibliothek, Berlin.

———. *Musikalische Vorstellung Einiger Biblische Historien* (Leipzig, 1720). In *Denkmäler deutscher Tonkunst,* vol. 4. Edited by Karl Päsler. Leipzig: Breitkopf und Härtel, 1901.

———. Preface to *Texte zur Leipziger Kirchen-Music* (Leipzig, 1710). Reprinted in B. F. Richter, "Eine Abhandlung Joh. Kuhnau's." *Monatshefte für Musik-Geschichte* 34 (1902): 148–54.

Kysar, Robert. *John, the Maverick Gospel.* Atlanta: John Knox Press, 1976.

Leaver, Robin. *Bach's Theological Library.* Neuhausen-Stuttgart: Hänssler, 1983.

———. "Bach und die Lutherschriften seiner Bibliothek." *Bach-Jahrbuch* 61 (1975): 124–32.

———. *J. S. Bach and Scripture: Glosses from the Calov Bible Commentary.* St. Louis: Concordia Publishing House, 1985.

———. *J. S. Bach as Preacher: His Passions and Music in Worship.* St. Louis: Concordia Publishing House, 1984.

Lester, Joel. "Major-Minor Concepts and Modal Theory in Germany, 1592–1680." *Journal of the American Musicological Society* 30 (1977): 208–57.

———. "The Recognition of Major and Minor Keys in German Theory, 1680–1730." *Journal of Music Theory* 22 (1978): 65–103.

Lippman, Edward. "Stil." Part 2, "Begriffsgeschichte." In *Die Musik in Geschichte und Gegenwart,* vol. 12, cols . 1307–15. Kassel: Bärenreiter, 1965.

Loewenich, Walter von. *Luther's Theology of the Cross.* Translated by Herbert J. A. Bouman. Minneapolis: Augsburg Publishing House, 1976.

———. *Luther und das Johanneische Christentum.* Munich: Chr. Kaiser Verlag, 1935.

Lott, Walter. "Zur Geschichte der Passionskomposition von 1650–1800." *Archiv für Musikwissenschaft* 3 (1921): 285–320.

———. "Zur Geschichte der Passionsmusiken auf Danziger Boden." *Archiv für Musikwissenschaft* 7 (1925): 297–328.

Lowinsky, Edward. *Secret Chromatic Art in the Netherlands Motet.* New York: Columbia University Press, 1946.

———. "Secret Chromatic Art Re-examined." In *Perspectives in Musicology,* edited by Barry S. Brook, Edward O. D. Downes, and Sherman Van Solkema, 91–135. New York: Norton, 1972.

———. *Tonality and Atonality in Sixteenth-Century Music.* Berkeley and Los Angeles: University of California Press, 1961.

Luther, Martin. *The Bondage of the Will (De servo arbitrio).* In *Luther and Erasmus: Free Will and Salvation.* Translated and edited by Philip S. Watson, 99–334. Philadelphia: The Westminster Press, 1969.

———. *Commentary on Psalm Eight.* Translated and edited by Jaroslav Pelikan. In vol. 12 of *Luther's Works (Selected Psalms I),* edited by Jaroslav Pelikan. St. Louis: Concordia Publishing House, 1955.

———. "Commentary on Psalm 130." Translated by Arnold Guebert. In vol. 14 of *Luther's Works,* edited by Jaroslav Pelikan, 189–94. St. Louis: Concordia Publishing House, 1958.

———. *A Commentary on St. Paul's Epistle to the Galatians.* Revised and edited by Philip S. Watson. London: James Clarke and Co., 1953.

———. *D. Martin Luthers Werke.* Vol. 52. Weimar, 1915.

———. *The Freedom of a Christian, 1520.* In vol. 31 of *Luther's Works (Career of the Reformer I),* edited by Harold J. Grimm. Philadelphia: Muhlenburg Press, 1957, pp. 333–77. Reprinted in *Martin Luther: Selections from His Writings.* Edited and with an introduction by John Dillenberger, 42–85. Garden City, N.Y.: Doubleday, 1961.

———. *Lecture on Psalm 90 (1534–1535).* Translated by Herbert J. A. Bouman. In vol. 11 of *Luther's Works,* edited by Hilton C. Oswald. St. Louis: Concordia Publishing House, 1976.

———. *Lectures on Isaiah, Chapters 1–39.* Translated by Herbert J. A. Bouman. In vol. 16 of *Luther's Works,* edited by Jaroslav Pelikan. St. Louis: Concordia Publishing House, 1969.

———. *Luther: Early Theological Works.* Edited and translated by James Atkinson. Philadelphia: The Westminster Press, 1962.

———. *Luther: Lectures on Romans.* Newly translated and edited by Wilhelm Pauck. Philadelphia: The Westminster Press, 1961.

———. *Luther's Works.* 55 vols. Edited by Jaroslav Pelikan and Heinz Lohmann. St. Louis: Concordia Publishing House, and Philadelphia: Fortress Press, 1955–1986.

———. *A Meditation on Christ's Passion.* Translated by Martin H. Bertram; edited by Martin O. Dietrich. In vol. 42 of *Luther's Works,* edited by Helmut J. Lehmann, 7–14. Philadelphia: Fortress Press, 1969.

———. *A Sermon on Preparing to Die.* Translated by Martin H. Bertram; edited by Martin O. Dietrich. In vol. 42 of *Luther's Works,* edited by Helmut J. Lehmann, 97–115. Philadelphia: Fortress Press, 1969.

———. "Two Kinds of Righteousness." Translated by Lowell J. Satre. In vol. 31 of *Luther's Works,* edited by Harold J. Grimm, 297–306. Philadelphia: Fortress Press, 1957.

Mahrenholz, Christhard. *Luther und die Kirchenmusik.* Kassel: Bärenreiter, 1937.

Maniates, Maria Rika. *Mannerism in Italian Music and Culture, 1530–1630.* Chapel Hill: University of North Carolina Press, 1979.

Marshall, Robert. *The Compositional Process of J. S. Bach.* 2 vols. Princeton, N.J.: Princeton University Press, 1972.

———. *Kritischer Bericht* to *Johann Sebastian Bach. Neue Ausgabe sämtlicher Werke* I/19. Kassel: Bärenreiter, 1989.

———. *The Music of Johann Sebastian Bach: The Sources, the Style, the Significance.* New York: Schirmer Books, 1989.

Mattheson, Johann. *Behauptung der himmlischen Musik aus den Grunden der Vernunft, Kirchenlehre und Heiligen Schrift.* Hamburg, 1747.

———. *Das beschützte Orchestre* (Hamburg, 1717). Facsimile ed. Leipzig: Zentralantiquariat der deutschen demokratischen Republik, 1981.

———. *Critica musica. Des fragende Componisten/Erstes Verhör/über eine gewisse Passion* (Hamburg, 1724). Facsimile ed. Amsterdam: F. Knuf, 1964.

———. *Das forschende Orchestre.* Hamburg, 1721.

———. *Der Musicalische Patriot* (Hamburg, 1728). Facsimile ed. Leipzig: Zentralantiquariat der deutschen demokratischen Republik, 1975.

———. *Das neu-eröffnete Orchestre.* Hamburg, 1713.

———. *Der Volkommene Kapellmeister* (Hamburg, 1739). Facsimile ed. Edited by Margarete Reimann. Kassel: Bärenreiter, 1954.

———. *Grosse General-Bass Schule.* Hamburg, 1731.

———. *Kleine General-Bass Schule.* Hamburg, 1735.

Mazzeo, Joseph Anthony. *Renaissance and Seventeenth-Century Studies.* New York: Columbia University Press, 1964.

Mendel, Arthur. *Kritischer Bericht* to *Johann Sebastian Bach. Neue Ausgabe sämtlicher Werke.* II/4. Kassel: Bärenreiter, 1974.

———. "More on the Weimar Origin of Bach's 'O Mensch, bewein.' " *Journal of the American Musicological Society* 17 (1964): 203–6.

———. "Traces of the Pre-History of Bach's St. John and St. Matthew Passions." In *Festschrift Otto Erich Deutsch,* edited by Walter Gerstenberg, 31–48. Kassel: Bärenreiter, 1963.

Meyer, U. "Johann Sebastian Bachs theologische Äusserungen." *Musik und Kirche* 47 (1977): 112–18.

———. "Zahlenalphabet bei J. S. Bach? Zur antikabbalistischen Tradition im Luthertum." *Musik und Kirche* 51 (1981): 15–19.

Minear, Paul S. "J. S. Bach and J. A. Ernesti: A Case Study in Exegetical and Theological Conflict." In *Our Common History as Christians: Essays in Honor of Albert C. Outler,* edited by John Deschner, L. T. Howe, and K. Penzel, 131–55. New York: Oxford University Press, 1975.

———. "Matthew, Evangelist, and Johann, Composer." *Theology Today* 30 (1973): 243–55.

Monteverdi, Claudio. Preface to *Madrigali Guerrieri et Amorosi . . . Libro Ottavo* (Venice, 1638). Facsimile in *Tutte le opere.* Vol. 7, pt. 1. Edited by G. Francesco Malipiero. Translated in Oliver Strunk, *Source Readings in Music History,* 413–15. New York: Norton, 1950.

Monteverdi, Giulio Cesare. *Dichiaratione della lettera stampata nel quinto libro de suoi madrigali.* In *Scherzi musicali . . . raccolti da Giulio Cesare Monteverdi* (1607). Reprinted in G. Francesco Malipiero, *Claudio Monteverdi.* Milan: Fratelli Treves editori, 1929, 83–84. Translated in Oliver Strunk, *Source Readings in Music History,* 411–12. New York: Norton, 1950.

Morley, Thomas. *A plaine and easie introduction to practical musicke* (London, 1597). Facsimile reprint of 2d ed. (1963) edited by R. Alec Harman. New York: Norton, 1973.

Moser, H. J. *Die Passion von Schütze bis Frank Martin.* Wolfenbüttel, 1967.

———. "Zum Bau von Bachs Johannespassion." *Bach-Jahrbuch* 29 (1932): 155–57.

Muffat, Georg. *An Essay on Thoroughbass.* Edited with an introduction by Hellmut Federhofer. In *Musicological Studies and Documents.* American Institute of Musicology, 4. Tübingen: C. L. Schultheiss and Chr. Gulde, 1961.

Müller-Schwefe, Hans-Rudolf. "Bachs Kantaten als Auslegung des Wortes Gottes." *Musik und Kirche* 30 (1960): 81–94.

Nettl, Paul. *Luther and Music.* Translated by Frida Best and Ralph Wood. New York: Russell and Russell, 1948.

Neumann, Werner, ed. *Kritischer Bericht* to *Johann Sebastian Bach. Neue Ausgabe sämtlicher Werke* I/36 (*Festmusiken für das Kurfürstlich-Sächsische Haus*). Kassel: Bärenreiter, 1962.

Neumann, Werner, and Hans-Joachim Schulze, eds. *Bach-Dokumente I. Schriftstücke von der Hand Johann Sebastian Bachs*. Kassel: Bärenreiter, 1963.

————, eds. *Bach-Dokumente II. Fremdschriftliche und gedruckte Dokumente zur Lebensgeschichte Johann Sebastian Bachs, 1685–1750*. Kassel: Bärenreiter, 1969.

The New English Bible. General editor, Samuel Sandmel. *The Apocrypha*, edited by Arnold H. Tkacik. New York: Oxford University Press, 1972.

Opitz, Martin. *Buch von der Deutschen Poeterey* (Brieg, 1624). Edited by Cornelius Sommer. Stuttgart: Reklam, 1970.

Palisca, Claude. "The Beginnings of Baroque Music: Its Roots in Sixteenth-Century Theory and Polemics." Ph.D. diss., Harvard University, 1953.

Pelikan, Jaroslav. *Bach among the Theologians*. Philadelphia: Fortress Press, 1986.

————. *Jesus Through the Centuries*. New Haven: Yale University Press, 1985.

————. *Luther the Expositor: Introduction to the Reformer's Exegetical Writings*. Companion volume to *Luther's Works*. St. Louis: Concordia Press, 1959.

Penna, Lorenzo. *Li Primi Albori Musicali*. Bologna, 1672.

Petzoldt, Martin. "Die theologische Bedeutung der Choräle in Bachs Matthäus-Passion." *Musik und Kirche* 53 (1983): 53–63.

————. "Zwischen Orthodoxie, Pietismus und Aufklärung: Überlegungen zum theologiegeschichtlichen Kontext Johann Sebastian Bachs." In *Bach-Studien 7: Johann Sebastian Bach und die Aufklärung*, edited by Reinhard Szeskus, 66–108. Leipzig: Breitkopf and Härtel, 1982.

————, ed. *Bach als Ausleger der Bibel: Theologische und musikwissenschaftliche Studien zum Werk Johann Sebastian Bachs*. Göttingen: Vandenhoeck und Ruprecht, 1985.

Pontio, Pietro. *Ragionamento di Musica* (Parma, 1588). Facsimile ed. Edited by S. Clerycx. Kassel: Bärenreiter, 1959.

Poos, Heinrich. " 'Christus Coronabit Crucigeros'—Hermeneutischer Versuch über einen Kanon Johann Sebastian Bachs." *Theologische Bach-Studien I*. Edited by Walter Blankenburg and Renate Steiger, 67–97. Neuhausen-Stuttgart: Hänssler-Verlag, 1987.

Praetorius, Michael. *Syntagma Musicum*. I and III. Wolffenbüttel, 1619. Facsimile reprint edited by Wilibald Gurlitt. Kassel: Bärenreiter, 1958.

Prautzsch, Ludwig. *Vor deinen Thron tret ich hiermit. Figuren und Symbole in den letzten Werken Johann Sebastian Bachs*. Neuhausen-Stuttgart: Hänssler-Verlag, 1980.

Prenter, Regin. *Spiritus Creator*. Translated by John M. Jensen. Philadelphia: Muhlenberg Press, 1953.

Rifkin, Joshua. "The Chronology of Bach's *St. Matthew Passion.*" *The Musical Quarterly* 61 (1975): 360–81.

Sauerländer, Willibald. "Die Jahreszeiten: Ein Beitrag zur allegorischen Landschaft beim späten Poussin." *Münchner Jahrbuch der bildenden Kunst* 7 (1956): 160–84.

Scheibe, Johann Adolph. *Compendium Musices* (MS). In Peter Benary, *Die deutsche Kompositionslehre des 18. Jahrhunderts. Jenaer Beiträge zur Musikforschung,* vol. 3, edited by Heinrich Besseler. Leipzig: Breitkopf and Härtel, 1961.

Scheide, William H. *Johann Sebastian Bach as a Biblical Interpreter.* Princeton Pamphlets No. 8. Princeton Theological Seminary. Princeton, N.J.: 1952.

Schellhous, Rosalie Athol. "Form and Spirituality in Bach's *St. Matthew Passion. Musical Quarterly* 71 (1985): 295–326.

Schering, Arnold. "Bach und das Symbol, insbesondere die Symbolik seines Kanons." *Bach-Jahrbuch* 22 (1925): 53–59.

———. "Bach und das Symbol, 2: Das 'Figürliche' und 'Metaphorische.' " *Bach-Jahrbuch* 25 (1928): 119–37.

———. "Bach und das Symbol. 3. Studie: Psychologische Grundlegung des Symbolbegriffs aus Christian Wolffs *Psychologia empirica.*" *Bach-Jahrbuch* 34 (1937): 89–95.

Schmitz, Arnold. *Die Bildlichkeit der wortgebundenen Musik Johann Sebastian Bachs. Neue Studien zur Musikwissenschaft I.* Mainz: B. Schotts Söhne, 1950.

Schnapp, Friedrich. "Das Notenrätsel des Bach-Pokals und seine Deutung." *Bach-Jahrbuch* 35 (1938): 87–94.

Schönberg, Arnold. "Bach." In *Style and Idea,* edited by Leonard Stein with translations by Leo Black, 393–97. Berkeley and Los Angeles: University of California Press, 1975.

Schrade, Leo. "Bach: The Conflict between the Sacred and the Secular." *Journal of the History of Ideas* 7 (1946): 151–94. Reprint. New York: Merlin Press, n.d.

Schulze, Hans Joachim, ed. *Bach-Dokumente.* Vol. 3. *Dokumente zum Nachwirken Johann Sebastian Bachs, 1750–1800.* Leipzig: Breitkopf und Härtel, 1972.

Schulze, Otto Friedrich. "Ein Bach-Pokal im Eisenacher Bach-Museum." *Musica* 21 (1967): 261–64.

Schütz, Heinrich. Preface to *Psalmen Davids* (1619). In vol. 23 of *Neue Ausgabe sämtlicher Werke.* Edited by Wilhelm Ehmann. Neue Schütz Gesellschaft. Kassel: Bärenreiter, 1971.

Schweitzer, Albert. *J. S. Bach, le musicien-poète.* Paris, 1905. German ed. 1908. English translation from the German by Ernest Newman with alterations and additions by the author. London: Breitkopf und Härtel, 1911. Reprint. Boston: Bruce Humphries, 1962.

Siegele, Ulrich. "Bachs Endzweck einer regulierten und Entwurf einer wohlbestallten Kirchenmusiik." In *Festschrift Georg von Dadelsen,* edited by Thomas Kohlhase, 148–80. Neuhausen-Stuttgart: Hänssler Verlag, 1978.

———. "Bachs Ort in Orthodoxie und Aufklärung." *Musik und Kirche* 51 (1981): 3–14.

———. *Bachs theologischer Formbegriff und das Duett F-Dur.* Neuhausen-Stuttgart: Hänssler Verlag, 1978.

Smallman, Basil. *The Background of Passion Music.* New York: Philosophical Library, 1957. New ed. New York: Dover Publications, 1970.

Smend, Friedrich. "Bachs Kanonwerk über 'Vom Himmel hoch da komm ich her.' " *Bach-Jahrbuch* 30 (1933): 1–30. Reprinted in *Bach-Studien,* edited by Christoph Wolff, 90–109. Kassel: Bärenreiter, 1969.

———. "Bachs Matthäus-Passion." *Bach-Jahrbuch* 25 (1928): 1–95.

———. "Die Johannes-Passion von Bach." *Bach-Jahrbuch* 23 (1926): 105–28.

———. *Joh. Seb. Bach: Kirchen-Kantaten.* 2d edition. 6 vols. Berlin: Christlicher Zeitschriftenverlag, 1950.

———. *J. S. Bach bei seinem Namen gerufen. Eine Noteninschrift und ihre Deutung.* Kassel: Bärenreiter, 1950. Reprinted in *Bach-Studien,* edited by Christoph Wolff, 176–94. Kassel: Bärenreiter, 1969.

———. "Luther und Bach." *Bach-Jahrbuch* 37 (1947): 5–49.

———. "Der Pokal im Eisenacher Bach-Museum." *Bach-Jahrbuch* 42 (1955): 108–12.

———. "Die Tonartenordnung in Bachs Matthäus-Passion." *Zeitschrift für Musikwissenschaft* 12 (1929–1930): 336–41.

Spener, Philipp. *Pia Desideria.* Translated and edited by Theodore G. Tappert. Philadelphia: Fortress Press, 1964.

Spitta, Philipp. "Die Arie 'Ach, mein Sinn' aus J. S. Bach's Johannes-Passion." *Vierteljahrsschrift für Musikwissenschaft* 4 (1888): 471–78.

———. *Johann Sebastian Bach.* Translated by Clara Bell and J. A. Fuller-Maitland. London: Novello, 1889. 2 vols. Reprint. New York: Dover Publications, 1951.

Steiger, Lothar, and Renate Steiger. *Bachs Kantaten zum Sonntag Estomihi: Eine theologisch-musicalische Auslegung.* Neuhausen-Stuttgart: Hänssler Verlag, 1984.

Steiger, Renate. "Bach und Israel." *Musik und Kirche* 50 (1980): 15–22.

———. "Die Einheit des Weihnachtsoratoriums von J. S. Bach." Parts 1, 2. *Musik und Kirche* 51 (1981): 273–88; 52 (1982): 9–15.

———. "Methode und Ziel einer musikalischen Hermeneutik im Werke Bachs." *Musik und Kirche* 47 (1977): 209–24.

———. " 'O schöne Zeit! O Abendstunde!': Affekt und Symbol in J. Bachs Matthäuspassion." *Musik und Kirche* 46 (1976): 1–13.

———. " 'Die Welt ist euch ein Himmelreich': Zu J. S. Bachs Deutung des Pastoralen." *Musik und Kirche* 41 (1971): 1–8, 69–79.

Stein, Arnold A. *John Donne's Lyrics*. Minneapolis: University of Minnesota Press, 1962.

Stiller, Günther. *Johann Sebastian Bach and Liturgical Life in Leipzig*. Translated by Herbert J. A. Bouman, Daniel F. Poellot, and Hilton C. Oswald; edited by Robin Leaver. St. Louis: Concordia Publishing House, 1984.

Szeskus, R., ed. *Bach-Studien 7: Johann Sebastian Bach und die Aufklärung*. Leipzig: Breitkopf und Härtel, 1982.

Tappert, Theodore G., trans. and ed. *The Book of Concord*. Philadelphia: Fortress Press, 1959.

Terry, Charles Sanford. "A Bach Relic." *The Musical Times* 76 (December 1935): 1075–78.

———. *Bach's Orchestra*. 2d ed. London: Oxford University Press, 1958.

———. *Bach. The Passions, Book II: 1729–31*. 2 vols. London: Oxford University Press, 1928.

———. "The Christmas Oratorio: Original or Borrowed?" Parts 1–3. *The Musical Times* 71 (October 1930): 887–89; (November 1930): 982–86; (December 1930): 1073–76.

Tovey, Donald Francis. *Beethoven*. Edited by Hubert J. Foss. London: Oxford University Press, 1944.

Trautmann, Christoph. " 'Calovii Schriften 3. Bände' aus Johann Sebastian Bachs Nachlass und ihre Bedeutung für das Bild des lutherischen Kantors Bach." *Musik und Kirche* 39 (1969): 145–60.

Turner, William. *Sound Anatomiz'd, in a Philsophical Essay on Music*. London, 1724. Facsimile ed. New York: Broude Bros., 1974.

Vicentino, Nicola. *L'antica musica ridotta alla moderna prattica*. Rome, 1555.

Walter, Bruno. *Of Music and Music-Making*. Translated by Paul Hamburger. New York: Norton, 1961.

Walther, Johann Gottfried. *Musicalisches Lexicon* (Leipzig, 1732). Facsimile ed. Edited by Richard Schaal. Kassel: Bärenreiter, 1953.

———. *Praecepta der musicalischen Composition* (MS, 1708). Edited by Peter Benary. Leipzig: Breitkopf und Härtel, 1955.

Warnke, Frank J. *Versions of Baroque*. New Haven: Yale University Press, 1972.

Weiss, Dieter. "Zur Tonartengliederung in J. S. Bachs Johannes-Passion." *Musik und Kirche* 40 (1970): 33.

Wellek, René. "The Concept of Baroque in Literary Scholarship." In *Concepts of Criticism*, edited by Stephen G. Nichols, Jr., 69–127. New Haven: Yale University Press, 1963.

————. *A History of Modern Criticism, 1750–1950.* Vol. 1. *The Later Eighteenth Century.* Cambridge: Jonathan Cape Ltd., 1955.

Werckmeister, Andreas. *Cribrum Musicum oder Musicalisches Sieb.* Quedlinburg and Leipzig, 1700. Facsimile ed. Hildesheim and New York, 1970.

————. *Harmonologia Musica.* Frankfurt and Leipzig, 1702. Facsimile ed. Hildesheim and New York: Georg Olms, 1970.

————. *Hypomnemata Musica.* Quedlinburg, 1697. Facsimile ed. Hildesheim and New York: Georg Olms, 1970.

————. *Musicae mathematicae hodegus curiosus.* Frankfurt and Leipzig, 1686.

————. *Musicalische Paradoxal-Discourse* (Quedlinburg, 1707). Facsimile ed. Hildesheim and New York: Georg Olms, 1970.

Werker, Wilhelm. *Die Matthäus-Passion.* Leipzig: Breitkopf und Härtel, 1923.

————. *Studien über die Symmetrie im Bau der Fugen und die motivische Zusammengehörigkeit der Präludien und Fugen des Wohltemperierten Klaviers von J. S. Bach.* Leipzig: Breitkopf und Härtel, 1922.

Werthemann, Helen. *Die Bedeutung der alttestamentlichen Historien in Johann Sebastian Bachs Kantaten.* Tübingen: J. B. Mohr, 1960.

————. "Zum Text der Bach-Kantate 21, 'Ich hatte viel Bekümmernis in meinem Herzen.'" *Bach-Jahrbuch* 51 (1965): 135–43.

Whittaker, W. Gillies. *The Cantatas of Johann Sebastian Bach.* 2 vols. London: Oxford University Press, 1959.

Wilhelmi, Thomas. "Bachs Bibliothek. Eine Weiterführung der Arbeit von Hans Preuss." *Bach-Jahrbuch* 65 (1979): 107–29.

Wittkower, Rudolf. *Architectural Principles in the Age of Humanism.* New York: Norton, 1971.

Wolff, Christoph. "Bach's *Handexemplar* of the Goldberg Variations: A New Source." *Journal of the American Musicological Society* 39 (1976): 224–41.

————. "The Last Fugue: Unfinished?" *Current Musicology* 19 (1975): 71–77.

————. "Ordnungsprinzipien in den Originaldrucken Bachscher Werke." In *Bach-Interpretationen,* edited by Martin Geck, 154–64. Göttingen: Vandenhoeck und Ruprecht, 1969.

————. *Der stile antico in der Musik Johann Sebastian Bachs.* Wiesbaden: Breitkopf und Härtel, 1968.

————. "Zur Chronologie und Kompositionsgeschichte von Bachs Kunst der Fuge." *Beiträge zur Musikwissenschaft* (1983): 130–42.

Wolin, Richard. *Walter Benjamin: An Aesthetic of Redemption.* New York: Columbia University Press, 1982.

Wustmann, Rudolf. "Matthäuspassion, erster Teil." *Bach-Jahrbuch* 6 (1909): 129–43.

——. "Tonartensymbolik zu Bachs Zeit." *Bach-Jahrbuch* 8 (1911): 60–74.

——. "Zu Bachs Texten der Johannes- und der Matthäus-Passion." *Monatsschrift für Gottesdienst und kirchliche Kunst* 15 (1910): 126–31, 161–65.

Zacconi, Lodovico. *Prattica di Musica*. Vol. I. Venice, 1592.

Zarlino, Giuseffi. *Sopplimenti Musicali*. Venice, 1588.

Catabasis (*continued*)
  St. Matthew Passion, 162–63,
  376–77, 399–400. *See also*
  Anabasis
Cavalieri, Emilio de', 256
Chafe, Eric 258n. 3
Chamber instrumentation: in
  Leipzig cantatas, 239, 243–
  47, 252; in Weimar cantatas,
  146–48
Chiastic design: in "Actus
  Tragicus," 120
Christus Victor: tradition of in
  St. John Passion, 276
Chromaticism: in *The Art of
  Fugue*, 52–63; in Bach's
  work, 34–35, 42, 132, 210;
  in Cantata 186, 234–36
Circle of fifths, in *St. John
  Passion* choruses, 298–99,
  300–301
Circle of keys: emergence of,
  21–22; of Johann David
  Heinichen, 65–72; in *St.
  Matthew Passion*, 391–99
Conzelmann, Hans: on salva-
  tion history, 93

Dahlhaus, Carl, 70, 79, 88; on
  durus and *mollis,* 73; on Monteverdi, 69n. 13; *System,* 67;
  on Webern and Bach, 3n. 5
Descent/ascent (tonal): in the
  cantatas, 151, 153–85; in *St.
  Matthew Passion, 400–403.
  See also* Luther, Martin:
  "analogy of faith"
Donne, John, 148, 219
Dreyfus, Laurence: on early
  music performance, 3n. 6
Dualism, in Bach, 4–5, 9
Dürr, Alfred: on Cantata 12,
  137n. 24; on Cantata 60,
  193–94; on Cantata 106, 95,
  99, 115; on Cantata 121, 173;
  on Cantata 150, 132; on
  Cantata 176, 212n. 23; on
  Cantata 186, 149n. 33; on
  Christmas Oratorio, 267; on

dating Bach's *Passion* performances, 302n. 28; on dating
  Cantata 213 and *Christmas
  Oratorio,* 255n. 1; on obbligato organ in the cantatas,
  245n. 14; on *St. John Passion,*
  302n. 31, 326n. 21; on *St.
  Matthew Passion,* 372; on
  "troped-motto" cantatas, 92
Durus, and *mollis:* in Bach's
  music, 40; in the cantatas,
  172, 195, 201, 263; in *St.
  Matthew Passion,* 396. *See
  also* Dahlhaus, Carl; Werckmeister, Andreas

E major: key association in the
  cantatas, 152n. 1
E minor: key association,
  152n. 1
Eagleton, Terry, 10n. 31
Eggebrecht, Hans Heinrich:
  on *The Art of Fugue,* 51–52,
  54, 57, 59, 61, 63
Ego eimi (I am): in *St. John
  Passion,* 286–87
Enlightenment: and Bach, 4, 8
Erasmus: debate with Luther
  over free will, 166–67
Ernesti, J. A., 248n. 18
Eschatology, in John, 278–79

F minor: association in the
  cantatas, 152n. 1
Federhofer, Helmut:
  Schenkerian interpretation
  of Christoph Bernhard,
  20n. 57
Fenner, Joachim: on Bach
  goblet, 29–30, 33n. 7
Flor, Christian, 369
Franck, Salomo, 137, 225,
  228–29, 303
Frei, Hans W., 12n. 40
Freiesleben, Gerhard, 297
Freyse, Conrad: on Bach gob-
  let, 29n. 2, 33n. 9

G sharp minor: association in
  the cantatas, 152n. 1

Gadamer, Hans-Georg, 4,
  8n. 22, 9
Gasparini, F.: on keys and
  genera, 75
Geier, Martin, 95
Gerhard, Johann, 356, 377
Glarean, Heinrich, 71
Glöckner, Andreas, 337n. 2
Gluck, Christoph Willibald
  von, 236
Goethe, Johann Wolfgang
  von: symbol and allegory,
  6n. 17, 7
Gryphius, Andreas, 78–79

Hamann, Johann Georg, 259
Handel, George Frederick,
  256; Bach's text for opening
  chorus of *Brockes Passion* of,
  313
Handschin, Jacques, 70
Heinichen, Johann David, 21;
  on circle of keys, 65–72; on
  key characteristics, vii; on
  sharp and flat genera, 66, 73–
  74, 78, 103; on *toni intermedii,*
  78
Hermeneutics: relation to
  allegory in Lutheran tradition, 10–19
"Herzlich tut mich
  verlangen": in Cantata 25,
  167–68; in Cantata 106, 99,
  110, 115; in Cantata 127,
  165–66; in Cantata 150, 132;
  in Cantata 161, 187–88; in
  motet "Jesu, meine Freude,"
  127; in *St. Matthew Passion,*
  339, 372–78, 381–84, *398*
"Herzliebster Jesu, was hast du
  gebrochen?", role of chorale
  in *St. Matthew Passion,* 350,
  372, 378–79
Historicism and Bach, 4
Hocke, Gustav René, 19
Holborn, Hans Ludwig,
  348n. 22

Jameson, Fredric: on allegory
  and symbol, 115n. 50

Janowka, Thomas Balthasar: on keys, 75

Jansen, Martin, 1n. 2, 127n. 6

Jeremiah, 170, 212

"Jesu, deine Passion," chorale in *St. John Passion*, 282n. 14

John, gospel of, 142–43, 221–23, 248–49; chiastic patterns in, 308–9; forensic imagery in, 310–11; glorification in, 282–85; as key to Bach's *St. John Passion*, 276, 307–15; numerology in, 309; structure of passion narrative, 307–10

Keiser, Reinhard: *St. Mark Passion*, 337–38, 340, 342–44, 366n. 7, 375

Key structure: classified into types, 151–53

Kircher, Athanasius, 43n. 34, 74, 76; on circle of fifths, 66, 69; on Phrygian mode, 223n. 31; on style, ix, 20, 24

Krebs family (Johann Ludwig, Johann Tobias, Johann Carl): as possible donors of Bach goblet, 29–30

Kreuzweis antiphony in *St. Matthew Passion*, 362

Kuhnau, Johann, 12, 23, 66, 70, 104, 261n. 5; on allegory and hermeneutics in musical composition, 6, 8–9, 10–11; *Biblical Histories*, 11, 112n. 48; on modes and cadences, 68; on modulation, 81

Kysar, Robert, 243n. 8

Lassus, Orlando: *Prophetiae Sibyllarum*, 70

Leidensethik, in Lutheranism, 191–93

Library of J. S. Bach: titles and title pages, 37. *See also* Calov Bible

Loewenich, Walter von, 108, 228nn. 3–4, 243n. 10, 248,

266n. 12; on Luther and John's gospel, 279

Lowinsky, Edward, 76

Lully, Jean Baptiste: *Alceste,* 77

Lute: in *St. Matthew Passion,* 356–57

Luther, Martin: "analogy of faith," 13, 103; antithesis in Scripture, 14; chorale "Aus tiefer Not," 52, 218–19; chorale "Mit Fried' und Freud'," 100–101, 108, 117, 172–73; on death, 96–102, 317, 396; and Erasmus, 166–67, 228, 406; on faith, 108; on faith and history, 93, 170; figurative interpretation of the veil of the Temple, 323; on flesh and spirit, 127, 234, 394–96; *The Freedom of a Christian*, 314–15; God's "proper" and "alien" work, 104; God's time, 96–97; *Hauspostille,* 351–52, 354, 367; hermeneutic principles, 10, 13–15, 22, 91; "hidden God," 102; incarnational theology, 230; on Isaiah, 107; and John's gospel, 279, 283, 315; on Law and Gospel in Scripture, 13, 317; on love, 358; on music, 38–39, 52, 71, 126, 146, 267; Passion Sermon, 35, 109, 135–37, 142, 198–99, 218, 276–77, 339, 346–59, 399–403, 412; on philosophy and reason, 227n. 2; on Psalm 8, 283; on Psalm 130, 219–21; on theology of the cross, 14–16, 228, 403

Maniates, Maria Rika, 71n. 22

Marshall, Robert, 17n. 11

Mattheson, Johann, 72, 329, 396n. 5; on ambitus, 68; on circle of keys, 66–67; *Critica Musica,* 314n. 4; description of Allemande, 357; on genera, 75; on key characteris-

tics, vii, 76–77, 85–89, 195–96, 391; on rhetoric, 7; on sense and intellect, 4n. 9, 21

Matthew, gospel of, 277, 377, 410

Meder, Johann, 369

Mendel, Arthur, 275n. 2, 302n. 29, 362n. 2, 364n. 5

Metaphysical tradition: in German baroque music theory, 8–9, 39

Minear, Paul, 12n. 40, 248n. 18, 344

Monogram, Bach's initials in, 27–28, 36

Monteverdi, Claudio, 70, 81, 256–57; on *oratio* versus *harmonia*, 8; *stile concitato,* 76; "Zefiro torna e'l bel tempo rimena," 77

Morley, Thomas: on style, 20n. 59

Müller, Heinrich: relationship of *St. Matthew Passion* texts to sermons of, 35, 302–3, 338, 344, 346–49, 352–53, 356, 366–67, 379; and *Symbolum,* 16, 18

Number symbolism, 7, 22, 43–45; in *The Art of Fugue,* 54, 58–59; in Cantatas 75 and 76, 248–50; in *St. John Passion,* 287, 291, 319–20; in *St. Matthew Passion,* 352

"O Lamm Gottes unschuldig": in *St. Matthew Passion,* 368–71, *369,* 392–93, 397–99, *398;* in seventeenth-century Passion tradition, 277

Oboes da caccia: in *St. Matthew Passion,* 348–54

Opitz, Martin, 11

Organ obbligato: in Bach's cantatas, 189, 191–92, 245–46

Orthodoxy (Lutheran): and love in *St. Matthew Passion*

theory, 8; on musical herme-
neutics, 11–12
Werker, William, 1n. 2
Werthemann, Helene, 97n. 20
Whittaker, W. Gillies: on
Cantata 9, 163
Winterfeld, Carl von, 406n. 7
Wittkower, Rudolf: on pro-
portion in Renaissance archi-
tecture and music theory, 21

Wolff, Christoph, 131n. 12; on
dating *The Art of Fugue*,
61n. 44
Wustmann, Rudolf, 339

Zacconi, Lodovico: on intrin-
sic/extrinsic effects in music,
20, 25
Zarlino, Giuseffi: on style,
20n. 59

Ziegler, Marianne von: librettist of Cantata 87, 154; librettist of Cantata 176, 212

Designer: Steve Renick
Compositor: A-R Editions, Inc.
Text: 10/13 Bembo
Display: Bembo
Printer: Malloy Lithographing
Binder: John H. Dekker & Sons